Book Four

Winter

The Lunar Chronicles

WRITTEN BY

Marissa Meyer

SQUARE
FISH

Feiwel and Friends
NEW YORK

SQUARE
FISH

An imprint of Macmillan Publishing Group, LLC
175 Fifth Avenue, New York, NY 10010
fiercereads.com

Square Fish and the Square Fish logo are trademarks of Macmillan and are
used by Feiwel and Friends under license from Macmillan.

Our books may be purchased in bulk for promotional, educational, or business
use. Please contact your local bookseller or the Macmillan Corporate and
Premium Sales Department at (800) 221-7945 ext. 5442 or by e-mail at
MacmillanSpecialMarkets@macmillan.com.

Library of Congress Cataloging-in-Publication Data Available

ISBN 978-1-250-00723-0 (paperback)   ISBN 978-1-250-06875-0 (ebook)

Originally published in the United States by Feiwel and Friends
First Square Fish edition, 2018
Book designed by Rich Deas
Square Fish logo designed by Filomena Tuosto

5   7   9   10   8   6   4

AR: 5.9 / LEXILE: 800L

*For Jesse, who turns every day
into a happily ever after.*

BOOK

One

The young princess was as beautiful

as daylight. She was more beautiful even

than the queen herself.

One

WINTER'S TOES HAD BECOME ICE CUBES. THEY WERE AS COLD as space. As cold as the dark side of Luna. As cold as—

"...security feeds captured him entering the AR-Central med-clinic's sublevels at 23:00 U.T.C...."

Thaumaturge Aimery Park spoke with a serene, measured cadence, like a ballad. It was easy to lose track of what he was saying, easy to let all the words blur and conjoin. Winter curled her toes inside her thin-soled shoes, afraid that if they got any colder before this trial was over, they would snap off.

"...was attempting to interfere with one of the shells currently stored..."

Snap off. One by one.

"...records indicate the shell child is the accused's son, taken on 29 July of last year. He is now fifteen months old."

Winter hid her hands in the folds of her gown. They were shaking again. She was always shaking these days. She squeezed her fingers to hold them still and pressed the bottoms of her feet into the hard floor. She struggled to bring the throne room into focus before it dissolved.

The throne room, in the central tower of the palace, had the most striking view in the city. From her seat, Winter could see Artemisia Lake mirroring the white palace and the city reaching for the edge of the enormous clear dome that sheltered them from the outside elements—or lack thereof. The throne room itself extended past the walls of the tower, so that when one passed beyond the edge of the mosaic floor, they found themselves on a ledge of clear glass. Like standing on air, about to plummet into the depths of the crater lake.

To Winter's left she could make out the edges of her stepmother's fingernails as they dug into the arm of her throne, an imposing seat carved from white stone. Normally her stepmother was calm during these proceedings and would listen to the trials without a hint of emotion. Winter was used to seeing Levana's fingertips stroking the polished stone, not throttling it. But tension was high since Levana and her entourage had returned from Earth, and her stepmother had flown into even more rages than usual these past months.

Ever since that runaway Lunar—that *cyborg*—had escaped from her Earthen prison.

Ever since war had begun between Earth and Luna.

Ever since the queen's betrothed had been kidnapped, and Levana's chance to be crowned empress had been stolen from her.

The blue planet hung above the horizon, cut clean in half. Luna was a little more than halfway through the long night, and the city of Artemisia glowed with pale blue lampposts and glowing crystal windows, their reflections dancing across the lake's surface.

Winter missed the sun and its warmth. Their artificial days were never the same.

"How did he know about the shells?" Queen Levana asked. "Why did he not believe his son to have been killed at birth?"

Seated around the room in four tiered rows were the families. The queen's court. The nobles of Luna, granted favor with Her Majesty for their generations of loyalty, their extraordinary talents with the Lunar gift, or pure luck at having been born a citizen of the great city of Artemisia.

Then there was the man on his knees beside Thaumaturge Park. He had not been born lucky.

His hands were together, pleading. Winter wished she could tell him it wouldn't matter. All his begging would be for nothing. She thought there would be comfort in knowing there was nothing you could do to avoid death. Those who came before the queen having already accepted their fate seemed to have an easier time of it.

She looked down at her own hands, still clawed around her gauzy white skirt. Her fingers had been bitten with frost. It was sort of pretty. Glistening and shimmering and *cold, so very cold* . . .

"Your queen asked you a question," said Aimery.

Winter flinched, as if he'd been yelling at her.

Focus. She must try to focus.

She lifted her head and inhaled.

Aimery was wearing white now, having replaced Sybil Mira as the queen's head thaumaturge. The gold embroidery on his coat shimmered as he circled the captive.

"I am sorry, Your Majesty," the man said. "My family and I have served you for generations. I'm a janitor at that med-clinic and I'd heard rumors . . . It was none of my business, so I never cared, I never listened. But . . . when my son was born a shell . . ." He whimpered. "He is my *son*."

"Did you not think," said Levana, her voice loud and crisp,

"there might be a reason your queen has chosen to keep your son and all the other ungifted Lunars separate from our citizens? That we may have a purpose that serves the good of *all* our people by containing them as we have?"

The man gulped hard enough that Winter could see his Adam's apple bobbing. "I know, My Queen. I know you use their blood for . . . experimentation. But . . . but you have *so many*, and he's only a baby, and . . ."

"Not only is his blood valuable to the success of our political alliances, the likes of which I cannot expect a janitor from the outer sectors to understand, but he is also a shell, and his kind have proven themselves to be dangerous and untrustworthy, as you will recall from the assassinations of King Marrok and Queen Jannali eighteen years ago. Yet you would subject our society to this threat?"

The man's eyes were wild with fear. "Threat, My Queen? He is a *baby*." He paused. He did not look outright rebellious, but his lack of remorse would be sending Levana into a fury soon enough. "And the others in those tanks . . . so many of them, children. Innocent *children*."

The room chilled.

He knew too much. The shell infanticide had been in place since the rule of Levana's sister, Queen Channary, after a shell sneaked into the palace and killed their parents. No one would be pleased to know their babies had not been killed at all, but instead locked away and used as tiny blood-platelet-manufacturing plants.

Winter blinked, imagining her own body as a blood-platelet-manufacturing plant.

Her gaze dropped again. The ice had extended to her wrists now.

That would not be beneficial for the platelet conveyor belts.

"Does the accused have a family?" asked the queen.

Aimery bobbed his head. "Records indicate a daughter, age nine. He also has two sisters and a nephew. All live in Sector GM-12."

"No wife?"

"Dead five months past of regolith poisoning."

The prisoner watched the queen, desperation pooling around his knees.

The court began to stir, their vibrant clothes fluttering. This trial had gone on too long. They were growing bored.

Levana leaned against the back of her throne. "You are hereby found guilty of trespassing and attempted theft against the crown. This crime is punishable by immediate death."

The man shuddered, but his face remained pleading. It always took them a few seconds to comprehend such a sentence.

"Your family members will each receive a dozen public lashings as a reminder to your sector that I do not tolerate my decisions being questioned."

The man's jaw slackened.

"Your daughter will be given as a gift to one of the court's families. There, she will be taught the obedience and humility one can assume she has not learned beneath your tutelage."

"No, please. Let her live with her aunts. She hasn't done anything!"

"Aimery, you may proceed."

"*Please!*"

"Your queen has spoken," said Thaumaturge Aimery. "Her word is final."

Aimery drew an obsidian knife from one of his bell-shaped

sleeves and held the handle toward the prisoner, whose eyes had gone wide with hysteria.

The room grew colder. Winter's breath crystallized in the air. She squeezed her arms tight against her body.

The prisoner took the knife handle. His hand was steady. The rest of him was trembling.

"Please. My little girl—I'm all she has. *Please.* My Queen. Your Majesty!"

He raised the blade to his throat.

This was when Winter looked away. When she always looked away. She watched her own fingers burrow into her dress, her fingernails scraping at the fabric until she could feel the sting on her thighs. She watched the ice climb over her wrists, toward her elbows. Where the ice touched, her flesh went numb.

She imagined lashing out at the queen with those ice-solid fists. She imagined her hands shattering into a thousand icicle shards.

It was at her shoulders now. Her neck.

Even over the popping and cracking of the ice, she heard the cut of flesh. The burble of blood and a muffled gag. The hard slump of the body.

The cold had stolen into her chest. She squeezed her eyes shut, reminding herself to be calm, to breathe. She could hear Jacin's steady voice in her head, his hands gripping her shoulders. *It isn't real, Princess. It's only an illusion.*

Usually they helped, these memories of him coaxing her through the panic. But this time it seemed to prompt the ice on. Encompassing her rib cage. Gnawing into her stomach. Hardening over her heart.

She was freezing from the inside out.

Listen to my voice.

Jacin wasn't there.

Stay with me.

Jacin was gone.

It's all in your head.

She heard the clomping of the guards' boots as they approached the body. The corpse being slid toward the ledge. The shove and the distant splash below.

The court applauded with quiet politeness.

Winter heard her toes snap off. One. By. One.

"Very good," said Queen Levana. "Thaumaturge Tavaler, see to it that the rest of the sentencing is carried out."

The ice was in her throat now, climbing up her jaw. There were tears freezing inside their ducts. There was saliva crystallizing on her tongue.

She raised her head as a servant began washing the blood from the tiles. Aimery, rubbing his knife with a cloth, met Winter's gaze. His smile was searing. "I am afraid the princess has no stomach for these proceedings."

The nobles in the audience tittered—Winter's disgust of the trials was a source of merriment to most of Levana's court.

The queen turned, but Winter couldn't look up. She was a girl made of ice and glass. Her teeth were brittle, her lungs too easily shattered.

"Yes," said Levana. "I often forget she's here at all. You're about as useless as a rag doll, aren't you, Winter?"

The audience chuckled again, louder now, as if the queen had given permission to mock the young princess. But Winter couldn't respond, not to the queen, not to the laughter. She kept her focus on the thaumaturge, trying to hide her panic.

"Oh, no, she isn't quite as useless as that," Aimery said. As Winter stared, a thin crimson line drew itself across his throat, blood bubbling up from the wound. "The prettiest girl on all of Luna? She will make some member of this court a happy bride someday, I should think."

"The prettiest girl, Aimery?" Levana's light tone almost concealed the snarl beneath.

Aimery slipped into a bow. "Prettiest only, My Queen. But no mortal could compare with your perfection."

The court was quick to agree, offering a hundred compliments at once, though Winter still felt the leering gazes of more than one noble attached to her.

Aimery took a step toward the throne and his severed head tipped off, thunking against the marble and rolling, rolling, rolling, until it stopped at Winter's frozen feet.

Still smiling.

She whimpered, but the sound was buried beneath the snow in her throat.

It's all in your head.

"Silence," said Levana, once she'd had her share of praise. "Are we finished?"

Finally, the ice found her eyes and Winter had no choice but to shut them against Aimery's headless apparition, enclosing herself in cold and darkness.

She would die here and not complain. She would be buried beneath this avalanche of lifelessness. She would never have to witness another murder again.

"There is one more prisoner still to be tried, My Queen." Aimery's voice echoed in the cold hollowness of Winter's head. "Sir Jacin Clay, royal guard, pilot, and assigned protector of Thaumaturge Sybil Mira."

Winter gasped and the ice shattered, a million sharp glittering bits exploding across the throne room and skidding across the floor. No one else heard them. No one else noticed.

Aimery, head very much attached, was watching her again, as if he'd been waiting to see her reaction. His smirk was subtle as he returned his attention to the queen.

"Ah, yes," said Levana. "Bring him in."

Two

THE DOORS TO THE THRONE ROOM OPENED, AND THERE HE was, trapped between two guards, his wrists corded behind his back. His blond hair was clumped and matted, strands of it clinging to his jaw. It appeared to have been a fair while since he'd last showered, but Winter could detect no obvious signs of abuse.

Her stomach flipped. All the warmth the ice had sucked out of her came rushing back to the surface of her skin.

Stay with me, Princess. Listen to my voice, Princess.

He was led to the center of the room, devoid of expression. Winter jabbed her fingernails into her palms.

Jacin didn't look at her. Not once.

"Jacin Clay," said Aimery, "you have been charged with betraying the crown by failing to protect Thaumaturge Mira and by failing to apprehend a known Lunar fugitive despite nearly two weeks spent in said fugitive's company. You are a traitor to Luna and to our queen. These crimes are punishable by death. What have you to say in your defense?"

Winter's heart thundered like a drum against her ribs. She

turned pleading eyes up to her stepmother, but Levana was not paying her any attention.

"I plead guilty to all stated crimes," said Jacin, drawing Winter's attention back, "*except* for the accusation that I am a traitor."

Levana's fingernails fluttered against the arm of her throne. "Explain."

Jacin stood as tall and stalwart as if he were in uniform, as if he were on duty, not on trial. "As I've said before, I did not apprehend the fugitive while in her company because I was attempting to convince her I could be trusted, in order to gather information for my queen."

"Ah, yes, you were spying on her and her companions," said Levana. "I do recall that excuse from when you were captured. I also recall that you had no pertinent information to give me, only lies."

"Not lies, My Queen, though I will admit I underestimated the cyborg and her abilities. She was disguising them from me."

"So much for earning her trust." There was mocking in the queen's tone.

"Knowledge of the cyborg's skills was not the only information I sought, My Queen."

"I suggest you stop playing with words. My patience with you is already thin."

Winter's heart shriveled. Not Jacin. She could not sit here and watch them kill Jacin.

She would bargain for him, she decided, though the plan came with a flaw. What did she have to bargain with? Nothing but her own life, and Levana would not accept that.

She could throw a fit. Go into hysterics. It would hardly be a stretch from the truth at this point, and it might distract them for a time, but it would only delay the inevitable.

She had felt helpless many times in her life, but never like this.

Only one thing to be done, then. She would throw her own body in front of the blade.

Oh, Jacin would *hate* that.

Ignorant of Winter's newest resolve, Jacin respectfully inclined his head. "During my time with Linh Cinder, I uncovered information about a device that can nullify the effects of the Lunar gift when connected to a person's nervous system."

This caused a curious squirm through the crowd. A stiffening of spines, a tilting forward of shoulders.

"Impossible," said Levana.

"Linh Cinder had evidence of its potential. As it was described to me, on an Earthen, the device will keep their bioelectricity from being tampered with. But on a Lunar, it will prevent them from using their gift at all. Linh Cinder herself had the device installed when she arrived at the Commonwealth ball. Only when it was destroyed was she able to use her gift—as was evidenced with your own eyes, My Queen."

His words carried an air of impertinence. Levana's knuckles turned white.

"How many of these hypothetical devices exist?"

"To my knowledge, only the broken device installed in the cyborg herself. But I suspect there still exist patents or blueprints. The inventor was Linh Cinder's adoptive father."

The queen's grip began to relax. "This is intriguing information, Sir Clay. But it speaks more of a desperate attempt to save yourself than true innocence."

Jacin shrugged, nonchalant. "If my loyalty cannot be seen in how I conducted myself with the enemy, obtaining this information and alerting Thaumaturge Mira to the plot to kidnap Emperor Kaito, I don't know what other evidence I can provide for you, My Queen."

"Yes, yes, the anonymous tip Sybil received, alerting her to Linh Cinder's plans." Levana sighed. "I find it very convenient that this comm you *claim* to have sent was seen by no one other than Sybil herself, who is now dead."

For the first time, Jacin looked off balance beneath the queen's glare. He still had not looked at Winter.

The queen turned to Jerrico Solis, her captain of the guard. Like so many of the queen's guards, Jerrico made Winter uncomfortable, and she often had visions of his orange-red hair going up in flames and the rest of him burning down to a smoldering coal. "You were with Sybil when she ambushed the enemy's ship that day, yet you said before that Sybil had mentioned no such comm. Have you anything to add?"

Jerrico took a step forward. He had returned from their Earthen excursion with a fair share of bruises, but they had begun to fade. "My Queen, Thaumaturge Mira seemed confident we would find Linh Cinder on that rooftop, but she did not mention receiving any outside information—anonymous or otherwise. When the ship landed, it was Thaumaturge Mira who ordered Jacin Clay to be taken into custody."

Jacin's eyebrow twitched. "Perhaps she was still upset that I shot her." He paused, before adding, "While under Linh Cinder's control, in my defense."

"You seem to have plenty to say in your defense," said Levana.

Jacin didn't respond. It was the calmest Winter had ever seen a prisoner—he, who knew better than anyone the horrible things that happened on this floor, in the very spot where he stood. Levana should have been infuriated by his audacity, but she seemed merely thoughtful.

"Permission to speak, My Queen?"

The crowd rustled and it took a moment for Winter to discern who had spoken. It was a *guard*. One of the silent ornamentations of the palace. Though she recognized him, she didn't know his name.

Levana glowered at him, and Winter imagined her calculating whether to grant the permission or punish the man for speaking out of turn. Finally, she said, "What is your name, and why do you dare interrupt these proceedings?"

The guard stepped forward, staring at the wall, always at the wall. "My name is Liam Kinney, My Queen. I assisted with the retrieval of Thaumaturge Mira's body."

A questioning eyebrow to Jerrico; a confirming nod received. "Go on," said Levana.

"Mistress Mira was in possession of a portscreen when we found her, and though it was broken in the fall, it was still submitted as evidence in the case of her murder. I wonder if anyone has attempted to retrieve the alleged comm."

Levana turned her attention back to Aimery, whose face was a mask that Winter recognized. The more pleasant his expression, the more annoyed he was. "In fact, we did manage to access her recent communications. I was about to bring forward the evidence."

It was a lie, which gave Winter hope. Aimery was a great liar, especially when it was in his best interests. And he hated Jacin. He would not want to give up anything that could help him.

Hope. Frail, flimsy, pathetic *hope*.

Aimery gestured toward the door and a servant scurried

forward, carrying a shattered portscreen and a holograph node on a tray. "This is the portscreen Sir Kinney mentioned. Our investigation has confirmed that there was, indeed, an anonymous comm sent to Sybil Mira that day."

The servant turned on the node and a holograph shimmered into the center of the room—behind it, Jacin faded away like a phantom.

The holograph displayed a basic text comm.

Linh Cinder plotting to kidnap EC emperor.
Escape planned from north tower rooftop, sunset.

So much importance pressed into so few words. It was just like Jacin.

Levana read the words with narrowed eyes. "Thank you, Sir Kinney, for bringing this to our attention." It was telling that she did not thank Aimery.

The guard, Kinney, bowed and stepped back into position. His gaze flickered once to Winter, unreadable, before attaching again to the far wall.

Levana continued, "I suppose you will tell me, Sir Clay, that this was the comm you sent."

"It was."

"Have you anything else to add before I make my verdict?"

"Nothing, My Queen."

Levana leaned back in her throne and the room hushed, everyone awaiting the queen's decision.

"I trust my stepdaughter would like me to spare you."

Jacin didn't react, but Winter winced at the haughtiness in her stepmother's tone. "Please, Stepmother," she whispered, the words clumping on her dry tongue. "It's *Jacin*. He is not our enemy."

"Not *yours*, perhaps," Levana said. "But you are a naïve, stupid girl."

"That is not so. I am a factory for blood and platelets, and all my machinery is freezing over ..."

The court burst into laughter, and Winter recoiled. Even Levana's lips twitched, though there was annoyance beneath her amusement.

"I have made my decision," she said, her booming voice demanding silence. "I have decided to let the prisoner live."

Winter released a cry of relief. She clapped a hand over her mouth, but it was too late to stifle the noise.

There were more giggles from the audience.

"Have you any other insights to add, Princess?" Levana said through her teeth.

Winter gathered her emotions as well as she could. "No, My Queen. Your rulings are always wise and final, My Queen."

"This ruling is not finished." The queen's voice hardened as she addressed Jacin again. "Your inability to kill or capture Linh Cinder will not go unpunished, as your incompetence led to her successful kidnapping of my betrothed. For this crime, I sentence you to thirty self-inflicted lashings to be held on the central dais, followed by forty hours of penance. Your sentence shall commence at tomorrow's light-break."

Winter flinched, but even this punishment could not destroy the fluttery relief in her stomach. He was not going to die. She was not a girl of ice and glass at all, but a girl of sunshine and stardust, because Jacin wasn't going to die.

"And, Winter ..."

She jerked her attention back to her stepmother, who was eyeing her with disdain. "If you attempt to bring him food, I will have his tongue removed in payment for your kindness."

She shrank back into her chair, a tiny ray of her sunshine extinguished. "Yes, My Queen."

Three

WINTER WAS AWAKE HOURS BEFORE LIGHT BRIGHTENED THE
dome's artificial sky, having hardly slept. She did not go to
watch Jacin receive his lashings, knowing that if he saw her, he
would have kept himself from screaming in pain. She wouldn't
do that to him. Let him scream. He was still stronger than any
of them.

She dutifully nibbled at the cured meats and cheeses brought
for her breakfast. She allowed the servants to bathe her and
dress her in pale pink silk. She sat through an entire session
with Master Gertman, a third-tier thaumaturge and her long-
standing tutor, pretending to try to use her gift and apologizing
when it was too hard, when she was too weak. He did not seem
to mind. Anyway, he spent most of their sessions gazing slack-
jawed at her face, and Winter didn't know if he would be able to
tell if she really did glamour him for once.

The artificial day had come and gone; one of the maidser-
vants had brought her a mug of warmed milk and cinnamon and
turned down her bed, and finally Winter was left alone.

Her heart pounded with anticipation.

She slipped into a pair of lightweight linen pants and a loose top, then pulled on her night robe so it would look like she was wearing her bedclothes underneath. She had thought of this all day, the plan taking form in her mind, like tiny puzzle pieces snapping together. Willful determination had stifled any hallucinations.

She fluffed her hair to look as if she'd woken from a deep slumber, turned off the lights, and climbed up onto her bed. The dangling chandelier clipped her brow and she flinched, stepping back and catching her balance on the thick mattress.

Winter braced herself with a breath full of intentions.

Counted to three.

And screamed.

She screamed like an assassin was driving a knife into her stomach.

She screamed like a thousand birds were pecking at her flesh.

She screamed like the palace was burning down around her.

The guard stationed outside her door burst inside, weapon drawn. Winter went on screaming. Stumbling back over her pillows, she pressed her back against the headboard and clawed at her hair.

"Princess! What is it? What's wrong?" His eyes darted around the dark room, searching for an intruder, a threat.

Flailing an arm behind her, Winter scratched at the wallpaper, tearing off a shred. It was becoming easier to believe she was horrified. There were phantoms and murderers closing in around her.

"Princess!" A second guard burst into the room. He flipped on the light and Winter ducked away from it. "What's going on?"

"I don't know." The first guard had crossed to the other side of the room and was checking behind the window drapes.

"Monster!" Winter shrieked, bulleting the statement with a sob. "I woke up and he was standing over my bed—one of—one of the queen's soldiers!"

The guards traded looks and the silent message was clear, even to Winter.

Nothing's wrong. She's just crazy.

"Your Highness—" started the second guard, as a third appeared at the doorway.

Good. There were only three guards regularly stationed in this corridor between her bedroom and the main stairway.

"He went that way!" Cowering behind one arm, Winter pointed toward her dressing closet. "Please. Please don't let him get away. Please find him!"

"What's happened?" asked the newcomer.

"She thinks she saw one of the mutant soldiers," grumbled the second guard.

"He was here," she screamed, the words tearing at her throat. "Why aren't you protecting me? Why are you standing there? *Go find him!*"

The first guard looked annoyed, as if this charade had interrupted something more than standing in the hallway and staring at a wall. He holstered his gun, but said, with authority, "Of course, Princess. We will find this perpetrator and ensure your safety." He beckoned the second guard and the two of them stalked off toward the closet.

Winter turned to the third guard and fell into a crouch. "You must go with them," she urged, her voice fluttery and weak. "He is a monster—enormous—with ferocious teeth and claws that will tear them to *shreds.* They can't defeat him alone, and if they fail—!" Her words turned into a wail of terror. "He'll come for me, and there will be no one to stop him. No one will save me!" She pulled at her hair, her entire body quivering.

"All right, all right. Of course, Highness. Just wait here, and . . . try to calm yourself." Looking grateful to leave the mad princess behind, he took off after his comrades.

No sooner had he disappeared did Winter slip off the bed and shrug out of her robe, leaving it draped over a chair.

"The closet is clear!" one of the guards yelled.

"Keep looking!" she yelled back. "I know he's in there!"

Snatching up the simple hat and shoes she'd left by the door, she fled.

Unlike her personal guards, who would have questioned her endlessly and insisted on escorting her into the city, the guards who were manning the towers outside the palace hardly stirred when she asked for the gate to be opened. Without guards and fine dresses, and with her bushel of hair tucked up and her face tucked down, she could pass for a servant in the shadows.

As soon as she was outside the gate, she started to run.

There were aristocrats milling around the tiled city streets, laughing and flirting in their fine clothes and glamours. Light spilled from open doorways, music danced along the window ledges, and everywhere was the smell of food and the clink of glasses and shadows kissing and sighing in darkened alleyways.

It was like this always in the city. The frivolity, the pleasure. The white city of Artemisia—their own little paradise beneath the protective glass.

At the center of it all was the dais, a circular platform where dramas were performed and auctions held, where spectacles of illusion and bawdy humor often drew the families from their mansions for a night of revelry.

Public humiliations and punishments were frequently on the docket.

Winter was panting, both frazzled and giddy with her success, as the dais came into view. She spotted him and the yearning inside her weakened her knees. She had to slow to catch her breath.

He was sitting with his back to the enormous sundial at the center of the dais, an instrument as useless as it was striking during these long nights. Ropes bound his bare arms and his chin was collapsed against his collarbone, pale hair hiding his face. As Winter neared him, she could see the raised hash marks of the lashings across his chest and abdomen, scattered with dried blood. There would be more on his back. His hand would be blistered from gripping the lash. *Self-inflicted*, Levana had proclaimed the punishment, but everyone knew Jacin would be under the control of a thaumaturge. There was nothing *self-inflicted* about it.

Aimery, she heard, had volunteered for the task. He had probably relished every wound.

Jacin raised his head as she reached the edge of the dais. Their eyes clashed, and she was staring at a man who had been beaten and bound and mocked and tormented all day and for a moment she was sure he was broken. Another one of the queen's broken toys.

But then one side of his mouth lifted, and the smile hit his startling blue eyes, and he was as bright and welcoming as the rising sun.

"Hey, Trouble," he said, leaning his head back against the dial.

With that, the terror from the past weeks slipped away. He was alive. He was home. He was still Jacin.

She pulled herself onto the dais. "Do you have any idea how

worried I've been?" she said, crossing to him. "I didn't know if you were dead or being held hostage, or if you'd been eaten by one of the queen's soldiers. It's been driving me mad not knowing."

He quirked an eyebrow at her.

She scowled. "Don't comment on that."

"I wouldn't dare." He rolled his shoulders as much as he could against his bindings. His wounds gapped and puckered with the movement and his face contorted in pain, but it was brief.

Pretending she hadn't noticed, Winter sat cross-legged in front of him, inspecting the wounds. Wanting to touch him. Terrified to touch him. That much, at least, had not changed. "Does it hurt very much?"

"Better than being at the bottom of the lake." His smile turned wry, lips chapped. "They'll move me to a suspension tank tomorrow night. Half a day and I'll be good as new." He squinted. "That's assuming you're not here to bring me food. I'd like to keep my tongue where it is, thank you."

"No food. Just a friendly face."

"Friendly." His gaze raked over her, his relaxed grin still in place. "That's an understatement."

She dipped her head, turning away to hide the three scars on her right cheek. For years, Winter had assumed that when people stared at her, it was because the scars disgusted them. A rare disfigurement in their world of perfection. But then a maid told her they weren't disgusted, they were in awe. She said the scars made Winter interesting to look at and somehow, odd as it was, even more beautiful. *Beautiful.* It was a word Winter had heard tossed around all her life. A beautiful child, a beautiful girl, a beautiful young lady, so beautiful, *too* beautiful . . . and the stares that attended the word never ceased to make her want to don a veil like her stepmother's and hide from the whispers.

Jacin was the one person who could make her feel beautiful without it seeming like a bad thing. She couldn't recall him ever using the word, or giving her any compliments, for that matter. They were always hidden behind careless jokes that made her heart pound.

"Don't tease," she said, flustered at the way he looked at her, at the way he always looked at her.

"Wasn't teasing," he said, all nonchalance.

In response, Winter reached out and punched him on the shoulder.

He flinched, and she gasped, remembering his wounds. But Jacin's chuckle was warm. "That's not a fair fight, Princess."

She reeled back the budding apology. "It's about time I had the advantage."

He glanced past her, into the streets. "Where's your guard?"

"I left him behind. Searching for a monster in my closet."

The sunshine smile hardened into exasperation. "Princess, you can't go out alone. If something happened to you—"

"Who's going to hurt me here, in the city? Everyone knows who I am."

"It just takes one idiot, too used to getting what he wants and too drunk to control himself."

She flushed and clenched her jaw.

Jacin frowned, immediately regretful. "Princess—"

"I'll run all the way back to the palace. I'll be fine."

He sighed, and she listed her head, wishing she'd brought some sort of medicinal salve for his cuts. Levana hadn't said anything about medicine, and the sight of him tied up and vulnerable—and shirtless, even if it was a bloodied shirtless— was making her fingers twitch in odd ways.

"I wanted to be alone with you," she said, focusing on his face. "We never get to be alone anymore."

"It's not proper for seventeen-year-old princesses to be alone with young men who have questionable intentions."

She laughed. "And what about young men who she's been best friends with since before she could walk?"

He shook his head. "Those are the worst."

She snorted—an actual snort of laughter that served to brighten Jacin's face again.

But the humor was bittersweet. The truth was, Jacin touched her only when he was helping her through a hallucination. Otherwise, he hadn't deliberately touched her in years. Not since she was fourteen and he was sixteen, and she'd tried to teach him the Eclipse Waltz with somewhat embarrassing results.

These days, she would have auctioned off the Milky Way to make his intentions a little less honorable.

Her smile started to fizzle. "I've missed you," she said.

His gaze dropped away and he shifted in an attempt to get more comfortable against the dial. Locking his jaw so she wouldn't see how much every tiny movement pained him. "How's your head?" he asked.

"The visions come and go," she said, "but they don't seem to be getting worse."

"Have you had one today?"

She picked at a small, natural flaw in the linen of her pants, thinking back. "No, not since the trials yesterday. I turned into a girl of icicles, and Aimery lost his head. Literally."

"Wouldn't mind if that last one came true."

She shushed him.

"I mean it. I don't like how he looks at you."

Winter glanced over her shoulder, but the courtyards surrounding the dais were empty. Only the distant bustle of music and laughter reminded her they were in a metropolis at all.

"You're back on Luna now," she said. "You have to be careful what you say."

"You're giving *me* advice on how to be covert?"

"Jacin—"

"There are three cameras on this square. Two on the lampposts behind you, one embedded in the oak tree behind the sundial. None of them have audio. Unless she's hiring lip-readers now?"

Winter glared. "How can you know for sure?"

"Surveillance was one of Sybil's specialties."

"Nevertheless, the queen could have killed you yesterday. You need to be careful."

"I know, Princess. I have no interest in returning to that throne room as anything other than a loyal guard."

A rumble overhead caught Winter's attention. Through the dome, the lights of a dozen spaceships were fading as they streaked across the star-scattered sky. Heading toward Earth.

"Soldiers," Jacin muttered. She couldn't tell if he meant it as a statement or a question. "How's the war effort?"

"No one tells me anything. But Her Majesty seems pleased with our victories . . . though still furious about the missing emperor, and the canceled wedding."

"Not canceled. Just delayed."

"Try telling her that."

He grunted.

Winter leaned forward on her elbows, cupping her chin. "Did the cyborg really have a device like you said? One that can keep people from being manipulated?"

A light sparked in his eyes, as if she'd reminded him of something important, but when he tried to lean toward her, his binds held him back. He grimaced and cursed beneath his breath.

Winter scooted closer to him, making up the distance herself.

"That's not all," he said. "Supposedly, this device can keep Lunars from using their gift in the first place."

"Yes, you mentioned that in the throne room."

His gaze burrowed into her. "*And* it will protect their minds. She said it keeps them from . . ."

Going crazy.

He didn't have to say it out loud, not when his face held so much hope, like he'd solved the world's greatest problem. His meaning hung between them.

Such a device could heal her.

Winter's fingers curled up and settled under her chin. "You said there weren't any more of them."

"No. But if we could find the patents for the invention . . . to even know it's possible . . ."

"The queen will do anything to keep more from being made."

His expression darkened. "I know, but I had to offer something. If only Sybil hadn't arrested me in the first place, ungrateful witch." Winter smiled, and when Jacin caught the look, his irritation melted away. "Doesn't matter. Now that I know it's possible, I'll find a way to do it."

"The visions are never so bad when you're around. They'll be better now that you're back."

His jaw tensed. "I'm sorry I left. I regretted it as soon as I realized what I'd done. It happened so fast, and then I couldn't come back for you. I'd just . . . abandoned you up here. With her. With *them.*"

"You didn't abandon me. You were taken hostage. You didn't have a choice."

He looked away.

She straightened. "You weren't manipulated?"

"Not the whole time," he whispered, like a confession. "I chose to side with them, when Sybil and I boarded their ship." Guilt washed over his face, and it was such an odd expression on him Winter wasn't sure she was interpreting it right. "Then I betrayed them." He thumped his head against the sundial, harder than necessary. "I'm such an idiot. You should hate me."

"You may be an idiot, but I assure you, you're quite a lovable one."

He shook his head. "You're the only person in the galaxy who would ever call me *lovable*."

"I'm the only person in the galaxy crazy enough to believe it. Now tell me what you've done that is worth hating you for."

He swallowed, hard. "That cyborg Her Majesty is searching for?"

"Linh Cinder."

"Yeah. Well, I thought she was just some crazy girl on a suicide mission, right? I figured she was going to get us all killed with these delusions of kidnapping the emperor and overthrowing the queen . . . to listen to her talk, anyone would have thought that. So I figured, I'd rather take a chance and come back to you, if I could. Let her throw her own life away."

"But Linh Cinder did kidnap the emperor. And she got away."

"I know." He shifted his attention back to Winter. "Sybil took one of her friends hostage, some girl named Scarlet. Don't suppose you know—"

Winter beamed. "Oh, yes. The queen gave her to me as a pet, and she's being kept in the menagerie. I like her a great deal."

Her brow creased. "Although I can't tell if she's decided to like me or not."

He flinched at a sudden unknown pain and spent a moment re-situating himself. "Can you get her a message for me?"

"Of course."

"You have to be careful. I won't tell you if you can't be discreet—for your own sake."

"I can be discreet."

Jacin looked skeptical.

"I *can*. I will be as secretive as a spy. As secretive as *you*." Winter scooted a bit closer.

His voice fell, as if he were no longer certain those cameras didn't come with audio. "Tell her they're coming for her."

Winter stared. "Coming for ... coming here?"

He nodded, a subtle dip of his head. "And I think they might actually have a chance."

Frowning, Winter reached forward and tucked the strands of Jacin's sweat- and dirt-stained hair behind his ears. He tensed at the touch, but didn't pull away. "Jacin Clay, you're speaking in riddles."

"Linh Cinder." His voice became hardly more than a breath and she tilted closer yet to hear him. A curl of her hair fell against his shoulder. He licked his lips. "She's Selene."

Every muscle in her body tightened. She pulled back. "If Her Majesty heard you say—"

"I won't tell anyone else. But I had to tell you." His eyes crinkled at the corners, full of sympathy. "I know you loved her."

Her heart thumped. "My Selene?"

"Yes. But ... I'm sorry, Princess. I don't think she remembers you."

Winter blinked, letting the daydream fill her up for one hazy moment. Selene, alive. Her cousin, her friend? *Alive.*

She scrunched her shoulders against her neck, casting the hope away. "No. She's dead. I was *there*, Jacin. I saw the aftermath of the fire."

"You didn't see *her.*"

"They found—"

"Charred flesh. I know."

"A pile of girl-shaped ashes."

"They were just ashes. Look, I didn't believe it either, but I do now." One corner of his mouth tilted up, into something like pride. "She's our lost princess. And she's coming home."

A throat cleared behind Winter and her skeleton nearly leaped from her skin. She swiveled her torso around, falling onto her elbow.

Her personal guard was standing beside the dais, scowling.

"Ah!" Heart fluttering with a thousand startled birds, Winter broke into a relieved smile. "Did you catch the monster?"

There was no return smile, not even a flush of his cheeks, which was the normal reaction when she let loose that particular look. Instead, his right eyebrow began to twitch.

"Your Highness. I have come to retrieve you and escort you back to the palace."

Righting herself, Winter clasped her hands in front of her chest. "Of course. It's so kind of you to worry after me." She glanced back at Jacin, who was eyeing the guard with distrust. No surprise. He eyed everyone with distrust. "I fear tomorrow will be even more difficult for you, Sir Clay. Do try to think of me when you can."

"*Try*, Princess?" He smirked up at her. "I can't seem to think of much else."

Four

CINDER LAY ON THE GROUND, STARING UP AT THE RAMPION'S vast engine, its ductwork, and revolving life-support module. The system blueprints she'd downloaded weeks ago were overlaid across her vision—a cyborg trick that had come in handy countless times when she was a working mechanic in New Beijing. She expanded the blueprint, zooming in on a cylinder the length of her arm. It was tucked near the engine room's wall. Coils of tubing sprouted from both sides.

"That has to be the problem," she muttered, dismissing the blueprint. She shimmied beneath the revolving module, dust bunnies gathering around her shoulders, and eased herself back to sitting. There was just enough space for her to squeeze in between the labyrinth of wires and coils, pipes and tubes.

Holding her breath, she pressed her ear against the cylinder. The metal was ice cold against her skin.

She waited. Listened. Adjusted the volume on her audio sensors.

What she heard was the door to the engine room opening.

Glancing back, she spotted the gray pants of a military

uniform in the yellowish light from the corridor. That could have been anyone on the ship, but the shiny black dress shoes . . .

"Hello?" said Kai.

Her heart thumped—every single time, her heart thumped.

"Back here."

Kai shut the door and crouched down on the far side of the room, framed between the jumble of thumping pistons and spinning fans. "What are you doing?"

"Checking the oxygen filters. One minute."

She placed her ear against the cylinder again. There—a faint clatter, like a pebble banging around inside. "*Aha.*"

She dug a wrench from her pocket and set to loosening the nuts on either side of the cylinder. As soon as it was free, the ship fell eerily quiet, like a humming that became noticeable only after it stopped. Kai's eyebrows shot upward.

Cinder peered into the cylinder's depths, before sticking her fingers in and pulling out a complicated filter. It was made of tiny channels and crevices, all lined with a thin gray film.

"No wonder the takeoffs have been rocky."

"I don't suppose you could use some help?"

"Nope. Unless you want to find me a broom."

"A broom?"

Raising the filter, Cinder banged the end of it on one of the overhead pipes. A dust cloud exploded around her, covering her hair and arms. Coughing, Cinder buried her nose in the crook of her elbow and kept banging until the biggest chunks had been dislodged.

"Ah. A broom. Right. There might be one up in the kitchen? . . . I mean, the galley."

Blinking the dust from her eyelashes, Cinder grinned at him. He was usually so self-assured that in the rare moments when he was flustered, it made all of her insides swap wrong side up. And he was flustered a lot lately. Since the moment he'd woken up aboard the Rampion, it was clear that Kai was twelve thousand kilometers outside of his element, yet he adapted well in the past weeks. He learned the terminology, he ate the canned and freeze-dried meals without complaint, he traded his fancy wedding clothes for the standard military uniform they all wore. He insisted on helping out where he could, even cooking a few of those bland meals, despite how Iko pointed out that—as he was their royal guest—*they* should be waiting on *him*. Thorne laughed, though, and the suggestion seemed to make Kai even more uncomfortable.

While Cinder couldn't imagine him abdicating his throne and setting off on a lifetime of space travel and adventure, it was rather adorable watching him try to fit in.

"I was kidding," she said. "Engine rooms are supposed to be dirty." She examined the filter again and, deeming it satisfactory, twisted it back into the cylinder and bolted it all in place. The humming started up again, but the pebble clatter was gone.

Cinder squirmed feetfirst out from beneath the module and ductwork. Still crouching, Kai peered down at her and smirked. "Iko's right. You really can't stay clean for more than five minutes."

"It's part of the job description." She sat up, sending a cascade of lint off her shoulders.

Kai brushed some of the larger chunks from her hair. "Where did you learn to do all this, anyway?"

"What, *that*? Anyone can clean an oxygen filter."

"Trust me, they can't." He settled his elbows on his knees and let his attention wander around the engine room. "You know what all this does?"

She followed the look—every wire, every manifold, every compression coil—and shrugged. "Pretty much. Except for that big, rotating thing in the corner. Can't figure it out. But how important could it be?"

Kai rolled his eyes.

Grasping a pipe, Cinder hauled herself to her feet and shoved the wrench back into her pocket. "I didn't learn it anywhere. I just look at things and figure out how they work. Once you know how something works, you can figure out how to fix it."

She tried to shake the last bits of dust from her hair, but there seemed to be an endless supply.

"Oh, you just *look* at something and figure out how it works," Kai deadpanned, standing beside her. "Is that all?"

Cinder fixed her ponytail and shrugged, suddenly embarrassed. "It's just mechanics."

Kai scooped an arm around her waist and pulled her against him. "No, it's impressive," he said, using the pad of his thumb to brush something off Cinder's cheek. "Not to mention, weirdly attractive," he said, before capturing her lips.

Cinder tensed briefly, before melting into the kiss. The rush was the same every time, coupled with surprise and a wave of giddiness. It was their seventeenth kiss (her brain interface was keeping a tally, somewhat against her will), and she wondered if she would ever get used to this feeling. Being *desired*, when she'd spent her life believing no one would ever see her as anything but a bizarre science experiment.

Especially not a boy.

Especially not *Kai*, who was smart and honorable and kind, and could have had any girl he wanted. *Any* girl.

She sighed against him, leaning into the embrace. Kai reached for an overhead pipe and pressed Cinder against the main computer console. She offered no resistance. Though her body wouldn't allow her to blush, there was an unfamiliar heat that flooded every inch of her when he was this close. Every nerve ending sparked and thrummed, and she knew he could kiss her another seventeen thousand times and she would never grow tired of it.

She tied her arms around his neck, molding their bodies together. The warmth of his chest seeped into her clothes. It felt nothing but right. Nothing but perfect.

But then there was the feeling, always lurking, always ready to cloud her contentment. The knowledge that this couldn't last.

Not so long as Kai was engaged to Levana.

Angry at the thought's invasion, she kissed Kai harder, but her thoughts continued to rebel. Even if they succeeded and Cinder was able to reclaim her throne, she would be expected to stay on Luna as their new queen. She was no expert, but it seemed problematic to carry on a relationship on two different planets—

Er, a planet and a moon.

Or whatever.

The point was, there would be 384,000 kilometers of space between her and Kai, which was a *lot* of space, and—

Kai smiled, breaking the kiss. "What's wrong?" he murmured against her mouth.

Cinder leaned back to look at him. His hair was getting longer, bordering on unkempt. As a prince, he'd always been groomed to near perfection. But then he became an emperor. The weeks since his coronation had been spent trying to stop a war, hunt down a wanted fugitive, avoid getting married, and endure his own kidnapping. As a result, haircuts became a dispensable luxury.

She hesitated before asking, "Do you ever think about the future?"

His expression turned wary. "Of course I do."

"And . . . does it include me?"

His gaze softened. Releasing the overhead pipe, he tucked a strand of hair behind her ear. "That depends on whether I'm thinking about the good future or the bad one."

Cinder tucked her head under his chin. "As long as one of them does."

"This is going to work," Kai said, speaking into her hair. "We're going to win."

She nodded, glad he couldn't see her face.

Defeating Levana and becoming Luna's queen was only the beginning of an entire galaxy's worth of worries. She so badly wanted to stay like this, cocooned in this spaceship, together and safe and alone . . . but that was the opposite of what was going to happen. Once they overthrew Levana, Kai would go back to being the emperor of the Eastern Commonwealth and, someday, he was going to need an empress.

She might have a blood claim to Luna and the hope that the Lunar people would choose *anyone* over Levana, even a politically inept teenager who was made up of 36.28 percent cybernetic and manufactured materials. But she had seen the prejudices of the people in the Commonwealth. Something told her they wouldn't be as accepting of her as a ruler.

She wasn't even sure she wanted to be empress. She was still getting used to the idea of being a princess.

"One thing at a time," she whispered, trying to still her swirling thoughts.

Kai kissed her temple (which her brain did not count as #18), then pulled away. "How's your training going?"

"Fine." She disentangled herself from his arms and glanced around the engine. "Oh, hey, while you're here, can you help me with this?" Cinder scooted around him and opened a panel on the wall, revealing a bundle of knotted wires.

"*That* was a subtle change of subject."

"I am not changing the subject," she said, although a forced clearing of her throat negated her denial. "I'm rewiring the orbital defaults so the ship's systems will run more efficiently while we're coasting. These cargo ships are made for frequent landings and takeoffs, not the constant—"

"Cinder."

She pursed her lips and unplugged a few wire connectors. "Training is going *fine*," she repeated. "Could you hand me the wire cutters on the floor?"

Kai scanned the ground, then grabbed two tools and held them up.

"Left hand," she said. He handed them to her. "Sparring with Wolf has gotten a lot easier. Although it's hard to tell if that's because I'm getting stronger, or because he's ... you know."

She didn't have a word for it. Wolf had been a shadow of his former self since Scarlet had been captured. The only thing holding him together was his determination to get to Luna and rescue her as soon as possible.

"Either way," she added, "I think he's taught me as much about using my Lunar gift as he's going to be able to. From here on, I'll have to wing it." She examined the mess of wires, aligning it with a diagram over her retina display. "Not like that hasn't been my primary tactic this whole time." She furrowed her brow and made a few snips. "Here, hold these wires and don't let them touch."

Edging against her, Kai took hold of the wires she indicated. "What happens if they touch?"

"Oh, probably nothing, but there's a small chance the ship would self-destruct." Pulling out two of the fresh-cut wires, she began to twist them together into a new sequence.

Kai hardly breathed until she'd taken one of the threatening wires out of his grip. "Why don't you practice on me?" he said.

"Practice what?"

"You know. Your mind-manipulation thing."

She paused with the cutters hovering over a blue wire. "Absolutely not."

"Why?"

"I said I'd never manipulate you, and I'm sticking with that."

"It isn't manipulation if I know you're doing it." He hesitated. "At least, I don't think so. We could use a code word, so I'll know when you're controlling me. Like . . . what were those called again?"

"Wire cutters?"

"Like *wire cutters*."

"No."

"Or something else."

"I'm not practicing on you." Slipping the cutters into her pocket, she finished splicing the rest of the wires and relieved Kai of his duty. "There, we'll see how that goes."

"Cinder, I have nothing better to do. Literally, *nothing* better to do. My time on this ship has taught me that I have zero practical skills. I can't cook. I can't fix anything. I can't help Cress with surveillance. I know nothing about guns or fighting or . . . Mostly, I'm just a good talker, and that's only useful in politics."

"Let's not overlook your ability to make every girl swoon with just a smile."

It took Kai a moment to hear her over his frustration, but then his expression cleared and he grinned.

"Yep," she said, shutting the panel. "That's the one."

"I mean it, Cinder. I want to be useful. I want to help."

She turned back to face him. Frowned. Considered.

"*Wire cutters*," she said.

He tensed, a trace of doubt clouding his expression. But then he lifted his chin. Trusting.

With the slightest nudge at Kai's will, she urged his arm to reach around her and pull the wrench from her back pocket. It was no more difficult than controlling her own cyborg limbs. A mere thought, and she could have him do anything.

Kai blinked at the tool. "That's wasn't so bad."

"Oh, Kai."

He glanced at her, then back to the wrench as his hand lifted the tool up to eye level and his fingers, no longer under his control, began to twirl the wrench—over one finger, under the other. Slow at first, then faster, until the gleaming of the metal looked like a magic trick.

Kai gaped, awestruck, but there was an edge of discomfort to it. "I always wondered how you did that."

"Kai."

He looked back at her, the wrench still dancing over his knuckles.

She shrugged. "It's too easy. I could do this while scaling a mountain, or . . . solving complex mathematical equations."

His eyes narrowed. "You have a *calculator* in your head."

Laughing, she released her hold on Kai's hand. Kai jumped back as the wrench clattered to the ground. Realizing he had control of his own limb again, he stooped to pick it up.

"That's beside the point," said Cinder. "With Wolf, there's some challenge, some focus required, but with Earthens . . ."

"All right, I get it. But what *can* I do? I feel so useless, milling around this ship while the war is going on, and you're all making plans, and I'm just waiting."

She grimaced at the frustration in his tone. Kai was responsible for billions of people, and she knew he felt like he had abandoned them, even if he hadn't been given a choice. Because *she* hadn't given him a choice.

He was kind to her. Since that first argument after he'd woken up aboard the Rampion, he was careful not to blame her for his frustrations. It was her fault, though. He knew it and she knew it and sometimes it felt like they were caught in a dance Cinder didn't know the steps to. Each of them avoiding this obvious truth so they didn't disrupt the mutual ground they'd discovered. The all-too-uncertain happiness they'd discovered.

"The only chance we have of succeeding," she said, "is if you can persuade Levana to host the wedding on Luna. So right now, you can be thinking about how you're going to accomplish that." Leaning forward, she pressed a soft kiss against his mouth. (*Eighteen.*) "Good thing you're such a great talker."

Five

SCARLET PRESSED HER BODY AGAINST THE STEEL BARS, straining to grasp the tree branch that dangled just outside her cage. Close—*so close.* The bar bit into her cheek. She flailed her fingers, brushing a leaf, a touch of bark—*yes!*

Her fingers closed around the branch. She dropped back into her cage, dragging the branch closer. Wriggling her other arm through the bars, she snapped off three leaf-covered twigs, then broke off the tip and let go. The branch swung upward and a cluster of tiny, unfamiliar nuts dropped onto her head.

Scarlet flinched and waited until the tree had stopped shaking before she turned the hood of her red sweatshirt inside out and shook out the nuts that had attacked her. They sort of looked like hazelnuts. If she could figure out a way to crack into them, they might not be a bad snack later.

A gentle scratching pulled her attention back to the situation. She peered across the menagerie's pathway, to the white wolf who was standing on his hind legs and batting at the bars of his own enclosure.

Scarlet had spent a lot of time wishing Ryu could leap over

those bars. His enclosure's wall was waist high and he should have been able to clear it easily. Then Scarlet could pet his fur, scratch his ears. What a luxury it would be to have a bit of contact. She had always been fond of the animals on the farm—at least until it was time to slaughter them and cook up a nice *ragoût*—but she never realized how much she appreciated their simple affection until she had been reduced to an animal herself.

Unfortunately, Ryu wouldn't be escaping his confinement any sooner than Scarlet would. According to Princess Winter, he had a chip embedded between his shoulder blades that would give him a painful shock if he tried to jump over the rail. The poor creature had learned to accept his habitat a long time ago.

Scarlet doubted she would ever accept hers.

"This is it," she said, grabbing her hard-earned treasure: three small twigs and a splintered branch. She held them up for the wolf to see. He yipped and did an enthusiastic dance along the enclosure wall. "I can't reach any more. You have to take your time with these."

Ryu's ears twitched.

Rising to her knees—as close to standing as she could get inside her cage—Scarlet grabbed hold of an overhead bar, took aim with one of the smaller twigs, and threw.

Ryu chased after it and snatched the stick from the air. Within seconds, he pranced back to his pile of sticks and dropped the twig on top. Pleased, he sat back on his haunches, tongue lolling.

"Good job, Ryu. Nice show of restraint." Sighing, Scarlet picked up another stick.

Ryu had just taken off when she heard the padding of feet down the path. Scarlet sat back on her heels, instantly tense, but relieved when she spotted a flowing cream-colored gown between the stalks of exotic flowers and drooping vines. The princess rounded the path's corner a moment later, basket in hand.

"Hello, friends," said Princess Winter.

Ryu dropped his newest stick onto the pile, then sat down, chest high as though he were showing her proper respect.

Scarlet scowled. "Suck-up."

Winter tilted her head in Scarlet's direction. A spiral of black hair fell across her cheek, obstructing her scars.

"What did you bring me today?" Scarlet asked. "Delusional mutterings with a side of crazy? Or is this one of your good days?"

The princess grinned and sat down in front of Scarlet's cage, uncaring that the path of tumbled black rock and ground covers would soil her dress. "This is one of my best days," she said, settling the basket on her lap, "for I have brought you a treat, with a side of news."

"Oh, oh, don't tell me. They're moving me to a bigger cage? Oh, please tell me this one comes with real plumbing. And maybe one of those fancy self-feeders the birds get?"

Though Scarlet's words were laced with sarcasm, in truth, a larger cage with real plumbing would have been a vast improvement. Without being able to stand up, her muscles were becoming weaker by the day, and it would be heaven if she didn't have to rely on the guards to lead her into the next enclosure, twice a day, where she was graciously escorted to a trough to do her business.

A *trough*.

Winter, immune as ever to the bite in Scarlet's tone, leaned forward with a secretive smile. "Jacin has returned."

Scarlet's brow twitched, her emotions at this statement pulling in a dozen directions. She knew Winter had a schoolgirl's crush on this Jacin guy, but Scarlet's one interaction with him had been when he was working for a thaumaturge, attacking her and her friends.

She'd convinced herself that he was dead, because the alternative was that he killed Wolf and Cinder, and that was unacceptable.

"And?" she prodded.

Winter's eyes sparkled. There were times when Scarlet felt like she'd hardened her heart to the girl's impeccable beauty—her thick hair and warm brown skin, her gold-tinged eyes and rosy lips. But then the princess would give her a look like *that* and Scarlet's heart would skip and she would once again wonder how it was possible this wasn't a glamour.

Winter's voice turned to a conspiratorial whisper. "Your friends are alive."

The simple statement sent the world spinning. Scarlet spent a moment in limbo, distrusting, unwilling to hope. "Are you sure?"

"I'm sure. He said that even the captain and the satellite girl were all right."

Like a marionette released, she drooped over her knees. "Oh, thank the stars."

They were *alive*. After nearly a month of subsisting on dogged stubbornness, finally Scarlet had a reason to hope. It was so sudden, so unexpected, she felt dizzy with euphoria.

"He also said to tell you," Winter continued, "that Wolf misses you very much. Well, Jacin's words were that he drove everyone rocket-mad with his pathetic whining about you. That's sweet, don't you think?"

Something cracked inside Scarlet. She hadn't cried once since she'd come to Luna—aside from tears of pain and delirium when she was tortured, mentally and physically. But now all the fear and all the panic and all the horror welled up inside her and she couldn't hold it back, couldn't even think beyond the on-slaught of sobs and messy tears.

They were alive. They were all alive.

She knew Cinder was still out there—word had spread even to the menagerie that she had infiltrated New Beijing Palace and kidnapped the emperor. Scarlet had felt smug for days when the gossip reached her, even if she didn't have anything to do with the heist.

But no one mentioned accomplices. No one said anything about Wolf or Thorne or the satellite girl they'd been trying to rescue.

She swiped at her nose and pushed her greasy hair off her face. Winter was watching Scarlet's show of emotion like one might watch a butterfly shucking its cocoon.

"Thank you," said Scarlet, hiccuping back another sob. "Thank you for telling me."

"Of course. You're my friend."

Scarlet rubbed her palm across her eyes and, for the first time, didn't argue.

"And now for your treat."

"I'm not hungry." It was a lie, but she'd come to despise how much she relied on Winter's charity.

"But it's a sour apple petite. A Lunar delicacy that is—"

"One of your favorites, yeah, I know. But I'm not—"

"I think you should eat it." The princess's expression was in-nocent and meaningful all at once, in that peculiar way she had. "I think it will make you feel better," she continued, pushing a box through the bars. She waited until Scarlet had taken it from her, then stood and made her way across the path to Ryu. She crouched to give the wolf a loving scratch behind his ears, then leaned over the rail and started gathering up his pile of sticks.

Scarlet lifted the lid of the box, revealing the red marble-like candy in its bed of spun sugar. Winter had brought her many treats since her imprisonment, most of them laced with painkillers. Though the pain from Scarlet's finger, which had been chopped off during her interrogation with the queen, had faded to a distant memory, the candies still helped with the aches and pains of life in such cramped quarters.

But as she lifted the candy from the box, she saw something unexpected tucked beneath it. A handwritten message.

Patience, friend. They're coming for you.

She closed the box fast before the security camera over her shoulder could see it, and shoved the candy into her mouth, heart thundering. She shut her eyes, hardly feeling the crack of the candy shell, hardly tasting the sweet-and-sour gooeyness inside.

"What you said at the trial," said Winter, returning with a bundle of sticks in her arms and laying them down where Scarlet could reach them. "I hadn't understood then, but I do now."

Scarlet swallowed too quickly. The candy went down hard, bits of shell scratching her throat. She coughed, wishing the princess had brought some water too. "Which part? I was under a lot of duress, you might recall."

"The part about Linh Cinder."

Ah. The part about Cinder being the lost Princess Selene. The true queen of Luna.

"What about it?" she said, bristling with suspicion. Had Jacin said something about Cinder's plans to reclaim her throne? And whose side was he on, if he spent weeks with her friends but had now returned to Levana?

Winter considered the question for a long time. "What is she like?"

Scarlet dug her tongue into her molars, thinking. What was Cinder like? She hadn't known her for all that long. She was a brilliant mechanic. She seemed to be honorable and brave and determined to do what needed to be done . . . but Scarlet suspected she wasn't always as confident as she tried to appear on the outside.

Also, she had a crush on Emperor Kai as big as Winter had on Jacin, although Cinder tried a lot harder to pretend otherwise.

But Scarlet didn't think that answered Winter's question. "She's not like Levana, if that's what you're wondering."

Winter exhaled, as if a fear had been released.

Ryu whined and rolled onto his back, missing their attention.

Winter grabbed a stick from the pile and tossed. The wolf scrambled back to his feet and raced after it.

"Your wolf friend," Winter said. "Is he one of the queen's?"

"Not anymore," Scarlet spat. Wolf would never belong to the queen again. Not if she could help it.

"But he *was*, and now he has betrayed her." The princess's tone had gone dreamy, her eyes staring off into space even after Ryu returned and dropped the stick beside his bars, beginning a new pile. "From what I know of her soldiers, that should not be possible. At least, not while they are under the control of their thaumaturge."

Suddenly warm, Scarlet unzipped her hoodie. It was filthy with dirt and sweat and blood, but wearing it still made her feel connected to Earth and the farm and her grandmother. It reminded her that she was human, despite being kept in a cage.

"Wolf's thaumaturge is dead," she said, "but Wolf fought against him even when he was alive."

"Perhaps they made a mistake with him, when they altered his nervous system."

"It wasn't a mistake." Scarlet smirked. "I know, they think they're so clever, giving soldiers the instincts of wild wolves. The instincts to hunt and kill. But look at Ryu." The wolf had lain down and was gnawing at the stick. "His instincts lean as much toward playing and loving. If he had a mate and cubs, then his instincts would be to protect them at all costs." Scarlet twirled the cord of her hoodie around a finger. "That's what Wolf did. He protected me."

She grabbed another stick from the pile outside her cage. Ryu's attention was piqued, but Scarlet only ran her fingers over the peeling bark. "I'm afraid I'll never see him again."

Winter reached through the bars and stroked Scarlet's hair with her knuckles. Scarlet tensed, but didn't pull away. Contact, any contact, was a gift.

"Do not worry," said Winter. "The queen will not kill you so long as you are my pet. You will have a chance to tell your Wolf that you love him."

Scarlet glowered. "I'm not your pet, just like Wolf isn't Levana's anymore." This time, she did pull back, and Winter let her hand fall into her lap. "And it's not that I *love* him. It's just . . ."

She hesitated, and again Winter listed her head and peered at Scarlet with penetrating curiosity. It was unnerving, to think she was being psychoanalyzed by someone who frequently complained that the castle walls had started bleeding again.

"Wolf is all I have left," Scarlet clarified. She threw the stick halfheartedly across the path. It landed within paw's reach of

Ryu and he simply stared at it, like it wasn't worth the effort. Scarlet's shoulders slumped. "I need him as much as he needs me. But that doesn't make it love."

Winter lowered her lashes. "Actually, dear friend, I suspect that is *precisely* what makes it love."

Six

"THESE TWO NEWSFEEDS INCLUDE STATEMENTS FROM THAT waitress, Émilie Monfort," said Cress, trailing her fingers along the netscreen in the cargo bay, pulling up a picture of a blonde-haired girl speaking to a news crew. "She claims to be overseeing Benoit Farms and Gardens in Scarlet's absence. Here she makes a comment about the work getting to be a lot for her, and joked that if the Benoits don't return soon she might have to start auctioning off the chickens." Cress hesitated. "Or, maybe it wasn't a joke. I'm not sure. Oh, and here she talks about Thorne and Cinder coming to the farm and scaring her witless."

She glanced over her shoulder to see whether Wolf was still listening. His eyes were glued to the screen, his brow set, as silent and brooding as usual. When he said nothing, she cleared her throat and clicked to a new tab. "As far as the finances are concerned, Michelle Benoit did own the land outright, and these bank statements show that the property and business taxes continue to be automatically deducted. I'll set up payments to go through to the labor android rentals too. She missed last month's payment, but I'll make it up, and it looks like she's been a loyal customer long enough the missed payment didn't interrupt their work." She enlarged a grainy photo. "This satellite imagery is from thirty-six hours ago and shows the full team of androids and two human foremen working this crop." She shrugged and turned to face Wolf. "The bills are being paid, the animals are being tended, and the crops are being managed. Any accounts that were expecting regular deliveries are probably annoyed at Scarlet's absence, but that's the worst of it right now. I estimate it can go on being self-sustaining for . . . oh, another two to three months."

Wolf didn't take his forlorn stare from the satellite image. "She loves that farm."

"And it will be there waiting for her when we get her back." Cress sounded as optimistic as she could. She wanted to add that Scarlet was going to be fine, that every day they were getting closer to rescuing her—but she bit her tongue. The words had been tossed around so much lately they were beginning to lose their meaning, even to her.

The truth was that no one had any idea if Scarlet was still alive, or what shape they would find her in. Wolf knew that better than anyone.

"Is there anything else you want me to look up?"

He began to shake his head, but stopped. His eyes flashed to her, sharp with curiosity.

Cress gulped. Though she'd warmed to Wolf during her time aboard the ship, he still sort of terrified her.

"Can you find information about people on Luna?"

Her shoulders sank with an apology. "If I could have found out about her by now, I—"

"Not Scarlet," he said, his voice rough when he said her name. "I've been wondering about my parents."

She blinked. *Parents?* She had never imagined Wolf with parents. The idea of this hulking man having once been a dependent child didn't fit. In fact, she couldn't imagine any of the queen's soldiers having parents, having once been children, having once been loved. But of course they had—once.

"Oh. Right," she stammered, smoothing down the skirt of the worn cotton dress she'd taken from the satellite, what felt like ages ago. Though she'd spent a day wearing one of the military uniforms found in her crew quarters, a lifetime spent barefoot and in simple dresses had made the clothes feel heavy and cumbersome. Plus, all of the pants were way too long on her. "Do you think you might see them? When we're on Luna?"

"It's not a priority." He said it like a military general, but his expression carried more emotion than his voice. "But I wouldn't mind knowing if they're still alive. Maybe seeing them again, someday." His jaw flexed. "I was twelve when I was taken away. They must think *I'm* dead. Or a monster."

The statement resonated through her body, leaving her chest vibrating. For sixteen years, *her* father had thought she was dead too, while she'd been told that her parents had willingly sacrificed her to Luna's shell infanticide. She'd barely been reunited with her father before he died of letumosis, in the labs at New Beijing Palace. She'd tried to mourn his death, but mostly she mourned the idea of having a father at all and the loss of all the time they should have had to get to know each other.

She still thought of him as Dr. Erland, the odd, curmudgeonly old man who had started the cyborg draft in the Eastern Commonwealth. Who had dealt in shell trafficking in Africa.

He was also the man who helped Cinder escape from prison.

So many things he'd done—some good, some terrible. And

all, Cinder had told her, because he was determined to end Levana's rule.

To avenge his daughter. To avenge *her*.

"Cress?"

She jolted. "Sorry. I don't... I can't access Luna's databases from here. But once we're on Luna—"

"Never mind. It doesn't matter." Wolf leaned against the cockpit wall and clawed his hands into his unkempt hair. He looked like he was on the verge of a meltdown, but that was his normal look these days. "Scarlet's the priority. The only priority."

Cress considered mentioning that overthrowing Levana and crowning Cinder as queen were decent-size priorities too, but she dared not.

"Have you mentioned your parents to Cinder?"

He cocked his head. "Why?"

"I don't know. She mentioned not having any allies on Luna... how it would be useful to have more connections. Maybe they would help us?"

His gaze darkened, both thoughtful and annoyed. "It would put them in danger."

"I think Cinder might intend to put a lot of people in danger." Cress worried at her lower lip, then sighed. "Is there anything else you need?"

"For time to move faster."

Cress wilted. "I meant more like ... food, or something. When did you last eat?"

Wolf's shoulders hunched closer to his ears, and the guilty expression was all the answer she needed. She'd heard rumors of his insatiable appetite and the high-octane metabolism that kept him always fidgeting, always moving. She'd hardly seen any of that since coming aboard the ship, and she could tell that Cinder, in particular, was worried about him. Only when they were discussing strategies for Cinder's revolution did he seem rejuvenated—his fists flexing and tightening like the fighter he was meant to be.

"All right. I'm going to make you a sandwich." Standing, Cress gathered her courage, along with her most demanding voice, and planted a hand on her hip. "And *you* are going to eat it without argument. You need to keep up your strength if you're going to be of any use to us, and Scarlet."

Wolf raised an eyebrow at her newfound gumption.

Cress flushed. "Or . . . at least eat some canned fruit or something."

His expression softened. "A sandwich sounds good. With . . . tomatoes, if we have any left. Please."

"Of course." Drawing in a deep breath, she grabbed her portscreen and headed toward the galley.

"Cress?"

She paused and turned back, but Wolf was looking at the floor, his arms crossed. He looked about as awkward as she usually felt.

"Thank you."

Her heart expanded, ballooning with sympathy for him. Words of comfort sprang to her tongue—*She'll be all right. Scarlet will be all right*—but Cress stuffed them back down.

"You're welcome," she said, before turning into the corridor.

She had nearly reached the galley when she heard Thorne call her name. She paused and backtracked to the last door, left slightly ajar, and pressed it open. The captain's quarters were the largest of the crew cabins and the only room that didn't have bunks. Though Cress had been inside plenty of times to help him with the eyedrop solution Dr. Erland made in order to repair Thorne's damaged optical nerve, she never lingered long. Even with the door wide open, the room felt too intimate, too personal. There was a huge map of Earth on one wall, filled with Thorne's handwritten notes and markers indicating the places he'd been and the places he wanted to go, along with a dozen to-scale models of different spaceships scattered across the captain's desk, including a prominent one of a 214 Rampion. The bed was never made.

The first time she'd been in that room she asked Thorne about the map and listened, captivated, while he talked about the things he'd seen, from ancient ruins to thriving metropolises, tropical forests to white-sand beaches. His descriptions had filled Cress with longing. She was happy here on the spaceship—it was roomier than her satellite had been, and the bonds she was forming with the rest of the crew felt like friendship. But she had still seen so little of Earth, and the thought of seeing those things, while standing at Thorne's side, their fingers laced together . . . the fantasy made her pulse race every time.

Thorne was sitting in the middle of the floor, holding a portscreen at arm's length.

"Did you call me?" she asked.

A grin dawned on his face, impishly delighted. "Cress! I thought I heard your footsteps. Come here." He circled his whole arm, like he could draw her forward with the vacuum it created.

When she reached his side, Thorne flailed his hand around until he found her wrist and pulled her down beside him.

"It's finally working," he said, holding up the port again with his free hand.

Cress blinked at the small screen. A net drama was playing, though the feed was muted. "Was it broken?"

"No, the *solution*. It's working. I can see"—releasing her wrist, he waved a finger in the screen's direction—"kind of a bluish light. And the lights in the ceiling." He tilted his head back, eyes wide and pupils dilated as they tried to take in as much information as they could. "They're more yellow than the screen. That's it, though. Light and dark. Some blurry shadows."

"That's wonderful!" Although Dr. Erland believed Thorne's eyesight would begin to improve after a week or so, that week had come and gone with no change. It had now been nearly two weeks since the solution had run out, and she knew the wait had tried even Thorne's relentless optimism.

"I know." Crushing his eyes shut, Thorne lowered his head again. "Except, it's kind of giving me a headache."

"You shouldn't overdo it. You might strain them."

He nodded and pressed a hand over both eyes. "Maybe I should wear the blindfold again. Until things start to come into focus."

"It's up here." Cress stood and found the blindfold and the empty vial of eyedrops nestled among the model ships. When she turned around, Thorne was looking at her, or through her, his brow tense. She froze.

It had been a long time since he *looked* at her, and back then they'd been scrambling for their lives. That had been before he cut her hair too. She sometimes wondered how much he remembered about what she looked like, and what he would think when he saw her again . . . practically for the first time.

"I can see your shadow, sort of," he said, cocking his head. "Kind of a hazy silhouette."

Gulping, Cress folded the blindfold into his palm. "Give it

time," she said, pretending the thought of him inspecting her, seeing every unspoken confession written across her face, wasn't terrifying. "The doctor's notes said your optical nerve would continue to heal for weeks on its own."

"Let's hope it starts healing faster after this. I don't like seeing blurs and shadows." He twisted the blindfold between his fists. "One of these days, I just want to open my eyes and see you."

Heat rushed into her cheeks, but the depth of his words hadn't sunk in before Thorne laughed and scratched his ear. "I mean, and everyone else too, of course."

She smothered the start of a giddy smile, cursing herself for getting her hopes up again, for the thousandth time, when Thorne had made it quite clear he saw her as nothing more than a good friend, and a loyal member of his crew. He hadn't tried to kiss her again, not once since the battle atop the palace rooftop. And sometimes she thought he might be flirting with her, but then he'd start flirting with Cinder or Iko and she'd remember that a touch here or a smile there wasn't special to him like it was to her.

"Of course," she said, moving back toward the door. "Of course you want to see everyone."

She stifled a sigh, realizing she was going to have to train herself not to stare at him quite as often as she was used to, otherwise there would be no chance of hiding the fact that, despite all his attempts to persuade her otherwise, she was still hopelessly in love with him.

Seven

JACIN AWOKE WITH A JOLT. HE WAS DAMP AND STICKY AND smelled like sulfur. His throat and lungs were burning—not painfully, but like they'd been improperly treated and they wanted to make sure he knew about it. Instinct told him he was not in immediate danger, but the fuzziness of his thoughts set him on edge. When he peeled his eyes open, blaring overhead lights burst across his retinas. He grimaced, shutting them again.

Memories flooded in all at once. The trial. The lashings. The forty mind-numbing hours spent tied to that sundial. The mischievous smile Winter shared only with him. Being carted to the med-clinic and the doctor prepping his body for immersion.

He was still at the clinic, in the suspended-animation tank.

"Don't move," said a voice. "We're still disconnecting the umbilicals."

Umbilicals. The word sounded far too bloody and organic for this contraption they'd stuck him in.

There was a pinch in his arm and the tug of skin as a series of needles were pulled from his veins, then a snap of electrodes as sensors were pried off his chest and scalp, the cords tangling in his hair. He tested his eyes again, blinking into the brightness. A doctor's shadow hung over him.

"Can you sit?"

Jacin tested his fingers, curling them into the thick gel substance he was lying on. He grasped the sides of the tank and pulled himself up. He'd never been in one of these before—had never been injured enough to need it—and despite the confusion upon first waking, he already felt surprisingly lucid.

He looked down at his body, traces of the tank's blue gel-like substance still clinging to his belly button and the hairs on his legs and the towel they'd draped across his lap.

He touched one of the jagged scars that cut across his abdomen, looking as if it had healed years ago. Not bad.

The doctor handed him a child-size cup filled with syrupy orange liquid. Jacin eyed the doctor's crisp lab coat, the ID tag on his chest, the soft hands that were used to holding portscreens and syringes, not guns and knives. There was a pang of envy, a reminder that this was closer to the life he would have chosen, if he'd been given a choice. If Levana hadn't made the choice for him when she selected him for the royal guard. Though she'd never made the threat aloud, Jacin had known from the beginning that Winter would be punished if he ever stepped out of line.

His dream of being a doctor had stopped mattering a long time ago.

He shot back the drink, swallowing his thoughts along with it. Dreaming was for people with nothing better to do.

The medicine tasted bitter, but the burning in his throat began to fade.

When he handed the cup back to the doctor, he noticed a figure hovering near the doorway, ignored by the doctors and nurses who puttered around the storage cells of countless other tanks, checking diagnostics and making notations on their ports.

Thaumaturge Aimery Park. Looking smugger than ever in his fancy bright white coat. The queen's new favorite hound.

"Sir Jacin Clay. You look refreshed."

Jacin didn't know if his voice would work after being immersed in the tank, and he didn't want his first words to the thaumaturge to be a pathetic croak. He cleared his throat, though, and it felt almost normal.

"I am to retrieve you for an audience with Her Majesty. You may have forfeited your honored position in service to the royal entourage, but we still intend to find a use for you. I trust you are fit to return to active duty?"

Jacin tried not to look relieved. The last thing he wanted was to become the personal guard to the head thaumaturge again—especially now that Aimery was in the position. He embraced a particular loathing for this man, who was rumored to have abused more than one palace servant with his manipulations, and whose leering attentions landed far too often on Winter.

"I trust I am," he said. His voice was a little rusty, but not horrible. He swallowed again. "May I request a new uniform? A towel seems inappropriate for the position."

Aimery smirked. "A nurse will escort you to the showers, where a uniform will be waiting. I will meet you outside the armory when you're ready."

THE VAULTS BENEATH THE LUNAR PALACE WERE CARVED FROM years of emptied lava tubes, their walls made of rough black stone and lit by sparse glowing orbs. These underground places were never seen by the queen or her court, hence no one worried about making them beautiful to match the rest of the palace with its glossy white surfaces and crystalline, reflection-less windows.

Jacin sort of liked it down in the vaults. Down here, it was easy to forget he was beneath the capital at all. The white city of Artemisia, with its enormous crater lake and towering spires, had been built upon a solid foundation of brainwashing and manipulation. In comparison, the lava tubes were as cold and rough and natural as the landscape outside the domes. They were unpretentious. They did not do themselves up with lavish decorations and glitz in an attempt to conceal the horrible things that happened inside their walls.

Even still, Jacin moved briskly toward the armory. There was no residual pain, just the memory of each spiked lash and the betrayal of his own arm wielding the weapon. That betrayal was something he was used to, though. His body hadn't felt entirely his own since he became a member of the queen's guard.

At least he was home, for better or worse. Once again able to watch over his princess. Once again under Levana's thumb.

Fair trade.

He cleared Winter from his thoughts as he turned into the armory. She was a danger to his hard-earned neutrality. Thinking about her tended to give him an unwanted hitch in his lungs.

There was no sign of Aimery, but two guards stood at the barred door and a third sat at the desk inside, all wearing the gray-and-red uniforms of royal guards identical to Jacin's but for the metallic runes over the breast. Jacin ranked higher than any of them. He'd worried he would lose his position as a royal guard after his stint with Linh Cinder, but evidently his betrayal of her counted for something after all.

"Jacin Clay," he said, approaching the desk, "reporting for re-instatement under the order of Her Majesty."

The guard scanned a holograph chart and gave a terse nod. A second barred door filled up the wall behind him, hiding shelves of weaponry in its shadows. The man retrieved a bin that held a handgun and extra ammunition and pushed it across the desk, through the opening in the bars.

"There was also a knife."

The man scowled, as if a missing knife were the biggest hassle of his day, and crouched down to peer into the cupboard.

Jacin dropped the gun's magazine, reloading it while the man riffled through the cabinet. As Jacin was tucking the gun into his holster, the man tossed his knife onto the desk. It skidded across, off the surface. Jacin snatched it from the air just before the blade lodged itself in his thigh.

"Thanks," he muttered, turning.

"Traitor," one of the guards at the door said beneath his breath.

Jacin twirled the knife beneath the guard's nose and sank it into the scabbard on his belt without bothering to make eye contact. His early rise through the ranks had earned him plenty of enemies, morons who seemed to think Jacin had cheated somehow to earn such a desirable position so young. When really the queen just wanted to keep a closer eye on him and, through him, Winter.

The click of his boots echoed through the tunnel as he left them behind. He turned a corner and neither flinched nor slowed when he spotted Aimery waiting by the elevator.

When he was six steps away, Jacin came to a stop and clapped a fist to his chest.

Stepping aside, Aimery swooped his arm toward the elevator doors. The long white sleeve of his coat swung with it. "Let's not keep Her Majesty waiting."

Jacin entered without argument, taking up his usual spot beside the elevator's door, arms braced at his sides.

"Her Majesty and I have been discussing your role here since your trial," said Aimery once the doors had closed.

"I'm eager to be of service." Only years of practice disguised how abhorrent the words tasted in his mouth.

"As we wish to once again have faith in your loyalty."

"I will serve in whatever way Her Majesty sees fit."

"Good." There was that smile again, and this time it came with a suspicious chill. "Because Her Royal Highness, the princess herself, has made a request of you."

Jacin's gut tightened. There was no way to stay indifferent as his thoughts started to race.

Please, please, you hateful stars—don't let Winter have done something stupid.

"If your service meets with Her Majesty's expectations," Aimery continued, "we will return you to your previous position within the palace."

Jacin inclined his head. "I am most grateful for this opportunity to prove myself."

"I have no doubt of it, Sir Clay."

Eight

THE ELEVATOR DOORS OPENED INTO THE QUEEN'S SOLAR—AN octagonal room made up of windows on all sides. The cylindrical elevator itself was encapsulated in glass and stood at the room's center so that no part of the view would be obstructed. The décor was simple—thin white pillars and a glass dome overhead, mimicking the dome over the city. This tower, this very room, was the highest point in Artemisia, and the sight of all those buildings white and glittering beneath them, and an entire jewelry case of stars overhead, was all the decoration the room required.

Jacin had been there dozens of times with Sybil, but never for his own audience with the queen. He forced himself to be unconcerned. If he was worried, the queen might detect it, and the last thing he wanted was for anyone to question his loyalty to the crown.

Though an elaborate chair was set on a raised platform, the queen herself was standing at the windows. The glass was crystal clear and showed no hint of reflection. Jacin didn't know how they'd managed to make glass like that, but the palace was full of it.

Sir Jerrico Solis, the captain of the guard and technically Jacin's superior, was also there, but Jacin didn't spare him a glance.

"My Queen," said Aimery, "you requested Sir Jacin Clay."

Jacin dropped to one knee as the queen turned. "You may stand, Jacin. How good of you to come."

Now, wasn't that sweet.

He did stand, daring to meet her gaze.

Queen Levana was horrifically beautiful, with coral-red lips and skin as pristine as white marble. It was all her glamour, of course. Everyone knew that, but it didn't make any difference. Looking at her could steal the breath of any mortal man.

However—and Jacin kept this thought very, very quiet in his head—the princess could steal both their breath *and* their heart.

"Sir Clay," said the queen, her voice a lullaby now compared with the harshness from the trial. "Aimery and I have been discussing your surprising yet joyful return. I would like to see you reinstated to your previous position soon. Our guard is weaker without you."

"I am yours to command."

"I've taken into consideration the comm you sent to Thauma-turge Mira prior to her death, along with two years of loyal service. I've also had a team looking into your claims about this . . . *device* Linh Garan invented, and it seems you were correct. He unveiled a prototype he called a bioelectrical security device at an Earthen convention many years ago. As it happens, this discovery has also solved a mystery that my pack of special operatives in Paris had encountered earlier this year. We now know that Linh Cinder was not the only person to have had this device installed—but that her longtime protector, a woman named Michelle Benoit, had one too. We can only guess how many more might still exist."

Jacin said nothing, though his heart was expanding at this news. Cinder had seemed sure no more of these devices had been made, but maybe she was wrong. And if she was wrong … if there were more of them out there … he could get one for Winter. He could save her.

"No matter," said Levana, gliding a hand through the air. "We're already finding ways to ensure no such invention will ever come to the Earthen market. The reason I called you here was to discuss what is now to become of *you*. And I have a special role in mind, Sir Clay. One that I think you will not find disagreeable."

"My opinion means nothing."

"True, but the opinions of my stepdaughter do yet carry some weight. Princess Winter may not have been born with my blood, but I think the people acknowledge that she is a part of my family, a true darling among the court. And I did love her father so." She said this with a small sigh, though Jacin couldn't tell whether it was faked or not. She turned away.

"You know I was there when Evret was murdered," Levana continued, peering at the full Earth through the windows. "He died in my arms. His last plea was that I would take care of Winter, our sweet daughter. How old were you when he died, Jacin?"

He forced his shoulders to relax. "Eleven, Your Majesty."

"Do you remember him well?"

He clenched his teeth, not knowing what she wanted him to say. Winter's father and Jacin's father had both been royal guards and the closest of friends. Jacin had grown up with plenty of admiration for Evret Hayle, who had kept his position even after marrying Levana, then a princess. He stayed a guard even after Queen Channary died and Selene disappeared and Levana ascended to the throne. He often said he had no desire to sit on the throne beside her, and even less to sit around drinking wine and getting fat among the pompous families of Artemisia.

"I remember him well enough," he finally said.

"He was a good man."

"Yes, Your Majesty."

Her gaze slipped down to the fingers of her left hand. There was no wedding band there—at least, not that she was allowing him to see.

"I loved him very much," she repeated, and Jacin would have believed her if he believed she was capable of such a thing. "His death nearly killed me."

"Of course, My Queen."

Evret Hayle had been murdered by a power-hungry thaumaturge in the middle of the night, and Jacin still remembered how devastated Winter had been. How inadequate all of his attempts to comfort or distract her. He remembered listening to the sad gossip: how Evret had died protecting Levana, and how she had avenged him by plunging a knife into the thaumaturge's heart.

They said Levana had sobbed hysterically for hours.

"Yes, well." Levana sighed again. "As I held him dying, I promised to protect Winter—not that I wouldn't have regardless. She *is* my daughter, after all."

Jacin said nothing. His reserves of mindless agreements were running low.

"And what better way to protect her than to instate as her guard one whose concern for her well-being matches my own?" She smiled, but it had a hint of mocking to it. "In fact, Winter herself requested you be given the position as a member of her personal guard. Normally her suggestions are rooted in nonsense, but this time, even I have to acknowledge the idea has merit."

Jacin's heart thumped, despite his best efforts to remain disconnected. *Him?* On Winter's personal guard?

It was both a dream and a nightmare. The queen was right—no one else could be as trusted as he was to ensure her safety. In many ways, he'd considered himself Winter's personal guard already, with or without the title.

But being her guard was not the same as being her friend, and he already found it difficult enough to walk the line between the two.

"The changing of her guard happens at 19:00," said the queen, swaying back toward the windows. "You will report then."

He wet his throat. "Yes, My Queen." He turned to go.

"Oh, and Jacin?"

Dread slithered down his spine. Locking his jaw, he faced the queen again.

"You may not be aware that we have had . . . difficulties, in the past, with Winter's guard. She can be difficult to manage, given to childish games and fancies. She seems to have little respect for her role as a princess and a member of this court."

Jacin pressed his disgust down, down, into the pit of his stomach, where even he couldn't feel it. "What would you have me do?"

"I want you to keep her under control. My hope is that her affection for you will lend itself to some restraint on her part. I am sure you're aware that the girl is coming to be of a marriageable age. I have hopes for her, and I will not tolerate her bringing humiliation on this palace."

Marriageable age. Humiliation. Restraint. His disgust turned to a hard pebble, but his face was calm as he bowed. "Yes, My Queen."

WINTER STOOD WITH HER EAR PRESSED AGAINST THE DOOR
of her private chambers, trying to slow her breathing to the point of dizziness. Anticipation crawled over her skin like a thousand tiny ants.

Silence in the hallway. Painful, agonizing silence.

Blowing a curl out of her face, she glanced at the holograph of Luna near her room's ceiling, showing the progression of sunlight and shadows and the standardized digital clock beneath it. 18:59.

She wiped her damp palms on her dress. Listened some more. Counted the seconds in her head.

There. Footsteps. The hard, steady thump of boots.

She bit her lip. Levana had given her no indication if Winter's request would be accepted—she didn't even know if her stepmother was going to *consider* the request—but it was possible. It was *possible.*

The guard who had been standing statuesque outside her chambers for the past four hours, relieved of duty, left. His footsteps were a perfect metronome to those that had just arrived.

There was a moment of shuffling as the new guard arranged himself against the corridor wall, the last line of defense should a spy or an assassin make an attack on the princess, and the first person responsible for whisking her away to safety should the security of Artemisia Palace ever be compromised.

She squeezed her eyes shut and fanned her fingers against the wall, as if she could feel his heartbeat through the stone.

Instead she felt something warm and sticky.

Gasping, she pulled away, finding her palm stained with blood.

Exasperated, she used the bloody hand to push her hair back, although it instantly tumbled forward again. "Not now," she hissed to whatever demon thought this was an appropriate time to give her visions.

She closed her eyes again and counted backward from ten. When she opened them, the blood was gone and her hand was clean.

With a whistled breath, Winter adjusted her gown and opened the door wide enough to poke her head out. She turned to the statue of a guard outside her door, and her heart swelled.

"Oh—she said yes!" she squealed, whipping the door open the rest of the way. She trotted around to face Jacin.

If he'd heard her, he didn't respond.

If he saw her, he showed no sign of it.

His expression was stone, his blue eyes focused on some point over her head.

Winter wilted, but it was from annoyance as much as disappointment. "Oh, please," she said, standing toe-to-toe, chest-to-chest, which was not simple. Jacin's flawless posture made her feel as if she were tilting backward, a breath away from falling over. "That's not necessary, is it?"

Five complete, agonizing seconds passed in which she could have been staring at a mannequin, before Jacin took in a slow breath and let it out all at once. His gaze dropped to hers.

That was all. Just the breath. Just the eyes.

But it made him human again, and she beamed. "I've been waiting all day to show you something. Come here."

Winter danced around him again, retreating back into her sitting parlor. She skipped to the desk on the other side of the room, where she'd draped her creation with a bedsheet. Taking hold of two corners, she turned back to the door.

And waited.

"Jacin?"

She waited some more.

Huffing, she released the sheet and stalked back toward the hall. Jacin hadn't moved. Winter crossed her arms over her chest and leaned against her door frame, inspecting him. Seeing Jacin in his guard uniform was always bittersweet. On one hand, it was impossible not to notice how very handsome and authoritative he looked in it. On the other hand, the uniform marked him as the property of the queen. Still, he was particularly striking today, all freshly healed from his trial and smelling of soap.

She knew that he knew that she was standing there, staring at him. It was infuriating how he could do such a blasted good job of ignoring her.

Tapping a finger against the flesh of her elbow, she deadpanned, "Sir Jacin Clay, there is an assassin under my bed."

His shoulders knotted. His jaw tensed. Three more seconds passed before he stepped away from the wall and marched into her chambers without looking her way. Past the covered surprise on the desk and straight through to her bedroom. Winter followed, shutting the door.

As soon as he reached the bed, Jacin knelt down and lifted the bed skirt.

"The assassin seems to have gotten away this time, Your Highness." Standing, he turned back to face her. "Do let me know if he returns."

He marched back toward the door, but she stepped in front of him and flashed a coquettish smile. "I certainly will," she said, bouncing on her toes. "But as long as you're here—"

"*Princess.*"

His tone was a warning, but she ignored him. Backing away

into the parlor, she tore the sheet away, revealing a table-size model of their solar system, the planets suspended from silk strings. "Ta-da!"

Jacin didn't come closer as she started fidgeting with the planets, but he also didn't leave.

Winter nudged the painted spheres into a slow orbit, each one moving separate from the others. "I had the idea when the engagement was first announced," she said, watching Earth complete a full circle around the sun before dragging to a stop. "It was going to be a wedding gift for Emperor Kaito, before … well. Anyway, it's been a distraction while you were gone." Lashes fluttering, she risked a nervous glance up at Jacin. He was staring at the model. "It helps, you know, to focus on something. To think about the details."

It helped keep her thoughts in order, helped keep her sanity. She'd started having the hallucinations when she was thirteen, a little more than a year after she'd made the decision to never again use her glamour, to never again manipulate someone's thoughts or emotions, to never again fool herself into believing such an unnatural use of power could be harmless. Jacin, not yet a guard, had spent many hours with her, distracting her with games and projects and puzzles. Idleness had been her enemy for years. It was in those moments when her mind was most focused on a task, no matter how trivial, that she felt safest.

Making the model without him hadn't been as much fun, but she did enjoy the sensation of being in control of this tiny galaxy, when she was in control of so very little of her own life.

"What do you think?"

With a resigned sigh, Jacin stepped forward to examine the contraption that gave each planet its own orbital path. "How did you make it?"

"I commissioned Mr. Sanford in AR-5 to design and build the framework. But I did all the painting myself." She was pleased to see Jacin's impressed nod. "I hoped you might be able to help me with Saturn. It's the last one to be painted, and I thought—I'll take the rings, if you want to do the planet . . ." She trailed off. His expression had hardened again. Following his fingers, she saw him batting Luna around the Earth—the way Mr. Sanford had given Luna its own little orbit around the blue planet was nothing short of brilliant, in Winter's opinion.

"I'm sorry, Highness," said Jacin, standing upright again. "I'm on duty. I shouldn't even be in here, and you know that."

"I'm quite sure I *don't* know that. It seems you can guard me even better from in here than out there. What if someone comes in through the windows?"

His lips quirked into a wry smile. No one was going to come in through the windows, they both knew, but he didn't argue the point. Instead, he stepped closer and settled his hands on her shoulders. It was a rare, unexpected touch. Not quite the Eclipse Waltz, but her skin tingled all the same.

"I'm glad to be on your guard now," he said. "I would do anything for you. If you did have an assassin under your bed, I would take that bullet without a second thought, without anyone having to manipulate me."

She tried to interrupt him, but he talked over her.

"But when I'm on duty, that's all I can be. Your guard. Not your friend. Levana already knows I'm too close to you, that I care about you more than I should—"

Her brow drew together, and again she tried to interject, thinking *that* statement deserved further explanation, but he kept talking.

"—and I am not going to give her anything else to hold

over me. Or you. I'm not going to be another pawn in her game. Got it?"

Finally, a pause, and her head was swimming, trying to hold on to his declaration—*what do you* mean *you care about me more than you should?*—without contradicting his concerns.

"We are already pawns in her game," she said. "I have been a pawn in her game since the day she married my father, and you since the day you were conscripted into her guard."

His lips tensed and he moved to pull his hands away, the extended contact overstepping a thousand of his professional boundaries, but Winter reached up and wrapped her hands around his. She held them tight, bundling both of their hands between them.

"I just thought . . ." She hesitated, her attention caught on how much bigger his hands were compared with the last time she'd held them. It was a startling realization. "I thought it might be nice to step off the game board every now and then."

One of Jacin's thumbs rubbed against her fingers—just once, like a tic that had to be stifled.

"That would be nice," he said, "but it can't be while I'm on duty, and it really can't be behind closed doors."

Winter glanced past him, at the door she'd shut when he'd come in to check for a fictional assassin. "You're saying that I'm going to see you every day, but I have to go on pretending like I don't see you at all?"

He pried his hands away. "Something like that. I'm sorry, Princess." With a step back, he morphed seamlessly into the stoic guard. "I'll be in the corridor if you need me. *Really* need me."

After he'd gone, Winter stood gnawing at her lower lip, unable to ignore the momentary bits of elation that had slipped into the cracks of an otherwise disappointing meeting.

I care about you more than I should.

"Fine," she murmured to herself. "I can work with that."

She gathered up the little compact of paints, a few paint-brushes, and the fist-size model of Saturn waiting for its kaleido-scope of rings.

This time, Jacin started a little when she emerged in the corridor. The first time he'd been expecting her, but this must have been a surprise. She bit back a grin as she walked around to his other side and slid down the wall, planting herself on the floor next to him with crisscrossed legs. Humming to herself, she spread her painting supplies out before her.

"What are you doing?" Jacin muttered beneath his breath, though the hallway was empty.

Winter pretended to jump. "Oh, I'm so sorry," she said, peering up at him. "I'm afraid I didn't see you there."

He scowled.

Winking, she turned her attention back to her work, dipping a paintbrush into rich cerulean blue.

Jacin said nothing else. Neither did she. After the first ring was completed, she leaned her head against his thigh, making herself more comfortable as she picked out a sunburst orange. Over-head, Jacin sighed, and she felt the faintest brush of fingertips against her hair. A hint, a suggestion of togetherness, before he became a statue once more.

Nine

"EVAPORATED MILK . . . KIDNEY BEANS . . . TUNA . . . MORE TUNA . . . oh!" Cress nearly toppled headfirst into the crate as she reached for the bottom. She grabbed a jar and emerged victorious. "Pickled asparagus!"

Iko stopped digging through the crate beside her long enough to shoot her a glare. "You and your taste buds can stop bragging anytime now."

"Oh, sorry." Pressing her lips, Cress set the jar on the floor. "Good thing we opened this one. The galley was starting to look pretty scarce."

"More weapons in here," said Wolf, his shoulders knotted as he leaned over another one of the crates. "For a planet that's seen a century of world peace, you manufacture a lot of guns."

"There will always be criminals and violence," said Kai. "We still need law enforcement."

Wolf made a strangled sound, pulling everyone's attention toward him as he lifted a handgun from the crate. "It's just like the one Scarlet had." He flipped the gun in his palms, running his thumbs along the barrel. "She shot me in the arm once."

This confession was said with as much tenderness as if Scarlet had given him a bouquet of wildflowers rather than a bullet wound.

Cress and the others traded sorrowful looks.

Kai, who was standing nearest to Wolf, dropped a hand onto his shoulder. "If she's in Artemisia," he said, "I will find her. I promise."

A slight dip of his head was the only indication Wolf had heard him. Turning, he handed the gun, handle first, to Cinder, who was sitting cross-legged in the center of the cargo bay, organizing what weaponry they had found. It was an impressive haul. It was a shame that when it came to fighting Lunars, weapons in the hands of their allies could be as dangerous as weapons in the hands of their enemies.

"This one's all medical supplies and common medicines," said Iko. "If we could find one with replacement escort-droid vertebrae and synthetic-tissue paneling, we'd be getting somewhere."

Cress smiled sympathetically. Iko was wearing the silk wrap top she'd worn to impersonate a member of the palace staff during the emperor's kidnapping, and its high collar almost covered the damage that had been done to her bionic neck and clavicle during the fight on the rooftop—but not quite. She'd gotten creative with scraps of miscellaneous fabric to hide the rest of her injury, which was as much as they could do until Cinder had the parts to finish her repairs.

"Is this what I think it is?" Having returned his focus to his own crate, Kai held up a carved wooden doll adorned with bedraggled feathers and four too many eyes.

Cinder finished unloading the handgun and set it next to the others. "Don't tell me you've actually seen one of those hideous things before."

"Venezuelan dream dolls? We have some on display in the palace. They're incredibly rare." He examined its back. "What is it doing here?"

"I'm pretty sure Thorne stole it."

Kai's expression filled with clarity. "Ah. Of course." He nestled the doll back into its packaging. "He'd better plan on giving all this stuff back."

"Sure I'll give it back, Your Majesticness. For a proper finder's fee."

Cress swiveled around to see Thorne leaning against the cargo bay wall.

She blinked. Something was different about him. The blindfold he'd been wearing since his eyesight had begun to return weeks ago was now around his neck, and he was exceptionally clean-cut, like he'd gotten a closer shave than usual, and he was . . .

Electricity jolted down her spine.

He was *looking* at her.

No. Not just looking. There was an intense inspection behind that gaze, along with a curious bewilderment. He was surprised. Almost . . . *captivated*.

Heat rushed up her neck. She gulped, sure that she was imagining things.

Worldly, confident Captain Thorne could never be captivated by plain, awkward *her*, and she'd been disappointed by such wishful thinking before.

One corner of Thorne's mouth lifted. "The short hair," he said, with half a nod. "It works."

Cress reached up, grasping at the wispy ends that Iko had trimmed into something resembling a hairstyle.

"Oh!" said Iko, launching to her feet. "Captain! You can see!"

Thorne's attention skipped over to the android seconds before she launched herself over Cress and into his arms. Thorne stumbled against the wall and laughed.

"Iko?" Thorne said, holding her at arm's distance and drinking her in. The dark, flawless skin, the long legs, the braids dyed in varying shades of blue. Accepting the scrutiny, Iko gave a twirl. Thorne clicked his tongue. "Aces. I really know how to pick them, don't I?"

"Sight unseen," said Iko, flipping her braids off her shoulder.

Deflating, Cress began filling up her arms with canned goods. Definitely wishful thinking.

"Excellent," said Cinder, standing up and brushing off her hands. "I was beginning to worry we wouldn't have a pilot for when it's time to take Kai back to Earth. Now I just have to worry about not having a competent one."

Thorne leaned against the crate Cress was organizing. She froze, but when she dared to peer up through her lashes, his attention was on the other side of the cargo bay. "Oh, Cinder, I've missed seeing your face when you make sarcastic comments in an attempt to hide your true feelings about me."

"Please." Rolling her eyes, Cinder started organizing the guns against the wall.

"See that eye roll? It translates to 'How am I possibly keeping my hands off you, Captain?'"

"Yeah, keeping them from *strangling* you."

Kai folded his arms, grinning. "How come no one told me I had such steep competition?"

Cinder glared. "Don't encourage him."

With flushed cheeks, gritted teeth, and three stacks of cans cradled in her arms, Cress spun toward the main corridor—and sent the top can of peaches sailing off the stack.

Thorne snatched it from the air before Cress could gasp.

She froze, and for a moment it was there again—the way he was looking at her, causing the world to blur and her stomach to swoop. It was a good catch, to be sure, and she couldn't help but wonder if he'd been paying more attention to her than she thought.

Thorne beamed at the peaches. "Lightning-fast reflexes. Still got them." He took some canned corn off the stack. "Want help?"

She fixated on the cans. "No-thank-you-I've-got-it." Her words were all rushed and full of nerves as another blush flamed across her face. It occurred to her she'd been blushing from the moment he walked in, with his cavalier smile and his eyes that saw right through her.

She wanted to climb into one of those crates and pull down the lid. He hadn't had his eyesight back for five minutes and already she'd turned back into the anxious, giddy, flustered girl she'd been when they met.

"All right," Thorne said slowly, nestling the cans back into her arms. "If you insist."

Cress dodged around him and made her way to the galley. It was a relief to dump the food onto the counter and take a moment to stabilize herself.

So he could see again. It didn't change anything. He didn't think she was irresistible when he first saw her over that D-COMM link ages ago, and he wasn't going to think she was irresistible now. Especially not when Iko was right there. Android or not, she was the one with pearly teeth and coppery eyes and . . .

Cress sighed, halting the envy before it could go any further. It wasn't Iko's fault Thorne wasn't interested in a tiny, skittish girl. In fact, she was happy for Iko, who took more delight in her new body than most humans ever did.

Cress just wished she could have half her confidence. If she had the guts to throw herself into Thorne's arms, to wink and make flirtatious comments and pretend like none of it mattered . . .

Except it *did* matter, or it would have, if she dared try it.

Just friends, she reminded herself. They were only friends, and would only be friends from here on out. It was a friendship that was to be cherished, as she cherished all the friendships she'd made aboard this ship. She wouldn't ruin it by wishing things could be more. She would be grateful for what affection she *did* have.

Cress let out a slow breath and stood straighter. It wouldn't be so hard, pretending this was all she wanted. Imagining she was satisfied with his companionship and platonic fondness. Now that he could see again, she would be extra vigilant in making sure any of her deeper feelings didn't show through.

Thorne was her friend and her captain, and nothing more.

When she returned to the cargo bay, the lightheartedness had dissipated. Hearing her, Thorne glanced over his shoulder, but she fixed her eyes resolutely on Kai.

"I understand this is sooner than we'd expected," Kai was saying, "but now that Thorne can finally see again, what are we waiting for? We can leave tomorrow. We could leave *now.*"

Cinder shook her head. "There's so much to do. We still have the video to edit, and we haven't confirmed which route we're going to take to the outer sectors, and—"

"All things you don't need *my* help for," interrupted Kai. "All things you can be working on while I'm doing my part. People are dying every day. My people are being attacked at this very *moment,* and I can't do anything for them up here."

"I know. I know it's hard—"

"No, it's *torture.*" Kai lowered his voice. "But once you take me back, I can talk to Levana. Negotiate a new cease-fire and start putting our plan into motion—"

"Get to Scarlet sooner," said Wolf.

Cinder groaned. "Look, I get it. It's been a really long month and we're all anxious to move forward, it's just . . . our strategy—"

"Strategy? Look at us—we're spending our time unpacking *pickled asparagus.*" Kai shoved a hand through his hair. "How is this a good use of our time?"

"Every day we wait, our chances of success get better. Every day, more of her army is heading to Earth, leaving Levana and the capital unprotected. The weaker she is, the better chance we have of this revolution succeeding." She pointed at the netscreen, even though it was turned off. "Plus, the Union has been fighting back. She's lost a lot of soldiers already and maybe she's beginning to feel a little concerned?"

"She's not concerned," said Wolf.

Cinder frowned. "Well, at least she may have realized this war won't be won as easily as she'd hoped, which means she'll be that much more thrilled to hear Kai has returned and the wedding is back on. She'll be eager to reschedule it right away." She looped her fingers around her left wrist, where skin met metal.

Cress bit her lip, watching the fear and nerves flash across Cinder's face. Though she always did her best to hide it, Cress knew Cinder wasn't always as brave as she pretended. It was sort of comforting to think they might have this in common.

Kai's shoulders dropped and his voice lost its desperation when he took a step closer to her. "I understand you want to feel like you're ready—like we're all ready. But, Cinder . . . we're never going to feel that way. At some point, we have to stop planning and start doing. I think that time is now."

It took her a moment, but she finally met his gaze, then shifted to look at each of them in turn. Though Thorne was their captain, they all knew Cinder was the one that held them together.

"We're all risking our lives," she said. "I just don't want to risk them unnecessarily. I want to make sure we're prepared to—" She froze, her eyes unfocusing. Cress recognized the look from when Cinder was seeing something on her retina display.

Blinking rapidly, Cinder turned back to Kai, stunned. "Ship, turn on cargo bay netscreen, Commonwealth newsfeed."

Kai frowned. "What's going on?"

The netscreen flickered to life. It showed Kai's chief adviser— Konn Torin—standing at a podium. Before the audio signal could connect, though, Cinder said, "I'm so sorry, Kai. Your palace is under attack."

Ten

THEY WATCHED THE NEWSFEED IN SILENCE, THE CAMERAS
trembling as android-manned hovers circled the palace below.
Many of the gardens were smoking from fires set by the queen's
soldiers, statues toppled and the massive gate torn to shreds, but
the palace itself remained untouched. So far the single regiment
of the Commonwealth's military stationed at the palace had
kept the enemy at bay while they waited for reinforcements to
arrive.

The siege on New Beijing Palace went against the strategies
the wolf soldiers had been using throughout the war. They had
become infamous for their guerilla attacks and scare tactics, as
concerned with making the people of Earth terrified of them as
they were with winning actual battles. To date, there had been
no real *battles* at all—only skirmishes and surprise attacks, resulting in too much bloodshed and too many nightmares.

The wolf soldiers moved in packs, stealthy and quick. They
caused havoc and destruction wherever they went, then disappeared before the Earthen military could catch up to them.
There was speculation that they were moving through the

sewers or disappearing into the wilderness, leaving a trail of blood and severed limbs in their wake. They were fond of leaving at least one witness alive in the aftermath to report on their brutality.

Again and again, their message was clear. *No one is safe.*

Earth had killed their share of the Lunar soldiers, as well as some of the thaumaturges that led each pack. They weren't invincible, as Earthen leaders pointed out again and again. But after 126 years of peace, the Earthen Union was unprepared to wage a war, especially one so unpredictable. For generations, their militaries had become more decorated social service workers than anything else, providing manual labor in impoverished communities and running supplies when natural disasters struck. Now, every country was scrambling to conscript more soldiers into their forces, to train them, to manufacture weaponry.

All the while, the Lunar soldiers decimated whole neighborhoods, leaving only the echo of their bloodthirsty howls behind.

Until now.

This attack on New Beijing Palace was the first time, as far as anyone could tell, multiple packs had come together in one orchestrated attack, and in broad daylight too. Cinder wondered if they were getting cocky, or if they were trying to make a statement. She tried to take solace in the fact that there were more wolf-mutant bodies lying on the palace grounds than she'd ever seen in one place—surely this battle would hurt their numbers, at least in New Beijing. But it was little comfort, when their blood was mixed with that of Earthen soldiers and one of the palace's towers was smoldering.

"The palace has been evacuated," said a journalist, speaking over the catastrophe in the video, "and all human officials and servants have been moved to safety. The secretary of defense commented in a speech only twenty minutes ago that they are not speculating at this time how long this siege might last, or how much destruction might be incurred. So far, military experts estimate upward of three hundred Commonwealth soldiers have been lost in this attack, and close to fifty Lunars."

"I feel so useless," Iko said, her tone deep with a misery only an android could understand. Iko was by no means a typical android, but she still managed to harbor one distinguishable trait all androids had been programmed with: the need to be useful.

On Cinder's other side was Kai, stricken. No doubt he was experiencing his own sense of uselessness. No doubt it was tearing him apart.

"The military will hold them," Cinder said.

He nodded, but his brow was drawn.

Sighing, she let her gaze travel from Kai to Wolf, Thorne to Cress to Iko. All watching the screen, determined and angry and horrified. Her attention swung back to Kai. He was veiling his emotions well, but she knew it was killing him. Watching his home burn. Having never had a home she cared about, at least not until she'd come aboard the Rampion, Cinder couldn't imagine the pain he was in.

She clenched her teeth, thinking of all their calculations, all their plans.

Kai was right. She would never feel ready, but they couldn't sit around doing nothing forever.

Thorne had his sight back.

Wolf had told her about his parents—laborers who had worked in factories and regolith mines all their lives. If they were alive, he thought they might be willing to offer them shelter on Luna. They might be allies.

The queen was making the boldest move she'd made since

the war started, which either meant she was getting overconfident or she was getting desperate. Either way, Cinder didn't want Luna to win this battle. She didn't want them to have control of New Beijing Palace, even if it was merely symbolic. It was the home of the Commonwealth's royal family. It belonged to Kai, not Levana. *Never* Levana.

"We have had word," said the journalist, "that the radical political group calling themselves the Association for Commonwealth Security has issued yet another statement calling for the forced abdication of Emperor Kaito, once again insisting that he cannot be the ruler we need in these troubled times, and that so long as he remains in the hands of terrorists, it is impossible for him to have the country's welfare as his primary concern. Though the ACS ideology has been largely ignored in mainstream politics, a recent net-based poll has indicated that their opinions are growing in popularity among the general public."

"Terrorists?" said Iko, looking around the group. "Does she mean *us*?"

Cinder dragged a frustrated hand down her face. Kai would be a great leader, *was* a great leader, but he hadn't yet been given the chance to prove himself. It made her stomach churn to think that his reign could be cut short, and all because of her.

She wanted to hug Kai and tell him they were idiots. They had no idea how much he cared about his country's welfare.

But that's not what he needed to hear.

Her retina display switched between her most-watched feeds. Body counts; death tolls; footage from the plague quarantines; teenagers standing in line outside recruitment centers, too many of them looking almost giddy to join the fight and defend their planet from this invasion. Levana in her sheer white veil.

She sent the feeds away.

Kai was watching her. "It's time, Cinder."

Time to say good-bye. Time to move ahead. Time to let go of the little utopia they'd cocooned themselves in.

"I know," she said, her voice sad and heavy. "Thorne, let's get ready to take Kai home."

Eleven

"THOUGHT I MIGHT FIND YOU DOWN HERE."

Cinder peeked around the side of the podship. Kai was loitering in the doorway, hands in his pockets, dressed again in his wedding finery.

She brushed some loose strands of hair off her forehead. "Just doing some basic maintenance," she said, disconnecting the power cell gauge from the podship and closing the hatch. "Making sure it's ready for your big return. I figured it was enough risk letting Thorne be your pilot; the least I could do is make sure the transport is in good condition."

"I wish you were coming with us."

"Yeah, me too, but we can't risk it."

"I know. It's just nice to have a mechanic on board. In case anything, you know . . . breaks." He scratched his ear.

"Oh, *that's* why you want me there. How flattering." Cinder wrapped the cord around the gauge and returned it to a cabinet bolted to the wall.

"That, and I'm going to miss you." His voice had gone soft, and it warmed the base of her stomach.

"With any luck, we'll see each other again soon."

"I know."

Cinder peeled off her work gloves and shoved them into her back pocket. There was still a tinge of panic at the action—her brain reminding her, out of habit, that she wasn't supposed to remove the gloves in front of anyone, especially Kai—but she ignored it. Kai didn't blink at the unveiling of her cyborg hand, like he didn't even notice it anymore.

She knew *she* was thinking about it less and less. Sometimes she was even surprised upon seeing a flash of metal in the corner of her eye when she went to pick something up. It was strange. She'd always been aware of it before, mortified that someone might see it.

"Are you scared?" she asked, pulling a wrench from her tool belt.

"Terrified," he said, but with a nonchalance that made her feel better about her own insides being wound into tight little knots. "But I'm ready to go back. I'm sure Torin is about to have a heart attack. And . . ." He shrugged. "I'm a little homesick."

"They'll be glad to have you back." Cinder knelt beside the ship, checking the bolts on the landing gear. She fit the wrench onto one, two, three bolts—none were loose. "Do you know what you're going to say to Levana?"

Kai crouched beside her, elbows braced against his knees. "I'm going to tell her I've fallen for one of my captors and the wedding is off."

Cinder's arm froze.

He smirked. "At least, that's what I wish I could tell her."

She blew a lock of hair out of her face and finished checking the bolts, before moving to the other side of the ship to repeat the process.

"I'm going to tell her I had nothing to do with the kidnapping," said Kai, donning what Cinder had come to think of as his *emperor voice*. "I'm in no way affiliated with you or the crew and I did my best to bargain for a quick release. I was a victim, held hostage, unable to escape. I'll probably make up something about inhumane treatment."

"Sounds about right."

"Then I'll *beg* her to marry me. Again." His lip curled with disgust.

Cinder couldn't blame him. The more she thought of it, the more she wanted to hijack this podship and head for Mars.

"When I see you again," said Kai, "I'll have clothes for everyone and new plating for Iko. If you think of anything else you need, Cress thinks she can get me an encrypted comm." He inhaled deeply. "Whatever happens, I'm on your side."

The sentiment both encouraged her and sent a shock of anxiety through her nerves. "I'm sorry to put you in so much danger."

"You're not," he said. "She was already going to kill me."

"You could try sounding a little more concerned when you say that."

"What is there to be concerned about?" His eyes glinted. "You're going to rescue me long before that happens."

Finished with the bolts, she stood and shoved the wrench back into her belt.

"Cinder . . ."

She froze, disconcerted at the serious edge in his voice.

"There's something I have to say before I go. In case—"

"Don't. Don't you even think this will be the last time we see each other."

A wistful smile touched his mouth, but quickly fled again. "I want to apologize."

"For suggesting this might be the last time we see each other? Because that *is* cruel, when here I am, trying to get some work done, and—"

"Cinder, listen to me."

She clenched her jaw shut and allowed Kai to take her shoulders, his thumbs tender against her collarbone. "I'm sorry about what happened at the ball. I'm sorry I didn't trust you. I'm sorry I . . . I said those things."

Cinder looked away. Though so much had changed between them since that night, it still felt like an ice pick in her heart when she remembered the way he'd looked at her, and his horrified words: *You're even more painful to look at than she is.*

"It doesn't matter anymore. You were in shock."

"I was an idiot. I'm ashamed at how I treated you. I should have had more faith in you."

"Please. You barely knew me. Then to find out all at once that I'm cyborg and Lunar . . . I wouldn't have trusted me either. Besides, you were under a lot of stress and—"

He tipped forward and kissed her on the forehead. The gentleness stilled her.

"You were still the girl who fixed Nainsi," he said. "You were still the girl who warned me about Levana's plans. You were still the girl who wanted to save her little sister."

She flinched at the mention of Peony, her younger stepsister. Her death was a wound that hadn't fully healed.

Kai's hands slipped down her arms, interlacing with her fingers—flesh and metal alike. "You were trying to protect yourself, and I should have tried harder to defend you."

Cinder gulped. "When you said I was even more painful to look at than Levana . . ."

Kai inhaled sharply, like the memory of the words hurt him as much as it hurt her.

"...do I ...did I look like her? Does my glamour look like hers?"

A crease formed between his brows, and he stared at her, into her, before shaking his head. "Not exactly. You still looked like *you*, just ..." He struggled for a word. "Perfect. A flawless version of you."

It was clear that it wasn't meant as a compliment.

"You mean, an unnatural version of me."

After a hesitation, he said, "I suppose so."

"I think it was instinct," she said. "I didn't realize I was using a glamour. I just knew I didn't want you to know I was a cyborg." A wry chuckle. "It seems so silly now."

"Good." He tugged her close again. "We must have made progress."

His lips had just brushed hers when the door opened.

"Got everything we need?" said Thorne, chipper as ever. Iko, Cress, and Wolf filed in after him.

Kai dropped Cinder's hands and she took a step back, adjusting her tool belt. "The pod's ready. Triple-checked. There shouldn't be any surprises."

"And the guest of honor?"

"I have everything I came with," said Kai, indicating his rumpled wedding clothes.

Iko stepped forward and handed Kai a box labeled PROTEIN OATS. "We have a gift for you too."

He flipped it over to the child's game printed on the back. "Yum?"

"*Open it,*" said Iko, bouncing on her toes.

Prying open the top, Kai turned it over and dumped a thin

silver chain and a medallion into his palm. He lifted it up to eye level, inspecting the rather tarnished insignia. "'The American Republic 86th Space Regiment,'" he read. "I can see why it made you think of me."

"We found it in one of the old military uniforms," said Iko. "It's to remind you that you're one of us now, no matter what happens."

Kai grinned. "It's perfect." He looped the chain around his neck and tucked the medallion under his shirt. He gave Cress a quick farewell embrace, then pulled Iko into a hug. Iko squeaked, frozen.

When Kai pulled away, Iko looked from him, to Cinder, then back. Her eyes suddenly rolled up into her head and she collapsed onto the floor.

Kai jumped back. "What happened? Did I hit her power button or something?"

Frowning, Cinder took a step closer. "Iko, what are you doing?"

"Kai hugged me," said Iko, eyes still closed. "So I fainted."

With an awkward laugh, Kai turned to face Cinder. "You're not going to faint too, are you?"

"Doubtful."

Kai wrapped his arms around Cinder and kissed her, and though she wasn't used to having an audience, Cinder didn't hesitate to kiss him back. An impractical, uncalculating part of her brain told her to not let go. To not say good-bye.

The light mood was gone when they separated. He set his brow against hers, the tips of his hair brushing her cheeks. "I'm on your side," he said. "No matter what."

"I know."

Kai turned to face Wolf last. He lifted his chin and adjusted his fine shirt. "All right, I'm ready when you—"

The punch hit Kai square in the cheek, knocking him back into Cinder. Everyone gasped. Iko jerked upward with a surprised cry as Kai pressed a hand against his face.

"Sorry," said Wolf, cringing with guilt. "It's better when you don't see it coming."

"I somehow doubt that," said Kai, his words slurred.

Cinder pried his hand away to examine the wound, which was flaming red and already beginning to swell. "You didn't break the skin. He's fine. It'll bruise up nicely by the time he's back on Earth."

"Sorry," Wolf said again.

Kai gave his head a shake and didn't complain when Cinder pressed a kiss against his cheek. "Don't worry," she whispered. "It's weirdly attractive."

His laugh was wry, but appreciative. He kissed her one last time before hurrying into the podship, like he might change his mind if he stayed for another moment.

"Do I get a good-bye kiss too?" said Thorne, stepping in front of Cinder.

Scowling, Cinder shoved him away. "Wolf's not the only one who can throw a right hook around here."

Thorne chuckled and raised a suggestive eyebrow at Iko.

The android, still on the floor, shrugged apologetically. "I would love to give you a good-bye kiss, Captain, but that lingering embrace from His Majesty may have fried a few wires, and I'm afraid a kiss from you would melt my central processor."

"Oh, trust me," said Thorne, winking at her. "It would."

For an instant, while the joke was still written across his face, Thorne's gaze flickered hopefully toward Cress, but Cress was captivated by her own fingernails.

Then the look vanished and Thorne was marching to the pilot's side of the shuttle.

"Good luck," said Cinder, watching them adjust their harnesses.

Thorne gave her a quick salute, but it was Kai she was worried about. He tried to smile, still rubbing his cheekbone, as the doors sank down around them. "You too."

Twelve

KAI WATCHED THORNE'S HANDS, SEEMINGLY COMPETENT, AS they toggled a few switches on the podship's control panel. They emerged from the Rampion's dock and dove toward planet Earth. Thorne tapped some coordinates into the computer and Kai was surprised at the jolt of longing he felt to see the satellite imagery of the Commonwealth appear on the screen.

The plan was for Thorne to leave Kai at one of the royal safe houses—far enough from civilization that the podship should go undetected, if they were quick about it, but close enough to the city that Kai would be retrieved within an hour of alerting his security staff to his return.

"This must be weird for you," Thorne said, dragging his fingers across a radar screen. "Your cyborg girlfriend being a wanted outlaw and your fiancée's niece and all that."

Kai grimaced, which made his cheek start smarting again. "Honestly, I try not to think about the details." He shifted his gaze toward the Rampion as it receded fast from the viewing window. "Does she really call herself my girlfriend?"

"Oh, I wouldn't know. We haven't spent an evening gossiping and painting each other's toenails since the kidnapping."

Glaring, Kai leaned back against the headrest. "I'm already uncomfortable with you piloting this ship and being in control of my life. Try not to make it worse."

"Why does everyone think I'm such a bad pilot?"

"Cinder told me as much."

"Well, tell Cinder I'm perfectly capable of flying a blasted pod-ship without killing anyone. My flight instructor at Andromeda—which is a very prestigious military academy in the Republic, I will have you know—"

"I know what Andromeda Academy is."

"Yeah, well, my flight instructor said I was a natural."

"Right," Kai drawled. "Was that the same flight instructor who wrote in your official report about your inattentiveness, refusal to take safety precautions seriously, and overconfident attitude that often bordered on . . . what was the word she used? 'Fool-hardy,' I think?"

"Oh, yeah. Commander Reid. She had a thing for me." The radar blinked, picking up a cruiser in the far distance, and Thorne deftly changed directions to keep them out of its course. "I didn't realize I had a royal stalker. I'm flattered, Your Majesty."

"Even better—you had an entire government team assigned to digging up information on you. They reported twice daily for over a week. You did run off with the most-wanted criminal in the world, after all."

"And your girlfriend."

Kai smothered both a smile and a glare. "And my girlfriend," he conceded.

"It took them a week, huh? Cress could have laid out my whole biography within hours."

Kai pondered this. "Maybe I'll offer her a job when this is all over."

He expected it, and he wasn't disappointed—the irritated twitch beneath Thorne's eye. He hid it easily, though, his expression morphing into nonchalance. "Maybe you should."

Kai shook his head and looked away. Earth filled up the viewing window, a kaleidoscope of ocean and land. He gripped his harness, knowing they were hurtling through space at terrifying speeds, yet feeling like he was suspended in time for one still, quiet moment.

He let his shoulders settle, awed by the sight. The next time he would be up here—if all went according to plan—he'd be on his way to Luna.

"You know what's really strange to think about?" Kai said, as much to himself as to Thorne. "If Levana hadn't tried to kill Cinder when she was a kid, I might be engaged to *her* right now. She would already be queen. We could be plotting an alliance together."

"Yeah, but she would have been raised on Luna. And from what I can tell, being raised on Luna really messes people up. She wouldn't be the cuddly cyborg we've all come to adore."

"I know. I could have despised her as much as I despise Levana, though it's difficult to imagine."

Thorne nodded, and Kai was relieved he didn't say something obnoxious as the podship slipped into a bank of clouds. The light around them began to bend and brighten as they entered the first layers of Earth's atmosphere. The friction made the ship tremble and beads of water slicked back off the view window, but it wasn't long before they'd broken through. The Pacific Ocean sparkled beneath them.

"I suppose this is all pretty weird for you too," said Kai. "A wanted criminal, piloting a kidnapped political leader back to the country you first escaped from."

Thorne snorted. "The weird part is I'm not getting any ransom money out of it. Although, if you're feeling generous . . ."

"I'm not."

Thorne scowled.

"Well, maybe a little. You're set to serve time in three countries, right? The Commonwealth, America, and Australia?"

"Don't remind me. One would think the whole unionization thing would mean we could have a little consistency in our judicial systems, but, *no*, you commit crimes in three different countries and everyone wants to help dole out the punishment."

Kai pinched his lips, giving himself one last chance to reconsider. He'd only had the idea a few days ago, and his word would be gold once he said it aloud. He didn't want to set an unfair precedent as his country's leader, but at the same time—this felt *right*. And what was the point of being emperor if he couldn't sometimes do something just because it felt right?

"I might come to regret this," he said, dragging in a deep breath, "but, Carswell Thorne, I pardon all of your crimes against the Eastern Commonwealth."

Thorne whipped his focus toward Kai. The podship surged forward and Kai gasped, grabbing hold of his harness.

"Whoops, sorry." Thorne leveled the ship's nose and resumed their steady flight. "That was a, uh . . . an air . . . doldrum. Thing. But you were saying?"

Kai exhaled. "I'm saying you can consider your time served,

for the Commonwealth, at least. If we both survive this, when it's all over, I'll make it official. I can't do anything about the other countries, though, other than put in a good word for you. And to be honest, they'll probably think I'm crazy. Or suffering from Stockholm syndrome."

"Oh, you are *definitely* suffering from Stockholm syndrome, but I won't hold it against you. So—right. Great. Can I get this in writing?"

"No," said Kai, watching the podship controls as Thorne had his attention pinned on him again. "And the deal is only valid if we *both survive.*"

"Mutual survival. Not a problem." Grinning, Thorne checked their course and made a few adjustments to his flight instruments as Japan appeared on the horizon.

"Also, I have one condition. You have to return everything you stole."

Thorne's grin started to fizzle, but he locked his hands around the console and brightened again. "Dream dolls and some surplus uniforms? Done."

"And?"

"And . . . and that's pretty much it. Aces, you make it sound like I'm a kleptomaniac or something."

Kai cleared his throat. "And the ship. You have to give back the ship."

Thorne's knuckles whitened. "But . . . she's my ship."

"No, she belongs to the American Republic. If you want a ship of your own, then you're going to have to work for it and buy one like everybody else."

"Hey, Mr. Born-into-Royalty, what do you know about it?" But Thorne's defensiveness faded as quickly as it had come, ending in a grumpy sulk. "Besides, I did work for it. Thievery isn't easy, you know."

"You're not really arguing with me about this, are you?"

Thorne clenched his eyes shut, and every muscle in Kai's body tensed, but then Thorne sighed and opened them again. "You don't get it. The Rampion and I have been through a lot together. I may have stolen her at first, but now it does feel like she belongs to me."

"But she *doesn't* belong to you. And you can't expect the rest of your crew to want to stay on in a stolen ship."

Thorne guffawed. "My crew? Let me tell you what's going to become of my crew when this is over." He ticked off on his fingers. "Cinder will be the ruling monarch of a big rock in the sky. Iko will go wherever Cinder goes, so let's assume she becomes the queen's hairdresser or something. You—are you a part of the crew now? Doesn't matter, we both know where you're going to end up. And once we get Scarlet back, she and Wolf are going to retire to some farm in France and have a litter of baby wolf cubs. *That's* what's going to become of my crew when this is done."

"It sounds like you've put some thought into this."

"Maybe," said Thorne, with a one-shoulder shrug. "They're the first crew I've ever had, and most of them even call me Captain. I'm going to miss them."

Kai squinted. "I notice you left out Cress. What's going on between you two, anyway?"

Thorne laughed. "What? Nothing's going on. We're ... I mean, what do you mean?"

"I don't know. She seems more comfortable around you than anybody else on the ship. I just thought ..."

"Oh, no, there's nothing like ... we were in the desert together for a long time, but that's it." He ran his fingers absently over the podship controls but didn't touch anything. "She used to have a crush on me. Actually"—he chuckled again, but it was more strained this time—"she thought she was in love with me when we first met. Funny, right?"

Kai watched him from the corner of his eye. "Hilarious."

Thorne's knuckles whitened on the controls, then he glanced at Kai and started to shake his head. "What is this, a therapy session? It doesn't matter."

"It sort of matters. I like Cress." Kai shifted in the harness. "I like you too, despite my better judgment."

"You'd be surprised how often I hear that."

"Something tells me Cress might still like you too—against *her* better judgment."

Thorne sighed. "Yeah, that pretty much sums that up."

Kai cocked his head. "How so?"

"It's complicated."

"Oh, it's *complicated.* Because I have no idea what that's like." Kai snorted.

Thorne glared at him. "Whatever, Doctor. It's just, when Cress thought she was in love with me, she was actually in love with this other guy she'd made up in her head, who was all brave and self-less and stuff. I mean, he was a real catch, so who could blame her? Even I liked that guy. I kind of wish I *was* that guy." He shrugged.

"Are you so sure you're not?"

Thorne laughed.

Kai didn't.

"You're kidding, right?"

"Not really."

"Um, hi, I'm Carswell Thorne, a convicted criminal in your country. Have we met?"

Kai rolled his eyes. "I'm saying maybe you should stop putting so much energy into lamenting the fact that Cress was wrong about you, and start putting your energy into proving her right, instead."

"I appreciate the confidence, Your Imperial Psychologist, but we're way beyond that. Cress is over me and . . . it's for the best."

"But you do like her?"

When Thorne didn't respond, Kai glanced over to see Thorne's attention fixed on the cockpit window. Finally, Thorne responded, "Like I said, it doesn't matter."

Kai looked away. Somehow, Thorne's inability to talk about his attraction to Cress spoke so much louder than an outright confession. After all, he had no trouble making suggestive commentary about Cinder.

"Fine," he said. "So what *is* Cress going to do once this is all over?"

"I don't know," said Thorne. "Maybe she will go work for you on your royal stalking team."

Below, the blur of land became beaches and skyscrapers and Mount Fuji and, beyond it, an entire continent, lush and green and welcoming.

"I don't think that's what she would want, though," Thorne mused. "She wants to see the world after being trapped in that satellite her whole life. She wants to travel."

"Then I guess she should stay with you after all. What better way to travel than by spaceship?"

But Thorne shook his head, adamant. "No, believe me. She deserves a better life than this."

Kai leaned forward to better get a view of his home spreading out before them. "My point exactly."

Thirteen

"WHEN DID YOU LEARN TO *EMBROIDER?*" JACIN SAID, PICKING through the basket that hung on Winter's elbow.

She preened. "A few weeks ago."

Jacin lifted a hand towel from the collection and eyed the precise stitches that depicted a cluster of stars and planets around the towel's border. "Were you getting any sleep?"

"Not very much, no." She riffled through the basket and handed him a baby blanket embroidered with a school of fish swimming around the border. "This one's my favorite. It took four whole days."

He grunted. "I take it the visions were bad that week."

"Horrible," she said lightly. "But now I have all of these gifts." She took the blanket back from him and tucked it among the rest of the colorful fabrics. "You know keeping busy helps. It's when I'm idle the monsters come."

Jacin glanced at her from the corner of his eye. He had been her guard for weeks now, but rarely did they get to talk so casually or walk side by side like this—it was expected that guards keep a respectful distance from their charges. But today Winter had dragged him along to AR-2, one of the domes adjacent to the central sector. It was mostly high-end shops set among residential neighborhoods, but this early in the day all of the shops were still closed and the streets empty and peaceful. There was no one to care about propriety.

"And all these gifts are for the shopkeepers?"

"Shopkeepers, clerks, household servants." Her eyes glimmered. "The overlooked machine of Artemisia."

The lower classes, then. The people who dealt with the trash and cooked the food and ensured all the needs of Luna's aristocracy were met. They were rewarded with lives much more enviable than the laborers in the outer sectors. Full stomachs, at the least. The only downfall was that they had to live in Artemisia, surrounded by the politics and mind games of the city. A good servant was treated like a prized pet—spoiled and fawned over when they were wanted, beaten and discarded when they'd overstayed their usefulness.

Jacin had always thought that, given a choice, he'd rather take his luck to the mines or factories.

"You've been visiting them a lot?" he asked.

"Not as much as I'd like to. But one of the milliner's assistants had a baby and I've been meaning to make her something. Do you think she'll like it?"

"It'll be the nicest thing the kid has."

Winter gave a joyful skip as she walked. "My mother was a great seamstress, you know. She was becoming quite popular among the dress shops when—well. Anyway, she embroidered my baby blanket. Levana tried to throw it out, but Papa was able to stash it away. It's one of my most prized possessions." She fluttered her lashes and Jacin felt his lips twitch at her, rather against his will.

"I knew she was a seamstress," he said, "but how come I've never seen this special blanket of yours?"

"I was embarrassed to tell you about it."

He laughed, but when Winter didn't join him, the sound fizzled away. "Really?"

Winter shrugged, grinning her impish grin. "It's silly, isn't it? Holding on to a baby blanket, of all things?" She took in a deep breath. "But it's also my namesake. She embroidered a scene from Earth's winter, with snow and leafless trees and a pair of little red mittens. Those are like gloves, but with all the fingers joined together."

Jacin shook his head. "Embarrassed to show me. That's the stupidest thing I've ever heard."

"Fine. I'll show you, if you want to see it."

"Of course I want to see it." He was surprised how much her confession stung. He and Winter had shared everything since they were kids. It had never occurred to him she might harbor something like this, especially something so important as a gift from her mother, who had died in childbirth. But his mood brightened when he remembered—"Did I tell you I saw snow when I was on Earth?"

Winter stopped walking, her eyes going wide. "Real snow?"

"We had to hide the spaceship in Siberia, on this enormous tundra."

She was staring at him like she would tackle him if he didn't offer up more details.

Smirking, Jacin hooked his thumbs over his belt and rocked back on his heels. "That was all."

Winter smacked him in the chest. "That is not *all*. What was it like?"

He shrugged. "White. Blinding. And really cold."

"Did it glisten like diamonds?"

"Sometimes. When the sun hit it right."

"What did it smell like?"

He cringed. "I don't know, Win—Princess. Sort of like ice, I guess. I didn't spend much time outside. Mostly we were stuck on the ship."

Her gaze flickered with the almost slip of her name, something like disappointment that gave Jacin a shot of guilt.

So he smacked her back lightly on the shoulder. "Your parents did well. You're named after something beautiful. It's fitting."

"*Winter,*" she whispered. Her expression turned speculative, the lights from a dress shop highlighting the specks of gray in her eyes.

Jacin tried not to be awkward when he looked away. There were times when she stood so close that he was amazed at his own ability to keep his hands to himself.

Moving the basket to her other arm, Winter started walking again. "Not everyone thinks I'm beautiful."

He scoffed. "Whoever told you that, they were lying. Or jealous. Probably both."

"*You* don't think I'm beautiful."

He snorted—somewhat uncontrollably—and laughed harder when she glared at him.

"That's funny?"

Schooling his expression, he mimicked her glare. "Keep saying things like that and people will start to think you've gone crazy."

She opened her mouth to refute. Hesitated. Nearly ran into a wall before Jacin scooped her back into the center of the narrow alley.

"You've never once called me beautiful," she said after his hand had fallen back to his side.

"In case you haven't noticed, you have an entire country of people singing your praises. Did you know they write poetry about you in the outer sectors? I had to listen to this drunk sing a whole ballad a few months back, all about your *goddess-like perfection*. I'm pretty sure the galaxy doesn't need my input on the matter."

She ducked her head, hiding her face behind a cascade of hair. Which was just as well. Jacin's cheeks had gone warm, which made him both self-conscious and irritated.

"*Your* input is the only input that matters," she whispered.

He stiffened, cutting a glance to her that she didn't return. It occurred to him that he may have led them into a topic he had no intentions of exploring further. Fantasies, sure. Wishes, all the time. But reality? No—this was taboo. This would end in nothing good.

She was a princess. Her stepmother was a tyrant who would marry Winter off to someone who was politically beneficial for her own desires.

Jacin was the opposite of politically beneficial.

But here they were, and there she was looking all pretty and rejected, and why had he opened his big, stupid mouth?

Jacin sighed, exasperated. With her. With himself. With this whole situation. "Come on, Princess. You know how I feel about you. *Everyone* knows how I feel about you."

Winter stopped again, but he kept walking, shaking his finger over his shoulder. "I'm not saying these things and looking at you at the same time, so keep up."

She scurried after him. "How do you feel about me?"

"No. That's it. That's all I'm saying. I am your *guard*. I am here to protect you and keep you out of trouble, and that's it. We are not swapping words that will result in a whole lot of awkward nights standing outside your bedroom door, got it?"

He was surprised at how angry he sounded—no, how angry he *felt*. Because it was impossible. It was impossible and unfair, and he had spent too many years in the trenches of unfairness to get riled up about it now.

Winter strode beside him, her fingers clenched around the basket handle. At least she wasn't trying to catch his eye anymore, which was a small mercy.

"I *do* know how you feel about me," she finally said, and it sounded like a confession. "I know that you are my guard, and you are my best friend. I know you would die for me. And I know that should that ever happen, I would die immediately after."

"Yeah," he said. "That's pretty much it." The sound of a nearby coffee grinder rumbled through the stone walkway, and the smell of baking bread assaulted his senses. He braced himself. "Also, I think you're sort of pretty. You know. On a good day."

She giggled and nudged him with her shoulder. He nudged her back and she stumbled into a flower planter, laughing harder now.

"You're sort of pretty too," she said. He threw a scowl at her, but it was impossible to hold on to when she was laughing like that.

"Your Highness!"

They both paused. Jacin stiffened, his hand going to his gun holster, but it was only a young girl watching them from the doorway of a little shop. A soap-filled bucket stood untouched at her feet and her eyes were as big as the full Earth.

"Oh, hello," said Winter, adjusting her basket. "Astrid, isn't it?"

The girl nodded, heat climbing up her cheeks as she gaped at the princess. "I—" She glanced toward the shop, then back to Winter. "Wait here!" she squealed, then dropped a rag into the bucket with a wet plop and rushed through the door.

Winter cocked her head to one side, her hair tumbling over her shoulder.

"You know that kid?"

"Her mother and father run this florist." She ran her fingers along a trailing vine in the window box.

Jacin grunted. "What does she want?"

"How should I know? I wish I'd brought them something . . ."

The girl reappeared, now with two younger boys in tow. "See? I told you she'd be back!" she was saying. The boys each paused to stare at Winter, their jaws hanging. The youngest was gripping a ring of twigs and dried flowers in both hands.

"Hello," said Winter, curtsying to each one. "I don't believe we've had the pleasure of meeting. I'm Winter."

When the boys couldn't find the courage to speak, Astrid answered, "These are my brothers, Your Highness, Dorsey and Dylan. I told them you bought flowers from our shop before and they didn't believe me."

"Well, it's true. I bought a posy of blue belldandies and kept them on my nightstand for a week."

"Wow," Dorsey breathed.

Winter smiled. "I'm sorry we can't stay to take a look through your shop this morning, but we're off to visit the milliner's assistant. Have you been to see the new baby yet?"

All three of them shook their heads. Then Astrid nudged the younger boy, Dylan, with her elbow. He jumped, but still couldn't bring himself to speak.

"We made something for you," said Astrid. "We've been waiting for you to come back. It's just . . . it's just from the leftovers, but . . ." She nudged her brother again, harder this time, and he finally held up the ring of flowers.

"What is this?" asked Winter, taking it into her hands.

Jacin frowned, then jolted as he realized what it was.

The older boy answered, "It's a crown, Your Highness. Took us almost a week of scrounging to get all the pieces." His cheeks were flushed bright red.

"I know it's not much," said the girl, "but it's for you."

The younger boy, having divested his gift, blurted suddenly, "You're *beautiful*," before ducking behind his brother.

Winter laughed. "You're all too kind. Thank you."

A hazy light caught Jacin's eye. Glancing upward, he spotted a nodule in the eaves of the next shop—a tiny camera watching over the shops and servants. There were thousands of identical cameras in sectors all over Luna, and he knew the chances of anyone minding the footage from a dull morning in AR-2 was unlikely, but a threatening chill still crept down his spine.

"The crown is lovely," Winter said, admiring the tiny white sprigs of flowers. She settled it on top of her thick black curls. "As splendid as the queen's jewels. I shall cherish it always."

With a growl, Jacin snatched the crown off her head and dropped it into the basket. "She will cherish it just as well in there," he snapped, his tone a warning. "The princess is busy. Go back inside, and don't go bragging about this to all your friends."

With frightened squeaks and wide eyes, the children couldn't have scurried back into the florist shop any faster. Grabbing Winter's elbow, Jacin dragged her away, though she soon ripped her arm out of his grip.

"Why did you do that?" she demanded.

"It looked bad."

"Accepting a gift from a few children? Honestly, Jacin, you don't have to be so mean."

"You could stand to be a little less *nice*," he spat back, scanning the walls and windows but not seeing any more cameras. "Putting it on your head. Are you insane?" She scowled at him and he scowled unapologetically back. "You're lucky no one saw." He gestured to the basket. "Cover it up before I rip it apart and bury it in one of these planters."

"You're overreacting," Winter said, though she did tuck a few of her hand towels around the mess of branches.

"You're not a queen, Princess."

Her gaze met his again, aghast. "I do not wish to be queen."

"Then stop accepting *crowns*."

Huffing, Winter turned away and marched on ahead—like a true princess would march ahead of her guard.

Fourteen

KAI WAITED UNTIL THORNE'S PODSHIP WAS A GLINT IN THE distance before he pulled out the portscreen Cinder had given him. Without an official ID chip confirming his identity, his comm to Royal Adviser Konn Torin was intercepted by the palace communications mainframe. The face of a young intern appeared.

"New Beijing Palace. How may I...direct..." Her eyes widened.

Kai smiled. "Emperor Kaito, for Royal Adviser Konn Torin, please."

"Y-yes, Your Majesty. Of course. Right away." Her cheeks bloomed red as she scrambled to redirect the commlink. Soon her image was replaced with Torin's.

"Your Majesty! Is it—are you—one moment. I'm stepping out of a meeting with the cabinet—are you all right?"

"I'm fine, Torin. But I'm ready to come home."

He heard the click of a door. "Where are you? Are you safe? Do you need—"

"I'll tell you everything when I get back. Right now I'm at our safe house on the Taihang terraces, and I'm alone. If you could alert the palace guard—"

"Right away, Your Majesty. We'll be there right away."

Torin suggested they keep the link open, afraid someone else would come for Kai before his own security team reached him. Although Cinder had ensured that the portscreen itself was untraceable, the link wasn't set up for direct communications and it was possible Lunars were listening in. But Kai knew Luna had lost their best method of surveillance when they'd lost Cress, so he insisted he was fine, he would be *fine*, before terminating the link.

He needed a moment to think before the whole galaxy spun out of control again.

Clipping the port to his belt, Kai climbed onto one of the large rocks overlooking the valley. He folded his legs beneath him, surprised at how calm he felt staring out at the terraces, plateaus that curled around the lush mountains, the teasing sparkle of a river winding at their feet. He could have gone inside the safe house to wait, but the weather was warm and there was a breeze that smelled like jasmine and it had been far too long since he'd admired the beautiful country he'd been born to.

After weeks aboard the Rampion, with its recycled air and reprocessed water, he was glad to be home.

And though he'd never seen Luna or its biodomes filled with artificial forests and man-made lakes, he was beginning to understand why Levana might want to dig her claws into Earth too.

Little time had passed when Kai heard the hum of engines. He kept his eye on the horizon, waiting for the podships. When they arrived, they arrived in force—a dozen military ships surrounding the safe house, many with guns drawn, and any number of personnel scanning the landscape for signs of a threat.

Squinting against the sunlight, Kai pushed his hair off his brow while the largest ship landed not far from the house. Uniformed officers poured out, establishing a perimeter and scanning for nearby life-forms, all jabbering into their headphones and holding ominous guns at the ready.

"Your Imperial Majesty," barked a gray-haired man, leading a team of four men up to him. "We are glad to see you, sir. Permission to conduct a security clearance scan?"

Kai pulled himself off the rock and handed the portscreen to one of the officers, who secured it in a crime evidence bag. He held out his arms while another officer dragged a scanner down his limbs.

"All clear. Welcome home, Your Majesty."

"Thank you. Where is Konn—"

A bang sent half a dozen personnel spinning toward the safe house, barking and leveling their guns at a cellar door that had burst open.

Konn Torin emerged, more harried than Kai had ever seen him. "Royal Adviser Konn Torin," he yelled, holding up his hands. His gaze flashed once over the guns, then landed on Kai near the edge of the plateau. His shoulders drooped with relief and as soon as one of the officers had scanned his wrist and confirmed his identity, Torin did something he had never done before.

He rushed toward Kai and hugged him.

The embrace was as quick as it was unexpected, before Torin pulled away and held Kai at arm's length, examining him. Kai was surprised to find he was slightly taller than Torin. That couldn't have happened in the past few weeks. Maybe he'd been taller for months and had never noticed. Having known Torin since he was a child, it was difficult to change his perception of him now.

Cinder told him that Torin had informed her of Kai's second

tracking chip. Maybe he was full of more surprises than Kai gave him credit for.

"Your face!" said Torin. "What did they do to you? She *promised* me—"

"I'm fine," said Kai, squeezing Torin's arm. "It's just a bruise. Don't worry about it."

"Don't worry—!"

"Your Majesty," interrupted the gray-haired man, "it may help to avoid media attention if you return through the safe house sublevels. We'll send a team to escort you."

Kai glanced around. A number of palace guards had emerged to join the flocking military. "If I'd known that was an option, I would have skipped this whole charade."

The officer didn't react.

"Yes, fine. Thank you for your thoroughness. Let's go."

Torin fell into step beside him, along with way too many guards, as they were ushered toward the cellar door.

"Nainsi will have tea waiting for you, and the chefs have been ordered to prepare refreshments for your return," said Torin. "The press secretary is drafting up a statement for the media, but you'll want to be briefed on the palace's official position regarding the security breach and kidnapping before we release anything."

Kai had to duck his head entering the house's basement. It was tidy, despite a few cobwebs in the corners, and as they headed into the passageways beneath the mountains they got brighter and cleaner.

"What's the status on the palace?" asked Kai.

"The enemy soldiers have not yet breached the palace walls. Our tactical analysts believe that if they do overrun the palace and discover there are no people to kill, they will redirect their attention to elsewhere. So far, we've found that these soldiers do not seem interested in general destruction or theft, only killing."

"Unless Levana is using the palace to make a statement. It would suggest they're winning."

"That is a possibility."

They rounded a corner and in the distance Kai could make out activity—talking and footsteps and the buzz of machinery. His entire staff was crammed into this labyrinth of rooms and hallways. He almost wished he'd stayed up on the terrace.

"Torin, what about the families of all these people? Are they safe?"

"Yes, sir. The families of all government officials were relocated to the palace within forty-eight hours of the first attacks. They are all here."

"And what about the people who aren't government officials? The chefs? The . . . the housekeepers?"

"I'm afraid we didn't have room for everyone. We would have brought down the whole city if we could."

Kai's gut clenched. He would have brought the whole *country* with him, if he could.

"Of course," he said, forcing himself not to dwell on the things he couldn't change. "Do I have an office down here? I need Nainsi to set up a meeting. This afternoon, if possible."

"Yes, Your Majesty. There are also private rooms set aside for the royal family. I'm having them made up now."

"Well, there's only one of me, and I only need one room. We can find something more useful to do with the rest of them."

"Of course. Who is Nainsi to contact for this meeting?"

He inhaled deeply. "My fiancée."

Torin's pace slowed and Kai thought he might come to a

complete stop, but Kai pulled his shoulders back and kept marching down the corridors. One of the guards ahead of them was yelling again—"Clear the way! Clear the way!"—as curious staff and officials emerged from doorways. Rumors were spreading fast and as Kai met the eyes of those he passed, he saw joy and relief cross their faces.

He gulped. It was strange to think how many people were worried about him—not just the people he saw every day, but citizens throughout the Commonwealth—waiting to hear if the kidnappers would return their emperor safely, having no idea that Linh Cinder was the last person in the world who would hurt him. It made him feel a little guilty for having enjoyed his time aboard the Rampion as much as he had.

"Your Majesty," said Torin, lowering his voice as he caught up with him again, "I must advise you to reconsider your arrangement with Queen Levana. We should at least discuss the best course of action before we make any hasty decisions."

Kai cut a glance toward his adviser. "Our government is being run out of an enormous bomb shelter and there are Lunar mutants beating down the doors of my palace. I'm not making hasty decisions. I'm doing what has to be done."

"What will the people think when they hear you intend to follow through with a marriage to the woman who is responsible for hundreds of thousands of deaths?"

"Millions. She's responsible for *millions* of deaths. But that doesn't change anything—we still need her letumosis antidote, and I'm hoping she'll accept the terms of a new cease-fire while we confirm alliance details."

One of the guards gestured toward an open door. "Your office, Your Majesty."

"Thank you. I require a moment of privacy with Konn-dàren, but if an android comes by with some tea, let her in."

"Yes, sir."

He stepped into the office. It was less lavish than his office in the palace, but not uncomfortable. Without windows, the room was filled with artificial light, but bamboo matting on the walls gave the space some warmth and helped deaden the sound of Kai's footsteps on the concrete floor. A large desk with a netscreen and half a dozen chairs took up the rest of the space.

Kai froze when his eyes landed on the desk and he started to laugh. On the corner of the desk sat a small, grime-filled cyborg foot. "You're kidding," he said, picking it up.

"I thought it was becoming a token of good luck," said Torin. "Although in hindsight, I can't imagine what led me to think that."

Smiling in amusement, Kai set Cinder's abandoned foot back down.

"Your Majesty," continued Torin, "what did you mean when you said Levana is already responsible for *millions* of deaths?"

Kai leaned against the desk. "We thought this war began when her special operatives attacked those first fifteen cities, but we were wrong. This war began when letumosis was manufactured in a Lunar laboratory and brought to Earth for the first time. All these years, she's been waging biological warfare on us, and we had no idea."

Though Torin was skilled at disguising his emotions, he couldn't hide his growing horror. "You're certain of this?"

"Yes. She wanted to weaken us, in population and resources, before she struck. I also suspect her ploy to offer an antidote as a bargaining chip was designed to create an immediate dependency on Luna—once she became empress."

"And you don't think this changes anything? Knowing it's all been a strategy to coerce you into this alliance, you still plan on going through with it? Your Majesty, there must be another way. Something we haven't considered yet." Torin's expression tightened. "I should inform you that in your absence, we've had a team focused on designing a new class of military-grade weaponry that will be able to penetrate even the biodomes on Luna."

Kai held his gaze. "We're building bombs."

"Yes. It's been a slow process. No Earthen military has built or harbored such weapons since the end of the Fourth World War, and there are unique modifications required to weaken Luna. But we believe that with Luna's limited resources and dependency on the domes to protect them—the success of a few bombs could mean a swift end to the war."

Kai stared down at his desk. All of Luna's population lived beneath specially designed biodomes that provided them with breathable atmosphere and artificial gravity and the ability to grow trees and crops. Destroying one of those protective barriers would kill everyone inside.

"How long before these weapons are ready?" he asked.

"We've finished the first prototype, and hope to have the first batch complete in four to six weeks. The fleet of spaceships required to transport the weapons is ready now."

Kai grimaced. He didn't want to say it, but he despised the thought of reducing Luna's cities to rubble. Already he had begun to think of Luna as belonging to Cinder, and he didn't want to destroy the kingdom that could someday be hers. But if it could end the war, and protect Earth ...

"Keep me informed of any developments," he said, "and have the space fleet ready at a moment's notice. This is a last resort. First, we will try to reach a peaceful resolution. Unfortunately, that begins with appeasing Levana."

"Your Majesty, I beg you to reconsider. We are not *losing* this war. Not yet."

"But we aren't winning it, either." Kai's lips twitched upward. "And one thing has changed. Until now, Levana has been calling all the shots, but for the first time, I might be a step ahead of her."

Eyes narrowing, Torin took a step closer. "This isn't about an alliance at all, is it?"

"Oh, I fully intend to form an alliance with Luna." Kai glanced at the cyborg foot again. "I just intend to put a different queen on the throne first."

Fifteen

THE COMMUNICATION LINK TOOK AGES TO CONNECT, WHILE Kai stood before the netscreen with his hands clasped behind his back and his heart thudding louder than the Rampion's engine. He hadn't bothered to change from the white silk wedding shirt he'd been wearing when he'd been kidnapped, though it was wrinkled and had a tiny hole where Cinder's tranquilizer dart had punctured it. Still, he thought Levana might appreciate that contacting her was his first priority—above a fresh change of clothes, above even alerting the Earthen media to his return.

He was going to use every tactic he could think of to get on her good side. Anything to make this believable.

Finally, *finally*, the small globe in the corner stopped turning and the netscreen brightened, revealing Levana in her sheer white veil.

"Could it be my dear young emperor?" she cooed. "I had all but given you up for lost. What has it been, more than a month, I believe? I thought for sure your captors had murdered and dismembered you by now."

Kai smiled, pretending she'd made an amusing joke. "A few bumps and scratches here and there, but nothing so horrible as all that."

"I see," Levana mused, tilting her head. "That bruise on your cheek looks recent."

"More recent than some of the others, yes," said Kai. Pretending his time aboard the Rampion had been a trial, barely endured, was the first step in his strategy. "Linh Cinder made it clear from the start that I was a prisoner aboard her ship, not a guest. Between you and me, I think she was still bitter I'd had her arrested at the ball."

"How savage."

"I'm considering myself lucky for now. I was finally able to negotiate my freedom. I've just returned to New Beijing. Informing you of my return was my highest priority."

"And to what do we owe this happy occasion? I suspect those negotiations must have been cumbersome."

"My kidnappers had many demands. A monetary payout, of course, and also that I call off the ongoing search for the fugitives, both Linh Cinder and Carswell Thorne."

The veil fluttered as Levana adjusted her hands on her lap. "They must have believed their capture was imminent," she said, her tone unimpressed. "Although I can't see how that would be, given that you could not apprehend them whilst they were *in your own palace.*"

Kai's smile remained poised. "Nevertheless, I agreed to it. However, I made no guarantees for the rest of the Union, nor Luna. I expect these criminals will be found and brought to justice for their crimes, including my own assault and kidnapping."

"I expect they will," said Levana, and he knew she was

mocking him, but for the first time the knowledge didn't crawl beneath his skin.

"They had one additional demand." Behind his back, Kai squeezed his hands together, forcing his nervous energy into them. "They insisted that I refuse to follow through with the alliance terms you and I had agreed upon. They asked that the wedding not be allowed to continue."

"Ah," said the queen, with a spiteful laugh, "now we get to the reason that contacting me was such a high priority. I am sure it killed you to agree to such egregious terms."

"Not really," he deadpanned.

Levana leaned back, and he could see her shoulders trembling. "And why should these criminals concern themselves with intergalactic politics? Are they not aware that they are already responsible for starting a war between our nations? Do they not believe I will find a way to sit upon the Commonwealth throne regardless of your selfish bargain?"

Kai gulped painfully. "Perhaps their interest has to do with Linh Cinder's claim that she is the lost Princess Selene."

A silence crackled between him and the netscreen, still as ice on a pond.

"She seems to think," Kai continued, "that should we proceed with this wedding and coronation, it will weaken what claim she might have on the Lunar throne."

"I see." Levana had reclaimed her composure and her flippant, whimsical tone. "I had wondered if she would fill your head with falsehoods. I imagine you were a captive audience."

He shrugged. "It's a pretty small spaceship."

"You believe these claims of hers to be fact?"

"Honestly?" He steeled himself. "I don't care one way or the other. I have over five billion people living under my protection, and for the past month, every one of them has gone to bed wondering if this would be the night their home was attacked. If this was the night their windows would be broken, their children pulled from their beds, their neighbors mutilated in the streets, all by your . . . by these *monsters* you've created. I can't—" He grimaced. This pain, at least, did not have to be faked. "I can't let this continue, and Linh Cinder, whether or not she is the lost princess, is not the one in charge of the Lunar military right now. I don't care about Lunar politics and family dynamics and conspiracy theories. I want this to end. And you're the one with the power to end it."

"A heartrending speech, young emperor. But our alliance is over."

"Is it? You seem convinced that I would bow to the whims of criminals and kidnappers."

She said nothing.

"You had my word long before I gave it to Linh Cinder. Therefore, I feel my agreement with you takes precedence. Wouldn't you agree?"

The veil shifted by her hands, like she was fidgeting with something. "I see that your time away has not diminished your impressive skills at diplomacy."

"I hope not."

"You're telling me that you wish to proceed with our previous arrangement?"

"Yes, under the same terms. We both agree to a cease-fire on all Earthen land and space territories, effective immediately. Upon your coronation as empress of the Eastern Commonwealth, all Lunar soldiers will be removed from Earthen soil, and you will allow us to manufacture and distribute your letumosis antidote."

"And what assurances can you give me that our wedding won't be subjected to the same mortifying spectacle as the last one? Surely your cyborg and her friends won't be pleased when they learn you've ignored their demands."

"I'm afraid I haven't had time to develop a plan. We'll increase security, of course. Bring in military reinforcements—I know how much you admire them."

Levana scoffed.

"But Linh Cinder has proven herself to be resourceful. One option would be to hold the ceremony in secret, and not release the proof of the wedding until after the coro—"

"No. I will not leave any question in the minds of the Earthen people that I am your wife, and their empress."

Kai's clenched his teeth to keep from gagging at the words. *Your wife. Their empress.* "I understand. We can consider other locations to host the ceremony, something more remote and secure. A spaceship, perhaps? Or even . . ."

He hesitated, trying to look appalled at his own unspoken thought.

"Or even what?"

"I was just . . . I doubt this would appeal to you. It would require a lot of work, and I don't know if it's even plausible . . . but, why not host the wedding on Luna? It would be impossible for Linh Cinder to interfere then."

Here, he paused, and tried not to seem like he was holding his breath.

The silence grew thick between them. Kai's heart began to pound.

It was too much. He'd made her suspicious.

Kai started to chuckle, shaking his head. "Never mind, it was a stupid idea." His mind whirred for another angle he could take.

"I'm sure we'll find a suitable location on Earth. I just need some time to—"

"You *are* clever, aren't you?"

His heart skipped. "Excuse me?"

The queen tittered. "Somewhere remote, somewhere secure. My darling emperor, of *course* we should host the wedding on Luna."

Kai paused, waited, then exhaled slowly, keeping his expression neutral. Another moment, and he remembered to even be skeptical. "Are you sure? We already have everything set up on Earth. All the transportation and accommodations, the catering, the announcements—"

"Don't be ridiculous." She fluttered her fingers behind the veil. "I don't know why I didn't think of it sooner. We will host the ceremony here in Artemisia. We have plenty of space for accommodations, and I have no doubt you will be pleased with the hospitality we can offer."

Kai pursed his lips, worried to dissuade her from the idea, and equally worried to appear too enthusiastic.

"Is this a problem, Your Imperial Majesty?"

"I don't doubt Artemisia is . . . lovely. But now that I'm considering it, I'm concerned this might alienate those guests who would have been privileged to attend the wedding here on Earth. In particular, the leaders of the Earthen Union."

"But of course the invitation will be extended to all Earthen diplomats. I would be disappointed if they didn't attend. After all, our union will be a symbol of peace, not only between Luna and the Commonwealth, but between Luna and all Earthen nations. I can extend the invitation to each of our Earthen guests personally, if you think that would be appropriate."

He scratched behind his ear. "With all due respect, there may be some ... *hesitation* from the Union leaders. If I may be blunt, how can you guarantee that we—*they* won't be walking into a trap? You've made no attempts to disguise your threats against Earth and there are suspicions that you might still use your status as empress as a launchpad for, well ..."

"World domination?"

"Precisely."

Levana tittered. "And what do you fear, exactly? That I might assassinate the heads of the Earthen Union while they're here, as a way of paving an easier path to taking control of their silly little countries?"

"*Precisely.*"

Another giddy laugh. "My dear emperor, this is an offer of peace. I want to earn the trust of the Union, not alienate them. You have my word that *all* Earthen guests will be treated with the utmost courtesy and respect."

Kai slowly, slowly let his shoulders relax. Not that he believed her for a minute, but it didn't matter. She had acted how he'd hoped she would.

"In fact," continued Levana, "as a show of my goodwill, I will agree to your request of an immediate cease-fire throughout the Union, and that cease-fire will be upheld in every Earthen territory whose leaders accept our invitation to attend the wedding here in Artemisia."

Kai flinched.

That was one way to increase attendance.

He rubbed his palms down the wrinkled fabric of his shirt. "I can't argue with the point that Artemisia is more secure than any place we could choose on Earth. I will discuss this with the leaders of the Earthen Union immediately."

"Please do, Your Majesty. As I'm sure the change of location will not be a problem, I'll begin making preparations for your visit, and our matrimonial and coronation ceremonies."

"Right, and . . . on that note. When would you like—"

"I suggest the eighth of November for our wedding and celebratory feast, followed by both coronations on the day following the new moon. We can schedule it to coincide with our sunrise—it is a beautiful time here on Luna."

Kai blinked. "That's . . . my days might be a little off, what with the whole hostage thing, but . . . isn't that only a week away?"

"Ten days, Your Majesty. This alliance has been deterred for too long. I do not believe anyone wishes to see my patience tried further. I do *so* look forward to receiving you and your guests." She dipped her head in a courteous farewell. "My ports will be ready to receive you."

Sixteen

THE AUDIO FEED DISCONNECTED WITH A SOFT CLICK, LEAVING the cargo bay in silence. Sitting atop one of the now-empty storage crates, Cress glanced around, taking in Cinder's tense shoulders as she stared at the blank netscreen, the way Wolf was tapping his fingers against his elbows, and Iko, who was still focused on the portscreen on her lap, trying to figure out her next move in the game she and Cress had been playing for the last hour.

"He did it," mumbled Cinder.

"Of course he did," said Iko, without looking up. "We knew he would."

Turning her back on the screen, Cinder scratched idly at her wrist. "The eighth is a lot sooner than I'd expected. I bet Earthen leaders will start departing within the next forty-eight hours."

"Good," said Wolf. "The wait is driving me crazy."

No, the separation from Scarlet was driving him crazy, Cress knew, but no one said anything. Maybe the wait was driving them all a little crazy.

"Jester to A1!" Iko finally announced. Beaming, she held the port out to Cress.

"King to C4, and I claim all rubies," said Cress, without hesitation.

Iko paused, looked down at the screen, and deflated. "How are you so good at this?"

Cress felt a rush of pride behind her sternum, although she wasn't sure if such a talent was impressive or embarrassing. "I played this a lot when I was bored on the satellite. And I got bored a lot."

"But my brain is supposed to be superior."

"I've only ever played against a computer if that makes you feel better."

"It doesn't." Iko crinkled her nose. "I want that diamond." Setting the port back into her lap, she fisted her hand around a ponytail of braids, once again deep in concentration.

Cinder cleared her throat, drawing Cress's focus, but not Iko's. "Kai will have a fleet with him. It's imperative we know which ship he's on."

Cress nodded. "I can find out."

"This plan will work," said Wolf forcefully, like he was threatening the plan itself. He started to pace between the cockpit and medbay. His and Cinder's anxiety made Cress more nervous than anything.

This was it, their only chance. Either it worked, or they failed.

"Crown-maker to A12."

It took Cress a moment to switch her thoughts back to the game. Iko had made the move she expected her to, the same move her computer aboard the satellite would have made.

Cress sacrificed her Jester, then proceeded to sneak her Thief across the board, snatching up every loose emerald, until even Iko's coveted diamond wouldn't win her the game.

"Ah! Why didn't I see that?" Growling, Iko pushed the portscreen away. "I never liked this game anyway."

"Podship detected," said the Rampion's monotone voice. Cress jumped, every muscle in her body tightening. "Captain Thorne is requesting permission to dock. Submitted code word: *Captain is King.*"

She exhaled, relieved not only that they hadn't been spotted by an enemy ship, but that Thorne was back. All the worry she'd been harboring since he and Kai had left rose to the surface of her skin and evaporated with a single breath.

"Permission granted," said Cinder, a fair amount of relief in her tone as well. She crossed her arms over her chest. "Step one complete. Kai is back on Earth, the wedding is rescheduled to take place on Luna, and Thorne has returned safely." She rocked back on her heels, a crease between her eyebrows. "I can't believe nothing went wrong."

"I would wait until you're sitting on a throne before making statements like that," said Wolf.

Cinder twisted her lips. "Good point. All right, everyone." She slapped her hands together. "Let's get started on any last-minute preparations. Cress and Iko, you're in charge of making final edits to the video. Wolf, I need you to—"

The door to the sublevel hatch burst open, crashing against the wall. Thorne heaved himself up the ladder and immediately rounded on Cinder, who took a startled step back.

"*You painted my ship?*" he yelled. "Why—what—why would you do that?"

Cinder opened her mouth, but hesitated. She had clearly expected a different sort of greeting. "Oh. That." She glanced around at Cress, Wolf, and Iko, like asking for backup. "I thought—wow, that was a long time ago. I guess I should have mentioned it."

"*Mentioned* it? You shouldn't have—! You can't go around painting someone else's ship! Do you know how long it took me to paint that girl in the first place?"

Cinder squinted one eye shut. "Judging from how precise and detailed it was, I'm going to guess . . . ten minutes? Fifteen?"

Thorne scowled.

"All right, I'm sorry. But the silhouette was too recognizable. It was a liability."

"A liability! *You're* a liability!" He pointed at Wolf. "He's a liability. Cress is a liability. We're *all* liabilities!"

"Am I one too?" asked Iko. "I don't want to be left out."

Thorne rolled his eyes and threw his hands into the air. "Whatever. It's *fine.* Not like it's *my* ship anyway, is it?" Growling, he dragged a hand through his hair. "I do wish you would have said something before I had a heart attack thinking I'd just hailed the wrong ship."

"You're right. Won't happen again." Cinder attempted a nervous smile. "So . . . how did it go?"

"Fine, fine." Thorne waved the question away. "Despite my inherent distrust of authority figures, I'm starting to like this emperor of yours."

Cinder raised an eyebrow. "I don't know if I should be relieved or worried."

Cress bit her cheek, burying an amused smile. She'd sensed some discomfort from Thorne when Kai had come aboard—after all, "Emperor" outranked "Captain" by just about anyone's standards—but she'd also noticed how Thorne stood a little straighter in Kai's presence, like he wanted the emperor to be impressed by him and his ship and his crew . . . just a little.

Shrugging off his jacket, Thorne draped it over the nearest crate. "Anything exciting happen while I was away?" For the first time, his gaze darted past Cinder and Iko to land on Cress, and the look was so sudden and focused she became instantly flustered. Tearing her gaze away, she set to inspecting the metal wall plating.

"The wedding is back on," said Cinder. "It will take place in Artemisia on the eighth, with the coronation to follow two days later at Lunar sunrise."

Thorne's eyebrows jumped upward. "Not wasting any time. Anything else?"

"Levana agreed to a cease-fire," said Wolf, "but we're waiting to hear if it's been implemented."

"Also, Cress destroyed me in a game of Mountain Miners," said Iko.

Thorne nodded, as if these two announcements carried the same weight. "She is a genius."

Cress's blush deepened, frustratingly. It had been easier to pretend she wasn't in love with him when he couldn't tell how often her gaze attached to him, how she blushed at every stray compliment.

"Yeah, but I'm an *android*."

Thorne laughed, all anger over the painted ship gone. "Why don't you play Android Assault then? Maybe that'll give you an upper hand."

"Or Robot Resistance," suggested Cinder.

Thorne snapped his fingers. "*Yes*. Vintage quality." His eyes were twinkling, all calm and confident in that way that always made Cress feel more calm and confident too, just from being near him and knowing he was brave and capable and—

And he was looking at her. Again.

She looked away. Again.

Stupid, stupid, stupid.

Mortified, she found herself fantasizing about crawling down to the podship dock and getting sucked out into space.

"We should get started," Cinder said. "Pack what supplies we think we'll need, prepare the ship for extended neutral orbit."

"You mean abandonment," said Thorne, the lightness fading from his tone.

"I've already adjusted the wiring for the most efficient settings. It will be fine."

"You know that's not true. Without Cress disrupting the signals, it won't be long before the ship is found and confiscated."

Cinder sighed. "It's a risk we have to take. How about, once I'm queen, I'll use my royal coffers or whatever to buy you a new ship?"

Thorne glowered. "I don't want a new ship."

Cress felt a pang of sympathy. They were all sad to be leaving the Rampion. It had been a good home for the short time it sheltered them.

"You know, Thorne," said Cinder, speaking softly, like she didn't want to say what she was about to say, "you don't have to come with us. You could take us to Kai, then come back to the Rampion and . . . you know we would never give you away." She took in a deep breath. "I mean it. For all of you. You don't have to go with me. I know the danger I'm putting you in, and that you didn't know what you were signing up for when you joined me. You could go on with your lives, and I wouldn't stop you. Wolf, Cress, returning to Luna must feel like a death sentence to you both. And, Iko—"

Iko held up a hand. "You need a system debug if you're suggesting that I would abandon you now."

Thorne grinned. His self-assured, one-sided grin. "She's right. It's sweet of you to worry, but there's no way you can pull this off without us."

Pressing her lips, Cinder didn't argue.

Cress stayed silent, wondering if she was the only one who was briefly tempted by Cinder's offer. Returning to Luna *was* like sentencing themselves to death—especially a shell like her, who should have been killed years ago. Undermining Levana from the safety of space was one thing. But walking right into Artemisia . . . it was almost like asking to be killed.

But Thorne was right. Cinder needed them. All of them.

She shut her eyes and reminded herself to be brave.

"Besides," added Iko, breaking the tension, "our captain is still holding out for that reward money."

The others laughed and a smile fluttered over Cress's lips, but when she opened her eyes, Thorne wasn't laughing with the rest of them.

In fact, he looked suddenly uncomfortable, his shoulders tense. "Well, you know, some people might say that doing the right thing is a reward in itself."

The cargo bay fell still. Cress blinked.

Uncertainty stretched between them.

With a nervous chuckle, Thorne added, "But those people die poor and destitute, so who cares what they think?" He brushed away his own words. "Come on, freeloaders. Let's get to work."

Seventeen

KAI STARED OUT THE WINDOW, WATCHING THE CLOUDS swirl over the continent below. He sought out the Great Wall snaking across the Commonwealth and smiled to think his ancestors had built something even the Fourth World War couldn't destroy.

He hoped this wouldn't be the last time he saw his beautiful country.

He knew the danger he was putting himself in, along with countless representatives from the rest of the Union. He hoped Levana had been truthful when she said she meant them no harm. He hoped this wasn't about to turn into a bloodbath in which the naïve Earthens made for easy prey.

He hoped, but hoping did little to comfort him. He didn't trust Levana. Not for a moment.

But this was the only way to give Cinder the chance she needed to face Levana and start her rebellion. Cinder's success would rid them all of Levana and her tyranny. No more plague. No more war.

Stars, he hoped this worked.

Burying a sigh, he cast his restless gaze around the sitting room of his royal ship. If it weren't for the breathtaking view of Earth, Kai would have had no idea he was aboard a spaceship at all. The décor held all the old-world decadence of the palace: ornate lanterns and gilt wallpapers and a theme of flying bats carved into the crown moldings. Long ago, bats had been a symbol of good luck, but over the years they had come to symbolize safe travels through the darkness of space.

Torin caught his eye from an upholstered chair on the other side of the room, where he was busy reading his portscreen. He had insisted on coming to Luna, asserting that the Chair of National Security, Deshal Huy, would be capable of acting as head of the Commonwealth in their absence. Torin's place was beside Kai—for whatever it was worth.

"Is something wrong, Your Majesty?"

"Not so far." He rubbed his palms on his thighs. "You told the pilots I want to be informed if any ships hail us?"

"Of course. I wish I could tell you they found it to be a reasonable request, but they seemed understandably suspicious."

"Just as long as they do it."

"And you're sure this is a good idea?"

"Not in the slightest." The ship turned and Earth was no longer visible through the window. Kai turned away. "But I trust her."

Torin set down his port. "Then I have no choice but to trust her as well."

"Hey, you're the one who told her about my second tracking chip."

"Yes, and I have since wondered if that was the biggest mistake I've ever made."

"It wasn't." Kai rolled his shoulders, trying to relax. "Cinder can do this."

"You mean, Selene can do this."

"Selene. Cinder. She's the same person, Torin."

"I must disagree. To the world, Linh Cinder is a dangerous felon who kidnapped a world leader and instigated a war, while Princess Selene could be the solution to all our problems with Luna. By helping Linh Cinder, the world will think you're nothing but an infatuated teenager. By helping Selene, you're making a brave stand against our country's enemies and doing what you believe is best for the Commonwealth's future."

A wisp of a smile jotted across Kai's lips. "Whatever the world thinks, they *are* the same person. I want what's best for Cinder, and I want what's best for my country. Conveniently, I believe those are the same thing."

It had been a relief to tell Torin everything—the only person he trusted to keep his secrets. Cinder's identity, the real reason they were going to Luna, the revolution she planned to start there, and Kai's role in it all. Though Torin expressed concern that Kai was risking far too much, he hadn't tried to talk him out of it. In fact, Kai wondered if Torin wasn't developing a little bit of faith in Cinder as well, even if he tried to hide it behind cold cynicism.

Torin returned his attention to his portscreen, and Kai sat watching through the window, his heart skipping every time he spotted another ship against the backdrop of space.

Hours passed like days. Kai tried to take a nap, to no avail. He read over his wedding vows without comprehending a word. He paced back and forth, and drank half a cup of tea that someone brought him—except it wasn't as good as Nainsi would have made, which made him miss his trusted android assistant. He'd come to rely on her practical, no-nonsense conversation, but Levana was adamant that no androids would be allowed on Luna, so he was forced to leave Nainsi behind.

He set the tea aside, his stomach writhing with nerves. He should have heard from Cinder by now. Something had gone wrong, and here he was flying an entire fleet of Earth's most powerful people right into Levana's clutches and it would all be for nothing and—

"Your Majesty?"

His head snapped up. The ship's first mate stood in the doorway.

"Yes?"

"We've been hailed by the American Republic's secretary of defense. It seems they're having technical issues with their ship's computer mainframe and have requested permission to board and complete the trip to Artemisia with us."

Kai exhaled.

"The captain suggests we send one of the military escorts to assist them. I'm happy to put them in touch—"

"That won't be necessary," said Kai. "We have the room. Let them board." Though a dozen province representatives and some journalists from the Commonwealth media were already aboard, the ship was nowhere near capacity.

The officer frowned. "I do believe it's a matter of security, not space. Due to their technical difficulties, we've been unable to obtain a proper ID on the ship or its officers. Their vid-comm is also malfunctioning. Our visual of the ship does confirm it as a Republic military ship, Rampion class, but beyond that we're forced to take them at their word, and I'm sure I don't need to remind Your Majesty that . . . your kidnappers were also in a Rampion."

Kai pretended to consider his point. "The Rampion I was held hostage aboard had the silhouette of a lady painted on its port side. Is there such a marking on the secretary's ship?"

The officer relayed the question into a comm-chip on his collar, and a moment later confirmed that no such lady was visible. Only black paneling on the boarding ramp.

"There you have it," said Kai, attempting nonchalance. "We will accept our American allies on board, assuming their podships are in working order. In fact, why don't I come down to the dock to greet them, as a show of political goodwill?"

"I'll come as well," said Torin, setting his port aside.

The first mate looked like he wanted to object but, after an uncertain moment, clicked his heels together and nodded. "Of course, Your Majesty."

EVEN THE WAITING ROOM OUTSIDE THE PODSHIP DOCK WAS luxurious and Kai found himself tapping his foot on thick carpet while machinery hummed in the surrounding walls. The ship's captain had joined them, waiting to greet their guests before returning to the bridge, and he and the first mate stood with impeccable posture in their unwrinkled uniforms.

The screen beside the sealed doors announced that the dock was safe to enter.

The captain went first, Kai right behind him. There were six of their own podships waiting, and empty spaces for three more. The Rampion's shuttle had taken the farthest spot and sat with its engines powering down.

The two doors rose simultaneously and five people emerged—America's secretary of defense, one assistant, one intern, and two security agents.

The captain shook the secretary's hand, welcoming the newcomers aboard, followed by a series of diplomatic bows.

"Thank you for your hospitality. We do apologize for any inconvenience this may have caused," said the secretary, as Kai tried to figure out who this was beneath the illusion. He guessed Thorne and Wolf were the security agents, but the glamour being cast for the Republic's secretary was perfect, straight down to the mole on the right side of her chin. The assistant and intern were equally convincing. It was impossible to distinguish them from Cinder, Iko, and Cress.

"Evidently," added the assistant, gaze flashing in Kai's direction, "this all could have been avoided if the ship's mechanic had remembered to bring a pair of *wire cutters*."

Kai's mouth twitched. That one, then, was Cinder. He tried to imagine her beneath the glamour, smug over her use of their new "code word." He refrained from rolling his eyes at her.

"It's no inconvenience at all," said Kai, focusing on the secretary. "We're glad we could be of assistance. Do you need us to send anyone to retrieve your ship?"

"No, thank you. The Republic has already sent a maintenance crew, but we didn't want to be delayed longer than necessary. We do have a party to get to, you know."

The secretary winked, very un-diplomat-like. Iko, then.

Remembering Cinder's warning—that it would be tiring for her to not only glamour herself but also manipulate the perception of her four comrades, and she didn't know how long she'd be able to maintain it—Kai gestured toward the exit. "Come with me. We have a sitting room where we'll all be comfortable. Can I offer you some tea?"

"I'll have a whiskey on the rocks," said one of the security personnel.

Cinder-the-assistant cast a cold glare at the man. *Thorne.*

"We're fine," said Cinder. "Thank you."

"Right this way." Kai and Torin led their guests away from the docking bay, dismissing the captain and first mate. No one spoke until they'd made their way back to his private rooms.

When Kai faced his guests again, the disguises were gone and the reality of seeing five known criminals in his sitting room reminded him that he'd just put everyone aboard this ship in a great amount of danger.

"Is this room secure?" asked Thorne.

"It should be," said Kai. "We use it for international conferencing and—"

"Cress?"

"On it, Captain." Cress pulled a portscreen from her back pocket and went to the control panel built into the wall, running whatever system check she'd devised.

"This is Konn Torin, my head adviser. Torin, you remember Cin—"

"Wait," said Cinder, holding up a hand.

Kai paused.

Nine long, silent seconds passed between them, before finally Cress unplugged her portscreen. "All clear."

"Thank you, Cress," said Thorne.

Cinder lowered her hand. "Now we can talk."

Kai raised an eyebrow. "Right. Torin, you remember Cinder and Iko."

Torin nodded at them, his arms crossed, and Cinder returned the nod, laced with an equal amount of tension. "I told you I'd return him safely," she said.

A flicker of irony passed over Torin's face. "You promised no harm would come to him. In my opinion, that includes physical injury."

"It was just one punch, Torin." Kai shrugged at Cinder. "I tried to explain it was all a part of the charade."

"I understand perfectly, but forgive me for being defensive." Torin scrutinized their new guests. "Though I'm grateful Kai has been returned, it seems this ordeal is hardly over. I hope you know what you're doing, Linh Cinder."

Kai expected her to make some self-deprecating remark about how Torin wasn't the only one, but instead, after a long silence, Cinder asked, "How much does he know?"

"Everything," said Kai.

She turned back to Torin. "In that case, thank you for your help. May I introduce you to the rest of our team: Iko you've met, and this is our ship's captain, Carswell Thorne, our software engineer, Cress Darnel, and my security officer . . . Wolf."

As Torin greeted their guests with more respect than was required, given the circumstances, Kai's attention lingered on Cinder. She stood ten full paces away from him, and as much as Kai wanted to cross the room and kiss her, he couldn't. Maybe it was Torin's presence. Maybe it was knowing they were on their way to Luna, where he would be married. Maybe he was afraid their time spent on the Rampion had been a dream, too fragile to survive in reality.

Though he'd seen her three days ago, it felt like a lifetime. A wall had been erected between them during that absence, though he wasn't sure what had changed. Their relationship was precarious. Kai felt like if he breathed the wrong way, he might destroy everything, and he could see the same uncertainty mirrored in Cinder's face.

"Oh, look," said Iko, crossing to the row of windows. Luna was emerging in their view, bright white and pocked with a thousand craters and cliffs. They were close enough to see the biodomes, sunlight glinting off their surfaces.

Kai had never in his life dreamed he would step foot on Luna. Seeing it now, the inevitability of his fate made his stomach squeeze tight.

Cinder turned to Kai. She was doing a good job of hiding her anxiety, but he was learning to recognize it beneath her squared shoulders and determined looks. "I hope you have something for us?"

Kai gestured at a cabinet against the wall.

Iko was the first one there, yanking open the doors with effervescent enthusiasm, but it wilted fast when she saw the clothes Nainsi had gathered. The stack was a mix of browns and grays and dull whites, linens and cottons. Simple, utilitarian clothing.

"That looks right," said Wolf, who had been the most helpful in describing what the people of Luna's outer sectors might wear.

While they eyed the clothes and began deciding who got which pieces, Kai crossed to another cabinet and pulled out a sheet of fiberglass android plating and a tub of synthetic skin fibers. "And this is for Iko. Plus everything Cinder should need to install it."

Iko squealed and launched herself across the room. Kai braced himself for another hug, but instead she was all over the new plating, marveling at the supplies. Cinder wasn't far behind.

"These are perfect," said Cinder, examining the fibers. Her eyes glinted teasingly. "You know, if this emperor thing doesn't work out, you might have a future career in espionage."

He gave her a wry look. "Let's make sure this emperor thing works out, all right?"

Cinder's face softened and she smiled for the first time since they'd boarded. Dropping the fibers back into their tub, she hesitated for a moment, before taking the last few steps toward Kai and wrapping her arms around him.

He shut his eyes. Just like that, the wall was gone. His arms were eager to pull her against him.

"Thank you," Cinder whispered, and he knew it wasn't for the clothes or the android parts. The words were weighted with faith and trust and sacrifices Kai wasn't ready to think about just yet. He squeezed her tighter, pressing his temple against her hair.

Cinder was still smiling when she extricated herself from the embrace, though it was laced with determination. "Time is running out," she said. "I suggest we go over the plan, one more time."

Eighteen

WINTER LET THE MAID STYLE HER HAIR, PULLING THE TOP
half into a thick braid threaded with strands of gold and silver
and leaving the rest to cascade around her shoulders. She let the
maid pick out a pale blue dress that grazed her skin like water
and a strand of rhinestones to accent her neck. She let the maid
rub scented oils into her skin.

She did not let the maid put any makeup on her—not even to
cover the scars. The maid didn't put up much of a fight. "I suppose you don't need it, Highness," she said, bobbing a curtsy.

Winter knew she had a sort of exceptional beauty, but she
had never before been given a reason to enhance it. No matter
what she did, gazes would follow her down the corridors. No
matter what she did, her stepmother would snarl and try to hide
her envy.

But since Jacin confessed he was not immune to her appearance, she had been looking forward to this chance to dress up in
new finery. Not that she expected much to come from it other
than a heady satisfaction. She knew it was naïve to think Jacin
might ever do something as crazy as profess his love for her. If he

did love her at all. Which she was confident he did, he *must*, after all these years . . . yet, his treatment of her had had a distant quality since he joined the royal guard. The professional respect he maintained too often made her want to grab his lapels and kiss *him*, just to see how long it would take for him to thaw.

No, she did not expect a confession or a kiss, and she knew all too well a courtship was out of the question. All she wanted was an admiring smile, one breathless look that would sustain her.

As soon as the maid had gone, Winter peeked into the corridor, where Jacin stood at his post.

"Sir Clay, might I solicit your opinion before we go to greet our Earthen guests?"

He waited two full breaths before responding. "At your service, Your Highness."

He did not, however, remove his attention from the corridor wall.

Smoothing down her skirt, Winter situated herself in front of him. "I wanted to know if you thought I looked sort of pretty today?"

Another breath, this one a bit louder. "Not funny, Princess."

"Funny? It's an honest question." She bunched her lips to one side. "I'm not sure blue is my color."

With a glower, he finally looked at her. "Are you *trying* to drive me crazy?"

She laughed. "Crazy loves company, Sir Clay. I notice you haven't answered my question."

His jaw tightened as he returned his focus to some spot over her head. "Go look for compliments elsewhere, Princess. I'm busy protecting you from unknown threats."

"And what a fine job you're doing." She tried to hide her disappointment as she headed back into her chambers, patting Jacin on the chest as she passed. But with that touch, his hand gathered up a fistful of her skirt, anchoring her beside him. Her heart flipped, and despite all her bravado, Jacin's piercing gaze made her feel tiny and childish.

"Please stop doing this," he whispered, more pleading than angry. "Just . . . leave it alone."

She gulped, and thought to feign ignorance. But, no—ignorance was what she feigned for everyone else. Not Jacin. Never Jacin. "I hate this," she whispered back. "I hate having to pretend like I don't even see you."

His expression softened. "I know you see me. That's all that matters. Right?"

She gave a slight nod, though she wasn't sure she agreed. How lovely it would have been to live in a world where she didn't have to pretend.

Jacin released her and she slipped into her chambers, shutting the door behind her. She was surprised to find herself lightheaded. She must have been holding her breath when he'd stopped her and now—

She froze a few steps into the sitting room. Her gut tightened, her nostrils filling with the iron tang of blood.

It was all around her. On the walls. Dripping from the chandelier. Soaking into the upholstered cushions of the settee.

A whimper escaped her.

It had been weeks since she had one of the visions. None had haunted her since Jacin's return. She'd forgotten the overwhelming dread, the swoop of horror in her stomach.

She squeezed her eyes shut.

"J-Jacin?" Something warm splattered on her shoulder, no doubt staining the beautiful blue silk. She took a step back and felt the area rug squish wetly beneath her feet. "Jacin!"

He burst through the door, and though she kept her eyes pressed tight, she could imagine him behind her, weapon drawn.

"Princess—what is it?" He grabbed her elbow. "Princess?"

"The walls," she whispered.

A beat, followed by a low curse. She heard his gun being replaced in its holster, then he was in front of her, his hands on her shoulders. His voice dropped, becoming tender. "Tell me."

She tried to swallow, but her saliva was thick and metallic. "The walls are bleeding. The chandelier too, and it got on my shoulder, and I think it's staining my shoes, and I can smell it, and taste it, and why—" Her voice unraveled all at once. "Why does the palace hurt so much, Jacin? Why is it always dying?"

He pulled her against him, cradling her body. His arms were stable and protective and he was not bloody and he was not broken. She sank into the embrace, too dazed to return it, but willing to accept the comfort. She buried herself in the security of him.

"Take a breath," he commanded.

She did, though the air was clouded with death.

She was glad to let it out again.

"It's all in your head, Princess. You know that. Say it now."

"It's all in my head," she murmured.

"Are the walls bleeding?"

She shook her head, feeling the press of his ranking pin against her temple. "No. They don't bleed. It's all in my head."

His hold tightened. "You're all right. It will pass. Just keep breathing."

She did. Again and again and again, his voice coaxing her through each breath until the smell of blood gradually subsided.

She felt dizzy and exhausted and sick to her stomach, but glad her breakfast hadn't come up. "It's better now. It's gone."

Jacin exhaled, like he'd been forgetting to breathe himself. Then, in a strange moment of vulnerability, he craned his head and kissed her on the shoulder, right where the nonexistent drop of blood had fallen before. "That wasn't so bad," he said, with a new lightness. "No windows at least."

Winter cringed, remembering the first time she saw the castle walls bleeding. She'd been so distraught and desperate to get away she tried to throw herself from the second-floor balcony—Jacin barely got to her in time to pull her back.

"Or sharp utensils," she said, carrying it off as a joke. The time she'd stabbed a dozen holes into her drapes trying to kill the spiders that were crawling over them, once stabbing her own hand in the process. It had not been a deep wound, but Jacin took care to keep sharp objects away from her ever since.

He pushed to arm's length, inspecting her. She forced a smile, then realized it wasn't forced after all. "It's over. I'm all right."

His eyes warmed and for the briefest of moments she thought—*this is it, this is when he will kiss me*—

There was a cough from the doorway.

Jacin recoiled.

Winter spun around, heart thundering.

Aimery stood in the open door, his expression dark. "Your Highness."

Catching her breath, Winter tucked a curl behind her ear—it must have fallen loose from the braid. She was warm all over. Flustered and nervous and aware that she should be embarrassed, but she was more annoyed at the interruption than anything else.

"Thaumaturge Park," she said with a cordial nod. "I was having one of my nightmares. Sir Clay was assisting me."

"I see," said Aimery. "If the nightmare has receded, I suggest he return to his post."

Jacin clicked his heels and left wordlessly, though it was impossible to tell if it was by his own volition or if Aimery was controlling him.

Still trying to compose herself, Winter fluttered a smile at the thaumaturge. "It must be time to leave for the docks?"

"Nearly," he said, and, to her surprise, he turned and shut the door to the corridor. Her fingers twitched defensively, but not out of concern for herself. Poor Jacin would hate to be left stranded on the other side, unable to protect her should anything happen.

Which was an inane thought. Even if Jacin was present, he could do nothing against a thaumaturge. Winter often thought this was a weakness in their security. She never trusted the thaumaturges, yet they were given so much power within the palace.

After all, a thaumaturge killed her father, and she never got over this fact. To this day, a long sleeve caught from the corner of her eye too often made her startle.

"Was there something you needed?" she asked, trying to appear unconcerned. She was still recovering from the vision. Her stomach was in knots and warm sweat clung to the back of her neck. She wanted to lie down for a minute, but she didn't want to appear any weaker than she already did. Than she already *was*.

"I have come to pose a rather interesting proposition, Your Highness," said Aimery. "One I have been thinking on for some time, and that I hope you will agree is beneficial to us both. I have already suggested the idea to Her Majesty, and she has voiced her approval, on the condition of your consent."

His voice was both slippery and kind. Always when she was in Aimery's presence Winter wished to both cower away and curl up sleepily beneath his steady timbre.

"Forgive me, Aimery, my brain is still muddled from the hallucination and I'm having difficulties understanding you."

His gaze slipped over her, lingering on her scars and on her curves, and Winter was glad she didn't involuntarily shudder.

"Princess Winter Blackburn." He slinked closer. She couldn't resist taking a step back before she managed to stop herself. Fear was a weakness in the court. Much better to act unperturbed. Much safer to act crazy, when in doubt.

She wished she had not told him the nightmare was over. She wished the walls had gone on bleeding.

"You are a darling of the people. Beloved. *Beautiful.*" His fingers stroked beneath her chin, with the delicacy of a feather. This time, she did shudder. "Everyone knows you will never be queen, but that does not mean you cannot wield your own sort of power. An ability to appease the people, to bring them joy. They admire you greatly. It is important that we show the people your support for the royal family and the court that serves them. Don't you agree?"

Her skin had become a mess of goose bumps. "I have always shown support for the queen."

"Certainly you have, my princess." His smile was lovely when he wanted it to be, and the loveliness of it curdled her stomach. Again, he looked at her scars. "But your stepmother and I agree it is time to make a grand statement to the people. A symbolic gesture that shows where you fit into this hierarchy. It is time, Princess, for you to take a husband."

Winter's muscles went taut. She had thought it might be coming to this, but the words in his mouth were repulsive.

She pressed her lips up into a smile. "Of course," she said. "I will be glad to give consideration to my future happiness. I have been told there are many suitors who have posed an interest. As soon as my stepmother's wedding and coronation ceremonies are complete, I'll enjoy looking at the potential suitors and carrying out courtships."

"That will not be necessary."

Her smile was plaster. "What do you mean?"

"I have come to request your hand, Your Highness."

Her lungs convulsed.

"We are perfectly matched. You are beautiful and adored. I am powerful and respected. You are in need of a partner who can protect you with his gift to offset your own disabilities. Think of it. The princess and the queen's head thaumaturge—we will be the greatest envy of the court."

His eyes were shining and it became clear he had been imagining this for a long time. Winter had often thought Aimery might be attracted to her, and this knowledge had been the seed for countless nightmares. She *knew* how he treated the women he was attracted to.

But she had never imagined he would seek a marriage, above the families, above even a potential Earthen arrangement—

No. Now that Levana would be an Earthen empress, it wouldn't matter if Winter could make a match with the blue planet as well. Instead, to marry her weak, pathetic stepdaughter off to a man with such an impressive ability to control the people . . .

It was a smart match, indeed.

Aimery's grin crawled into her skin. "I see I have left you speechless, my princess. Can I take your shock for acquiescence?"

She forced herself to breathe and look away—demure, not disgusted. "I am ... flattered by your offer, Thaumaturge Park. I do not deserve the attentions of one as accomplished as yourself."

"Don't pretend to be coy." He cupped her cheek and she flinched. "Say yes, Princess, and we can announce our engagement at tonight's feast."

She stepped away from his touch. "I am honored, but ... this is so sudden. I need time to consider. I ... I should speak with my stepmother and ... and I think ..."

"Winter." His tone had a new harshness, though his face remained gentle, even impassive. "There is nothing to consider. Her Majesty has approved the union. It is now only your acceptance that is needed to confirm our engagement. Take my offer, Princess. It is the best you will receive."

She glanced at the door, seeking what solace she didn't know. She was trapped.

Aimery's eyes darkened. "I hope you aren't expecting that guard to ask for your hand. I hope you aren't harboring some childish fantasy that to deny *me* is to accept *him*."

She clenched her teeth, smiling around the strain. "Don't be silly, Aimery. Jacin is a dear friend, but I have no intentions toward him."

He scoffed. "The queen would never allow such a marriage."

"I just said—"

"What is your answer? Do not toy with words and meanings, Princess."

Her head swam. She would not—could not—say yes. To Aimery? Cruel, deceitful Aimery, who smiled when there was bloodshed on the throne room floor?

But to say no would not do either. She did not care what they might do to her, but if she endangered Jacin with her refusal, if Aimery believed Jacin was the *reason* for her refusal . . .

A knock prolonged her indecision.

Aimery growled, "What?"

Jacin entered, and though he wore no expression, as usual, Winter detected a resentful shade of red on his cheeks.

"Her Highness has been summoned to join the queen's entourage in meeting with our Earthen guests."

Winter crumbled with relief. "Thank you, Sir Clay," she said, skirting around Aimery.

Aimery grabbed her wrist before she was out of reach. Jacin's hand went to his gun, but he didn't draw.

"I will have an answer," Aimery said under his breath.

Winter placed her hand on top of Aimery's, imagining herself unconcerned. "If you must have it now, then I'm afraid the answer must be no," she said, with a flippancy that denied her true feelings. "But give me time to consider your offer, Thaumaturge Park, and perhaps the answer will be different when next we speak of it."

She gave his knuckles a gentle tap and was thankful when he released her.

The look he gave to Jacin as they passed, though, spoke not of jealousy, but murder.

Nineteen

IT TOOK A HEROIC AMOUNT OF EFFORT FOR KAI TO PRETEND like he wasn't sick with nerves. The ship settled with a thud that made him jump. Torin's presence beside him, at least, was stabilizing, and he could hear the anxious whispers of the Commonwealth ambassadors as they waited to debark the ship's common room. He could sense five stowaways hidden aboard the ship—even though he didn't know where, so there was no chance he could give their location away with a stray glance.

If anyone was going to draw suspicion, it would be him. Only he and Torin knew about Cinder and her allies, and Torin's expression was as unperturbed as ever. The ship's crew was too busy with their arrival procedures to question the disappearance of America's secretary of defense, and none of the other passengers knew they'd taken guests aboard in the first place.

Whereas Kai couldn't stop thinking about these people—his friends—and what he was helping them do. Invade Luna. Start a rebellion. End a war.

He also couldn't stop counting the thousands of things that could go wrong.

He needed to focus. This would only work if Levana believed Kai was determined to finalize their marriage alliance, once and for all. He had to make her think she had won.

The ramp started to descend. Kai took in a deep breath and held it, trying to clear his mind. Trying to convince *himself* he wanted this marriage and this alliance to succeed.

Artemisia's royal port was glowing up from the floor in a way that immediately made him disconcerted. The walls themselves were rocky and black, but lit with thousands of tiny lights like a starry night sky. The port contained dozens of ships in various sizes, mostly Lunar ships that glimmered uniformly white, painted with unfamiliar runes and displaying the royal seal. Kai also recognized Earthen emblems among the ships—some Earthen guests had already begun to arrive. Seeing them gathered together filled him with dread.

Movement drew his gaze and Kai spotted Levana herself gliding along the wide platform that circled the docks. She was surrounded by her entourage: the ever-smug Head Thaumaturge Aimery Park stood to her right and a girl in a pale blue dress followed behind the queen, her head lowered and her face obstructed by an abundance of curly black hair. There were five additional thaumaturges and at least a dozen more guards. It made for an impressive amount of security—overkill, in Kai's opinion.

Was Levana expecting something to go wrong? Or was this a show of intimidation?

Bracing himself, Kai descended the ramp to meet the queen. His own entourage, including ten of his own guards, followed behind.

"Your Majesty," said Kai, accepting Levana's proffered hand. He bowed to kiss it.

"Always so formal," Levana said in that cloying voice that made his skin crawl. "We cannot refer to each other in such droll terms forever. Perhaps I shall henceforth call you My Beloved, and you shall call me your Sweet."

Kai hovered over her hand, hatred blistering his skin where it touched hers. After a drawn-out moment, he released her and straightened. "*Your Majesty*," he started again, "it is an honor to be welcomed to Luna. My ancestors would have been filled with pride to witness such an occasion."

"The pleasure is my own." Levana's gaze slinked over the ambassadors gathered on the ship's ramp. "I hope you will find our hospitality agreeable. If you need for anything, please let one of the servants know and they will see that you are well taken care of."

"Thank you," said Kai. "We're all curious about the famed luxuries of the white city."

"I've no doubt of it. I'll have some servants brought to unload your belongings and have them taken to your rooms."

"That won't be necessary. Our crew is already unloading the ship." He gestured over his shoulder. A second loading ramp had been lowered out of the cargo bay. He had made sure to tell the captain he wanted the crew to make this a top priority. He wanted to be sure the ship was emptied of both people and cargo as soon as possible, so Cinder and the others wouldn't be trapped in the docks for too long.

"How efficient," Levana said. "In that case, your ambassadors may follow Thaumaturge Lindwurm to our guest suites." She indicated a black-coated man. "I'm sure they would like to rest from such a long journey."

Within moments, Kai's following of nervous companions

were being led to a set of enormous arched doors that glittered with a depiction of a crescent moon over Earth. Though the presence of his Earthen companions had offered no security at all, Kai still felt abandoned as he, Torin, and his guards remained behind.

"I hope you won't think it rude that I didn't offer full introductions to your guests," said Levana. "My stepdaughter is easily distressed, and too many new faces could unnerve her." She floated a hand out to her side, like she was conducting a symphony. "But do allow me to introduce *you*, at least, to my stepdaughter, Princess Winter Hayle-Blackburn of Luna."

"Of course. I've heard so much . . . about . . . you."

Kai trailed off as the princess lifted her head and peered at him through a fringe of thick lashes. It was a brief look, barely a glance, but that was all it took for a rush of heat to climb up Kai's neck and into his ears. He had heard of the princess's legendary beauty. Beauty that was not created by a glamour, they said, unlike Levana's. The rumors weren't exaggerated.

Clearing his throat, Kai forced a composed smile. "I'm honored to meet you, Your Highness."

The princess's eyes were teasing as she stepped beside the queen and lowered into a curtsy with the grace of a dancer. When she rose again, Kai noticed her scars for the first time. Three uniform scars cut down her right cheek. These, too, were legendary, along with the tale of how out of envy Levana had forced the princess to mutilate her own face.

The sight twisted his stomach.

Princess Winter offered him a docile, close-lipped smile. "The honor is mine, Your Imperial Majesty." Drifting closer, she pressed a light kiss to Kai's bruised cheek. His insides turned to goo. He had the presence of mind to be grateful Cinder wasn't witnessing this exchange, because something told him he'd never hear the end of it.

The princess stepped back and he was able to breathe again. "With our introductions complete, I feel it is safe for us to drop any future formalities. After all, with your upcoming nuptials, you're practically my father."

Kai reeled back, his jaw dropping open.

Silent laughter glimmered in the princess's gaze as she took her spot behind her stepmother again. She seemed neither distressed *nor* unnerved.

The queen gave her stepdaughter an annoyed look, before gesturing to the man on her other side. "You will of course remember my head thaumaturge, Aimery Park."

Snapping his mouth shut, Kai inclined his head, though the thaumaturge offered only his signature smugness in return. "Welcome to Luna," he drawled.

Scanning the rest of the entourage, Kai recognized two of the guards too. Seeing the queen's captain of the guard was no surprise, but his teeth clenched when he spotted the blond guard who had been like a shadow to Sybil Mira when she'd been a guest in New Beijing.

Distrust twisted his insides. Cinder had thought this guard was an ally, but she now suspected he'd betrayed them to Sybil when they were trying to make their escape from the palace. His presence here, in uniform again, confirmed her suspicions.

No matter, he thought. Cinder had succeeded, despite his betrayal.

Levana grinned, like she detected the rebelliousness of Kai's thoughts, despite all his attempts to appear complacent. "I believe that leaves only one matter of business to tend to before we show you to your rooms." She snapped her fingers, and two of her thaumaturges and six guards snapped to attention. "Search their ship."

Despite all his attempts at normalcy, Kai couldn't keep away the panic that flared in his chest. "Excuse me?" he said, swiveling his head as the entourage marched past him. "What are you doing?"

"My dear beloved, you didn't think I would blindly trust your word after you've shown so much sympathy to my enemies, did you?" She laced her fingers together. They might have been discussing the weather. "In monitoring your fleet, we noted that you took aboard some passengers from the American Republic, but it seems they're too shy to show themselves."

Kai's stomach sank as one of her guards pulled him and Torin behind the queen, and he was left to watch helplessly as Levana's men boarded his ship. If his own guards thought to offer any protection, they were already under Lunar control.

Kai tightened his fists. "This is absurd. The Americans were with that group you just sent away. There's nothing on that ship but luggage and wedding gifts."

The queen's face hardened. "For your sake, Emperor Kaito, I hope that's true. Because if you came here to betray me, I'm afraid this will be a remarkably unpleasant visit."

Twenty

CINDER WAS PRESSED INTO THE CORNER OF A STORAGE closet, her heart pounding in the darkness. Faint strips of light spilled through the slots in the door, allowing her to make out the profiles and bright eyes of her companions. She could hear the shuffling and thumping as the cargo bay was unloaded beneath their feet.

She tried to think of this like a homecoming. She had been born here—this moon, this city. Here, her birth had been celebrated. Here, she would have been raised to be a queen.

But no matter how she tried to think of it, she did not feel like she was home. She was hiding in a closet with the very real possibility that she would be killed the moment someone recognized her.

She glanced at her companions. Wolf was beside her, jaw tense and brow set in concentration. Against the opposite wall, Iko was crouched down with both hands over her mouth, like the need to be quiet was torture. In the hollow silence, Cinder could detect a subtle hum coming from the android, a hint at the machinery beneath her synthetic skin. Her neck was fixed now—Kai had brought exactly what Cinder needed.

Standing beside Iko, Thorne had one arm draped around Cress's shoulders, his free hand scratching at his jaw. Tucked against him, Cress seemed paler than usual, her anxiety evident even in the darkness.

They were a ragtag group in the drab clothing Kai had brought them, including a black knit hat to cover Iko's blue hair and heavy gloves for Cinder's cyborg hand. Putting them on had dredged up a number of memories. There had been a time when she wore gloves everywhere, when she'd been so ashamed of being cyborg she refused to let her prostheses show. She couldn't recall when that had changed, but now the gloves felt like a lie.

A blue glow drew her attention back to Cress, who had turned on a portscreen and was pulling up a diagram of Artemisia's royal port. "We're in good position," she whispered, tilting the screen to show them. There were three exits from the port— one that led into the palace above them, one that connected to the city's public spaceship docks, and one that led down to the maglev tunnels, which was their destination. The maglev tunnels made up a complex underground transit system, linking all of Luna's sectors together. Cinder had studied the system so many times she would have had it memorized even without having the map downloaded to her brain-machine interface. To her, the system resembled a spiderweb and the capital city of Artemisia was the spider.

Cress was right. The pilots had settled the ship close to the exit that would take them down to the maglev tunnels. It was the best they could have hoped for.

Yet she couldn't deny how tempting it was to abandon the

plan, to forget patience, to try to end it here, now. She was at Levana's doorstep. She was *so close*. Her body was wound up tight, ready to storm the palace—an army of one.

She glanced at Wolf. His fists flexed, in and out, in and out. There was murder in his eyes. *He* would have stormed the palace with her, she knew, in hopes that Scarlet was there. But they didn't even know whether Scarlet was still alive.

But it was desperation goading her, not confidence. Even if she got past Levana's security and somehow managed to kill her, she would end up dead as well. Then some other Lunar would step in to take the throne and Luna would be no better off than it had been before.

She shoved the temptation down into the pit of her stomach. This wasn't about assassinating Levana. This was about giving the citizens of Luna a voice and ensuring it was heard.

She tried to distract herself by going over their plan again in her head. This was the most dangerous part, but she hoped Levana and her security team would be so busy with the arriving Earthen guests they wouldn't notice a handful of dockworkers slipping out of the royal port. Their goal was to make it to Sector RM-9 where they hoped to find Wolf's parents and be offered temporary shelter from which to start the next phase of their plan—informing the people of Luna that their true queen had returned.

If they could make it there undetected, Cinder knew they had a chance.

The clomp of feet startled her. It was too loud—like someone was on the same level as they were, not down below in the cargo bay. She traded frowns with her companions. A distant door was slammed shut and she heard someone yelling orders. More scuffling followed.

"Is it just me," whispered Thorne, "or does it sound like some-one is searching the ship?"

His words mirrored her thoughts exactly. Comprehension turned fast into horror. "She knows we're here. They're looking for us."

She looked around at her companions, their expressions ranging from terrified to eager and all of them, she realized with a start, looking back at her. Awaiting instruction.

Outside their confined closet, the voices grew louder. Something crashed against the floor.

Cinder tightened her gloved fists. "Wolf, Thorne, the second a thaumaturge sees either of you they'll try to control you." She licked her lips. "Do I have permission to take control of you first? Just your bodies, not your minds."

"I've been waiting for you to admit you wanted my body," said Thorne. He laid a hand on the gun at his waist. "Be my guest."

Wolf looked less enthusiastic, but he gave her a sharp nod.

Cinder slipped her will into Thorne as easily as slicing through a block of tofu. Wolf's energy was more chaotic, but she'd spent so much time training with him aboard the Rampion that his energy, too, offered little resistance. Cinder felt their limbs as if they were an extension of her own. Though she knew she was doing it for their own protection, keeping them from being turned into weapons for the enemy, she couldn't help feeling like manipulating them was a betrayal of their trust. It was an unfair balance of power—their safety was now her responsibility.

She thought of Levana, forcing her guard to take a bullet for her at the royal ball, and wondered if she would ever make that same decision with one of her friends.

She hoped she would never have to.

A voice echoed in the nearby corridor: "Nothing in the engine room. You—split up. Search these corridors and report back."

They were close, and if there was a thaumaturge, she knew it wouldn't be long before he or she was near enough to detect the bioelectricity coming from this storage closet. She pictured the ship's layout and tried to formulate a plan, but there was little hope now of slipping away without announcing their presence.

They would have to fight their way out of the ship. They would have to fight all the way to the maglev shuttles.

"Cinder," Thorne whispered. His body was statue still, waiting for Cinder's command. "Send me out there."

Cress's head snapped up, but he didn't return the look.

Cinder frowned. "What?"

"Send me as a decoy, out the main ramp and away from the maglev doors. I'll draw them off long enough for you to get out through the cargo bay."

"Thorne . . ."

"Do it." His eyes flashed. He still wouldn't look at Cress. "We made it to Luna. You don't need a pilot here, or a captain."

Her pulse thundered. "You don't have to—"

Outside someone called, "Press room is clear!"

"Stop wasting time," Thorne said through his teeth. "I'll lead them away and circle back to you."

She knew he was being overconfident, but Cinder found herself nodding at the same time Cress started shaking her head.

"My control of you will be intermittent inside the ship, but if I can find you, I'll reclaim you as soon as we're all outside." *If they don't claim you first,* she thought, unwilling to speak it out loud.

Controlling an Earthen like Thorne was easy, but wresting control away from a thaumaturge was significantly more difficult.

"Got it." Thorne's jaw tensed.

"Be careful," Cress said, more a squeak than a whisper, and Thorne's attention alighted on her for the briefest of moments . . .

Before Cinder kicked open the door and sent Thorne bolting into the corridor. He collided with the wall, but pushed himself off and careened to the left. His arms and legs pumped as he raced toward the main deck. It wasn't long before he was out of her reach. Too much steel divided them. Cinder lost control, and Thorne was on his own.

Seconds after her grasp on him had snapped, they heard a crash. Thorne had broken something.

Cinder hoped it wasn't some priceless Commonwealth artifact.

In the next chamber, a stampede of feet raced after him. When Cinder reached out with her thoughts, she couldn't feel any bioelectricity other than Wolf's. This side of the ship had been cleared.

She tipped her head into the corridor. No sign of anyone aboard. On the other side of the ship, she heard yelling.

Cinder ran in the opposite direction she'd sent Thorne. The others hurried after her—down two levels on a narrow, spiraling stairwell, through an industrial galley that made the kitchen on the Rampion feel like a child's play set, and along a utilitarian corridor dividing the podship docks. They paused above the hatch that would drop them into the cargo bay. Cinder could still hear shuffling and the crank of machinery below, but she had no way of knowing if it was the Earthen workers unloading the cargo, or Lunars inspecting it.

Whoever it was, they didn't have time to wait for them to leave.

Cinder loaded a bullet into her projectile finger. They'd found plenty of ammunition aboard the Rampion, but she couldn't help wishing Kai had been able to procure more tranquilizer darts for her on Earth.

Too late. No time to think.

Wolf popped open the hatch and jumped down first. Cinder once again took control of his body, in case there were Lunars down there, but she had nothing to do with the growl or flash of teeth.

Cinder swung herself down beside him. The floor clanged as Iko dropped next, followed by the tentative thuds of Cress's footsteps on the ladder.

Three figures that had been inspecting the crates swung around to face them. Cinder registered the uniforms of a black-coated thaumaturge and two Lunar guards at the same moment a gun fired.

Her left leg kicked out from under her, the shock wave vibrating up through her hip and into her spine. The bullet had hit her metal thigh.

Cress cried out and froze on the ladder, releasing the rungs only when Iko grabbed her and yanked her off. Cinder urged Wolf's legs to move. They scurried behind a pallet loaded with Commonwealth merchandise just as another bullet pinged on the wall overhead. A third hit the crate, splintering the wood on the other side.

The firing stopped.

Cinder pressed her back to the crate, reorienting herself. She stretched out her thoughts, finding the Lunars' bioelectricity sizzling in the room, but of course the guards were already under the thaumaturge's control.

The ramp that would let them escape from the ship was on the opposite side of the cargo bay.

Eerie silence fell, leaving Cinder jumpy as she strained to listen for footsteps coming toward them. She expected the Lunars would try to surround them. Their weapons wouldn't stay quiet for long.

Wolf's limbs were still for once, and it occurred to Cinder that *she* was holding him so still. Only his expression was alive. Fierce, wild. He was her best weapon, but under her control he would be clunky and awkward—not half as brutal as he could be on his own. Their training aboard the Rampion had focused on stopping an enemy. Disarming them. Removing a threat.

She wished now they would have spent more time practicing how to turn people into weapons. It was a skill that Levana and her minions excelled at.

Wolf met her gaze, and a thought occurred to her. Cinder was controlling his body, but not his mind or his emotions. What if she changed tactics? She could still protect him from the thaumaturge's power while allowing him to do what he did best.

"Get the thaumaturge," she whispered, then released Wolf's body and snatched at his thoughts instead. She fed him a vision of the first terrible thing that came to mind: the fight aboard the Rampion between them and Sybil Mira. The day Scarlet had been taken.

Wolf vaulted over the crate. Gunshots blared, bullets pinged, the walls shook.

Iko roared and launched herself past Cinder, tackling a guard who appeared in the corner of Cinder's vision. His gun fired; the bullet struck the ceiling. Iko punched him and his head cracked against the metal floor. His body stopped flailing, unconscious.

Cinder jumped to her feet, holding her cyborg hand like a gun, and spotted the second guard creeping around to their other side. His face was blank—unafraid. Then, as she watched, it cleared. His eyes focused on Cinder, bewildered.

The thaumaturge had lost control of him.

The moment was fleeting. The guard snarled and aimed his gun at Cinder, but he was too late. Already she had a grip on his bioelectricity. With a thought, she sent him spiraling into uncon-sciousness. He dropped to his knees and collapsed face-first to the floor with a crunch. Blood spurted from his nose. Cinder recoiled.

A scream echoed through the bay.

Cinder could no longer see Wolf, and terror struck her. In tak-ing control of the guard, she'd forgotten about protecting Wolf's mind from—

The screaming stopped, followed by a thud.

A second later, Wolf appeared from behind a shelf stacked with suitcases, snarling and shaking out his right fist.

Pulse thrumming, Cinder turned to see Iko with her arm wrapped around an extra-pale Cress.

They ran for the ramp, and Cinder was grateful that it was lowered to face away from the palace entrance. As they crept downward, she scanned their surroundings, with both her eyes and her Lunar gift. In this wide-open space, she could sense a cluster of people in the distance and she could tell there were both Earthens and Lunars in the mix.

Their route to the maglev doors, at least, was unblocked. If they were careful, they could stay hidden behind this row of ships.

At least, until one of those Lunars picked up on Wolf's sizzling energy and questioned what a modified soldier was doing here.

She waved her arm and they skimmed around the side of the ramp. A breath passed while Cinder waited for a sign they'd been noticed. When none came, they darted to the next ship, and the next. Every thump of their feet pounded in her ears. Every breath sounded like a windstorm.

A shout startled her and together they ducked behind the landing gear of an elaborately painted ship from the African Union. Cinder held her hand at the ready, the bullet still loaded in her finger.

"Over there!" someone yelled.

Cinder peered around the telescoping legs of the spacecraft and spotted a figure bolting between ships. Thorne, running away from them at full speed.

Not yet controlled by a Lunar.

Heart leaping, Cinder reached out for his mind, hoping to get to him before one of the Lunars on the other side of the dock ...

Success.

Like with Wolf, she thrust an idea into his head.

Get back here.

Startled, Thorne tripped and fell, rolled a couple times, and sprang again to his feet. Cinder flinched with guilt, but was relieved when Thorne changed directions. He skirted around a couple podships, dodging a volley of bullets from a cluster of guards that had emerged from the main ramp of Kai's ship.

"I've got him," said Cinder. "Come on."

Keeping half her focus on Thorne, the rest on her own careful movements, Cinder stayed close to Wolf as they ducked in and out of the safety of the spacecraft, weaving their way to the wide platform that stood shoulder height around the perimeter of the docks. Their exit loomed before them. Enormous double doors carved in mysterious Lunar runes. A sign above them indicated the way to the maglev platform.

They reached the last ship. They'd run out of shelter. Once they were on the platform, they would be on raised, wide-open ground.

Cinder glanced back. Thorne was on his stomach beneath the tail of a solo-pilot pod. He waved at them to go ahead, to hurry.

"Iko, you and Cress go first," said Cinder. If they were seen, they at least couldn't be manipulated. "We'll cover you."

Iko put herself between Cress and the palace doors and they ran for the short flight of steps. Cinder swung her embedded gun from side to side, searching for threats, but the guards were too focused on finding Thorne to notice them.

A hiss drew her attention back to the platform. Iko and Cress were at the doors, but they were still shut.

Cinder's stomach dropped.

They were supposed to open automatically.

But—no. Levana had been expecting them. Of course she had taken precautions to ensure they wouldn't be able to escape.

Her face contorted, desperation crashing into her. She struggled to come up with another way out. Would Wolf be strong enough to pry open the doors? Could they fire their way through?

As she racked her brain, a new expression came over Cress, replacing her wide-eyed terror with resolve. Cinder followed her gaze to a circular control booth that stood between the maglev and palace entrances. Before Cinder could guess her plan, Cress had dropped to her hands and knees and started crawling along the wall.

A gun fired. Cress flinched but kept going.

It was followed by another shot, and another, each making Cinder duck down farther. With the third shot there was a shatter of glass.

Cinder spun around, her heart in her throat, and sought out Thorne. He hadn't moved, but now he was holding a handgun, and had it aimed behind him. He'd shot out a window on Kai's ship.

He was causing another distraction, trying to draw more attention to himself, to keep it away from Cress.

Throat dry as desert sand, Cinder looked back to see that Cress had made it to the booth. She was clutching her portscreen, the fingers of her other hand dancing over an invisi-screen. Iko was still by the doors, crouched into a ball, ready to spring up and run at the slightest provocation.

Beside Cinder, Wolf was focused on Thorne, ready to rush into the fight the second one broke out.

Footsteps came pounding down the ramp of Kai's ship and additional Lunar guards swarmed the aisles. It wasn't the guards that concerned Cinder, though. They wouldn't be skilled enough to detect Thorne in their midst. It was their thaumaturges that worried her, but she couldn't find them.

Doors whistled. Wolf grabbed Cinder's elbow before she could turn around and dragged her up to the platform.

Cress had gotten the doors open.

Iko was already on the other side, her back against a corridor wall, waving them on. She had drawn her own gun for the first time and was searching for a target.

"There!"

Wolf and Cinder pounded up the stairs. A bullet pinged against the wall, and she ducked and stumbled through the doors. They slammed into the wall beside Iko.

Cinder looked back, panting. Their pursuers had given up trying to catch them off guard and were now running toward them at full speed. But Thorne had a head start, and he, too, had given up secrecy for speed. Cinder fed images into his mind—his legs running fast as a gazelle's, his feet barely touching the ground. She was too afraid that to turn him into a puppet would only slow him down, but the mental encouragement seemed to work. His speed increased. He bounded up the stairs in two steps.

Over his shoulder, Cinder finally saw the thaumaturge, a woman with short black hair and a red coat.

Gritting her teeth, she raised her arm and fired. She didn't know where she'd hit her, but the woman cried out and fell.

Thorne threw himself across the threshold as the guards reached the base of the platform steps. The doors slammed shut behind him.

Thorne collapsed against the wall, holding his chest. His cheeks were flushed, but his eyes were bright with adrenaline as he looked around at the group. At Cinder, at Iko, at Wolf.

The growing smile vanished. "Cress?"

Cinder, still gasping for her own breath, shook her head.

His jaw fell slack with horror. He pushed himself off the wall and lunged for the doors, but Wolf jumped in front of him, pinning Thorne's arms to his sides.

"Let me go," Thorne growled.

"We can't go back," said Wolf. "It's suicide."

To punctuate his words, a volley of bullets struck the doors, their loud clangs echoing down the corridor they were now trapped in.

"We're not leaving her."

"Thorne—" started Cinder.

"No!" Wriggling one arm free, Thorne swung, but Wolf

ducked. In half a heartbeat, Wolf had spun around and pinned Thorne to the wall, one enormous hand at Thorne's throat.

"She gave us this chance," Wolf said. "Don't waste it."

Thorne's jaw flexed. His body was taut as a cable, ready to fight, though he was no match for Wolf. Panic was etched into every line of his face, but slowly, slowly, his erratic breaths started to even.

"We have to go," said Cinder, almost afraid to suggest it.

Thorne's focus shifted to the closed doors.

"I could stay?" suggested Iko, her tone uncertain. "I could go back for her?"

"No," said Cinder. "We stay together."

Thorne flinched and Cinder realized the cruelty of her words too late. Their group was already divided.

She inched forward to settle a hand on Thorne's arm, but thought better of it. "We'd still be out there if it wasn't for her. We'd *all* be captured, but thanks to Cress, we're not. She saved us. Now, we have to *go*."

He squeezed his eyes. His shoulders slumped.

His whole body was trembling, but he nodded.

Wolf released him and they ran.

BOOK
Two

The huntsman took pity on her and said,

"Run away into the woods, child, and never come back."

Twenty-One

AT SOME POINT DURING THE EXCITEMENT FOLLOWING
Emperor Kaito's arrival, Jacin had placed himself in front of
Winter—ever her protector—and she gathered up the back of
his shirt's material in one fist. His presence was part comfort,
part annoyance. He kept blocking her view.

Her sight was clear as daybreak, though, as she watched four
figures dash through the exit that led down to the maglev shuttles. The doors slammed shut to a volley of gunfire. Though they
had been too far away to see clearly, Winter was certain one of
them was Linh Cinder.

Her dear missing cousin, Princess Selene.

"Follow them!" Levana shouted. The guards who had been
sent to search the emperor's ship were at the exit within seconds, trying to pry the doors open, but they wouldn't budge.

Levana wheeled around to face Sir Jerrico Solis. "Send one
team through the palace to the lakeside entrances, another
through the city. Try to cut them off at the platform."

Jerrico clasped a hand to his fist and was gone, summoning
eight other guards to follow.

"Aimery," Levana barked, "see to it that all shuttles leaving Artemisia are stopped. Have them searched, along with all connecting tunnels and platforms. They are not to make it out of the city. And find out how they were able to get through those doors!"

Aimery bowed. "I have already summoned the technician. We will have the entire system locked down."

Nostrils flaring, Levana straightened her spine and turned to face the emperor. He was standing near the back of their small group—alone, but for a handful of Earthen guards and his adviser. Yet he didn't look afraid. Winter thought he should have looked afraid, but his lips were pressed together in a strained effort not to smile.

Winter cocked her head, inspecting him. He seemed proud. Borderline smug. She began to feel guilty for having teased him before.

"Stowaways," he said, once he had Levana's attention. His shoulders twitched in an unconcerned shrug. "What an unexpected surprise."

Levana's face was fiercely beautiful. Breathtaking in her viciousness. "You have brought a known enemy into the heart of my country. In a time of mutual cease-fire, you have committed an act of treason."

Kai didn't flinch. "My loyalty lies with the Eastern Commonwealth and with Earth. Not with Luna, and certainly not with you."

Levana's eyes narrowed. "You seem confident that I won't have you killed for this."

"You won't," he said with, as her stepmother guessed, an overabundance of confidence. Winter squirmed, suddenly afraid for him. "At least," Kai amended, "not yet."

One perfect eyebrow lifted. "You're right," said Levana. "Perhaps I will kill your adviser instead. Surely he was aware of this blatant betrayal of my trust."

"Do with me as you see fit," said the adviser, as unshaken as Kaito. "*My* loyalties lie only with my emperor."

Kai's cheek twitched. "If you harm any one of your Earthen guests as either a punishment or a threat to me, I will refuse to continue with this wedding."

"Then I will no longer have any reason to keep you alive."

"I know," said Kai, "but you also won't get to be empress."

Their gazes warred with each other while Winter, Jacin, and the other guards watched. Winter's heartbeat was erratic as she waited for the queen's order to have Emperor Kaito killed—for his insolence as much as for his role in bringing Linh Cinder to Artemisia.

The doors to the palace opened and a guard entered, escorting one of their technicians.

"My Queen, you summoned?"

Aimery stepped forward. "There had been strict orders that the exits out of this port were to be locked, but it seems there has been a malfunction. Her Majesty demands to know what went wrong, and be assured it won't happen again."

The technician bowed and scurried around the platform toward the control panel that monitored the exits and the massive spaceship-holding chamber beyond the port doors.

Winter was watching him when her eye caught on a slip of movement. She frowned, sure she saw someone ducking in between some of the Earthen cargo.

Or as sure as she could be of anything she saw, which was not very sure at all.

Her stepmother rounded again on the emperor and flicked

her arm toward him, irritated with his presence. "Take the Earthens to their quarters," she said, "and keep them there."

The emperor and his entourage put up no resistance as the guards shuffled them away with more force than was necessary. Kai didn't look in Winter's direction, but as he passed she could see he was no longer hiding his grin. He might have become a prisoner of the queen, but clearly he saw this as a victory.

The guards' clomping footsteps had faded when the technician shouted, "My Queen!" His fingers were dancing over the screens, his face set with panic. Levana swept toward him. The rest of her entourage trailed after, and though Jacin moved to keep himself in front of Winter, she dodged around him and skipped ahead, ignoring his low growl. She scanned the stacks of crates and luggage again, but there was no sign of the mysterious figure she'd imagined before.

"What?" Levana snapped.

The technician didn't turn away from the controls. On the nearest screen, Winter could see a map of the shuttle system and a flashing error message in the corner. Jacin appeared again at her side and cast her a cool glare for leaving the circle of his protection. She ignored him.

"It's—" the technician started. He swiveled to another screen.

"I suggest you find your tongue before I disable it permanently," said Levana.

The technician shuddered and turned back to face them, though his hands lingered uselessly over the screens. "The system is . . ."

Levana waited.

Winter became very worried for this man's life.

". . . inaccessible, My Queen. I can't . . . I can't access the shuttle schedules, the manual overrides . . . even the entrances to the main platform have been locked. With . . . with the exception of the corridor connecting it to these docks, which alone was left unimpeded."

Levana, lips pressed into a firm line, said nothing.

"The system has been hacked?" said Aimery.

"Y-yes, I think so. It could take hours to reconfigure the access codes . . . I don't even know what they *did*."

"Are you telling me," said Levana, "that you cannot even put a stop to the shuttles leaving the city?"

The technician had gone pale. "I will keep trying, Your Majesty. I'll have much better access to the system from the palace control room, so I'll just—"

"Do you have an apprentice?" said the queen. "Or a partner in your trade?"

The hair stood up on Winter's neck.

The technician stammered, "Th-there are three of us . . . here in the palace . . . but I have the most experience, with over twenty years of loyal service and—"

"Kill him."

A guard removed the gun from his holster. Winter turned her head away, and though it was a petty thought, she was glad it wasn't Jacin being forced to do the murder. If he had still been guard to the head thaumaturge, it very well could have been.

"Please, My Que—"

Winter jumped as the shot rang through her head, followed by a sound she was all too familiar with. A whimper. Coming from behind a stack of cargo bins.

Behind her, the crackle of wiring and splinter of plastic suggested the bullet had struck one of the screens as well. The guard holstered his gun.

Aimery turned to the queen. "I will contact Jerrico and see if his teams have managed to gain access to the platform, and alert him that their way may be impeded."

"Thank you, Aimery. Also alert the other two technicians to the problem with the shuttle system."

Aimery pulled out his portscreen and stepped away from their group, toward the edge of the platform. He was overlooking the piled cargo crates, and though his attention was on his port, Winter was searching for another sign of life below.

There. A foot, she thought, curling in against a large trunk.

Winter gasped delightedly and laced her fingers beneath her chin. Everyone spun to her, startled at her presence, which was not uncommon. "Do you think the Earthens brought us gifts, Stepmother?"

Without waiting for a response, she lifted her skirts and trotted toward the cargo, climbing over the uneven stacks of crates and bins until she reached the lower level.

"Winter," Levana snapped. "What are you doing?"

"Looking for presents!" she called back, giggling. Jacin's shadow fell over her from above. She could picture his expression down to the annoyed twitch in his brow, and she knew that from where he stood with the rest of the queen's entourage, he could not see what she was seeing.

A girl with cropped blonde hair and terrified blue eyes was curled into a tight ball. Her back was pressed up against a crate, her whole body trembling.

Winter lifted her head and beamed, first at Jacin, then her stepmother, doing her best not to look at the spray of blood on the far wall. "This one says it has wine from Argentina! It must be from the Americans. We can toast to such an eventful afternoon."

She leaned over the shaking girl and unlatched the crate with a loud clack. She pried up the lid. "Oh, drat, the box lied. It's only packing fluff." Holding the lid with one hand, she started pulling out the shredded paper as quickly as she could, scattering it over the floor at her feet. The girl gawked up at her.

Her stepmother's voice had turned to ice. "Sir Clay, please escort your charge from the premises. She is embarrassing herself."

Her words carried too much weight, but Winter didn't try to decipher them. She was busy nudging at the girl with her toe, gesturing for her to get into the crate.

Jacin's boots thumped against the cargo as he descended toward her. Winter grabbed the girl's elbow and tugged, spurring the girl into action. She scrambled onto her knees, gripped the edge of the crate, and hauled herself inside—the noise muffled by Winter's crumpling of the paper.

Without waiting to see whether the girl was comfortable, Winter dropped the lid shut as Jacin dropped down beside her. Her grin brightened at him. "Oh, good, you're here! You can help me carry this paper up to my room. What a thoughtful gift from the Americans, don't you think?"

"Princess—"

"I agree, Jacin. A box full of paper is a bit messy for a wedding gift, but we shan't be ungrateful." She scooped up an armful of the paper and pranced toward the palace entrance, not once daring to look back.

Twenty-Two

CINDER WAS USED TO SENSING WOLF'S ENERGY—TIRELESS and agitated and steaming off him like heat waves over pavement. But it was a new thing coming from Thorne, who was normally unshakable. As they ran down an endless staircase, deeper and deeper into Luna's underground, Thorne's energy was every bit as palpable as Wolf's. Angry, terrified, burdened with guilt. Cinder wished she could turn off her Lunar gift so she wouldn't have to deal with her companions' tirade of emotions in addition to her own.

They'd lost Cress. Levana knew of Kai's betrayal. Already their group was fragmented and her plan was falling to pieces.

The steps leveled off into a long, narrow corridor lined with robed statues, each holding a glowing orb that cast swells of light onto the arched ceiling. The floor was fitted with thousands of tiny black and gold tiles, creating a pattern that swirled and ebbed like the Milky Way. It would have been a marvel to behold if they had the time to appreciate it, but Cinder's thoughts were too tumultuous. Listening for sounds of pursuit. Picturing Cress's face, determined in spite of her fear. Trying to plan their next move, and what they would do if the maglevs failed—for Levana must know where they were heading.

At the end of the corridor they came to another spiraling staircase carved from dark, polished wood. The rails and steps were undulating and uneven, and it took Cinder two flights—gripping the rails to keep from falling headfirst in her hurry—to realize the staircase was carved to resemble an enormous octopus that was allowing them passage on its looping tentacles.

So beautiful. So strange. Everything made with such striking craftsmanship and detail. And all this in just some tunnels hundreds of feet beneath the moon's surface. She couldn't imagine how stunning the palace itself must be.

They reached another set of double doors inset with an artfully rendered map showing the entirety of the maglev system.

"This is the platform," said Iko, the only one of them not panting.

"I'll go out first," said Cinder. "If anyone is out there, I'll use a glamour to make them see us as members of Levana's court. Any thaumaturges we kill on sight. Everyone else we ignore."

"What about guards?" said Iko.

"Guards are easy to control. Let me deal with them." She adjusted the scratchy gloves Kai had given her, then opened her thoughts, prepared to detect the bioelectricity off anyone who might have been on the platform. She pressed her palm against the doors. At her touch, they divided into four sections that spiraled into the walls. Cinder stepped onto the platform.

Empty.

She couldn't imagine it would be that way for long.

Three shimmering white shuttles waited on the rails. They ran for the first one. Cinder let the others climb in first, ready to call up a glamour at the first sign of someone approaching, but the platform remained silent. Wolf grabbed Cinder and dragged her in with them.

"How do we work this thing?" Iko cried, pounding at the control screen. The shuttle remained open and motionless. "Shut door! Move! Get us out of here!"

"It won't work for you," said Wolf, leaning past Iko to press all five fingertips against the screen. It lit up and the doors glided shut.

It was a false sense of protection, but Cinder couldn't help a breath of relief.

A tranquil voice filled the shuttle. "Welcome, Alpha Ze'ev Kesley, Lunar Special Operative Number 962. Where shall I take you?"

He glanced at Cinder.

She stared at the screen, sifting through the possibilities. Giving directions to RM-9 was a sure way of leading Levana straight to them. She pulled up the map of Luna on her retina display, trying to strategize the best route, one that would lead Levana off their track.

"WS-1," said Thorne. He was slumped on the floor between the two upholstered benches, his hands draped over his knees, his head against the wall. Between the disheartened expression and collapsed posture, he was almost unrecognizable. But at his voice, the shuttle rose up on the magnetic force beneath the rails and started racing away from Artemisia.

"Waste salvage?" Iko said.

Thorne shrugged. "I thought it would be good to have a Plan B in case something like this happened."

After a short silence, in which Iko's internal workings hummed, she said, "And Plan B is to go to the waste salvage sector?"

Thorne looked up. His voice was neutral as he explained, "It's a short trip from Artemisia, so we won't be giving Levana too much time to regroup and send people after us before we get out of this shuttle. And it's one of the most connected sectors on Luna, given that everyone has waste. There are fifteen maglev tunnels branching out from that one platform. We can go on foot for a ways, throw them off our course, then start doub—"

"Don't say it," said Cinder. "We don't know if we'll be recorded in here."

Thorne shut his mouth and nodded.

Cinder knew he'd been about to say they could start doubling back toward RM-9. She focused in on sector WS-1 on the map in her head, and Thorne was right. It was a smart plan. She couldn't believe she hadn't thought of it herself. "Good call, Thorne."

He shrugged again, without enthusiasm. "Criminal mastermind, remember?"

Cinder sagged onto the bench beside Wolf, allowing her body a brief respite from the pumping adrenaline. "The system recognized you."

"Every Lunar citizen is in the database. I've only been missing for a couple of months—I figured they wouldn't have had my identity removed yet."

"Do you think they'll notice if a special operative who's supposed to be on Earth suddenly shows up again?"

"I don't know. But as long as we're traveling by shuttle, using my identity will draw less attention than yours. And without Cress here to break into it . . ."

Thorne flinched and pressed his forehead into the shuttle wall. They sat in silence for a long time, the lack of Cress's presence filling up the hollow spaces around them.

Only in her absence did Cinder realize how much they'd been

relying on Cress. She could have sneaked them through the mag-lev system without having to input any identities. And Cress had been confident that, once they arrived in RM-9, she could disable any surveillance equipment that might give them away. Plus there was the all-important matter of infiltrating Luna's broadcasting system to share Cinder's message with Luna's citizens.

But knowing how much Cress's loss impacted their objectives was nothing compared to the horror Cinder felt. Cress would be tortured for information on their whereabouts and then almost certainly killed.

"She's a shell," Cinder said. "They can't detect her bioelectricity. As long as she stays hidden, she'll be—"

"Don't," said Thorne.

Cinder stared at his whitened knuckles and struggled for something meaningful to say. Her grand plan of revolution and change had just begun and already she felt like a failure. This seemed worse than failing the people of Luna, though. She'd failed the people she cared about most in the universe.

Finally, she whispered, "I'm so sorry, Thorne."

"Yeah," he said. "Me too."

Twenty-Three

JACIN WAS EXTRA BROODY AS WINTER LED HIM INTO THE elevator.

"Why do I have a bad feeling about this?" he grumbled, eyeing Winter suspiciously.

"You have a bad feeling about *everything*," she said, nudging him with her shoulder. It was a playful gesture, one that always made her giddy to have returned. This time, it was not returned. She frowned. "I forgot something down in the ports. It will only take a moment."

She fluttered her lashes at him.

He scowled and looked away. He was in guard mode. Uniform. Posture. Inability to hold eye contact for more than half a second.

Guard Jacin was not her favorite Jacin, but she knew it was only a disguise, and one that was forced upon him.

She was itching to tell him the truth from the instant they'd left the ports. She was stricken with anxiety over the fate of the girl she'd ushered into that crate. Was she still in hiding? Did she try to run and rejoin her friends? Had she been found? Captured? Killed?

This girl was an ally of Linh Cinder's, and perhaps a friend of her Scarlet's as well. Fear for her life turned Winter into a pacing, fidgety mess for the two hours that she'd forced herself to wait in her chambers, so as not to draw attention to her return to the docks. Her awareness of the palace surveillance system kept her from telling the secret to even Jacin. It had been a difficult secret to retain.

But if she'd been acting odd, even Jacin didn't ask her about it. No doubt the day's excitement was plenty reason enough for her agitation.

"What was it?" Jacin asked.

Winter peeled her focus from the descending indicator above the elevator door. "Pardon?"

"What did you forget in the ports?"

"Oh. You'll see."

"Princess—"

The doors swished open. She grabbed his arm and pulled him through the lavish gallery where Artemisians could await their transport. This level was abandoned, just as she'd hoped. Though it had been easy for Winter to gain access to the ports from the guard in the palace above—it had taken little more than a pout and defiantly ignoring Jacin's groan—the ports were supposed to be off-limits for the duration of the Earthens' visit. *For the security of their ships and belongings*, Levana had said, but Winter knew it was really to prevent anyone from trying to leave.

The ports were quiet when they stepped onto the main platform. The glowing floor made the ships' shadows appear monstrous on the high ceilings, and the cavernous walls echoed every footstep, every breath. Winter imagined she could hear her own thunderous heartbeat ricocheting back to her.

She took off around the platform with Jacin following at a fast clip. She couldn't help glancing toward the control booth, and though there remained a broken screen and a few dark stains on the wall, the technician's body was gone. To her knowledge, his replacements were still in the palace's main control center trying to regain access to the malfunctioning system.

Her attention swept down to the lower level and endless relief filled her to see the cargo untouched. Though the ambassadors' personal luggage had been taken to their suites, their gifts and trade goods had been left behind for retrieval at a later date.

Winter spotted the box of Argentinian wine. Her pace quickened.

"Stars above," Jacin grumbled. "If you dragged me down here for more packing paper—"

"*Paper,*" said Winter, scrambling unladylike over the cargo boxes, "is a most difficult resource to obtain. The lumber sectors have enough demand for building supplies. I once had to trade a pair of silk slippers for half a dozen greeting cards, you know."

It was only partly true. Most of the paper goods available in Artemisia's shops were made from pulped bamboo, which was one of the few resources that grew with abundance in the agriculture sectors. But bamboo also contributed to textile and furniture manufacturing, and even that paper was in limited supply.

Winter was fond of paper. She liked the crisp, tactile way it crinkled beneath her fingers.

Jacin sat down on a plastic bin, his legs dangling over the edge. In the serene solitude of the docks, Guard Jacin had withdrawn. "You want to turn packing paper into greeting cards?"

"Oh, no," she said. "I have no interest in the paper."

One eyebrow rose. "The wine, then?"

Winter unlatched the shipping crate. "Not the wine, either."

She held her breath and heaved open the lid. It clattered against the next bin and Winter found herself staring into a large shipping crate with a layer of tight-packed wine bottles and loose bits of paper and no sign of the girl.

Her heart plummeted.

"What?" Jacin leaned forward to peer into the box. His face took on a layer of concern. "Princess?"

Her lips parted, then snapped shut again. She turned in a slow circle, examining the crates stacked all around her. The girl could have sneaked into any of them.

Or she could have run.

Or she could already have been found by someone else.

Jacin dropped down from his perch and grabbed her elbow. "What's wrong?"

"She's gone," Winter murmured.

"*She?*"

"There was—" She hesitated. Her gaze darted up to one of the many inconspicuous cameras along the dock's perimeter. Though the queen would have demanded them to be disabled while she was there, Winter had no idea if or when they'd been reinstated.

Jacin bristled, with impatience but also worry. Checking for the cameras was the first sign someone was going against the queen's wishes. After a quick sweep of the ceiling, he shook his head. "No indicator lights. They're still off." He was frowning as he said it, though. "Tell me what's going on."

Winter swallowed. "There was a girl. I think she came with Linh Cinder and her companions. I saw her sneaking around these crates while the queen was arguing with the technician, so I hid her in here. But . . . now she's gone."

Jacin rocked back on his heels. Winter expected him to chastise her for doing something so dangerous and right in front of the queen, no less. But instead, after a long hesitation, he asked, "What did she look like?"

"Small. Short blonde hair. Afraid." Remembering the girl's terrified expression made Winter shiver. "Maybe she tried to rejoin her companions. Or . . . or maybe she's back on the emperor's ship?"

Jacin's gaze had unfocused. "Cress," he whispered, turning around. He released Winter's elbow and bounded back up the crates, vaulting onto the platform overhead.

"What? Jacin?" She lifted her skirt over her knees and hurried after him. By the time she'd managed to get back up onto the platform, Jacin was in the control booth, yanking open cabinets filled with wires and cords and computer parts that Winter didn't comprehend.

He found the girl behind the third door he opened, her body curled into such a tight ball Winter couldn't believe she hadn't suffocated. Her wide eyes attached to Jacin and widened, impossibly, further.

Winter staggered to a halt as Jacin reached into the cabinet and pulled the girl out. The girl yelped, trying to regain her footing as Jacin shoved the door shut behind her. She pried her arm out of his grip and backed against the wall, trembling like a caged animal.

Rather than reaching for her again, Jacin took a step back and pinched the bridge of his nose. He cursed. "Princess, you have got to stop collecting these rebels."

Ignoring him, Winter drifted toward the girl, her hands placating. "We won't hurt you," she cooed. "It's all right."

The girl spared her a hasty glance before turning back to Jacin. Terrified, but also angry.

"My name is Winter," she said. "Are you hurt?"

"We can't stay here," said Jacin. "The cameras will be coming on again any minute. It's a miracle they haven't already."

The girl continued to stare at him with her timid ferocity.

"Wait." Jacin laughed. "You disabled them, didn't you?"

The girl said nothing.

Winter swiveled her attention from her to Jacin. "*She* disabled them?"

"This girl used to be the queen's best-kept secret. She can find her way around any computer system." He crossed his arms, his stern expression softening into an almost smile. "You're the one who's been messing with the shuttles too."

The girl's lips thinned into a line.

"What's your name?" asked Winter.

When the girl still didn't respond, Jacin answered, "Her name is Cress. She's a shell and one of Linh Cinder's allies." He scratched his temple. "I don't suppose you have a plan as to what we're supposed to do with her?"

"We could sneak her up to the guest wing? I'm sure the Earthen emperor would watch over her. He did help them get here, after all."

Jacin shook his head. "He's under too much security. We'd never get her close. Besides, the fewer people who know you helped her, the less chance of Levana finding out."

The girl—Cress—seemed to be relaxing as it became apparent Winter and Jacin weren't going to have her executed. Winter smiled at her. "I've never met a shell before. What a marvelous gift. I can't sense you at all, like you're not even there, even though you're standing right in front of me." Her grin broadened. "That would drive my stepmother mad."

"It *was* a shell who killed the last king and queen," said Jacin. "Maybe we can turn her into an assassin."

Winter turned to him, aghast. "Does she *look* like an assassin?"

He shrugged. "Does she look like she's capable of disabling our entire maglev system?"

"I didn't disable it." Cress's voice was meek, but Winter was so surprised to hear her speak, she might as well have shouted. "I changed the access parameters so the queen couldn't shut it down."

Jacin stared at her. "But you could disable it, if you wanted to."

After a beat, the girl dropped her gaze to the floor.

"We have to find someplace to keep her," said Winter, tugging on a curl of hair. "Somewhere safe."

"Why?" said Cress. "Why are you helping me?"

Winter didn't know if she was asking her or Jacin, but Jacin answered first with a grumbled "Good question."

Winter shoved him hard in the shoulder. He barely shifted.

"Because it's the right thing to do. We're going to protect you. Aren't we, Jacin?"

When Jacin said nothing, Winter shoved him again. "Aren't we?"

Jacin sighed. "I think we can sneak her into the guard quarters. It's not far and we won't have to go into the main part of the castle."

With obvious disbelief, Cress said, "*You're* going to protect me?"

"Rather against my will," said Jacin, "but it looks like it."

"For as long as we can," said Winter. "And, if the opportunity arises, we'll do our best to reunite you with your friends."

For the first time, Cress's defenses began to slip. "They got away?"

"It would seem so. They haven't been found yet, as far as I can tell."

"But the queen won't stop looking," added Jacin, as if either of them weren't aware.

Cress had stopped trembling. Her expression became thoughtful as she stared at Jacin. Finally, she asked, "I don't suppose the guard quarters have access to the royal broadcasting network?"

Twenty-Four

THEIR PROGRESS THROUGH LUNA'S OUTER SECTORS WAS slow and tedious. Sometimes taking maglev shuttles, sometimes walking through the tunnels, sometimes using Wolf's identity to send a shuttle on without them before skipping to a different platform and heading in the opposite direction. Sometimes they split up and rejoined one another a couple of sectors over, to confuse any security personnel looking for a group of two men and two women traveling together.

They kept their heads down. Iko kept her hair hidden beneath her cap. Cinder fidgeted with her gloves to be sure her metal hand wouldn't be seen on any of the cameras. Though they avoided what surveillance cameras they could, she knew they couldn't miss them all. She hoped there were so many surveillance feeds on Luna they couldn't possibly all be monitored.

Though they occasionally ventured up to the surface in order to switch to a different shuttle line, they avoided it when they could. Wolf warned them that most of the outer sectors were manned by armed guards. Though they were meant to be there for the security of the people, it seemed they spent more time punishing anyone who dared to speak out against the crown. The few times they did sneak up into the surface domes, they managed to go unassaulted in their disguises and cowed postures, but Cinder knew it wouldn't be long before security measures were increased all over Luna.

They barely talked. Cinder spent the hours mulling over the battle in the docks, folding every misstep over in her head again and again, trying to determine a way she could have gotten them all away safely, trying to rescue Cress, trying to keep Kai out of Levana's clutches.

She never found a good solution.

The constant churning of her thoughts threatened to drive her mad.

The farther they traveled from Artemisia, the more their surroundings changed. It began to feel like they'd stepped into a different world altogether. Judging from how opulent the royal docks were, Cinder had constructed an image in her head of how beautiful all of Luna must be. But it soon became clear that the outer sectors received none of the capital's luxuries. Each platform they passed held new signs of neglect—crumbling stone walls and flickering lights. Graffiti scribbled onto the tunnel walls spoke of unrest.

SHE'S WATCHING . . . , read one message, painted in white upon the black cave walls. Another asked, **HAVE YOU SEEN MY SON?**

"How would we know if we had?" Iko asked. "They didn't leave a description."

"I think it's meant to be thought provoking," said Cinder.

Iko frowned, looking unprovoked.

They stopped when they heard a shuttle approaching or when they had to wait for a platform to clear, relishing their brief respites before moving on. They had brought a couple packs of food rations—not knowing when they would have an opportunity to find more—and Cinder doled them out in small increments, even though no one was all that hungry.

Though Cinder knew she couldn't be the only one whose back was sore and legs were aching, no one complained. Iko alone kept a graceful bounce to her step, having been fully charged before they left Kai's ship.

By shuttle, this trip should have lasted only a couple of hours. By the time they finally arrived at their destination, Cinder's internal clock told her they had left Artemisia over nineteen hours ago.

When they emerged from the darkened tunnel onto the shuttle platform of RM-9: REGOLITH MINING, the elaborate beauty of Artemisia felt like a distant dream. Gone were the glistening tiles and intricate statues, gone were the polished woods and glowing orbs. This platform was dark and cold and tasted of still, sterile air. Every surface was covered in a layer of dust, years of footprints pressed into it. Cinder brushed her hand across a wall and her fingers came away coated in gray.

"Regolith dust," said Wolf. "It covers everything out here."

Iko pressed both of her palms against one wall. When she pulled away, two handprints remained, perfect, yet lacking the normal creases of a human palm.

"Doesn't seem healthy," Thorne muttered.

"It's not." Wolf swiped at his nose, like the dust was tickling him. "It gets in your lungs. Regolith sickness is common."

Cinder clenched her teeth and added *unhealthy living and work conditions* to her long list of problems she was going to address when she was queen.

Iko smeared her dust-covered hands on her pants. "It feels abandoned."

"Everyone's working, either in the mines or the factories."

Cinder checked her internal clock, which she had synced with Lunar time before leaving the Rampion. "We have about eight minutes before the workday ends." She turned to Wolf. "We can wait here, or we can try to find your parents' house. What do you want to do?"

He looked conflicted as he peered up a set of narrow, uneven steps. "We should wait here. There aren't many reasons for people to be on the streets during work hours. We'd be too obvious." He gulped. "Besides, they might not be there. My parents might be dead."

He tried to say it with nonchalance, but he failed.

"All right," said Cinder, stealing back into the shadows of the tunnel. "How far are we from the factories?"

Wolf's brow was drawn, and she could see him straining to remember the details of his childhood home. "Not far. I remember them all being clustered near the dome's center. We should be able to blend in with the laborers as soon as the day ends."

"And the mines?"

"Those are farther away. There are two mine entrances on the other side of the dome. Regolith is one of the few natural resources Luna has, so it's a big industry."

"So . . . ," started Thorne, scratching his ear, "your best resource is . . . rocks?"

Wolf shrugged. "We have a lot of them."

"Not just rock," said Cinder, as her net database fed her an abundance of unsolicited information. "Regolith is full of metals and compounds too. Iron and magnesium in the highlands, aluminum and silica in the lowlands." She chewed the inside of her cheek. "I figured all of the metal would have had to come from Earth."

"A lot of it did, ages ago," said Wolf. "We've become experts at recycling the materials that were brought up from Earth during colonization. But we've also learned to make do. Most new construction uses materials mined from regolith—stone, metal, soil . . . Almost the entire city of Artemisia was built from regolith." He paused. "Well, and wood. We grow trees in the lumber sectors."

Cinder stopped listening. She had already educated herself as well as she could on Luna's resources and industries. Though, for their purposes, she'd spent most of her time researching Lunar media and transportation.

It was all controlled by the government, of course. Levana didn't want the outer sectors to have easy communication with one another. The less interaction her citizens had with each other, the more difficult it would be for them to form a rebellion.

A series of chimes pealed through the tunnel, making her jump. A short melody followed.

"The Lunar anthem," said Wolf, his expression dark, as if he had long harbored a deep hatred for the song.

The anthem was followed by a pleasant female voice: *"This workday has ended. Stamp your times and retire to your homes. We hope you enjoyed this workday and look forward to your return tomorrow."*

Thorne grunted. "How considerate."

Soon they could hear the drumming footsteps of exhausted workers pouring into the streets.

Wolf cocked his head, indicating it was time, and led them up the steps. They emerged into artificial daylight, where the dome's curved glass blocked out the glow of stars. This sector was not much of an improvement over the tunnels below. Cinder was staring at a patchwork of browns and grays. Narrow streets and run-down buildings that had no glass in their windows. And dust, dust, so much dust.

Cinder found herself shrinking away from the first sparse groups of people they saw—instinct telling her to stay hidden—but no one even glanced at them. The people they passed looked weary and filthy, hardly talking.

Wolf rolled his shoulders, his gaze darting over the buildings, the dust-covered streets, the artificial sky. Cinder wondered if he was embarrassed they were seeing this glimpse into his past, and she tried to imagine Wolf as a normal child, with parents who loved him and a home he grew up in. Before he was taken away and turned into a predator.

It was impossible to think that every member of Levana's army, every one of those mutants, had started out this way too. How many of them had been grateful to be given the chance to get away from these sectors with the dust that coated their homes and filled their lungs?

How many had been devastated to leave their families behind?

The graffiti echoed back at her: *Have you seen my son?*

Wolf pointed down one of the narrow streets. "This way. The residential streets are mostly in the outer rings of the sector."

They followed, trying to mimic the dragging feet and lowered heads of the laborers. It was difficult, when Cinder's own adrenaline was singing, her heartbeat starting to race.

The first part of her plan had already gone horribly wrong. She didn't know what she would do if this failed too. She needed Wolf's parents to be alive, to be allies. She needed the security they could offer—a safe place to hide while they figured out what they were going to do without Cress.

It was as far ahead as she could think.

Find a sanctuary.

Then she would start worrying about revolutions.

They hadn't gone far from the maglev tunnel when Cinder spotted the first guards, in full uniform, each clutching ominous guns in their arms. Unlike the civilians, their noses and mouths were covered to protect them from the dust.

Cinder shivered at the sight of them and cast her attention around, searching for the signature aura of a thaumaturge. She had never known a guard to be far from one, but she didn't sense any here.

How was it possible that a few weak-minded guards could hold such power over hundreds of gifted civilians? Though she guessed the Lunars in these outer sectors wouldn't be nearly as strong as Levana or her court, surely they could manipulate a few guards?

No sooner had she questioned it than the answer came to her.

These guards may not have a thaumaturge with them, but the threat was still there, implied in their very presence. The people of this sector could revolt. They could have these guards killed or enslaved easily. But such an act of defiance would bring the wrath of the queen down on them. The next guards that came would not be without the protection of a thaumaturge, and retribution would not be merciful.

When they passed by the guards, Cinder made sure to keep her face turned away.

They shuffled through the dome's center, where a water fountain stood in the middle of a dust-covered courtyard, forcing the crowd to flow around it. The fountain was carved into the figure of a woman, her head veiled and crowned, clear water pouring from her outspread hands as if she were offering life itself to the people who crossed her path.

The sight of it made the blood freeze in Cinder's veins. Levana had been queen for barely over a decade, yet she'd already put her mark on these far-reaching sectors.

Such a beautiful, serene fountain, but it felt like a threat.

They followed the dispersing crowd through blocks of factories and warehouses that smelled of chemicals, before the industrial buildings gave way to houses.

Though *houses* was a relative term. More like shacks, these homes were as unplanned and patched together as the overcrowded Phoenix Tower Apartments in New Beijing. Now Cinder understood what Wolf meant by how they had become experts at recycling materials. Every wall and roof looked like it had been cut and chopped and resoldered and rebolted and twisted and reconfigured again. As there was no weather to rust or corrode the materials, they were left to deteriorate at the hands of people. Houses pulled apart and reconstituted as families moved and changed and grew. The entire neighborhood was a ramshackle assortment of metal sheets and wood panels and stray materials left abandoned in the spaces between, waiting to be given a new use.

Wolf froze.

Nerves humming, Cinder scanned the nearby windows and opened the tip of her pointer finger in preparation for an attack. "What is it?"

Wolf didn't speak. Didn't move. He was focused on a house down the street, unblinking.

"Wolf?"

His breath rattled. "It might be nothing, but I think . . . I thought I smelled my mother. A soap that seemed familiar . . . though I didn't have these senses last time I saw her. It might not . . ."

He looked burdened and afraid.

He also looked *hopeful.*

A few of the shanties had flower boxes hung from their windows, and some of them even had live flowers. The house Wolf was staring at was one of them—a messy cluster of blue daisies spilling over the rough-hewn wood. They were a spot of beauty, simple and elegant and completely at odds with their dreary surroundings.

They paused in front of the house. There was no yard, only a spot of concrete in front of a plain door. There was one window but it had no glass. Instead, faded fabric had been tacked around its frame.

Wolf was rooted to the ground, so it was Thorne who shouldered past him and gave a quick rap against the door.

With the fabric alone acting as a sound barrier, they could hear every creak of the floors within as someone came to the door and opened it a timid crack. A small woman peeked out, alarmed when she saw Thorne. She was naturally petite but unnaturally gaunt, as if she hadn't had a complete meal in years. Brown hair was chopped short, and though she had olive-toned skin like Wolf's, her eyes were coal black, nothing like his striking green.

Thorne flashed his most disarming smile.

It had no obvious effect.

"Mrs. Kesley?"

"Yes, sir," she said meekly, her gaze sweeping out to the others. She passed over Wolf first, then Cinder and Iko, before her eyes rounded, almost comically. She gasped and looked at Wolf again, but then her lips turned down with distrust.

"My name," Thorne said, with a respectful tilt of his head, "is Captain Carswell Thorne. I believe you may know—"

A strangled sound escaped the woman. Her shock and

suspicion multiplied by the second, warring against each other as she stared at her son. She pulled open the door the rest of the way and took one hesitant step forward.

Wolf had become a statue. Cinder could feel the anxiety rolling off him in waves.

"Ze'ev?" the woman whispered.

"Mom," he whispered back.

The uncertainty cleared from her eyes, replaced with tears. She clapped both hands over her mouth and took another step forward. Paused again. Then she strode the rest of the way and wrapped her arms around Wolf. Though he dwarfed her in every way, he looked suddenly small and fragile, hunching down to fit better into her embrace.

Wolf's mother pulled away far enough to cup his face in her hands. Taking in how handsome and mature he'd become, or maybe wondering about all the scars.

Cinder spotted a tattoo on her forearm, in the same place where Wolf had one marking him as a special operative. His mother's, though, was stamped simply RM-9. It reminded Cinder of how someone might mark their pet, to be returned home in case it got lost.

"Mom," Wolf said again, choking down his emotions. "Can we come inside?"

The woman raked her attention over the others, pausing briefly on Iko. Cinder wondered if she was confounded by Iko's lack of bioelectricity, but she didn't ask. "Of course."

With those simple words, she extracted herself from Wolf and ushered them inside.

They found themselves in a tiny room with a single rocking chair and a sofa, a seam ripped open to reveal yellow stuffing inside. A fist-size holograph node was stuck in the center of one wall and a squat table was pushed beneath it. There was a drinking glass full of more blue daisies.

One doorway led to a short hall where Cinder assumed there were bedrooms and the washroom. A second door offered a glimpse into an equally small kitchen, the shelves and counters overflowing with dishes.

It looked like it hadn't been dusted in a year. But then, so did the woman.

Wolf hunched in the room as if he no longer physically fit inside it, while his mother gripped the back of the chair.

"Everyone," said Wolf, "this is my mother, Maha Kesley. Mom—this is Iko and Thorne and . . . Cinder." He chewed on the words like he wanted to say more, and Cinder knew he was debating whether or not to tell his mom her *true* identity.

Cinder did her best to look friendly. "Thank you for welcoming us. I'm afraid we've put you into a lot of danger by coming here."

Maha stood a little straighter, still wary.

Thorne had his hands in his pockets, as if he was afraid to touch anything. "Will your husband be home soon?"

Maha stared at him.

"We don't want any surprises," Cinder added.

Maha pursed her lips. She looked at Wolf, and Cinder knew. Wolf tensed.

"I'm sorry, Ze'ev," said Maha. "He died four years ago. There was an accident. At the factory."

Wolf's expression gave away nothing. Slowly, his head bobbed with acceptance. He'd seemed more surprised to see his mother alive than to learn of his father's death.

"Are you hungry?" said Maha, burying her shock. "You were always hungry ... before. But I suppose you were a growing boy then ..."

The words hung between them, filled with a lost childhood, so many years.

Wolf smiled, but not enough to show his sharp canine teeth. "That hasn't changed much."

Maha looked relieved. She tucked a stray hair behind her ear and bustled toward the kitchen. "Make yourselves comfortable. I think I might have some crackers."

Twenty-Five

JACIN FELT HEAVY WITH DREAD AS HE ENTERED THE THRONE room. The seats reserved for the members of the court were empty. Only the queen sat on her throne, with Aimery at her side. Not even their personal guards were with them, which meant that whatever this meeting was about, Levana didn't trust anyone to know of it.

Cress, he thought. She knew about Cress. He'd been hiding her in his private quarters, keeping her safe like he'd promised Winter he would, but he knew it couldn't last forever.

How had Levana found out?

A screen had been brought into the room, a large flat netscreen like the ones they used for two-dimensional Earthen media, only this one was more elaborate than anything Jacin had seen on Earth. It was set on an easel and framed in polished silver, bands of roses and thorns surrounding the screen as if it were a piece of art. The queen sparing no expense, as usual.

Queen Levana and Thaumaturge Park both wore dark expressions as Jacin came to a stop and clicked his heels together, trying not to think of the last time he'd stood in this spot. When he was sure he would be killed, and Winter would have to watch.

"You summoned, My Queen?"

"I did," Levana drawled, running her fingers over the arm of her throne.

He held his breath, racking his brain for some way he could explain Cress's presence that didn't incriminate Winter.

"I have been thinking a great deal about our little dilemma," said the queen. "I desire to put my trust in you again, as I did when you were under Sybil's care, yet I haven't been able to convince myself that you serve *me*. Your queen. And not ..." She whisked her fingers through the air, and her beautiful face took on something akin to a snarl. "Your *princess*."

Jacin's jaw tensed. He waited. Waited for her to accuse him of sheltering a known traitor. Waited for his punishment to be declared.

But the queen seemed to be waiting too.

Finally he dipped his head. "All due respect, Your Majesty, my becoming Princess Winter's guard was your decision. Not mine."

She shot him a sultry look. "And how very upset you seemed about it." Sighing, Levana rose to her feet and walked behind Winter's usual chair. She smoothed her fingers along the top of the upholstery. "After much deliberation, I have devised a test of sorts. A mission to prove your loyalty once and for all. I think, with this mission completed, there will be no qualms about placing you back into the service of my head thaumaturge. Aimery is eager to have your skills under his command."

Aimery's eyes glinted. "Quite."

Jacin's brows knit together and it dawned on him slowly that this wasn't about Cress at all.

He would have felt relief, except, if it *wasn't* about Cress . . .

"I told you before of my promise to my husband, Winter's father," Levana continued. "I told him I would protect the child to the best of my ability. All these years, I have held to that promise. I have taken care of her and raised her as my own."

Though he tried, Jacin could not stifle a surge of rebellion at these words. She had raised Winter as her own? No. She tortured Winter by making her attend every trial and execution, though everyone knew how she hated them. She had handed Winter the knife that disfigured her beautiful face. She had mocked Winter relentlessly for what she saw as her mental "weaknesses," having no idea how strong Winter had to be to avoid the temptation of using her glamour, and how much willpower it had taken her to suppress it over the years.

A wry smile crept over Levana's bloodred lips. "You do not like when I speak of your darling princess."

"My queen may speak of whomever she pleases." The response was automatic and monotone. It would make no difference to try to deny he cared for Winter, not when every person in this palace had witnessed their childhood antics, their games, and their mischief.

He'd grown up beside Winter because their fathers were so close, despite how improper it was for a princess to be climbing trees and playing at sword fights with the son of a lowly guard. He remembered wanting to protect her even then, even before he knew how much she needed protecting. He also remembered trying to steal a kiss from her, once—only once—when he was ten and she was eight. She laughed and turned away, scolding him. *Don't be silly. We can't do that until we're married.*

No, his only defense was to pretend he didn't care that

everyone knew it. That their taunts didn't bother him. That every time Levana mentioned the princess, his blood didn't turn to ice. That he wasn't terrified Levana would use Winter against him.

Levana stepped off the raised platform. "She has been given the best tutors, the finest clothes, the most exotic of pets. When she makes a request of me, I have tried my best to see it done."

Though she paused, Jacin did not think she was expecting a response.

"Despite all this, she does not belong here. Her mind is too weak for her to ever be useful, and her refusal to hide those hideous scars has made her a laughingstock among the court. She is making a mockery of the crown and the royal family." She set her jaw. "I did not realize the extent of her disgrace until recently. Aimery offered his own hand in marriage to the girl. I could not have hoped for a better match for a child who has no royal blood." Her tone became snarling and Jacin felt her studying him again, but he'd recaptured control of himself. She would get no rise from him, not even on this topic.

"But, no," said the queen at last. "The child refuses even this generous offer. For no other reason, I can fathom, than to jilt my most worthy counselor and bring further humiliation on this court." She tilted her chin up. "Then there was the incident in AR-2. I trust you remember?"

His mouth turned sour. If he had not been so careful to hide his mounting dread, he would have cursed.

"No?" Levana purred when he said nothing. "Allow me to spark your memory."

Her fingers glided across the netscreen. It flickered to life inside its elaborate frame, showing footage of a quaint little row of shops. He saw himself, smiling at Winter. Nudging her with his shoulder, and letting her nudge him back. Their eyes taking glimpses of each other when the other wasn't looking.

His chest felt hollowed out. Anyone could see how they felt about each other.

Jacin watched, but he didn't have to. He remembered the children and their handmade crown of twigs. He remembered how beautiful Winter had looked as she put it on her head, unconcerned. He remembered ripping it away and stuffing it into the basket.

He had hoped the whole incident would go unnoticed.

He'd known better. Hope was a coward's tool.

His attention shifted back to the queen, but she was scowling at the imagery, loathing in her eyes. His gut churned. She had mentioned a special mission for him that would prove his loyalty, yet all she'd talked about was Winter and what an embarrassment she'd become.

"I'm disappointed in you, Sir Clay." Levana rounded on him. "I thought I could trust you to keep her under control, to make sure she didn't do anything to embarrass me and my court. But you failed. Did you think it was proper for her to go gallivanting around the city, playing at being a queen before her loyal subjects?"

Jacin held his ground, already resigning himself to death. She had brought him here to have him executed after all. He was grateful she had decided to spare Winter the sight.

"Well? You have nothing to say in your defense?"

"No, My Queen," he said, "but I hope you'll allow me to speak in *her* defense. The children gave her a gift as thanks for purchasing some flowers from the florist. They were confused— they didn't understand what it would suggest. The princess meant nothing by this."

"Confused?" Levana's gaze turned brittle. "The children were *confused*?" She cackled. "And how much confusion am I to tolerate? Am I to ignore the sickening way they idolize her? How they talk about her *beauty* and her *scars* as if they were a badge of honor, when they have no idea how weak she is! Her illness, her delusions. She would be crushed if she ever sat on a throne, but they don't see that. No—they think only of themselves and their pretty princess, giving no thought to all I've done to bring them security and structure and—" She spun away, her shoulders trembling. "Am I to wait until they put a real crown on her head?"

Horror filled up Jacin's chest and this time he couldn't disguise it.

She was psychotic.

This he'd known, of course. But he'd never seen her vanity and greed and envy enflame her like this. She'd become irrational, and her anger was directed at Winter.

No—Winter and *Selene*. That's where this was coming from. There was a girl claiming to be her lost niece and Levana felt threatened. She was worried that her grip on the throne was loosening and she was overcompensating with paranoia and tightening control.

Jacin placed a fist to his chest. "My Queen, I assure you the princess is not a threat to your crown."

"Would you not bow to her?" said Levana, spinning back to face him with venom in her eyes. "You, who love her so dutifully? Who are so loyal to the royal family?"

He forced down a gulp. "She is not of royal blood. She can never be queen."

"No. She *will* never be queen." She swayed toward him, and he felt like he was being encircled by a python, smothered and choked. "Because you are my loyal servant, as you have so vehe-mently proclaimed. And you are going to kill her."

Jacin's tongue ran dry as moon rock. "No," he whispered.

Levana raised an eyebrow.

"I mean—My Queen." He cleared his throat. "You can't . . ." He looked at Aimery, who was half smiling, pleased with this deci-sion. "Please. Ask her to marry you again. I'll talk to her. I'll make sure she agrees. She can still be useful—it's a good match. She's just nervous—"

"You dare to question me?" said Levana.

His pulse thundered. "Please."

"I offered my hand to the princess as a kindness," said Aimery, "to protect her from the offers of far less sympathetic suitors. Her refusal has demonstrated how ungrateful she is. I would no longer take her if she begged me."

Jacin clenched his jaw. His heart was racing now and he couldn't stop it.

The queen's attention softened, full of honey and sugar. She was close to him. Close enough that he could grab his knife and cut her throat.

Would his arm be faster than her thoughts? Would it be faster than Aimery's?

"Dearest Sir Clay," she mused, and he wondered if she'd de-tected his desperation. "Do not think I am unaware of what I am asking you to do and how difficult it will be for you. But I am being *merciful.* I know you will be quick. She will not suffer at your hands. In this way, I also fulfill my promise to her father, don't you see?"

She was insane. Absolutely insane.

The worst of it was that he thought she might actually believe what she was saying.

His fingers twitched. A drop of sweat slipped down his neck.

"I can't," he said. "I won't. Please . . . please spare her. Take away her title. Turn her into a servant. Or banish her to the outer sectors, and you'll never hear from her again, I promise you . . ."

With a withering glare, Levana turned away and sighed. "How many lives would you sacrifice for hers?" She strolled toward the screen. The video was paused now, showing the three children in the doorway. "Would you rather I had these children killed instead?"

His heart kicked, trying to free itself from his rib cage.

"Or what about . . ." She turned back to him, tapping a finger against the corner of her mouth. "Your parents? If I recall correctly, Sir Garrison Clay was transferred to a guard post in one of the outer sectors. Tell me, when was the last time you spoke to them?"

He pressed his lips together, frightened that any admission could be turned against him. He had not seen or spoken to his parents in years. Just like with Winter, he had been sure the best way to protect his loved ones was to pretend he didn't love them at all, so they could never be used against him. Just as Levana was using them now.

How had he failed like this? He couldn't protect anyone. He couldn't save anyone—

He knew his face was contorted with panic, but he couldn't stifle it. He wanted to fall to his knees and plead for her to change her mind. He would do anything, *anything* but this.

"If you refuse me again," Levana said, "it will be clear that your loyalty is false. You will be executed for treason and your parents will follow. Then I will send Jerrico to deal with the princess, and I do not think he will be as gentle with her as you would have been."

Jacin choked back his misery. It would do him no good.

The thought of Jerrico—the smug and brutal captain of the guard—being given this same order made his blood run cold.

"Will you complete this task for me, Sir Clay?"

He bowed his head to hide his despair, though the show of respect nearly killed him.

"I will. My Queen."

Twenty-Six

FOR THE FIRST TIME SINCE SHE HAD ABANDONED IT, CRESS found herself missing her satellite. Jacin's private quarters were smaller than her satellite had been. The walls were so thin that she dared not even sing to pass the time. And when she needed to use the facilities, she had to wait for Jacin to get off his shift so he could sneak her in and out of the washroom that was shared between the guards and their families, all of whom lived in this underground wing of the palace. Once she crossed paths with another person, and while it was only a guard's wife who smiled kindly at her without any sign of suspicion, the encounter left Cress shaken.

She sensed the queen and her court all around her. She was aware at every moment that one person recognizing her for a shell would mean death. Perhaps torture and interrogation first. She was sick with anxiety for her own safety and terrified for the fate of her friends. She was frustrated that Jacin never had any news about them.

She told herself this was a good sign. Jacin would know if they'd been found. Wouldn't he?

Cress distracted herself doing what she could to help Cinder's cause with the limited resources available to her in Jacin's quarters. She still had her portscreen, and though she dared not send any comms, knowing how easily they could be traced, she was able to connect to the queen's broadcasting system via the holograph node embedded in Jacin's wall. The nodes were everywhere on Luna—as common as netscreens on Earth, and the feeds as easily hacked. She still had Cinder's prerecorded video stored in her port but she was afraid to do anything with it without knowing whether Cinder and the others were ready. Instead she spent her time interrupting propaganda messages from the queen and trying to come up with some way she could indicate to her friends that she was alive and relatively safe. She could never think of anything that wasn't either too obvious or too obscure though, and she was too timid to do anything that could alert the queen to her presence.

She wished again and again that she had access to the same technology she'd had in the satellite. She felt more cut off from the world than she ever had—with no media to view but that approved by the crown. No way to send a direct communication. No access to Luna's surveillance network or security systems and, hence, no way to fulfill the duties Cinder had given her. As the hours merged into days, she grew more anxious and addled, itching to get out of this enclosed space and *do* something.

She was altering the soundtrack from a royal message about their "brave victories against the weak-minded Earthens," when hard-soled footsteps in the hall made her pause.

They stopped outside Jacin's door. Cress disconnected her portscreen, threw herself off Jacin's cot, and scurried underneath it, pressing herself as close to the wall as possible. Outside, she heard the input of a code and fingerprint check on the lock. The door opened and shut.

She held her breath.

"Just me," came Jacin's voice, sounding as disillusioned as ever.

Exhaling, Cress crawled out from her hiding spot. She stayed on the floor, her back pressed against the cot's side. The cot was the only place to sit in this tiny room and she felt guilty taking it from Jacin—although she couldn't recall him ever sitting in her presence. He had even slept on the floor since her arrival, without any discussion of it.

"Any news?" she asked.

Jacin leaned against the door, his shadowed eyes caught on the ceiling. He seemed strangely disheveled. "No."

Cress pulled her knees into her chest. "What's wrong?"

Still entranced by the ceiling, he muttered, "You disabled the cameras in the dock."

She blinked.

"Could you do it again? To any cameras in the palace?"

She reached for her hair. The habit of fidgeting with it was hard to break, though it had been short for weeks now. "If I had access to the system. Which I don't."

He opened his mouth, paused, shut it again.

Cress frowned. Jacin was rarely chatty, but this was unusual even for him.

Finally, he said, "I could get you access to the system."

"Why are we disabling cameras?"

His chest rose and his focus traveled down the bare stone walls and landed on Cress. "You're leaving. You, Winter, and that redhead girl are leaving the palace. Tonight."

Cress hauled herself to her feet. "What?"

"Winter can't stay here, and she won't leave without that friend of hers. You help me get them out of here, and it's your ticket too." He started to massage his temple. "You know where

Cinder was heading, right? You can find her. She'll keep Winter safe. She *better* keep her safe."

Suspicion crawled up her spine at the mention of Cinder. Was this a trick? Was he trying to get information from her to be sold to the queen for his own gains? He'd done it before.

"It will look suspicious if a bunch of camera feeds go down at once," she said.

He nodded. "I know, but hopefully you'll be gone before anyone notices."

She gnawed on her lip. She could put them on a timer, try to make the blackouts seem like random power failures or a system glitch, but even that had the potential for being discovered.

Jacin had started to pace. She could see his thoughts churning. A plot was forming in his head, though she couldn't begin to guess how he planned to sneak them out of the palace without anyone seeing them—especially when Princess Winter was so recognizable.

"What happened?" said Cress. "Did Levana find out about me?"

"No. It was something else." He was pinching the bridge of his nose now. "She's going to have Winter killed. I have to get her out of here. I think I know a way. I can set it up, but ..." His eyes turned pleading. "Will you help me?"

Cress's heart squeezed. In the little time she'd known Jacin, he had struck her as cold, heartless, even cruel at times. But now he was fringed at the edges, ready to tear apart.

"By disabling the cameras?" she asked.

He nodded.

She looked at her portscreen. Though she'd detached it from the holograph node when she scuttled beneath the cot, the connector cable was still dangling from its side. This was her chance.

She could get away from the palace, away from this city and all its dangers. She could be with her friends again. She could be safe, *tonight.*

The temptation engulfed her. She had to get out of here.

But when she turned her face up toward Jacin again, she was shaking her head.

Bewilderment flashed across his face.

"It will be safest for the princess and Scarlet if"—she swallowed, but her saliva stuck in her throat—"if I stay behind."

"What?"

"Our best chance for the tampering to go unnoticed will be if I operate the system failure manually. I can turn the cameras off for short bursts, make them look like random power outages. A full blackout would draw too much attention, and blacking out just a portion of them would give the queen a clue as to which way Winter and Scarlet went. But if I disable and restart random sections of the surveillance system at the same time ... I can make it look like a coincidence." She tapped a finger against her lower lip. "I could set up a distraction too. Maybe an alarm in another part of the palace, to draw people away from them. And all the door locks in the major thoroughfares can be altered remotely too."

She was growing confident in her decision. She would stay behind to give Winter and Scarlet the best chance for escape.

"You're insane," said Jacin. "Do you *want* to die in this palace?"

She stiffened. "Levana doesn't know I'm here. As long as you keep me hidden ..."

"As soon as Levana learns I let Winter go, she'll kill me."

She clenched her fists, annoyed that he was punching holes in her newfound courage. "Scarlet was captured during an attempt to rescue me. And Winter protected me, even though she didn't have to, and I know it put her in a lot of danger. This is how I can repay them both."

Jacin stared and she could see the moment he accepted her decision. It was their best chance and he had to know it. He turned away, his shoulders starting to fall. "I was Sybil's pilot for over a year," he said. "I knew about you for over a year, and I did nothing to help you."

His confession stabbed her in the chest. She'd always thought Sybil had come alone, never realizing she had a pilot with her until it was too late. Maybe Jacin *could* have helped her, even rescued her.

They would never know.

He didn't apologize. Instead, he set his jaw and met her eye again. "I will protect Winter with my life. Second only to her, I promise to protect you too."

Twenty-Seven

SCARLET WAS WORKING ON THIS NEW THING SHE LIKED TO call *not reacting*.

It was a skill that by no means came to her naturally. But when she was the one locked inside a cage and her enemy was the one on the outside, jabbering and giggling and generally being buffoons, *not reacting* seemed like a better habit than screaming obscenities and trying to smack them through the bars.

At least it carried a bit more dignity.

"Can't you get her to do a trick?" asked the Lunar woman, holding an umbrella of owl feathers over one shoulder, though Scarlet couldn't guess what she was protecting herself from. According to Winter, they had another six days to go before they saw real sunshine again, and there was no rain on Luna at all.

The woman's companion leaned over, resting his hands on his knees, and peered at Scarlet through the bars. He was wearing orange sunglasses. Again, Scarlet didn't know why.

Scarlet, cross-legged on the ground, her hands folded and her hood pulled up past her ears, peered back.

I am a vision of tranquility and indifference.

"Do something," he ordered.

Scarlet blinked.

He glared at her. "Everyone says Earthens are supposed to be cute and amusing. Why don't you do a dance for us?"

Her insides writhed, wanting more than anything to show this man how *cute and amusing* she could be. Outside, however, she was statuesque.

"Are you mute, or just stupid? Don't they teach you how to address your betters down on that rock?"

I am the essence of peace and calm.

"What's wrong with her hand?" said the woman.

The man glanced down. "What's wrong with your hand?"

Her fingers didn't so much as twitch. Not even the half-missing one.

The woman yawned. "I'm bored and Earthens smell bad. Let's go look at the lions."

The man straightened, arms akimbo. Scarlet could see him calculating something in his tiny head. She didn't think he would try to use his gift on her—no one had manipulated her since she'd been brought to the menagerie and she was beginning to suspect her status as one of the princess's pets was protecting her from *that* torture, at least.

He took a step forward. Behind him, Ryu growled.

It was a test of willpower for Scarlet to smother a grin. That wolf had really grown on her lately.

Though the woman glanced back at the wolf's enclosure, the man kept his attention pinned on Scarlet. "You're here to entertain us," he said, "so *do something*. Sing a song. Tell a joke. Something."

For my next trick, I will win a staring contest with the moron in orange sunglasses.

Snarling, the man grabbed the umbrella from his girlfriend and closed it. Holding on to the curved handle, he pushed the pointy end through the bars and jabbed Scarlet in the shoulder.

Ryu barked.

Scarlet's hand whipped upward, her fist wrapping around the feathered fabric. She yanked it toward her and the man stumbled against the cage. She shoved the umbrella's handle up toward his face. He screamed and reeled back, his glasses clattering to the ground. Blood spurted from his nose.

Scarlet smirked long enough to shove the umbrella out onto the path—there was no point keeping it, as the guards would just take it away. She stifled her smug expression and returned her face to neutral.

This not-reacting thing was working out better than she'd expected.

After cursing and screaming and getting blood all over his shirt, the man grabbed his girlfriend and the umbrella and stormed away, back toward the menagerie's entrance. They were probably going to rat her out to the guards. She would probably miss a meal or two for her misbehavior.

It was totally worth it.

She met Ryu's yellow gaze across the way and winked. In response, the wolf raised his nose and howled, a short, joyful sound.

"You've made a friend."

She started. A guard was leaning against a large-leafed tree, arms crossed and eyes steely. He wasn't one of her normal guards, though there was an air of familiarity to him. She wondered how long he'd been standing there.

"We animals have to stick together," she said, but then resolved that was as much as he would get out of her. She was not here to entertain the spoiled Lunar aristocrats, and she was *certainly* not going to entertain one of the queen's brainless minions.

"Guess it makes sense you'd like that one. He's related to your boyfriend."

Her heart thumped. A sense of foreboding stirred in her chest.

Pushing himself off the tree, the guard strolled in front of Ryu's enclosure. One hand was resting at his belt, on the hilt of a large knife. The wolf froze, standing on all fours like he hadn't decided whether to trust this stranger or not.

"This one's father was the wolf they first gathered DNA from when they started experimenting with the soldiers. The queen's prized arctic wolf. Once an alpha male." He turned to Scarlet. "But you need a pack to be an alpha, don't you?"

"I wouldn't know," she deadpanned.

"Take my word for it." He listed his head, inspecting her. "You don't know who I am."

He said it at the same moment her memory clicked. The blond hair, the uniform, his creepy knowledge of Wolf.

Her recognition only made her more wary.

"Sure I do. I can't get the princess to shut up about you."

She watched him carefully, curious if Winter's feelings were even half mutual, but he gave nothing away.

He was handsome, sure enough. Broad shouldered and chisel jawed. But he wasn't what she'd been expecting. His posture spoke of condescension, his expression disinterest. He was all brambles and icicles as he strode toward her cage.

He was about as opposite of warm, spacey, babbling Winter as she could imagine.

Jacin didn't crouch or bend down and it was a strain on Scarlet's neck to look up at him. Her dislike increased.

"I trust she told you about your friends."

Winter had told her they were alive. That they were coming for her. That Wolf missed her very much.

Now, meeting the infamous Jacin, she couldn't envision him being the one to make that report.

"I got the message."

Scarlet wondered if he expected a thank-you, which he wasn't going to get, given that he was here on Luna, wearing that uniform. Whose side was he on?

Scarlet huffed and leaned back on her elbows. It may not have been as dignified, but she wasn't about to let this guy intimidate her into a permanent neck ache. "Is there something you needed?"

"Winter thinks you're a friend."

"That makes one of us."

After a beat, he revealed a crack in his armor. The tiniest of smiles.

"What?" she asked.

Rocking back on his heels, Jacin rested his hand on the knife again. "I wasn't sure what kind of girl could make a special op go ballistic over her. I'm glad to see it's not the stupid kind."

She curled her hands into fists. "Also not the kind that buys into empty flattery."

Wrapping a hand around one of the bars, Jacin finally crouched so they were at eye level. "You know why you're still alive?"

She gritted her teeth and answered, somewhat begrudgingly, "Because of Winter."

"That's right, firework. Try not to forget it."

"It's hard to forget when I'm locked up in her cage, *sunshine*."

The corner of his mouth crinkled with restrained amusement,

but it vanished just as fast. Unnerving. He nudged his chin toward her hand. "When was the last time someone checked that for infection?"

"I know what infection looks like." She resisted the urge to hide her wounded finger, but there was no way she was showing this guy her finger stub. "It's fine."

He made a noncommittal sound. "They say you're a decent pilot."

She scowled. "What is this, a job interview?"

"Have you ever flown a Lunar ship before?"

For the first time, he had her full attention, but her curiosity was crowded with suspicion.

"Why?"

"They're not much different from Earthen ships. Little different layout of the flight controls, smoother liftoff generally. I think you could figure it out."

"And why would it matter if I can fly a Lunar ship?"

His gaze cut through her, saying more than his words. He stood. "Just be ready."

"Be ready for *what*? And why do you care about me, anyway?"

"I don't," he said, so casual Scarlet had to believe him. "But I do care about the princess, and she could use an ally." He looked away. "A better ally than me."

Twenty-Eight

WINTER'S HEART FLUTTERED AS SHE PUSHED OPEN THE
massive glass door to the menagerie. Sounds of wildlife spilled
into the corridor—squawking birds in their palatial cages, monkeys chattering from overhead vines, white stallions neighing in
distant stables.

She shut the door before the heat could escape and scanned
the forked pathways, but there was no sign of Jacin. The menagerie took up several acres of this wing of the palace, a labyrinth
of barred cages and glass enclosures. It was always humid and
perfumed with exotic flowers, an aroma that barely covered up
the animal scent.

It was her favorite place—had been even before Scarlet had
lived there. She always felt at home with the animals, who knew
nothing of mind control and manipulation. They didn't care if
she was beautiful or if she was the queen's stepdaughter or if
she was going mad. She could not remember ever having an
episode of madness inside these walls, surrounded by her
friends. Here, she was calmer. Here, she could pretend that she
was in control of her own senses.

She tucked an unruly curl behind her ear and moved away from the door. She passed the chilled home of the arctic fox, who was curled atop a birch log, hiding his face behind a bristled tail. The next cage held a mother snow leopard and her litter of three prancing cubs. On the opposite side of the mossy path was a sleeping white owl. It peeped its huge eyes open as Winter passed.

She spotted Ryu's enclosure ahead, but he must have been sleeping in his den, as the wolf was nowhere to be seen. Then there was Scarlet, the one creature in the menagerie that was not made up of all-white fur or feathers, and she wore the distinction with defiance in her red hair and the hooded sweatshirt she never took off despite the humidity. She was sitting with her knees pulled up to her chest, staring at the flowering moss outside her cage.

She startled as Winter came closer.

"Hello, friend." Winter knelt in front of Scarlet's cage.

"Hello, crazy," said Scarlet. It sounded like an endearment. "How are the castle walls today?"

Winter hummed thoughtfully. She'd been so distracted she'd hardly been paying attention to the walls. "Not as bloody as usual," she determined.

"That's something." Scarlet pulled her curls to one side. Her hair was dark with grease and grime, extinguishing the fiery redness that had once reminded Winter of a comet's tail. She'd also lost too much weight since her captivity. Winter felt a pang of guilt. She should have brought a snack.

Scarlet's gaze raked over Winter with a tinge of suspicion, taking in the fluttery dress that sparkled a bit more than usual. "You look . . ." She paused. "Never mind. What's the occasion?"

Winter knotted her hands together. "Jacin asked me to meet him here."

Scarlet nodded, unsurprised. "Yeah, he came by a bit ago." She tilted her chin toward the path. "He went that way."

Winter stood again, knees shaking. Why was she nervous? This was Jacin, who had seen her covered in mud and scratches when they were children, who had bandaged her wounds when she got a scrape, who had held her when the visions were closing in, his whispers dragging her back to reality.

But something had been different when he asked her to meet him here.

For once, he seemed anxious.

She spent half the night wondering what it could mean, and her imagination always pulled her back to one possibility, one glittering hope.

He was going to tell her that he loved her. He didn't want to pretend anymore, despite the politics, despite her stepmother. He couldn't go another day without kissing her.

She shivered.

"Thank you," she murmured to Scarlet. Adjusting her skirt, she headed down the path.

"Winter?"

She paused. Scarlet was clutching the bar nearest her face. "Be careful."

Winter cocked her head. "What do you mean?"

"I know you like him. I know you trust him. But just . . . be careful."

Winter smiled. Poor, untrusting Scarlet. "If you insist," she said, turning away.

She spotted him as soon as she'd rounded the corner of Ryu's enclosure. Jacin was standing on a bridge that overlooked the menagerie's central pond and burbling waterfalls. A family of six swans was clustered beneath him as he tossed bread crumbs from his pockets.

He was wearing his uniform, ready to start his shift as her personal guard. His hair was so pale in the menagerie's hazy light that for a sinking moment Winter imagined he was one of Levana's animals—one of her pets.

She brushed the thought away as Jacin looked up. His expression was dark and her giddiness faded. So this was not a romantic meeting after all. Of course it wasn't. It never was.

This disappointment did not, however, chase away the fantasy of how badly she wanted him to press her against these caged walls and kiss her until she could think of nothing else.

She cleared her throat and came to stand beside him. "This is quite clandestine," she said, nudging him with her shoulder as he emptied the bread from his pockets.

Jacin hesitated, before nudging her back. "The menagerie is open to the public, Highness."

"Yes, and the doors will be locking in five minutes. No one's here."

He glanced over his shoulder. "You're right. I suppose it is clandestine."

A new whisper of hope stirred between her ears. Maybe. *Maybe* . . .

"Walk with me," Jacin said, ducking off the bridge.

She followed him around the pond. His attention was glued to the ground, one hand brushing against the handle of his knife. Ever the guard.

"Was there something . . . ?"

"Yeah," he whispered, as if pulling himself from deep thoughts, "there's a thing or two."

"Jacin?"

He massaged his brow. Winter couldn't recall the last time he'd looked so unsure of himself. "In fact, there are a whole lot of things I'd like to say to you."

Her heart ricocheted. Struggling through the topsy-turvy thoughts in her head, all she managed to say was a baffled "oh?"

Jacin's eyes flickered to her, but didn't linger, darting instead down the path. They crossed another ivory-carved bridge. Most of the swans had gone their separate ways, but one was floating after them still, dipping its head into the water. On the other side of the path were albino hares that watched them pass with red eyes and twitching noses.

"Ever since we were kids, all I ever wanted was to protect you."

Her lips tingled. She wished he would stop walking so she could see his face. But he didn't stop, guiding her past rocky out-croppings and drooping, heavy-headed flowers.

"Knowing you were there at the trial, all I could think was, I have to survive this. I'm not going to make her sit there and watch me die."

"Jacin—"

"But I was stupid to think I could protect you forever. Not from her."

His tone turned harsh. Winter's emotions were shredded from the constant flipping of this conversation.

"Jacin, what is this about?"

He took in a shaky breath. They'd come full circle and she could see that Ryu was awake now, prowling behind his bars.

Jacin stopped walking, and Winter tore her gaze from the wolf. She was pinned beneath Jacin's ice-blue stare. She gulped.

"She wants to kill you, Princess."

Winter shivered, first with the intensity of his words, and second with their meaning. She supposed such a declaration should have shocked her, but ever since Levana had given her these scars, she had been expecting this.

Her disappointment over Jacin *not* bringing her here to confess his love was more potent than the knowledge her stepmother wanted her dead.

"What have I done?"

He shook his head, the deep sadness returning. "Nothing that you could help. The people love you so much. Levana's just realized *how* much. She thinks you could be a threat to her crown."

"But I could never be queen," she said. "The bloodline. The people would never—"

"I know." His expression was sympathetic. "But it doesn't matter."

She drew back, hearing his words again. Spoken with such certainty. *She wants to kill you, Princess.*

"She told you this?"

A sharp, single nod.

Bright spots flickered in her vision. She stepped backward, grasping the rail of Ryu's enclosure. Behind her, she heard a growl, followed by Ryu's nose against her fingers. She hadn't realized he was there.

"She asked you to do it."

His jaw clenched. Guiltily, he glanced at the wolf. "I'm so sorry, Princess."

When the world stopped spinning, she dared to look up at the camera over his shoulder. She rarely paid the cameras much attention, but now she wondered if her stepmother was watching, waiting to see her stepdaughter murdered so she could protect her throne from an imaginary threat.

"Why would she do that to you?"

He laughed, like someone had stabbed him in the chest and he had no other choice but to find it amusing. "To *me*? Really?"

She forced herself to stand tall. Recalling her breathless anticipation of this meeting, she thought of what a naïve, silly girl she'd been.

"Yes," she said, firmly. "How could she be so cruel, to ask *you*, of all people?"

His face softened. "You're right. It's torture."

Tears started to mist her eyes. "She threatened someone, didn't she? She's going to have someone killed if you don't do this."

He didn't respond.

She sniffed, blinking the tears away. He didn't have to tell her. It didn't really matter who it was. "It's selfish of me, but I'm glad it's you, Jacin." Her voice shook. "I know you'll make it quick."

She tried to imagine it. Would he use his knife? A gun? She had no idea what was the fastest way to die. She didn't want to know.

Jacin would have had to ask these same questions. All the night before. All that day. He must have been planning how to do it, dreading this meeting as much as she'd been yearning for it.

Her heart broke for him.

Behind her, Ryu started to growl.

"Winter ..."

It had been so long since he'd called her by her name. Always *Princess*. Always *Highness*.

Her lip quivered, but she refused to cry. She wouldn't do that to him.

Jacin's fingers curled around his knife.

It *was* torture. Jacin looked more afraid than when he'd stood on trial. More pained now than when his torso had been stripped raw from the lashings.

This was the last time she would ever see him.

This was her last moment. Her last breath.

Suddenly, all of the politics and all of the games stopped mattering. Suddenly, she felt daring.

"Jacin," she said, with a shaky smile. "You must know. I cannot remember a time when I didn't love you. I don't think such a time ever existed."

His eyes filled with a thousand emotions. But before he could say whatever he would say, before he could kill her, Winter grabbed the front of his shirt with both hands and kissed him.

He thawed much quicker than she'd expected. Almost instantly, like he'd been waiting for this moment, he grabbed her hips and pulled her against him with a possessiveness that overwhelmed her. His lips were desperate and starved as he leaned into the kiss, pressing her against the rail. She gasped, and he deepened the kiss, threading one hand into the hair at the nape of her neck.

Her head swam, muddled with heat and a lifetime of desire.

Jacin's other hand abandoned her hip. She heard the ring of steel as the knife was pulled from its scabbard. Winter shuddered and kissed him harder, filling it with every fantasy she'd ever had.

Jacin's hand slipped out of her hair. His arm encircled her. He held her against him like they couldn't get close enough. Like he meant to absorb her body into his.

Releasing his shirt, Winter found his neck, his jaw. She felt the tips of his hair on her thumbs. He made a noise and she couldn't tell if it was desire or pain or regret or a mix of everything. His arm tensed against her back. His weight shifted as he raised the knife.

Winter squeezed her eyes tight.

Having seen so many deaths in her life, she had the distant thought that this was not such a horrible way to go.

His arm jerked downward and Winter gasped, the rush of air separating them. Her eyes flew open. Behind her, Ryu yelped, but the sound turned to a betrayed whimper.

Jacin's eyes were open too, blue and regretful.

Winter tried to back away but he held her firm. She had nowhere to go anyway, pinned between him and the railing as she was. Over his shoulder, a camera's light glowed against the ceiling. Her breaths were ragged. Her head spun. She couldn't tell her heartbeat from Jacin's.

Jacin. Whose cheeks were flushed and whose hair was a mess. Jacin, who she had finally dared to kiss. Jacin, who had kissed her back.

But if she'd expected to see desire in his face, she was disappointed. He had frozen again.

"Do me a favor, Princess," he whispered, his breath warm against her mouth. "The next time someone says they're going to kill you, don't just *let them.*"

She stared at him, dazed. What had he done?

Winter's knees gave out. Jacin caught her, sliding her down the enclosure's bars. Her hand landed in something warm and wet seeping out from underneath the short wall.

"You're all right, Princess," Jacin murmured. "You're all right."

"Ryu?" Her voice broke.

"They'll think the blood is yours." He was explaining something, but she didn't understand. "Wait here. Don't move until I turn out the lights. Got it? Princess?"

"Don't move," she whispered.

Jacin pulled away and she heard the knife being ripped from the wolf's flesh. The body sagged against the bars. Jacin cupped her scarred cheek, studying her to be sure she wasn't mid-breakdown, to be sure she'd understood, but all she could comprehend was the warm stickiness soaking through her skirt. Blood was flooding the pathway. Gallons and gallons of blood were suddenly dripping from the glass ceiling, splattering on her arms, filling up the pond.

"*Winter.*"

She gaped at Jacin, incapable of speaking. The memory of the kiss clouded over with something awful and unfair. Ryu. Sweet, innocent Ryu.

"Until the lights go out," he repeated. "Then I want you to get your redhead friend and get off this damned game board." Jacin's thumbs rubbed against her skin, stirring her from her shock. "Now play dead, Princess."

She sagged, finding relief in the command. They were playing a game. A game. Like when they were kids. *It's a game and the blood isn't real and Ryu—!*

She scrunched her face against the tears. A sob stayed locked in her throat. Jacin propped her against the cage wall and then his warmth was gone. The heaviness of his boots thudded away, leaving a path of sticky footprints in his wake.

Twenty-Nine

SCARLET'S FROWN FELT ETCHED INTO HER FACE AS SHE STARED down the empty pathway of the menagerie. Winter had gone that way what felt like hours ago, and Scarlet knew no guests were supposed to be in the menagerie this late. Probably those rules didn't apply to princesses, though. Maybe Winter was getting that romantic tryst she'd wanted, after all.

But something didn't feel right about it. Scarlet could have sworn she'd heard Ryu emerge from his den, but he hadn't yet come to see her, as was his normal routine. And she'd heard a noise—something that reminded her of the sound a goat makes during slaughter. Something that sent chills down her limbs, despite the menagerie's warmth and her zipped-up hoodie.

Finally, footsteps. Scarlet wrapped her hands around the bars.

She knew her suspicions were right as soon as the guard came into view, a knife clutched in one hand. Her heart pounded. Even from this distance she could see darkness on the blade. Even not knowing Jacin, she could read the regret on his face.

Her knuckles whitened on the bars.

"What did you do?" she said, choking back the fury that wanted to explode out of her, but would have nowhere to go. "Where's Winter?"

His gaze didn't waver as he came to stand outside her cage, and Scarlet didn't shrink back from him, despite the knife and the blood.

"Hold out your hand," he said, crouching.

She sneered. "Do you know what happens to people around here who 'hold out their hand'?"

He stabbed the point of the knife into the soft moss and, before Scarlet could move, reached for her wrist and twisted so hard a scream of pain arced up her shoulder. Scarlet gasped and her hand betrayed her, opening, palm up. It wasn't mental manipulation, just a plain old dirty trick.

Scarlet tried to rip her arm back through the bars, but his grip was iron. Changing tactics, she pressed her body against the cage and clawed at his face, but he hovered out of reach.

Dodging a second swipe of Scarlet's nails, the guard removed his scabbard from his belt and tipped it over. A tiny cylinder dropped into her palm.

He released her. Scarlet's fingers curled around the cylinder instinctively, her body shuddering back out of the guard's reach.

"Plug that into the security port of a Lunar ship and it will allow royal access. You can figure out the rest. There's also a message from a friend of yours encoded in there, but I suggest you wait until you're far away before worrying about that."

"What's going on? What did you do?"

He slammed the knife into the scabbard and, to her surprise, tossed it at her. She flinched, but it landed harmlessly in her lap.

"You need to find Artemisia Port E, Bay 22. Repeat it."

Her pulse was hammering. She looked down the path again,

expecting Winter's black curly hair and glittering dress and the uncanny grace of her walk to appear any second. Any second . . .

"*Repeat it.*"

"Port E, Bay 22." She wrapped her fingers around the knife's handle.

"I suggest going through the gamekeepers' halls first. Winter will know the way from there. We'll do what we can about the security, but try not to do anything stupid. And if you're tempted to try and leave Luna, fight it. You'll just draw attention, and that little pod isn't equipped for far distances anyway. Act like you're going to pick up a delivery in RM-9. That's where your boyfriend grew up. Understand?"

"No."

"Just get away from Artemisia. Port E, Bay 22. Sector RM-9." He stood. "And when you see that princess of yours, tell her to hurry up."

Scarlet dragged her attention back to him, thinking, *Winter? Winter had better hurry up?* But then she realized he was talking about the other princess. Selene. Cinder.

Jacin rounded the cage to the side with the barred door and pressed his thumbprint into the pad, identifying himself. He entered a code. Scarlet heard the telltale release of the lock, the clunk of the bolt. Her nerves hummed.

"Count to ten." Without looking at her, Jacin turned and walked away.

Everything in her screamed to shove that door open and race down the pathway to find Winter, but she refrained. Her fingers twitched. He had given her a weapon and an escape. She didn't know what was going on, but something told her that *not reacting* for ten measly seconds wasn't going to kill her.

On the count of four, she shoved the small cylinder into her hoodie's pocket. On five, she tucked the knife into the back of her torn and disgusting jeans. On six, she neared the bars again and pressed her face against them. On seven, she screamed, "*Winter!* Are you—"

On eight, the lights went out, plunging her into blackness.

Scarlet froze. That *jerk*. Was this supposed to make it easier? Was this supposed to be helpful? Was this—

Oh. The cameras.

Huffing, Scarlet checked that the knife was secure and pushed open the cage door. She scrambled through it and used the bars to pull herself to her feet. Her legs wobbled from lack of use. She steadied herself and stepped out onto the moss.

First, see if the princess was dead.

Second, find out where the hell Port E was.

"Winter?" she hissed, shuffling across the path. The enclosure wall seemed farther than she remembered, her own muddled senses playing tricks on her. Finally her hand found the railing and she used it to guide her way down the path. "Ryu?"

The wolf didn't answer. Another oddity.

Above the artificial jungle canopy and the glass wall, stars could be seen twinkling in abundance, and Scarlet's eyes adjusted to the dim light they provided. As she rounded a corner, she could make out only the shadows of tree boughs overhead and her own hand in front of her face.

She squinted. There was something white in the pathway, which could have been any number of albino animals that had their run of the place, but Scarlet's instincts told her exactly what it was. *Who* it was.

"Winter!" She jogged the rest of the way, her hand skimming the rail. The princess's shape took form, slumped across the bars. Something dark pooled beneath her. "Oh, no—oh, no—*Princess!*"

She collapsed to her knees, tilting Winter back and feeling around her throat.

"The walls are bleeding."

The faint, near-delirious words sent a wave of relief over Scarlet. Winter's heartbeat was strong when she found it. "Where are you hurt?"

"The blood . . . everywhere . . . so much blood."

"Winter. I need you to talk to me. Where did he hurt you?" She ran her hands over the princess's arms, shoulders, throat, but the blood was all beneath her. Her back then?

"He killed Ryu."

Scarlet froze.

The princess sobbed and fell forward, pressing her forehead into the crook of Scarlet's neck. "He was trying to protect me."

Scarlet didn't know if she meant the wolf or the guard. "You're all right," she said, more confirmation for herself. She glanced around. The menagerie disappeared in blackness, but she could hear the gurgle of a waterfall, the prowling of small paws, the leaves of a tree shaking as some creature scurried through it. She caught sight of the bundle of white fur behind Winter and her heart twinged, but she quickly smothered the feeling.

Like with her grandmother, there would be time to mourn later. Right now, she was getting them out of here.

Her brain clicked into overdrive.

Guards were always posted at the menagerie doors, and they would no doubt become suspicious when Princess Winter didn't return. Unless Jacin had something up his sleeve for them, but either way, Scarlet wasn't about to traipse out into the middle of the queen's palace.

She looked past Ryu. On the far wall she could make out the vague outline of the door that led into the gamekeepers' hallways, corridors used to feed the animals and maintain their cages. Jacin had suggested this route, and much as he got under her skin, she had no reason to question him.

"Come on." She hauled Winter to her feet.

The princess peered down at her hands and started to shake. "The blood ..."

"Yes, yes, the walls are bleeding, I get it. Look. Over there. Focus." Scarlet grabbed Winter's elbow and spun her around. "See that door? That's where we're heading. Here, I'll give you a boost." She knitted her fingers together, but Winter didn't move. "*Winter.* I am giving you five seconds to get your act together and decide to help me out, or else I am leaving you behind with your dead wolf and your bleeding walls. Got it?"

Winter's lips were parted and her expression dazed, but after three seconds she nodded. Or, her head dipped and Scarlet thought her eyelashes may have fluttered a little, which she was going to count.

"Good. Now step into my hands and get over that rail."

The princess did as she was told. The act was clumsy, which was at odds with every movement Scarlet had ever seen her make. As Winter collapsed into the wolf's enclosure, the reality of the situation crashed down around Scarlet.

That guard had given them a chance to escape. They were making a run for it.

Adrenaline rushed through her veins. Scarlet checked the knife one more time, then grasped the rail and hauled herself over.

She landed with a grunt and sprang back up, running for the door. It swung open, and to her relief, no alarms sounded. She glanced back to see the princess stooped over Ryu's body, but before Scarlet could yell for her, the princess lifted her chin, swiped her bloodied palms on her skirt, and followed.

Thirty

THE FEEDING HALLS WERE PITCH-BLACK. SCARLET PAUSED TO listen for footsteps or voices, but there was nothing but the muffled chatter of birds they'd left behind. The smell reminded her of the farm, a heady combination of feed and hay and manure. She oriented herself. Going right would lead her farther into the menagerie, but left might land them back in the palace—hopefully in some sort of servants' quarters. With one hand on the wall, she grabbed Winter's wrist and took off. Her fingers skimmed over closed doors and she used what she knew of the menagerie to count them. *This must be the stag. This could be the snow leopard. Is this is the arctic fox?*

They turned a corner and a blinking light caught her eye—hazy and distant. She headed toward it and found a control panel embedded in the wall, where one could control the menagerie's lights and temperature and automatic feeders.

Beside the panel, barely seen in its faint light, was a door.

She pressed the unlock mechanism, hoping beyond hope that this door didn't lead to the lion. Nothing happened.

Cursing, Scarlet pressed the unlock mechanism again. Nothing.

Then the control panel pinged, startling her, and a message scrolled across the top.

BE CAREFUL, SCARLET.

Her jaw fell. "What—?"

Before she could question it, she heard the door unlock. Trembling, she reached for the handle. The door slid open.

She flinched at the onslaught of light and pulled Winter against the wall, but a glance told her this well-lit hallway was equally desolate. Narrow and plain. If Scarlet had to guess what a servants' hall looked like, this would be it.

She listened and heard nothing.

She looked up and her heart jumped.

A camera was rotating on the ceiling, scanning the hallway, back and forth. But no sooner had Scarlet spotted it than it froze. Its power light dimmed and went out. Startled, Scarlet leaned farther into the hallway and saw a second camera some fifty paces away just as it, too, shut off.

What had Jacin said? Something about handling the security? But . . . *how?*

Fumbling for Winter's elbow, Scarlet dragged her into the hallway. "Do you know where we are?"

"Near the guest wing."

Well, that was something. At least Scarlet didn't have to worry about them *starting out* hopelessly lost.

"We're trying to get to Artemisia Port E. You know where that is, right?"

"*E . . .*," murmured Winter. "*E* for *execution. Earth. Evret. Emperor.*" She pondered a moment longer. "*E* for *escape.*"

Scarlet groaned. "*E* for *unhelpful.*"

"No, that does not work."

Scarlet spun on her and the princess came to a hasty stop. The back of her skirt was dark with blood, and smears of it covered her arms, her legs, even her face. In fact . . .

Looking down, Scarlet saw that she had a fair amount of it on herself, as well. This would not help to make them inconspicuous.

"The docks, Winter," she said, glowering at the princess. "Do you know where they are or not?"

The princess scrunched up her face and pressed her bloodied palms against her cheeks and for a moment Scarlet thought she was going to cry.

"No. Yes. I don't know." Her breaths shortened, her shoulders beginning to quake.

"*Princess,*" warned Scarlet.

"I think so. The docks . . . yes, the docks. With the mushrooms."

"Mushrooms?"

"And the shadows that dance. Port E. *E* for *escape.*"

"Yeah, *E* for *escape.*" Scarlet could feel her hope slipping through her fingers. There was no way this was going to work. "How do we get there?"

"We take the rail. To the edge of the city."

"The rail. All right. How do we get there?"

"Down, down, down we go."

Scarlet could feel her patience unraveling. "And how do we go down?"

Winter shook her head, apology swimming in her amber

eyes. Scarlet would have wanted to hug her if she hadn't simultaneously wanted to strangle her.

"Fine. I'll figure it out. Come on." She took off down the hallway, hoping they would stumble across a flight of stairs or an elevator. Servants had to get around quickly, didn't they? Surely they would find—

She rounded a corner and screeched, nearly colliding with a girl, a maid who couldn't have been more than fourteen years old. Winter crashed into Scarlet and she grasped the princess's arm, adrenaline thundering in her ears. The maid stared at Scarlet for a heartbeat, then at the princess, covered in blood, then dropped into a nervous curtsy, clutching the linens in her arms.

"Y-your Highness," she stammered.

Clenching her teeth, Scarlet grabbed the knife out of the scabbard and lunged for the girl, pinning her against the wall with the blade against her throat.

The girl squeaked. The linens tumbled around their feet.

"We need to get to the rail that will take us to the docks. Quickest way there. Now."

The girl started to shake, her eyes round.

"Do not be afraid," said Winter, her voice singsong and delicate. "She will not hurt you."

"Like hell I won't. How do we get to the docks?"

The girl raised a finger. "D-down this hallway, to the right. The stairs go down to the sh-shuttle platform."

Pulling away, Scarlet grabbed a white tablecloth from the fallen stack and ushered Winter down the hall without looking back.

The corridor ended in a T. Scarlet turned right and found an alcove that dropped into a bright stairwell. Once the door had shut behind them, Scarlet shook out the tablecloth and draped it around Winter, doing her best to knot it into something that resembled a cloak, hiding the blood and the princess's recognizable beauty. Deeming her work passable, she grabbed Winter's hand and headed down the steps. As they reached the second landing, the walls changed to rough gray-brown stone. They were underground, in the sublevels of the palace.

Three floors down they emerged onto a platform lit by glowing sconces. Before them were silent magnetic rails. Scarlet approached the ledge, peering each way down the tunnel.

She spotted a second doorway, arched and trimmed with phosphorescent tiles. The entry into the palace corridors, as opposed to the dull servants' entrance.

Something clicked. The magnets started to hum. Heart launching into her throat, Scarlet held out her arm and backed Winter against the wall. A bullet-shaped shuttle emerged from the tunnel and glided to a stop on the tracks. Scarlet held still, hoping whoever it was wouldn't see them, wouldn't even glance their way.

The shuttle door lifted with a hiss of hydraulics and a giggling noblewoman stepped out, wearing a flamboyant emerald-green gown that glittered with jeweled peacock feathers. A man followed in a tunic stitched with runes similar to those worn by the thaumaturges. He reached over and squeezed the woman's backside. She squealed and swished him away.

Scarlet didn't breathe until they'd stumbled to the door and their laughter faded in the stairwell.

"That was not her husband," Winter whispered.

"I really don't care." Scarlet lunged toward the shuttle. "Open!"

The shuttle didn't move. The door didn't open.

"Open, you stupid piece of junk!" Digging her fingers into the crack of the door, Scarlet tried to pry it open. Her injured finger throbbed for the first time in days. "Come on. What's wrong with this thing? How do we—"

The door opened, nearly knocking Scarlet off balance. A robotic voice said, "Transport to Artemisia Port E."

Goose bumps rushed along her skin, but she urged Winter inside, silently thanking whatever invisible ally was helping them. Climbing in after Winter, Scarlet collapsed onto a bench. The door breezed shut, sealing them inside. As the shuttle lifted and began to glide down the tracks, Winter added, "For escape."

Scarlet swiped her damp forehead with a dirty sleeve. When she felt her panic settle down enough to speak, she asked, "What happened back there? In the menagerie?"

The strength that had entered Winter's eyes just as quickly extinguished. "The queen sent him to kill me," she said, "but he killed Ryu instead."

Scarlet unzipped her hoodie, trying to cool her burning skin. "Why does the queen want to kill you?"

"She believes I am a threat to her crown."

Scarlet snorted, an exhausted sound that didn't carry half as much derision as it should have. "Really? Has she ever heard you talk?"

Winter turned questioning eyes on her.

"Because you're *crazy*," explained Scarlet. "Not exactly queen material. No offense."

"I cannot be queen because I am not of royal descent. Her Majesty is only my stepmother. I have none of her blood."

"Right, because that's what's important in a ruler."

Though there were two monarchies in the Earthen Union— the United Kingdom and the Eastern Commonwealth—Scarlet had grown up in Europe, a democracy made up of checks and

balances, voter ballots, and province representatives. She generally figured, to each his own, and clearly the countries of the
Union were doing something right to have gotten through
126 years of world peace.

But that wasn't the case with Luna. Something was broken
with their system.

The shuttle began to slow. Scarlet glanced toward the window as the rocky black cave opened up to an enormous spaceship port bustling with activity. The tiled floor glowed, casting
the shadows of countless ships against the dark walls. But this
dock was crowded and huge, with several more sets of maglev
tracks bringing in more shuttles every second. Cargo was being
unloaded on another set of tracks, food and goods coming in
from the outer sectors, by men who yelled at one another in ab-
breviated orders that sounded like another language.

"Bay 22," Scarlet reminded herself as their shuttle door
opened. "Try to fit in."

Winter glanced at her, a moment of perfect clarity and even
humor in the look.

She was right. They were filthy. They were bloody. Winter was
a well-loved princess who was prettier than a bouquet of roses
and crazier than a headless chicken.

Fitting in would be a miracle.

"You could use your glamour," Scarlet suggested.

The connection severed and Winter turned away. "No. I
couldn't." She stepped out onto the platform.

Scarlet followed, relieved that she didn't see anyone wearing
rich finery and donning ridiculous headpieces. This was a place
for trade and cargo, not aristocrats, but that didn't mean they
were safe. Already she could sense the workers pausing, looking
again, staring.

"You mean you won't," said Scarlet.

"I mean I won't," agreed the princess.

"Then at least keep your head down." Scarlet adjusted the tablecloth material over Winter's hair as they moved away from the rails.

The port was enormous, stretching far into the distance. Hundreds of dark alcoves lined either side, numbers carved above them. Scarlet scanned the cargo as they passed, her eye catching on words of war.

SMALL ARMS AMMUNITION
DELIVER: LUNAR REGIMENT 51, PACK 437
THAUM LAIGHT, ALPHA GANUS
STATIONED: ROME, ITALY, EF, EARTH

Ammunition. These were weapons destined for Earth to aid in Luna's war efforts.

Don't react, she told herself, fists clenching. Every fiber in her body yearned to find a weapon and set fire to every crate in this port.

Don't react. Do not react.

Steadying her breath, she forged ahead, Winter trailing beside her. She caught E7 stenciled on a wall to her left, E8 on her right. Almost there.

It took every ounce of willpower not to sprint to Bay 22.

"Can I help you?"

They paused. A worker stepped toward them wearing filthy coveralls. "What are you ..." He caught himself, his gaze landing on Winter, or what he could see of her down-turned face. "I ... forgive me. Your Highness?"

Winter looked up. Color flooded into the man's cheeks.

"It is you," he breathed. "I didn't ... can I help you, Your Highness?"

Scarlet bristled. No one else had noticed them yet. She grabbed the man's arm before he bowed. "Her Highness does not wish to be gawked at. If you want to help, you can escort us to Bay 22."

Anxiety flashed across the man's face and he nodded, as if he were afraid of her. Maybe he thought she was a thaumaturge in training.

"Y-yes, of course. Right this way."

Scarlet released him and shot Winter a cool glare, gesturing for her to hide her face again. The man's stride was stiff as he led them past hovering cargo platforms and crates on complicated tracks. Scratching his neck with his free hand, he glanced twice over his shoulder.

"Is something wrong?" said Scarlet, steel in her tone.

"N-no. I'm sorry."

"Then stop looking at her."

He opened his mouth and Scarlet thought he wanted to mention the blood or the grime or Winter's very existence, but then he shut it again and kept his head down.

Some of the alcoves they passed had heavy metal doors over them, but most were open, showing docked ships within.

"See?" Winter whispered. "Mushrooms, and the shadows that dance."

Scarlet followed her gesture. The spacecrafts' shadows on the walls did look something like dancing mushrooms. Sort of. If she tilted her head and squinted just right.

"Bay 22, Your Highness."

Scarlet glanced at the number over the arched door and the podship enclosed within. It was a two-person carrier, inset with the gold insignia of the royal court.

"Thank you," said Scarlet. "That will be all."

The man's eyebrows stitched together. "Will ... will you need an escort back?"

Scarlet shook her head and linked her elbow with Winter's again, but had only taken two steps when she paused. "Tell no one you saw us," she told the man. "But if someone asks, tell them we glamoured you into helping us. Understand?"

His round eyes fell on Winter, who smiled warmly. His blush deepened.

"I'm not so sure you didn't," he muttered.

Rolling her eyes, Scarlet hauled the princess toward the ship. She checked that the man was gone before she opened the pilot's side door and nudged Winter inside. "All the way over, unless you plan on flying this thing."

Winter complied without question. Scarlet removed the knife from her waistband and settled it between them. She shut the door and the noise of the docks silenced in the vacuum-sealed ship.

Scarlet exhaled, willing her hands to stop shaking. Willing the mess of controls in front of her to come into focus. She examined the cockpit, noting what was similar to the delivery ship she'd flown since she was fifteen and what was different.

"I can do this," she whispered, pressing her fingers against the main screen. It brightened. The controls lit up.

SECURITY CLEARANCE UNDETERMINED

She stared at the message. She had to read it four times before the meaning of the words sank in. She half expected their phantom helper to override the ship's security and start the engines for her too. When nothing happened, she remembered the cylinder Jacin had given her. She fished it from her pocket and popped off its cap, holding her breath as she jammed it into the corresponding security port.

An icon whirled over the message.

And whirled.

And whirled.

Her stomach tightened. A drop of sweat slid down the back of her neck.

CLEARANCE GRANTED. WELCOME, ROYAL GUARD JACIN CLAY.

Scarlet whooped, dizzy with relief. She jogged a few switches. The engine hummed and the ship lifted up on the magnetic force beneath the ports, steady and sure. Outside their alcove, a series of cargo ships were making their way toward the sealed chamber that separated Artemisia's Port E from the emptiness of space. They could slip in right behind them and no one would stop a royal ship, no one would even question—

"Wait," said Winter as Scarlet nudged the podship forward.

Scarlet's heart dropped. "What?" she said, scanning the port for a thaumaturge, a guard, a threat.

Winter reached over and pulled the pilot's harness over Scarlet's head. "Safety first, Scarlet-friend. We are fragile things."

Thirty-One

WINTER WAS MESMERIZED BY SCARLET'S CONFIDENT HANDS as they skimmed over the ship's controls. Behind the ship, enormous iron doors slammed shut, locking them in a vacuum-sealed chamber with a dozen other ships waiting to be released from Artemisia's underground port. Tearing her attention away from Scarlet and the twinkling instruments, Winter glanced over her shoulder at the interlocking doors—so ancient they looked almost like they had existed on the moon even before colonization.

Now they divided her from the ports, the city, the palace.

And Jacin.

Scarlet was all nerves, tapping her fingers across the instruments. "How long is this going to take?"

"I don't know. I've only ever left Artemisia on the maglev rails."

"They just have to seal a couple doors, right?" Scarlet reached overhead and toggled a few switches. The lights inside the ship faded to black. "This would be a bad time for someone to look over and recognize you. They'd probably think I was kidnapping you."

"You are, in a manner."

"*No.* I'm saving you from your psychotic stepmother. There's a difference."

Winter pulled her attention away from the doors and scanned the nearby ships. Most seemed to be cargo ships. She wondered how many were taking supplies for the war efforts on Earth or carrying more of the queen's soldiers. Still, most would be headed to the outer sectors for deliveries or to load up on goods to be brought back to the capital. It was much faster to fly than to take the maglev shuttles halfway around the moon.

"Are we going to Earth?"

Scarlet's frown deepened. "Jacin said this ship wouldn't make it that far. He said to go to Sector RM-9."

Jacin. Brave Jacin. Always protecting her.

She'd abandoned him.

Scarlet tugged on one of the drawstrings of her hoodie, the end frayed and dirty. "Jacin said this sector we're going to is where Wolf grew up. His family might still be there."

Winter trailed her fingers along her harness and sang to herself, "*The Earth is full tonight, tonight, and the wolves all howl, aa-ooooooooooh . . .*"

"We need an ally. Someone we can trust. Maybe I can persuade Wolf's parents to shelter us. Hide us, until we come up with a better plan, and in the name of all the stars, *what is taking so long?*"

Winter blinked at her. "*Aa-ooooh?*"

Scarlet huffed. "Would you focus? We need to find someplace we can hide from the queen."

"She will find us anywhere. We will not be safe."

"Don't say that. The people like you, don't they? They'll protect you. Us."

"I do not wish to put them in danger."

"You need to get over that mode of thinking right now. This is us against her, Winter. From now on, I need you to think like a survivalist."

Winter took in a shuddering breath, jealous of the embers that burned inside Scarlet. She felt hollow and cold on the inside. Easily shattered.

Scarlet popped one of her sweatshirt's drawstrings into her mouth and gnawed on the plastic end. "RM-9," she muttered to herself. "What does RM-9 mean?"

"Regolith Mining Sector 9. That is a dangerous sector."

"Dangerous? Dangerous how?"

"Regolith sickness. Many deaths."

Scarlet's mouth quirked. "Sounds like the sort of place Levana wouldn't look for you." Scarlet clicked on a screen and opened up a map. "Perfect."

The second set of massive doors began to slide apart, disappearing into the black cavern walls. Faint light spilled in.

"Scarlet?"

"What?" Scarlet looked up and gasped. "*Finally.*"

As the gap between the doors grew, Winter saw they were in a cave built into the side of a crater. Beyond its rim lay the rocky wasteland of Luna, its jagged rocks and pockmarked surface as unwelcoming as a black hole.

"Jacin saved us both," she whispered, her chest aching.

Scarlet harrumphed and guided the ship forward, falling in line with the others. Ahead, the boosters on the ships nearest the exit flamed and thrust them into space. "He could have been a little more forthcoming with information. But, yeah. Remind me to thank him someday."

"Levana will kill him." She looked down. There was dried blood beneath her fingernails, smearing her dress, drenching her slippers. She blinked, and the bloodstains began to seep through the fabric, spreading.

Winter let out a weak breath. *It's not real, Princess.*

"I'm sure he stayed behind for a reason," said Scarlet. "He must have a plan."

Their ship reached the front of the line and the whole galaxy opened up before them. A bold smile curled on Scarlet's lips. "Here we go."

As Scarlet's fingers flew over the controls and the podship hummed around them, Winter glanced back one last time. There was a jerk. Her stomach flipped and then they were soaring out of the holding bay and Scarlet was laughing and the crystal dome that housed Artemisia was beneath them and growing smaller and smaller and ...

Winter sobbed and pressed a hand to her mouth.

"Hey, hey, none of that," said Scarlet, not bothering to hide her own effusive joy. "We made it, Winter, and I'm sure Jacin will be fine. He seems tough."

Winter's neck began to ache from being twisted in her seat, but she didn't want to tear her gaze away from Artemisia, not even as the palace and the buildings blurred together and the lights twinkled and went out, invisible beneath the dome's surface.

"She will kill him."

"I know you're worried, but *look*. We are out of that star-forsaken city. We're alive and we're free, so stop moping."

Winter rested her cheek against her chair's back. More tears were threatening to escape, but she held them back, focusing instead on her ragged breaths.

After a long silence, she felt a hand settle over hers.

"I'm sorry," said Scarlet. "That wasn't fair. I know you like him."

Winter swallowed. "I love him like I love my own platelet-manufacturing plant."

"Your own *what*?"

"I don't know. My heart, I think. My body. I love him, every part of him."

"Fine, you love him. But, Winter, he seemed to know what he was doing."

"Protecting me," Winter whispered. "He's always protecting me." She was startled by the unexpected scent of blood invading her lungs. She looked down and gasped.

"What? What's wrong?"

Winter held the fabric of her dress away from her stomach. The blood had soaked the shimmering white material, turning it dark red. Even the cloth they'd taken from the servant was covered. The stench was so thick she could taste it.

"Winter?"

"It—it's nothing," she stammered, trying to imagine it away. The blood dripped down her legs.

"You're hallucinating, aren't you?"

Winter leaned back against the seat. She wrapped her fingers around the straps of her harness. *It's all in your head, Princess. It isn't real.* "I'm fine. It will go away soon."

"Honestly," Scarlet snapped, "why don't you just use your glamour? Why let it drive you crazy like this?"

"I won't." Winter choked down another difficult breath.

"I get that, but *why*?"

· 267 ·

"It is a cruel gift. I wish I hadn't been born with it."

"Well, you *were* born with it. Look at you, Winter. You're a mess. Why don't you just—I don't know—make me think your hair is orange or something? Something harmless?"

"It's never harmless." The harness constricted. Her fingernails clawed at the straps.

"If *I* had the gift," continued Scarlet, ignorant of the harness's choking hold, the gushing blood, "I would have shown those snotty imbeciles a thing or two. See how *they* like being asked to do tricks."

Winter's hands were wet and slick and sticky.

"My grandfather was Lunar," said Scarlet. "I never met him, but I do know he died in an insane asylum. I have to assume because he made the same choice you're making now. He was down on Earth and trying to hide what he was, so maybe he had a reason. But you? Why do this to yourself? How does it make anything better?"

"It does not make anything worse."

"It makes *you* worse. Why can't you just . . . do *good* things with it?"

Winter laughed against the strain of the delusion. "They all believe they are doing good." Her head fell to the side and she watched Scarlet with her bleary eyes. "My stepmother is not only powerful because the people fear her, she is powerful because she can make them *love* her when she needs them to. We think that if we choose to do only good, then we are only good. We can make people happy. We can offer tranquility or contentment or love, and that must be good. We do not see the falsehood becoming its own brand of cruelty."

The ship trembled and their speed increased. Luna blurred beneath them.

"Once," Winter continued, pushing the words out of her lungs. "Once I believed with all my heart that I was doing good. But I was wrong."

Scarlet's gaze darted to her, then back to the landscape. "What happened?"

"There was a servant who tried to kill herself. I stopped her. I forced her to change her mind. I made her *happy*. I was so sure I was helping her." Her breaths came in strangled gasps, but she kept talking, hoping to push through the hallucination if she ignored it enough. "But all I did was give her more time to be tortured by Aimery. He was quite fond of her, you see."

Scarlet went quiet, but Winter dared not look at her.

"The next time she tried to take her life, she succeeded. Only then did I realize that I hadn't helped her at all." She swallowed, hard. "That day I swore to never manipulate anyone again. Even if I believed I was doing good—for who am I to presume what is good for others?"

The harness tightened again, pressing against Winter's sternum, cutting against her ribs. The blood was spilling over it now. Soon it would be sloshing around her ankles. The harness would cut right through her, chopping her into girl-shaped pieces. Razor wire slicing through her flesh.

Winter shut her eyes.

Stay with me, Princess.

After a suffocating silence, Scarlet murmured, "It just seems like there should be a way to manage it, without . . . *this*."

The harness tightened, forcing the air out of her lungs. With a whimper, she tilted her head back to avoid it pressing against her windpipe.

"What—*Winter*?"

Stars danced behind her eyelids. Her lungs burned. Blood

dripped off the curls of her hair and soaked into the harness straps. She stopped fighting it and let her body slump forward. The straps crushed her sternum, snapped her ribs.

Scarlet cursed, but the sound was distant and muffled.

Hands thumped against her like mittened fingers, leaning her back against the seat and feeling her throat. She heard her name but it was far away, trying to reach her across a whole sea of stars and everything was fading fast . . .

There was a series of loud clicks and the whir of the harness being reeled into the ship's roof.

Winter collapsed into Scarlet's arms, both of them crumpled over the center console. Scarlet struggled to lift Winter's head and open her air passage while keeping the ship from colliding with Luna's jagged terrain.

Air rushed back into Winter's lungs. She gasped, swallowing it down hungrily. Her throat was still stinging, but the aches in her chest were fading into the lost depths of the hallucination. She coughed and forced her eyes open. The blood had receded, and now only the remnants of Ryu's death were left, dried and smeared on her skirt.

"Are you all right?" Scarlet cried, half hysterical.

Winter met her bewildered face, still dizzy from the loss of air, and whispered, "The harness tried to kill me."

Dragging a hand through her hair, Scarlet fell back into the pilot's seat. Through the window, half a dozen distant domes were growing larger—a slow growth, giving way to the subtle impression of buildings underneath.

"The harness didn't do anything," Scarlet growled. "It's your brain that's the problem."

Winter started to giggle, but it was cut short by sobs. "Y-you're right," she stammered, hearing Jacin's voice in her head.

Stay with me, Princess. Stay with me—

But she was already so far away.

"MY QUEEN, WE HAVE BEEN EXPERIENCING MINOR GLITCHES in the surveillance system. Random power failures that have been occurring throughout the palace."

Levana stood before the grand windows of her solar, listening to the third-tier thaumaturge present his daily report, though she was lacking her usual focus. Her thoughts were a maze of distractions. Despite using every resource available to her and demanding that her security team review hours and hours of footage from the outer sectors, Linh Cinder and her companions had yet to be found. Wedding preparations were underway, but she had been too livid to even look at her husband-to-be since he'd arrived.

Now she had Winter to concern herself with. The ungrateful wretch of a princess had been nothing but an embarrassment to her since the day Levana had married her father. If Jacin succeeded, she would never again have to listen to her mindless mutterings. She would never again have to defend her from the mocking laughter of the court. She would never again have to see the looks of desire following the doltish girl down the palace corridors.

Levana wanted the princess gone. She wished to let go of the resentment that had plagued her for so long. Her life was beginning anew, finally, and she deserved this fresh beginning without the cumbersome girl dragging her down, reminding her of a too-painful past.

But if Jacin failed . . .

Levana couldn't stomach another failure.

"My Queen?"

She turned to the thaumaturge. "Yes?"

"The technicians need to know how you would like them to proceed. They estimate an hour or two will be required to locate the source of these system glitches and restore the defaults. They might need to disable portions of the system while they're working on it."

"Will this take them away from the search for the cyborg?"

"It would, Your Majesty."

"Then it can wait. The cyborg is our top priority."

He bowed. "We will keep you updated on further developments."

Aimery gestured toward the door. "That will be all. Thank you for the report."

The thaumaturge swept away, but another figure was standing inside the elevator when the doors opened.

Levana straightened at the sight of Jacin Clay. There was a shadow across his face, a loathing that he normally worked so hard to disguise. Levana's gaze slipped down to his hands. They were covered in blood. There was a stain on the knee of his pants too, dried black.

He stepped off the elevator, but Jerrico stopped him in his tracks, a palm on Jacin's chest.

"Sir Clay?" she said.

"It's done." His tone carried all the horror that the simple words concealed.

A smile tickled Levana's mouth. She spun away to hide it—an act of generosity. "I know it could not have been easy for you," she said, hoping sympathy carried in her voice. "I know how you cared for her, but you have done the right thing for your crown and your country."

Jacin said nothing.

When she could school her face again, Levana turned back. Aimery and Jerrico were impassive, while Jacin looked like he would rip out Levana's still-beating heart if he had the chance.

She took pity on him, choosing to forgive these rebellious instincts. He had loved the girl, after all, hard as it was to fathom.

"What did you do with the body?"

"I took it to the menagerie's incinerator, where they take the deceased animals." None of his anger faded as he recounted the task, though he made no movement toward Levana. Still, Jerrico did not relax. "I killed the white wolf, too, to cover the blood, and left the wolf's body behind. The gamekeepers will think it was a random attack."

Levana frowned, her mood dampening. "I did not tell you to destroy the body, Sir Clay. The people must see proof of her death if she is no longer to be a threat to my throne."

His jaw tightened. "She was *never* a threat to your throne," he growled, "and I wasn't about to leave her there to be pecked apart by whatever albino scavengers you keep down there. You can find some other way to break the news to the people."

She pressed her lips against a sour taste in her mouth. "So I shall."

Jacin swallowed, hard, regaining some composure. "I hope you won't mind that I also disposed of a witness, *My Queen*. I thought it would be contrary to your objectives if word got out that a royal guard had murdered the princess. People might question if it was under *your* order, after all."

She bristled. "What witness?"

"The Earthen girl. I didn't think anyone would miss her."

"Ah, her." With a scoff, Levana brushed her hand through the air. "She should have been dead weeks ago. You have done me a service by ridding me of her." She tilted her head, examining him. It was amusing to see so much emotion revealed when it was normally so impossible to aggravate him. "You've exceeded my expectations, Sir Clay." She placed a hand on his cheek. A muscle twitched beneath her palm and she tried to ignore the glower searing into her. His anger was expected, but he would soon realize it was for the best.

If he didn't, she could always force him to.

Levana felt lighter already, knowing she would never have to see her stepdaughter's face again.

She dropped her hand and floated back to the windows. Beyond the curved dome she could see the barren landscape of Luna, white craters and cliffs against the black sky. "Is there anything else?"

"Yes," said Jacin.

She raised an eyebrow.

"I wish to resign from the royal guard. I ask to be reassigned to the sector where my father was sent years ago. This palace holds too many memories for me."

Levana's face softened. "I am sure it does, Jacin. I am sorry that I had to ask this of you. But your request is denied."

His nostrils flared.

"You have proven yourself to be loyal and trustworthy, traits I would be remiss to lose. You may take leave for the rest of today, with my gratitude, but tomorrow you will report for your new assignment." She grinned. "Well done, Jacin. You are dismissed."

Thirty-Two

CINDER WAS LOSING HER MIND. THEY HAD BEEN HIDING IN Maha Kesley's tiny shack for days. Wolf and his mother, Thorne, Iko, and herself, all crammed into little rooms, tripping over one another every time they tried to move. Though they didn't move much. There was nowhere to go. They were afraid to be heard through the small, glassless windows, so they communicated mostly in hand signals and messages tapped out on their one remaining portscreen. The silence was horrendous. The stillness was suffocating. The waiting, agony.

She thought often of Cress and Scarlet and wondered if either of them was alive.

She worried about Kai as the wedding loomed ever closer.

There was guilt too. Not only had they put Maha in danger by being there, they were also eating far too much food, having already burned through the measly packs they'd brought with them. Maha said nothing about it, but Cinder could tell. Food was strictly rationed in the outer sectors, and Maha was barely able to feed herself.

They spent their days trying to rework their plan, but after all the plotting they'd done aboard the Rampion, Cinder was disheartened to be back at square one. The video they'd recorded remained unused—copies of it downloaded not only to the portscreen, but to Cinder's and Iko's internal computers too. It didn't matter how many copies of it they had. Without Cress being there to tap into the broadcasting system, the video was useless.

They discussed starting a grassroots movement. Maha Kesley could spread the word of Selene's return to the laborers in the mine and let the news spread from there. Or they could send messengers through the tunnels, scrawling messages on the tunnel walls. But these were slow strategies, with too much risk for miscommunication and little chance the news would spread far.

There was a reason Levana kept her people isolated from one another. There was a reason no one had attempted a cohesive rebellion yet, not because they didn't want to. It was clear from the government-sanctioned propaganda that Levana and her ancestors had sought to brainwash the Lunar people into a belief that their rule was righteous and fated. It was equally clear from the tunnel graffiti and the people's downcast eyes that they no longer believed it, if they ever had.

Any spark of defiance may have been starved and threatened out of them, but the more Lunars Cinder saw, the more she believed she could reignite them.

All she needed was a way to *talk* to them.

Maha had gone to the maglev platform to wait in line for her weekly rations, leaving the rest of them staring at a holographic map of Luna. It had been over an hour, but few suggestions had been posed.

Cinder was beginning to feel hopeless, and all the while, the clock was ticking. To the wedding. To the coronation. To their inevitable discovery.

An unexpected chorus of chimes made Cinder jump. The map faded, the feed overridden by a mandatory message being broadcast from the capital. Cinder knew that the same message would be playing on a dozen embedded screens on the dome outside, making sure that every citizen saw it.

Head Thaumaturge Aimery Park appeared before them, handsome and arrogant. Cinder recoiled. The holograph made it seem as though he were in the room with them.

"Good people of Luna," he said, "please stop what you are doing and listen to this announcement. I am afraid we have tragic news to impart. Earlier today, Her Royal Highness, Princess Winter Hayle-Blackburn, stepdaughter of Her Majesty the Queen, was found murdered in the royal menagerie."

Cinder's brow furrowed and she traded frowns with her companions. She knew little about the princess, only that she was said to be beautiful and the people loved her, which must mean Levana hated her. She had heard of the princess's scarred face, a punishment inflicted by the queen herself, or so the rumors went.

"We are reviewing security footage in an attempt to bring the murderer to justice, and we will not rest until our beloved princess is avenged. Though our devoted queen is devastated at this loss, she wishes to proceed with her wedding ceremony as scheduled, so we might have joy in this time of sadness. A funeral procession for Her Highness will be scheduled for the coming weeks. Princess Winter Hayle-Blackburn will be missed by us all, but never forgotten."

Aimery's face disappeared.

"Do you think Levana killed her?" Iko asked.

"Of course I do," Cinder said. "I wonder what the princess did to anger her."

Thorne folded his arms. "I'm not sure you have to *do* anything to earn Levana's wrath."

He looked ragged, unshaven and weary, even more so than the day Cinder had met him in New Beijing Prison. Though no one had dared to talk about abandoning Cress, Cinder knew he was taking her loss harder than any of them. She'd sensed from the moment they were reunited in Farafrah that Thorne felt a responsibility toward Cress, but for the first time she was beginning to wonder if his feelings didn't go deeper than that.

Wolf's head suddenly snapped up, his eyes locking on the fabric-covered window.

Cinder went rigid, ready to load a bullet into her finger or use her Lunar gift to defend herself and her friends—whatever this unseen threat called for. She felt the tension rise around her. Everyone falling silent, watching Wolf.

His nose twitched. His brow drew closer, doubtful. Suspicious.

"Wolf?" Cinder prodded.

He sniffed again and his eyes brightened.

Then he was gone—hurling himself past the group and tearing open the front door.

Cinder jumped to her feet. "Wolf! What are you—"

Too late. The door slammed shut behind him. She cursed. This was *not* the time for her mutant wolf ally to start running around and drawing attention to himself.

She yanked on her boots to chase after him.

SCARLET LANDED THE SHIP IN A TINY UNDERGROUND PORT that had only two ancient delivery ships already inside. Once the chamber had been sealed, two blinding lightbulbs lit up the ceiling, one of them with a sporadic flicker. Scarlet got out first, scanning every corner, inspecting beneath each ship. Empty.

There were two enormous freight elevators and three stairwells leading to the surface, labeled RM-8, RM-9, RM-11.

Every surface was covered in dust.

"You coming?" she called to Winter, who had made it so far as opening the podship door. The princess's hair was a tangled mess and her skirt crusted with blood. The tablecloth they'd stolen had slipped down around her shoulders. Whereas the escape had filled Scarlet with adrenaline, it had left Winter drained. Her head bobbed as she pulled herself out of the ship.

Scarlet planted her hands on her hips, her patience stretched to near breaking. "Do I have to carry you?"

Winter shook her head. "You don't think we were followed?"

"I'm hoping no one has figured out we're missing yet." Scarlet read the signs again, the letters almost undetectable beneath the dust. "Not that we have a whole lot of options at this point, even if we were followed."

Scarlet turned back and tightened the tablecloth around Winter's waist so it looked like an ill-fitting skirt, covering the blood, then she unzipped her hoodie and helped Winter into the sleeves. She tucked the princess's voluminous hair back and pulled the hood over her face as well as she could. "Not great, but better than nothing."

"Do you think he's dead yet?"

Scarlet paused in the middle of zipping up the hoodie again. Winter peered back at her, looking small and vulnerable.

She sighed. "He's smart and he's strong. He'll be all right." She tugged the zipper up to Winter's throat. "Come on."

When they emerged on the surface, protected beneath the

enormous dome, Scarlet paused to get her bearings. She had looked up the Kesley address on the ship's database, though the series of numbers and letters made no sense to her.

The spaceship port was meant for freight and this entrance was situated between two warehouses, one wall lined with carts that were heaped to overflowing with chipped black rock. Not far away was an enormous cavern opening up into what looked like a mine or rock quarry. *Regolith Mining*, the sector map had said.

Were Wolf's parents miners? Would Wolf have become a miner, too, if he hadn't been conscripted into the army? It was impossible to imagine a life in which he lived here, on this moon, beneath this dome, and never came to Earth. Never met her.

"This doesn't appear to be residential," she muttered.

"Residences are usually in the outer rings of each sector," said Winter.

"Outer ring. Right." Scarlet scanned the squat warehouses. "Which way is that?"

Winter pointed up at the dome that encapsulated them. Even with the surrounding buildings, it was clear where the dome's highest point was and where it rounded out toward the edges.

Scarlet turned away from the dome's center.

As they walked, she tried to cobble together a plan. First, find where the people lived. Second, figure out how their homes were addressed and find the home of Wolf's parents. Third, stumble through an awkward conversation in which she tried to explain to them who she was and why they had to shelter her and Winter.

When the industrial buildings gave way to ramshackle homes, Scarlet was relieved to see address numbers painted on the concrete in front of each building, faded from years of foot traffic. "A-49, A-50," she murmured to herself, quickening her pace. The next circle of houses were labeled with *B*s. "Easy enough. The Kesley house was D-313, right? So we'll head to the row of *D*s and . . ."

She glanced back.

Winter was gone.

Cursing, Scarlet spun in a full circle, but there was no sign of the princess. "You can't be serious," she growled, backtracking her steps. She'd been so immersed in finding the house, she couldn't recall hearing Winter beside her since she'd left the warehouses behind. She'd probably wandered off, strung along by some hallucination . . .

Scarlet paused, catching sight of the princess down an alley. She was wedged between two factories and mesmerized by a metal shaft that poked out of one of the buildings. Broken white rock tumbled out of it into a cart below.

The red hood was still pulled over the princess's face and a great cloud of dust was billowing around her, but she didn't seem to notice.

Huffing, Scarlet squared her shoulders and started marching toward her, ready to drag the crazy girl away by her hair if she had to. She hadn't crossed half the distance, though, when Winter's head snapped around, away from Scarlet.

Scarlet's pace slowed, dread pulsing through her as she, too, heard the footsteps. Pounding footsteps, like someone was running at full speed toward them.

She reached for the knife Jacin had given her.

"*Winter*," she hissed—but either she was too far away, or the noise of the clattering rock and machinery was too loud. "*Winter!*"

A man barreled around a corner, heading straight for the

princess. Winter tensed half a second before he reached her. Grabbing Winter's elbow, he yanked back the red hood.

Scarlet gasped. Her knees weakened. The man stared at Winter with a mixture of confusion and disappointment and maybe even anger, all locked up in eyes so vividly green Scarlet could see them glowing from here.

She was the one hallucinating now.

She took a stumbling, uncertain step forward. Wanting to run toward him, but terrified it was a trick. Her hand tightened around the knife handle as Wolf, ignoring how Winter was trying to pull away, grabbed her arm and smelled the filthy red sleeve of Scarlet's hoodie, streaked with dirt and blood.

He growled, ready to tear the princess apart. "Where did you get this?"

So desperate, so determined, so *him*. The knife slipped out of Scarlet's hand.

Wolf's attention snapped up to her.

"Wolf?" she whispered.

His eyes brightened, wild and hopeful.

Releasing Winter, he strode forward. His tumultuous eyes scooped over her. *Devoured* her.

When he was in arm's reach, Scarlet almost collapsed into him, but at the last moment she had the presence of mind to step back. She planted a hand on his chest.

Wolf froze, hurt flickering across his face.

"I'm sorry," said Scarlet, her voice teetering with exhaustion. "It's just . . . I smell so awful, I can hardly stand to be around *myself* right now, so I can't even imagine what it's like for you and your sense of sm—"

Batting her hand away, Wolf dug his fingers into Scarlet's hair and crushed his mouth against hers. Her protests died with a muffled gasp.

This time, she did collapse, her legs unable to hold her a second longer. Wolf fell with her, dropping to his knees to break Scarlet's fall and cradling her body against his.

He was here. He was *here*.

She was crying when she broke away, and part of her hated that, and part of her felt like it was long overdue. "How?"

"I smelled you." Wolf was grinning so wide she could see the sharp teeth he normally tried to hide. It had been a long time since she'd seen him so happy.

Actually . . . she wasn't sure if she'd ever seen him so happy.

She started to laugh, though it was born out of delirium. "Of course you did," she said. "I really need a bath."

He pushed a lock of Scarlet's dirty hair away from her cheek, following the gesture with his eyes, still beaming. He ran a thumb across her shoulder, down her arm, and lifted her hand—the one with the bandaged finger. A moment of fury dulled his smile, but it was brief, and then he was examining her face again. "Scarlet," he whispered. "*Scarlet.*"

With a sob, she settled her head into the crook of his neck. "If this is a Lunar trick, I am going to be *furious.*"

A thumb brushed against her ear. "You called them swine."

Her brow furrowed. "What?"

Wolf pulled back and cupped her face in his gigantic hands, still beaming. "In the tavern in Rieux, when all those men were making jokes about Cinder at the ball. You called them swine and you got up on the bar and defended her even though she was Lunar, and that was the moment I started to fall in love with you."

Heat rushed into her cheeks. "Why are you . . . ?"

"No Lunar would know that." His grin turned impish. "So I can't be a Lunar trick."

Her lips parted in understanding, and another sniff turned into a laugh. "You're right." She thought back, to a time before she knew about mutant soldiers and missing Lunar princesses. "When you came to the farm and I thought I would have to shoot you. You told me to aim for the torso because it's a bigger target, then laughed when I said your head looked big enough to me." She dug her fingers into his shirt. "That's when I . . ."

He kissed her again, molding their bodies together.

A high-pitched whistle sounded over the clattering rocks, startling her. Pulling away, she saw Cinder and Thorne—the source of the whistle—along with a dark-skinned girl with blue hair who had her hands pressed dreamily against her cheeks.

It was such a welcome sight, Scarlet started crying again. Disentangling herself from Wolf's arms, she hobbled to her feet. He was quick to join her, one arm encircling her shoulders. "I can't believe it. You're here. On *Luna.*"

"We're here," agreed Thorne. "And if you'd bothered to RSVP, we would have brought you a snack." His eyes skimmed down her body. "When was the last time you ate?"

Scarlet glanced down. Her clothes hung from her bones, her muscles withered to almost nothing in the tiny cage. Still, he didn't need to point it out.

"You look lovely," said the blue-haired girl. "A little rough around the edges, but it adds character."

"Um, thanks," said Scarlet, swiping the tears from her cheeks. "And you are . . . ?"

The girl bounced on her toes. "It's me, Iko! The captain found me a real body."

Scarlet's eyebrows jotted upward. This was Iko? Their *spaceship*?

Before she could reply, a sweet singing voice floated through the alley.

"*The parakeets sing ta-weet-a-weet-a-weet, and the stars twinkle all the night . . .*"

Four pairs of eyes swiveled toward the cart that was now full of shimmering white rock, though the shaft from the building had fallen silent. At some point, Winter had crawled behind it, wedging herself between the cart and the wall. Scarlet could see the top of the red hood pulled over Winter's hair.

"*And the monkeys frolic a-eet-eet-eet, while the rockets fly on by . . .*"

Cinder approached the cart with her brow drawn and rolled it away. Winter was curled up on her side, facing the wall and drawing little designs into the dust. The tablecloth had fallen open, revealing her blood-covered skirt.

"*And the Earth is full tonight, tonight, and the wolves all howl, aa-ooooooooooh . . .*"

The dainty howl faded away.

Scarlet could feel everyone's curious gazes switching between her and the princess. She cleared her throat. "She's harmless," she said. "I'm pretty sure."

Winter rolled onto her back so she was staring at Cinder upside-down.

Cinder's eyes widened. The others crept forward.

After three slow blinks, Winter rolled onto her stomach and pushed herself up to her knees. She turned down the hood, letting her thick hair tumble out around her shoulders. "Hello."

Scarlet started laughing again. She remembered what it was like seeing the princess for the first time. Her full lips, delicate shoulders, huge eyes flecked with shavings of gray, all paired with the unexpected scars on her right cheek that *should* have made her less stunning but didn't.

It occurred to Scarlet that Wolf hadn't seemed to notice. She felt a little twinge of pride.

"*Stars,*" whispered Iko. "You're beautiful."

A loud click echoed through the alley. "Drop your glamour," demanded Thorne, aiming a gun at the princess.

Scarlet's pulse hiccuped. "Wait—" she started, but Cinder had already put a hand on his wrist and was pressing the gun back down.

"It's not a glamour," she said.

"*Really?*" Thorne leaned toward Cinder and whispered, "Are you *sure?*"

"I'm sure."

This statement was followed by another long, heady silence, during which Winter passed her sweetest smile between each of them.

Thorne clicked the safety on and shoved the gun back into its holster. "Holy spades, you Lunars have good genes." An awkward pause followed, before he added, "Who is she?"

"This is Winter," said Scarlet. "Princess Winter."

Thorne guffawed and pushed a hand into his hair. "Are we running a boardinghouse for misplaced royalty around here, or what?"

"Princess Winter?" said Cinder. "They just announced that you were murdered."

"Jacin faked the murder," said Scarlet, "and helped us escape."

Cinder's eyes flashed toward her, surprised. "Jacin?"

Scarlet nodded. "The guard who attacked us aboard the Rampion."

A shadow fell over Cinder's expression. She looked away.

"She's just so pretty." Iko sighed, feeling her own face for comparison.

Scarlet glared. "She can hear."

Cocking her head, Winter held out a hand toward Thorne. His eyes widened and it seemed an automatic response to help her to her feet.

He was blushing when Winter took her hand away and adjusted her skirt. "You are all very kind," she said, but it was Cinder that her attention had landed on. She studied the cyborg, curious. Cinder scrunched her shoulders in tight to her body. "And you," said Winter, "are my long-lost cousin and very dear friend. I could not believe it until now, but it *is* true." Winter took Cinder's hands into hers. "Do you remember me?"

Cinder slowly shook her head.

"It's all right," said Winter, and her expression said that it *was* all right. "My memories are hazy too, and I'm a year older. Still, I hope we can be good friends again." She interlaced their fingers. "This hand is unusual," she said, lifting the titanium-plated one. "Is it made of ashes?"

"Is it made . . . I'm sorry, what?"

"Don't," said Scarlet, waving a hand. "I find it's better if you don't ask."

The princess grinned again. "Forgive me. You are no longer only my friend or my cousin, and this is no way to greet you." She dropped into a dancer's curtsy and placed a kiss on Cinder's metal knuckle. "My Queen, it is my honor to serve you."

"Er—thank you?" Cinder pried her hand away and hid it behind her back. "That's kind, but you don't have to do that. Again. Ever."

Thorne cleared his throat. "We need to get back to the house. We've already risked drawing enough attention, and she . . ." He looked at Winter. There was an edge to his expression, like he didn't trust anyone who was more attractive than he was. ". . . will *definitely* draw attention."

Thirty-Three

WOLF HELPED SCARLET CLEAN AND BANDAGE HER WOUNDED finger without asking her to tell him what, exactly, had happened. Though his expression had said he was ready to tear out Queen Levana's jugular, his hands had been breathlessly gentle. Afterward, Scarlet insisted she be given time to bathe, and though Wolf had looked borderline devastated, the time apart was worthwhile. The tiny washroom in his childhood home was by no means luxurious, but it was a far cry from the trough she'd had in the menagerie, and she felt brand-new when she emerged. She and Winter were given new clothes out of Maha Kesley's meager stash while theirs were washed, though Scarlet was already anxious to have her hoodie back. It had become her own personal armor.

"I can't believe you kidnapped Prince Kai," she said, untacking the curtain on the front window to peek outside. Blue daisies in a window box were a solitary spot of color.

"Emperor Kai," Wolf corrected. He was leaning against the wall, holding the hem of her shirt in his fingers. Winter was taking her turn in the washroom while the others had crowded into the kitchen, trying to cobble together enough food for everyone. Scarlet had heard someone mention *rations*, and it occurred to her that this tiny household wasn't meant to support guests, especially so many. Wolf's mom would be back soon from collecting that week's supply of food, but of course, that was meant for only one woman.

Scarlet tried to imagine what this must be like for Wolf. To return home more than a decade after being taken away, a grown man with scars and fangs and the blood of countless victims on his hands.

And now . . . with a girl.

Scarlet was trying not to think about meeting his mother—it all felt too strange.

"Emperor, right." She retacked the curtain. "That's weird to say, after eighteen years of listening to celebrity gossip feeds go on and on about 'Earth's favorite prince.'" She claimed one of the lumpy sofa cushions, curling her legs beneath her. "I had a picture of him taped to my wall when I was fifteen. Grand-mère cut it off a cereal box."

Wolf scowled.

"Of course, half the girls in the world probably had that same picture from that same cereal box."

Wolf scrunched his shoulders against his neck, and Scarlet grinned, teasing. "Oh, no. You're not going to have to fight him for pack dominance now, are you? Come here." She beckoned him with a wave of her hand and he was at her side in half a second, the glower softening as he pulled her against his chest.

His brazenness was new—so different from the shyness she'd grown accustomed to. On the Rampion, Wolf was always pattering around his feelings, like he didn't want to risk the tentative trust they'd started to rebuild since Paris.

Now, when he kissed her or put his arms around her, Scarlet felt like he was staking a claim. Which normally would have sent her on a tirade about relationship independence, except she felt like she'd claimed *him* a long time ago. The moment she'd expected him to choose her over his pack, the moment she'd dragged him aboard that ship and taken him away from everything he'd ever known, she'd made the decision for them both. He was hers now, just like she was his.

Except she wondered if everything had changed between them, once again. She'd figured he would come back to the farm with her when all this was over, but now he'd been reunited with his mom, the only family he had left. Scarlet could no longer assume she was the most important thing to him, and she knew it wouldn't be fair to ask him to choose between her and the family he'd been taken away from. Not now, and maybe not ever.

In the kitchen, a cupboard slammed, saving her from thoughts she wasn't ready for. Not when she'd just found him again. She heard Thorne say something about freeze-dried cardboard and Iko accuse him of being insensitive to those without any taste buds at all.

Scarlet nestled her head against Wolf's shoulder. "I was so worried about you."

"*You* were worried?" Wolf angled her away from him. "Scarlet—they took you, and I couldn't do anything about it. I didn't know if you were dead, or if they were ..." He shuddered. "I would have killed every one of them to get to you. I would have done anything to get you back. Knowing that we were coming here was the only thing that kept me sane." His brow creased. "Though there were a couple times when I went a little insane anyway."

Scarlet nudged him with her elbow. "That shouldn't sound as romantic as it does."

"Dinner is served," said Thorne, coming out of the kitchen with a plate in each hand. "And by dinner, I mean soggy brown rice and oversalted meat on stale crackers. You Lunars sure know how to live it up."

"We were trying to only take things from the pantry," said Cinder, as she and Iko filed into the front room, though there was hardly enough space for everyone. "There isn't much in the way of fresh food, and Maha's already given us enough."

Scarlet glanced at Wolf. "I assumed you'd never had tomatoes or carrots before because those things couldn't be grown here on Luna, but that's not the case, is it? They just don't ship them to the outer sectors."

He shrugged, without a hint of self-pity. "I don't know what they can and can't grow in the agriculture sectors. Whatever it is, I'm sure it can't compete with Benoit Farms and Gardens." His eyes twinkled, and Scarlet—to her own surprise—started to blush again.

"You two are giving me a stomachache," Thorne griped.

"I'm pretty sure that's the meat," said Cinder, ripping a piece of dried mystery meat with her teeth.

The food wasn't appetizing, but it was no worse than what she'd gotten in the menagerie, and Scarlet ate her small share with relish. Winter emerged from the washroom, her dark ringlets still dripping and the too-short pants and ill-fitted blouse doing nothing to lessen her beauty. A hush fell over the group as she joined them, kneeling on the floor around the small table and scanning the food with sad, distant eyes.

Scarlet spoke first, pushing a couple of crackers across the table. "I know it's not what you're used to," she said, "but you have to eat something."

Offense flashed across Winter's face. "I'm not particular." Her expression softened as she stared at the crackers. "I just hadn't realized how much I'd been given. I knew conditions were bad in the outer sectors, but not as bad as this. Others have gone hungry so my stomach might be full each night." Sighing, she sat back on her heels and folded her hands in her lap. "I'm not hungry, anyway. Someone else can have mine."

"Winter—"

"I'm not hungry." Her voice was sterner than Scarlet had ever heard it. "I couldn't eat it if I tried."

Scarlet frowned, but let it go. Wolf eventually ate the crackers, looking guilty about it.

"You said Jacin told you where to find us?" said Cinder. Her shoulders were tense, and it had been clear from the moment Scarlet had explained what she could about their escape that Jacin wasn't popular with her friends. "How did he know?"

"I would imagine," said Winter, "that your miniature friend told him."

"Our miniature friend?" asked Cinder.

Winter nodded. "Cress, isn't it?"

Silence expanded over them, drawing all the oxygen from the room.

Thorne leaned forward first. "*Cress?* You've seen Cress?"

"I haven't seen her in days, but Jacin was keeping her safe."

"Oh! That reminds me." Scarlet dug out the small cylinder. "Jacin gave this to me and said it had a message from a friend in it. Maybe he meant her—Cress?"

Thorne snatched it away before she'd finished talking and

flipped the cylinder over in his palm. "What is it? How do we work it?"

Cinder grabbed it away from him and inserted it into the holograph node on the wall. A holograph flickered to life in the center of the room.

Scarlet wouldn't have recognized the queen's hacker, having only seen her once through a comm link. The girl's long, unruly hair had been chopped short and her skin, though still pale, had at least seen the sun in the recent past.

Thorne launched himself from his seat, circling the room to put himself in front of the holograph as she began to speak.

"Hello, everyone. If you're seeing this, our good friends from the palace must have found you. I wish I could have joined them. My current guardian gave me the option of leaving, but I had to stay behind to assist with their travels. I know you'll understand. I wanted you to know I'm all right, though. I'm safe and unhurt, and I know you'll come for me. When you do, I'll be ready. Until then, I promise to be careful and stay hidden." She paused. A fleeting smile crossed her lips, like proof of her courage, though her eyes stayed anxious. After a deep breath, she continued, "My absence has probably changed some things for you, and I know you were relying on me for help with some of your plans. I've built a program into this file. Insert this cylinder into the universal port in the dome's broadcast receiver and follow the prompts I've set up for you. On the chance this could fall into the wrong hands, I have locked the program with the same passcode we used on the ship." Her lashes dipped, and there was that weak smile again. "I hope this message reaches you safely. I ... I miss you." She opened her mouth to say more, but hesitated and shut it again. A second later, the message ended.

They stared at the empty air where Cress had been. Scarlet

knew for sure now that the girl had been the one watching over her and Winter during their escape. She had saved them, and sacrificed her own safety to do it.

"Brave, stupid girl," Thorne muttered. He sank back down to the floor, his expression torn between relief and increased distress.

"She's still with Jacin, then," said Cinder. "I guess . . . I'm grateful for what he's done, but . . . I don't like him knowing where we are, or being responsible for Cress. I don't trust him."

Winter stared at her, aghast. "Jacin is a good person. He would never betray you, or Cress."

"Too late," said Thorne. "He already did once."

Winter laced her fingers together. "He regrets betraying you. It was never his intention. He only . . . he had to come back to Luna. For me."

Iko made a noise that was probably meant to be a snort. Scarlet cocked her head to inspect the android. What had been endearing tics when she had been the Rampion's control system were a little disconcerting in her humanoid body.

"It's true," Winter insisted, her eyes crinkling at the corners. "I understand why you don't trust him, but he's trying to make amends. He wants to see you back on your throne as much as anyone."

"He did save my life," added Scarlet. Then, after a pause, she shrugged. "Probably just because he needed me to save *her* life, but still, it has to count for something."

Thorne crossed his arms and said grudgingly, "I wish he would have tried a little harder to send Cress with you."

"At least we know she's alive," said Cinder.

Thorne grunted. "All we know is she's still in Artemisia and under the protection of a guy who betrayed us once. The princess thinks he's on our side? Fine. But that doesn't change the fact he sold us out in New Beijing, and I don't doubt he'll do it again if it means saving his own skin."

"On the contrary, he cares very little for his own skin." Winter's voice was sharp, her shoulders trembling. "It is my safety alone that he cares about, and I will never be safe again so long as my stepmother is the queen." She turned to Cinder. "I believe he will do anything he can to help your revolution succeed. We both will."

A long silence was followed by Thorne grumbling, "I still plan on punching him if I ever see him again."

Scarlet rolled her eyes.

Cinder tapped her fingers against the table. "I don't understand why Levana tried to have you killed *now*. She has Kai. She's getting what she wants."

"I believe she's afraid of losing her grip on Luna," said Winter, "especially with the rumors that our true queen is still alive. She's become paranoid, afraid of every potential threat."

Cinder shook her head. "But you're not her real daughter. Isn't there some superstition about bloodlines?"

"Yes. Only a person of royal blood can sit on Luna's throne. It is believed that should a person of nonroyal blood ascend to the throne, the gift bestowed upon our people will cease to exist. There have been countless studies proving this."

Scarlet laughed. "Let me guess—the studies were paid for by the royal family."

"Does it matter?" said Winter. "Whether the people believe it or not, my stepmother is frightened. She's desperate to maintain her power. That is why she tried to kill me."

"Good," said Cinder. "People make mistakes when they're desperate, and trying to kill you could be a big one." She leaned back on her hands. "From what I can tell, the people adore you. If they knew Levana tried to have you murdered, it could be just the thing to persuade them to choose me over her. Listen, Your Highness—we have a video. If Cress's program works, we'll be able to play it across all outer sectors. It will tell the people who I am and ask them to join me in ending Levana's reign." She inhaled. "I'd like to include a message from you, to show the people you're alive and tell them Levana was the one who tried to have you killed. Having your support would mean a lot. To them, and to me."

Winter held her gaze for a long time, considering, before she sighed. "I'm sorry, but I can't. Levana would find out, and she can't know I'm alive."

"Why not?" said Scarlet. "The people care about you. They deserve to know the truth."

"Jacin was ordered to kill me," said Winter, her voice growing weak, "and he went through a lot of trouble to make it look like he succeeded. I won't endanger him by announcing the truth. The longer she goes on believing that Jacin is loyal to her, the safer he'll be." She looked up again. "The safer your Cress will be too."

Thorne looked away.

"I'm sorry that I can't help you with this. For what it's worth, you *do* have my support, even if it must be a secret." Winter slumped. Scarlet could see her withdrawing into herself and her worries over Jacin's safety. She wished she could offer some comfort, but she had spent enough time under Levana's thumb to know there was nothing she could say that would make Winter feel any better.

"All right," Cinder conceded. "I understand. We'll just have to hope the video succeeds without you."

The front door opened and they all started. Scarlet spun

around as a woman shut the door behind her. She wore coveralls dusted with regolith particles and was carrying a worn wooden box full of food. She had Wolf's dark hair and olive-toned skin, but she also had the bone structure of a bird. Wolf could have crushed her with his fingertips.

Scarlet felt weird for having such a thought.

Everyone relaxed. Everyone but Scarlet and Wolf, whose arm turned to iron around her.

Leaning against the door, Maha surveyed the room with a fluttery smile. "They were giving out *sugar*," she chirped, "in cele-bration of the queen's upcoming ..." She trailed off, noticing Scarlet with Wolf's arm across her shoulders.

Winter stood up, drawing Maha's surprise to her. Scarlet scrambled to her feet, but Maha's attention was caught on the princess now. Her jaw had fallen.

Winter curtsied. "You must be Mother Kesley. I am Princess Winter Hayle-Blackburn, and I'm frightfully sorry about the crackers."

Maha stared, speechless.

"I hope you don't mind our intrusion into your hospitality. Your wolf cub welcomed us. He's surprisingly tender, given the teeth. And the muscles." Winter raised her eyes to the chipping plaster around the door. "He rather reminds me of another wolf I once knew."

Scarlet grimaced.

"Your ... Your Highness," stammered Maha, looking like she wasn't sure if she should be afraid or honored.

"Mom," said Wolf, "this is Scarlet. She's the one we told you about—that was taken off our ship by the thaumaturge. She'd been held prisoner in the palace, but she's ... she escaped. This is her. This is Scarlet."

Maha had not yet managed to pull up her jaw. "The Earthen."

Scarlet nodded. "Mostly. My grandfather was Lunar, but I never met him. And I have no ... um, gift."

With that statement, it occurred to Scarlet that Maha probably *did* have the gift. They all did to some degree, didn't they? Even Wolf had had it, before the scientific tampering took it away.

But it was impossible to imagine this petite woman abusing it like it was abused in the capital. Was that naïve? How hard it must be to navigate society here, never knowing who was controlling and who was being controlled.

"Hello, Scarlet," said Maha, composing herself enough to smile. "Ze'ev failed to mention he was in love with you."

Scarlet could feel her cheeks turning as red as her hair.

Thorne muttered, "How could you not tell?"

Cinder kicked him.

Wolf gripped Scarlet's hand. "We didn't know if she was alive. I didn't want to tell you about her if ... if you never met her ..."

Scarlet squeezed his hand. He squeezed back.

In the back of her head, she heard her grandma's voice, reminding her of her manners. "I'm so pleased to meet you. I ... um. Thank you for your hospitality."

Maha set the box of rations by the door and crossed the tiny room, wrapping Scarlet up in a hug. "I look forward to getting to know you." Releasing Scarlet, she turned back to Wolf and settled her hands on his shoulders. "When they took you away, I feared you would never know love at all." She embraced him, and her smile was as bright as a bouquet of blue daisies. "This has all been so much. So very much."

"Are we almost done with the gushing and the weeping?" said Thorne, massaging his temple. "When do we start planning a revolution again?"

This time, it was Iko that kicked him.

"I knew you were in love with him." Winter tapped her fingers against her elbow. "I can't understand why no one ever listens to me."

Scarlet glared, but there was no ire behind it. "You're right, Winter. It's a complete mystery."

Thirty-Four

LINH PEARL STEPPED OFF THE ELEVATOR, CLUTCHING THE strings of her purse against her shoulder. She was shaking—livid with rage. Since Cinder had made that spectacle at the ball and been revealed to be not only an insane cyborg but an even more insane Lunar, Pearl's world had crumbled around her.

At first it had been minor inconveniences—annoying, but tolerable. With no servant cyborg and no money to hire new help, Pearl was now expected to help around the apartment. Suddenly she had "chores." Suddenly her mother wanted her to help with the shopping and to cook her own meals and even do the dishes when she'd finished, even though it had been *her* stupid decision to sell off their only functioning android.

But that she could have lived with, if her social life hadn't simultaneously splintered along with her dignity. Overnight, she had become a pariah.

Her friends had dealt with it well enough at first. Filled with shock and sympathy, they flocked around Pearl like she was a celebrity, wanting to know everything. Wanting to offer their condolences, knowing that her adopted stepsister had been such a terror. Wanting to hear every horrific story of their childhood. Like a girl who'd barely escaped death, she had been the center of all their conversations, all their curiosity.

That had dwindled, though, when Cinder escaped from prison and remained at large for too long. Her name became synonymous with traitors and it was dragging Pearl down with it.

Then her mother—her ignorant fool of a mother—had unknowingly aided Cinder in the kidnapping of Emperor Kai by giving her their wedding invitations.

She'd traded them for napkins. *Napkins.*

And it had baffled her. Hours before they were to attend the royal wedding, already dressed in their finest, her mother had torn the apartment apart, frantically digging through every drawer, crawling on her hands and knees to peer beneath the furniture, searching every pocket in her wardrobe. Cursing and swearing over and over that she'd had them, she'd seen them *just that morning*, when that awkward woman from the palace had brought them and explained the mishap and *where could they have gone?*

They missed the wedding, naturally.

Pearl had screamed and cried and hidden in her room to watch the newsfeeds—the live footage that had gone from talk of wedding traditions and palace décor to a devastating account of an assault on the palace and the disappearance of Emperor Kai.

Linh Cinder was behind it all. Her monstrous stepsister, once again, had ruined everything.

It had taken two days for the palace's security team to trace the invitations of a Bristol-dàren (who had been at home in

Canada, enjoying a bottle of fine wine) back to the actual invitations that had been given to Linh Adri and her daughter, Linh Pearl. Only then did her mother understand. Cinder had made her out to be an idiot.

That had been the last straw for Pearl's friends.

"*Traitors*," Mei-Xing had called them, accusing Pearl and her mother of helping the cyborg and putting Kai in danger.

Furious, Pearl had stormed out, screaming that they could believe whatever they wanted for all she cared. She was the victim in all of this, and she didn't need so-called friends to throw these accusations at her. She had enough to deal with as it was.

She'd expected them to chase after her, apologies in tow.

They didn't.

She walked all the way home with her fists clenched at her sides.

Cinder. This was all Cinder's fault. Ever since Peony—no, ever since *their dad* had caught the plague and been taken away from her. Everything was Cinder's fault.

Karim-jiě, their neighbor in 1816, didn't move aside as Pearl barreled past. Her shoulder smacked the woman against the wall and Pearl paused long enough to glare at her—was the old hog turning blind now, as well as lazy?—but she was met with a haughty snort.

This reaction, too, was one Pearl had seen too often since the ball. Who was this woman to look down on Pearl and her mother? She was nothing but an old widow whose husband had died from a love of drink, and who now sat in her garbage-smelling apartment with a sad collection of ceramic monkeys.

And *she* thought she was better than *Pearl*?

The whole world had turned against her.

"So sorry," Pearl said through her teeth, stomping ahead to her own apartment.

The door was opened slightly, but Pearl didn't give it any thought until she shoved it open and it banged against the wall.

She froze.

The living room had been torn apart. Even worse than when her mother had been searching for those stupid invitations.

The pictures and plaques had all been shoved off the fireplace mantel, the brand-new netscreen was lying facedown on the floor, and the urn containing Peony's ashes . . .

Pearl's stomach plummeted. The door came back to hit her shoulder.

"Mom?" she said, darting across the hall.

She froze. A scream crawled up her throat but died in a petrified squeak.

He was leaning against the living room's far wall. Though he had the form of a man, he stood with hunched shoulders and enormous clawed hands. His face had been disfigured into a snout with teeth that jutted between his lips and dark, glassy eyes sunk back in his face.

Pearl whimpered. Instinct prompted her to take a step back, though instinct also told her it was useless.

A hundred horrific stories, from newsfeeds to whispered gossip, filled her head.

The killings were random, people said.

The Lunar monsters could be anywhere at any time. No one could discern any pattern or logic to their strikes. They might swarm a crowded office building one day and kill every soul on the ninth floor, but leave the rest alone. They might kill one child asleep in their bed, but not their brother across the room. They might dismember a man as he dashed from a hover to his front door, then ring the doorbell so a loved one would find him still bleeding on the step.

The terror of it was in the randomness. The brutality and the senseless way they chose their victims, while leaving so many witnesses to spread the fear.

No one was safe.

No one was ever safe.

But Pearl never thought they would come here, to their inconsequential apartment, in such a crowded city . . .

And—and the war was in cease-fire. There hadn't been any attacks in days. Why now? Why *her*?

A whine squeezed through her throat. The creature smirked and she realized his jaw had been working when she'd come in. Like he'd been helping himself to a snack.

Mom.

Sobbing, she turned to run.

The door slammed shut. A second creature blocked her way.

Pearl collapsed to her knees, sobbing and shaking. "Please. *Please.*"

"You sure we can't eat her?" said the one by the door, his words barely discernible beneath a gruff, raspy tone. He grabbed Pearl's arm and hauled her back to her feet. She screamed and tried to cower away, but his grip was merciless. He peeled the arm away from her body, extending it so he could get a good view of her forearm. "Just a taste? She looks so *sweet.*"

"Yet smells so sour," said the other.

Pearl, through her hysteria, smelled it too. There was warm dampness between her legs. She wailed and her legs gave out again, leaving her to dangle from the monster's hold.

"Mistress said to bring them unharmed. You want to take a nibble, go ahead. Her wrath, your head."

The one holding Pearl pressed his wet nose against her elbow and sniffed longingly. Then he let the arm fall and scooped Pearl over one shoulder. "Not worth it," he said with a growl.

"I agree." The second beast came closer and pinched Pearl's face in his massive, hairy hand. "But maybe we'll get to sample her when they're done."

Thirty-Five

"THERE'S THE GUARDHOUSE," SAID THORNE, CROUCHED IN AN alleyway between Iko and Wolf. For the hundredth time since they'd left Maha's house, he checked his pocket for the cylinder containing Cress's message.

"I had higher expectations," said Iko.

Just like everything in this sector, the guardhouse was drab and covered in dust. It was also made of stone and lacking windows, which made it one of the more impenetrable buildings Thorne had seen. One uniformed guard stood watch at the door, a rifle laid across his arms and a helmet and dust mask obscuring his face.

Inside would be weaponry, dome maintenance equipment, a cell to hold lawbreakers before sending them for trial in Artemisia, and a small control center for accessing the dome's power grid and security system. Most important, this was where the receiver-transmitter was housed that connected this sector to the government-run broadcasting network.

"How much time do we have?" he asked.

"Estimated two minutes, fourteen seconds until the next patrol guard comes into view," said Iko.

"Wolf, you're up."

There was a flash of razor-sharp teeth before Wolf straightened and strolled out from the alley. Thorne and Iko ducked out of sight.

A harsh voice ordered, "Stop and identify yourself."

"Special Operative Alpha Kesley. I'm here on orders from Thaumaturge Jael to check your weapons inventory."

"You're special op? What are you doing out—" A gasp was followed by a short scuffle and thump. Thorne braced himself for the blare of a gunshot, but it never came. When silence reigned, he and Iko peered around the corner again.

Wolf was already dragging the guard's unconscious form to the door and holding his fingertips against the screen. Thorne and Iko rushed to join him just as the door popped open. They dragged the guard inside.

The interior of the guardhouse wasn't much of an improvement over the exterior. Slightly less dusty, but still dim and uncomfortable. In this main room, a large desk took up most of the space, separating them from two barred doors in the back wall.

Thorne wasted no time in ripping off the itchy linen shirt he'd been wearing to fit in with the miners. Squatting beside the guard, he started unbuttoning the uniform's shirt. Though the guard was a bit stockier than he was, it looked like it would fit.

"I don't suppose you need help with that?" Iko said, sounding too hopeful as she watched Thorne work the guard's limp arms out of his sleeves.

Thorne paused to glare at her and, remembering the cylinder, dug it out and pressed it into her fist. "You get to work."

Iko gave him a quick salute and threw herself behind the desk. Soon, Thorne could hear her lighthearted humming as she found the universal port and inserted the cylinder. A screen pinged, and Iko proclaimed proudly, "Code word: Captain is King!"

Thorne's lips twitched as he tugged the guard's shirt over his head.

"It worked! I'm in!" said Iko. "Uploading the program now."

Wolf helped Thorne tie on the awkward shoulder armor.

"Just about done and . . . that's it. Selecting sectors to receive altered programming, and uploading Cinder's video into the holding queue . . . Wow, Cress couldn't have made this any easier."

Thorne grunted, not wanting to hear how great of a job Cress had done in helping them from afar. He wished she would have just sent herself.

He dropped the dust mask over his face to hide his grimace and wedged his feet into the guard's boots. He raised questionable eyebrows at Wolf.

Wolf nodded. "Passable."

"Give me at least four more minutes," said Iko.

"Got it. Two knocks means trouble, three means coast is clear." Thorne grabbed the guard's rifle. He heard Wolf cracking his knuckles as he slipped back through the door to take up the guard's post. The grim-faced, shoulders-back posture came easily and he was glad that, for once, his military training was coming in handy.

He counted off six seconds before the guard patrolling this portion of the dome came into view. He strolled past Thorne with his own gun held over his shoulder, searching for errant civilians or laborers who should have been working.

If the guard looked at him, Thorne didn't know it. He kept his own gaze pinned to the horizon, stoic and serious.

The guard passed by.

Behind the dust mask, Thorne smirked.

CINDER WISHED SHE HAD MORE FLOOR SPACE IN WHICH TO pace. Her nerves were a wreck as she waited to hear from Iko.

"Are you all right?" Scarlet asked, sitting cross-legged on the rocking chair. She was fidgety too, toying with the drawstring of her freshly cleaned hoodie.

"I'm fine," Cinder lied. The truth was that she was as tense as a coiled spring, but she didn't want to talk about it. They'd already talked their strategy to death. Everything that could go right. Everything that could go wrong.

The people would answer her call, or they wouldn't. Either way, she was about to show Levana her hand.

In the kitchen, Princess Winter was humming an unfamiliar song. She'd hardly stopped moving since her arrival the evening before. She'd dusted, swept, beat rugs, reorganized cabinets, and folded laundry, and done it all with the grace of a butterfly. All her work was making Cinder feel like a bad houseguest.

Cinder wasn't sure what to make of the princess. She both admired and questioned Winter's decision to not use her glamour. Life had been simpler before Cinder had use of her own gift, and she'd too often been terrified to think she was becoming more and more like Levana. But at the same time, now that she had her gift, she couldn't imagine giving it up, especially seeing the toll it was taking on the princess's sanity.

But to write off the princess as merely crazy didn't feel right, either. She was quirky and strange and ridiculously charismatic. She also seemed to honestly care about the people around her and she showed glimpses of intelligence that would have been easy to overlook. While she exuded humbleness, Cinder didn't think she was as ignorant of her own charms as she pretended to be.

She wished she could remember her from when they were children, but all her memories consisted of flames and burning coals and seared flesh. There was nothing about a friend, a cousin. It had never even occurred to her she might have such a connection from her brief life on Luna—she'd assumed everyone in the palace would be her enemy.

A comm popped up on her retina display.

Cinder froze, read it, and released a heavy breath. "They're in position. The video is set to play one minute following the end of the workday announcement across all outer sectors. Thorne is standing watch. No alarms raised—yet."

Cinder placed a hand over her knotted stomach. This was the moment all her preparations had been for.

A thousand horrors clouded her mind. That they wouldn't believe her. That they wouldn't follow her. That they wouldn't *want* her revolution.

As far as she could tell, this would be the first time Luna's outer sectors would be exposed to a message that wasn't crown-sanctioned propaganda or fearmongering. Every bit of media they had came from the crown, from public executions that villainized anyone who dared criticize the queen, to documentaries on the royal family's generosity and compassion. Sectors could be singled out for individual broadcasts or all set to receive one message at once, although Cinder suspected the queen rarely did mass communications. Rather, the rich communities of Artemisia might see coverage on the most elite parties of the season while laborers in the outer sectors saw reports on food shortages and reduced rations. Without any way to communicate between themselves, though, how were they to know any different?

Cinder was about to hijack Levana's most valuable brainwashing tool—more powerful even than her glamour. For the first time, the people in the outer sectors would hear a message of truth and empowerment. For the first time, they would be united.

She hoped.

A familiar chime blared outside, followed by Luna's anthem and the woman's polite voice sending the workers home from the workday.

Cinder wrapped her arms around herself, squeezing tight in an effort to keep from dissolving. "That's it," she said, looking at Scarlet. They had discussed at length whether or not Cinder should risk being out in the sector when her message played. Her companions had all encouraged her to wait and let the video do its job without putting herself at risk, but she knew in that moment that waiting wasn't an option. She had to be there to see their reaction, in this sector at least, if she couldn't see the reactions anywhere else.

Scarlet's lips turned down. "You're going out there, aren't you?"

"I have to."

Scarlet rolled her eyes, though she didn't look surprised. She stood and glanced toward the kitchen, where Winter's humming had become dramatic and overwrought. "Winter?"

The princess appeared a moment later, her hands covered in wall putty.

Scarlet settled her hands on her hips. "What are you doing?"

"Patching up the house," said Winter, as if it were obvious. "So it won't fall apart."

"Right. Well, good job. Cinder and I are going to watch the video. If anyone comes to the house, hide. Don't leave, and try not to do anything crazy."

Winter winked. "I shall be a vestibule of unhampered sanity."

With an exasperated shake of her head, Scarlet turned back to Cinder. "She'll be fine. Let's go."

The clock in Cinder's head was counting down the minutes, and she and Scarlet had barely left the house when the dome darkened overhead. In the distance she could see the first laborers heading home from the factories. They all paused and looked up, waiting to hear whatever bad news the queen had for them now.

A series of building-size squares flickered across the surface of the dome and sharpened into one image, duplicated a dozen times in every direction—Cinder's face plastered half a dozen times across the sky.

Cinder grimaced at the sight. When they had recorded the video aboard the Rampion, she felt bold and resolute. She hadn't bothered to dress up, preferring the people to see her as she was. In the video she was wearing the same military-issued T-shirt and cargo pants she'd found aboard the Rampion ages ago. Her hair was in the same ponytail she always wore it in. Her arms were crossed over her chest, her cyborg hand on full display.

She looked nothing at all like her regal, glamorous, powerful aunt.

"Cinder," Scarlet hissed. "Shouldn't you be using your glamour?"

She started and called up the glamour of the plain teenage girl she'd used during the trek from Artemisia. It would keep anyone in the sector from recognizing her at least, though it wouldn't protect her from camera footage.

She hoped Levana would have a lot of footage to be examining after this.

Her likeness in the sky began to speak.

"Citizens of Luna, I ask that you stop what you're doing to listen to this message. My name is Selene Blackburn. I am the daughter of the late Queen Channary, niece to *Princess* Levana, and the rightful heir to Luna's throne." She had practiced the words a thousand times and Cinder was relieved she didn't sound like a complete idiot saying them. "You were told that I died thirteen years ago in a nursery fire, but the truth is that my aunt, Levana, did try to kill me, but I was rescued and taken to Earth. There, I have been raised and protected in preparation for the time when I would return to Luna and reclaim my birthright.

"In my absence, Levana has enslaved you. She takes your sons and turns them into monsters. She takes your shell infants and slaughters them. She lets you go hungry, while the people in Artemisia gorge themselves on rich foods and delicacies." Her expression turned fierce. "But Levana's rule is coming to an end. I have returned and I am here to take back what is mine."

Chills skittered down Cinder's arms at hearing her own voice sound so capable, so confident, so *worthy.*

"Soon," the video continued, "Levana is going to marry Emperor Kaito of Earth and be crowned the empress of the Eastern Commonwealth, an honor that could not be given to anyone less deserving. I refuse to allow Levana to extend her tyranny. I will not stand aside while my aunt enslaves and abuses my people here on Luna, and wages a war across Earth. Which is why, before an Earthen crown can be placed on Levana's head, I will bring an army to the gates of Artemisia."

Above, her smile turned devious and unflinching.

"I ask that you, citizens of Luna, be that army. You have the power to fight against Levana and the people that oppress you. Beginning now, tonight, I urge you to join me in rebelling against this regime. No longer will we obey her curfews or forgo our rights to meet and talk and be heard. No longer will we give up our children to become her disposable guards and soldiers. No longer will we slave away growing food and raising wildlife, only to see it shipped off to Artemisia while our children starve around us. No longer will we build weapons for Levana's war. Instead, we will take them for ourselves, for *our* war.

"Become my army. Stand up and reclaim your homes from the guards who abuse and terrorize you. Send a message to Levana that you will no longer be controlled by fear and manipulation. And upon the commencement of the royal coronation, I ask that all able-bodied citizens join me in a march against Artemisia and the queen's palace. Together we will guarantee a better future for Luna. A future without oppression. A future in which any Lunar, no matter the sector they live in or the family they were born to, can achieve their ambitions and live without fear of unjust persecution or a lifetime of slavery.

"I understand that I am asking you to risk your lives. Levana's thaumaturges are powerful, her guards are skilled, her soldiers are brutal. But if we join together, we can be *invincible.* They can't control us all. With the people united into one army, we will surround the capital city and overthrow the impostor who sits on my throne. Help me. Fight for me. And I will be the first ruler in the history of Luna who will also fight for you."

The video focused on Cinder's indomitable expression for a heartbeat and cut out.

Thirty-Six

"WOW," SCARLET WHISPERED. "GOOD SPEECH."

Cinder's heart was thundering. "Thanks. Kai wrote most of it."

She peered down the empty row of houses. The few people she had spotted before were still milling around, staring up at the dome. More miners and factory workers should have returned by now, but the streets stayed empty. The dome was a vacuum of silence.

It should have frightened Cinder, knowing that she had made her first move. She had been running for so long. Levana had kept her on the defensive since the moment she'd seen her at the Commonwealth ball.

No more. She felt energized. *Ready.* Far from looking like a fool in the video, she had sounded like a queen. She sounded like a *revolutionary*. She sounded like she could actually pull this off.

"Come on," said Scarlet, marching ahead. "Let's go see what's happening."

Cinder hurried after her. They heard shouting coming from the central square and the distant citizens were drifting toward the residential streets, though they frequently paused to look back. As Cinder and Scarlet got closer, the shouting turned into barking orders.

The sector guards had shoved their way into the loitering crowd, gripping long, slender clubs in their fists.

"Move along," a guard shouted. All but his eyes were concealed beneath his helmet and face mask. "Four minutes to curfew! Loitering is strictly prohibited, and no video is changing that."

Cinder and Scarlet ducked behind a delivery cart.

The citizens were clustered into small groups, their hair and uniforms covered in regolith dust. A few had their sleeves rolled up, revealing the RM-9 tattoos on their forearms. Most lowered their eyes when the guards approached them, recoiling at the prospect of those clubs being turned on them. But few seemed to be leaving.

One guard grabbed a man by his elbow and shoved him away from the bubbling fountain at the dome's center. "Get along, all of you. Don't make us file a report of misconduct."

Gazes shifted between the tired workers. The crowd was thinning. Their tired shoulders drooping as they dispersed. Groups dissolved without even an angry word shouted back at the guards.

Cinder's heart squeezed.

They weren't fighting.

They weren't defending themselves.

They were cowed by their oppressors every bit as much as before.

Disappointment swarmed over her and she stumbled, slouching against the cart. Had she not been persuasive enough? Had she failed to convey how important it was that they all stand up, unified and resolute? Had she failed?

Scarlet laid a hand on her shoulder. "It's only one sector," she said. "Don't be discouraged. We don't know what else is happening out there."

Though her words were kind, Cinder could see her frustration mirrored on Scarlet. It might be true—they *didn't* know what was happening in the rest of the sectors and they had no way of knowing. What she saw here, though, did little to give her confidence.

"Don't touch me!" a man yelled.

Cinder glanced around the cart. A guard was staring down a skinny man with sickly pale skin. Despite the gaunt bent to his body, the man stood before the guard with clenched fists.

"I will not return to my home in recognition of curfew," he said. "Threaten to report me all you like—after a video like that, the queen and her minions are going to have their hands full rounding up people guilty of much bigger crimes than staying out a few extra minutes."

Two other guards stopped ushering the people away and moved toward the man. Their gloved hands tightened on their clubs.

The remaining workers stopped to watch. Curious. Wary. But also, Cinder thought—angry.

The first guard loomed over the man. His voice was muffled behind the mask, but his arrogance was clear. "Our laws are for the protection of all people, and no one will be exempt from them. I suggest you go home before I'm forced to make an example of you."

"I'm perfectly capable of making an example of myself." The man snarled at the guards that were converging around him, then at the people who had hesitated at the edges of the square. "Don't you get it? If the other sectors saw that video too—"

The guard wrapped his free hand around the back of the

man's neck and shoved him down, forcing the man onto his knees. His words were cut off with a strangled grunt.

The guard raised his club.

Cinder pressed a hand over her mouth. She reached out with her gift, but she was too far away to stop it, too far to control him.

The other two guards joined in, their clubs falling onto the man's head, back, shoulders. He fell onto his side and covered his face, screaming from the force of the blows, but they wouldn't relent—

Cinder gritted her teeth and took a step into the road, but another voice cut through the man's cries before she could speak.

"Stop!" a woman screamed. She shoved her way through the crowd.

One of the guards did stop. No, he *froze*.

The other two hesitated, seeing their companion with his club held halfway through a swing. The woman's face was contorted in concentration.

"Unlawful use of manipulation," bellowed another guard. He grabbed the woman and pulled her arms behind her back. Before he could bind them, though, another miner had stepped forward—an elderly man with his back bent under years of work. His gaze was sharp, though, as he raised one hand.

The guard's body turned to stone.

Another civilian stepped forward. Then another, their expressions made of grim determination. One by one, the guards dropped their clubs. One by one, their bodies were claimed by the people.

A young boy rushed toward the man who had been beaten. He lay limp on the ground, groaning in pain.

The woman who had stepped forward first snarled at the

guards. "I don't know if that girl was Princess Selene or not, but I do know she's right. This might be our only chance to stand together, and I, for one, refuse to be afraid of you anymore!" Her face was strained, full of resentment.

As Cinder watched, the guard she was controlling reached for the knife at his belt and lifted it, pressing the blade against his own throat.

Horror cascaded over her like ice water.

"No!" Cinder screamed. She ran forward, releasing the glamour of the plain girl. "Don't! Don't kill them!" Barreling into the center of the crowd, Cinder held her hands toward the gathered civilians. Her pulse was racing.

She was met first with rage, the remnants of years of tyranny and yearning for revenge turned to disgust at her interruption.

But then, slowly, there was recognition, matched with confusion.

"I understand these men have been the queen's weapons. They have abused and degraded you and your families. But *they* are not your enemies. Many guards were removed from their loved ones and forced into the queen's employment against their will. Now, I don't know about these guards, specifically, but killing them without offering a fair trial or showing any mercy will only further the cycle of distrust." She met the eyes of the woman who held the guard and his knife in thrall. "Don't become like the queen and her court. Don't kill them. We'll take them prisoner until further notice. We might still find a use for them."

The guard's arm began to lower, removing the knife's imminent threat. He was watching Cinder, though, not the woman. Maybe he was relieved that she'd intervened. Maybe he was embarrassed at his lack of power. Maybe he was plotting to kill all of these rebellious citizens the moment he had a chance.

It occurred to her that this same scenario could be playing out in countless other sectors, without her there to stop it. She wanted the people to defend themselves from Levana's regime but she hadn't considered how she might also be sentencing thousands of guards to death.

She tried to tamp down the sting of guilt, telling herself this was war now, and wars came with casualties. But it didn't make her feel much better.

She approached the fountain and stepped up onto the edge. The water sprayed against her calves.

The crowd around her had grown and was still growing. People who had wandered off to their residences returned in force, drawn by the commotion and the spreading whispers of rebellion. With the guards subdued, their heads were lifted.

She imagined hundreds of thousands, even *millions* of Lunars gathering together like this, daring to envision a new regime.

Then a man's voice shouted, "It's a trick! This is Levana testing us! She'll slaughter us all for this."

The crowd rustled, made nervous by the accusation. Their eyes roved over Cinder's face, her clothes, the metal hand she wasn't hiding. She felt like she was at the ball again, the center of unwanted attention, forging ahead with single-minded resolve and the knowledge that she couldn't turn back now, even if she wanted to.

"This isn't a trick," she said, loud enough that her words echoed off the nearest factory walls. "And it isn't a test. I am Princess Selene, and the video you just saw was broadcast to almost every sector on Luna. I *am* organizing a rebellion that will span the entire surface of Luna—starting here. Will you join me?"

She hoped to be met with cheers, but uncomfortable silence greeted her instead.

The elderly man she'd seen before cocked his head. "But you're only a kid."

She glared at him, indignant, but before she could speak a familiar face emerged in the crowd. Maha came to stand before her. Despite her small stature, she carried every ounce of Wolf's fearlessness in her stance.

"Didn't you hear the video? Our true queen has returned! Will we cower in fear and ignore this one chance we have to make a better life for ourselves?"

The old man gestured toward the sky. "One pretty speech will not make for an organized rebellion. We have no training and no weapons. We have no time to prepare. What do you expect us to do—march into Artemisia with shovels and pickaxes? We'll be slaughtered!"

It was clear from the scattered frowns and bobbing heads that he wasn't alone in his thoughts.

"What we lack in training and time," said Maha, "we'll make up for in numbers and determination, just like Selene said."

"'Numbers and determination'? You'll take two steps into Artemisia and her thaumaturges will have you cutting open your own throats before you even *see* the palace."

"They can't brainwash all of us!" someone yelled from the crowd.

"Exactly," agreed Maha. "Which is why we have to do this now, when all of Luna can move forward together."

"How do we even know the other sectors will fight?" said the man. "Are we expected to risk our lives for some fantasy?"

"Yes!" Maha screamed. "Yes, I will risk my life for this fantasy. Levana took both of my sons away from me and I could do nothing to protect them. I couldn't stand up to her, even though it killed me to let them go. I will not waste this chance now!"

Cinder could tell her words meant something to the gathered civilians. Eyes dropped to the ground. A handful of children, covered in the same dust as everyone else, were pulled into the shelter of their parents' arms.

The man's face tightened. "I have wished for change my whole life, which is precisely how I know it's not going to be that simple. Levana may not be able to send manpower into every sector if we all riot at once, but what will stop her from halting the supply trains? She can starve us into submission. Our rations are already too low as it is."

"You're right," said Cinder. "She could cut your rations and halt the supply trains. But not if we control the maglev system. Don't you see? The only way this can work is if we all band together. If we refuse to accept the rules Levana has forced on us."

She caught sight of Scarlet in the crowd, then Iko, too, with Wolf and Thorne. Thorne was wearing a guard uniform but had taken off the helmet and face mask. She hoped his open grin would be enough to halt anyone's misplaced hatred.

Their presence bolstered her.

She tried to meet the eyes of as many citizens as she could. "I have no doubt the other sectors are dealing with the same fears you have. I suggest we select volunteers to act as runners to your neighboring sectors. We'll tell them that I'm here and that everything I said on that video is true. I will be marching into Artemisia, and I will reclaim my birthright."

"And I will be with you," said Maha Kesley. "I believe you are our true queen, and we owe you our allegiance on that alone. But as a mother reunited with her son, I owe you so much more."

Cinder smiled at her, grateful.

Maha returned it. Then she dropped to one knee and bowed her head.

Cinder tensed. "Oh, Maha, you don't have to . . ." She trailed off as, all around her, the crowd started to follow suit. The change was gradual at first but spread like ripples in a pond. Her friends alone stayed standing, and Cinder was grateful for their lack of reverence.

Her fears started to melt away. She didn't know if her video had persuaded *every* civilian to join her cause, and maybe not even *most* of them.

But the sight before her was proof that her revolution had begun.

Thirty-Seven

KAI STOOD WITH HIS ARMS CROSSED, GLARING AT THE window of his lavish guest suite but seeing nothing of the beautiful lake or city below. He had not managed to appreciate any of the luxuries of his fine prison, despite the suite being larger than most houses in the Commonwealth. Levana was feigning respect, giving him accommodations complete with an enormous bedroom and closet, two sitting parlors, an office, and a washroom that, at first glance, had seemed as though it had an actual pool in it, before Kai realized it was the bathtub.

Breathtaking, to be sure. It was even more luxurious than the guest suites in New Beijing Palace, though Kai and his ancestors had prided themselves on how they welcomed and treated their diplomatic guests.

The effect was ruined, however, by the fact that the double doors leading onto his outdoor balcony remained locked and Lunar guards were posted outside his chambers day and night. He had fantasized about breaking one of the windows and trying to scale down the wall of the palace—it was probably what Cinder would have done—but what was the point? Even if he avoided breaking his neck, he had nowhere to go. Though it pained him to think it, his place was here, beside Levana, doing his best to keep her occupied with wedding and coronation rubbish.

Which was not going well, given that he hadn't seen Levana or any of her cohorts since they'd locked him in here after the ambush in the docks. The only visitors he'd had were mute servants bringing him overflowing platters of extravagant food that went largely untouched.

With an exasperated growl, he started pacing again, sure he would wear a hole through this stone floor before this ordeal was over.

He had succeeded in getting Cinder and the others to Luna, which had been his primary role in their planning, but it hadn't gone smoothly and he was going mad not knowing what had happened. Had they gotten away? Was anyone hurt?

Even without a D-COMM link, he would have been tempted to send a comm to Iko or Cinder just to know what was happening, but Levana had confiscated his portscreen. It was maddening, but given the risk of a comm being traced, possibly for the best.

His anxiety would have been quelled if he could have moved forward with his other objectives. In addition to distracting Levana, he had also been tasked with gathering information about Scarlet Benoit, but he could learn nothing, *nothing*, while trapped in here.

It was like being stuck on the Rampion again, but a hundred times worse.

A bell echoed through his suite.

He bolted through the main parlor and yanked open the door.

A liveried servant stood on the other side, a boy a few years younger than Kai. He was flanked by four Lunar guards.

"I am not a prisoner," Kai started, wedging his foot into the door in case it was slammed shut as it had been countless times before. The servant stiffened. "I am the emperor of the Eastern Commonwealth, not some common criminal, and I will be treated with diplomatic respect. I have the right to hold counsel with my adviser and cabinet officials and I demand to hear Queen Levana's reasons for detaining us in this manner!"

The servant's mouth worked, speechless, for a moment, before he stammered, "I-I have been s-summoned to escort you to Her Majesty."

Kai blinked, momentarily baffled, but he quickly gathered himself. "It's about time. Take me to her immediately."

The servant bowed and stepped back into the corridor.

Kai was marched through the palace feeling even more like a prisoner with the guards spread out at his back, though no one touched him. He did his best to observe the palace layout, picking out memorable landmarks when he could—an interesting sculpture, an intricate tapestry. Over a sky bridge and down a long, narrow corridor where holographic portraits were lined up like a gauntlet.

His feet stumbled once when he saw the last holograph. He had to look twice to be sure he wasn't losing his mind.

The final holograph was a woman who looked, at first glance, just like Cinder.

His heart pounded, but as the holograph turned toward him, he realized his mistake. This was a mature version of Cinder, with flirtatious eyes and a vixen's smile. Her cheekbones were more pronounced, her nose a bit narrower. In fact, the real similarities lay not between this woman and the Cinder he knew, but between her and the Cinder he'd seen at the base of the ballroom steps.

He checked the plaque, confirming his suspicions. QUEEN CHANNARY BLACKBURN.

Cinder's unintentional glamour, painfully beautiful as it had been, looked so much like her mother.

"Your Majesty?"

He startled and whipped his attention away. He said nothing to the servant as he left the swaying holograph behind.

He had expected to be taken to the throne room, but as they walked through an iron-grated door and into a far less luxurious hallway, he grew suspicious. On his left they passed an elaborate vault door.

"What's in there?"

Expecting to be ignored, he was surprised when the servant answered, "The crown jewels and regalia."

The crown jewels. In New Beijing they stored priceless artifacts and heirlooms in one of the most secure underground vaults. There they kept gemstones the size of eggs, millennia-old gold-plated swords, even the crowns of the emperor and empress when they weren't in use.

It was clear that this wing was not open for general palace tours. Where were they taking him?

They turned another corner and Kai was ushered through a door into some sort of computer control center, full of invisi-screens and holograph nodes. Maps and surveillance videos were flickering on every wall and there were at least thirty men and women analyzing the abundance of feeds and compiling the ongoing data.

Before he could begin to make sense of what they were doing, he was shoved through a door into an adjacent room. The door was shut, locking him behind soundproof glass.

His gaze swept around the new space. A backdrop on one wall showed the city of Artemisia and Earth off the horizon. Two elaborate thrones sat before it.

The rest of the room was full of enormous standing lights and recording equipment. It reminded him of the media room in New Beijing Palace, but without any seats set up for journalists.

Levana stood behind one of the thrones, her hands rested on its back. She was dressed in a shimmering black gown hung with a silver sash. A brooch on the sash had a delicate gold filigree and rhinestones that read *Princess Winter, Though Gone, Never Forgotten*.

Kai's lips curled in disgust. This bit of gossip, at least, had reached him in his captivity. Princess Winter had been murdered. Some were saying it was by a guard, some were saying a jealous lover. But after seeing the way Levana had snarled at her stepdaughter, Kai couldn't help having his own theories.

Thaumaturge Aimery stood by the door, along with the red-haired captain of the guard. An unfamiliar man was fiddling with one of the lights.

Though Levana's mouth was smiling, her eyes were vicious.

Something had happened.

Kai planted his feet and shoved his hands into his pockets, hoping to come across as composed but formidable. "Hello, *my sweet*," he drawled, recalling the sycophantic endearments she'd mentioned in the ports.

Levana gave him a withering look, which spoke volumes. If

she wasn't willing to fake amusement, then something had gone horribly wrong.

Which he hoped meant something had gone horribly right.

"I was promised that I would be treated as a diplomatic guest," he said. "I wish to hold counsel with Konn Torin and the rest of the Earthen delegates and to be allowed access to roam the palace and city. We are not your prisoners."

"Unfortunately, I am not taking demands today." Levana's long nails dug into the back of her false throne. "You are, however, going to help me with a little project. Are we ready?"

The man was holding up pieces of paper in varying tones of white. "One more moment, My Queen."

Kai raised an eyebrow. "I'm not helping you with anything until you grant my requests and answer my questions."

"My dear groom-to-be, you gave up your rights to diplomatic courtesy when you brought those criminals into my home. Sit down."

Kai experienced a heartbeat's worth of defiance before his legs moved of their own accord and he collapsed into one of the thrones. He glared at the queen.

"I'm told," he pressed, "that you took an Earthen prisoner during a time of cease-fire. A citizen of the European Federation by the name of Scarlet Benoit. I demand to know if there is any truth to these rumors and where the girl is now."

Levana started to laugh. "I assure you there is no Earthen prisoner by that name here."

Her laughter set Kai's teeth on edge and her statement did nothing to convince him. Was Levana implying that Scarlet was dead? Or no longer in the palace? Or no longer in Artemisia at all?

Levana grabbed a veil from a mannequin's head and draped it over herself. Aimery stepped forward and settled the queen's crown on her head. When Levana turned back, her glamour was no longer visible. Having grown accustomed to her beautiful face, Kai had forgotten how this blank veil had filled him with horror for so long.

"What are we doing here?" Kai asked.

"Filming a little video," came Levana's voice. "There has been some confusion in the outer sectors of late, and I thought it pertinent to remind the people of their true loyalties, and all the great things you and I are going to accomplish once we are husband and wife."

He studied her, but could see little beneath the veil.

She was telling him so little, but she was telling him enough. Cinder's video had played. Levana was on the defensive. It had to be.

"What do you expect me to say?"

Levana clicked her teeth and took the throne beside him. "Nothing at all, darling. I will do the talking for you."

Dismay kicked behind his sternum. He tried to jolt to his feet, but his legs had become stone. He wrapped his hands around the chair's arms, digging his nails into the polished wood. "I don't think—"

His tongue halted.

The technician counted down on his fingers and a light glowed on the cameras before him.

Kai's body relaxed. His hands released the chair's arms and settled in his lap. His posture was poised but natural, his gaze soft. He was smiling as he looked into the camera's lens.

On the inside, however, he was furious. He was screaming and threatening Levana with every law regarding intergalactic policies he could think of. None of it mattered. His tirade was apparent to no one but himself.

"My good people," said Levana, "it has come to my attention that you have been accosted by an impostor claiming to be our beloved Princess Selene, who was tragically lost to us thirteen years ago. It has distressed me greatly that this girl, whose real name is Linh Cinder and who is a wanted criminal both on Luna and on Earth, has dared to take advantage of this painful episode in our history, particularly when we are still in mourning over the death of my stepdaughter. It breaks my heart to inform you that this girl's claims are nothing but lies meant to confuse you and manipulate you into joining her even when your good sense, when not so manipulated, would refuse to participate."

She gestured to Kai. "I wish to introduce you all to my future husband, His Imperial Majesty, Emperor Kaito of Earth's Eastern Commonwealth. He has a reputation of being a most fair and compassionate ruler, and I have no doubt he will be a great king to us as well. Together, we will unite our countries with a union built on admiration and mutual respect."

Inside, Kai gagged.

Outside, he turned love-struck eyes toward his bride.

"You may not know," Levana continued, "that His Majesty has had many personal dealings with Linh Cinder, this criminal who is masquerading as Her Highness, Princess Selene. I wanted you to hear his opinion of the girl so you might make decisions based on facts, and not emotional responses. Please grace him with your full attention."

Kai faced the camera again and the words that came out of his mouth would later have him scrubbing his own tongue.

"Citizens of Luna, it is my honor to address you as your future king, and my greatest sadness that my introduction to you must be on such tumultuous grounds. As your queen has stated, I have had many interactions with Linh Cinder, and I know with certainty she is not what she claims to be. The truth is that she is a violent criminal, responsible for countless thefts and murders on planet Earth. After developing an obsession with me, she even attempted to assassinate my beloved bride-to-be, your queen, during our annual peace festival in New Beijing. When that attempt failed, she went so far as to kidnap me on the day that had been intended as our wedding, proceeding to hold me hostage against my will and under inhumane conditions until I promised to give up on this union between Earth and Luna and agree to marry her, instead. It is only thanks to Luna's brave soldiers and Her Majesty's indomitable spirit that I was safely released. Unfortunately, Linh Cinder has not given up. She continues to live a fantasy in which she is Princess Selene, returned from the dead, in hopes that she might win my affection. Her instability and recklessness have made her a dangerous felon and a threat, not only to my safety, but to the well-being of all who come in contact with her. I would urge you all, if you see Linh Cinder, to report her to officials immediately. Do not speak to her. Do not approach her. As your future king, I am now most concerned with *your* safety, and it is my hope that Linh Cinder will be found and brought to Artemisia where she can be met with the justice her crimes deserve."

By the time he had finished speaking, Kai felt like he would have ripped out his own tongue if given the chance.

Levana started again, "Of course, if ever there was found to be any truth to the rumors that my dear niece, Selene, had survived all those years ago, I would joyfully welcome her into my heart and home and place Luna's crown myself upon her head. Sadly, it is not to be. Selene lies with the stars, and I alone must maintain the security and livelihoods of our people. I know times are difficult. It is with great sadness that I watch our food production diminish year after year, and our limited resources fail to meet the needs of our growing populace. Which is why it has been the topmost priority of my regime to secure this alliance with Earth, so that our future might be brighter and our people taken care of for generations to come. This, my people, is the future that I alone can offer you. Not this cyborg, this impostor, this fraud." As her tone dipped toward resentment, Levana paused and regathered herself. Her voice carried a smile again as she finished, "I am your queen and you are my people. It is my great privilege to guide us all into a bright new future."

The technician stopped the recording and Kai's body throbbed as control was returned to him. He bolted to his feet and rounded on Levana. "I am not a brainless instrument to be used for your propaganda."

Levana removed the crown and veil and passed them to Aimery. "Be calm, my beloved. You spoke so eloquently. No doubt the people were impressed."

"Cinder will know it was fake. She'll know you were controlling me."

Levana's eyes flashed. "What do I care what *Cinder* thinks? Her opinion, like yours, means nothing." She snapped her fingers at the guard. "I am finished with him. You may take him back."

Thirty-Eight

AS SOON AS THE EMPEROR HAD BEEN LED AWAY BY THE contingent of guards, Levana swept out of the studio into the control room. "Have that video edited and set to play in all sectors where the cyborg's message went out. Monitor those feeds carefully. I want hourly reports on how each broadcast is being received. What is the current status of the outer sectors?"

"We are seeing minor upheavals in thirty-one sectors," said a woman. "Mostly civilians have been refusing to respect curfew laws, and there have been some attacks on sector guards."

A man added, "We're also seeing an increase of thefts in two agricultural sectors. Laborers returned to the fields and have been harvesting food rations for their own use. Guards have been incapacitated in both sectors."

Levana huffed. "Send added security to all sectors showing signs of insurgence. We must quell this immediately. And find that cyborg!"

She stood watching the flicker of surveillance videos for a moment, though her thoughts were far away. As her blood boiled, she found herself back in New Beijing, watching the girl rush past her in that tawdry silver ball gown. She saw her trip on the ballroom steps and tumble down toward the gardens. Her hideous metal foot snapped off at the ankle and the full force of her glamour surged over her, crackling like electricity, rolling off her body like heat waves in the desert.

In her unpracticed state, the girl had done nothing more than call up an exaggeratedly beautiful version of herself, and in so doing, she had turned herself into Channary. Her mother. Levana's tormentor.

Levana could still see her like a photograph imprinted forever in her memory. Hatred she had not felt in years surged through her veins. Fury sparked in her vision, white and blinding.

Selene. She was meant to die thirteen years ago, yet here she was, disastrously alive. And just as Levana had feared back then, she would take everything from her. Everything that Levana had worked so hard for.

It made her sick. Why couldn't Selene have died, easily, mercifully, the way she'd planned? When she had coaxed that young nanny into setting fire to the princess's playhouse, it should have ended it all. No niece. No princess. No future queen.

But she'd been tricked. Selene was alive and attempting to take her throne from her.

Her attention refocused on the screens. "These are my people," she whispered. "My blood and my soul. *I* am their queen."

Aimery appeared at her side. "Of course you are, Your Majesty. The cyborg has no idea what it is to be queen. What choices one must live with. What sacrifices must be made. When she is gone, the people will recognize that you have always been the one to rightly sit upon our throne."

"'When she is gone,'" Levana repeated, grasping at the words. "But how will I ever know that she is gone if I cannot *find* her?"

It was infuriating. She had known the cyborg was a threat from the moment she recognized her on Earth. But for her to attempt to turn Levana's citizens against her was a blow she couldn't fathom. The thought of their love turning to biased hatred stole the air from her lungs and left her feeling hollowed out to her core.

That was the cyborg's plan too. To turn as many people's minds against Levana as she could, knowing that large numbers would be her greatest advantage. Levana could control hundreds, perhaps thousands of her citizens when she had a need to do it. With her thaumaturges behind her, they could control entire sectors, entire *cities.*

But even she had limits.

She shook her head. It mattered not. The people would not revolt against her. The people *loved her.*

She rubbed two fingers against her brow. "What will I do?"

"My Queen," said Aimery, "perhaps I can offer a bit of good news."

Releasing her breath, she turned to the thaumaturge. "Good news would be very welcome indeed."

"I received an interesting report from your laboratories this morning, but had not had a chance to share their discoveries in the wake of the cyborg's broadcast. However, it has been confirmed that we are capable of duplicating the mutated letumosis microbes that were recovered from the body of Dr. Sage Darnel on Earth, and that our immunity to the original disease has in fact been compromised by this mutation."

It took Levana a moment to change the direction of her thoughts. "And the antidote?"

"Still effective, though there is a much shorter window in which it can be used."

Levana tapped her fingers against her lower lip. "That *is* interesting."

Years ago, Levana had unleashed this plague on Earth, and she would soon embrace the results. Earth was weak and desperate. Desperate to cure the plague. Desperate to end the war.

When she gave them the antidote, they would be unspeakably grateful to their new empress.

She had never expected her lab-created disease to mutate in the wild, though. Now, no one was immune, not even her own people. What a strange, miraculous thing.

"Thank you, Aimery. This could be the answer I've been seeking. If the people do not see their errors and come crawling back to my good graces, I may have to employ new means of persuasion. It would break my heart to see my people suffering, but that is one of those difficult decisions a queen finds herself making from time to time."

Her heart fluttered as she imagined the people filling up the courtyard beyond the palace walls and kneeling before her, tears on their faces. They would worship her for having saved them. She would save them all with her goodness and charity.

Oh, how they would adore her, their savior, their rightful queen.

"Your Majesty!"

She pivoted toward the voice. A woman had stood up and was adjusting an invisi-screen. "I think I've found something."

Levana shoved past Aimery to get a better view. The screen showed the central square of an outer sector—regolith mining, perhaps, judging by the dust that covered every surface, smudging even the camera lens. The fountain depicting her likeness could be seen in the footage, a thing of beauty in their drab world.

The square was full of people, a rarity in itself. Her mandated curfew ensured that the people focused on their work and their rest without being tempted to converge with their neighbors during off-work hours.

"Is this live?" she asked.

"No, My Queen. This was filmed not long after the end of the workday." She hastened through the footage, and Levana squinted to try to make sense of it. Guards, civilians, a just punishment, and then . . .

"Pause the video."

The woman did, and Levana found herself staring into the face that had haunted her for months. If there had been any doubt, the monstrous metal hand dispelled it.

"Where is this?"

"Regolith Mining 9."

Levana's lips curled upward.

The cyborg was hers.

"Aimery, assemble a team for immediate deployment to this sector. Linh Cinder is to be arrested and brought to me for a public trial and execution. Use whatever methods you see fit to detain her." Her vision bled with loathing as she stared at the screen. The haughty girl with her ignorant words and her proud displays. "We are not to tolerate any sympathizing with her or her allies. This uprising must be brought to an end."

BOOK

Three

"Your stepmother will soon know you are here,"

warned the kindly dwarfs. "Do not let anyone in."

Thirty-Nine

LEVANA'S REBUTTAL VIDEO WAS PLAYING FOR THE THIRD TIME that hour. Cinder was doing her best to ignore it, but every time Kai started speaking the sound of his voice made her jump, only to be reminded all over again that he wasn't here. He was under Levana's control, as Levana had so deftly illustrated.

From her spot around a worktable on the third floor of a regolith factory, Cinder could see most of one of the screens embedded on the dome. It showed a contented Levana and a peaceful Kai. So *happy* together. There was one moment when Kai turned to Levana and smiled all dreamy-like that made Cinder's skin crawl. For the billionth time, she wished Cress was with them. She would have known how to turn it off.

Cinder turned away from the video to concentrate. She had no way of knowing how Levana's message was being received across Luna, just as she had no way of knowing how *her* video was being received. The best she could do was move forward.

She was gathered among her allies—Iko, Thorne, Wolf, and Scarlet. Wolf's mother was there, too, along with a handful of sector residents who had been nominated to represent the others. They had worked through the night, plotting and orga-nizing, too energized to sleep.

Two runners had returned that morning from neighboring mining sectors and were reporting good news. The guards had been restrained, their weaponry confiscated, and the people would join Cinder on her march to Artemisia. Additional mes-sengers had taken on the dangerous assignment of traveling through the mines, lava tubes, and maglev tunnels to confirm the truth of Cinder's video and rally as many sectors as they could to the cause.

It was a promising start.

The rest of the sector residents had been sent home after Cinder encouraged them to get some rest. In truth, she needed space from their curiosity and awestruck whispers. Space to think.

When they regathered, she would divide the people into teams and assign each team a task. Though some volunteers had already been put on watch guarding the maglev platforms, she would soon have to establish a rotation to make sure they stayed alert. Some groups would be tasked with gathering what food and medical supplies they could find, another would watch the guardhouse, and still others would be sent to ransack the mines for potential weapons and tools. Wolf promised to spend time training any able-bodied citizens in basic combat techniques, to commence that afternoon.

She stared up at the holographic map of Luna, her brow drawn, as Wolf indicated what routes he thought they should take to the capital. Everyone agreed they should come at the city from as many directions as possible to force Levana to divide her own defenses against them.

"We should avoid Research and Development, and also

Technical Services," Wolf said, pointing out two sectors in Artemisia's near vicinity. "Most people there will be Levana supporters."

"RD-1 seems easy enough to get around." Cinder spun the holograph for a better view. "But TS-1 and 2 are right in our path if we're going to hit these agricultural sectors on the way."

"Maybe we don't avoid them," said Thorne. "Is there some way we can blockade the platforms under those sectors, trapping anyone inside? It would allow us safe passage through, and also keep anyone from sneaking up behind us afterward and trapping us in these tunnels."

Cinder tapped a finger against her lower lip. "That might work, but what do we block them with?"

"Doesn't this sector manufacture building materials?" asked Scarlet, gesturing to a sector labeled GC-6: GENERAL CONSTRUCTION. "Maybe they'll have something we can use."

Cinder turned to one of the miners. "Can I appoint you to look into that?"

He clapped a hand to his heart in proud salute. "Of course, Your Majesty. We can take some of the mining carts to transport the materials too."

"Perfect." Trying not to feel awkward about the Your Majesty part, Cinder turned back to the group.

Wolf stiffened—a small change that sent an alarm through Cinder.

"What is it?"

He started to shake his head, but stopped, his frown deepening. His piercing eyes turned toward the window. The screens on the dome had once again fallen silent.

"I thought I . . . I smelled something."

Hair prickled on the back of Cinder's neck. If it had been

anyone other than Wolf, she would have laughed. But his senses were uncanny, and his instincts hadn't led them astray yet.

"What sort of something?" she asked.

"I can't place it. There are a lot of bodies here, a lot of scents. But there was something..." His fists tightened. "Someone is near. Someone who was also on the rooftop in New Beijing."

Cinder's heart thumped—*Kai!*

But, no, Wolf would have recognized Kai for sure.

It had to be one of the royal guards who had attacked them.

Iko grabbed the portscreen—a device that had stunned and awed the civilians—and shut off the holograph.

A shrill scream echoed through the streets outside.

Cinder ran for the window, pressing her body against the wall, ready to duck out of view. Thorne plastered himself to the wall beside her. "You should hide," he whispered.

"So should you."

Neither of them moved.

She watched the scene below, trying to make sense of it as horror built inside her. Countless guards were marching through the streets, along with at least half a dozen thaumaturges that she could see.

A white coat drew her attention and her stomach sank. Thaumaturge Aimery stood on the edge of the central fountain, right where Cinder had stood before. He carried himself like a prince with his beautiful face and proud stance.

More reinforcements kept pouring in from the narrow streets that stretched out from the square like spokes on a wheel. Far too many reinforcements to quell a simple uprising in a non-threatening mining sector.

Cinder's gut knotted.

They knew she was here.

The guards were dragging the people out of their homes, corralling them into uniform lines around the fountain. She recognized the man who had been beaten by the guards, still bruised and limping. There was the old woman who had been stockpiling what she could of her meager rations for years and who had already offered to give it up to those who would be fighting in Artemisia. And there was the twelve-year-old boy who had trailed Iko around all morning with a swoony expression on his face.

"They're rounding up everyone in the sector," whispered Maha, peering out of the next window. "No doubt they'll search these buildings too." Her expression was fierce as she stepped back. "You should all hide. The rest of us will give ourselves up. They might not search these upper floors if they think everyone is accounted for."

Cinder gulped. "They won't stop looking."

Maha squeezed her hand. "Then hide well."

She wrapped Wolf in a tight embrace. He bent down to accept it, his knuckles going white as he held her.

They heard the factory door bang open on the first floor. Cinder jumped. She wanted to grab Maha and force her to stay, but Maha extricated herself from her son's embrace and walked away with her head up. The remaining citizens followed. Without a word from Cinder, it seemed they had unanimously agreed that keeping her safe was the priority.

A chill washed down her spine as she watched them go.

It wasn't long before she heard orders shouted by the guards, and Maha's calm voice stating that they were unarmed and coming down voluntarily. A moment later she saw them being shoved out toward the crowd in the square with guns pointed at their backs.

Scarlet gasped. "What about Winter?"

Cinder turned wide eyes on her. They had left the princess at Maha's house, thinking it was the safest place for her, but now . . .

"I can go," said Iko. "They won't be able to detect me like they would any of you."

Cinder pressed her lips in a firm line, debating. She wanted Iko here with her, as her only ally that couldn't be manipulated. But that also made her the best choice for securing the princess.

She assented. "Be careful. Sneak out through the loading bay."

Iko gave a brief nod and then she, too, was gone.

Cinder was shaking as she looked around at Thorne, Wolf, and Scarlet. From this far up she wasn't able to feel the bioelectricity of the thaumaturges down in the crowd, so she was confident they couldn't feel her and her friends up here, either, but that did little to comfort her.

They had come for her, she knew it. She had nowhere to go. Nowhere to hide.

What was more, she wasn't sure she *wanted* to hide. These people had put their trust in her. How could she abandon them?

Aimery's voice reached her ears. Though he didn't yell, the sound carried upward, echoing off the hard surfaces of the factory walls. Cinder adjusted her audio interface to be sure she caught every word.

"Residents of Regolith Mining Sector 9," he said, "you have been gathered here to face the consequences of your unlawful behavior. In harboring and aiding known criminals, you are all guilty of high treason against the crown." He paused, allowing the full impact of his words to settle. "The sentence for this crime is death."

Cinder's body was wound tight as she peeked through the window again. The people who had been gathered into orderly groups were forced to their knees. There were over two thousand residents, minus only those who had been sent as messengers into the neighboring sectors. Their kneeling bodies filled up the streets as far as she could see.

He wouldn't kill all of them. He wouldn't dare reduce Luna's labor force so severely.

Would he?

Aimery studied those gathered before him, while the statue of Levana watched over them like a proud mother. Two guards stood to either side of the fountain. Cinder recognized the red-haired guard and wondered if this was the one Wolf had scented before. The rest of the guards were spread out in their helmets and armor, boxing in the civilians with guns at the ready. The other thaumaturges remained interspersed throughout the crowd, arms tucked into their sleeves.

Cinder stretched her thoughts out as far as she could. Reaching, reaching for Aimery's energy. If she could take control of just him, she could force him to offer mercy. He could order these people to be let go.

But no. He was too far away.

It frustrated her, knowing that Levana would have been able to stretch her gift that far. Levana could have easily controlled Aimery from up here—probably could have controlled all of them from here. Cinder didn't care that her aunt had a lifetime of practice over her. She should have been as strong. She should have been capable of protecting the people who would protect her.

Panting, she turned her attention to the nearest guards, those stationed beneath the window. She could detect them, at least, but they were already under the control of one of the thaumaturges.

Panic simmered through her. She had to *think*.

She still had five bullets in her hand. Thorne and Scarlet were both armed too. She was confident she could hit one of the nearest guards and maybe even a thaumaturge, but the attempt would give away their location.

Plus, as soon as Aimery realized they were under attack, he would start using the sector residents as shields.

She didn't know if she could risk it.

She didn't know if she had a choice.

"However," said Aimery, his dark gaze fixed on the crowd, "Her Majesty is prepared to offer you all amnesty. Each one of you will be spared." His lips turned upward in a kind smile. "All you must do is tell us where you're keeping the cyborg."

Forty

CINDER SHOVED A KNUCKLE INTO HER MOUTH, BITING DOWN hard to keep from screaming. She could feel her companions' eyes on her, but she dared not look at them.

"You *cannot* go out there." Scarlet's whisper was harsh, no doubt seeing the indecision scrawled across Cinder's face.

"I can't let them die for me," she whispered back.

A hand grabbed her and jerked her away from the window. Wolf glared down at her. Sweet and vicious Wolf, whose mother was down there, with *them*.

She half expected him to give her away himself, but instead he grabbed Cinder's shoulders, squeezing tight. "No one is dying for *you*. If anyone dies today it will be because they finally have something to believe in. Don't you even think about taking that away from them now."

"But I can't—"

"Cinder, get yourself together," said Thorne. "You are the heart of this revolution. If you give yourself up now, it's over. And you know what? She'll probably kill all those people down there any-way just to make sure this doesn't happen again."

A gunshot made her yelp. Wolf clamped his hand over Cinder's mouth, but she ripped herself away and threw herself back at the window.

White spots crowded into her vision. Then red as fury blinded her.

In the square below, a man's body was sprawled out at Aimery's feet, blood splattered across the ground. Cinder didn't know who it was, but that didn't matter. Someone was dead. Someone was dead because of *her*.

Aimery scanned the stricken faces of those closest to him, smiling pleasantly. "I will ask you again. Where is Linh Cinder?"

They all kept their eyes pinned to the ground. No one looked at Aimery. No one looked at the growing pool of blood. No one spoke.

Inside her head, Cinder was screaming. The gunshot still echoed in her skull, her audio interface repeating it again and again and again. She pressed her hands over her ears, shaking, furious.

She would kill Aimery. She would *destroy* him.

A body pressed against her back. Scarlet wrapped her arms around Cinder, tucking her face into the crook of Cinder's neck. To restrain her, she thought, as much as to comfort her.

She didn't pull away, but she was not comforted.

Below, Aimery signaled to a woman seven rows back, a strategically random choice that would ensure no one felt safe. Another shot fired from one of the guards. The woman convulsed and crumpled against the person beside her.

A shudder pulsed through the crowd.

Cinder sobbed. Scarlet held her tighter.

How long would it go on? How many would he kill? How long could she stand to wait up here and do nothing?

"All it takes is one person to tell me her location," said Aimery, "and this will all be over. We will leave you to your peaceful lives."

Something damp fell on Cinder's neck. Scarlet was crying, shaking every bit as hard as she was. But her arms didn't loosen.

She wanted to look away, but she forced herself not to. Their bravery left her both speechless and horrified. She found herself wishing someone would betray her just so it would end. Just so the choice would no longer be hers.

Thorne took her hand and squeezed. Wolf formed a barrier to her other side, all three of them acting both as her jailers and her life raft. She knew they shared her horror, but none of them could understand the responsibility she felt clawing at her from the inside. These people trusted her to fight with them, to give them the better future she'd promised.

Did it matter that they were willing to die for her cause? Did it matter that they would sacrifice their own lives so she might succeed?

She didn't know.

She didn't know.

All she saw were blinding sparks. All she heard were gunshots pulsing through her head.

Aimery pointed at another victim and Cinder's knees weakened. It was the young boy who had been so smitten with Iko.

Cinder sucked in a breath, prepared to cry out, to stop it, to *scream*—

"No!"

Aimery held up his hand. "Who was that?"

A girl a few rows behind the boy had begun to cry hysterically. "No, please. Please, leave him alone." She was about Cinder's age. A sister, she guessed.

New tension rolled through the crowd. A few nearby people cast the girl betrayed looks, but Cinder knew it wasn't fair. This girl didn't know Cinder. Why should she protect her over someone she loved?

Aimery raised an eyebrow. "Are you prepared to give up the cyborg's location?"

"Maha Kesley," the girl stammered. "The cyborg was being housed by Maha Kesley."

With a flick of Aimery's fingers, the guard who had targeted the boy lowered his gun. "Where is this Maha Kesley?"

Maha stood up before anyone was forced to betray her, a pillar in the kneeling crowd. "I'm here."

Wolf took in a shaky breath.

"Come to the front," said Aimery.

Maha's slender shoulders were back as she walked among her friends and neighbors. A change had occurred in the short time Cinder had known her. On that first day she had seemed beaten, heavy shouldered, afraid. The woman who stood defiantly before the queen's head thaumaturge was someone new.

It made Cinder even more terrified for her.

"What is the number of your residence?" Aimery asked.

Maha gave it with a steady voice.

Aimery gestured at the captain of the guard and a female thaumaturge. They stepped away, signaling for one additional guard to join them as they headed toward Maha's house.

Aimery's attention had returned to Maha. "Have you been sheltering the cyborg Linh Cinder?"

"I do not know that name," said Maha. "The one cyborg I know is named Princess Selene Blackburn and she is the true queen of Luna."

The crowd rustled. Chins lifted. Shoulders squared. If anyone had forgotten why they were risking their lives for a stranger, Maha's statement reminded them.

Aimery smirked. Cinder's blood iced over.

As she watched, Maha raised both of her hands over her head so everyone could see. Then she grabbed her right thumb and yanked it back, hard.

Cinder heard the pop even from here, followed by Maha's cry. She didn't know if Aimery had forced her to break her thumb or merely dislocate it, and she didn't care. She made a decision.

In another moment, she had slipped into the minds of her friends and forced them to back away from her.

She spun around. Scarlet, Thorne, and Wolf gawked at her, dismayed.

Wolf recovered first. "Cinder, don't—"

"It's the people's revolution now, not mine. Wolf, you're coming with me. I'll keep your mind under control but not your body, just like we did in Artemisia. Thorne, Scarlet, stay here and target Aimery and the other thaumaturges, but don't shoot unless you have a clear shot, otherwise you're just giving away your location."

"Cinder, *no*," Scarlet hissed, but Cinder was already leaving her and Thorne behind, forcing Wolf to follow in her tracks.

He growled.

"I have to, Wolf," she said as they rushed down the staircase to the second landing. Outside, muffled by thick factory walls, she heard another cry of pain from Maha. "I can't do nothing."

"He'll kill you."

"Not if we kill him first." She raced down the last staircase and braced herself. She checked that she had control of Wolf's bioelectricity so no thaumaturge could claim him, then pushed through the factory doors. A third scream from Maha felt like a knife in Cinder's chest. One look told her that Maha's first three fingers were bent at crippling angles. Tears were on her pain-clenched face.

"Here I am," Cinder bellowed. "You found me. Now let her go."

In one uniform movement, all the guards swiveled, turning their weapons on Cinder. She sucked in a breath, prepared to be riddled with bullets, but no one fired.

Across the sea of prostrated laborers, Aimery grinned. "So the impostor has finally graced us with her presence."

She clenched her fists and started toward him. The guns followed. So did Wolf, his energy crackling. "You know very well that my claims are true," she said. "It's the only reason Levana is so determined to have me killed." She stretched out her thoughts to the people surrounding her, but none of their minds were available to her. She had expected as much.

She had a trained killer at her side and two skilled shooters at her back. It would have to be enough.

She reached the front row of the gathered civilians. "You came here for me, and here I am. Leave these people alone."

Aimery cocked his head. His gaze swooped over Cinder, from head to toe and back up, making her feel like easy prey. She knew how she looked in her drab clothing, with her metal hand and clunky boots, her messy ponytail, and most likely, a hearty amount of dust smudged across her face. She knew that she did not look like a queen.

"Imagine how differently this could have gone," he said, stepping down from the fountain's ledge, "if you had chosen to claim the minds of these people before our arrival. Instead, you left them adrift on the ocean of their own weaknesses. You turned them into targets and then did nothing to protect them. You are not suited to be a ruler of Luna."

"Because I would rather my people know freedom than constant manipulation?"

"Because you are not capable of making the decisions a queen must make for the good of all her people."

She gritted her teeth. "The only people who have benefited from Levana's regime are the greedy aristocrats in Artemisia. Levana's not a queen. She's a tyrant."

Aimery bowed his head, almost like he was agreeing with her. "And you," he whispered, "are nobody at all."

"I am the true ruler of Luna." Though she put as much conviction behind the words as she could, they fell flat. Within moments, the arrival of the queen's head thaumaturge had undone all the progress she'd made in this sector. With a flick of his fingers Aimery had taken away all her power and prostrated the people before him.

"You are a child playing at war games," said Aimery, "and you're too naïve to see you've already lost."

"I'm *surrendering* to you," she said. "And if that means I have to lose so these people can go free, so be it. What *you* don't seem to realize is that this isn't about me. It's about the people who have lived in oppression for far too long. Levana's rule is coming to an end."

Aimery's smile grew. Behind him, the fountain gushed and spat.

Wolf's energy surged behind her, hackles raised.

Aimery opened his arms to the crowd. "Let it be known that on this day, the impostor princess surrendered to Her Majesty the Queen. Her crimes will be dealt with swiftly and justly." His eyes glimmered. "However, I promised that *your* lives would be spared if any one of you were to give up the cyborg's location." He clicked his tongue. "It is a great shame no one came forward sooner. I do not like to be kept waiting."

A shot fired. A shock wave pulsed through Cinder's body.

She didn't know where it came from. She saw blood, but didn't know who had been hit.

Then Maha's legs collapsed and she fell face-first onto the hard ground. Her three deformed fingers remained stretched out over her head.

Still reeling from the concussion of the gunshot, Cinder stared at Maha's body, unable to breathe. Unable to move.

She heard Wolf's intake of breath. His energy crystallized into something still and fragile.

The world stilled, balancing on a needle point. Silent. Incomprehensible.

Another gun fired, this shot from much farther away, and the noise shoved the world off its axis. Aimery crowed and stumbled back as a spot on his thigh soaked through with blood. His eyes blazed up toward the factory. Another shot hit the fountain behind him.

Wolf roared and leaped forward. The nearest guard blocked his path, but was too slow to shoot. Wolf batted him away like an annoying gnat and rushed for Aimery, teeth bared.

A cacophony of noise and bodies erupted. Every citizen that should have been on Cinder's side instead surged to their feet and grappled for her and Wolf. Cinder's body was slammed to the ground. She lost sight of Wolf. More gunshots.

Throwing a punch to someone's jaw, she rolled once and scrambled back to her feet. She spotted a red coat, raised her hand, and fired. She waited long enough to see the thaumaturge buck back before she was searching for another target, but she didn't get off another shot as dozens of hands grabbed her, pulled her, wrestled her to the ground.

Cinder thrashed against their hold, blowing a lock of hair from her face. She spotted Wolf. He, too, was pinned to the ground, though it had taken a dozen men to do it. Every limb was held in place, his cheek pressed into the dust. The bodies of two guards and one miner lay not far away.

Aimery loomed above him, panting, his constant smile nowhere to be seen. He had one hand pressed over the wound in his leg. "The shots are coming from that factory. Send a team to search it, and bind these two before they try anything else."

Cinder strained against the arms holding her. If she could raise her arm, take one clean shot—

Her arms were yanked behind her, her wrists bound. She screamed as her shoulder was pulled just shy of dislocation. She was hauled back to her feet, coughing on dust, her entire body throbbing.

She glanced around, searching for an ally, but only blank faces greeted her.

She sneered, defiant, as she and Wolf were forced to kneel in front of Aimery's livid face. She was dizzy with her own hatred, but as her thoughts settled, she was hit with the full force of Wolf's agony beside her.

He was in anguish, his emotions splintering, and Cinder remembered that the body of the miner beside him was his mother.

Cinder shuddered and had to look away. She spotted the red-coated thaumaturge she'd shot, not moving, and another in a black uniform also lying not far away.

That was all. Two thaumaturges and two guards killed,

Aimery injured. That was all she had gotten from Maha's sacrifice, and the brave deaths of two other innocent civilians.

Cinder was more angry than afraid, feeding on Wolf's devastation and the horror of all the blank faces around her, all these people used like marionettes.

She believed what she'd said before. Levana could kill her, but Cinder had to believe her death wouldn't be the end. This revolution no longer belonged to her.

Forty-One

"THEY'RE COMING," SAID SCARLET, SNARLING AS SHE BACKED away from the window. Her first shot had been low, hitting Aimery's thigh when she'd been aiming for his head. Her second shot had hit the fountain, useless, before the crowd had been too thick to keep firing. She had heard at least three shots coming from Thorne but didn't know if he'd had any more success.

Cinder and Wolf were like hogs in a slaughterhouse down there, and she and Thorne would be close behind if they didn't get out, now.

Thorne grabbed the helmet he'd stolen from the guard and pulled it over his head, transforming from her friend to her enemy. She hoped the transformation was as convincing to the Lunars. "Give me your gun," he said. She hesitated only briefly before handing it over. Thorne pocketed it and grabbed her elbow, dragging her toward the staircase.

They were on the first landing when footsteps stampeded through the bottom level.

"Found one!" Thorne yelled, making her jump. He held his gun to Scarlet's head as he dragged her to the bottom of the stairs. Four guards surrounded them. "There were two gunmen. The other might have run, but check the top floors to be sure. I've got this one."

Scarlet pretended to thrash against his hold as Thorne dragged her past the guards, oozing authority. The guards charged up the stairs. The second they were gone, Thorne swiveled around and released her. They ran for the back exit, dashing into the alley behind the factory.

Already the brawl was over, judging from the dreadful silence that filled the dome.

Thorne turned away from the factory, but Scarlet grabbed his arm. "Wait."

He looked back, his gaze harsh, but maybe that was the effect of the face mask.

"We have to try to help them," she said.

His brow wrinkled. "You saw how easily they took down Cinder and Wolf, and you think *we* can do something to help them?"

She didn't. She honestly didn't.

But if she didn't even try . . .

"Give me my gun," she said, holding out her hand.

Thorne stared at her.

"Give me my gun."

With a huff, he pulled the gun from his waistband and shoved it into her palm. Scarlet spun away, not sure if he would follow. He did.

When they turned the first corner she could see the square. The citizens who had risen up to attack Cinder and Wolf were all kneeling again, placid, as if the fight hadn't even happened.

Scarlet wondered how long it would take those guards to

search the factory. She wondered if she was crazy not to turn and run.

The gun was warm in her hand, the handle leaving imprints in her skin. There had been a time when holding a weapon had offered a sense of protection, but that comfort was compromised knowing how easily Lunars could turn the weapon against her.

Still, if she could get close enough she could get off a shot or two, and this time she wouldn't miss.

How close could she get before they detected her? Would the size of the crowd help to hide her, or would she be caught up in the same brainwashing trick as soon as she got too close? She didn't know how it worked or how vulnerable she would be. She was wishing now that she had asked Cinder more about it when she'd had the chance.

They moved stealthily, Thorne silent behind her.

She stopped when she could pick out Wolf and Cinder among their enemies. They both had their hands bound behind them now. Wolf's shoulders were hunched. He was looking at the ground.

No, she realized with a shudder. He was looking at Maha.

Fury ignited in her gut. They had taken everything from Wolf. His freedom, his childhood, his entire family, and he had done nothing, *nothing*, to deserve it.

She wanted to avenge him. To take him away from this horrible dust-mottled place. To offer him a life of blue skies and tomatoes and peace.

Scarlet tightened her grip on the gun, feeling the familiar press of the trigger.

But she was too far away. She had a better chance of hitting an ally than an enemy from here.

Heart thumping, Scarlet scrutinized the narrow alley,

estimating how many steps she could take and still stay hidden. There was a doorway set into the factory wall she could duck into, but being seen wasn't her biggest concern, not when Lunars could *sense* her.

Letting out a slow breath, she raised the gun and lined up the sights, targeting Aimery's heart. She held her aim for three breaths before she huffed and lowered the weapon again. She'd been right before. Too far away.

Again, she considered moving closer. Again, she hesitated.

Then she noticed a shift in Wolf's posture. His head turned in her direction.

It was a subtle change, almost unremarkable. He didn't look at her. He didn't make any move to suggest he had picked out her scent among all these people, but Scarlet knew he had. There was a tension to his shoulders that hadn't been there moments before.

Her heart somersaulted. She imagined being caught. Wolf, watching, as they put a gun to her head. Wolf, powerless, as she was handed another hatchet. Wolf, whose mother had just been killed in front of him while he could do nothing to stop it.

Scarlet's body shook as the memory of her grandmother's death hit her like a hammer to her skull. The despair that had engulfed her. All the fury and hatred and the certainty thumping into her again and again that she should have been able to stop it.

But she couldn't have stopped it.

Just like Wolf couldn't have protected Maha. Just like he wouldn't be able to protect *her.*

She couldn't do that to him.

Scarlet scrunched up her face, choking back a violent scream. *Don't react, Scarlet,* she told herself. *Don't react.*

She lowered the gun and stepped back. She looked up at

Thorne, and though there was pain etched into his brow, too, he nodded in understanding.

Aimery's calm voice drifted toward them. "Linh Cinder will be tried and no doubt executed for her crimes against the crown. It is by the queen's mercy alone that I will spare the rest of your lives. But take note that anyone caught speaking of the cyborg and her treasonous plots or conducting any sort of rebellious activity will receive a swift punishment."

Scarlet glanced back in time to see a guard shove Wolf hard between the shoulder blades, and he and Cinder were led away.

"PRINCESS!" IKO SAID, KEEPING HER VOLUME AS LOUD AS SHE dared, which wasn't all that loud considering. "Princess, where are you?" She backtracked through the house, scouring each room for the third time. Winter was not in any cabinets or closets. She was not under Maha's bed. She was not in the tiny shower or . . .

Well, that was it. Those were the only hiding places.

It was a really small house and Winter wasn't there.

Iko returned to the living room, feeling the rumble of her fan in her chest, air escaping through the porous fibers in her back. She was still overheated from the run through the sector, dodging in and out of abandoned homes in an attempt to be discreet.

Had Winter already been found? Was she too late?

She didn't have the answers. She forced herself to pause and organize the information she *did* have.

Levana's minions were in RM-9. They had rounded up every citizen and she was relatively certain it wasn't to throw them a party.

Cinder and the others were still in that factory, as far as she knew, and she would have no way of knowing if they were safe until she saw them again.

She did not know where Princess Winter was.

She considered her options. Sneaking back to the factory to rejoin Cinder seemed like a logical next step, but she would be endangering herself by doing so. This didn't bother her so much as her fear of falling into enemy hands. Lunars didn't seem to know much about android data systems, but if they managed to dissect her programming they would find a lot of confidential information about Cinder and her strategies.

She could wait for her friends to return, safe and unharmed, but this option went against her most basic programming. She *despised* being useless.

She was still debating when she heard heavy footsteps outside the front door. Iko startled and ran into the kitchen, tucking herself beneath a counter.

The door banged open. Someone entered and Iko picked out the slight auditory differences in the footsteps. Three intruders were inside the house.

They stopped in the main room.

A male voice said, "The database confirms this as the residence of Maha Kesley."

A short silence was followed by a female voice. "I sense someone, but their energy is faint. Perhaps muffled behind a barrier of some sort."

Iko frowned. Surely they couldn't sense *her*? Cinder had always insisted that Iko could not be detected by the Lunar gift, given that she didn't produce bioelectricity.

"In my experience with the cyborg," said a third voice, also male, "she does not always react as one would expect to mind control and manipulation. Perhaps she is capable of disguising her energy as well?"

"Perhaps," said the woman, though she sounded doubtful. "Kinney, search the perimeter and neighboring homes. Jerrico, check the bedrooms."

"Yes, Mistress Pereira."

The footsteps scattered. The front door shut again.

It was a small house. Only moments had passed before the woman entered the tiny kitchen and Iko saw the fluttering sleeves of a red thaumaturge coat. She came to stand in the center of the closet-size kitchen, so close Iko could have touched her. But she didn't look down or bother to open any of the cupboards.

From her crouched position, Iko stared up at the woman's profile. Her gray hair was cut in a bob, and though she was one of the older thaumaturges Iko had seen, she was still beautiful, with sharp cheekbones and full lips. Her hands were tucked into her sleeves.

She stood still for a long moment, her brow drawn. Iko suspected she was searching for more traces of bioelectricity, and it became clear she was not about to notice Iko beside her.

Iko held still, glad she didn't have to stifle her breathing—good stars above, when she'd been trapped in the spaceship closet with Cinder and the others, the noise of their combined breaths had been *earsplitting*.

But then her fan kicked in again.

The woman glanced down and started.

Iko raised a hand in greeting. "Hello."

The thaumaturge studied her for a long, long moment, before she stammered, "A *shell*?"

"Close." Iko snatched a dish towel off the counter and lunged for the woman. A yelp escaped before Iko pressed the towel against her face, stifling the scream. The thaumaturge thrashed, but Iko held her firm against the wall, biting back her instinctive apology as she watched the woman's face pale, her eyes widen in panic.

"Just pass out," Iko said, trying to sound comforting, "and I'll let you go."

"Hey!"

She snapped her head around as a royal guard spotted them through the kitchen window. He ran for the back door and swung it open and . . .

Holy stars almighty.

She'd always thought Kai was the most attractive human specimen she'd ever seen, but this man was devastingly beautiful, with tan skin and roguish wavy hair, and he was . . .

He was . . .

Pointing a gun at her.

Iko yanked the thaumaturge in front of her at the same moment he pulled the trigger. The bullet hit the woman somewhere in her torso and she collapsed, already weak from Iko's suffocation.

Iko dropped the woman and hurled herself over the body, grappling for the guard's gun. He swung her around, knocking her back into the counter. The impact reverberated through Iko's limbs. The guard yanked the gun away and swung his opposite fist toward Iko's face. Her head snapped back and she stumbled two, three steps, before colliding with the stove. The guard cursed, shaking out his hand.

Iko was just thinking that she should have installed some martial arts programming when a second gunshot jolted through her audio receptors. She flinched and clamped her hands over her ears, dialing down the volume even though it was too late.

When her thoughts cleared, she saw the guard staring at her with an open mouth and saucer-wide eyes, his hands still gripping the gun. "What . . . what *are* you?"

She looked down. There was a hole in her chest, revealing sparking wires and frayed synthetic skin tissue. She groaned. "I just had that replaced!"

"You're . . ." The guard took a step back. "I'd heard of Earthen machines that could . . . that were . . . but you . . ." His face contorted, and Iko had spent enough time analyzing facial muscles to recognize this expression as complete, unbridled disgust.

Indignation flared inside her, probably seeping out through the new hole in her chest. "It's not polite to stare, you know!"

A form appeared in the door leading to the main room. Another guard, and this one Iko recognized as one from Levana's personal entourage. He had been part of the team that had accosted them on the rooftop in New Beijing. "What happened?" he barked, taking in the fallen thaumaturge and the pretty guard's lowered weapon and Iko.

Recognition flitted through his eyes and he grinned. "Nice find, Kinney. I guess this trip wasn't as pointless as I thought." He stepped over the thaumaturge's body.

Iko raised her fists, trying to recall all those fighting pointers Wolf had given Cinder.

"Where's the cyborg?" asked the guard.

Iko snarled at him. "Bite me."

He raised an eyebrow. "Tempt me."

"Sir Solis," said the other guard, Kinney, "she's not . . . it isn't human."

"Clearly," he drawled, glancing at the bullet hole in her chest cavity. "I guess we'll have to get creative with how we extract information from her. I mean, *it*."

He swung for her. Iko ducked and swung back, but he trapped her easily. Before her processor could catch up, he had her hands locked behind her back. Iko struggled, trying to stomp on the arch of his foot, but he evaded every attempt. He was laughing as he bound her hands and spun her back to face him.

"All that Earthen technology," he said, pulling aside the fabric of her shirt to pick at the destroyed skin fibers, "yet you're somehow still completely worthless."

Hot anger turned her vision red. "I'll show you worthless!"

Before she could show him anything, though, a banshee's scream filled the kitchen and a kitchen knife slashed toward Jerrico's shoulder. He gasped and dodged. The blade cut through his sleeve, leaving a bright red gash. Iko stumbled back.

Jerrico spun around and slammed the attacker against the wall, holding her throat in one hand while the other wrestled for her wrist, securing her knife hand.

Winter didn't let go of the knife or her wild-eyed loathing. She brought her knee up, right between his legs. Jerrico grunted and pulled her away from the wall, just to slam her back again. This time, Winter wheezed, the air pushed out of her lungs.

"Kinney, watch the android," Jerrico said through his teeth.

Iko swiveled her attention from Princess Winter to the too-handsome-to-be-such-a-jerk guard, but Kinney no longer cared about her. His face was horrified as Jerrico held the princess by her throat. "That's Princess Winter! Unhand her!"

A humorless laugh erupted from Jerrico. "I know who it is, idiot. Just like I know she's supposed to be dead."

"I heard she was dead too, but clearly she's not. Release her."

Rolling his eyes, Jerrico turned and dragged Winter off the wall. "No, she's *supposed* to be dead. The queen ordered her to be killed, but it seems like someone didn't have the stomach for it." Winter slumped forward but he dragged her back up, holding her against his chest. "What a lucky catch. I've been waiting to have you alone for years, but that annoying Sir Clay was always hanging around like a vulture on dead meat." Jerrico dragged his thumb along Winter's jaw. "Doesn't look like he's here now, does it, Princess?"

Winter's lashes fluttered. Her eyes were dazed as she looked at Kinney. "You . . ."

"Hey." Jerrico forced her chin around to face him. "You're my prize, Princess. So what reward do you think I'll get for bringing your dead body to the queen? I don't think she'll care what state it's in, and as an added bonus, I can prove that your boyfriend is a traitor after all."

Iko yanked at her hands, trying to disconnect her thumbs from their sockets and shimmy out of the cords, but she couldn't get enough leverage with her arms so tightly bound.

She was about to throw herself forward and ram into Jerrico's spine with all the force her metal skull could muster when Winter collapsed, as limp as a rag doll.

Jerrico startled, barely able to regain his hold on her. In the same moment, Winter plunged the forgotten knife into his side.

Jerrico yelled and released her. Winter stumbled out of his grip, but he grabbed her wrist and yanked her back, then backhanded her across the face. Winter fell. Her head crashed into the edge of the counter.

Iko screamed as the princess's body crumpled to the floor.

With a stream of curses, Jerrico wrapped his hand around the knife handle, but didn't pull it from the wound. His face was as red as his hair as he snarled at the princess. "What a stupid, crazy—"

He hauled back his foot to kick her, when Kinney raised his gun and fired. The shot knocked Jerrico against the wall.

Iko recoiled. No matter how many brawls and fights she found herself in, she was always stunned at how much more horrible the reality was than the net dramas. Even the death of such a despicable guard, his face contorted in disbelief as the life drained out of it, made her grimace.

The silence that followed felt like it had taken over the whole sector and Iko questioned if that last gunshot had permanently damaged her audio.

The guard was staring at the gun in his hand as if he'd never seen it before. "That's the first time I pulled the trigger myself." Inhaling deeply, he set his gun on the counter and crouched over Princess Winter. He reached back to inspect her head. His fingers came away bloodied.

"She's breathing," he said, "but she might have a concussion."

Iko's processor stumbled. "Whose side are you on?"

He looked up. His nose twitched as he took in the bullet hole again, but his gaze didn't linger on it. "We were told the princess was dead. I thought another guard killed her."

Iko arranged the folds of her shirt to cover her wound. "A guard named Jacin was ordered by the queen to kill her, but he helped her escape instead."

"Jacin Clay."

She narrowed her eyes. "Why did you help us?"

With a tense brow, Kinney eased the princess back onto the floor. There was blood everywhere. From the thaumaturge. From Jerrico. From Winter.

"I helped *her*," said Kinney, as if the distinction was important. He found the dish towel Iko had started to suffocate Mistress Pereira with and tied it around Winter's head, bandaging the wound as well as he could. When he finished, he stood and picked up the bloodied knife.

Iko stepped back.

He paused. "Do you want me to cut those cords or not?"

She searched his face, wishing she didn't feel so compelled to keep staring at it. "Yes, please?"

She turned around and he made quick work of freeing her. She half expected to find split skin fragments when she held up her hands, but the blade hadn't so much as nicked her.

"Here's what's going to happen," said Kinney, gesturing to the gun still on the counter. Iko could tell he didn't like looking at her. He kept finding reasons to look away. "I'm going to make up a report telling them you wrestled the gun away from me and killed Mistress Pereira and Sir Solis, then managed to get away. I'm not going to tell them anything about seeing the princess. They don't even have to know she's still alive." He pointed at her nose, daring to hold her gaze for longer than half a second. "And you are going to get her far away from here. Keep her hidden."

She planted her hands on her hips. "And here we were just keeping her holed up in a tiny little house in a completely random mining sector. Why didn't it ever occur to us to try and *keep her hidden*?"

Kinney's face was unreadable for a long moment before he asked, "You understand sarcasm?"

"Of course I understand sarcasm," she spat. "It's not like it's theoretical physics, is it?"

The guard's jaw worked for a moment, before he shook his head and turned away. "Just take care of her." He checked on the princess one more time and then he was gone.

Forty-Two

CINDER AND WOLF WERE TAKEN TO AN UNDERGROUND cargo port crowded with battered delivery ships and three royal pods, which explained why the arrival of their enemies hadn't set off any alarms. Cinder had only posted watch at the maglev platform.

She berated herself, hoping she would someday have a chance to learn from this mistake.

With her wrists shackled, Cinder felt like her arms might come out of their sockets. Though Wolf walked behind her, she could sense his energy—ragged and lethal. Shuddering with fear for Scarlet. Hollow and devastated over what they had done to Maha.

A royal guard was waiting. His hair was disheveled but his expression was empty.

"Report," said Aimery. He was walking with a limp and Cinder fantasized about kicking him right where the bullet had entered.

"Mistress Pereira and Sir Solis are dead."

Aimery lifted an eyebrow. He seemed nothing but curious at this unexpected statement. "How?"

"We were ambushed inside the Kesley house by an Earthen android," said the guard.

Cinder's heart leaped.

"A brawl ensued. The android was immune to mental manipulation, nor did bullets do much to affect her. She . . . *it* suffocated Mistress Pereira, after which I engaged it in hand-to-hand combat. It disarmed me and used my gun to shoot both Sir Solis and our thaumaturge. While the android was distracted, I managed to lodge my knife into its back, severing its . . . spine, of sorts. That successfully disabled it."

A headache pulsed behind Cinder's eyes, the sign of tears that would never come. First Maha, now Iko . . .

"With the threat removed, I conducted a thorough search of the rest of the house and surrounding properties," the guard continued. "I found no other accomplices."

It was the smallest relief. Winter, at least, had not been discovered, and as far as Cinder could tell, neither had Thorne or Scarlet.

Aimery stared a long time at the guard, as if he were searching for a flaw in the story. "What became of the android?"

"I found and destroyed what I believe was its power source," said the guard. "I threw what was left into the public trash compactor."

"No!" Cinder staggered, but the guard behind her hefted her back to her feet.

The guard cast her the briefest of glances, before adding, "I left the bodies behind. Shall I return for them?"

Aimery waved a careless hand. "We will send a crew."

New clomping emanated from the stairwell. Still shuddering from the news of Iko's loss, Cinder barely managed to lift her head. She glimpsed Wolf, watching her. Though his eyes were sympathetic, his jaw was tense with anger.

They had both lost someone dear to them today.

Cinder felt like she was suffocating, like her ribs were tightening around her lungs, but she pulled strength from Wolf's presence. Her fury started to build. Her sorrow became dry kindling, quick to ignite.

She found her footing again, and though she couldn't extricate herself from the guard's hold, she made herself stand tall.

The footsteps turned into a black-coated male thaumaturge and more guards.

"We have not found any more accomplices, or discerned who was firing on us from the factory windows," the new thaumaturge said. "It's possible they've retreated to a different sector. They might reattempt the insurgence elsewhere."

Aimery dismissed the thaumaturge's concern with a smile. "Let them try. We are not afraid of our own people." His dark eyes settled on Cinder. "This little rebellion is over."

Cinder lifted her head, but a low growl stole Aimery's attention away from her. He turned to Wolf, whose sharp canines were bared. He looked feral and bloodthirsty, ready to tear their captors apart.

In response, Aimery laughed. Stepping forward, he cupped Wolf's chin in his fingers and squeezed until Wolf's cheeks puckered. "Besides, how could we ever lose when we have beasts such as this at our disposal?" Releasing Wolf's chin, Aimery slapped him tenderly on the cheek. "Alpha Kesley, isn't it? I was there for the queen's tournament, the day you won your position in your pack. It seems you've been led astray by these Earthens. What shall we do about that?"

Wolf watched the thaumaturge with a hatred that could have burned the skin off his bones.

Without warning, one of his knees gave way and he knelt before Aimery. Cinder flinched, feeling the shock as if it were ricocheting through her own joints. In another moment, Wolf had bowed his head.

It was sickening to watch. All that strength. All that fury. Reduced to nothing more than a marionette. It was even more sickening because she knew how much mental strength and focus it took to force Wolf to do *anything.* She'd barely begun to master such a skill, yet Aimery showed no sign of difficulty at all.

"There's a good dog," said Aimery, patting Wolf's head. "We will take you before Her Majesty and let her decide the punishment for your betrayal. Does that suit you, Alpha Kesley?"

Wolf's voice was throaty and robotic as he answered, "Yes, Master."

"As I thought." Aimery cast his attention to the rest of his entourage. "Should there be any lingering pockets of rebellion, ensure they are swiftly stamped out. There is to be a royal wedding tomorrow, and we will not tolerate any more disturbances."

After the other thaumaturges had bowed and scattered, Aimery tucked his hands into his sleeves and turned back to Cinder. "Which only leaves the question of what shall be done with you."

She held his gaze. "You could bow before me as your true queen."

Aimery's lips curled upward. "Kill her."

It happened so fast. One of the guards whipped the gun from

his holster, held it against Cinder's forehead, released the safety, squeezed the trigger—

Cinder sucked in a final breath.

"Stop. I've changed my mind."

Just as quickly, the gun was stashed back at the guard's waist.

Cinder sagged, her head spinning from the rush of fear.

"My queen has requested the pleasure of deciding your fate herself. I think I will suggest she offer your head to Emperor Kaito as a wedding gift."

"Thaumaturge Park?"

He turned to the red-coated woman who had spoken. She had her palm on the side paneling of a small podship.

"This is a royal pod," she said, "and it looks to have arrived recently." She held up her hand. "Hardly any dust. Odd for it to be way out here."

Aimery made a disinterested sound. "I am not surprised there are thieves about, but it could help us locate the missing rebels. Run a search on its tracking number and see what you find."

He gestured to some of the guards. Cinder and Wolf were marched into his ship and forced onto separate benches. No words were spoken as the engines started to rumble.

Within moments, they were heading back toward Artemisia.

Aimery kept giving orders, something about medical care and bullet wounds, designating a new captain of the guard and informing the queen of casualties and prisoners. Cinder's thoughts became muddled and she found herself staring at the profile of the guard who had killed Iko. *"Disabled it,"* he'd said. Thrown it into a *trash compactor.*

The visions rolled through her head again and again. A knife ripping through Iko's spine. Maha's broken fingers. The sector residents kneeling at Aimery's feet.

Her hatred warmed. Simmered at first, low in her gut. But by the time Artemisia came into view, she was boiling.

The ship dropped into Artemisia's underground port. The ramp was lowered and a guard hauled her up with a squeeze so painful she had to bite back a cry of pain. Wolf's heavy steps labored behind her.

She was greeted with a slew of new threats. A dozen guards, their bioelectricity as malleable as factory-new personality chips, and three more thaumaturges, whose mental strength always had a certain iron rigidity to it.

Her finger twitched and she wondered how quickly she could have a bullet loaded in her finger and how long it would take to kill them all. She was back in Artemisia. If she escaped, she could go rogue—a lone assassin hunting down the queen.

It was just a fantasy. Her hands were still bound.

She squeezed her cyborg hand into a useless fist instead.

"Thaumaturge Park?"

Cinder peered at the guard who had killed Iko.

"Sir Kinney."

"Permission to seek immediate medical attention?"

Aimery's attention darted down to the blood on his uniform. There was a lot of it, though Cinder couldn't tell where, exactly, he'd been hurt. "Fine," he said. "Report back as soon as you are cleared for service."

The guard fisted a hand against his chest, then paced off in the opposite direction.

Cinder and Wolf were shoved away from the docks and into a maze of corridors. Not knowing what else to do, Cinder tried to focus on where they were taking her. She counted her steps, creating a rudimentary map in her head and piecing it together with what she knew of the queen's palace.

They were led to an elevator bank, flanked by more guards. There was a pause in which Aimery conversed with another thaumaturge, and though Cinder adjusted her audio interface, she could only pick up a few words—*alpha* and *soldier* at first. Then *insurgence* and *RM-9* and *cyborg*.

Aimery gestured and they started pulling Wolf away, down a separate corridor.

"Wait," said Cinder, panic flooding her veins. "Where are you taking him?"

Wolf growled and strained against his captors, but any fight was tempered beneath the mind control.

"Wolf! *No!*" Cinder stumbled forward, but arms held her back. The bindings burned against her wrists. "*Wolf!*"

It was for nothing. They turned a corner and Wolf was gone, leaving Cinder panting and shaking. She felt wetness on her right wrist where the cords had cut into the skin. She wasn't so naïve to think she and Wolf could have made a successful stand against their enemies, but she hadn't imagined being parted from him so soon. She might never see him again. She might never see *any* of them again.

As she was forced into the elevator, it occurred to Cinder that, for the first time since this had all begun, she was alone.

"I'm sorry we aren't able to give you a private tour," said Aimery, "but we're rather preoccupied with wedding preparations. I'm sure you understand."

The elevator doors shut and they began to descend. And descend. Cinder felt like she was being taken to her tomb.

When the doors opened again, she was prodded forward with a jab in her back. She was taken through a dim corridor, with rough walls and the smell of stale air and urine and bodies. Her nose wrinkled in disgust.

"I hope you'll find your accommodations acceptable for such a *distinguished* guest as yourself," Aimery continued, as if the scent didn't bother him. "I understand you're already accustomed to prison cells."

"I wouldn't say that," said Cinder. "The last one could only hold me for a day."

"This one will be much more suited to you, I'm sure."

This prison of rocks and caves was nothing like the modern structure in New Beijing. This was dreary and suffocating, and worst of all, Cinder had no blueprint for it. She had no accurate map, no plan, no means of judging her location in relation to ... well, anything.

They paused and there was the jangling of keys and the creak of ancient metal hinges. An old-fashioned padlock. How quaint.

If she could reach it from within the cell, she could have that picked in under thirty seconds.

The thought offered a twitch of hope, at least.

As the door opened, the smell intensified. Her lungs tried to expel the air as soon as they took it in.

"You will remain here until Her Majesty the Queen has time to see to your trial and execution," said Aimery.

"Can't wait," Cinder muttered.

"Of course, you'll want to use the time to get reacquainted."

"Reacquainted?"

A guard cut away the bindings on her wrists and shoved her forward. Her shoulder hit the edge of the iron door as she stumbled into the cell, catching herself on a rough wall.

Someone whimpered and she froze. She wasn't alone.

"Do enjoy your stay ... *Princess.*"

The door slammed shut, the noise of it vibrating through Cinder's bones. The cell was small with a high, barred window in the iron door that allowed just enough light from the hallway that she could make out a bucket on the floor. The source of the rank smell.

Two people were huddled together in the far corner.

Cinder gaped at them, willing her eyes to adjust. She turned on the built-in flashlight in her hand. The two figures shuddered and cowered behind their arms.

Recognition hit her like a right hook and she fell against the wall.

Adri.

Pearl.

"You can't be serious."

Her stepmother and stepsister were quaking with fear and staring up at her with wide eyes. Cinder couldn't begin to imagine why they were here—what Levana wanted with them.

Then it hit her.

She would be stuck here, with them, until her execution.

She dragged a hand down her face, hating Levana so very, very much.

Forty-Three

IN WINTER'S DREAM, SHE WAS STANDING IN THE KITCHEN OF a little farmhouse on Earth, or what her imagination thought a farmhouse on Earth must be like. She knew it was Scarlet's home, though she'd never been there. She stood at a sink overflowing with dirty dishes. It was vital that she get them all clean before everyone came home, but every time she lifted a plate from the suds it shattered in her hands. Her fingers were bleeding from all the shards, turning the bubbles red.

When the seventh plate cracked in her hands, she stepped back from the sink with an overwhelming sense of failure. Why could she never do anything right? Even this simple task turned to disaster at her touch.

She fell to her knees and began to weep. The blood and soap puddled in her lap.

A shadow fell across her and she looked up. Her stepmother stood in the doorway, acres of fields and Earth's blue, blue sky laid out behind her. She was holding a bejeweled comb in her hand, and though she was beautiful, her smile was cruel.

"They love you," said Levana, as if they'd been in the middle of a conversation. She came into the kitchen. The hem of her regal gown trailed through the soapy water on the floor. "They protect you. And what have you ever done to deserve that?"

"They love me," Winter agreed, though she wasn't sure who they were talking about. The people of Luna? Cinder and her allies? Jacin?

"And they will all pay the price for their adoration." Coming around behind her, Levana began brushing the comb through Winter's curls. The touch was gentle. Motherly, even. Winter wanted to weep with longing—how she had yearned for a mother's touch—but there was fear in her too. Levana had never been so kind. "They will come to know all your weaknesses. They will learn how flawed you truly are. Then they will see how you never deserved any of this."

A sharp pain stitched into her skull as one of the comb's tines dug into Winter's scalp. She gasped. Her head started to throb.

A growl drew her attention back to the door. Ryu was standing with his paws spread in defense, his teeth bared.

Levana stopped brushing. "And what do *you* care? She betrayed you too. She allowed that guard to sacrifice your life for hers. You cannot ignore her selfishness."

Ryu prowled closer. His yellow eyes flashed.

Levana dropped the comb and stepped back. "You are an animal. A killer. A *predator*. What do you know of loyalty or love?"

Ryu hushed and lowered his head as if chastised. Winter's heart opened to him. She could tell he missed her. He wanted to play fetch, not be berated by the queen's cruel words.

Winter raised her hand to her stinging scalp. Her hair was damp. She looked down at the fallen comb and saw that the pool of dishwater had become thick with blood.

"You are wrong," she said, turning her face up to the queen.

"*You* are the killer. You are the predator. You know nothing of loyalty or love." She held her hand out to Ryu, who sniffed it, before settling his warm head down on her knee. "We may be animals, but we will never again live in your cage."

WHEN SHE OPENED HER EYES, THE FARMHOUSE WAS GONE, replaced with shabby walls and furniture and window curtains covered in regolith dust. Her eyelids flickered as she tried to ward off the heavy drowsiness and a throbbing headache. She could still smell the pool of blood, and her scalp still ached from where the comb had punctured it.

No, from where she had hit the corner of the table.

Someone had laid her out on the sofa. Her feet dangled off the edge.

"Hey, crazy."

Winter pushed her hair out of her face and found a towel wrapped around her head. She looked up at Scarlet, who had brought a dining chair into the front room and was sitting on it backward with her arms settled on its back. She was wearing her hooded sweatshirt again. Most of the stains were gone but it still looked worn and ragged. So did she, actually. Her eyes were rimmed with red, her face blotchy and flushed. Her usual ferocity had dulled to bitter exhaustion.

"Iko told us what happened," she said, her voice withered and cracked. "I'm sorry I wasn't here, but I'm glad she was."

Winter sat up. Iko sat cross-legged on the floor, picking at a thread of skin fiber that had been torn open in her chest. Thorne was standing with his back against the main door. He was wearing the partial uniform of a Lunar guard and she had to look twice to be sure it was him. She listened, but the house was otherwise silent.

Winter felt a flush of dread. "Where are the others?"

"The sector was attacked," said Thorne. "They took Wolf and Cinder and they . . . they killed Maha."

Scarlet wrapped her arms tighter around the back of the chair. "We can't stay here. We moved the bodies of that guard and thaumaturge into the back bedroom, but I bet someone will come for them."

"The guard who helped us," said Iko, "told me to take Her Highness into hiding. I know he meant to take her out of this sector, but where else can we go? I've been reviewing the maps of Luna and the only places that seem like they might offer more security are underground. At least we would be away from people, and surveillance isn't as strict in the tunnels and mines, but it doesn't seem like a perfect solution, either."

"There is no perfect solution," said Winter, sinking against the sofa's lumpy cushion. "The queen will find me anywhere I go. She finds me even in my dreams."

"You're not the only one having nightmares," Thorne muttered. "But there's still a chance that a lot of angry civilians are going to show up in Artemisia four days from now, demanding a new regime. Is there any chance Cinder will still be alive by then?"

They traded glances, but there was not much optimism.

"Official executions take place in Artemisia Palace," said Winter. "That's where they'll take her."

"Why not just kill her here?" asked Scarlet. "Why go through the trouble?"

Thorne shook his head. "Levana wants to execute her in a way that will show the futility of this uprising."

"You think she plans on broadcasting it?" said Iko.

"I guarantee she does," said Winter. "The queen is fond of public executions. They are an effective way to break the will of any citizens who might be feeling rebellious."

Thorne rubbed his brow. "She'll kill her soon, then. Tonight, maybe, or tomorrow. Nothing like an execution on your wedding day."

Winter drew her knees to her chest, squeezing them tight. The day had started so hopeful for her companions. The broadcast had gone as planned, the people had been answering her call. But now it was over. Levana was still the queen, dear Selene would soon be dead, and Jacin too, if he wasn't already.

"Stop it."

She lifted her head—not so much at Thorne's command, but at the hardened tone beneath it. Scarlet and Iko, too, looked up.

"Stop acting discouraged, all of you. We don't have time for it."

"You are not discouraged?" Winter asked.

"It's not in my vocabulary." Thorne pushed himself off the door. "Iko, did we break into that guardhouse and broadcast Cinder's message across all of Luna?"

"Yes, Captain."

"And, Scarlet, did I rescue you and Wolf when the entire city of Paris was under siege?"

She raised an eyebrow at him. "Actually, I'm pretty sure Cinder—"

"Yes, I did." He pointed at Iko. "Did I rescue you and Cinder from that prison cell and fly us all to safety aboard the Rampion?"

"Well, at the time, I wasn't exactly—"

"Aces, Iko, just answer the question."

Scarlet drummed her fingers. "What's your point?"

"My point is that I am going to figure this out, like I always do. First, we're going to find a way to get into Artemisia. We're going to find Cress and rescue Cinder and Wolf. We're going to over-throw Levana, and by the stars above, we are going to make Cin-der a queen so she can pay us a lot of money from her royal coffers and we can all retire very rich and *very alive*, got it?"

Winter started to clap. "Brilliant speech. Such gumption and bravado."

"And yet strangely lacking in any sort of actual strategy," said Scarlet.

"Oh, good, I'm glad you noticed that too," said Iko. "I was wor-ried my processor might be glitching." She felt for the back of her head.

"I'm working on that part," Thorne growled. "For now, we need to get out of this sector. I'll think better once I'm not worried about more thaumaturges surrounding us. Besides, if we're going by maglev tunnel, it's a long walk back to Artemisia."

"One flaw in this not-really-a-plan?" said Scarlet, jutting her thumb toward Winter. "We're not taking *her* back there. That's the opposite of keeping her hidden."

Winter untied the towel around her head. There was a spot of blood, but not much. She wondered if her headache would ever ease. "You're right. I will go underground, as Iko suggested."

"You're not a mole," said Scarlet. "You can't just *go under-ground*. Where will you go? What will you do? Are there people down there? Do you need to take supplies? What if—"

"Ryu was in my dream too." Winter folded the towel on her knee. "He was trying to protect me from the queen. I think he's forgiven me for what happened."

Scarlet guffawed, a harsh and delirious sound. "Are you even listening? Don't you get it? Cinder and Wolf are gone! Levana has them. She's going to torture them and kill them and . . ." Sobbing, Scarlet lowered her head between her trembling shoulders. "No one cares about your stupid dreams and your stupid delusions. They're *gone.*" She wiped her nose with the back of her hand. She was not pretty when she cried, and Winter liked this about her.

Tipping forward, she rested her hand on Scarlet's shoulder. Scarlet didn't shake her away.

"I do understand," she said. "It would not be safe for me to return to Artemisia, but that doesn't mean I can't help Selene and my people. I, too, have a not-really-a-plan."

Scarlet peered up at her with bloodshot eyes. "I'm afraid to ask."

"Thorne and Iko will go to Artemisia and try to save Selene and Wolf and Jacin and Cress, while you and I disappear underground, into the lava tubes and the shadows, and there we shall raise an army of our own."

"Oh, we're going to go underground and raise *an army*, are we?" Scarlet sniffed and threw her hands into the air. "Why do I even bother talking to you? You are not helping. You are the capital *U* of *Unhelpful.*"

"I am serious. There are killers and there are animals and there are predators yearning to be free. You know this, Scarletfriend. You have already freed one." Winter stood and placed a hand on the wall for balance, then skirted around the small table.

Scarlet rolled her eyes, but it was Iko who spoke. "The barracks," she said. "The barracks where Levana keeps her soldiers are in the lava tubes."

Thorne's gaze swiveled from Iko to Winter. "Her soldiers? You mean, her *mutant wolf* soldiers? Are you insane?"

Winter started to giggle. "I might as well be," she said, placing a hand on Thorne's cheek. "For everyone tells me so."

Forty-Four

"THE QUEEN'S ON EDGE," JACIN SAID AS HE STRAPPED HIS GUN holster on over his uniform. "She's keeping quiet about it, trying to pretend like nothing's happening so the families won't panic. But you can tell something's changed."

Cross-legged on the cot, Cress was cradling her portscreen against her chest. The temptation grew by the hour to send a comm to Thorne and the others. Her curiosity was killing her, and the separation from them had left her anxious and lonely. But she wouldn't risk the signal being traced. She wouldn't put them in any more danger than they already were—or herself, for that matter.

Still. Being so disconnected was agony.

"You don't know if the video played?" she asked.

Jacin shrugged and went through a process of checking the gun's ammunition and safety with practiced movements. He tucked it into the holster.

"I know the queen recorded an impromptu broadcast of her own. I guess she dragged the emperor out for it too, but it didn't broadcast in Artemisia, so I don't know what it said. It could have just been wedding announcement garbage."

Cress licked her lips. "If I could have access to the security center again, I could find out—"

"No."

She glared at him, and was met with a finger jutting toward her nose. "We already risked enough. You're staying here." Turning away, he adjusted his shoulder armor, looking once again like the queen's loyal servant. "Long shift tonight—I'm on duty for the entire wedding and celebratory feast. But most of us are, so it should be quiet around here at least."

Cress sighed. There had been a time when the quiet and solitude would have been comforting. That was what she'd been accustomed to aboard the satellite, after all. But now it made her feel even more like a prisoner.

"Bye," she muttered, before adding half-jokingly, "Bring me back some cake."

Jacin paused with his hand on the door. His face softened. "I'll do my best."

He pulled open the door, and froze.

Cress's heart leaped into her throat.

Another guard stood in the hall, his hand raised to knock. His attention flitted from Jacin to Cress.

Recovering faster than Cress, Jacin crossed his arms and leaned against the doorjamb, blocking the guard's view of her. "What do you want?"

"Who's she?" the guard asked.

"That's *my* business."

"Oh, please." The guard shoved aside Jacin's arm, forcing his way into the small room. Cress pushed her back against the wall, squeezing the portscreen so hard she heard the plastic creak in protest. "Lots of guards might take mistresses, but not you."

The door shut behind him.

Cress was watching the stranger when she heard the click of a gun's safety releasing.

The guard froze, his back to Jacin. His gaze turned surprised as he raised both hands to the side of his head.

"Who said anything about a mistress?" Jacin growled.

Cress swallowed. This guard was unfamiliar, with dark eyes and wavy hair cut above his ears. She didn't remember him from the ambush at the docks, but she couldn't be sure.

"Not the welcome I was expecting," said the guard.

Jacin kept the gun aimed at his back. "I don't like people knowing my business." His face was calm. So calm it terrified Cress almost as much as a stranger's presence. "Kinney, isn't it?"

"That's right."

"I never got to thank you for vouching for me at the trial."

"Don't mention it."

"Take his weapons."

It was a long moment before Cress realized Jacin was talking to her. She gasped and scrambled off the bed. The guard, Kinney, didn't move as she took his gun and knife and backed away again, glad to set the weapons down.

"I'd rather not kill you," said Jacin, "but you're going to have to give me a really good reason not to."

Kinney's eyebrow twitched. He was looking at Cress again. He seemed curious, but not as afraid as he should have been. "I saved your life."

"Covered that already."

"How about the sound from the gun will bring every guard running?"

"Most are already on duty. I'll take the risk."

Cress thought she detected a smile, but then Kinney turned around to face Jacin. "Then how about because I saved Princess Winter's life?"

Jacin's eyes narrowed.

"There are rumors of rebellion in the outer sectors. I just got back from a raid on RM-9, and while searching the house of a known rebel sympathizer, I was pretty shocked to run into none other than the princess herself. I believed her dead just like everyone else." He cocked his head. "It must kill you, to have everyone thinking you killed her out of some petty jealousy. I admit, I believed it. I've been half-tempted to kill you myself, for retribution, and I know I'm not the only one."

A muscle twitched in Jacin's jaw.

"Sorry I misjudged you." Kinney lowered his arms and hooked his thumbs over his belt. Jacin didn't move. "I know you care for her more than any of us."

When the silence stretched painfully thin between them, Cress asked, "So . . . she's alive?"

Kinney glanced back at her and nodded. "I told her to go into hiding. As far as I know, everyone else still thinks she's dead."

Jacin sounded like he had sand in his throat when he asked, "Did she look all right?"

Kinney's lips curved with amusement. "I'd say she looked a lot better than just all right, but then you'd probably shoot me after all."

Frowning, Jacin lowered his gun, but didn't put it away. "So you saw her. That doesn't explain how you saved her life."

"Jerrico was there too. I guess he knew about the queen ordering her to be killed. He wanted to kill her and drag her body back here, so I shot him."

Though he tried to sound nonchalant about it, Cress heard his tone waver just a bit.

"Did you kill him?" Jacin asked.

"Yes."

They stood in a face-off for a long time before Jacin said, "I hated that man."

"Me too."

Jacin's muscles slowly began to unwind, though his expression was still suspicious. "Thanks for telling me. I'm . . . I've been worried about her."

"That's not why I'm here. I came to warn you. We saw a royal podship out there that shouldn't have been there, and I'm willing to bet it'll be traced back to you. If I figured it out, she will too. The queen might think Winter is dead now, but she's going to find out the truth soon enough." He paused. "Who did she threaten to kill if you didn't do it?"

Jacin gulped. "No one."

"Yeah, right." Kinney glanced at his weapons lying beside Cress but didn't move to pick them up. "She ordered my little sister to be killed once, after I released a maid who'd stolen a pair of the queen's earrings."

Cress's eyes widened. Jacin, however, looked unsurprised.

"Well, whoever it was," Kinney continued, "you're both going to end up dead if you don't stop wasting time and get the hell out of here before Levana finds out you lied to her." He turned to Cress. "Can I have my weapons back now? I have about five minutes to report for duty."

After a hesitation, Jacin nodded and put his own gun away. He was still frowning as Kinney reclaimed his gun and knife. "Why are you risking your neck for me . . . again?"

"It's what the princess would want." Kinney crossed back to

the door, careful not to bump into Jacin as he passed him. "Her Highness persuaded the queen to give my sister the maid's position instead of killing her, so I owe her a lot." He tipped his head toward Cress. "Whoever you are, I never saw you."

Jacin didn't try to stop him as he slipped out the door.

Cress's heart was still hammering. "I'm glad you didn't kill him," she whispered.

"I'm undecided, myself." His gaze slid around the room, evaluating what, Cress couldn't tell. "We'll wait until the wing is mostly cleared, but then it's time to leave."

She clutched the portscreen, both excited and terrified to be leaving her prison, and her sanctuary.

"Jacin, *did* Levana threaten to hurt someone, if you didn't kill Winter?"

"Of course she did. That's how she operates."

Her heart cracked, for him, for Winter, for victims she didn't even know. "Who?"

He turned away and started rummaging through a drawer, but she could tell the action was just to occupy himself. "No one," he said. "No one important."

Forty-Five

"**DON'T THEY HAVE ANY NEWSFEEDS ON THIS STAR-FORSAKEN** rock?" Kai grumbled, sliding his fingers along the base of the holograph, Luna's version of the ever-present netscreen.

"We are in a dictatorship, Your Majesty," said Torin, his arms folded as he stared out the window, toward the sparkling lake below. "Do you believe the newsfeeds would be reliable even if they had them?"

Ignoring him, Kai swiped his finger again.

He had sent a message to the queen that morning that the wedding would, unfortunately, have to be postponed if he wasn't allowed to meet with his adviser prior to the ceremony, as his adviser was the one most educated on the vows and customs that would cement the wedding as a recognized political union.

Somewhat to his surprise, she assented.

It was a relief to see Torin again and assure himself that his adviser hadn't been harmed, but that relief was matched with his growing frustration and restlessness. The queen's broadcasting networks were his newest cause for complaint. They seemed to contain a whole lot of mindless drivel and nothing useful at all.

"I want to know what's going on out there," he said, flipping off the holograph. "I know it's started. I know Cinder's done something."

Torin shrugged, somewhat apologetically. "I have no more answers than you do."

"I know. I don't expect you to. It's just so frustrating to be stuck here when she's—when they're all out there! Doing... whatever it is they're doing!" He joined Torin at the window and clawed a hand into his hair. "How can the people here stand to be cut off from the rest of the country? Without any media, they have no way of knowing what's happening in the other sectors. Doesn't it drive them crazy?"

"I would think not," said Torin. "Look at the splendor they are able to enjoy, thanks to the labor of the outer sectors. Do you think the people here want their illusion of paradise destroyed by witnessing the squalor in the rest of the country?"

Kai scowled. He'd known that already, and he regretted how naïve his question sounded. But he couldn't understand it. He still remembered the day Nainsi told him the statistics of poverty and homelessness in the Commonwealth, back when he was ten years old. Nainsi had impressed upon him how *good* the numbers were. How, even though the numbers had crept upward since the spread of letumosis, they still remained lower than they had been in the decades following World War IV. Even still, Kai had gone a week of near-sleepless nights, thinking of all those people, *his* people, who had nowhere to sleep and no food to eat, while he was so comfortable and cared for in his palace. He had even written up a proposal about how they could lease out parts of the palace to the citizens with the most need, offering up half of his own private quarters if that would help, but while his father had promised to read the proposal, Kai doubted he'd ever taken it seriously.

He could recognize, now, how childish the proposal had been, but he still couldn't imagine not wanting to do anything to help the citizens of the Commonwealth, just like he couldn't imagine how the members of Levana's court could lack compassion for the people who had built the paradise they got to enjoy.

"Your face has healed well," said Torin. "I'm sure it will be hardly noticeable in the wedding photos."

It took Kai a moment to comprehend him. "Oh—right." Reaching up, he felt for his cheek, where Wolf had punched him. It was only sore to the touch now, and without any mirrors to see himself, he'd forgotten all about it.

"I guess that ruse didn't do me much good," he muttered, shoving his hands into his pockets.

"It was a valiant effort, nevertheless," said Torin. "Speaking of your time away, have you seen the report from the American military that came through this morning?"

He spun around. "Of course not—she took my portscreen."

Torin grimaced sympathetically. "Right. I will leave you with mine."

"Thank you, Torin. What report?"

"It appears they've found your friends' ship orbiting in space, abandoned. They're towing it back to the Republic now to begin searching it for evidence to be used against your kidnappers. Once they're found, of course."

Kai rubbed the back of his neck. "They knew it would happen, but still, Thorne won't be happy when he finds out."

"It *was* a stolen ship. Regardless of whose side he's on now, the man is a thief and a deserter. I find it difficult to be sympathetic to his loss."

Kai couldn't keep down a wry smile. "I don't disagree, but when we see Thorne again, maybe I should be the one to break this news to him."

He let his gaze travel out to the edge of the lake, where the water met with the encompassing dome. It looked like the end of the world out there. Civilization inside a perfect capsule, all sparkling and pristine. Beyond it, nothing but wasteland. On the horizon he could see the edge of another dome and he wondered which it was.

He had chosen his words carefully. *When* they saw Thorne again, not *if*. Because that's how he had to think about all of his allies, his friends. That's how he had to think about Cinder if he was going to make it through this. He wondered where she was right now, how far she'd gone. Was she safe?

A tap at the door startled Kai, but the surprise was suffused with dread. "So it begins," he muttered. "Enter."

It wasn't a wedding stylist, though, but one of his own guards in the doorway, holding a small package wrapped in strips of colored velvet. "Pardon the interruption. This was delivered by a servant as a wedding gift from Her Majesty the Queen. We've tested it for chemicals or explosives and have deemed it safe to open." He held the package toward Kai.

"You mean she doesn't intend to blow me up before the ceremony?" said Kai, taking the box. "How disappointing."

The guard looked like he wanted to crack a smile, but he resisted. Bowing again, he retreated into the corridor.

Kai made quick work of the wrappings, eager to be done with whatever new torment Levana had devised for him. He was picturing a very tiny ball and chain as he lifted the box's lid.

He froze. The blood drained from his head, seeping all the way down to his feet.

A cyborg finger was settled onto a bed of white velvet. Grease was smudged into the knuckle joints and disconnected wires jutted out one side.

His stomach twisted.

"She has Cinder," he said, passing the box to Torin. Dazed, he paced back to the windows, his thoughts muddled with denial. This *gift* answered so many of his questions, and he realized that Torin was right.

Sometimes, it was better to be ignorant.

IT HAD BEEN AGES SINCE LEVANA COULD REMEMBER FEELING such contentment.

Her bothersome niece was once again in captivity and, soon, would be no more bother at all.

Her annoying stepdaughter was dead and she would never again have to listen to her mutterings or indulge her inane wishes.

In mere hours, she would be married to the emperor of the Eastern Commonwealth, and in a few short days she would be given a crown and the title of empress. It would not be long before all of Earth was hers. Resources. Land. A place for her people to enjoy the beauty and luxuries Earthens took for granted.

She imagined the history texts centuries from now, telling the story of the Lunar queen who had conquered the blue planet and begun a new era. An era ruled by those most worthy.

She hardly felt the weight of the jewels that were clipped to her gown's sleeves and draped across her collar. She hardly noticed the servants as they shuffled around her, adjusting the skirt of her wedding dress, flouncing the crinoline, making final adjustments to the bodice's fit.

Without a mirror, Levana knew she was beautiful. She was the most beautiful queen Luna had ever known, and Kaito was lucky to have such a bride.

She was smiling to herself when she finally dismissed the servants.

"Stunning, My Queen."

She turned to see Aimery in the doorway.

"What liberties you take to enter without announcing yourself," said Levana, though there was little venom to her tone. "I am preparing for my wedding ceremony. What do you want?"

"I do not wish to be a distraction. I understand this is a momentous occasion, for all of us. But I wanted to put your mind at ease regarding tonight's . . . special guest. The cyborg will be brought to the throne room during the feast as requested. Everything is arranged."

"I am happy to hear it. What a surprise her presence shall be for my new husband." She rubbed her thumb over the base of her ring finger as she spoke, feeling the worn stone band. It was a constant memory of her first husband, Winter's father. He would always be her only love, and she had sworn long ago that this ring would never be removed from her finger.

Concealing it was as much second nature to her now as the glamour of her red lips and serene voice.

"There is one other bit of news I must bring to your attention," said Aimery, "though it remains under investigation, and I do not wish for it to upset you so near your wedding hour."

"As long as the cyborg is in our custody," Levana said around a smile, "nothing more can upset me."

"I am glad to hear it, My Queen. For we discovered something suspicious on our visit to the mining sector. There was a royal podship docked there and upon further inspection we've found the ship was chartered to none other than Sir Jacin Clay."

Levana turned to give Aimery her full attention. "Go on."

"We have documentation of this ship leaving Artemisia forty-seven minutes after the death of Princess Winter. Of course, Sir Clay was still here, in the palace, at that time, and we do not know who was piloting it. It also seems suspicious that, no matter who was aboard that ship, they would find themselves in the same sector as the cyborg and her companions."

Though Aimery's expression was neutral, it was easy to discern his suspicions.

"We have video footage of Winter's death, do we not?"

"We do, My Queen. However, as you might recall, we were experiencing technical difficulties that day, with sporadic power outages affecting surveillance throughout the palace. Allow me."

He approached the netscreen Levana had long ago commissioned to be put into the stunning frame that had once housed her sister's mirror, before all mirrors were destroyed. A moment later, Levana was watching Jacin and Winter inside the menagerie. The wolf prowled behind them. Winter kissed the guard with such passion it made Levana snarl. Then Jacin raised the knife and plunged it into her back. Winter's body slumped and he lowered her to the ground with all the gentleness of a man in love. Blood began to pool beneath her.

The video ended.

She raised an eyebrow. "She is dead, then."

"Perhaps. But I have concerns that this death might have been staged. You see, this is where the video ends—we have no footage of Jacin removing the body or killing the wolf to cover his tracks, as he claims to have done. It does seem a convenient time for this camera, in particular, to have stopped functioning."

Levana inhaled sharply. "I see. Detain Sir Clay in a holding cell for now. I will question him after tonight's feast."

"I had already taken the liberty of having the guard sent for, Your Majesty, and I'm afraid he has gone missing."

This, more than anything, gave her pause. "Missing?"

"He was to report for duty two hours ago, but he has not been seen. Of those guards we have spoken to, no one claims to have seen him since he finished last night's shift."

Levana's gaze unfocused as she glanced out her windows, toward her beautiful lake, her beautiful city.

Jacin had run.

Only guilty men run.

It had to mean that Winter was alive.

Her teeth clenched with loathing—not only for her stepdaughter's continued existence, but at the audacity of a weak-minded guard to play her for a fool. But she forced herself to breathe and let the hatred ebb from her knotted shoulders.

"No matter," she said. "The princess is dead so long as the people believe she is dead. This changes nothing. I have much more important matters to tend to."

"Of course."

"Should Jacin Clay be found, he is to be killed on sight. Any word of the princess and I wish to be informed immediately."

Aimery bowed. "Yes, My Queen. I will leave you to your preparations. Congratulations on your coming happiness."

Levana's smile was not forced. *Her coming happiness.* She liked the sound of that very much.

Aimery turned to go.

Levana gasped. "Wait, one more thing."

Aimery paused.

"Jacin Clay's parents are to be executed for treason—publicly, as a reminder that such betrayals will not be tolerated. Have the guards in their sector do it now, so their deaths won't taint tonight's wedding broadcast." She smoothed the front of her bodice. "Jacin will know that the fault of their deaths lies with him."

Forty-Six

KAI WASN'T SURE HOW HE'D ENDED UP DRESSED LIKE A groom again. He said nothing as the stylists fidgeted with his hair and clothes. He couldn't have picked any of them out of a lineup once they'd gone.

Cinder was dead. That, or Levana was keeping her somewhere. He didn't know which would be worse.

Cinder.

Her name whispered over and over in his thoughts, each time a fresh thorn in his flesh.

Brave, determined Cinder. Smart, resourceful, sarcastic Cinder.

He refused to believe that she was dead. What did a finger indicate, really? He trudged through every faint possibility. It was a fake finger Levana had crafted to torment him. Or Cinder had lost it in a battle but the rest of her had gotten away. Or . . . surely there must be some other explanation. She couldn't be dead.

Not *Cinder.*

His brain was muddled, like the afternoon had been spent in a hazy dream. A hazy *nightmare.*

Whether or not the finger meant what he feared it meant, he would soon be married to Levana. After everything—all their planning, all their hopes. It was all ending this way, just as Levana had intended from the start.

"What am I doing?" he asked when Torin returned from changing into his own dress clothes.

Unless it was a thaumaturge using a glamour to impersonate Torin . . .

He slammed shut his eyes.

He *hated* it here.

Torin sighed and came to stand beside him. Earth was hanging above them—almost full amid the star-filled sky.

"You are stopping a war," said his adviser, "and obtaining an antidote."

Kai had used those same arguments so many times they'd begun to lose their meaning. "It wasn't supposed to go this way. I'd thought . . . I'd really thought she stood a chance."

A hand landed on his shoulder. Comforting as it could be.

"You have not married her yet, Your Majesty. You can still say no."

A wry laugh escaped him. "With us all trapped here? She would slaughter us."

Coming here had been a mistake. In the end, his good intentions didn't matter. He had failed.

A thaumaturge entered, and though he was flanked by two of Kai's personal guards, everyone in the room knew the guards were merely ornamentation.

"I am to escort you to the grand ballroom," said the thaumaturge. "The ceremony is about to begin."

Kai wiped his hands down the front of his silk shirt. Rather than damp and clammy, they were dry. Bone dry and freezing cold. "All right," he said. "I'm ready."

Torin stayed at his side as long as he could, following their entourage through the palace's vast corridors until he was forced to go join the rest of the Commonwealth representatives and guests. It happened in a blur, and though Kai felt as if he were walking with iron shoes on his feet, they reached the ballroom too quickly.

He sucked in a breath, his disbelief interrupted by a jolt of panic.

When they had gone over the rehearsal the day before, it had felt like a joke. Like he was playing a game, and for once, he had the winning hand. But now, as the thaumaturge gestured for him to take his place at the altar set up at the front of the grand ballroom, and he caught sight of the hundreds of exotically dressed Lunars seated before him, it all came crumbling down.

This wasn't a game at all.

Prime Minister Kamin stood on the dais behind an ornate gold-and-black altar that was crowned with hundreds of small glowing orbs. She caught Kai's eye as he made his way onto the platform. Her expression was sympathetic. Kai wondered if she realized that Levana intended to conquer her country too, once her grasp was firm around the Commonwealth. Levana planned to conquer them all.

Inhale. Exhale. He turned away without returning Kamin's almost smile.

The crowd was larger than he'd imagined—easily a thousand people gathered in their evening finest. The contrast between the Earthens' muted colors and the Lunars' sparkles and fluorescents was laughable. An aisle stretched down the middle of the ballroom, defined by candelabras topped with more pale orbs, their light flickering like little flames. The aisle runner was black and set with rhinestones in mimicry of the night sky. Or, the always sky, as it was here on Luna.

A hush fell over the room, and Kai could tell it was not a normal hush. It was too controlled, too flawless.

His heart pounded, uncontrolled in its cage. This was the moment he'd been dreading, the fate he'd fought against for so long. No one was going to interfere. He was alone and rooted to the floor.

At the far back of the room, the massive doors opened, chorused with a fanfare of horns. At the end of the aisle, two shadows emerged—a man and a woman in militaristic uniforms carrying the flags of Luna and the Eastern Commonwealth. After they parted, setting the flags into stands on either side of the altar, a series of Lunar guards marched into the room, fully armed and synchronized. They, too, spread out when they reached the altar, like a protective wall around the dais.

Next down the aisle were six thaumaturges dressed in black, walking in pairs, graceful as black swans. They were followed by two in red, and finally Head Thaumaturge Aimery Park, all in white.

A voice dropped down from some hidden speakers. "All rise for Her Royal Majesty, Queen Levana Blackburn of Luna."

The people rose.

Kai clasped his shaking hands behind his back.

She appeared as a silhouette first in the lights of the doors, a perfect hourglass dropping off to a full billowing skirt that flowed behind her. She walked with her head high, gliding toward the altar. The dress was scarlet red, rich as blood, with dainty gold chains draped around her shoulders. It reminded Kai of a bloodred poppy, the petals full and drooping. A sheer gold veil covered her face and billowed like a sail as she walked.

When she was close enough, Kai could make out hints of her face through the veil. Her lips had been painted to match the dress and her eyes burned with victory. She strode onto the dais and paused at Kai's side. The skirt's hem pooled at her feet.

"You may be seated," said the disembodied voice.

The crowd shuffled into their seats. Prime Minister Kamin lifted her portscreen from the altar. "Ladies and gentlemen, Lunars and Earthens," she began, a hidden microphone carrying her voice over the crowd. "We gather today to witness a historical union of Earth and Luna—an alliance formed by trust and mutual respect. This is a significant moment in our history that will forever symbolize the enduring relationship of the people of Luna and the people of Earth."

She paused to let her words sink into the crowd. Kai wanted to gag.

The prime minister focused on the bride and groom. "We are here to witness the marriage of Emperor Kaito of the Eastern Commonwealth and Queen Levana Blackburn of Luna."

Kai met Levana's gaze through her veil. Her taunting smile chased all his denial away.

Cinder was captured or dead. The wedding would go on as planned; the coronation would take place in two days' time.

It was just him, now. The last line of defense between Levana and Earth.

So be it.

He set his jaw and returned his focus to their officiant. He gave a small nod. The wedding began.

Forty-Seven

"THE GROOM WILL NOW TAKE HIS RIBBON AND TIE IT THREE times around his bride's left wrist, symbolizing the love, honor, and respect that will forever bind their matrimony," said Prime Minister Kamin, unwinding a length of velvet ribbon from a spool. She picked up the polished silver scissors from the tray and snipped off the length of ribbon.

Kai tried not to make a face as Kamin laid the ribbon across his palms. It was shimmering and ivory, the color of the full moon, as opposed to the silky blue ribbon already wrapped around his own wrist, the color of Earth.

It felt like his consciousness was hovering above him, watching as his fingers wrapped the ribbon around Levana's bone-thin wrist—once, twice, three times—finishing it off with a simple knot. There was no grace to it and the ribbon was probably too loose, a side effect of his unwillingness to brush her skin with his fingertips. When she had tied his, she had practically given him a wrist massage that had made him squirm on the inside.

"I will now knot the two ribbons together," said Prime Minister Kamin, in her measured, serene voice. She had not faltered once during the ceremony. "This is to symbolize the unity of the bride and groom and also of Luna and the Eastern Commonwealth, which represents the planet of Earth on this, the eighth day of November in the 126th year of the third era." She took the ends of each ribbon between her fingers.

Kai watched with detached interest as her dark, slender fingers knotted the two ribbons together. She yanked on the ends, tightening the knot. Kai stared at it, feeling the disconnect in his mind.

He was not here.

This was not happening.

His hateful gaze betrayed him, flickering toward Levana's face. It was the briefest of looks, but she somehow managed to catch it. She smiled, and icicles stabbed at his spine.

This *was* happening. This was his bride.

Levana's lips twitched behind her veil. He could hear her voice, though she didn't open her lips, accusing him of an endearing, bashful crush, chastising his youth and innocence at such a moment. He couldn't tell if the voice was his own taunting imagination or something she was injecting into his thoughts.

And he would never know.

He was marrying a woman who would forever hold this power over him.

How different she was from Cinder. Selene. Her *niece*, though it didn't seem possible the two had anything in common, especially their ancestry.

Thinking of Cinder brought back the painful memory of the cyborg finger on a bed of silk and Kai shuddered.

The officiant paused, but Kai was already reconfiguring his expression. He let out a steady breath and gave her a subtle nod to continue.

Kamin reached for her portscreen, and Kai grasped at the momentary pause, trying to compose himself. He thought of the mutants murdering innocent civilians. He thought of his father dying in the palace quarantine while an antidote existed in Levana's control. He thought of all the lives he would be saving by stopping this war and obtaining the cure.

"We will now commence with the exchanging of vows, as set forth by the council of leaders of the Earthen Union, beginning with the groom. Please, repeat after me." Kamin glanced up to make sure Kai was paying attention. "I, Emperor Kaito of the Eastern Commonwealth of Earth ..."

He repeated, as accommodating as an android.

"...take as my wife and the future empress of the Eastern Commonwealth, Her Royal Majesty, Queen Levana Blackburn of Luna..."

He was out of his body again. Looking down. Listening to the words, but not understanding them. They held no meaning.

"...to rule at my side with grace and justice, to honor the laws of the Earthen Union as laid out by our forefathers, to be an advocate for peace and fairness among all peoples."

Did anyone believe a word of this rubbish?

"From this day forward, she will be my sun at dawn and my moon at night, and I vow to love and cherish her for all our days."

Who wrote these vows anyway? He'd never heard anything so ridiculous in his life.

But he said them, with no emotion and even less interest. Prime Minister Kamin gave him a nod, akin to a *well done*, and turned to Levana. "Now, the bride will repeat after me ..."

Kai tuned out Levana's voice, examining their bound wrists instead. Was the ribbon around his wrist growing tighter? His fingers were beginning to tingle with numbness. He was losing circulation. But the ribbon curled innocently against his skin.

Stars above, it was warm in here.

"...and I vow to love and cherish him for all our days."

Kai snorted. Loudly.

He'd meant for it to be kept inside, but it just slipped out.

Levana tensed and the officiant speared him with a sharp look.

Kai coughed in an attempt to smooth over the moment. "Sorry. There was something in my—" He coughed again.

Terse wrinkles formed around Kamin's mouth as she turned back to the queen. "Your Royal Majesty, do you hereby accept the terms of marriage set forth before you on this day, as both the rules of matrimony between two beings and also as the bond that will henceforth be forged between Luna and the Eastern Commonwealth, resulting in the political alliance of these two entities? If you accept, say 'I do.'"

"I do." Levana's voice was clear and sweet and sent a thousand piercing needles into Kai's chest.

His head was throbbing. From exhaustion, from disbelief, from misery.

"Your Imperial Majesty, do you hereby accept the terms of marriage set forth before you on this day, as both the rules of matrimony between two beings and also as the bond that will henceforth be forged between the Eastern Commonwealth and Luna, resulting in the political alliance of these two entities? If you accept, say 'I do.'"

He blinked at Prime Minister Kamin.

His heart was pulsating against his ribs, and her words were hollow echoes in his hollow head, and he had only to open his mouth and say *I do* and the wedding would be over and Levana would be his wife.

But his lips would not open.

I don't.

The muscles flexed in the prime minister's jaw. Her gaze hardened, prompting.

I can't.

He felt the hush of a thousand guests bearing down on him. He imagined Torin and President Vargas and Queen Camilla and all the others, watching, waiting. He pictured all of Levana's guards and thaumaturges and that smug Aimery Park and a thousand vain, ignorant aristocrats hanging on his silence.

He knew Levana could force him to say the words, but she didn't. Though he imagined a blast of icy air rolling off her with each passing second, she waited with all the others.

Kai pried open his lips, but his tongue was heavy as iron.

The officiant inhaled a patient breath and cast a worried glance to the queen, before fixating on Kai again. Her expression grew nervous.

Kai looked down at the scissors she'd used to cut the ribbons.

He moved fast, before he could question himself. His unbound hand shot forward, snatching the scissors off the altar. Blood rushed in his ears as he spun toward Levana, arm raised, and plunged the scissors toward her heart.

Cinder cried out, her arms flying up in defense. The point of the scissors sliced through the fabric of her elbow-length gloves before coming to a swift halt, pressed into the silver bodice of her ball gown. Kai's arm trembled with the effort to push through the control, but his hand was now carved from stone. Breath ragged, he looked up into Cinder's face. She looked like she had at the ball, in her tattered dress and stained gloves, her damp hair tumbling around her face. The only difference was the blue ribbon tying them together and, now, a single slit cut into the silk of her gloves.

Slowly, like molasses, blood began to seep through that cut, staining the fabric.

Cinder—no, *Levana*—saw the blooming cut and snarled. Her hold on Kai snapped and he stumbled back. The scissors clattered to the floor, ringing with a tone of finality.

"You dare to threaten me here?" Levana hissed, and though she tried to mimic Cinder's voice, Kai could tell the difference. "In front of both our kingdoms?"

Kai's attention was still on the blood leaking from her wounded arm.

He had done it. For a moment, he had gotten through the glamour, through the manipulation. It wasn't much, but he had actually hurt her.

"It wasn't meant to be a threat," he said.

Her eyes narrowed.

"We both know you intend to kill me the moment I'm no longer useful to you. I thought it was fair to let you know the feeling is mutual."

Levana glared, and it was unnerving to see such hatred on Cinder's face.

Vibrating with adrenaline, Kai looked back at the audience. Most of their guests were on their feet, their expressions a mix of shock and confusion. Near the front, Torin looked like he was ready to hurtle himself over two rows of seats to be at Kai's side the instant he was needed.

Kai held his gaze long enough, he hoped, to convey that he was all right. He had hurt her, Kai wanted to say. It was possible to hurt her. Which meant it was possible to kill her.

Setting his jaw, Kai turned back to face Prime Minister Kamin. She, too, was shaking, both hands gripping her portscreen.

"I do," he said, listening to his own proclamation echo around the altar.

The officiant's gaze darted between him and his bride, like she wasn't sure if she should proceed or not. But then Levana straightened her wedding gown—or Cinder's ball gown, as it was. Whatever reaction she was hoping to get from him by maintaining the glamour, he wouldn't—*couldn't*—give it to her.

When the silence had hovered for too long, Levana growled, "Get on with it then."

Kamin gulped. "By the power given to me by the people of Earth, I do now pronounce you . . . husband and wife."

Kai didn't even flinch.

"We ask that all video feeds be discontinued so the groom might kiss his bride."

Kai waited to be hit by a wall of dread, but even that was replaced with fervent determination. He imagined all the holographs on Luna fading away, and all the Earthen newsfeeds flickering to dead air. He imagined all his people watching, and the horror they must be feeling as those feeds were silenced.

He turned to Levana.

His bride.

His *wife*.

She was still impersonating Cinder, but the ball gown was replaced by the vibrant red wedding dress and sheer veil. She smiled deviously.

Ignoring her, he mechanically took her veil between his fingers and pulled it over her head.

"I thought you might prefer this look," she said. "Consider it a wedding gift."

Kai couldn't bring himself to react, no matter how much he wanted to reflect that haughtiness back to her. "In fact, I do." He craned his head toward her. "Selene is more beautiful than you could ever be."

He kissed her. An abrupt, passionless kiss that felt nothing at all like kissing Cinder.

A collective breath released from the audience.

Kai pulled away, putting a full body of open air between them. The audience started to applaud, politely at first, then growing more enthusiastic as if they were afraid their clapping might not be polite enough. Kai held out his elbow for Levana to take, their hands still bound, and together they turned to face the audience. From the corner of his eye, he saw Cinder's image melt away, her face replaced with Levana's, and he was glad she looked annoyed. It was the tiniest of victories, but he was glad for it.

They stood amid the thundering cheers, each of them seething.

Husband and wife.

Forty-Eight

CRESS HAD LONG AGO LOST TRACK OF WHERE THEY WERE OR what direction they were going. Jacin had dragged her through some complicated labyrinth of halls beneath the palace, down stairs and through maglev tunnels. Though it felt like they'd been walking for hours, she couldn't even be sure they'd left the boundaries of Artemisia Central, given how circuitous their route had been.

They were sneaking through a tunnel, staying close to the edges to avoid any shuttles, which had a tendency to sneak up too fast on their silent magnets, when the power cut out, plunging them into darkness. Cress gasped and reached for Jacin, but froze with her fingers inches away from where she expected him to be. Clenching her fist, she drew her hand back to her side.

Brave. She was *brave*.

In the distance, they heard the scream of a shuttle hitting the rails and careening to a stop.

A moment later, orange emergency lights illuminated the tracks at their feet and a voice echoed from invisible speakers. "This shuttle route has been discontinued until further notice. Please proceed to the next platform on foot and prepare for a security inspection. The crown apologizes for any inconvenience."

She glanced up at Jacin. "What does that mean?"

"My guess? That whatever Cinder's doing, it's working." He started walking again, picking their way more carefully with the reduced lighting. "They must be limiting transportation into the city."

Her nerves hummed. "Will we be able to get out?"

"We're almost to the station that receives eighty percent of our supply trains. They should still be operational, given how many guests Levana has to feed this week."

Cress trotted in his wake, hoping he was right. He hadn't been very forthcoming with his plan and she still had no idea where they were going. She wondered if he was right. Had Winter and Scarlet gotten her message to the others? Had they been able to broadcast the video? She had no answers. If Levana was aware of a potential uprising, she was keeping the knowledge to herself.

The tunnel became wider, the rails merging with two other tracks, and Cress was hit with a pungent smell that reminded her of the caravan she and Thorne had crossed the Sahara with. Dirt and animals.

Around the next bend in the tunnel, she could see a bright glow and hear the echoes of grating machinery and rumbling wheels. Jacin slowed his pace.

A massive platform came into view. A holographic sign was showing coverage of the royal wedding.

A dozen maglev tracks stretched in multiple directions, loaded with cargo trains. Most of their cars were hidden from view in the darkened tunnels, waiting to be relieved of their goods. Cranes and pulleys filled the dock and Cress imagined it would have taken countless laborers to man all the machinery, but the only personnel was a contingent of uniformed guards sweeping the cars ahead.

Jacin pulled Cress into the shadows of the nearest train. A second later, a silhouette passed up ahead and the beam of a flashlight jotted in their direction. Jacin and Cress ducked between the nearest cars, watching as the light beam flickered along the ground and disappeared.

"A6 is clear," someone yelled, followed by another: "A7, clear."

There was a pause, then the hum of magnets. The train swayed forward.

Jacin jumped onto the axle to keep from being caught on the tracks, hauling Cress up beside him. This time she did grab his arm as the train surged forward, then came to another stop. Car doors thudded open.

Jacin jumped down from the axle, dragging Cress with him. "Inspections," he whispered. "Making sure no one tries to sneak into the city."

"What about sneaking out of the city?"

He pointed toward the front of the train. "We need to get into one of the cars that was already searched. This train should be heading back to the agriculture sectors from here."

They sneaked over the axle to the opposite side of the car. Though there were platforms on both sides of the tracks, the second platform had only a single guard, pacing the perimeter with an assault rifle at the ready.

"All right, shortcake, when that guard has his back to us again, we're going to sneak forward as fast as we can. Once he starts to turn, crawl under the train and hold still."

Cress glared at the back of his head. "Don't call me shortcake."

Up ahead, someone yelled, "A8, clear! B1, clear!"

The guard turned away.

Jacin and Cress darted forward. Her heart was thumping as she kept one eye on the guard's back and his threatening gun, the other on the tracks beneath her feet. The guard started to pivot. Cress dropped to her hands and knees and scurried under the train car. Sweat matted her hair to the back of her neck.

"Over he—!"

A yell was cut off, followed by two loud thuds and the clang of metal on metal. The guard with the rifle turned and charged toward the tracks, vaulting over an axle. A gunshot. A grunt.

"*Freeze!*"

Another gunshot.

With the platform unexpectedly clear, Jacin shimmied out from beneath the train and waved for Cress to follow. Her elbows scraped against the hard ground as she pulled herself out. Jacin dragged her to her feet and they took off running toward the front of the train. The sounds of a struggle continued on the opposite platform.

They reached car A7 and plastered themselves to the side to catch their breath. Now they only had to sneak around to the other side and climb into the car without being seen—or shot, she thought—as another gunshot made her jump.

Cress looked back and her heart leaped into her throat.

A girl was on the ground, crawling beneath one of the train cars just like Cress had been seconds before. Though Cress could see very little of her, she couldn't mistake the abundance of silky braids dyed in varying shades of blue.

"Iko!"

Iko's head snapped up. Her eyes widened. The look was brief, though, as she turned her head toward something on the other side of the train. She started to scuffle forward, her belly pressed against the ground.

Jacin cursed, then launched himself past Cress. His own gun was already in his palm as he ran into the fray.

Cress followed, though with more hesitation, having no weapon of her own. She crouched down against the train car and inched her head forward.

Her throat dried.

Thorne.

He was wearing the uniform of a Lunar guard, but there was no mistaking him.

She clapped both hands over her mouth to keep from shouting his name. He was grappling with the guard from the platform. The rifle was nowhere to be seen. Four other guards and two flashlights, their beams spotlighting random spots on the tracks, were scattered across the platform. Cress noticed a spray of blood against one of the cars at the same moment Iko charged out from beneath the car and threw herself at a sixth guard who was trying to get a good shot at Thorne. It was an awkward tackle, though. Something seemed to be wrong with Iko's right arm.

The guard grabbed Iko and pinned her to the ground, wrapping his hands around her throat, oblivious that oxygen intake wasn't an issue.

Spotting an abandoned handgun a few steps away, Cress leaped for it. But the moment she picked it up and aimed it into the fight, her arms began to tremble. She had never fired a gun before.

She was attempting to still her hand enough to take aim when two successive gunshots echoed through her skull. The first knocked the guard off Iko; the second took out the guard wrestling with Thorne.

The world seemed to still, but for heavy breathing. The uncanny silence made her panting unbearably loud.

Upon confirmation that both guards were dead or incapacitated, Jacin dropped his gun back into its holster.

Thorne blinked at Jacin, shocked, as he stood and straightened his shirt. He looked about to say something when Iko screamed, "CRESS!" and shot forward, wrapping Cress in a one-armed embrace.

Cress stumbled, letting herself be held, even while her gaze sought out Thorne. His jaw hung as he stared at her. He was disheveled and bruised and breathless. He stumbled forward and engulfed both Cress and Iko in an enormous hug. Cress squeezed her eyes shut as hot tears began to cloud them. His arm around her shoulders. His bristled chin on her forehead. One of Iko's braids in her mouth.

She had never been so happy.

Jacin grunted. "We need to go."

Iko stepped back, but Thorne filled the space she'd left, cupping Cress's face in his hands. His eyes bored into her, full of disbelief. His thumb caught her first tear.

Suddenly, Cress found herself laughing and sniffling and laughing some more. She ducked her head and swiped at the tears. "No crying," she said. "It's dehydrating."

His arms wound around her again. She felt the rumble of his voice as he said, "It *is* you. Thank the stars."

"When I say we should go," said Jacin, "I mean *now*."

Thorne's arms tensed and, with one tight squeeze, he let her go and turned to face Jacin. A muscle twitched in his cheek. It was the only warning before Thorne's fist collided with Jacin's jaw. Cress gasped.

Jacin stumbled back, his hand coming up to feel the wound.

"That's for selling us out on Earth," said Thorne. "And this is for taking care of Cress." He pulled Jacin into a hug, burying his face in Jacin's shoulder.

Jacin rolled his eyes to the cavernous ceiling. "Don't make me regret that decision." He shoved Thorne away. "Your eyesight's back. Good. Let's search these men for weapons and get out of here."

With a nod, Thorne leaned over one of the bodies and unstrapped the knife from the guard's belt. To Cress's surprise, he handed it to Jacin, who hesitated only briefly before tucking it through his belt. "How did you know how to find us?" Thorne asked.

"We didn't. We were on our way out of here." Jacin frowned. "Where's Winter?"

"She and Scarlet went into hiding," said Iko. She was poking at her limp right arm, then tugging at her deadened fingers. "Well, sort of. It's complicated."

Thorne peered at the android. "What happened?"

Her lips bunched. "One of those guards stabbed me in the shoulder. I think it severed something important." She turned to show them a jagged cut in her upper back and sighed. "It's like this is 'Pick on Iko' day or something."

Cress pressed her lips in sympathy, but the reminder of Iko's cybernetic parts made her realize . . . "Where's Cinder?"

Thorne's face became shadowed, but before he could respond, a chime blared through the tunnel. Cress jumped.

The holographic screen on the wall brightened with Thaumaturge Aimery's face.

"People of Luna, I am pleased to make the announcement that the wedding ceremony is complete. Our honored ruler, Queen Levana, has sealed the marriage alliance with Emperor Kaito of Earth."

Iko grunted in a most unladylike way, drawing everyone's gaze to her. "I get stabbed and *she* gets to marry Kai. That just figures."

"The coronation ceremony," Aimery continued, "in which we will welcome Emperor Kaito as our honored king consort, and Her Majesty Queen Levana will be bestowed with the title of empress of Earth's Eastern Commonwealth, will take place two days hence at sunrise." Aimery's eyes took on an arrogant glint. "Our illustrious queen asks that the people of Luna partake in to-night's celebration. Tonight's wedding feast shall be broadcast across all sectors, during which we have a special trial planned for the festivities. This broadcast will be mandatory viewing for all citizens and shall commence in twenty minutes from the end of this announcement."

The video cut off.

"Special trial?" said Cress.

"It's Cinder," said Thorne, glowering at the holograph. "She has Cinder, and Wolf, too. We expect her to have them publicly executed as a way of quelling the insurrection."

A chill swept down Cress's spine. *Twenty minutes.* It would take longer than that to get back to the palace.

"We're going to rescue her," said Iko, as if it were the most natural thing in the world.

"Sorry," said Jacin, looking like he actually meant it. "But if we only have twenty minutes, we're already too late."

Forty-Nine

CINDER JABBED HER FINGER'S SCREWDRIVER INTO THE WALL beside the cell door. A thumbnail's worth of dust and rock chipped away, joining the pile at her feet. The lava rock was hard, but her titanium tools were harder, and her resolve was the hardest it had ever been.

She was angry. She was frustrated. She was afraid.

She was distraught over Maha's death, which kept replaying in her memory, making her want to jab the screwdriver into her own temple to make it stop. She had looked at the raid on RM-9 from every angle, torturing herself with what-ifs and implausible scenarios, trying to find some way to bring Maha back to life. To free herself and Wolf. To protect her friends. To defeat Levana.

She was aware of how futile it was.

Maybe Aimery was right. Maybe she should have controlled everyone in that sector from the start. It would have made her a tyrant, but it also would have kept them alive.

She was nauseated from the rank smell coming from the bucket against the wall. She was annoyed that Levana's goons had taken her best weapon—her cybernetic pointer finger with the gun attachment—and locked her up with her stepmother and stepsister, who had barely spoken since she'd arrived.

Rationally, she knew there was no way she could dig through to the door's hinges before the guards came for her. She knew she was working herself into a frenzy for no logical reason. But she couldn't bring herself to slump to the ground, defeated.

Like *they* were.

Another rock chip crumbled down the wall.

Cinder blew a lock of hair out of her face, but it fell right back down.

According to the clock in her head, she had been in this cell for over twenty-four hours. She had not slept. The wedding, she knew, would be over by now.

The thought tied her stomach into knots.

It occurred to her that if she had let Levana come and take her from New Beijing, this was where she would have ended up anyway. She still would have been executed. She was still going to die.

She'd tried to run. She'd tried to fight. And all she got for it was a spaceship full of friends who she'd now be taking down with her.

"Why did he call you Princess?"

Cinder paused, glaring at the pathetic scratch marks she'd made. It was Pearl who had spoken, her voice fragile as she broke their silence for the first time in hours.

Pushing the miscreant hair back with her sweat-dampened wrist, Cinder glanced at Pearl and Adri, not bothering to hide her disdain. She had already hardened herself to any sort of sympathy for them. Every time a twinge struck her, she called up the memory of Adri demanding that Cinder hobble around footless for an entire week, as a reminder that she "wasn't human." Or the time Pearl had thrown Cinder's toolbox into a crowded street, ruining the silk gloves Kai had given her.

She kept reminding herself that whatever was going to happen to them, they deserved it.

It didn't make her feel any better. In fact, thinking about it was making her feel cruel and petty, and also giving her a headache.

She shook it off.

"I'm Princess Selene," she answered, turning back to her work.

Pearl laughed, a short hysterical sound, full of disbelief.

Adri stayed silent.

The cell filled with Cinder's persistent *scrape scrape clatter, scrape scrape clatter.* Her pile grew larger, pebble by hard-earned pebble.

She was never getting out of here.

"Garan knew." Adri's voice was brittle.

Cinder froze again. Garan had been Adri's husband, the man who had made the decision to adopt Cinder. She'd barely known him.

She was annoyed when her own curiosity forced her to turn around. Switching the screwdriver for her flashlight, she beamed it toward her stepmother. "Excuse me?"

Adri flinched, both arms wrapped around her daughter. They hadn't moved from their corner. "Garan knew," she said again. "He never told me, but when he was taken away to the quarantines, he told me to take care of you. He said it as if it were the most important thing in the world." She fell quiet, like the presence of her dead husband was there, hanging over them all.

"*Wow,*" said Cinder. "You really excelled at that dying request, didn't you?"

Adri's gaze narrowed, full of a disgust Cinder was all too familiar with. "I will not tolerate you speaking to me this way when *my* husband—"

"*You* won't tolerate it?" Cinder yelled. "Should I tell you all the things I'm no longer going to tolerate? Because it's a *long* list."

Adri shrank back. Cinder had wondered if Adri might be afraid of her, now that she was Lunar and a wanted felon. Her reaction confirmed it.

"Why wouldn't Dad say something?" said Pearl. "Why wouldn't he tell us?"

"Maybe he knew you'd sell me for ransom the first chance you got."

Pearl ignored her. "And if you really are the princess, why are you in here?"

Cinder glared at her. Waited. Watched as understanding dawned across Pearl's face. "She wants to kill you, so she can stay the queen."

"Give the girl a treat," Cinder said.

"But what does it have to do with us?" Tears began to pool in Pearl's eyes. "Why are we being punished? We didn't do anything. We didn't *know.*"

Cinder's adrenaline and anger were slipping, exhaustion crawling into the spaces they'd left behind. "You gave me your invitations to the royal wedding, which allowed me to kidnap Kai, which drove Levana crazy. Thanks for that, by the way."

"How can you think only of yourself at a time like this?" Adri snapped. "How can you be so selfish?"

Cinder's hands curled into fists. "If I don't take care of myself, nobody will. That's something I learned early on, thanks to you."

Adri pulled her daughter closer and smoothed down her hair. Pearl slumped against her without a fight. Cinder wondered if she was in shock. Maybe they both were.

She turned back to the wall and carved a *C* into the stone. These walls were scored with hundreds of words, names, pleas, promises, threats. She considered adding a "+ K" but the idea of such whimsy made her want to beat her head against the iron door.

"You're a monster," Adri whispered.

Cinder smirked, without humor. "Fine. I'm a monster."

"You couldn't even save Peony."

At the mention of her younger stepsister a new bout of rage surged like a thousand sparking wires in Cinder's head. She spun back. "You think I didn't *try?*"

"You had an antidote!" Adri was screaming now too, her eyes wild, though she stayed hunkered over Pearl. "I know you gave it to that little boy. It saved his life. Chang Sunto!" She spat the name like poison. "You chose to save him over Peony. How could you? Did you taunt her with it? Did you give her false hope before you watched her die?"

Cinder gaped at her stepmother, her own anger eclipsed with a surprising jolt of pity. This woman was full of so much ignorance it was almost like she *wanted* to stay that way. She saw what she wanted, believed anything to support her limited view of the world. Cinder could still remember how she had felt running to the plague quarantines. How she'd desperately clutched the vial of antidote. How she'd been so hopeful she could save Peony's life, and so devastated when she failed.

She'd been too late. She still hadn't quite forgiven herself.

Adri would never know, would never understand. To her, Cinder was just a machine, incapable of anything but cruelty.

Five years she had lived with this woman, and never once had she seen Cinder as she was. As Kai saw her, and Thorne and Iko and all the people who trusted her. All the people who *knew* her.

She shook her head, finding it easier than she'd expected to dismiss her stepmother's words. "I'm done trying to explain myself to you. I'm done seeking your approval. I'm done with you."

Kicking at the pile of rock shavings, she jabbed the screwdriver into the wall at the same moment she heard footsteps.

Her jaw tightened. Her time was up. Turning, she reached Adri and Pearl in three long strides. They both shriveled away.

Cinder grabbed the front of Adri's shirt and pulled her upward.

"If you even *think* about telling them my foot can be as easily removed as that finger, I will force you to gouge out your own eyes with your fingernails if it is the last thing I do—do you understand me?"

Adri paled and gave a trembling nod before a man's voice sounded beyond the door.

"Open it."

Dropping her stepmother back into the corner, Cinder spun back.

The door opened and the cell filled with the corridor's light, a single guard, Thaumaturge Aimery, plus four additional thaumaturges dressed in a mix of red and black. *Five* of them. How flattering.

"Her Majesty has requested the pleasure of your company," said Aimery.

Cinder lifted her chin. "I can't promise my company will be as pleasant as she expects."

She strode toward them to show she wasn't afraid, but suddenly felt herself being thrown against the wall. The pain jolted down her spine, knocking the air from her lungs. It reminded her of all the sparring matches she'd had with Wolf aboard the Rampion, except a hundred times worse because Wolf always looked guilty afterward.

The guard who had thrown her wrapped his hand around Cinder's throat. Cinder scowled at him, even though she knew he was being controlled and her true attacker was one of the thaumaturges. The guard glared back.

"That was your first warning," said Aimery. "If you try to run, if you try to fight, if we sense you trying to use your gift, we will not bother with a second one."

The guard released her and Cinder slumped, bracing herself with locked knees. She rubbed her neck briefly before her wrists were yanked behind her back and bound.

The guard shoved her toward the door. There were four more guards in the hallway, weapons drawn. Unfortunately, they were already under the control of the thaumaturges. She had no hope for turning any of them to her side.

Yet.

But if anyone slipped for a moment, she wasn't going to bother with a *first* warning.

"Bring the Earthens too," Aimery said.

Adri and Pearl whimpered as they were hauled to their feet, but Cinder turned down her audio interface to drown them out. She didn't know why Levana wanted her stepmother and stepsister, but if she thought Cinder held some affection for them, she would be disappointed.

"Where are we going?" Cinder asked as she was shoved away from the cell.

There was a long silence, and she was sure she was being ignored, but eventually Aimery answered, "You are to be the guest of honor at Her Majesty's wedding feast."

She clenched her jaw. *Wedding feast.* "But I forgot my ball gown on Earth."

This time, it was one of the females who snickered. "Don't worry," she said. "You wouldn't want to get blood all over it anyway."

Fifty

CINDER FOUND HERSELF BEFORE A PAIR OF OMINOUS, ebony-black doors. They stood twice her height, and in a palace made almost entirely of glass and white stone, standing before them felt like standing at the edge of a black hole. They were minimally accented with two thick, black iron handles that arched halfway to the floor. The Lunar insignia had been carved into the wood in pristine detail, depicting the capital city of Artemisia and, in the distance, Earth.

Two guards pulled open the doors, and Cinder was facing a gauntlet of yet more thaumaturges and guards and now wolf-mutant soldiers as well. The sight of them made Cinder shudder. These were not special operatives like Wolf. These men had been transformed into something beastly and grotesque. The bones of their jaws were misshapen and reinforced to fit enormous canine teeth; their arms hung awkwardly at their sides, as if their spines were unaccustomed to the weight of their new muscles and extended limbs.

It occurred to her that they weren't unlike cyborgs. They were both made to be better than what they'd been born as.

They were both unnatural. Only, instead of being pieced to-gether with wires and steel, these creatures were a jigsaw of muscle tissue and cartilage.

The guard yanked on Cinder's elbow and she stumbled for-ward. The soldiers watched her with keen, hungry eyes.

Wolf had told her these soldiers would be different. Erratic and feral, craving nothing but violence and blood. A powerful Lunar, like the queen, could trick them into perceiving a glam-our, but that was it. Even the thaumaturges couldn't control their minds or bodies, but instead had to train the soldiers like dogs. Misbehave, and they were punished with pain. Do well, and they were rewarded. Only, the rewards Wolf had talked about didn't strike Cinder as all that appetizing.

Evidently, on Earth, each bloody kill made for its own reward. They were *eager* to go to war.

Cinder opened her mind to them, trying to sense their bioelectric pulses. Their energy burned white-hot and violent. Hunger and temptation writhed beneath their skin. She was dizzy with the mere thought of trying to control this much raw energy.

But she had to try.

Taking in a measured breath, Cinder reached for the mind of the last soldier. His energy was scalding and ravenous. She imag-ined it cooling, calming. She imagined the soldier looking at her and seeing not an enemy but a girl who needed rescuing. A girl who deserved his loyalty.

She caught the soldier's eye, and his mouth curled into a sick-ening grin around his jagged teeth.

Disheartened, Cinder pulled her attention away.

Nearing the end of the gauntlet, she tried to take in the rest of her surroundings. Lively chatter and laughter and the chaotic clinking of glasses. The aroma of food struck her like a cloud of steam released from a covered pot. Her mouth filled with saliva. Onions and garlic and braised meat and something peppery that stung her eyes—

Her stomach howled at her. Light-headedness crept over her brain like a fog. She hadn't eaten in over a day, and even that meal had been unsatisfying.

She gulped hard and tried to focus, surveying the room. To her right, enormous windows looked over a lake, bordered on each side by the curved wings of the white palace, like an enormous protective swan. The lake continued as far as she could see. The floor of the room jutted out like a balcony over the water. Although it made for an uninterrupted view, Cinder couldn't deny a feeling of dread curdling in her stomach. There was no rail to keep a person from falling off the edge.

The swell of conversation started to die out, but it was not until Cinder had breached the line of soldiers that she saw the audience to her left.

The orange light flickered in Cinder's vision and didn't go off, no matter where she looked. There were a lot of glamours here.

At the center was Levana, seated upon a massive white throne, the back of which was ornamented with the phases of the moon. She was wearing an elaborate red wedding gown.

Cinder's retina display began to pick up the queen's underlying features. It was like being at the ball again, the first time she'd laid eyes on the queen and had realized it might be possible for her optobionics to see beneath the glamour. But it wasn't an easy task. Her cyborg eyes were in conflict with her own brain and the queen's manipulation, and her mind couldn't figure out what it was seeing. The result was a stream of confused data, blurred colors, fragmented lines trying to piece together what was real and what was an illusion.

It was distracting, and already giving her a headache. Cinder blinked the data away.

Five tiers of seats arced around the throne, a crescent of on-lookers surrounding Cinder on every side except the one that dropped off to the lake. The Lunar court. Women wore large hats shaped like peacocks and one man had a purring snow leopard draped over his shoulders; dresses were made of gold chains and rubies, platform shoes had beta fish swimming in their heels, skin had been painted metallic silver, eyelashes dotted with rhinestones and fish scales . . .

Cinder had to squint against the dazzle of it all. Glamour, glamour, *glamour.*

A chair was pushed back. Cinder's heart jumped.

The bridegroom stood beside Levana's throne, wearing a white silk shirt with a red sash. *Kai.*

"What is this?" he said, his tone somewhere between horri-fied and relieved.

"This," said Queen Levana, her eyes full of mirth, "is our en-tertainment for the evening. Consider it my wedding gift to you." Beaming, she traced a knuckle down the side of Kai's face. *"Husband."*

Kai ducked away from her touch, redness climbing into his cheeks. Cinder knew it wasn't embarrassment or bashfulness, though. That was all fury. She could feel it in how the air crackled around him.

Levana twirled a fingernail through the air. "Tonight's pro-ceedings will be broadcast live, so my people can witness and join in the celebrations of this most glorious day. And also so they may know the fate of the impostor who dares to call herself *queen.*"

Ignoring her, Cinder examined the ceiling. There were no

cameras that she could see, but she knew Levana had a way of creating surveillance devices that were practically invisible.

Given that the queen wasn't wearing a veil, it was safe to assume any video footage would be focused on their "entertainment." Levana wanted the people to see Cinder's execution. She wanted them to lose hope for their revolution.

Levana raised her arms. "Let us begin the feast."

A line of uniformed servants traipsed single file from behind a curtain. The first knelt at the queen's feet and whisked a dome off a tray, holding it above his head. The queen's smirk grew as she selected a large, pink prawn and pulled the flesh between her teeth.

Another servant knelt before Kai, while the others surrounded the room and dropped to their knees before the audience, revealing trays of orange fish eggs and steamed oyster shells, braised tenderloin strips and stuffed peppers. Cinder realized that Kai was not the only Earthen in the room after all. She recognized his adviser, Konn Torin, seated in the second row, and the American president and the African prime minister and the Australian governor-general and . . . She stopped looking. They were all there, just as Levana had wanted.

Heart pounding, she scanned the servants, guards, and soldiers again, hoping that maybe Wolf, too, had been brought before the queen. But he wasn't here. Cinder, Adri, and Pearl were the only prisoners.

Worry gnawed at her. Where had they taken him? Was he already dead?

She swept her gaze back to Kai. If he had noticed the food, he ignored it. She could see his jaw working, wanting to question her presence, wanting to know what the queen was planning. She could see him trying to reason his way out of this, to come up with some diplomatic angle he could use to keep the inevitable from happening.

"Sit down, my love," said Levana, "or you'll be disrupting the view for our other guests."

Kai sat down too quickly for it to have been his own doing. He turned his smoldering glare on the queen. "Why is she here?"

"You sound angry, my pet. Are you displeased with our hospitality?"

Without waiting for a response, Levana tilted her chin up and swooped her gaze from Cinder to Adri and Pearl. "Aimery, you may proceed."

He paced to the front of the room, smirking at Cinder as he walked past her. Though his coat had been washed of blood, he was still walking stiffly to conceal his injured leg.

Aimery offered his elbow to Adri, who made a half-strangled, terrified sound. It took her a long time to accept it. She looked like she was going to be sick as Aimery led her to the center of the throne room floor.

All around them, the sounds of chewing and the licking of fingers persisted, as if the delicacies were every bit as interesting as the prisoners. The servants were still on their knees, holding the trays above their heads. Cinder grimaced. How heavy must those trays be?

"I present to the court Linh Adri of the Eastern Commonwealth, Earthen Union," said Aimery, releasing Adri's arm so she stood alone on her own trembling legs. "She is charged with conspiracy against the crown. The punishment for this crime is immediate death by her own hand, and that her child and dependent, Linh Pearl, be given as a servant to one of Artemisia's families."

Cinder's eyebrows shot upward. Until now she'd been

concerned with her own fate, and it hadn't occurred to her that Adri may have been brought there for any reason other than to annoy her.

She wanted to not care. She wanted to feel nothing but disinterest toward her stepmother's fate.

But she knew that, for all her many faults, Adri had not done anything to warrant a Lunar execution. This was a power play on Levana's part, nothing more, and it was impossible not to feel a tinge of pity for the woman.

Adri fell to her knees. "I swear to you I haven't done anything. I—"

Levana raised a hand and Adri fell silent. An agonizing moment followed in which Levana's expression was unreadable. Finally, she clucked her tongue, like chastising a small child. "Aimery, continue."

The thaumaturge nodded. "An investigation has shown that the two invitations with which Linh Cinder's accomplices were able to invade New Beijing Palace and kidnap Emperor Kaito had been given them by none other than this woman. The invitations were meant for herself and her teenage daughter."

"*No!* She stole them! *Stole* them! I would never give them to her. I would never help her. I hate her—*hate her!*" She sobbed again, her shoulders hunched so far now she was practically a ball on the floor. "Why is this happening to me? What have I done? I didn't ... She isn't mine ..."

Cinder was finding it easier not to care.

"You must calm yourself, Mrs. Linh," said Levana. "We will see the truth of your loyalties soon enough."

Adri whimpered, and made some attempt to compose herself.

"That is better. You have been the legal guardian of Linh Cinder for almost six years, is that correct?"

Adri's whole body was shaking. "It—it's true. But I didn't know what she was, I swear. My husband was the one who wanted her, not me. *She* is the traitor! Cinder is a criminal, and a dangerous, deceitful girl—but I thought she was just a cyborg. I had no idea what she was planning, or I would have turned her in myself."

Levana ran a fingernail over the arm of her throne. "Were you with Linh Cinder when she underwent her cyborg surgeries?"

Adri's lip curled in disgust. "Stars, no. Her operation was completed in Europe. I did not meet her until she was brought to New Beijing."

"Was your husband present for the operation?"

Adri blinked, flustered. "I . . . I don't think so. We never spoke of it. Although he was gone for a couple of weeks when he went to . . . to claim her. I knew he was going to see about a child who had been in a hovercar accident. Although *why* he saw fit to go all the way to Europe to be charitable I never could understand, and his philanthropy was rewarded with nothing but heartache. He contracted letumosis on that trip, died within weeks of returning, leaving me to care for my two young girls and this *thing* he left in my custody—"

"Why did you never seek to capitalize on his inventions after his death?"

Adri gawked openmouthed at the queen. "Pardon, Your Majesty?"

"He was an inventor, was he not? Surely he must have left you something of value."

Adri pondered this, maybe wondering why the Lunar queen would be interested in her deceased husband. Her gaze darted around the guards and Lunars. "N-no, Your Majesty. If there was anything of value, I never saw a single micro-univ from it." A shadow fell over her face. "He left us with nothing but disgrace."

Levana's voice ran ice cold. "You are lying."

Adri's eyes widened. "No! I'm not. Garan didn't leave us with anything."

"I have evidence to the contrary, Earthen. Do you think I'm a fool?"

"What evidence?" Adri shrieked. "I haven't—I swear to you—" But whatever she meant to swear was drowned out by a flood of sobs.

Cinder clenched her jaw. She didn't know what game Levana was playing, but she knew Adri's hysteria wouldn't make one bit of difference. She considered using her Lunar gift to stop Adri's uncontrolled sobbing so she could die with a bit of dignity, but she hardened her heart and did nothing. She might need her strength when it came time for her own trial. When it was her turn, she vowed to not dissolve into a trembling mess.

"Aimery?" said Levana, her words cutting over Adri's sobs.

"One of our regiments uncovered a box of paperwork in the storage space leased to Linh Adri in her apartment building."

Levana smirked. "Do you still wish to maintain your defense that there was nothing of value left from your husband? No important paperwork still kept in storage?"

Adri hesitated. Started to shake her head, but stopped. "I don't . . . I don't know . . ."

"The paperwork," said Aimery, "indicated a pending design patent for a weapon with the intended purpose of neutralizing the Lunar gift. We suspect this weapon was intended to be used against *you*, Your Majesty, and our people."

Cinder was struggling to keep up with Aimery's accusations. *A weapon with the intended purpose of neutralizing the Lunar gift.*

She barely refrained from rubbing the back of her neck, where Linh Garan's invention—a bioelectrical security device—had been installed into her wiring. Was that what they were talking about?

"Hold on," said Kai, his voice thundering. "Do you have this paperwork that allegedly proves her guilt?"

Aimery cocked his head. "It has already been destroyed, as a matter of royal security."

Kai's knuckles whitened on the arms of his chair. "You can't destroy evidence and then try to use it to condemn somebody. You can't expect us to believe you found this box of paperwork, during an illegal search, mind you, and it held the patents for a Lunar-targeted weapon, and that Linh Adri had some working knowledge of it. That is a *lot* of speculation. On top of that, you violated a number of articles in the Interplanetary Agreement when you apprehended an Earthen citizen without due cause *and* invaded private property."

Levana cupped her chin with one hand. "Why don't we argue about this later, darling?"

"Oh, you want to argue *later*? Would that be before or after you've killed an innocent Earthen?"

Levana shrugged. "That remains to be seen."

Kai sneered. "You can't—" He abruptly cut off, forced to hold his tongue.

"You will soon learn, dear, that I do not like to be told that I *can't*." Levana shifted her attention on Adri again. "Linh Adri, you have heard the charges against you. How do you plead?"

Adri stammered, "I-I'm innocent. I swear I would never . . . I didn't know . . . I . . ."

Levana sighed. "I want to believe you."

"*Please*," Adri begged.

Levana ate another prawn. Swallowed. Licked her blood-red lips. "I am prepared to offer you clemency."

A rustle of curiosity spread through the crowd.

"This decision is contingent on your disowning all legal interest to the orphan child, Linh Cinder, and swearing fealty to me, the rightful queen of Luna and the future empress of the Eastern Commonwealth."

Adri's head was already bobbing. "Yes. Yes, I do. Gladly, Your Grace. Your Majesty."

Cinder glared at the back of Adri's head. Not because her decision was any big surprise, but because she couldn't imagine it was going to be this easy. Levana was planning something and Adri was falling right into her hands.

"Good. All charges are absolved. You may pay your respects to your sovereign." Levana held out a hand, and Adri, after a moment's hesitation, scurried forward on her knees and placed a grateful kiss on the queen's fingers. She started sobbing again.

"Does the child not show any gratitude?" said Levana.

Pearl squeaked, but slowly shuffled forward and kissed Levana's hands.

A woman in the front row, her mouth full, clapped politely.

Levana nodded and two guards stepped forward to drag Adri and Pearl to the side of the room.

Cinder had already put thoughts of her stepmother aside, bracing herself, when Levana's attention landed on her. She made no attempts to withhold her delight as she said, "Let us continue with our second trial."

Fifty-One

CINDER LUMBERED TO THE SPOT WHERE ADRI HAD BEEN groveling moments ago. She planted her feet and readied herself with an exhale that was meant to be steadying, though it was impossible to ignore the fluttering of her pulse or the list of thirty different hormones her retina display told her were flooding her system. Her brain was acutely aware of her fear.

Two guards flanked her on either side.

"Our second prisoner, Linh Cinder," said Aimery, pacing in front of her, "has been charged with the following crimes: unlawful emigration to Earth, rebelliousness, assisting a traitor to the crown, conspiring against the crown, kidnapping, meddling in intergalactic affairs, obstruction of justice, theft, evading arrest, and royal treason. The punishment for these crimes is immediate death by her own—"

"No," said Queen Levana, smiling. It was clear she'd thought a lot about this moment. "It has proven to be too difficult to manipulate her, so an exception is to be made. Her punishment shall be immediate death by . . . oh, what shall it be? Poison? Drowning? *Burning?*"

Her eyes narrowed with the last word and Cinder had a stark memory—a nightmare she'd dreamed a hundred times. A bed of red-hot coals charring her skin, her hand and leg crumbling into ash.

"Dismemberment!" a man yelled. "Starting with those horrendous appendages!"

His suggestion was met with a roar of approval from the crowd. Levana allowed the tittering for a moment before she raised a hand for silence. "A rather vile suggestion, for a rather vile girl. I'll allow it."

Cheers exploded through the room.

Kai leaped to his feet. "Are you *savages*?"

Levana ignored him. "Another idea comes to mind. Perhaps the honor of enacting this punishment should be none other than my newest, most loyal subject. I do believe she is quite eager to please." Levana curled her fingers. "Linh Adri. Won't you step forward again?"

Adri looked about ready to faint. She took two uncertain steps forward.

"Here is an opportunity to prove that you are loyal to me, your future empress, and that you despise your once-adopted daughter as much as she deserves."

Adri gulped. She was sweating. "You . . . you want me to . . ."

"*Dismember* her, Mrs. Linh. I suppose you'll need a weapon? What would you like? I'll have it brought up. A hatchet perhaps, or an axe? A knife seems like it could get messy, but a nice sharp axe—"

"Stop this," said Kai. "It's revolting."

Levana leaned back in her chair. "I am beginning to think you do not appreciate your wedding gift, my dear. You are free to leave if these proceedings unsettle you."

"I won't let you do this," he hissed between his teeth, his face flushed.

Levana shrugged at Kai. "You can't stop me. And you won't stop the coronation. There is far too much at stake to risk it all for some girl . . . some *cyborg*. I know you'll agree."

Kai's knuckles whitened and Cinder imagined him striking the queen, or attempting some equally stupid thing.

"*Wire cutters*," she said, the tone of voice and the random declaration enough to draw everyone's attention back to her. Kai's brow furrowed, but only in that moment between confusion and when her manipulation hit. She felt for his energy, crackling and heated, and did her best to soothe it. "It's all right," she said, relieved to see his muscles relax.

He would probably be angry about this later.

Snarling, Levana shoved away the tray of appetizers and stood, knocking the servant onto his side. He scrambled away. "Stop manipulating my husband."

Cinder laughed, her gaze slipping back to the queen. "Don't be a hypocrite. You manipulate him all the time."

"He is *mine*. My husband. My king."

"Your prisoner? Your pet? Your trophy?" Cinder took a step forward, and a guard was there, a hand on her shoulder, holding her back, while another half-dozen guards jumped to attention. Cinder sniffed. It was nice to know she could make Levana jumpy, even with her hands bound. "It must be so rewarding to know that every relationship you have is based on a lie."

Levana's lip curled, and for a moment, a scrambled, inconsistent picture cascaded over Cinder's retina display. Something was wrong with the left side of Levana's face. One half-shut eyelid. Strange ridges along her cheek. Cinder blinked rapidly, wondering if Levana's anger was causing her to lose control of the glamour, or if this was her own optobionics trying to make sense of the anomaly before them.

She flinched at the overload of visual data, trying to disguise her loss of focus.

The guards started to relax as their queen did.

"You are the lie," said Levana, her voice level. "You are a fraud."

Cinder's attention was caught on the queen's mouth, usually so perfect and crimson red. But something was off now. A weird downward curl to one side that didn't fit the queen's usual apathetic smile.

There was damage there beneath the glamour. Scarring of some sort. Maybe even paralysis.

Cinder stared, her pulse thundering through her head. An idea, a hope, began to build in the back of her thoughts.

"Believe me, I've been called worse," she said, schooling her expression back into nonchalance, though she could tell it was too late. Levana had seen the change in her, or perhaps felt it. The queen was instantly guarded again, suspicious.

Levana could guard herself all she wanted. She could glamour everyone in this room—everyone in her kingdom.

But she couldn't fool Cinder. Or, rather, she couldn't fool Cinder's internal computer.

She stopped fighting the onslaught of data being pieced together by her brain-machine interface. The glamour was a biological construct. Using a person's natural bioelectricity to create tiny electric pulses in the brain, to change what they saw and thought and felt and did. But the cyborg part of Cinder's brain couldn't be influenced by bioelectricity. It was all machine, all data and programming and math and logic. When faced with a Lunar glamour or when a Lunar tried to manipulate her, the two parts of her brain went to war, trying to figure out which side should be dominant.

This time, she let the cyborg side win.

The chaotic jumble of information returned full force. Pieces scrambling to right themselves, like watching a puzzle made up of pixels and binary code work itself out in her head. Like bringing a camera into focus, every glamour in the room was replaced with truth. The purring snow-leopard shawl was nothing more than a faux-fur drape. The fishbowl shoes were nothing more than clear acrylic. Levana was indeed wearing an elaborate red gown, but there were places where it clung too tight or draped too loose, and the skin revealed on her left arm was . . .

Scar tissue. Not unlike Cinder's skin around her prostheses.

As the world righted itself and the patchwork reality stopped scrambling and flipping and seaming together, Cinder commanded her brain to start recording.

"I am guilty of the crimes you listed," she said. "Kidnapping and conspiracy and all the rest of it. But these are nothing compared to the crime you committed thirteen years ago. If there is anyone in this room who is guilty of royal treason, it is the woman sitting on that throne." She fixed her eyes on Levana. "*My* throne."

The crowd stirred and Levana smirked, feigning indifference though her hands were shaking, and the details of them were flicking between lithe, pale fingers, and a pinkie that was shriveled, and the constant changes were making it hard for Cinder to focus.

"You are nothing but a criminal," said Levana, her voice writhing, "and you will be executed for your crimes."

Cinder flexed her tongue, testing it, and raised her voice. "I am Princess Selene."

Levana leaned forward. "You are an impostor!"

"And I am ready to claim what's mine. People of Artemisia, this is your chance. Renounce Levana as your queen and swear fealty to me, or I swear that when I wear that crown, every person in this room will be punished for their betrayal."

"That is *enough*. Kill her."

At first, the guards did not move, and the brief hesitation was all the information Cinder needed. Levana, in her hysteria, had lost her mental grip on her protectors.

Before the thaumaturges could realize it had happened, Cinder slipped into their minds. Twelve royal guards. Twelve men who were, as Jacin had once told her, like brainless mannequins. Puppets for the queen to shuffle around as it pleased her. Twelve armed protectors, ready to obey her every whim.

Cinder's retina display flared with information—her accelerated heart rate, the offset of bioelectrical manipulation, the adrenaline flooding her veins. Time slowed. Her brain synapses fired faster than she could recognize them, information being noted and translated and stored away before she could interpret it. Seven thaumaturges: two in black stood behind the queen, the four who had taken Cinder from her cell stood near the doors, and Aimery. The nearest guard stood 0.8 meters to her left. Six wolf soldiers: the nearest 3.1 meters away; the farthest, 6.4 meters. Forty-five Lunars in the audience. Kai and his adviser and five Earthen leaders along with seventeen additional representatives from the Union. Thirty-four servants kneeling like statues, trying to sneak glances at the girl who claimed to be their queen.

Twelve guards, with twelve guns and twelve knives, all belonging to her.

Threats were weighed, balanced, measured. Dangers turned

into data, running through a mental calculator. The stiletto knife emerged from the tip of Cinder's finger.

Every Earthen dived off their seats to take cover, including Kai. Only afterward did she realize she'd forced them to do it.

Then she used eleven of the twelve guards to open fire.

Eleven guns went off, all aiming at the six wolf mutants, while the guard closest to Cinder drew his knife and hacked through the binds around her wrists. In her hurry, she felt the blade clang against her metal palm.

Her hands burst free. Her body and mind were in harmony, just as Wolf had taught her. Her brain ticked down the list of threats.

The wolf soldiers lunged for the guards as another round of bullets exploded around them.

The nearest servant leaped to his feet and charged at Cinder, as if to tackle her.

Cinder grabbed him and shoved him toward a thaumaturge. They collided with a series of grunts, collapsing to the floor.

"*Kill her!*" Levana's voice cracked.

More gunshots throbbed against Cinder's eardrums. Bodies scrambled and chairs screeched and Cinder lost track of where the guards were and if any wolf soldiers had fallen and two aristocrats were running at her from either side and she urged the guards to focus on the thaumaturges, the thaumaturges, *now.* There was another volley of bullets and the aristocrats cried out and crumpled and tried to scurry out of the fray as soon as they were released.

A wolf soldier grabbed Cinder from behind. Pain ripped through her shoulder, his canine teeth tearing at her flesh. She screamed. Hot blood dripped down her arm. Lifting her cyborg hand, she stabbed wildly and the blade connected with flesh. The soldier released her with a roar and she spun, kicking him away.

Shaking from head to toe, she sought to reclaim the minds of the guards, but in that second of distraction the room had been emptied of the guards' bioelectric waves. Ten of them were dead, ripped to shreds by the soldiers, who had turned on them with surprising ferocity, despite the bullet holes puncturing their chests and stomachs.

In the chaos, Cinder found Kai, who was staring at her, jaw hanging open.

She tore her eyes away and found the queen, still screaming and trying to cast around her orders, but the two remaining guards no longer belonged to her and the wolves did not care who they were attacking and the thaumaturges … dead. All dead. Cinder had killed them all. Except maybe Aimery, who she couldn't find in the chaos. She wanted him, but she wanted someone else more.

Clearheaded, Cinder bent down to retrieve a gun from one of the fallen guards. She lifted her arm, gritting her teeth against the searing pain in her shoulder, and aimed for the spot between the queen's eyes.

For a split second, Levana looked terrified.

Then Kai was between them, face slack from manipulation.

Sweat dripped into Cinder's eyes, blurring the world around her.

The heavy doors crashed open, followed by the sound of boots pounding in the hallway.

Reinforcements had arrived.

Heartened, Levana sent every remaining person in the room

charging at Cinder. The Earthens and the aristocrats may not have weapons, but there were a lot of hands and a lot of nails and a lot of teeth. The new guards would be close behind.

What had her sentence been? *Death by dismemberment.*

Cinder lowered the gun, pivoted, and ran. Past the puppet Lunars in their glittering clothes. Past the mindless servants and the dead thaumaturges and the splatters of blood and the fallen chairs and Pearl and Adri cowering in a corner. She sprinted toward the only escape—the wide-open balcony hanging above the water.

The pain in her shoulder throbbed and she used the reminder to run faster, her feet pounding against the hard marble.

She heard gunshots, but she had already jumped. The black sky opened up before her and she fell.

Fifty-Two

KAI WAS ROOTED TO THE GROUND, A STATUE SURROUNDED BY turmoil. Levana was screaming—no, *screeching*—her normally melodic voice turned harsh and unbearable. She was yelling orders—*Find her! Bring her back! Kill her!*—but no one was listening. There was no one left to listen.

Nearly all of the guards were dead. The thaumaturges, dead. The wolf soldiers, dead. A handful of servant and aristocrat bodies littered the floor as well, tossed among the blood and broken furniture, the victims of hungry hybrid soldiers let loose on an unsuspecting, unarmed crowd.

Beside him, Levana ripped the jeweled necklace off some Lunar woman and threw it at a servant girl who was cowering on the floor, splattered with blood. "You! Bring me more guards! I want every guard and thaumaturge in the palace in this room at once. And *you*—clean up this mess! What are you all standing there for?"

The servants dispersed, half crawling, half slipping toward the hidden exits in the walls.

Awareness began to burrow its way through the shock, and

Kai glanced around, spotting a group of Earthen leaders clustered in a corner. Torin was among them. He looked stricken. His suit was disheveled.

"Are you hurt?" Kai asked.

"No, sir." Torin made his way to Kai, gripping the backs of chairs to keep from slipping on the bloody floor. "Are you?"

Kai shook his head. "The Earthens—?"

"All accounted for. No one seems to be injured."

Kai tried to swallow, but his throat was too dry and the saliva got stuck until he tried a second time.

He spotted Aimery emerging from one of the servants' alcoves, the only surviving thaumaturge from the trials, though more had since arrived. The members of the court who hadn't yet run from the throne room were plastered to the back walls, sobbing hysterically or jabbering to one another as they tried to relive the traumatic event, piecing together their stories. Who had seen what and which guard had shot whom and did that girl really believe she was the lost princess?

Cinder, half-starved and surrounded by enemies, had caused so much destruction in so little time, right in front of the queen. It was unnatural. Impossible. Sort of amazing.

A laugh burbled up Kai's throat, trembling uncontrolled in his diaphragm. His emotions were shredded with fear and panic and awe. Hysteria hit him like a punch to the gut. He pressed a hand over his mouth as the crazed laughter spilled out, turning fast into panicked breaths.

Torin pressed a hand between his shoulder blades. "Majesty?"

"Torin," Kai stammered, struggling to breathe, "do you think she's all right?"

Though Torin looked doubtful, he answered, "She has shown herself to be quite resilient."

Kai started to make his way across the throne room, his wedding shoes leaving prints in the sticky blood. Reaching the edge, he peered down into the water. He had not been able to tell from his seat how far the drop was. Four stories, at least. His stomach flipped. He couldn't see to the opposite shore. In fact, the lake stretched out so far it seemed to run right into the dome's wall.

Though the air was still, the water was choppy and black as ink. He searched and searched for something to indicate a body, a girl, a sheen of a metal limb, but there was no sign of her.

He shivered. Could Cinder swim? Was her body even designed for swimming? He knew she'd taken showers aboard the Rampion, but to be fully submerged . . .

"Could she have survived?"

Kai jumped. Levana stood a few feet away with her arms crossed and nostrils flared. Kai moved away from her, spurred by the irrational fear that she was about to push him off the ledge. As soon as he backed away, though, he remembered she could still make him jump.

"I don't know," he said. To provoke her, he added, "That was some marvelous entertainment, by the way. I had high expectations, and you did not disappoint."

She snarled and he was glad he'd backed away.

"Aimery," she snapped. "Have the lake combed by morning. I want the cyborg's heart served to me on a silver platter."

Aimery bowed. "It will be done, Your Majesty." He nodded toward the group of thaumaturges that had arrived after all the action, who were all trying to look like the destruction of the throne room wasn't as shocking as it was. Four of them departed. "I am afraid I must inform Your Majesty that there has been a disturb—"

"*Clearly* there is a disturbance!" Levana bellowed. She jutted her red fingernail toward the lake. "You think I can't see that?"

Aimery pressed his lips. "Of course, My Queen, but there is something else."

Her gaze burned. "What else could there be?"

"As you know, the trial and execution tonight was live-broadcast to all sectors. It would appear that as a result of the cyborg's escape, the people are . . . they are rioting. In several sectors, it seems. SB-1 is the nearest that our security footage indicates, and there also appears to be a sizable crowd of civilians beginning to march toward Artemisia from as far away as AT-6."

"She did not escape." Levana's voice sounded thin and taut, about to splinter. Kai took another step away from her. "She is dead. Tell them she is dead. She could not have survived the fall. And find her! *Find her!*"

"Yes, My Queen. We will assemble a broadcast informing the people of Linh Cinder's death immediately. But we cannot guarantee that this alone will subdue the riots . . ."

"Enough." Levana shoved the thaumaturge out of her way and stormed toward her throne, planting herself before it. "Barricade the maglev tunnels in and out of Artemisia. Shut down the ports. No one is to enter or leave this dome until that cyborg has been found and the civilians of Luna have repented for their actions. If anyone tries to get through the barricades, shoot them!"

"Wait," said Europe's Prime Minister Bromstad, stalking toward Levana. The throne room had mostly emptied of Lunar aristocrats, leaving only the servants who were trying to rid the room of bodies and the Earthens who were trying not to look as shaken as they were. "You can't lock down the ports. You invited us to a wedding, not a war zone. My cabinet and I are leaving tonight."

Levana raised an eyebrow, and that simple, elegant gesture made every hair on Kai's neck stand on edge. She approached the prime minister, and though Bromstad held his ground, Kai could see him regretting his words. Behind him, the other leaders drew closer together.

"You want to leave tonight?" said Levana, the purr having returned to her inflections. "Well then. Allow me to help you with that."

A nearby servant, who had been attempting invisibility, stopped scrubbing the floor and instead picked up a stray serving fork. On her knees, head bowed, the servant handed the fork to Prime Minister Bromstad.

The second his hand closed around the fork's handle, fear surged through his face. Not just fear. But a fear in knowing that he was now holding a weapon, and Levana could make him do anything—*anything*—that she wanted to.

"Stop!" said Kai, grabbing Levana's elbow.

She sneered at him.

"As I said before, I will not make you my empress if you attack a leader of an allied country. Let him go. Let them all go. There's been enough bloodshed for one day."

Levana's eyes burned like coals, and there was a moment in which Kai thought she might kill them all and simply take Earth with her army, her pathway cleared with all the world leaders gone.

He knew the thought had crossed her mind.

But there were a lot of people on Earth—far more than on

Luna. She could not control them all. A rebellion on Earth would be much more difficult to secure if she tried to take it by force.

The fork clattered to the floor and the air left Bromstad in rush.

"She will not save you," Levana hissed. "I know you think she's alive and that this little rebellion of hers will succeed, but it won't. Soon, I will be empress and she will be dead. If she isn't already." Schooling her features, she slicked her hands down the front of her dress, like she could smooth out the disaster of the past hour. "I do not know that I will see you again, dear husband, until we stand together for our coronations. I am afraid the sight of you is making me ill."

Thanks to a warning look from Torin, Kai managed to withhold commentary on this unexpected disappointment.

With a snap of her fingers, Levana ordered one of the servants to have a bath drawn in her chambers and then she was gone, blood clinging to the hem of her gown as she swept from the throne room.

Kai exhaled, dizzy from it all. The queen's sudden absence. The iron tang of blood mixed with sharp cleaning chemicals and the lingering aroma of braised beef. The way his ears still echoed with gunfire and how he would never forget the image of Cinder launching herself off that ledge.

"Your Majesty?" said a shriveled, frightened voice.

Turning, he saw Linh Adri and Pearl crouched in a corner. Tears and dirt streaked their faces.

"Might we . . ." Adri gulped, and he could see the fluttering rise and fall of her chest as she tried to gather herself. "Might it be possible for you to . . . to send my daughter and me home?" She sniffed and brand-new tears pooled in her eyes. Scrunching up her face, she let her shoulders slump, her body barely supported in the corner of the room. "I'm ready . . . I want to go home now. Please."

Kai clenched his jaw, pitying the woman almost as much as he despised her. "I'm sorry," he said, "but it doesn't look like anyone is leaving until this is over."

Fifty-Three

THE WATER HIT HER LIKE CONCRETE. THE FORCE POUNDED through her body. Every limb vibrated, first with the hard slap of the water, then from its icy cold.

It swallowed her down. She was still reeling from the hit as the air left her lungs in a burst of froth and bubbles. Already her chest was burning. Her body rolled over like a buoy, her heavy left leg dragging her down.

A red warning light filled up the darkness.

LIQUID IMMERSION DETECTED. SHUTTING DOWN POWER SUPPLY IN 3 . . .

That was as far as the countdown got. Blackness pulled at the back of Cinder's brain, as if a switch had been turned off. Dizziness rocked her. She forced her eyes open and looked toward the surface, only able to orient herself because she could feel her leg pulling her down, down.

White sparks were creeping into the corners of her vision. Her lungs tightened, begging to contract.

Slippery weeds reached up to grasp at her, sliming her right calf where her pants had bunched around her knee. Willing herself to stay conscious, Cinder aimed her finger's flashlight into the blackness at her feet and tried to turn it on, but nothing happened.

With just enough light from the palace filtering through the muck and water, Cinder thought she detected a series of pale bones caught among the grasses. Her metal foot sank into a rib cage.

She jolted, surprise clearing her thoughts as the bones crushed beneath her.

Gritting her teeth, Cinder used every ounce of energy left to push herself off the lake bottom, struggling back toward the surface. Her left leg and hand weren't responding to her controls. They had become nothing but dead weights at the end of her limbs, and her shoulder screamed where the mutant soldier had dug his teeth into her flesh. It took every ounce of remaining energy to claw her way upward.

Her diaphragm twitched. Overhead, the glare on the surface grew brighter, lights flickering like a mirage over the surface. She felt the strength draining out of her, her waterlogged leg trying to drag her back down . . .

She burst through the surface with a sputter, sucking huge mouthfuls of air into her lungs. She managed to tread water for one desperate moment before she was pulled down again. Her muscles burned as she kicked, bobbing back up at the surface, straining to keep her head above the water.

As the flashes in her vision began to recede, Cinder swiped the water from her eyes. The palace towered above her, ominous and oppressive despite its beauty, stretching along either side of the lake. Without artificial daylight brightening the dome, she could see the spread of the Milky Way beyond the glass, mesmerizing.

On the balcony far above her, Cinder caught shadows moving. Then a wave crashed into her and she was underwater again, her body battered against the current. She lost her sense of direction, up or down. Panic burst again in her head, her arms flailing for control against the buffeting waves. Her shoulder throbbed. Only when she felt herself sinking did she reorient herself and flounder back to the surface.

She tried to swim away from the palace, toward the center of the lake, though there was no end in sight. She hadn't gone far before her muscles started to burn, and every joint on the left side of her body was screaming at the useless weights of her prosthetic limbs. Her lungs felt scratched raw, but she had to survive. She couldn't stop fighting—couldn't stop trying. Kai was still up there. All her friends were on Luna somewhere, needing her, and the people of the outer sectors were counting on her, and she had to keep pushing, pushing . . .

Holding her breath, Cinder ducked beneath the surface and tugged off her boots, letting them sink. It wasn't much, but she felt lightened enough to scramble against her body's lopsided weight, propelling herself through the waves.

The lake seemed never-ending, but every time she glanced back and saw how far the Lunar palace had receded into the distance, Cinder felt a new surge of strength. The shore was lit now by mansions and tiny boat docks. The far side of the lake had disappeared over the horizon.

She rolled onto her back, panting. Her leg was on fire, her arms made of rubber, the wound in her shoulder like an ice pick jammed into her flesh. She couldn't go any farther.

It occurred to her, as a wave crashed over her body and she almost didn't bother to reach for the surface, that she didn't know if she'd reserved enough energy to make it to the shore.

What if they were waiting for her there? She couldn't fight. Couldn't manipulate. She was done. A half-dead, beaten girl.

Cinder's head collided with something solid.

She gasped, her loss of propulsion sending her beneath the surface again.

She lashed out with her foot, forcing herself back up, and spat the water from her mouth. Her hands slapped against the hard, slick surface she'd run into. The dome.

She'd reached the edge of Artemisia.

The enormous curved wall acted like a dam, holding the lake back, while on the other side of the glass the crater continued for miles in each direction—dry and pocked and disturbingly, horrifyingly deep.

Bobbing against the glass, Cinder stared at the bottom of the crater hundreds of feet below. She felt like a fish in a fishbowl. Trapped.

She turned toward the shore, but couldn't make herself move. She was shivering. Her stomach was hollow. Her weighted leg pulled her down again and it took the strength of a thousand wolf soldiers for her to climb back to the surface. Water flooded her mouth and she spat as soon as her head broke through the waves, but it was useless.

She couldn't.

Dizziness rocked over her. Her arms flopped against the water. Her right leg gave out first, too tired for one more kick. Cinder gasped and she was dragged down, one hand sliding down the slimy glass wall.

There was a strange release as blackness engulfed her. A pride in knowing that when they combed the lake they would find her body way out here and they would know how hard she had fought.

Her body went limp. A wave pushed her back and she struck the wall, but hardly felt it. Then something was gripping her, dragging her upward.

Too weak to fight, Cinder let herself be carried. Her head broke into the air and her lungs expanded. She coughed. Arms wrapped around her. A body pressed her against the wall.

Cinder drooped forward, settling her head against a shoulder.

"Cinder." A man's voice, strained and vibrating through her chest. "Stop slacking off, would you?" He adjusted her in his arms, shifting her weight to cradle her in one elbow. "Cinder!"

She turned her bleary eyes up. Catching glimpses of his chin and profile and the wet hair plastered to his brow. She must have been delirious.

"Thorne?" The word stuck in her throat.

"That's Captain . . . to you." He gritted his teeth, straining to pull them toward the shore. "Aces, you're heavy. Oh, there you are! How nice of you . . . to help out . . ."

"Your mouth uses up a lot of energy," someone growled. *Jacin?* "Roll her onto her back so her body's not fighting against—"

His words turned into a sharp yell as Cinder's body slipped out of Thorne's hold, sinking into the comforting lull of the waves.

Fifty-Four

CRESS AND IKO STOOD GRIPPING EACH OTHER ON THE lakeshore, watching Thorne and Jacin dive beneath the surface. Cress was shivering—more from fear than cold—and while Iko's body didn't give off natural heat like a human being, there was a comfort that came from her solidarity. They waited, but there was no sign of Thorne or Jacin or Cinder. They'd been underwater for a long time.

Too long.

Cress didn't realize she was holding her breath until her lungs screamed. She gasped, the sensation more painful because she knew her companions would have been holding their breath for that long too.

Iko squeezed her hand. "Why haven't they—" She took a step forward, but paused.

Iko's body wasn't made for swimming and Cress had never been in a body of water larger than a bathtub.

They were useless.

Cress pressed a shaky hand over her mouth, ignoring the hot tears on her face. It had been far too long.

"There!" Iko cried, pointing. Two—no, three heads appeared over the dark, chopping waves.

Iko took another step. "She is alive, isn't she? She . . . she doesn't seem to be moving. Do you see her moving?"

"I'm sure she's alive. I'm sure they're all fine."

She glanced at Iko, but couldn't bring herself to ask the question she knew they'd all been thinking. The live broadcast of the wedding feast had shown them everything. The trial. The massacre. Cinder jumping from the ledge and plunging toward the lake below.

Could Cinder swim?

Everyone had thought it, but no one had asked.

Together, the four of them had sneaked through the city, grateful that the few Lunars they saw were too busy celebrating the queen's marriage to pay them any attention. Jacin had led the way, familiar with the city and the patterns of the lake, knowing where the bodies that fell into it from the throne room occasionally surfaced. There had been no hesitation between them—they all knew they had to find Cinder while Levana was reeling from the attack.

When they had caught sight of Cinder's dark form among the waves, there was a resounding gasp of joy and relief from the whole group, but they still had no idea what state Cinder would be in.

Was she alive? Was she injured? *Could she swim?*

When the trio in the water was close enough, Cress let go of Iko and waded out to join them. Together they pulled Cinder's body ashore, laying her down on the white sand.

"Is she alive?" Iko asked, half-hysterical. "Is she breathing?"

"Let's get her to that boathouse," Jacin said. "We can't stay out here."

Thorne, Jacin, and Iko shared the job of carrying Cinder's limp body while Cress ran ahead to hold the doors. Three row-boats were stacked on brackets against the two sidewalls, with a fourth laid out in the middle and covered with a tarp. She cleared a mess of oars and fishing equipment from the tarp, making a space for them to lay out Cinder's body, but Jacin laid her on the hard floor instead. Iko closed the doors, shrouding the room in darkness. Cress scrambled to switch on her portscreen for its ghostly blue light.

Jacin didn't bother to check for breath or a pulse before he leaned over Cinder and locked his hands together on top of her chest. His eyes hardened as he started to pump down on her sternum with quick, forceful movements. Cress winced at the sound of popping cartilage.

"Do you know what you're doing?" said Thorne, crouched on Cinder's other side. He coughed and wiped his mouth with his arm. "Do you need help? We learned this in boot camp...I remember...sort of..."

"I know what I'm doing," said Jacin.

And he *did* seem to know, as he tilted Cinder's head back and formed a seal over her mouth with his own.

Thorne didn't look comforted, but he didn't argue.

Kneeling at Cinder's feet, Cress watched in silence as Jacin started the compressions again. She remembered net dramas where the heroine was revived by the hero with mouth-to-mouth resuscitation. It had seemed so romantic. Cress had even had fantasies about drowning, dreams in which the press of a man's lips could breathe life back into her lifeless form.

The dramas had lied. There was a violence to this they hadn't shown. She grimaced as Jacin's hands flattened against Cinder's sternum for a third time, imagining she could feel the bruises on her own chest.

She felt suspended in time. Thorne took up sentinel by the doorway, peering out through a small, filthy window to keep watch. Iko wrapped her arms around her body and looked about ready to dissolve into impossible tears.

Cress was about to take Iko's hand again when Cinder jerked. She started to gag.

Jacin eased her head over to the side and water burbled out of her mouth, though not as much as Cress expected. Jacin held Cinder in place, keeping her airway clear, until she had stopped hacking. She was breathing again. Weak and shaky, but breathing.

Cinder opened her eyes and Jacin eased her into a sitting position. Her right arm flopped. Her hand found Jacin's arm and squeezed. She spat a few more times. "Good timing," she croaked.

Water was glistening on her lips and chin until Iko reached forward and wiped it away with her sleeve. Cinder looked at her and her eyes lightened, though her eyelids still drooped with exhaustion.

"Iko? I thought . . ." With a groan, she fell onto her back.

Iko squealed and made to collapse onto Cinder, but reconsidered. Instead, she scurried around Jacin so she could lift Cinder's shoulders and cradle her head in her lap. Smiling wearily, Cinder reached up to pet Iko's braids. Her cyborg hand was missing one of its fingers.

"We can't stay here," said Jacin, rubbing water droplets from his cropped hair. "They'll start the search closer to the palace, but it won't be long before they barricade the whole lake. We need to find someplace for her to recover."

"Any ideas?" asked Thorne. "We're not exactly in friendly territory."

"I need medical supplies," said Cinder, her eyes shut. "A soldier bit me. Should clean the wound before it's infected." She sighed, too exhausted to go on.

"I wouldn't mind a warm meal and a clothes dryer so long as we're making demands," said Thorne. Leaning forward, he stripped off his soaking wet shirt.

Cress's eyes widened, glued to him as he wrung the lake out of the shirt, water splattering on the concrete.

Jacin said something, but she didn't catch what.

Thorne pulled his shirt on again, a little more dry and wrinkled now, and Cress was able to breathe again.

"That might work," said Thorne, nodding at Cinder. "Think you can make it?"

"No," said Cinder. "I can't walk."

"It's not far," said Jacin. "I thought you were supposed to be tough."

Cinder scowled up at him. "I *can't* walk. The water did something to my interface." She paused. Wheezed. "My leg and hand aren't functioning. Lost net access too."

Four pairs of eyes shifted to the glistening metal foot. Cress was not in the habit of thinking of Cinder as cyborg—as something *other.* As someone who could just . . . stop functioning.

"Fine," said Jacin, turning to Thorne. "You want to carry her first, or shall I?"

Thorne raised an eyebrow. "Do you know how *heavy* she is?"

Cinder kicked him.

He huffed. "Fine. You first."

"ARE WE SURE ABOUT THIS?" CRESS WHISPERED. SHE WAS crouched behind a trellis covered in ivy, along with Cinder, Thorne, and Jacin, watching as Iko lifted the shining gold door knocker for the third time.

"I told you, they aren't home," said Jacin, annoyed at the precaution of having Iko scout out the pillared mansion before they went in. "This family is popular at court. They'll be staying at the palace all week."

After a fourth knock bore no result, Iko turned to them and shrugged.

Cress wrapped an arm around Cinder's waist—she was a good height to act as a crutch for her as they hobbled through the garden. Cinder's dead metal foot dragged a groove into the pathway of tumbled blue glass.

"What if it's locked?" asked Cress, glancing down the street, although they hadn't seen a single person. Perhaps this entire neighborhood was made up of popular members of the court. Perhaps this whole city was off having a raucous celebration at the palace.

"Then I'll pick it," said Thorne.

The door wasn't locked. They found themselves in a grandiose entryway with a curved staircase and a sea of gold and white tiles.

Thorne let out a low whistle. "This place is ripe for plundering."

Iko responded, "Can I go plunder the master closet?"

Jacin found an enormous vase full of flowers and set it on the floor inside the front door, so anyone who opened it would knock it over and shatter the vase into a hundred tiny pieces. Fair warning that it was time for them to leave.

It didn't take them long to find a kitchen that was bigger than Cress's satellite. Cress and Iko maneuvered Cinder onto a stool and helped her prop up her leg while Jacin rummaged through the pantry, emerging with an assortment of nuts and fruits.

"What do you think is wrong with you?" Iko asked.

Cinder smacked her palm against the side of her head, like she hoped to jog something back into place. "It's not a power issue," she said. "My eyes are working, at least. It's something in the connection between the brain-machine interface and my prostheses. It affected both my hand and leg at the same time, so it must be a primary connection. My control panel could have gotten waterlogged or something. Could be a few dead wires." She sighed. "I guess I should feel lucky. If my power cell had died, I'd be dead with it."

They mulled over this for a moment, picking at the food.

Thorne glanced back at the pantry. "Did you see any rice in there? Maybe we could fill Cinder's head with it."

Everyone stared at him.

"You know, to . . . absorb the moisture, or something. Isn't that a thing?"

"We're not pouring *rice* in my head."

"But I'm pretty sure I remember someone putting a portscreen in a bag of rice once after they'd put it through a clothes washer and—"

"*Thorne.*"

"Just trying to be helpful."

"What *do* you need to fix it?" asked Cress, then hunched down between her shoulders as all eyes turned toward her.

Cinder frowned, and Cress could see her working through different possibilities. Then she started to laugh, dragging her good hand through her tangled, still-damp hair. "A mechanic," she said. "A really good one."

Iko beamed. "That, we have. Plus, we're in a mansion. They

have tons of technology here. We just need to find you the parts and tools and you can talk me through fixing you. Right?"

Cinder pursed her lips. There were dark circles beneath her eyes and an unhealthy pallor to her skin. Cress had never seen her so worn down.

Iko cocked her head. She must have noticed it too, because she spent a moment studying Cinder, then everyone in their group. "You all look awful. Maybe you should rest for a while. I can keep watch."

They mulled over the idea for a minute, before Thorne said, "That's actually not a bad idea."

Iko shrugged. "Someone has to stay clearheaded in an emergency situation." Frowning, she added, "Although I never thought it would have to be me."

Thorne turned to Cinder. "You'll think more clearly after a nap."

She ignored him, staring at the counter. There was a dejected slump to her shoulders, a hollowness in her gaze.

"I don't think a nap is going to fix this," she said, lifting her cyborg hand. It hung limply from her wrist, a hole where one finger had been removed. "I can't believe this is happening. I can't fight like this, or start a revolution, or be a *queen*. I can't do anything like this. I'm broken. I'm literally *broken*."

Iko settled a hand on Cinder's shoulder. "Yeah, but broken isn't the same as unfixable."

Fifty-Five

"THIS WAS A BAD DECISION," SAID SCARLET.

Winter peered over at her. There was discomfort in Scarlet's face, a deep-etched line between her eyebrows.

Reaching over, Winter tugged at one of Scarlet's curls. "You have not turned back yet."

Scarlet batted her away. "Yeah, because I no longer have any idea where we are." Scarlet glanced over her shoulder. "We've been wandering around these caves for *hours.*"

Winter followed her look, but the cave was so dim they couldn't see very far before it disappeared into shadows lit only by the occasional glowing orb on the ceiling. Winter couldn't tell how far she and Scarlet had come through the underground lava tubes in search of the wolf soldiers—in search of an army—and she still didn't know how much farther they would have to go. Whenever she thought of turning back, though, she would imagine she heard a faint howl in the distance, compelling her to go on. Her dream of Ryu and Levana clung to her thoughts like sticky pollen, inciting her resolve again and again.

Levana believed she could control everyone on this moon. The people, the soldiers, Winter herself.

But she was wrong. Winter was sick of being manipulated, and she knew she couldn't be the only one. She would find soldiers to fight for her and together they would rid themselves of her stepmother and her cruelty.

They rounded another bend. The dark, gritty walls never changed. The ceiling was jagged, but the ground was worn smooth from years of foot traffic. And marching. Did the soldiers march? Winter wasn't sure. She had not paid much attention to her stepmother's army. She wished she'd taken more of an interest in what Levana was doing with these boys-made-soldiers. What she had been planning all along.

Otherwise, the cave looked like it had since it had first been carved out by molten lava billions of years ago. Back then, Luna had been a place of heat and transformation. It was difficult to fathom now in these cold, barren caverns, left to exist in quiet darkness.

When Earthens had first built their colony, they had made temporary homes of the vast interconnected lava tubes while the domes were under construction, and afterward converted them into storage and shuttle rails.

Only recently had they been used for something violent and grotesque.

"Secret barracks for a secret army," she whispered to herself.

"All right, time out." Scarlet stopped and settled her hands on her hips. "Do you even know where we're going?"

Winter tugged on a lock of her own hair this time, like a spring curled against her cheek. There was still a bump on her scalp where she'd hit her head, though the headache was mostly gone. "Many of the lava tubes that were not used for the shuttles were converted into underground training facilities. That is where the soldiers will be. At least, those who have not been sent to Earth."

Scarlet blinked, slowly. "And how many lava tubes are there under Luna's surface?"

Winter blinked, slowly, back. "I do not know. But did you know Luna started its life as a giant ball of magma, liquid and burning?"

Scarlet knotted her lips to one side. "How many wolf regiments are left on Luna?"

This time, Winter did not answer at all.

Exhaling, Scarlet rubbed at her brow. "I knew better. I knew better than to listen to you. *Winter.* We could be wandering down here for days and not see a single person. And even if we do find one of these regiments, or packs, or whatever they call themselves, they are most likely going to *eat us.* This is suicide!" She pointed back the direction they'd come. "We should be looking for allies, not enemies."

"You go back then." Winter continued down the endless tunnel.

Scarlet let out a bedraggled groan and stomped after her. "Thirty minutes," she said. "We are going to walk for thirty more minutes and if we haven't seen any evidence that we're getting closer, then we are turning around and going back, and I am not taking no for an answer. I'll club you over the head and drag you back if I have to."

Winter fluttered her lashes, amused by the thought. "We will find them, Scarlet-friend. They will join us. Your Wolf is proof that they are men, not monsters."

"I really wish you would stop comparing them with Wolf. Wolf is different. The rest of them . . . they *are* monsters. I met Wolf's pack in Paris, and they were brutal and terrible. And that was her special ops, and *they're* still mostly human! You can't reason with these monsters any more than you could a . . . a . . ."

"A pack of wolves?"

Scarlet glared. "Exactly."

"Ryu was my friend."

Scarlet threw her hands into the air. "What are you going to do, play *fetch* with them? You are thinking about this all wrong. They are under Levana's control, or whoever their thaumaturge is. They will do what they're told, and that will be to *eat us*."

"They were young boys forced into a difficult situation. They did not ask for this life, just as your Wolf didn't ask for it, but they have done what they needed to do to survive. If they are given the opportunity to break their binds of enslavement, I believe they will take it. I believe they will side with us."

Winter heard a distant, low howl, and shivered. Scarlet didn't seem to hear it, though, so she said nothing.

"You have no idea whose side they'll take. They've been so messed with, they'll side with whoever is offering them a bigger piece of steak." Scarlet hesitated. "What's wrong? Are you hallucinating right now?"

Winter forced a smile. "Not unless you are a figment of my imagination, but how could I ever be sure one way or the other? So I will go on believing you are real."

Scarlet looked unimpressed with her logic. "You know what these men become, don't you? You know they can never be normal again."

"I would think that you, of all people, would believe in their ability to change. Wolf changed because of his love for you. Why can they not change also?" She started walking again.

"Wolf is—it's not the *same*. Winter, I know you're used to

batting your eyelashes at everyone who walks by and expecting them to fall in love with you, but that's not going to happen here. They are going to laugh at you and mock you and then they are going to—"

"Eat me. Yes. I understand."

"You don't seem to be grasping the meaning behind the words. This isn't a metaphor. I'm talking about huge teeth and digestive systems."

"*Fat and bones and marrow and meat,*" Winter sang. "*We only wanted a snack to eat.*"

Scarlet grunted. "You can be so disturbing."

Winter hooked her elbow with Scarlet's. "Don't be afraid. They will help us."

Before Scarlet could mount another argument, a peculiar smell assaulted their senses, sharp and pungent. An animal smell, like in the menagerie, but different. Sweat and salt and body odor mingling in the cave's stale air, along with something rank, like old meat.

"Well," said Scarlet, "I think we found them."

A chill crawled down Winter's neck. Neither of them moved for a long while.

"If we can smell them," said Scarlet, "they can smell us."

Winter raised her chin. "I'll understand if you leave. I can go on without you."

Scarlet seemed to consider it, but then she shrugged. Her expression was reckless. "I'm beginning to think we're all going to end up wolf food anyway by the time this is over."

Facing her, Winter cupped Scarlet's face in both hands. "It is not like you to talk like that."

Scarlet clenched her jaw. "They took Wolf and they took Cinder, and as much as I want to see Levana ripped into tiny pieces and fed to her own mutants, I just don't think we have a whole lot of hope without them." She gulped, her resentment clouding over. "And I . . . I don't want to see this place. He was trained here too, you know. I'm afraid to see what he came from, what he . . . who he was."

"He is your Wolf now, and you are his alpha."

Scarlet laughed. "According to Jacin, you need a pack to be an alpha."

Jacin. The name brought sunshine and blood and kisses and growls rising to Winter's skin. She gave it a moment to sink back toward her bones, before she tilted Scarlet's head down and placed a kiss on the top of her flame-and-fury hair. "I will get you your pack."

Fifty-Six

THEY HADN'T GONE MUCH FARTHER BEFORE THEY DETECTED noise rumbling through the caverns. Low and thunderous, like a distant train. They came to another fork in the tunnel, and while one path led into further darkness and rock and nothingness, the other ran into a set of iron doors. Hinged into the regolith walls, the doors looked ancient. Their sole ornamentation was a faded label painted on the lower corner of each door— STOREROOM 16, SECTOR LW-12.

A tiny screen had been embedded into the wall beside the doors. It was old and outdated and the text kept flickering. *LUNAR REGIMENT 117, PACKS 1009-1020.*

The ground and walls thrummed with activity beyond those doors—laughter and shouting and thumping footsteps. For the first time since she'd embarked on this quest, Winter felt a flutter of nervousness in her stomach.

Scarlet glanced at her. "It isn't too late to go back."

"I disagree."

Sighing, Scarlet studied the screen. "Eleven packs, so around a hundred soldiers, give or take."

Winter hummed, a sound without commitment. A hundred soldiers.

Animals, killers, predators, or so everyone claimed. Had she truly gone mad to think she could change them?

Her eyes began to mist, surprising her. She had not realized that thinking of her own imbalance would sadden her, but the feel of her ribs crushing against her heart was unmistakable.

"Why did you follow me?" she asked, staring at the solid doors. "Knowing what's wrong with me. Knowing that I'm broken."

Scarlet scoffed. "That is an *excellent* question."

A loud thud was followed by hollers. The walls reverberated around them.

They had not been noticed. Scarlet was right. They could turn around and leave. Winter could admit she was delusional and no one should ever listen to her. She was adept only at making the wrong decisions.

"I couldn't let you go on your own," said Scarlet, most of the venom gone from her tone.

"Why?"

"I don't know. Call me crazy."

Winter shut her eyes. "I won't. You are not damaged like I am. You are not a hundred scattered pieces, blowing farther and farther away from each other."

"How would you know?"

Listing her head, Winter dared to look up again.

Scarlet leaned against the regolith wall. "My father was a liar and a drunk. My mother left when I was a kid and never looked back. I witnessed a man kill my grandmother and then rip out her throat with his teeth. I was kept in a cage for six weeks. I was forced to cut off my own finger. I'm pretty sure I'm falling in love with a guy who has been genetically modified and mentally programmed to be a predator. So all things considered, I'd say I have a fair amount of scattered pieces myself."

Winter felt her resolve crumbling. "You came with me because it was the quickest path to death, then."

A crease formed between Scarlet's eyebrows. "I'm not *suicidal*," she said, the sharpness returning to her tongue. "I came with you because—" She crossed her arms over her chest. "Because ever since my grandma took me in, I've heard people tell me she was crazy. A kooky, belligerent old woman, always good for a joke around town. They had no idea how brilliant she was. That crazy old woman risked everything she had to protect Cinder when she was a baby, and in the end, she sacrificed her own life rather than give up Cinder's secret. She was brave and strong, and everyone else was too closeminded to see it." She rolled her eyes, annoyed with her own frustration. "I guess I'm just hoping that despite all the absurd things you say, you might also be a little bit brilliant. That this time, you might be right." She held up her finger. "That said, if you're going to tell me how stupid this idea was to begin with and we should run like hell, then I'm right behind you."

Beyond the doors, something crashed, and there was a round of boisterous laughter. Then, a howl. A chorus of a dozen other voices rose up to meet it, sounding victorious.

A muscle twitched in Winter's jaw, but her lip had stopped trembling. She hadn't cried. She'd been too focused on Scarlet's words to remember to be upset. "I believe they were boys once and they can be boys again. I believe I can help them, and they will help me in return."

Scarlet sighed, sounding a little disappointed and a little resigned, but not surprised. "And I believe you're not as crazy as you want everyone to think you are."

Winter's gaze flitted toward Scarlet, surprised, but Scarlet didn't return it. She stepped forward and placed her palm on one of the heavy doors. "So, do we knock?"

"I do not think they would hear us." Another round of howls echoed through the cavern. Winter swiped her fingers across the screen, and the text changed.

SECURITY CLEARANCE IDENTIFICATION REQUIRED

She pressed the pads of her fingers onto the screen and it brightened, welcoming her. The doors began to open, creaking on ancient hinges. When Winter turned back, Scarlet was staring at her, aghast.

"You do realize you just alerted the queen to where you are, right?"

Winter shrugged. "By the time she finds us, either we will have an army to protect us, or we will have already become meat and marrow and bone."

She drifted through the doors and instantly froze.

Scarlet had been right. There were about a hundred men in the 117th Regiment of Levana's army, though *men* was a general term for what they'd become. *Soldiers* felt inadequate too. Winter had been hearing stories of her stepmother's army for years, but they were far more beastly than she had ever imagined, with malformed bodies, fur down the sides of their faces, and snarled lips curved around enormous teeth.

This storeroom, which had begun life as housing for the first colonists, was equipped to hold many more than a hundred people. The ceiling reached three stories high and was rough with divots and stalactites where air bubbles had formed and lava had dripped eons ago. Though the cavern was ancient and impenetrable, someone long ago had had the foresight to rein-force it with interspersed stone columns. Countless alcoves and more corridors stretched in every direction, leading to addi-tional barracks or training grounds.

Around the exterior were dingy lockers and open crates, many of which had been left wide-open and neglected. Benches and exercise equipment filled the remaining space: freestand-ing punching bags, chin-up bars, weights. Many of them had been shoved aside to make room for the main entertainment in the room's center.

The howls dissolved into cheering and whooping again. Ca-nine teeth flashed. Most of them were in some state of undress—missing shirts, bare feet, a stunning amount of hair in places that Winter wasn't certain were natural or not.

A shudder danced over her skin. Scarlet's words rang back to her: *They will do what they're told, and that will be to eat us.*

Scarlet was right. This had been a mistake. She was not bril-liant. She was losing her mind.

The doors slammed shut, making her jump. One man jerked around to face them. His gaze fell on Winter, skipped to Scarlet, then returned. First curious, then—inevitably—ravenous.

A sly smile curled one side of his mouth.

"Well, well," he mused. "Feeding time already?"

Fifty-Seven

THE MAN WHO HAD SPOKEN GRABBED THE NEAREST SOLDIER by the neck and tossed him toward the center of the circle. Shouts of surprise and anger rolled through the gathered men as a few toppled beneath their comrade's weight. Within seconds there was a furor of flying fists and snapping jaws. One man slashed at the one who had noticed them, sharpened fingernails drawing lines of blood across his chest. A second later, he was also picked up and hurled into the turmoil.

"*Manners*," someone yelled, loud enough that his voice shook through the walls, and Winter had a quick and searing vision of the dome of lava rock crumbling on top of them. It would start with a quaking of the walls, then a few dribbles of dust and pebbles, until a crack drove its way from one end of the cavern to the other, opening wide and—

"There are *ladies* in our presence," said the mutant who had first seen them. His nose crinkled at the word *ladies*.

The attention of a hundred hybrid soldiers landed on Winter and Scarlet. As eyebrows rose and thorny gazes raked over them, the men seemed to forget their brawl. They started to spread out. Lithe, muscular bodies creeping between the mess of equipment with agonizing patience. Noses twitching. Tongues tapping at sharp teeth.

Hair prickled at the back of Winter's neck and she found herself rooted to the floor, shocked by the sudden, breathable silence.

Once the crowd had dispersed, she could see that their focus had been on a fight between two of the soldiers, both of whom were bleeding and swollen and grinning, as intrigued as the rest. It was impossible to tell which of them had been winning the fight prior to the interruption.

There was an abundance of scars and faded bruises on all of the men, suggesting that such brawls were a common occurrence. A way to pass the time while waiting to be sent to Earth and take part in Levana's war.

Fear pulsed through Winter. What if she had been wrong?

"Hello, pretty ladies," said one of the soldiers, rubbing his whiskered jaw. "Are you lost?"

Winter shrank closer to Scarlet, but Scarlet pulled away, stepping forward to meet them. Scarlet was the brave one, the resilient one, proving it as she tilted back her head in mock defiance.

"Which one of you is in charge?" said Scarlet, fisting her hands on her hips. "We want to speak with your alpha."

A dull cackle spread through them.

"Which one?" said the first mutant. "Eleven packs, eleven alphas."

"The strongest one," said Scarlet, piercing him with a glower as fierce as any Winter had ever seen. "If you're not sure which one that is, we'll wait while you fight it out."

"Are you sure you don't want to take your pick, pretty lady?"

one asked as he prowled behind them, cutting off their exit—not that Winter had any hope of running. She could tell they were trying to intimidate her and Scarlet, and she could feel to her bones how well it was working. "I'm sure any of us would be happy to satisfy whatever needs you might have."

Scarlet glared at him from the corner of her eye. "I already have an alpha mate to satisfy my *needs*, and he could slaughter any one of you."

The man barked and a rough chuckle rumbled through the rest of them.

The first soldier stepped closer to Scarlet and his expression was intrigued again. "She's telling the truth," he said, silencing the laughter. "His scent is all over her. One of us." His eyes narrowed. "Or . . . a special operative?"

"Alpha Ze'ev Kesley," said Scarlet. "Heard of him?"

A beat. A smirk. "No."

Scarlet clicked her tongue. "Too bad. I can already tell he's both twice the man *and* twice the wolf of any of *you*. He could teach you a thing or two."

The man laughed again, amused. "I didn't realize they were letting our pack brothers take mates on Earth. More reason to anticipate our deployments."

Winter pressed her sweating palms against her sides, grateful that Scarlet held their attention. If she'd been forced to speak, her mouth would have spouted incoherent mutterings and they would have laughed at her one moment and sunk their teeth into her the next. Jaws clamping around her limbs. Teeth tearing her muscles from the bones.

"We're not here to discuss my love life, or yours," said Scarlet. "You seem to be the most chatty. Do you nominate yourself as the leader here?"

He tilted his head in a manner that reminded Winter of Ryu, how he would sometimes cock his ears when he heard the game-keeper arriving with a meal. "Alpha Strom, at your service." He dipped into a mocking bow. Though he wasn't larger than the others, he moved with an unnatural grace. Like Wolf. Like Ryu. "And at the service of the pretty thing, back there. I suggest you speak fast, pretty lady. I can hear my pack's stomachs growling."

One of the soldiers ran his tongue over his bottom lip.

Scarlet turned and gave Winter a *look*.

Shivering from head to toe, Winter reached for Scarlet, using her shoulder for balance.

The soldiers laughed.

"*Winter*," Scarlet hissed.

"I'm frightened, Scarlet."

Scarlet's expression turned to stone. "Perhaps you'd like to go outside and compose yourself and we can come back later," she said, speaking through clenched teeth.

Winter shuddered at Scarlet's anger, though she knew Scarlet had a right to it. Coming here had been *her* idea. If they both died here, it would be her fault.

But she wouldn't allow it. These were men, she reminded her-self. Men who deserved life and happiness as much as anyone.

Holding firm to that thought, she forced herself away from Scarlet and was grateful when the dizziness receded.

"I am Winter Hayle-Blackburn, Princess of Luna," she said, and could tell even in her own ears how faintly her voice car-ried. Not at all like Scarlet's. "I need your help."

Eyes flashed, delighted.

"In return, I wish to help you."

Amusement. Hunger. Less curiosity than she would have hoped.

She gulped.

"Queen Levana, my stepmother, has treated you with cruelty and unfairness. She has taken you from your families and acted as though you are nothing to her but scientific experiments. She has locked you away in these caves, for no other purpose than to be sent to Earth and fight in her war. And what will you be given for your service?" They all waited with their hard and sparkling eyes, watching Winter like she was their afternoon snack, still cooking on a spit. It was not unlike the looks she'd received from countless men in Levana's court.

"Nothing," she said, shoving her fear into the bottom of her stomach. "If you survive your battles, you'll come back here and be enslaved in these caverns until she needs you again. You will not be allowed to return to your families. You will not rejoin our society and live what lives you may once have dreamed of living, back before you were ... you were ..."

"*Monsters?*" suggested one of the men, grinning around the word.

"I do not believe you are monsters. I believe you have been given very few choices, and you are dealing with the consequences as well as you can."

A snort came from Alpha Strom. "Who knew we would be receiving such counsel from the princess herself today? Tell me, pretty highness ... does this therapy session come with refreshments?"

"Your friend, perhaps?" said another. "She smells delicious."

Scarlet crossed her arms, fingers digging into her elbows.

Winter squared her shoulders. "We came here to give you another choice. The people of Luna are planning a rebellion. In two days we will be marching into the central dome of Artemisia. We plan to overwhelm the queen and her court, to overthrow her and put an end to her tyranny. I ask that you join us. Fight on our behalf and help us end the rule that took you from your lives and turned you into soldiers. Ensure that you will never become prisoners, or experiments, or . . . *animals* created for Levana's amusement, ever again."

A silence settled over them, as if they were waiting to make sure she was finished. Winter searched for some indication they were even listening.

She felt like a lamb in their den.

"She has pretty words."

Winter turned toward the voice. It was one of the men who had been involved in the fight. Fresh blood had dried at the corner of his lip.

He tipped his head when he saw that he had her attention, his eyelids dipping suggestively. "Not quite as pretty as her face."

"Except for these scars."

She jumped and spun around. She hadn't heard this soldier step so close and now he was hovering over her. He dragged a sharp-tipped nail down her cheek. "Where'd these come from, pretty lady?"

She didn't—couldn't—answer.

An arm wrapped around Winter's shoulders, pulling her back. "Stop it," said Scarlet, tucking Winter behind her, though it was useless. They were surrounded. "Were you listening to her? You can call yourselves soldiers or wolf packs or whatever you want, but the truth is, you're nothing but slaves. Winter is offering you freedom. She's giving you a choice, which is more than Levana has ever offered. Will you help us or not?"

"You'll be slaughtered," someone whispered against Winter's ear.

She gasped and turned again, locking her back against

Scarlet's. The soldiers crept closer. Predators toying with their catch, luxuriating in the anticipation of the meal.

"A bunch of pathetic civilians are going to stand up against the queen?" another said. "They don't stand a chance."

And another. "Don't you know who the queen will call on to hold them back, if there are too many to manipulate?"

"*Us*," spoke a third. "Her army."

"You mean her lapdogs?" said Scarlet, and though her tone was mocking, her back was pressing against Winter just as forcefully. "Her *pets*?"

The soldiers' faces twitched.

"If you side with us," said Winter, "we can win. We *will* win."

"What will happen to us if we side with you and you lose?" said Alpha Strom.

One of them brushed a finger down Winter's throat. Her heart skipped.

"With you beside us," she said, her voice wavering, "we will not lose." Her eyes began to water from fear. "You can stop now. You've frightened us enough. I know you are not the vicious creatures you're pretending to be—that you've been trained and tormented and built to be. You are men. You are citizens of Luna. If you help me, if you fight for me . . . I can help you get your lives back. You can't tell me you don't want that!"

She could feel their breath on her now. She could see the colored flecks in their eyes. Smell the sweat and blood on their skin. One of the men was sucking on a knuckle as if he couldn't wait to taste her flesh.

They were a noose growing tighter.

Pulse hiccuping, Winter raised her hand to her throat where the soldier had touched her. She felt a prickly rope there. Tightening. *Squeezing.* She squeaked and tried to wrap her fingers around it, to form a barrier between the rope and her throat, but it was already too tight.

"Spoiled little princess," one of the soldiers hissed, stooping down so she could feel his breath on her cheek. Winter shivered and knew her gaze was watery and pleading. "We don't fight for princesses. We *play* with them."

Alpha Strom smirked. "Ready to play?"

Fifty-Eight

SCARLET PUSHED WINTER, HARD, SENDING HER SPRAWLING to the floor with a cry. Through a veil of hair she watched Scarlet elbow one of the mutants in his nose. She reached for the gun beneath her hoodie, but the soldiers were already grabbing her, pinning her arms to the side. The gun fell uselessly to the ground.

A dozen enormous hands pulled Winter back to her feet. She hung limp in their hold, her legs too weak to carry her. She was shaking from head to foot, and the men were flickering in her vision. Engineered soldiers one moment and a pack of wild wolves the next. Prowling and baring their enormous fangs.

Scarlet screamed something. A battle cry. She was struggling like a caged tigress, hair flying, teeth snapping, while Winter hung, weak and brittle and trying to block out the vision before it overwhelmed her. Her head was heavy as moon rock and spinning as fast as an asteroid in orbit. Burdened with the brutal knowledge that this was real. They were going to die. They were going to be *devoured*.

The tears came on fast and overflowed quickly, leaking down

her cheeks. "Why are you being so cruel? Ryu would not act like this. He would be ashamed of you."

"Hold it together, Winter," Scarlet growled.

The world hesitated. Dissolved into blackness before re-forming again. Winter knew she would collapse if they let her go, but she couldn't find grounding in her own strength.

"Wait—I have an idea!" she said brightly, lifting her head. "Let us play a different game. Like when Jacin and I would play house. This one can be our pet." Tipping forward, she tried to put her palm on the nearest soldier's nose, but he jerked away from her, surprised.

She blinked at him. Trying to remember who he was. *What* he was. "No? Would you rather play fetch?"

His face turned from baffled to angry in half a second. He sneered, his teeth taking up half his face.

"What's wrong with her?" someone spat.

"Or I'll be the pet, if you prefer it." She swayed against those holding her. "Sticks and bones, sticks and stones. We'll play for hours, but I'll never tire and I'll always come back, I'll always come back . . ." Her voice shattered. "Because Ryu always, always came back. Sticks and bones. Sticks and bones . . ."

"Lunar sickness," someone murmured. Winter sought him, finding a warm-skinned soldier who could have been handsome before he'd been made so very ugly. He looked at her with the same hunger as any of them, but there also might have been sympathy.

Winter couldn't remember what she'd said that was insane. What had they been talking about? Leaving? Weren't they leaving? She wanted to leave. Or perhaps they'd been making dinner plans, hosting a cocktail party.

"That's right," said Scarlet. She was panting. "She refuses to manipulate anyone or to use her glamour, even when it would be *highly* beneficial. Unlike the people you serve, obviously."

"It will not affect how she tastes," someone yelled.

Winter started to giggle. They had all become animals now. Even Scarlet had turned wolfish, with pointed ears and a fluffy tail and flaming red fur. She turned her own muzzle up to the cavernous ceiling and sang, *"And the Earth is full tonight, tonight, and the wolves all howl, aa-ooooooooooh . . ."*

One of the hands—paws?—on her forearm loosened.

She howled again.

"A princess of Artemisia," Alpha Strom muttered, "who does not use her gift? By choice?"

"She thinks it's wrong to control people," said Scarlet, "and she doesn't want to end up like the queen. You can see the toll it's taking on her."

Winter's voice cracked and she stopped howling. When she slumped again, the hands released her, letting her crash to her knees. She gasped in pain and looked around. Scarlet was once again Scarlet, and the men were once again soldiers. She blinked, and was grateful when the hallucination didn't return.

"I'm sorry," she said. "I did not mean to interrupt your meal."

Scarlet groaned. "When she says she'll never manipulate you, she means it. And she does plan on giving you your freedom back. I doubt you'll ever get such a promising offer again."

The grate of ancient hinges startled Winter. The soldiers pulled apart. The huge iron doors creaked open and the soldiers separated, filing into neat rows fast as an oiled machine. Scarlet took the opportunity to snatch up her gun again, tucking it against her side.

Beyond the doors stood eight thaumaturges, one in second-tier red, the rest in black.

The red-coated thaumaturge, a man with silver-gray hair, saw Winter and Scarlet and smiled viper-like at them.

"Hello, Highness. We heard you might be down here."

Some of the soldiers shifted aside, making a clear aisle between the thaumaturges and Winter.

"Hello, Thaumaturge Holt," Winter answered, rising onto her wobbly legs, though they were aching. She felt like she should be afraid of these men and women—normally the sight of their coats and embroidered runes filled her with anxiety and dread and a thousand memories of people dying on the throne room floor. But all her fear had been used up.

"When the system picked up on your identification, I thought it must be a mistake. I did not think even you would be crazy enough to come *here*." His gaze cut over the soldiers. "Were you not hungry? Or were the girls not appetizing enough for your tastes?"

"Oh, they were very hungry indeed," said Winter, struggling to her feet. "Isn't that right, alpha-friends, wolf-friends?" Her head swayed to one side. "But I had hoped they might protect me and fight for me, if I could remind them they were men once, men who did not wish to be monsters."

"Turns out," said Scarlet, "they're just Levana's trained dogs after all."

A handful of the soldiers cast them cool glares.

Thaumaturge Holt scoffed. "I'd heard about your sharp tongue." His gaze dipped toward the stubbed finger on Scarlet's hand. "Say and think what you want, Earth child. These soldiers know their duty. They were created to carry out Her Majesty's bidding, and they will do it without complaint."

"Is that so?"

Winter wasn't sure which of them had spoken, but the words were so full of loathing they made her skin crawl.

Holt glowered at the surrounding men, cocky and hateful. "I trust this isn't *dissension* I'm detecting, Regiment 117. Her Majesty would be disappointed if she heard some of her prized soldiers were showing disrespect to their masters."

"Prized puppies, you mean," muttered Scarlet. "Will they each be getting their own diamond collar too?"

"Scarlet-friend," Winter whispered, "you are being inconsiderate."

Scarlet rolled her eyes. "They are about to kill us, in case you hadn't noticed."

"Yes, we are," said Holt. "Men, you may kill these traitors."

Winter sucked in a breath, but Alpha Strom raised a hand—and none of the soldiers moved. "Interesting that you mentioned our masters before, as you seem to be missing a few."

The seven thaumaturges behind Holt remained as statues, staring into the ranks. Winter counted. There were eleven packs in this regiment. There would have to be eleven thaumaturges to control them.

"I will forgive your ignorance in this matter," Holt said through clenched teeth, "as you could not have known that our country is in upheaval. Some of our highest-ranking thaumaturges and guards and even soldiers, like you, were murdered today, along with an attempted assassination on our queen. So you *see*, we do not have time for discussions. I ordered you to kill these girls. If you refuse, I will do it myself, and you will be punished for failing to obey a direct order."

Winter felt the bodies around her shift, as they had when

they first surrounded her and Scarlet. Moving almost impercep-
tibly closer. Tightening a knot.

"Too bad you did all that tampering with our brains," said
Alpha Strom. "Otherwise you could have manipulated us, right?
Forced us to follow your command. Instead, you've turned us
into a bunch of wild animals."

"A pack of hungry wolves," someone growled.

"Killers," Winter whispered to herself. "Predators, all."

They moved around Winter and Scarlet like water around a
rock. Winter grabbed Scarlet's wrist and tugged her close, their
shoulders tight together.

"You didn't make me to be good at math," Strom continued,
"but by my count, you couldn't punish all of us, even if you
wanted to."

They had half circled around the thaumaturges, who were
showing uncertainty now.

"Enough," Holt snapped. "I order you to—"

The tension exploded before he could finish. The soldiers
converged on their masters, mouths snarling and enormous
hands ready to shred and claw and tear.

Like a sonic pulse, dozens of soldiers fell to the ground, writhing and grasping their heads. Knuckles whitened as they pressed
their fingertips against their scalps, screaming in pain. The few
left standing bounded over their fallen comrades with faces
twisted in rage.

Winter flinched, watching as Alpha Strom, who had fallen in
front of her, curled into a fetal position and screamed. But it was
cut short, and replaced with retching and a whimper, his eyes
shut tight as he tried to block out whatever was being done to
him.

That whimper cascaded into Winter like a memory. Ryu behind her. The sound of Jacin's knife. The warm, sticky blood.

Winter dropped to the ground and crawled toward Strom, rubbing her hands over his misshapen face, trying her best to soothe him. The tips of her fingers cracked, devastatingly cold.

The fight, if it could be called a fight, was over in seconds. Winter couldn't recall the thaumaturges even having the time to cry out. There was the crunch of bones, the tearing of tissue, and it was over. A quick glance confirmed eight bloody bodies inside the cavern's entrance, and a couple dozen soldiers standing over them, wiping the blood from their chins and digging the flesh from beneath their fingernails.

Winter's breath fogged in the air. The cold was in her stomach too, icing over.

Her fingers were still in Strom's hair when he suddenly grabbed her hand and threw it back at her.

Scarlet was there in a second, her elbows hooked under Winter's arms, pulling her away. All around them, those who had fallen were recovering from whatever torment their masters had inflicted on them. Their faces were glazed from pain, but there was also a satisfaction when they noticed the dead thaumaturges.

Strom pushed himself into a crouch and gave his head a shake. His piercing gaze found Winter. She curled against her fiery friend, shivering.

Strom's words were slurred when he spoke. "You have Lunar sickness because you cannot control people like they do?"

Winter glanced toward the thaumaturges, or what was left of them, and immediately regretted it. She looked down at her brittle fingertips instead. "Oh, I c-could," she stuttered through her numb lips. "But I know what it is I-like to be controlled as m-much as you do."

Strom stood, gaining his strength back faster than many of the others. He inspected Winter and Scarlet for a long while.

Finally, he said, "She will send more of her hounds to punish us for this. They will torture us until we are all begging before them like the dogs we are." Though his voice was rough, a smile crept across his vicious mouth. "But to know the taste and smell of thaumaturge blood is worth it."

One soldier howled in agreement and was soon joined by a chorus of howls, splitting through Winter's ears and making the cavern tremble. Alpha Strom faced the regiment and there was a moment of celebration—fists clasping fists and howls that went on and on.

Winter forced herself to stand, though she was still cold and trembling. Scarlet stayed at her side, a pillar.

Winter's voice was strong when she asked, "Are you now satiated?"

Strom turned back, and the raucous congratulations between his men began to fade. Their eyes still showed hunger as they raked over the two girls.

"Are your cravings filled?" asked Winter. "Is your hunger abated?"

"*Winter,*" Scarlet hissed. "What are you doing?"

She whispered back, "I am thawing out."

Scarlet frowned, but Winter took a step away from her. "Well? Are you satisfied?"

"Our hunger is never satisfied," one of the soldiers growled.

"I thought as much," said Winter. "I know you still want to eat my friend and me, for what a juicy, tasty snack we would be." She smiled, not as terrified by the prospect as she had been before.

"But if you choose to help us instead, perhaps you will soon be feasting on the queen herself. And won't her flesh be more satisfying than ours? More satisfying, even, than your dead masters in the doorway?"

A silence hovered over them. Winter watched the calculations behind their faces and listened to a few of them sucking on their teeth.

"Fight with me," she said, when enough time had passed and neither she nor Scarlet had been devoured. "I will not control you. I will not torture you. Help me end Levana's rule and we will all have our freedom."

Alpha Strom met the eyes of a handful of the soldiers—the other alphas, she presumed—before fixing a penetrating look on her. "I cannot speak for the entire regiment," he finally said, "but I will accept your offer. If you swear to never control us as they have done, my pack will fight for your revolution."

Some of the men nodded. Others growled, but Winter thought it was a growl of agreement.

In response, she lifted her nose to the cavern ceiling and howled.

Fifty-Nine

SCARLET WAITED UNTIL THIS NEW ROUND OF HOWLS ABATED, echoing off the cave walls, before throwing herself in front of Winter. "You understand," she said, shoving a finger at Strom, "that by agreeing to help us, you can only attack Queen Levana and the people who serve her. *No* civilians whatsoever, not even those obnoxious aristocrats, unless they pose a threat. Our goal is to dethrone Levana, not slaughter the whole city. And we're not giving you all a free meal ticket, either. We expect you to follow orders and make yourselves useful. That could mean training some of the people from the sectors in how to fight or use weapons, or it could mean carrying injured people out of the line of fire . . . I don't know. But it does *not* mean you get to run rampant through the streets of Artemisia destroying everything in sight. Can you agree to that?"

Strom held her gaze, his ferocity once again turning to amusement. "I understand why your mate chose you."

"I'm not looking for personal commentary," she spat.

Strom nodded. "We agree to your demands. And when Levana

is gone, we will be free men, able to pursue a life of our choosing."

"So long as that life follows the laws of society—yes. That's right."

Strom surveyed the crowd. If it wasn't for all the blood, it would look as if the killings of the thaumaturges had never happened. "Alpha Perry? Alpha Xu?"

One by one, he counted off the remaining Alphas, and one by one they accepted Scarlet and Winter's terms. When it was done, Winter turned to Scarlet with a weary yet endearing smile. "I told you they would join us."

Scarlet inhaled sharply. "We need to find out what's happening on the surface. Is there some way to communicate with the sectors? To tell them the revolution is going to happen, even if Cinder . . ."

She couldn't finish the sentence. She had no idea what had become of Cinder, or Wolf.

Wolf. Ze'ev. Her alpha mate.

Thinking of him cut a hole in her chest, so she wouldn't. She would believe he was alive, because he *had* to be alive.

"We have to head to the surface anyway," said Strom. "These lava tubes don't connect to the maglev tracks. Or—they do, but it will take us too far out of the way. Better to head up to the nearest sector and infiltrate the tunnels that way."

"Which sector is that?" asked Scarlet.

"LW-12," someone said. "Lumber and wood production. Dangerous work, lots of injuries. Doubt they'd be too sympathetic to Her Majesty."

"We might have luck obtaining weaponry there too," said another.

"How far is it?" asked Scarlet.

"This used to be the storeroom for LW-12." Strom pointed at the ceiling. "It's right over our heads."

ONCE THEY WERE BACK IN THE CAVES, IT TOOK FEWER THAN ten minutes before a man was prying open a metal door that led to a thin stairwell. It seemed like an endless amount of stairs. The confined space quickly become stifling and hot.

"Scarlet-friend?"

Winter's fragile voice set Scarlet on edge. Pausing, she glanced down the steps and saw the princess using the ancient rail on the wall to pull herself forward as much as her legs were pushing her. Her breathing was labored, and not from the climb.

"What's wrong?"

"I am a girl made up of ice and snow," whispered the princess. Her eyes unfocused.

Cursing, Scarlet scrambled around a group of soldiers to get to the princess. Everyone came to a stop, and Scarlet felt oddly touched at the concern she saw in a few of the soldiers' eyes.

Leave it to Winter to make a bunch of sadistic, hot-headed predators get all swoony over her. Though Scarlet didn't like to think that what she and Wolf had was built on Wolf's animal instincts, she couldn't help but wonder if the same sort of instincts were at play here. Now that they'd persuaded these men to join their cause, were they shifting away from predator-killers to predator-protectors? Perhaps they'd lived with violence and darkness for so long, a single crack in their armor was all it took to have them craving something more meaningful.

Or maybe it was just Winter, who could make a rock fall in love with her if she smiled at it the right way.

"Are you hallucinating?" Scarlet asked, pressing a hand to Winter's brow, although she wasn't sure what she was looking to find there. "You don't feel cold. Can you walk? Are you still breathing?"

Winter's gaze dropped downward. "My feet are encased in ice cubes."

"Your feet are fine. Try to walk."

With an absurd amount of effort, Winter hauled herself onto the next step. She paused again, gasping for breath.

Scarlet sighed. "Fine. You're a girl of ice and snow. Can somebody help her?"

The nearest soldier took Winter's wrist and pulled her arm across his shoulders, so she could use his body as a support to climb the stairs. Soon, he was carrying her.

They made it to the top, emerging into a steel holding tank that would have been used to keep in the artificial atmosphere while the domes were under construction. Then they were outside.

Or, as outside as one could ever be on Luna, which Scarlet felt was a sad representation.

"Is this supposed to be a forest?" she muttered, taking in the short, skinny trees in their perfect rows. Through the trunks in the distance she could see a vast area that had been recently cleared for timber, and to the other side, acres of young saplings.

Straight ahead, in the direct center of the dome, she could make out the shape of a water fountain, identical to the one from the mining sector, situated in a clearing among the trees. The grass looked untended around it.

Alpha Strom took the lead, heading away from the fountain and toward the residences on the perimeter. They could hear people. A lot of people. When they reached the main residential street, Scarlet saw dozens of civilians holding an assortment of weapons (mostly wooden sticks), standing in neat rows and being guided through a series of attack maneuvers. A barrel-chested, bearded man was walking through the rows, yelling things like, "Parry! Jab! There's someone behind you!"

Even Scarlet's untrained eye could see that the people's movements were jerky and uncoordinated, and the people were a sad lot—most as gaunt and hungry looking as those in the mining sector. Still, it was heartening to know the people were heeding Cinder's call.

Scarlet had the gut-wrenching thought that they could be sending these people to their deaths, but she shook it off.

A bewildered scream interrupted the training. They'd been spotted.

Scarlet and a hundred mutants emerged from the forest's shadows. The scream turned into a dozen more and the rows broke apart, pulled back. But the people didn't run. Instead, as Scarlet and the mountainous soldiers came nearer, the people lifted their weapons, trying to disguise their terror behind feigned courage. Or perhaps this was the truest courage there was.

The people had probably expected something like this. It would not be a surprise that Levana would punish them for this blatant show of rebellion. But a *hundred* soldiers must have been far beyond their expectations.

True to their word, the soldiers did not attack, just lumbered forward until they stood twenty paces from the first row of citizens.

Scarlet kept going, separating herself from the crowd.

"I know they're scary looking," she said, "but we're not here to hurt you. We're friends of Princess Selene's. And you might rec-ognize Her Highness, Princess Winter."

Winter's head rolled against the shoulder of the man who was holding her. "It is a most profound pleasure to meet you all," she murmured, sounding half-drunk. Scarlet was proud of her for making the effort.

The people tightened their grips around their staffs, or spears, or whatever those were supposed to be.

The bearded man pushed his way to the front of the crowd, looking both tough and anxious at once. "Princess Winter is dead."

"No, she's not," said Scarlet. "The queen tried to have her killed, but she failed. Everything she's told you has been a lie."

The man stared at Winter for a long time, his face contorted with suspicion.

"It's not a glamour," said Scarlet. "It really is her." She hesitated, rolling her eyes. "Not that I have any way to prove that. But if we wanted to kill you, why bother with this charade? Look, we're here to join you in your siege on Artemisia. These men have agreed to fight on our behalf."

The man studied her. "Who are you?"

"My name is Scarlet Benoit. I'm—" She struggled to think of what to call herself. The pilot? The alpha female?

"She's an Earthen," someone said. It annoyed her that they could tell so easily, like she was branded somehow.

"I'm a friend of Princess Selene's," she said. "And I'm a friend of Princess Winter's. And not very long ago I was a prisoner of Queen Levana. She took my finger"—she held up her hand—"and she took my grandmother, and now I intend to help Selene take *everything* from her." She gestured at the soldiers. "These men have chosen our side over Levana's, just like you have, and they're the best assets we've got. Maybe they can help with your combat training." She turned to Strom. "Right?"

Strom's expression, though, was not appeasing as he stepped up beside her. "We said we would help and we will, but we're not going to stand out here all night listening to negotiations with a bunch of lumberjacks. If they don't want us here, we'll find a sector that does."

Scarlet snorted. "Good luck."

He growled at her. Scarlet growled back.

Lips pressed into a thin line, the bearded man glanced from the nervous civilians with their sharpened sticks, to the brawny, fur-covered soldiers. "We've been sending messengers to the nearest sectors when we can, but it's difficult trying to coordinate the attack. The shuttles are all down. And we aren't warriors."

"Clearly," one of the soldiers grumbled.

Someone in the crowd hissed, "Tell them about the guards."

Scarlet raised her eyebrows as the crowd's fear was replaced with puffing chests and straightened spines. "Guards?"

"We've had a regiment of armed guards stationed here for years, and we've talked about trying to overwhelm them, even made plans for it before, but it always seemed pointless when Levana would just send more. But as soon as Selene's message came through . . ." He grinned back at his peers. "Our plan worked. We had them disarmed within minutes, and now they're locked up in one of the storerooms in the mill." He crossed his arms. "There were fatalities, but we knew there would be. We're willing to do what must be done, just like the people in RM-9. I believe Selene has given us what might be our only chance."

Scarlet blinked. "What about the people in RM-9?"

"They say Selene was there, and there was a woman housing

her. She was just a miner, no one special, like us, but she proved how brave we can be."

"Maha Kesley," whispered Scarlet.

The man jolted in surprise. "That's right." He glanced back at the gathered people, his jaw set. "She was killed for offering her home to our true queen, but her death won't be in vain, just like the deaths of all those who stood up to Levana in the past."

Scarlet nodded, though she was still reeling. Aimery had intended for Maha's death to act as a warning to anyone who sided with Cinder, but here, at least, it had the opposite effect.

Maha Kesley had become a martyr.

"You're right," she said. "Selene doesn't need you to be warriors. Maha Kesley certainly wasn't, but she was brave and believed in our cause. That resolve is what this revolution needs."

"A few more warriors wouldn't hurt," Strom muttered, grabbing a stick away from the nearest civilian, who shrank away. "Everyone—back in formation! Let's see if we can't make you look a little less pathetic."

Sixty

"THE RESIDENTS OF GM-3 HAVE OVERPOWERED THE GUARDS sent to quell the uprising that began in the factories yesterday afternoon," said Aimery, reciting the information from a portscreen as if this were business as usual. Levana allowed the charade, keeping her face calm as she listened to the report. Only her foot tapped against the glistening tiles of her solar, shaking with restrained fury. "We are sending a new regiment of guards, along with a thaumaturge this time. The uprising in WM-2 has been put down, with sixty-four civilian casualties and a loss of five guards. We are conducting a full census on the sector, but we estimate close to two hundred civilians escaped prior to the insurrection along with an unknown amount of stolen weaponry and ammunition. The guards in all neighboring sectors have been put on high alert."

Levana downed a long, thin breath. She paced to the massive windows overlooking the city. Her perfect, pristine, tranquil city. It seemed impossible that so much chaos was happening on her planet, not when everything here was so calm, so *normal*.

And all because of that cyborg and her wretched video and her stupid speeches.

"Sixteen agriculture sectors have refused to load the supply trains that were brought in," Aimery rambled on, "and we are told that one unguarded train carrying dairy products, many intended for this week's celebrations, was boarded by a group of civilians outside Sector AR-5 and stripped of supplies. We have been unable to retrieve any of those goods or apprehend the thieves at this time." He cleared his throat. "In Sector GM-19, the citizens have blockaded two of the three maglev platforms, and this morning they killed twenty-four guards sent to tear down the blockades. We are compiling a thaumaturge-controlled regiment to send there as well."

Levana rubbed a kink from her shoulder.

"In Sector SB-2—"

The elevator chimed in the center of the room, pulling Levana's attention away from the city. Thaumaturge Lindwurm swooped in and dipped into a hasty bow, his black sleeves scraping the floor.

"Your Majesty."

"If you are here to tell me that the outer sectors are in chaos and the people are in revolt, I am afraid you are sorely late." She snapped her fingers at the servant who stood beside the elevator doors. "Bring wine."

The servant scurried away.

"No, My Queen," said Lindwurm. "I have news from the barracks, Regiment 117."

"What? Are *they* in revolt too?" Levana cackled, though beneath her hysteria lurked a growing dread. Could that cyborg have turned her entire country against her with such ease?

"Perhaps, My Queen," said Lindwurm.

Levana spun toward him. "What do you mean, *perhaps*? They are my soldiers. They cannot revolt against me."

Lindwurm lowered his gaze. "Our security team received notice two hours ago that Princess Winter's identity had been tracked to the outside of those barracks."

Levana's smile vanished. "Winter?" She glanced at Aimery, who straightened, his own interest piqued. "So she *is* alive. But what would she be doing there?"

"The system picked up on her fingerprints being used to enter the barracks. After learning of the security breach, the eight remaining thaumaturges for Regiment 117 were sent to ascertain if the princess was posing a threat."

"I suppose it is too much to hope that they found the dear girl ripped to bloody shreds."

That's what they should have found. The beasts should have killed Winter without hesitation—it was what they were designed to do. But she suspected that was not the case.

"From what we can ascertain," said Lindwurm, "when the thaumaturges arrived, the soldiers turned on them and attacked. All eight are dead."

Her blood ran hot, pounding at her temples. "And Winter?"

"The princess and the soldiers have abandoned the barracks. Security feeds showed them entering the nearest surface sector—LW-12. It is one of the sectors in upheaval, but we have not been considering them a high-priority threat."

"You're telling me that *my* soldiers have sided with the girl?"

Lindwurm dipped his head.

The servant returned carrying a silver tray with a decanter and crystal glass. Levana could hear the decanter trembling against the glass's lip as her wine was poured. Levana barely felt the weight of the glass in her hand as she took it.

"Leave," she ordered, and the servant couldn't scramble away fast enough.

She glided back to the window. Her city. Her moon. The planet that she would someday rule hanging off the horizon, nearly full.

When she had given Jacin Clay the opportunity to earn back her favor by killing the princess, she had expected him to try something stupid, but she'd hoped he would realize how futile it was. She'd hoped he would choose to hasten Winter's death as painlessly as possible rather than risk a much more brutal sentencing. That was mercy, after all. *Mercy*.

But he'd failed. Winter was still alive and she was trying to take Levana's army away from her, just as she'd taken the people's adoration, just as Selene was ruining *everything*.

She tried to picture the scene. Docile, half-crazy Winter, batting her lashes at the brutal beasts, and them *falling for it*. Oh, how they would fawn over her. How they would fall to their knees and beg to do her bidding. How they would follow their beloved princess anywhere.

"My Queen," said Aimery, placing a fist against his chest, "I feel responsible that we failed to find the princess during our raid on RM-9. Please allow me this chance to atone for the error. I will go to this sector and see that the princess is dealt with. I will not fail again."

She turned to face him. "You intend to kill her, Aimery?"

A pause—a slight one, but there all the same. "Of course, My Queen."

Laughing, Levana took a draft of the wine. "It was not long ago when you asked to marry her. Do you think she is beautiful?"

He chuckled. "My Queen. Everyone thinks the princess is beautiful, but she is no match for Your Majesty. *You* are perfection."

"I have begun to wonder if perfection might be its own flaw." She smirked. "Though perhaps a flaw can contribute to perfection." She pinned Aimery beneath her glare and adjusted her glamour, drawing three sharp, bloodied scratches down her right cheek.

He gulped.

"I've known you for many years, Aimery. I know how you *like* them broken. You would have made a good match after all . . . you are as pathetic as she is." She hurled the goblet. Aimery ducked, blocking the glass with his forearm. It crashed to the floor, the wine spilling like a mix of water and blood, splattering on Levana's shoes. "You will have your chance to prove yourself, but not where Winter is concerned. It seems no one has the stomach to do what must be done—not you, not Jacin Clay, not even my beloved pets. I am sick to death of disappointment."

She turned her back. Her thoughts reeled with betrayal, disgust, and jealousy—yes, even jealousy. All over that insignificant child. The weak, fragile thing.

If only she had killed her years ago, before she became so beautiful. Before she had become a threat. She should have killed her the first time she'd seen her sleeping in her cradle. She should have killed her when she'd ordered Winter's hand to take that knife, when she'd thought for sure a slight disfigurement would erase all the whispers in the court, all the talk of her thirteen-year-old stepdaughter already vying for *most beautiful girl on Luna.*

If only she hadn't made that stupid promise to Evret, all those years ago. What were promises, anyway, when made to the dying?

As her breathing evened again, she erased the scars from her own flawless complexion.

Thaumaturge Lindwurm took in a loud breath to remind her of his presence. "My Queen, we shall compose a task force to deal with the princess and the deserting soldiers. Shall I direct them to kill the princess on sight?"

She glanced over her shoulder. "I am a good queen, am I not?"

Lindwurm tensed. "Of that, there is no doubt."

"I have held this country together. I have waged a war for them, so my people might have access to all that Earth has to offer. I have done it for *them*. Why are they doing this? Why do they love *her*, when she has done nothing to deserve it? If she wasn't so pretty, they would see her for what she is. Manipulative, conniving . . . she's made a mockery of everything we stand for."

Neither Aimery nor Lindwurm responded.

Drawing in a shuddering breath, Levana snapped, "Find another servant to bring me more wine."

Lindwurm bowed and retreated.

"Death is not good enough for her," Levana murmured to herself, pacing past Aimery. "Death was the merciful choice, because I made a promise to my husband, but she has lost her right to mercy. I want them all to see her as she is. As weak and pathetic on the outside as she is within."

Aimery's lips tightened. He looked smug, even when he was groveling. "Tell me how best I can serve you."

"This rebellion has gone on quite long enough. No food or supplies are to be sent to the outer sectors unless they are prepared to beg for forgiveness. It is time the citizens of Luna were reminded how lucky they are to have me." Her heart fluttered with anticipation. "And send for Dr. Evans. I have a special task for him."

"And the princess, My Queen?"

"Do not worry about your darling disfigured princess." Sneering, Levana leaned forward and dragged her thumb across Aimery's jaw, gathering a splattered drop of wine. "I will deal with her myself, as I should have done a long time ago."

BOOK
Four

"Are you afraid of poison?" asked the old woman.
"Here, I will cut the apple in two. You eat the red half,
and I shall eat the white."

Sixty-One

CINDER WAS FRUSTRATED BY HER OWN HELPLESSNESS. THEY'D moved into the mansion's recreational room. Until then, Cinder hadn't known mansions *came* with recreational rooms. She was doing her best to dictate to the others what needed to be done in order to extract the video she'd tried to take in the throne room, and how to fix her leg and brain-machine interface. But while they were running around gathering supplies, she was seated on a lavish sofa with her useless hunk-of-metal leg. She hated knowing she could have had everything working again easily enough if she was back in her workshop in New Beijing. If she had the right tools. If *she* wasn't the machinery that needed fixing.

She tried to be grateful. She had survived the queen's attempted execution and she hadn't drowned in Artemisia Lake. She was with her friends again and Iko hadn't been destroyed after all—had, in fact, been helped by one of Aimery's own guards, which confirmed what Jacin had told her once before. Not everyone in the palace was as loyal to Levana as she wanted to think.

On top of all that, she *might* have video footage of Queen

Levana that would show what lay beneath her glamour. It could be the best weapon they had against her and her mind control.

If the footage hadn't been destroyed in the water, that is.

"Thorne, pry off the back panel of that receiver, but *gently*. Jacin, what did you find in the security panel?"

"A bunch of wires." Jacin dumped a handful of wires and a databoard onto the floor.

Cinder nudged at the wires with her good foot. "A few of these should work. Help me turn this table over. It's similar to the holographic game boards we have on Earth, so I think..." She grabbed one of the table legs with her good hand, but her injured shoulder resisted when she tried to turn it over. Jacin grabbed it from her and did it himself, and Cinder felt a twitch developing in her left eye. She tried not to be resentful. It wasn't his fault she was still tender from where the wolf soldier had bitten her, and at least the numbing pain salve they'd found was performing miracles.

"There's not going to be blood when we open you up, is there?" said Thorne, carrying the receiver over to Cinder so she could pick through its inner workings. "I mean, we're talking strictly cybernetics, right?"

"Better be." She scanned the inner workings of the receiver while Thorne and Jacin disassembled the VR gaming table. The setup was different from anything they had on Earth—different-colored wires, different-size plugs and connectors, but it all functioned with similar technology and the same basic principles. "It's not so much surgery as ... maintenance. Our biggest concern is whether or not all the hardware will be compatible. The technology is similar, but it's changed enough since Luna and Earth stopped trading with each other that ... I guess we'll see." She glanced at the gaming table as Thorne pried off the side panel, revealing the inner workings. "Oh, perfect!" Leaning forward, she pried up the fiber mode converter. "We can use this."

Iko and Cress strolled into the room, Cress carrying a wooden box.

"They have a workshop out back," said Iko. She was wearing a shimmering pink shirt she'd found in the house, mostly to cover up the bullet hole in her torso and the slash in the back of her right shoulder. Cinder hoped that once she was fixed, she'd be able to at least make Iko's arm functional again too.

"I found everything on your list except the demagnetized three-pronged parts retriever. But I did find some tweezers in the bathroom?" She twirled the tweezers between her good fingers.

Twisting her mouth, Cinder took the tweezers and flicked a stray eyebrow hair from their tip. "We'll make them work." She surveyed the pile of tools and spare parts they'd accumulated from technology all over the mansion. Without being able to see inside her own head and offer an accurate diagnosis, it was difficult to know what they were going to need to fix her, but if it wasn't included in this pile, they had little hope of finding it here. "We'll need a lamp so you can see what you're doing. And what about a hand mirror? We can hold it up so I can see inside."

Jacin shook his head. "Not in this city."

Cinder scowled. "Right, fine. We're going to extract the data off the vid-chip first, then we'll focus on the retina display. My eyes are still communicating with my optical nerve, so my best guess is there's been a disruption of data transfer from my control panel to the display. Could be as simple as a damaged wire. Once we have that working, I should be able to run my internal diagnostics and figure out what's wrong with my hand and leg."

She pointed at a virtual reality viewing chair. "Drag that over here."

Jacin complied, and Cinder pulled herself into the chair, facing backward so she could drape her arms over the back. She rested her forehead on them. "Cress?"

"Ready when you are."

"All right. Let's see what we can find."

Iko brushed Cinder's hair off to one side and dug a fingernail into the latch in the back of Cinder's skull. Cinder felt the panel swing open.

"Oh, sure," said Thorne. "When *I* open her head panel, she yells at me. When Iko does it, she's a hero."

Cinder glared at him over her folded arms. "Would *you* like to do this?"

He grimaced. "Not even a little bit."

"Then back up and give them space to work." She laid her forehead down again. "All right, Iko. There's a cable insert on the left side of the control panel."

Someone turned on a lamp and bright light edged around her vision.

"I see it," said Iko. "Cress, you have that port?"

"And connector cable, right here."

Cinder heard them shuffling behind her, brushing more of her hair out of the way. There was a click, muffled inside her own head. A shudder coursed through her. It had been a while since an external device had been plugged into her processor. The last time had been when she'd drained her power source getting the Rampion into space, right after they'd escaped from New Beijing Prison. Thorne had had to recharge her with a pod-ship plug.

The time before that she'd been in a research lab, strapped to a table while a med-droid downloaded the statistics of her cybernetic makeup.

She really, really hated having things plugged into her head.

She forced herself to take deep breaths. It was only Iko and Cress. She knew what they were plugging into her and what data they were extracting. It was not a violation. It was not an invasion.

But it was impossible not to feel that way.

"The connection worked," said Cress. "There doesn't appear to be any obvious holes in the data, so this part of your programming wasn't affected by whatever cut off power to your limbs. I just need to find where it stores visual input and . . . here we go. Recordings . . . chronological . . . would it be the most recent . . . never mind, this must be it. Video, encrypted, one minute fifty-six seconds long. And . . . transferring."

Cinder's gut twisted. She was not squeamish in general, but whenever her panel was open it was impossible not to think about nameless, faceless surgeons hovering over her uncon-scious form. Connecting wires and synapses to her brain, regu-lating her electrical pulses, replacing part of her skull with a removable metal plate.

She squeezed her forearms until they began to hurt, trying to distract herself from the humming of her own internal work-ings and the sound of Cress's fingertips padding against the portscreen.

"Eighty percent," said Cress.

White spots flickered on the blackness of Cinder's eyelids. She breathed deeply, chastising herself. She was fine. This would have been a routine procedure if it had been her working on an android or another cyborg. She was *fine*.

The humming stopped and Cress said, "Done."

"Check it before you disconnect," said Cinder, gulping down a mouthful of sour saliva. "Make sure it's the right one."

"It's showing . . . a lot of people."

"There's Kai!" squealed Iko.

Cinder jerked her head up. She felt the pull of the cord still connected to the portscreen. "Show me," she said, even as brightness flooded her vision. She cringed, slamming her eyes shut again.

"Wait, hold still," said Cress. "Let me disconnect—"

That was the last Cinder heard.

NEW CONNECTIONS FOUND
REALITY MANUFACTURING CYBERHAND T200-L-
CUSTOM : FIVE UTILITIES UNRECOGNIZED :
STANDARD APPLICATIONS APPROVED
REALITY MANUFACTURING CYBERFOOT T60.0-L :
STANDARD APPLICATIONS APPROVED
REBOOTING IN 3 . . . 2 . . . 1 . . .

Cinder woke up on the sofa with the softest blanket she'd ever felt tucked around her shoulders. She squinted at the unfamiliar shadows on the ceiling, trying to shake off the bewilderment of waking up in a strange place and not being sure how she'd gotten there. Sitting up, she rubbed at her bleary eyes. The room was in disarray, tools and parts scattered around the carpet and tables.

DIAGNOSTICS CHECK COMPLETE. ALL SYSTEMS
STABILIZED. TWO NEW CONNECTIONS FOUND:
CYBERHAND T200

```
CYBERFOOT T60.0
RUN APPLICATION TEST NOW?
```

She raised her left hand in front of her face. The shiny finish it had when Dr. Erland had first given it to her was gone after two months of making repairs to the Rampion and living in a desert and a dip in Artemisia Lake.

Most baffling was that she had all five fingers, although the pointer—the gun finger Levana had removed—didn't quite match the others. The finish was different, it was too slender, and the angle of the first knuckle was crooked.

Cinder ran the application test and watched as her fingers curled down, one at a time. Flexed back. Tightened into a fist. The wrist swiveled from side to side.

Her foot went through a similar range of motions. She pulled back the blanket to watch.

```
BASIC APPLICATION TEST COMPLETE.
STANDARD APPLICATIONS APPROVED FOR USE.
FIVE UTILITIES UNRECOGNIZED.
```

Five utilities.

Inspecting her hand, Cinder sent the command for the tips of her fingers to open, which they did without problem. But when she tried to turn on the flashlight, to eject the knife or universal connector cable, or to spin the built-in screwdriver, nothing happened. She didn't bother trying to load a projectile into the replacement finger.

Still, she had use of the limb again, and she couldn't complain.

"You're awake!"

Iko traipsed into the room carrying a tray one-handed, with a glass of water and a plate of fried eggs, along with bread and jam.

Cinder's stomach started gnawing through its lining. "You cooked?"

"Just some skills left over from my Serv9.2 days." Iko set the plate in Cinder's lap. "But I don't want to hear a word about how delicious it is."

"Oh, I'm sure it's *awful*," Cinder said, shoveling a spoonful into her mouth. "*Tank oo, Iko.*" Her gaze landed on Iko's disabled arm. It was missing a finger. She swallowed. "For the attachment too."

Iko shrugged with her good shoulder. "You have a few escort-branded wires installed now too. The stuff from the gaming table didn't work."

"Thank you. That was really generous."

Iko pushed Cinder's feet aside and sat down. "You know how we androids are programmed to make ourselves useful and all that."

"Are you still an android?" Cinder said around a bite of toast. "Sometimes I forget."

"Me too." Iko ducked her head. "When we saw the feed of you jumping off that ledge, I was so scared I thought my wiring was going to catch fire. And I thought, *I will do anything to make sure she's all right.*" She kicked at a pile of stray screws on the carpet. "I guess some programming never goes away, no matter how evolved a personality chip gets."

Licking some jam from her fingertips, Cinder grinned. "That's not programming, you wing nut. That's friendship."

Iko's eyes brightened. "Maybe you're right."

"About time you woke up, lazy." Cinder glanced over her shoulder to see Thorne in the doorway. Cress and Jacin filed in behind him. "How's the hand?"

"Almost fully functional."

"Of course it's almost fully functional," said Iko. "Cress and I are geniuses." She flashed Cress a thumbs-up.

"I helped," said Thorne.

"He held the lamp," Iko clarified.

"Jacin did nothing," said Thorne, pointing.

"Jacin checked your pulse and breathing and made sure you weren't dead," said Iko.

Thorne snorted. "I could have done that."

"Why did I pass out?" Cinder interrupted.

Crouching beside the couch, Jacin felt for the pulse in Cinder's wrist. After a short silence, he let it drop down again. "Stress, probably, along with your physical reaction to having the portscreen connected to your"—he gestured to her general head area—"computer thing."

"And you call *me* squeamish," said Thorne.

Cinder squinted. "I passed out from stress? That's it?"

"I believe the princess term is *fainted*," said Thorne.

Cinder smacked him.

"With everything you've been through," said Jacin, "it's amazing you haven't had a meltdown. Next time you feel light-headed or are having trouble breathing, tell me *before* you pass out."

"The good thing," said Iko, "is that with you unconscious, Cress and I were able to run your full diagnostics. Two fixed connections, a new data cable, some reinstalled software, and good as new! Well, except—"

"My hand tools, I know." Cinder smiled. "But that's fine. I went five years without a built-in flashlight, I'll survive now."

"Yeah, that, but I think there might be some problems with your interface too. The diagnostics showed a few errors with net connectivity and data transfer."

Cinder's smile faded. She'd been dependent on her cyborg brain ever since she could remember, relying on her ability to download information, send comms, monitor newsfeeds. It was an uncomfortable feeling to be without it, like part of her brain had been erased.

"I'll just have to make do," she said. "I'm alive, and I have two working hands and two working feet. I've been in worse shape before." She glanced from Iko to Cress. "Thank you."

Cress ducked her head, while Iko tossed her braids over one shoulder. "Oh, you know. I used to apprentice for this brilliant mechanic in New Beijing. She may have taught me a thing or two."

Cinder laughed.

"Speaking of brilliant mechanics," Iko said, "do you think you have time to look at my arm now?"

Sixty-Two

WINTER SAT ON A ROUGH-HEWN BENCH, WATCHING THE LAST chips of ice thaw around her feet. She plunked her toes against the shallow puddle that had formed, amazed at how everything about it could be so real—the crackling, the cold—even when she knew it wasn't.

Sighing, she raised her head, weary as she was, to watch the haphazard training sessions happening all down the dusty street. Maneuvers and tactics, a hundred trained soldiers doing their best to build an army. She scanned the crowd for Scarlet's flaming hair, not sure where her friend had gone off to.

Instead of seeing Scarlet, her gaze caught on something else entirely. A head of pale hair near the back of the crowd.

Her heart lurched.

Inhaling a shaky breath, she pulled herself from the bench, but he was already gone.

Her gaze darted over all the faces, searching. Hoping.

She clenched her fists at her sides, willing away the sudden rush of euphoria. It was her desperation causing her to see phantoms. She missed him so much. She still didn't know if he was even alive. She supposed it was to be expected that she would see his face in every crowd, around every corner.

There—she saw it again. Sunshine-bright hair tucked back behind his ears. Broad shoulders disguised in the clothes of the sector laborers. Blue eyes that pinned her to the ground even as her entire body tingled. Air flooded her lungs. He was alive. He was *alive.*

But Jacin raised a finger to his lips, halting her before she could run to him. Ducking his head in an effort to minimize his height, he skirted around a group of laborers and slinked toward the forest. He glanced back once and, with a subtle jerk of his head, disappeared into the shadows.

Palms damp, Winter looked around for Scarlet, but she was nowhere to be seen. No one was watching her. She slipped away, newly energized, and traipsed in between the slender tree trunks.

She would circle around through the woods and meet Jacin halfway. She would throw herself into his arms and she didn't care if he thought it was appropriate or not.

Up ahead she could hear the bubble of the central fountain.

"Princess."

Winter startled. In her haste, she'd walked right past the old woman without even seeing her. Though she was an ancient creature with a crooked back, she had a liveliness to her expression. She was holding a basket filled with twigs and bark gathered from the forest floor.

"Yes, hello," Winter said in a rush, dipping into a quick curtsy. Her gaze was already traveling on, searching for blond hair and a teasing smile. She saw nothing. The trees were hiding him from her.

"You're looking for a handsome young man, I believe." The woman's wrinkles tightened into something like a smile.

Winter started to nod, but stopped herself. "Did someone come through here just now?"

"Just your prince, my dear. No need to be shy. He's very handsome, isn't he?" She herself stood no taller than Winter's collarbone, though that was partly due to the crook in her spine. Winter wondered how many years of hard work weighed upon those shoulders.

"He asked me to give you a message."

"He did? Jacin?" Winter glanced around again. "But where did he go?"

"He said not to follow him. That it's too dangerous, and he'll find you when it's safe again." She tilted her head, gazing down the row of orderly trees, to where the alphas were yelling their orders.

Winter tried to stifle her disappointment. He could not have waited for a smile, a kind word, a quick embrace? "Why aren't you with the others?"

The woman shrugged her shoulders, with some effort. "Someone said we could use wood scraps. I cannot do much, but I can assist in that way."

"Of course," said Winter. "We all must do what we can. Allow me to help you." She took the basket from the woman.

The woman held up a finger, her arm no longer burdened. "I almost forgot. Your prince left you a gift." Digging through the basket, she found a plain box buried beneath the twigs. "He said these are your favorites."

Winter's heart leaped as she took the box in her palm. She knew what it was without opening it and her heart expanded.

She couldn't imagine the trouble Jacin had gone through to get these for her. All so she would know he was thinking about her?

Unless there was more to it than that.

Unless there was a message.

Chewing the corner of her lips, she lifted the lid. There, inside, were two pristine sour apple petites, fresh from the confectioner's window.

"My, but those look tasty," said the old woman, craning her head to peer inside. "I haven't had one of those since I was a little girl. Apple, aren't they?"

"Yes." Winter held the box toward her. "Please, take one. With my gratitude for delivering them."

The woman pondered the offer. "If you insist . . . I suppose one little bite won't kill me. I'll take this one, if you're sure you don't mind. See, it has a crack in the shell, not fit for a princess." Her eyes were daring as she took the candy between her fingertips. "But only if you eat the other. It would be the greatest honor to share this bounty with Your Highness—the *beautiful* Princess Winter herself."

"You are too kind." Winter lifted the second candy from the box. She scanned the inner lining, hoping for some clue Jacin may have left for her, but she saw nothing.

Still. It was a gift. Not only the candies, but to have seen him from afar. To know he was all right.

She placed the candy between her teeth. The woman was watching her, mimicking her movements, and together they bit down. Winter felt the crack of the brittle shell before it melted against her tongue.

The old woman smiled, bits of crimson-colored filling stuck in her teeth. "This has been more satisfying than I could have imagined."

Winter swallowed. "I'm glad. It's been my pleasure to . . . to . . ."

She blinked, catching a tinge of familiarity in the way the woman watched her. At the particular curve of her grin—something haughty and brimming with contempt.

"Is something wrong, my dear child?"

"No. No. For a moment you reminded me of someone. But my eyes play tricks on me sometimes. They're not very reliable."

"Oh, sweet, stupid child." The kink in the woman's back began to straighten. "We are Lunars. Our eyes are never reliable."

Winter shriveled back. The basket slipped from her hold, crashing to the ground.

Before her, Levana shed the guise of the old woman, a snake shedding its skin.

"My researchers assured me the disease would act quickly," said the queen, her cold eyes roving over Winter's skin. Curious. Delighted.

Winter's thoughts spun, puzzling out the truth from the illusion. Her whole life had been spent puzzling out truths from illusions.

Where was Jacin? Why was Levana here? Was this another nightmare, a hallucination, a trick?

Her stomach kicked. She felt ill.

"The infected microbes are being absorbed into your bloodstream even at this very moment."

Winter placed a hand over her stomach, feeling the devoured candy roiling inside her. She pictured her heart, her arteries, her platelet-manufacturing plant. Little red soldiers marching down their conveyor belts. "Microbes?"

"Oh, don't worry. Young and able-bodied thing that you are, it should be an hour or two still before you begin to show symptoms. A rash of blood-filled blisters will erupt on your perfect

skin. The tips of your delicate fingers will shrivel and turn blue ..."
Levana grinned. "I do wish I could be here to witness it."

Winter peered through the forest, toward her allies. Levana would stop her if she tried to run. She wondered if she could get out a scream before Levana sewed shut her lips.

"Thinking of warning your friends? Don't worry. I'm going to let you go, little princess. I will let you return to them and infect them yourself. They made a mistake when they chose you over me, and that will be their undoing."

She faced her stepmother again. "Why do you hate me?"

"Hate you? Oh, child. Is that what you think?" Levana placed her cool fingers on Winter's cheek, over the scars she'd given her years before. "I don't hate you. I am merely annoyed at your existence." Her thumb caressed Winter's cheek. "From the day you were born, you had everything I ever wanted. Your beauty. Your father's love. And now, the adoration of the people. *My* people." She drew her hand away. "But not for long. Your father is dead. Your beauty will soon be tarnished. And now that you are a carrier of the blue fever, any citizen who comes close to you will soon come to regret it."

Winter's stomach dropped. She imagined she could feel the disease being absorbed through the lining of her stomach. Seeping into her veins. Each beat of her heart pushed it further through her system. It was a detached sort of knowledge. Of all the tortures she had seen her stepmother devise for others, there was something merciful about this death. A slow, calm acceptance.

"You could have their adoration too, you know," she said, watching as Levana's condescending smile hardened to her face. "If you were kind to them, and fair. If you didn't trick them into being your slaves. If you didn't threaten them and their loved ones for every minor crime. If you shared the riches and the comforts we have in Artemisia—"

Her tongue stilled.

"I am queen," Levana whispered. "*I* am the queen of Luna and I will decide the best way to rule my people. No one—not you, and not that hideous cyborg—will take this from me." She lifted her chin, nostrils flaring. "I must go tend to my kingdom. Good-bye, Winter."

Stumbling back, Winter turned toward the people. If she could see just one person, get off one warning . . .

But then the forest closed in around her and she collapsed, unconscious, to the ground.

Sixty-Three

"HAVE YOU SEEN WINTER?"

Alpha Strom finished demonstrating the upward-stab movement with the staff and handed it back to a young woman, before turning to face Scarlet. "I have not."

Scarlet scanned the hectic crowd for the thousandth time. "Me either, not for a long time. She has a tendency to wander off . . ."

Tilting his head back, Strom sniffed a few times at the air, then shook his head. "It seems she hasn't been around for a while now. Perhaps she's found somewhere to rest."

"Or perhaps she's poking out her own eye with a stick. I'm telling you, it's not good for her to be left alone."

Grumbling, Strom gestured at one of the beta members of his pack, then shambled toward a bench. He paused to sniff again, sending his keen eyes into the crowd, before turning and gazing into the forest.

"You're being creepy," said Scarlet.

"You asked for my help."

"Not *technically*."

When Strom headed into the shadows of the not-really-a-forest, Scarlet followed, though she couldn't imagine why Winter would have left everyone behind and wandered off all by her—

Never mind. She could imagine it after all.

"She came this way," Strom said, running his fingers over a tree's bark. He turned to the right and increased his speed. "I've picked up on her now."

Scarlet trotted along beside him.

"There."

She saw her at the same moment, and broke into a run before Strom did.

"*Winter!*" she screamed, dropping to her knees. Winter's body was sprawled out in the patchy grass. Scarlet rolled the princess onto her back and checked for a pulse, relieved to find one fluttering at Winter's neck.

A hand grabbed Scarlet's hood and dragged her back. She yelped, flailing to get away, but Strom ignored her pummeling fists. "Let me go! What are you doing?"

"She is sick."

"What?" Unzipping her hoodie, Scarlet scrambled out of the sleeves and fell at Winter's side again. "What are you talking about?"

"I can smell it on her," Strom growled. He didn't come any closer. "Diseased flesh. Vile."

Scarlet frowned up at him before refocusing on the princess. "Winter, wake up," she said, smacking the princess's cheek a few times, but Winter didn't even flinch. Scarlet pressed a hand to her forehead. She was clammy and hot. She felt the back of her head, wondering if the princess had hit her head again, but there was no blood and the only bump was from the fight at Maha's house. "Winter!"

Strom kicked something and it skipped through a tuft of grass and hit Scarlet's knee. Scarlet blinked and picked it up. A sour apple petite, one of the candies Winter had often brought to her in the menagerie, usually laced with painkillers. It had a bite taken out of it. Picking up Winter's hand, Scarlet found bits of melted candy shell stuck to her fingertips.

"Poison?"

"I don't know," said Strom. "She isn't dead—just dying."

"With some sort of disease?"

He gave a curt nod. "You should not be so close to her. It smells—" He looked like he might be sick.

"Oh, pull yourself together. All those muscles and teeth and you're afraid of a little cold?"

His expression darkened, but he didn't come any closer. In fact, after a second, he stepped back. "There is something wrong with her."

"Obviously! But what? And *how*?" She shook her head. "Look, I saw a little med-clinic on the main street. Can you carry her there? We'll have a doctor check her out. She might need her stomach pumped or—"

Scarlet's gaze landed on Winter's arm and she gasped. She skittered away from the princess's unconscious form, every instinct telling her to hold her breath. To clean the skin that had come in contact with the princess. To run.

"Now she listens."

Ignoring him, Scarlet cursed, loudly. "When you said she had a disease, I didn't think you meant she had the *plague*!"

"I do not know what this is," said Strom. "I have never smelled this before."

Scarlet hesitated a moment more, then let out a painful, frustrated sound, and forced herself to crawl back to Winter again.

She grimaced as she lifted Winter's arm to inspect the dark spots scattered across her elbow. The red-tinged rings around the bruises had swollen above the skin, puffed and glossy like blisters.

For as long as she could remember, the plague had worked in predictable stages, though how long they took to manifest varied by victim. Once the rash of bruise-colored rings marred a person's skin, they may have three days or three weeks still to live. But given that Winter hadn't been gone for more than an hour, the disease seemed to be working especially fast.

She scrutinized Winter's fingertips, relieved to see them pink and healthy—no tinge of blue. Blood loss to the extremities was the final symptom of the disease before death.

She scowled. Hadn't Cinder once told her that Lunars were immune to letumosis? This disease shouldn't even be here.

"It's called letumosis," she said. "It's a pandemic on Earth. It acts fast and no one survives. But ... Levana has an antidote. It's half the reason Emperor Kai is marrying her in the first place. We just ... we need to keep Winter alive long enough to get it. We have to keep her alive until the revolution is over. All right?"

She dragged a hand through her hair, but it got caught in a tangle of curls and she gave up before she'd reached the ends.

"That could be days, even weeks," said Strom. "She does not smell as though she has that much time."

"Stop talking about how she smells!" she screamed. "Yes, the disease is bad. It's—*horrible.* But we can't just leave her here. We have to *do* something."

Strom rocked back on his heels, eyeing the princess with disgust. Which was still better than the ravenous glint his eyes had had before. "She needs a suspension tank."

"A what?"

"We use them for healing after surgeries or severe injuries." He shrugged. "It may slow the progression of the disease."

"Where do we get one?"

"I expect they'll have one here. Dangerous work in this sector."

"Great. Let's go." Pushing herself to her feet, Scarlet dusted off her hands. Strom stared at her, then down at Winter. He didn't come any closer.

"Ugh. Fine." Crouching again, Scarlet grabbed Winter's arms and was about to haul her over one shoulder when Strom lumbered forward and lifted the princess into his arms.

"Well, aren't you a perfect gentleman," Scarlet muttered, grabbing her hoodie instead.

"Just hurry," he said, his face already strained in an effort to take shallow breaths.

They practically ran back toward the residences.

Scarlet burst out of the tree line, flushed and panting. Those who were gathered turned to watch as Strom emerged with Winter in his arms.

"The princess has been poisoned," said Scarlet. "She's ill with a fatal disease called letumosis. The queen has an antidote, but Winter will likely die if we don't slow the spread of the disease right away." She spotted the bearded man who had acted as the leader before. "Is there a suspension tank in this sector?"

"Yes, at the clinic. I don't know . . ." He glanced at a white-haired man who was emerging from the crowd.

The white-haired man approached Winter, felt for a pulse, and lifted her eyelids one at a time. A doctor, she guessed. "The tank isn't in use," he said, following his quick inspection. "It will take fifteen or twenty minutes to prep the tank and the girl for immersion."

Scarlet nodded. "Let's get on it, then."

The doctor led them through the crowd. The people parted, watching the princess with distraught expressions.

"Who would do such a thing?" someone whispered as Scarlet passed. "To the *princess*," another voice added.

"Does this mean we have a traitor among our people?" the doctor asked, his voice low.

Scarlet shook her head. "I don't think so. Whoever did this had to have access to the disease, somehow, and expensive candy. They must have sneaked in for Winter and left."

"Or they are still among us, wearing a glamour."

She sniffed. Stupid Lunars and their stupid glamours. Anyone could be an enemy. Anyone she passed could be a thaumaturge or one of those lousy aristocrats or the queen herself, and Scarlet wouldn't be able to tell the difference.

Still, why would anyone come all the way out here just to attack Winter but leave the rest of them alone, knowing they were planning to join Selene's revolution? Was this a warning? A threat? A distraction?

A sinking thought occurred to her. Perhaps they weren't leaving the rest of them alone at all. Letumosis was highly contagious, and it acted fast. In closed quarters, with recirculating air . . .

"Here," said the doctor, leading them into a building that was only slightly larger than the neighboring houses and just as rundown. A coffin-shaped tank stood against one wall, covered in dust and piled high with worn blankets. The doctor shoved the linens onto the floor. "There are beds in that room if you want to lay her down while I get it ready."

Strom seemed happy to do just that. His face was still contorted when he returned. "I am going to bring in some of my men to have the tank moved outside."

The doctor glanced up. "Outside?"

"The people admire her. They should be able to see her—a reminder of what we're fighting for."

The doctor blinked rapidly, but gave a small nod. "All right. It won't affect the treatment."

Strom left the clinic, his footsteps pounding on the short wooden porch.

"I am afraid," said the doctor, sounding very afraid indeed, "that we have only the one tank."

Scarlet held his gaze. "So?"

Lips tightening, he gestured at her. Scarlet followed the look to her own hands. Nothing. Nothing. Then she saw the red-ringed bruise on her upper arm and cursed.

Sixty-Four

HE DREAMED OF RAN, HIS YOUNGER BROTHER, AFTER HE'D become a monster. In the dream, he watched as Ran prowled around his prey, his muscles flexing beneath his skin, saliva gathering at the corners of his mouth. Ran's hand curled into a fist, then sprang open, revealing the fingernails he'd filed into sharp points. His eyes glinted with the knowledge that his prey had nowhere to run.

With a snarl, Ran dug his claws into the victim's sides and tossed her—*her.* The dream sharpened, the blurred shadow turning into a girl as she was thrown into a statue at the center of a dried fountain basin. She was bleeding, her red hair dark with grime, her eyes bloodshot with panic.

Wolf watched, but could do nothing. He was encapsulated in stone and only his thoughts were wild and alert, telling him again and again that he'd failed her.

The scene switched, and he was a boy meeting his pack for the first time. He was still trying to get used to the fact that they had taken his Lunar gift away from him and turned it into something unnatural. Something that would make him a better soldier for their queen. The rest of the boys eyed him with loathing and distrust, though he didn't know why. He was just like them. A pawn, a mutant.

Just like them.

The sound of a gunshot ricocheted in his head and he was standing in a crowded, dusty square. His mother collapsed beside him. Blood pooled under his feet. But they weren't his feet. They were enormous paws, prowling back and forth, and the scent of his mother's blood was in his nostrils—

The dream ended the same way it had begun. With the girl, beaten and covered in blood. She was on her hands and knees, scrambling to get away. She rolled onto her back. He could smell the blood on her. He could feel the horror rolling off her in torrents. He could see the hatred in her eyes.

This time, he was the predator. This time, she was looking at *him*.

He jolted awake. *Stop Ran. Kill the alpha. Run away. Save her. Find the old woman. Kill Jael and rip his still-beating heart from his chest. Find his parents. Join his pack. Tear their limbs from their sockets. Hide. Be brave. Protect her. Find her. Save her. Kill her—*

"A little help here!"

His eyes were open, but he couldn't see beyond blaring lights. Someone was holding down his arms. Multiple someones. Growling, he snapped his teeth at his captors, but caught only air.

"Stars above," someone grunted. "I've never seen one of them wake up like that before. Hand me that tranquilizer."

"No. Do not tranquilize him." This second feminine voice was soft and calm, yet spoke in demands. "Her Majesty has requested his presence."

Wolf got one arm loose. Cords snapped around him. Something scraped beneath the skin of his forearm, but he was too frazzled to pay it much attention. He snagged one of the blurred shapes by the throat and tossed him overhead. A scream was followed by a crash of metal.

"What—"

Wolf found the second person and wrapped both hands around their throat. *Just a snap . . .*

A shock of pain tore through his arms. He let go and the stranger stumbled back, gasping for air.

Wolf collapsed back onto the table. Though the pain had been brief, his left hand continued to twitch.

It wasn't a table at all, he realized. Shallow walls surrounded him. Dozens of tubes, many of which were still buried in his flesh. The tugging sensation he'd felt before was from needles still half-buried under his skin. Grimacing, he turned his face away, the sight churning his stomach.

Not more needles. Not another tank. Not more surgeries.

Footsteps approached and he glanced toward his feet. A form was silhouetted in the bright lights. A female thaumaturge in red, with pitch-black hair pulled into a bun. "Welcome back, Alpha Kesley."

Wolf swallowed, though the movement hurt his throat. Something felt wrong. Many things felt wrong. Something was on his face. A mask, or—

He reached for his mouth but the cords held him back, and this time he didn't fight them.

"Finish the reconstitution procedures," said the thaumaturge. "He is quite amicable now."

Another woman crept into view, rubbing her neck. She eyed Wolf warily as she started to remove the needles from his arms, then disconnected some probes that had been stuck to his scalp. He flinched at each one.

"Can you sit?" asked the lab technician.

Wolf braced his muscles and pushed himself upward. The task was easier than he'd expected. His brain was telling him he was weak, confused, delirious. But his body felt ready to fight. His nerves hummed with unspent energy.

The technician handed him a cup of orange liquid. He sniffed it first, his nose curling in distaste, then fit it to his lips.

He paused. Lowered the cup again.

Raising his free hand, he pressed it against his mouth. His nose. His jaw.

His body convulsed with horror.

It was done. After years of fighting to avoid becoming one of the queen's monsters, it had happened.

"Is something wrong, Alpha Kesley?"

He met the thaumaturge's gaze. She was watching him like one might watch a ticking bomb. Wolf knew he had no words to express all the confusion and bewilderment and the savage needs pulsing through his brains, needs he couldn't name. He didn't think he was capable of speaking, anyway. He drank the orange liquid.

The dream came back to him in sharp, scattered pieces. The girl's red hair. His brother's animalistic fury. His mother falling, dead, out of his reach.

Always back to the beautiful, quick-tongued girl. The memory of her was sharpest of all, because he so clearly remembered how she *loathed* him.

Memories and fears crowded together, shoving up against one another, and he could no longer tell truth from fiction. His head ached.

"What did you say was different about him from the others?" said the thaumaturge, walking around to Wolf's side.

The technician analyzed a screen built into the tank's side. "His brain patterns were more active than they usually are in the final stages of reengineering, and usually when they wake up they're just . . . hungry. Not violent. That comes later, once they've gotten their strength back."

"He seems to have plenty of strength."

"I noticed." The technician shook her head. "It could be from rushing the process. Normally we have them for at least a week. His mind and body have been through a lot in a short period of time, which could be causing the aggression."

"Is he fit to serve the queen?"

The technician peered at Wolf. He crumpled the cup in his fist. She gulped and slid back a step.

"As capable as any other soldier. I suggest getting some food into him before putting him on active duty. And of course, usually they spend months training with a thaumaturge after the surgeries are complete, so their master can learn their bioelectric patterns and how best to control them—"

"They are not made to be controlled."

The technician frowned. "I realize that. But they can be taught obedience. He's a loaded weapon. I wouldn't recommend bringing him into a room full of people without anyone first being able to handle him."

"Does it not look like I can handle him?"

The technician's attention danced from the thaumaturge to Wolf to the crumpled cup in his fist. She lifted her hands. "I'm just here to make sure their bodies don't reject the modifications."

Wolf ran a tongue along the sharp point of his canine tooth. It had taken him months to get used to the implants and now they felt all wrong again. Too big. Too sharp. There was a dull ache through his entire jaw.

The thaumaturge paced around the tank. "Alpha Ze'ev Kesley, you are once again a soldier in the queen's army. Unfortunately, your pack of special operatives disbanded after the first attack on Paris and we do not have time to get you reacquainted with a new one. For now, you will be serving as a lone wolf."

She smiled. Wolf did not.

"I am Thaumaturge Bement, but you will refer to me as Mistress," she continued. "You have been granted a great honor. The queen wishes you to be a part of her personal entourage during her coronation, in which she is to be crowned empress of the Eastern Commonwealth of Earth. As you have a history of rebellious tendencies, she feels your presence, serving as a loyal soldier, will send a message to any who would dare threaten the crown. Can you guess what that message is?"

Wolf said nothing.

Thaumaturge Bement's tone turned to a whispered threat. "Once the queen has claimed you, you are forever hers." She tapped her fingers against the rim of the tank. "Let's see if you can remember that this time."

She waited for a response. When there wasn't one, her eyes narrowed. "Have you forgotten your training? When you are addressed by your thaumaturge, your proper response is?"

"Yes, Mas—Mistress." It felt like the words were being pulled up from him, the words a reflex drilled into him from years and years under Thaumaturge Jael. *Rip his still-beating heart from his chest.*

Wolf cringed and his mouth started to water. He *was* hungry.

"Who do you serve, Alpha Kesley?"

Who did he serve?

The queen's beautiful face rose up in his memory, seated

upon her throne. Watching the packs fight to gain favor. *He* had desired to impress her. He had killed for her. He had been proud.

"I serve my queen," he said, his voice stronger.

"That's correct." Bement leaned over the tank, but Wolf didn't look away. He was salivating now. He could smell the blood pumping beneath the woman's skin, but a memory of pain darted down his spine when he thought of tasting her.

"I am told," she said, "that you took for yourself a mate while you were on Earth."

He tensed. Her red hair flashed through his thoughts.

"What would you do if you saw her today?"

He watched her being thrown against the statue. Crawling on her hands and knees. Staring at him with terrified, hate-filled eyes.

A growl rumbled deep in his throat. "Earthens have the sweetest flesh."

The thaumaturge's lips turned upward. "He'll do fine." Pushing away from the tank, she strode past the technician and her fallen companion. "Get him cleaned up. You know how Her Majesty likes to maintain appearances."

Sixty-Five

JACIN, CRESS, AND THORNE HAD GONE, LEAVING CINDER TO cobble her way through Iko's repairs. She knew immediately that she couldn't get Iko back to normal. Not only had Iko given up her finger and some of the wires required for hand dexterity, but they also didn't have the replacement parts or skin fibers to fix the tear in her shoulder or bullet hole in her chest. But Cinder managed to wrangle together a temporary skeletal patch and re-configure the joints so she would be able to move her elbow and wrist, at least. When Iko swooned with relief, Cinder knew ex-actly what she was feeling—having complete loss of a limb was a difficult thing to get used to.

While Cinder worked, Iko explained to her how they'd man-aged to sneak into Artemisia aboard a supply train, how most of the shuttle system was down and the trains were being searched, how Levana was nervous, if not downright terrified.

When she was done, Cinder told her about being transported back to Artemisia and how they'd separated her and Wolf. How he hadn't been at the trial, and how she had no idea where they'd taken him. She told Iko about seeing Kai in the throne room and how he looked unharmed, so far.

She asked if the broadcast had also shown Adri's trial.

"Adri?" Iko's lashes fluttered, for a beat, two beats, three, before she said, "I don't compute."

"Adri and Pearl are here, on Luna. Adri was put on trial before me—something about how she's been keeping design patents for a weapon that could neutralize the Lunar gift. I think Levana's found out about Garan's invention, the one that was installed on my spine."

Iko pressed her fingertips together in imitation of thoughtfulness. "I suppose it makes sense that Levana wouldn't want such a thing to exist."

"I know. It hadn't occurred to me before, but such a device would change the balance of power between Luna and Earth, if it could be manufactured. If we're ever going to have an alliance with Luna, a device like this would be the only way for Earthens to be sure they aren't being manipulated."

"That's genius," Iko said. "I always liked Garan. He was nice to me, even after they discovered my personality chip was faulty. He at least kept all my software updated. You know, until Adri had me disassembled." She paused. "The first time."

Cinder smiled to herself. The first time she'd seen Iko she'd been nothing more than a jumble of android parts thrown into a box, waiting to be put back together. Iko had been her first project, an attempt to prove her worth to her new stepfamily. She'd had no idea at the time that Iko would also become one of her dearest friends.

Her smile faded, turning to suspicion. "Iko, they stopped making software updates for Serv9.2s over a decade ago."

Iko tugged on one of her braids. "I never thought about that. You don't think he was trying to fix the bug that made me . . . *me*. Do you?"

"I don't know. I don't think so. He designed android systems, after all. I'm sure if he wanted to reprogram you to be a regular android, he could have done it." She hesitated. If Linh Garan hadn't been updating Iko's software or trying to fix her, what *had* he been doing? "I guess it doesn't matter. Garan invented this device, but it sounds like Levana destroyed all his notes. If my own software wasn't already damaged enough by Dr. Erland, I doubt that dip in the lake did it any good . . ." She trailed off, squinting at Iko.

"What?"

"Nothing." Cinder shook her head. There were too many problems to fix, too many puzzles to solve. The mystery of Garan's device would have to wait. "I just can't imagine how Levana would have even known about the device in the first place, that's all."

"I told her."

Cinder snapped her head toward the door, where Jacin was standing as still and quiet as the door frame itself, sporting a decent-size bruise on his jaw, compliments of Thorne. "*You* told her?"

"Information has value. I traded that piece for my life."

It was always difficult to read Jacin's emotions, but if Cinder had to guess, she would have thought he was incensed over making such a trade. She remembered telling Jacin about the device, ages ago, in the little oasis town of Farafrah. His face had taken on a curiosity that bordered on hunger when he learned there was an invention that could prevent a Lunar from using their gift and prevent their gift from driving them mad.

She stifled a gasp.

Winter.

Of course.

Jacin jerked his chin toward the hallway. "I hate to rush you, but the crown just released a new video that you might be interested in seeing. Evidently you're dead."

He and Iko led her to the mansion's home theater, with enormous lounging chairs that each had a built-in beverage dispenser on its side. Thorne and Cress were standing beside a larger-than-life holograph depicting Levana. She was wearing her veil, but the sound was muted. The enormity of it made Cinder recoil.

"Jacin says they found my body?"

Thorne gave her a passing glance. "That's the word, corpse girl. You were dredged up from the lake last night. They even have this mannequin thing with a painted metal hand and they keep showing a grainy photo of it. Stay around a while—you'll see. It keeps looping with this speech from Levana. They have the most boring entertainment on this rock."

"What is she saying?"

Thorne's voice pitched high in imitation of the queen. "The impostor of my beloved niece is vanquished . . . Let us put this messiness behind us while we go forward with the coronations . . . I am a psychotic, power-hungry nut basket and my breath smells really bad under this veil."

Cinder snickered. She tried to check the time with her internal clock before remembering it no longer worked. "How long until the coronation?"

"Nine hours," said Iko.

Nine hours. They'd been in this mansion for an entire day and night and Cinder had been asleep for most of it.

"There's also the ticker ..." Cress pointed to the holograph, where a list of sectors was trekking across the bottom, making a constant floating ring around Levana.

"That's the interesting part," said Thorne. "She's passed an edict that any sector found in violation of curfew or suspected of assisting 'the impostor' will be barricaded, to be dealt with on a case-by-case basis after the coronation. Then she goes on some spiel about repentance and begging their queen for mercy."

"It seems a lot of people were motivated by your stunt at the wedding feast," said Jacin. "The number of barricaded sectors keeps growing."

"How many?"

"Eighty-seven at last count," said Cress.

"Including RM-9," added Thorne, "and every sector in its immediate surroundings. Rather than discouraging the rebellion, the raid there seems to have angered people even more."

Eighty-seven at last count.

"And you think they've all ... that all these sectors ..." Cinder swallowed. Her head still felt foggy. "What do we think this means?"

"It means the queen is having a bad day," said Jacin.

Thorne nodded. "Some of it could be her own paranoia, but even when Iko and I were trying to get into Artemisia there were rumors of some sectors blockading their own tunnels to keep supplies out of the city, or looting their factories for weapons, that sort of thing. And that was before your trial. Of course, we don't know if the people believe you're really dead, but I'm not sure it matters at this point. If you're alive, then you're one hell of a revolutionary. If you're dead, then you're one hell of a martyr."

"It sort of matters to me," Cinder said, watching the ticker scroll by.

Eighty-seven sectors had been ready to fight for her—for themselves. From what she'd seen, each sector housed at least a thousand civilians, and sometimes many times that. That should be more than enough to overwhelm the capital and overthrow Levana . . .

Except all those people were trapped.

"Don't faint," said Thorne.

She looked at him. "What?"

"You look stressed out."

Glowering, Cinder started to pace. "Can we do something about these barricades? The people can't come to our aid if they're confined to their own sectors."

"Oh, sweetheart," said Thorne, "we are so far ahead of you. Cress?"

Cress pulled up the holograph of Luna they'd spent a lot of time studying aboard the Rampion—all the domes and subway tunnels laid out on the moon's rocky, cratered surface. She had been tagging the barricaded sectors as they were listed on Levana's broadcast. It was still only a fraction of all the sectors on Luna, but then, it was possible there were plenty more sectors in uprising that Levana didn't know about yet.

Levana was focusing on those sectors closest to Artemisia, which made sense. No wonder she was nervous—the revolution had already crept up to her doorstep.

Cress adjusted the holograph, zooming in on Artemisia, then the palace.

"The barricade controls are a part of the main security network that operates out of the palace's security center," said

Cress. "I could hack them remotely, but not without raising alarms. At least, not with the amount of time I have to do it. So . . ."

"We thought we'd break in," said Thorne. He had claimed one of the lounge chairs and kicked up his feet.

"Of course you did," said Cinder.

"We got into New Beijing Palace, we can get into this one. From there, Cress undoes the barricades on the outer sectors and schedules the security barriers around the central dome to open at the end of the coronation." He filled an expensive-looking goblet with a blue drink from the chair's dispenser and took a big gulp. "It's the best way to coordinate a surprise attack and make sure everyone is entering Artemisia at the same time, even if we have no way of communicating with one another."

Cress pulled back the holograph's focus, highlighting the eight maglev tunnels that were the only passages in and out of the city—excepting the spaceship ports.

Cinder massaged her wrist. "It's too risky to send you in. I'd rather Cress remove the barricades remotely, even if it does raise alarms."

"That makes two of us," said Thorne, "but that's not the only reason we need to get into the palace. We also need access to the queen's broadcast room if we want to do anything with that video of yours. Levana disabled all outside access to the system after your last stunt, so if we want to project it over the whole system, we have to do it from inside."

Cinder inhaled sharply. "Is the video . . . is it worth it?"

"Oh!" Iko clapped her hands to her face. "It's *horrifying*!"

Thorne grinned. "It's a jackpot."

"I'll load it on the projector," said Cress, turning toward the holograph node.

"Please, no," said Iko, "we don't need to see it that big again."

Cinder tapped her foot. "How are you proposing we get into the palace? I can glamour all four of us as coronation guests if we wanted to sneak in—"

"Cool those engines, jet plane," said Thorne. "You already have a job. While Cress and I are clearing the passages into the city, you, Iko, and Jacin are going to be stationed in these three sectors"—he indicated them on the holograph, three of the domes adjacent to Artemisia Central—"or at least in the tunnels underneath them, welcoming all those rebels you've stirred up and organizing what last-minute battle plan we can. In approximately nine hours, with any luck, this city is going to be under siege by a whole lot of angry Lunars. They're going to need someone to lead them."

"That's you," Iko clarified.

"But I thought this dome was cordoned off? How are we supposed to get out to those sectors if we're stuck in here?"

"There are storage units not far from here," said Jacin, "where some of the families keep recreational vehicles, including terrain speeders."

"Terrain speeders?"

"Vehicles made for going outside the domes. They can adjust to the unmodified gravity and atmospheric conditions and handle difficult terrain. Dunes. Craters. Rich people use them for sport. They're not as fast as ships, but we can bypass the shuttles and cut a direct route to the nearest sectors, anywhere that has external dock access. Levana won't care about a couple nobles out for a joyride."

"We're splitting up," said Cinder.

Iko wrapped an arm around Cinder's waist. "Only temporarily."

"It's our best hope for coordinating an attack," said Thorne, "and getting as many people in front of that palace as possible, which is the whole point, isn't it? Strength in numbers?"

Cinder's heart was galloping again, but she managed a nod. She was studying the holograph again when an anomaly caught her eye. "What's wrong with that sector?" she asked, pointing to one that was tinged red on the map.

Cress spun the holograph and brought the sector into focus. "LW-12, lumber and wood manufacturing. Quarantined?"

"Like a disease quarantine?" Cinder asked.

"That's all we need," Thorne muttered.

But Jacin was shaking his head. "It's been a long time since we had an outbreak of any sort of disease on Luna. There aren't many environmental influences that we can't control." He crossed his arms. "We do have measures in place in case something happens, though. With the domes confined like they are, it wouldn't take much to take down a whole community if a disease was bad enough."

"Could it be letumosis?" Iko asked, a tinge of fear vibrating in her voice.

"That's an Earthen disease," said Jacin. "We've never had any cases here."

"It's not just an Earthen disease," said Cinder. "Not anymore. Dr. Erland discovered a mutated strain in Africa, remember? Lunars may not be immune anymore, and ..." She gulped. "And a whole lot of Earthens just arrived on Luna. Anyone could be a carrier. One of the diplomats, or even one of us. We might not even know it."

Jacin gestured to the holograph. "Have any of you gone into a lumber sector lately?"

Cinder pressed her lips.

"That's what I thought. I doubt any of your political friends have, either. It's probably a coincidence."

"Actually," said Cress, pulling her wide-eyed gaze away from her portscreen, "one of us has been there." She input a new command, transferring the feed she was watching up to the holograph.

It was a collection of the queen's surveillance videos, all labeled LW-12. They were dark and grainy, but as Cinder's eyes adjusted she could see rows of trees in the outside shots and wood-paneled walls on the interiors. She focused on one of the more crowded feeds, which appeared to be inside a medical building, although it was nothing like the sleek, shiny laboratories of New Beijing.

There were so many people, taking up what few beds there were while others curled against walls or collapsed in corners.

Stepping closer to the image, Jacin enlarged one of the feeds, zooming in on a rash of blue-and-red rings across one patient's throat, then to the bloodstained pillow beneath another patient's head.

"It does look like letumosis," Cinder said, gut spasming with instinctive fear.

"Are those what I think they are?" asked Iko, pointing.

"Lunar soldiers," Cress confirmed, enlarging one of the outside feeds that showed dozens of mutant men standing among the citizens. Many seemed caught up in a fervent conversation. Cinder had never seen them when they weren't in attack mode, and if it wasn't for their deformed faces, they would have looked just like, well, really big, scary men.

Then she spotted someone who was even more shocking than the mutants. A girl with red hair and a hooded sweatshirt and hands settled stubbornly on her hips. "Scarlet!"

Very much alive and very much unafraid of the predators surrounding her. In fact, as she watched, Scarlet seemed to be bossing them around, pointing her finger toward the main doors of the clinic. Half a dozen of the soldiers nodded at her and left.

"I don't compute," said Iko.

Thorne laughed, as jovial as Cinder felt. "What's to compute? They did say they were going to build an army."

"Yes, but Scarlet wasn't with us in the desert. How could *she* be a carrier of the new strain of the disease?"

Cinder started. "You're right. She could have . . . picked it up from one of us?"

"None of you are sick."

She had no answer. She wished Dr. Erland was here, but he had died from the same disease he'd been trying to eradicate.

"What's that they're carrying out of the clinic?" asked Thorne.

Jacin crossed his arms. "A suspended-animation tank."

Four soldiers had the tank hefted between them, while others propped open the main doors of the med-clinic for them to pass through. Outside, hundreds of civilians had gathered—those who weren't already sick. The soldiers pushed them back to make room for the tank.

Jacin inhaled sharply and stepped up beside the holograph, bringing the feed into focus. He paused. Scrolled back. Zoomed in closer.

"Oh, no," Cinder whispered. Another familiar face was encapsulated beneath the tank's glass lid. Princess Winter.

Sixty-Six

THERE WERE NO MIRRORS IN THE LAB, NOT EVEN IN THE TILED room with the sterilizing shower Wolf had been taken to in order to wash the sticky gel out of his hair. He didn't need a mirror, though, to know what they'd done. He could see the difference in his bone structure when he looked at his hands and feet. He could feel the difference in his protruding mouth, his enlarged teeth, his malformed jaw. They'd altered his facial bone structure, making way for the row of implanted canine teeth. There was a new curvature to his shoulders and an awkward flex of his feet, which looked more like paws now, made for running and bounding at great speeds. His hands were enormous, now fixed with reinforced, claw-shaped fingernails.

He could even smell it inside himself. New chemicals and hormones pumping through his veins. Testosterone. Adrenaline. Pheromones. He wondered when the new fur would start sprouting over his skin, completing the transformation.

He was miserable. He was everything he had never wanted to be.

He was also starving.

A uniform had been left for him, similar to the uniform he'd worn as a special operative. A formality for his role at the coronation. Most of the bioengineered soldiers received far less distinguished clothing, being more animal than man.

And now he was one of them. He tried to temper his disgust. After all, who was he to pass judgment on his brothers?

Yet his emotions continued to fluctuate. Furious and burning one moment. Devastated and full of self-loathing the next.

This was his fate. This had always been his fate. He couldn't imagine how he had ever thought differently. Had he honestly believed he could be better? That he deserved more? He was destined to kill and eat and destroy. That was all he was entitled to.

Suddenly, his nose twitched.

Food.

Saliva rolled onto his tongue and he wicked it against his sharp teeth. Something in his stomach roiled, angry at its own hollowness.

He shuddered, remembering this hunger from back when he had first begun training as an operative. He had both craved and hated the slabs of barely cooked meat they were presented, and the way they had to fight for their own piece, confirming the pack's pecking order in the process. Even then, the hunger had not been this bad.

He swallowed, hard, and finished dressing.

His body had begun to shake when he opened the door and the aroma of the food burst in his nostrils. He was almost panting.

Thaumaturge Bement and the lab technician were still there, though the unconscious man had been removed. The technician shrank back when she saw Wolf's expression. She situated herself behind another suspension tank, filled with some other victim.

"That look must mean there's food in the building," she said.

"Indeed." The thaumaturge was leaning against a wall, perusing her portscreen. "They are in the elevator with it now."

"I didn't realize you were going to have him eat *here*. Have you ever seen one of them when they've first eaten?"

"I will handle him. Go about your business."

Casting one more hesitant glance at Wolf, the woman returned to checking the diagnostics screens on the tank.

There was a chime down the hallway and the aroma of food wafted a hundred times stronger still. Wolf gripped the door frame. His legs were weak with lust, his knees ready to give out beneath him.

A servant arrived, pushing a wooden cart draped with a white cloth. "Mistress," he said, bowing to the thaumaturge. He was dismissed.

Wolf's senses were being pummeled. His ears pricked at the hiss of steam. His stomach spasmed with desire. *Lamb.*

"Are you hungry?"

He snarled, growling at the thaumaturge. He could lunge at her now, have the woman torn to bits before she even knew what was happening. But something held him back. Some deep-seated fear. Memories of another thaumaturge breaking his will.

"I asked you a question. I know you're nothing but an animal now, but I still think you're smart enough to answer with a simple yes or no."

"Yes," Wolf grunted.

"Yes, what?"

Rage nearly blinded him, but it was shoved back down. Wolf grimaced against the uprise of hatred. "Yes, Mistress."

"Good. We do not have time to get to know each other and build the relationship of understanding a thaumaturge would normally form with her pack. But I did want to illustrate for you two main principles, in a way that your little animal brain can understand." She whisked off the white cloth, revealing a platter overflowing with seared meat and bones, cartilage and marrow.

Wolf shuddered with hunger, but also with disgust. Disgust at the meat, and disgust at his own cravings. An odd memory eclipsed this new urge. Something glossy and red and bursting with juice—*tomatoes.*

They're the best part, and they were grown in my own garden . . .

"The first thing you need to know as a member of Her Majesty's army is that a good dog will always be rewarded." The thaumaturge waved her arm over the food. "Go ahead. Take a bite."

He flapped his head, willing away the unfamiliar voice. It was that girl again. The red-haired girl who was so repulsed by him.

Wolf's legs moved of their own accord, drawing him toward the cart. His stomach yearned. His tongue lagged.

But as soon as he reached a clawed hand toward the platter, pain lanced through his gut. He doubled over in agony. His legs gave out and he crumpled to the floor, his shoulder smacking the edge of the cart and sending it crashing into the nearby wall. The pain dragged on and on, arcing through every limb, like a thousand daggers burying themselves in his flesh.

The thaumaturge smiled.

The pain relented. Wolf was left trembling on the ground, his cheeks damp from sweat or tears or both.

The torture wasn't new to him. He remembered it from his training before, with Jael. But he had not felt it since he'd become the alpha. A prized soldier. A good, loyal pup.

"And that," said the thaumaturge, "is what will happen should you disappoint me. Do we have an understanding?"

He nodded shakily, his muscles still twitching.

"*Do we have an understanding?*"

He coughed. "Yes. Mistress."

"Good." Taking the tray off the cart, the thaumaturge dropped it onto the floor beside him. "Now eat your meal like a good dog. Our queen awaits."

Sixty-Seven

KAI WAS BEGINNING TO UNDERSTAND WHY LEVANA HAD SET the time for the coronations as she had. The ceremony was coming at the end of Artemisia's long night—two weeks of darkness, broken up only with artificial light. This would be the first real sunrise Kai had seen since he'd been on Luna. A new dawn, a new day, a new empire.

It was all very symbolic.

He simultaneously longed for this day to be over, and wanted it to never come at all.

Standing amid the lapping waves of Artemisia Lake, staring at the blue-black water that spanned as far as he could see, Kai hoped Levana's new dawn would be very different than she expected, although his hope was spread thin. He didn't know if Cinder had survived the fall into the lake, or if the people of Luna would heed her call, or if they would succeed even if they tried.

At least he knew with certainty that the video footage of Cinder's reclaimed body was fake. Even from the distant, blurry footage, Kai could tell it wasn't her, but some dummy or an actor or some other poor victim dragged from the lake bottom and made to look like Cinder.

If they were faking her death, she hadn't been found.

She was alive. She *had* to be alive.

At least, with the coronation drawing closer, the queen had begun to relax some of the restrictions on Kai and the other Earthen guests. He was finally free to roam the palace and even venture down to the lakeshore, though every step was trailed by a pair of matching Lunar guards.

He'd spent his whole life surrounded by guards, though. It had gotten easier to ignore them.

She'd even let him have his portscreen back so he could check on the Earthen newsfeeds and confirm for them that all was well up here on Luna.

Ha.

The sand slipped out from beneath his feet as the surf pulled back into the lake. The world disintegrating beneath him. He was mildly curious whether this was moon rock pulverized to fine sand, or if it had long ago been imported from some white Earthen beach. So many times since coming here he had wished that he'd spent more time researching the history between Earth and Luna. He wanted to know what the relationship had been like when Luna was a peaceful colony, and, later, an allied republic. For years Earth had supplied Luna with building materials and natural resources, and Luna had returned valuable research in the fields of space exploration and astronomy. Knowing it had once been a beneficial relationship suggested it could be again.

But not with Levana.

Scanning the shore on either side of the lake, Kai watched the royal guards still searching, waiting for a bedraggled cyborg to wash ashore. Kai had also seen them patrolling the city streets from his window, and if they thought it was possible Cinder had survived and gone into hiding, then Kai would believe it was possible too.

Meanwhile, the palace was bustling with final preparations for the coronation. The aristocrats—or *families*—were very good at faking unadulterated merriment. Even the havoc from Cinder's failed execution had been swept away like a minor mishap, bound to happen from time to time. Everyone seemed happy to leave the manhunt to the guards while they commenced with their drinking and eating and revelries.

If they were at all concerned over Cinder's calls for revolution, they weren't showing it. Kai wondered if a single member of the court would take up arms against the people if it came to that, or if they would cower in their fancy mansions and wait for it to be over, happy to claim allegiance to whoever sat on the throne once the chaos had ended.

Thinking it, Kai shut his eyes and bit his tongue against a smirk, knowing the fantasy was petty. But *oh*, how he would love to see their faces if—when—Cinder became queen and informed the *families* that their indulgent way of life was coming to an end.

A throat cleared behind Kai, drawing his attention over his shoulder. Torin stood in a formal tuxedo, already dressed for the coronation though it was hours away.

"His Imperial Majesty, Emperor Rikan," Torin said. It was a code they had devised with the rest of the Earthen guests—to begin each meeting by mentioning some other person who had been present when they had first formally met. It had been Kai's idea, so they could always make sure they were speaking to the person they believed they were speaking to, rather than a Lunar using a tricky glamour.

Kai smiled at the mention of his father. He didn't remember meeting Torin, who had been a permanent fixture in the palace since before Kai's birth.

"My mother," he said, by way of reply.

Torin's gaze dropped down to Kai's bare feet and rolled-up slacks, but didn't linger. "Any news?"

"Nothing. You?"

"I spoke briefly with President Vargas earlier. He and the other American representatives feel threatened. They feel we're all being held hostage."

"Smart man." A wave crashed into Kai, and he swayed with it, curling his toes into the wet sand. "Levana believes she has us right where she wants us."

"Is she wrong?"

Kai frowned, and didn't respond. His silence was followed by a sigh.

Glancing back, Kai saw Torin untying his dress shoes and removing his socks. He rolled up his pant hems before coming to stand beside Kai in the surf.

"I told President Vargas that once Levana has the title of empress, she will feel less defensive and we'll be able to set rational boundaries around a new Earthen-Lunar alliance." He hesitated, before adding, "I didn't say anything about Princess Selene. I felt he would see any hope placed in her as nothing more than a fairy tale."

Kai bit the inside of his cheek and hoped that wasn't the case. He had been putting his faith in Princess Selene even before he'd found her. Even before he'd known she was the most capable, resourceful, determined person he'd ever met. Even before he'd started having fantasies of a royal Earthen-Lunar marriage that didn't involve Levana at all.

"Your Majesty," said Torin, with a tone that said he was about to broach a subject Kai wasn't going to like. Kai braced himself accordingly. "Have you given thought to what your next move will be should our hoped-for outcome not come to pass?"

"You mean if Cinder is dead and the people don't rebel and tomorrow morning I find myself stuck with an empress who wants to kill me and take control of my military and wage war on my allies until they all succumb to her will?"

Torin made a derisive sound in the back of his throat. "I suppose you have been thinking about it."

"It's crossed my mind a time or two." He peered at Torin from the corner of his eye, surprised to find that looking at his adviser felt like looking at an older, wiser version of himself. Not that they looked much alike—Torin had neat, gray-flecked hair, a longer nose, and thin, stern lips. But standing barefoot in the water, each with their hands in their pockets and their faces turned toward the lake, Kai thought it wouldn't be a bad thing to grow up to be as stable and capable as Konn Torin. Or as thoughtful and intelligent as Kai's father had been.

He checked that the Lunar guards were out of earshot before asking, "What's the status of the bombs that could weaken these biodomes?"

"I'm told we have a dozen built and ready for deployment, but it will be weeks before a second batch is complete. The most we could hope for at this point is to weaken them, but I don't think it would be enough to deter Levana completely."

"Unless we target the dome that she's in," said Kai.

Torin's lips twitched downward. "That is also the dome that *we* are in."

"I know." With a sigh, Kai curled his toes into the silt. "Prepare the fleet. I want a regiment of armed ships positioned in neutral space, as close to Luna as they can get without warranting concern. After the coronation, if Levana doesn't allow the other leaders to leave, we might be able to threaten her into consenting. I'd like everyone else off this moon as soon as possible."

"Everyone *else*? What about you?"

Kai shook his head. "I have to make sure Levana gives up the letumosis antidote. I don't know where she's keeping it, but if it's here in Artemisia, we can't risk it being destroyed. I need to make sure we retrieve it and get it to Earth as quickly as possible. I have to succeed at that, if nothing else."

"And once the antidote is secured," Torin said, "our priority must be your own safety. If she does mean to have you killed so she can assume control of the Commonwealth, we need to take steps to make sure it doesn't happen. We will have increased security around you at all times. And physical separation from the queen will be mandatory. I will not have her brainwashing you into committing self-harm."

Kai smiled, heartened somewhat by the protectiveness in Torin's voice. "All sound suggestions, Torin, but it won't be necessary."

Torin turned toward him, but Kai was looking at the horizon, where black water met black sky. Sunlight was glinting off some of the domes in the far distance, but the change from night to day had been so gradual Kai barely noticed. Lunar sunrises were an agonizingly slow affair.

"I almost killed her at the wedding. I was so close. I could have ended it all, but I failed."

Torin gave a frustrated snort. "You are not a murderer. I find it difficult to think of that as a personality flaw."

Kai opened his mouth, but Torin continued, "And if you *had* managed to kill her, it would have brought down the wrath of every thaumaturge and guard in that room. You would have gotten yourself killed, and no doubt every Earthen guest as well. I understand where the impulse came from, but I am glad you failed."

"You're right. Even so, it won't happen next time." Kai tucked his hands into his pockets and found the medallion there. The one Iko and Cress had given him aboard the Rampion, forever claiming him as a member of their crew, no matter what happened. He tightened his fist around it. "I'm not leaving Luna with this unresolved. She can't be allowed to rule Earth. If Cinder ... if Princess Selene fails, I won't."

"What are you saying?"

Kai faced Torin, though it was difficult to pull his feet from the sucking sand. "I can make myself useful to her long enough to obtain the antidote. She won't kill me right away, not if I can convince her I have information she wants—knowledge about our military procedures, resources ... Then, when the antidote has been safely relocated, I will order our military to bomb Artemisia."

Torin stepped back. "With you *in it?*"

He nodded. "It's the only way I can be sure Levana will be here when the attack happens. She won't be suspicious. As long as I'm here, she'll think she has control over us. With a single attack, we can remove her, the thaumaturges, and the most powerful members of her court. They won't be able to stop it. No brainwashing. No manipulation. There will be a lot of casualties, but we can try to keep the destruction to the central sectors, and once Luna is in disarray, Earth can offer assistance for reconstruction."

Torin had started shaking his head. His eyes were shut, as if he couldn't stand to listen to Kai's plan anymore. "No. You cannot sacrifice yourself."

"I'm already sacrificing myself. I won't let her have my country. There has been peace between the Earthen Union for over a century—I won't let my decisions be the end of that." He peeled back his shoulders. "Which is why it's so important that the Commonwealth be ruled by someone who is smart and fair. The Articles of Unification state that in the event that the last in line to the empire has reason to expect their death without first procuring an heir for the throne, they are to nominate one person to become the new emperor or empress, and the people shall nominate their choices and it will be put to a vote." He met Torin's gaze. "I nominated you before we left. Nainsi has my official statement. So . . ." He gulped. "Good luck with the election."

"I cannot . . . I won't . . ."

"It's already done. If you come up with a better plan, I'd love to hear it. But I will not let that woman rule the Commonwealth. I would be honored to die in service of my country." Kai glanced up at the palace and the throne room balcony jutting out over their heads. "Just as long as I can take her down with me."

Sixty-Eight

"WHY DOES CRESS ALWAYS GET TO WEAR THE BEST CLOTHES?"
Iko whined, crossing her arms while Cress practiced walking
back and forth in the ridiculously tall platform shoes. "Cress gets
to go to a royal wedding. Cress gets to go to a coronation. Cress
has *all* the fun."

"I'm not going to the coronation," said Cress, trying to look at
her feet without falling over. "We're just impersonating guests so
we can hack into the palace broadcast system."

"Cress gets to hack into the palace broadcast system."

"*Cress* is risking her life to do this." Cinder threw a pile of
shimmering accessories onto the bed. "Do any of these match?"

Iko flopped onto the bed and started pawing through the accessories with desire-filled eyes. "I think these gloves attach to
the wing-things," she said, followed by a pitiful sigh. "I wish my
outfit came with fingerless orange elbow-length gloves."

"These shoes are like stilts," said Cress, wobbling. "Isn't there
something more practical?"

"I don't think *practical* is in the Lunar vocabulary," said Cinder,
diving back into the closet, "but I'll look."

They'd managed to find a new pair of boots for Cinder, at least, who had lost hers in the lake. They'd found them stacked in a utility closet along with miscellaneous sporting equipment, or what Cress thought was sporting equipment. Unfortunately, there'd been nothing small enough to fit *her*, and Iko had insisted they wouldn't have matched her aristocratic outfit anyway.

"Tell me I don't look as ridiculous as I feel." Thorne appeared in the doorway, fidgeting with his cuffs.

Startled, Cress tripped and crashed into Iko, sending them both tumbling onto the floor.

Cinder poked her head out of the closet, surveyed the scene, and bunched up her lips. She disappeared again, muttering, "I'd better find some different shoes."

Thorne helped Cress and Iko back to their feet. "Maybe ridiculous is the theme of the day," he said, tilting his head to survey Cress's outfit, which was part cocktail dress, part butterfly costume. An orange tutu barely reached her mid-thigh and was gaudy enough when paired with a glitz-covered, form-fitting bodice. Two sheer swaths of material had been sewn onto the bodice's back and did in fact connect to the fingerless orange elbow-length gloves Iko relinquished, so when Cress spread her arms it gave the effect of a pair of black-and-yellow butterfly wings opening up behind her. To top it off, Iko had found a tiny blue hat in the accessories chest that had a pair of springs and feathered balls on top—what Cress assumed were meant to be the antennae.

"I do feel a little better now that I see what you're wearing." Thorne adjusted his bow tie. He was in a lean plum-toned suit that was surprisingly flattering on him despite having been dragged out of a stranger's closet. The bow tie had tiny threaded lights running through the fabric, making the collar of his white shirt glow in different shades of neon. He'd left on his own black military boots.

He looked absurd and sexy, and Cress had to force herself to look away.

"You'll fit right in, from what I could tell at the feast." Cinder emerged with a pair of more user-friendly shoes. "They were all wearing crazy things like this at the feast. I don't doubt that a lot of the clothing was glamour-made, but the fewer elements of your appearance you have to glamour, the easier it is to hold the illusion."

"Hey, Captain," said Iko, "stop checking out her legs."

Cress turned in time to see Thorne's appreciative grin. Shrugging, he adjusted the cuffs of his jacket. "I'm a connoisseur, Iko. Look how tall those shoes make her look." He hesitated. "Well, tall-ish."

Flushing, Cress inspected her bare legs.

Cinder rolled her eyes. "Here, Cress, try these on."

"Hm? Oh, right." She removed the torture devices and tossed them to Iko, who was all too thrilled to slip them onto her feet.

Within seconds, Iko was waltzing around the room's perimeter as if she'd been designed with those exact shoes in mind. "Oh, yes," she said. "I'm keeping these."

When Cress had fitted the replacement shoes onto her feet, Thorne flicked one of her antenna puff balls and draped an arm over her shoulders. "How do we look?"

Cinder scratched the back of her neck. Iko tilted her head from one side to the other, as if their appearance might improve from a different angle.

"I guess you look Lunar?" Cinder ventured.

"Nice." Thorne held up a hand for a high five. Cress awkwardly complied.

Cinder adjusted her ponytail. "Of course, any Lunar who's paying attention will be able to tell you're an Earthen and she's a shell. So be careful."

Thorne scoffed. "*Careful* is my middle name. Right after *Suave* and *Daring.*"

"Do you even know what you're saying half the time?" asked Cinder.

Thorne picked up the chip that they'd transferred Cinder's video onto and handed it to Cress. "Put this somewhere safe."

She stared, not sure what constituted safe. She had no pockets, no bag, and very little clothing in which to hide anything. Finally she tucked it inside her bodice.

Grabbing Cress's portscreen off the vanity, Thorne slid it into a pocket on the inside of his jacket, where she could also see the outline of his handgun. A small knife they'd taken from the kitchen vanished in his hands, so quick she wasn't sure where he'd put it.

"I guess that's it," said Cinder, scanning over Thorne's and Cress's outfits again. "Are we ready?"

"If anyone answers *no* to that question," said Jacin, appearing in the hallway with a scowl and tapping fingers, "I'm leaving without you."

Cress cast her gaze over her friends, realizing they were about to be separated. Again. Trepidation curled in the pit of her stomach.

She and Thorne would go off to the palace, while Cinder, Iko, and Jacin tried to save Winter and Scarlet and organize the people who would soon be infiltrating Artemisia.

She didn't want to leave them. She didn't want to say good-bye.

But Thorne's arm was over her shoulders, comfortable and solid. When he tugged on his lapel with his free hand and told the others, "We're ready," Cress didn't argue.

"THERE'S THE BACK ENTRANCE," SAID JACIN, POINTING AT A near-invisible door in the back of the medical and research clinic, half-hidden behind overgrown shrubberies. Iko popped up beside him in an attempt to see, but he flattened a hand on her head and forced her to duck down as two men in lab coats strolled by, both of them with their attention stuck to their portscreens.

Jacin scanned the yard one more time before darting out from their cover and ducking into the building's shadow. Through the dome's wall he could see the desolate landscape of Luna stretching into the distance.

He waved his arm, and Cinder and Iko scurried after him, crowding together in the shadows.

The door opened easily—no reason to lock doors in a building that was open to the public—but Jacin refused to feel relieved. There would be no relief for him until he knew Winter was safe.

They scurried into a dim corridor, the walls in need of a coat of paint. Jacin listened, but all he heard was a squeaky wheel and a clattering cart in some distant hallway.

"There's a maintenance room down there," he said, pointing, "and a janitorial closet on each floor. That door takes you to the main part of the building."

"How do you know all this?" Cinder whispered.

"I interned here for a few months before the queen decided I would make a decent guard."

He felt Cinder peering up at him, but he didn't meet the look.

"That's right," she murmured. "You wanted to be a doctor."

"Whatever." He paced to the screen beside the maintenance room and pulled up a mapped diagram of the clinic. A few red exclamation points glowed in different areas, with inserted notes. PATIENT RM 8: NON-TOXIC SPILL ON FLOOR. LAB 13: FAULTY LIGHT SWITCH.

"Here," said Cinder, pointing at the fourth floor of the diagram. DISEASE RESEARCH AND DEVELOPMENT.

There was a back staircase on the opposite side of the building—it would get them to the right floor, at least. Jacin hoped the research team had taken the day off to enjoy the coronation festivities. He didn't want any more complications, and he'd like to avoid killing anyone else if he could.

That didn't stop him from loosening his gun, though.

The climb to the fourth floor came with no surprises. Jacin cracked open the door and scanned the well-lit corridor. He could hear the gurgle of water tanks and the hum of computers and the constant growl of machinery, but no people.

Indicating for the others to stay close, he slipped out of the stairwell. Their shoes squeaked and thumped on the hard floors. Beside each door a screen lit up as they passed, indicating the purpose for each room.

AGRICULTURE: GEN MOD DEVELOPMENT AND
TESTING
BIOELECTRICAL MANIPULATION: STUDY #17
(CONTROL AND GROUPS 1-3)

GENETIC ENGINEERING: CANIS LUPUS SUBJECTS
#16-20
GENETIC ENGINEERING: CANIS LUPUS SUBJECTS
#21-23
GENETIC ENGINEERING: SURGICAL ALTERATION

"...increased manufac..."

Jacin froze. The feminine voice was from somewhere down the hallway, and was followed by the slamming of a door or cupboard.

"...be possible to sustain...resources..."

Another door opened, followed by footsteps.

Jacin grabbed for the nearest door, but it was locked. Behind him, Cinder tested another handle, sneering when it didn't open either.

"Here," Iko whispered, pulling open a door down the hall. Jacin and Cinder ducked in after her and shut the door, careful to not make a sound.

The lab was empty—or at least, empty of people. *Conscious* people. The walls were lined with shelves of suspended-animation tanks, filling up the space from floor to ceiling. Each tank hummed and gurgled, their insides lit with faint green lights that made the bodies look like frozen corpses. The far wall was full of even more tanks layered like shut drawers, making it a checkerboard of screens and statistics, glowing lights and the soles of feet.

Cinder and Iko ducked behind two of the tanks. Jacin backed himself against the wall so he would be hidden if the door opened and able to take anyone by surprise.

The first voice was met with another, male this time.

"... plenty in stock, but it would be nice if they gave us some indication that this was going to ..."

Jacin inhaled as the voice grew louder, until footsteps were right outside the door. But the footsteps and voices soon faded in the other direction.

Iko peeked around the base of the tank, but he held a finger to his lips. Cinder's face appeared a second later, questioning.

Jacin gave a cursory glance to the rest of the lab. Each of the suspension tanks had a small tube that connected it to a row of holding containers. Though most of the tubes were clear, a few of them were tinted maroon with slow-flowing blood.

"What is this place?" Cinder whispered. Her face was twisted with horror. She was staring at the unconscious form of a child, maybe a few years old.

"They're shells," he said. "She keeps them here for an endless supply of blood, which is used in producing the antidote."

When a shell was born and taken away, their families were told they were being killed as part of the infanticide laws. Years ago they had actually been kept in captivity—secluded dormitories where they were regarded as little more than useful prisoners. But one day those imprisoned shells had raised a riot and, unable to be controlled, managed to kill five thaumaturges and eight royal guards before they'd been subdued.

Since then they'd been considered both useful *and* dangerous, which had led to the decision to keep them in a permanent comatose state. They were no longer a threat and their blood could more easily be harvested for the platelets that were used for the letumosis antidote.

Few people knew the infanticide laws were fake and that their lost children were still alive, if barely.

Jacin had never been in this room before, though he'd known it existed. The reality was more appalling than he'd imagined. It occurred to him that if he'd succeeded in becoming a doctor and escaped his fate as a palace guard, he may have ended up in this same lab. Only, instead of healing people, he'd be using them.

Iko had gone back to the door. "I don't hear anyone in the hallway."

"Right. We should go." Cinder brushed her fingertips over the tank of the young child, her eyes crinkled with sadness, but also—if Jacin knew anything about her—a touch of determination. He suspected she was already planning the moment when she would come back here, and see them all freed.

Sixty-Nine

THE TWO PEOPLE THEY'D HEARD IN THE HALLWAY WERE nowhere to be seen. They soon found the door labeled DISEASE RESEARCH AND DEVELOPMENT, right where the diagram had told them it would be.

The lab was filled with designated stations—each one with a stool, a metal table, a series of organized vials and test tubes and petri dishes, a microscope, and a stand of drawers. Impeccably clean. The air tasted sterile and bleached. Holograph nodes hung on the walls, all turned off.

Two lab stations showed evidence of recent work—spotlights blaring on petri dishes and tools abandoned on the desks.

"Spread out," said Cinder.

Iko took the cabinets on the far side of the room; Cinder started pawing through open shelving; Jacin started in on the nearest workstation, scanning the labeled drawers. In the top drawer he found an outdated portscreen, a label printer, a scanner, and a set of empty vials. The rest were full of syringes and petri dishes and microscope lenses, still in protective wrapping.

He moved on to the second station.

"Is this it?"

Jacin's attention snapped to Iko, who was standing in front of a set of floor-to-ceiling cabinets with their doors thrown open, revealing row upon row and stack upon stack of small vials, each filled with a clear liquid.

Jacin joined her in front of the cabinets and lifted one vial from its tray. The label read EU1 PATHOGENIC BACTERIA—"LETUMOSIS" STRAIN B—POLYVALENT VACCINE. It was identical to the lid on the next vial, and the next.

Jacin's gaze traveled over the hundreds of trays. "Let's get a rolling cart from maintenance and fill it up with as many trays as we can. We probably won't need all this for one sector, but I'd rather it be in our possession than Levana's."

"I'll get the cart," said Iko, rushing for the door.

Cinder ran a finger across a row of vials, listening to them clink in their trays. "This right here is half the reason Kai is going through with this," she whispered, then clenched her jaw. "This could have saved Peony."

"This is *going* to save Winter." When he heard the cart in the hallway, Jacin started pulling trays off the shelves, and together they loaded the cart as high as they could, stacking tray upon tray of antidote. His pulse was racing. Every time he shut his eyes he could see her in that tank, clinging to survival. How long would the immersion protect her? How long did he have?

Iko had brought a heavy drop cloth from the maintenance closet too, and they draped it over the cart, tucking it around the edges of the trays to stabilize them for their journey.

They were pushing the cart toward the door when they heard the ding of the elevator. They froze. Jacin planted his hands across the covered vials to keep them from clinking.

"You don't seem to understand the predicament we're in,"

said a sharp feminine voice. "We need those guards returned to active duty immediately. I don't care if they're fully healed or not."

"Thaumaturge," Cinder whispered. Her eyes were closed, her face tense with concentration. "And two . . . I'm going to guess, servants maybe? Or lab technicians? And one other. Really weak energy. Possibly a guard."

"No offense taken," Jacin muttered.

"These orders have come from the queen herself, and we have no time to waste," continued the thaumaturge. "Stop making excuses and do your jobs."

Not trusting his own body if there was a thaumaturge nearby, Jacin drew his gun and pushed it into Cinder's hand.

She looked confused at first, but comprehension came fast. Her grip tightened.

Footsteps approached and Jacin wondered if the thaumaturge had already sensed *them*, frozen and waiting inside this laboratory. Maybe she thought they were just researchers.

That ruse would be up as soon as she saw them. If she walked past this lab. Or if she was *coming* to this lab.

But, no, a door opened down the hallway. He didn't hear it shut again, and there were no other exits. To get to either the stairs or the elevator, they'd have to go back the way they'd come.

"Maybe we can wait it out?" suggested Iko. "They have to leave eventually."

He scowled. *Eventually* wasn't soon enough.

"I'll take control of the guard and the other two," said Cinder, knuckles whitening. "I'll kill the thaumaturge, and wait until you're all clear before I follow you."

"You'll raise a lot of alarms," said Jacin.

Her gaze turned icy. "I've already raised a lot of alarms."

"I'll go," said Iko. Her chin was up, her face resolute. "They can't control me. I'll draw them off and find a place to hide until you come back. You have to get this antidote to Her Highness."

"Iko, no, we should stay together—"

Iko cupped Cinder's face. Her fingers still weren't functioning, so the touch looked awkward, like being petted by an oversize doll. "Like I said, I'd do anything to keep you safe. Besides, if anything happens to me, I know you can fix it."

Iko winked, then marched bravely out into the hallway. Jacin shut the door after her.

They heard Iko's measured footsteps beating down the hallway, then a pause.

"Oh, hello," came her cheery voice, followed by the sound of a chair screeching across the floor. "Oops, I didn't mean to startle you."

"What are—" The thaumaturge's voice cut out, then turned vile. "A *shell*?"

"Close," said Iko. "In case you don't recognize me, I happen to be good friends with Princess Selene. I'm willing to guess you've heard of—"

"Apprehend her."

"I guess you have."

There was a rush of footsteps, a crash of furniture, two gunshots that made Cinder flinch. "Stop her!" screamed the thaumaturge, farther away now.

A door slammed shut.

"That sounded like the stairwell," said Jacin.

Cinder's jaw was tight, her muscles taut, but she drew in a shaking breath and squared her shoulders. "We'd better get out of here before they come back."

Seventy

CRESS WAS RELIEVED TO FIND THAT SHE AND THORNE WERE not the only crazily clothed guests milling around the palace gates hours before the royal coronation. The entire city had come to partake in the festivities, as if Artemisians had nothing at all to fear from a possible insurgence or the crazed claims of a cyborg girl.

The palace's main entrance was surrounded by an imposing wall topped with sharp finials. The main gate was open, revealing a lush courtyard. The walkway was lined with an assortment of sculptures depicting mythical beasts and half-dressed moon gods and goddesses.

No one gave Cress or Thorne a second glance as they strolled through the open gates, joining the crowd of gathered aristocrats who were drinking from jeweled flasks and promenading between the statues. Between Cress's frilly orange skirt and Thorne's light-up bow tie, they fit right in.

Trying to avoid eye contact with the other guests, Cress let her gaze travel up the gilded arched doors of the palace. Like the gates, they were swung wide open, inviting the queen's guests to enter, although palace guards did stand on either side.

Her heart hammered.

It felt like she and Jacin had only just escaped.

She had been inside the palace a handful of times in her youth to perform different programming tasks for Sybil. She had been so eager to please back then. *Can you track the arrivals and departures between Sectors TS-5 and GM-2? Can you create a program that will alert us to specific phrases picked up from the recorders in the holograph nodes? Can you track the ships that come and go from the ports and ensure their destinations match the itineraries in our files?*

With each success, Cress had grown more confident. *I think so. I will try. Yes, Mistress, I can do that.*

That had been back when Cress still harbored hopes of one day being welcome here, before her imprisonment aboard the satellite. She should have known better when Sybil refused to ever bring her through this breathtaking main entrance, instead smuggling her in through the underground tunnels as something shameful and secret.

At least this time she was entering the palace beside an ally and a friend. If there was anyone in the galaxy she trusted, it was Thorne.

As if hearing her thoughts, Thorne pressed a hand against her lower back.

"Pretend you belong here," he murmured against her ear, "and everyone else will believe it."

Pretend you belong here.

She let out a slow breath and tried to mimic Thorne's swagger. Pretending. She was good at pretending.

Today, she was Lunar aristocracy. She was a guest of Her

Royal Majesty. She was on the arm of the most handsome man she had ever known—a man who didn't even have to use a glamour. But most important . . .

"I am a criminal mastermind," she murmured, "and I'm here to take down this regime."

Thorne grinned at her. "That's my line."

"I know," she said. "I stole it."

Thorne chuckled and strategically placed them behind a group of Lunars, close enough that they would appear part of the group, and they glided up the white stone stairs. The doors loomed larger and larger as they stepped into the palace's shadow. The chatter of the courtyard was replaced with the echo of stone floors and the resounding laughter of people with nothing to fear.

She and Thorne were inside the palace. As far as she could tell, the guards hadn't even looked at them.

Cress released her breath, but it snagged again as she took in the extravagance.

More aristocrats loitered in droves in the grand entrance, picking at trays of food that floated in the basins of crystal-blue pools. Everywhere were gilded columns and marble statues and flower arrangements that stood twice as tall as she was. Most breathtaking of all was a statue at the center of the hall depicting the ancient moon goddess, Artemis. It towered three stories tall and showed the goddess wearing a thorny crown atop her head and holding an arched bow, the arrow pointing toward the sky.

"Good day," said a man, stepping forward to greet them. Thorne's fingers dug into Cress's back.

The man wore the uniform of a high-ranking servant, though his dreadlocked hair was dyed in variegated green—pale foam green at the roots and deep emerald at the tips. Though Cress was on guard, waiting for suspicion or disgust, the man's face was pure joviality. Perhaps servants, like the guards, were chosen for having little talent with their gift, and he wasn't able to sense that Cress was nothing but a shell.

She could hope.

"We are glad you have come to enjoy the festivities on this most celebrated day," the man said. "Please enjoy the comforts our generous queen has laid out for her guests." He gestured to his left. "In this wing you are free to enjoy our menagerie, full of exotic albino animals, or listen to an assortment of musical performances that will be taking place in our grand theater throughout the day." He lifted his right arm. "This way there is an assortment of game rooms should you care to test the providence of luck, as well as our renowned companionship rooms—*not* that the gentleman is in need of further companionship. Of course, a variety of refreshments are available throughout the palace. The coronation ceremony will begin at sunrise and we ask that all guests begin to make their way to the great hall at half before. For the safety of all our guests, there will be no continued access to the corridors once the coronation has begun. If you require anything to make your day more pleasurable, please let me or another courtier know."

With a tilt of his head, he walked off to welcome another guest.

"What do you suppose he meant by 'companionship rooms'?" Thorne asked.

When Cress shot him a glare, he stood straighter and ran a finger in between his throat and his shirt collar. "Not that I'm tempted to . . . or . . . this way, right?"

"You two seem lost," someone purred.

Thorne spun around, tucking Cress behind him as he did. A man and a woman were standing not far away, eyeing Thorne as if he were on display in a candy shop window. Both of them wore rhinestone-studded suits.

The man dropped a pair of thick-framed glasses to the end of his nose, letting his gaze swoop over Thorne from head to foot and back up. "Maybe we can help you find your way?"

Thorne was quick to draw on his signature grin. "Flattered, ladies," he purred right back.

Cress frowned, but then, realizing the man must have glamoured himself as a woman, schooled her face into indifference. She couldn't let on to anyone that she wasn't affected by mind control.

"We're on something of a covert mission right now," Thorne was saying, "but we'll keep our eye out for you at the coronation."

"Ooh, a covert mission," swooned the woman, chewing on her pinkie nail. "I will want to hear *that* story later."

Thorne winked. "I will want to tell it." Wrapping an arm around Cress's shoulders, he led her away from the couple. When they had gone far enough that he was sure they wouldn't be overheard, Thorne let out a low whistle. "Holy spades. The women in this place."

Cress bristled. "You mean, the *glamours* in this place. One of them was a man."

Stumbling, Thorne looked down at her. "You don't say. Which one?"

"Um . . . the one wearing glasses?"

He glanced back over his shoulder, scanning the crowd for the couple. "Well played, Lunars," he murmured, duly impressed. He faced forward again. "Jacin said to take the third hallway, right?" He tugged her toward a curving hall, where floor-to-ceiling windows offered a breathtaking view of the front gardens.

"Try to keep in mind that they can make themselves look however they want to," said Cress. "No one in this palace is as beautiful as you think they are. It's all just mind control."

Thorne grinned and squeezed her closer against his side. "I'm fairly certain there's at least one exception to that rule."

Cress rolled her eyes. "Yeah. Thaumaturges."

He laughed and dropped his arm, though she wasn't sure what was funny.

They passed by a group of young men, and Cress watched, baffled, as they stumbled across the hallway. One of them shoved open a glass door and headed toward the lakeshore and expansive gardens. He nearly tumbled off the staircase that led down to the sprawling lawn.

Shaking her head, Cress faced forward again—and realized she was alone.

Every muscle tensed as she swiveled around, relieved to spot Thorne a few paces away. Not relieved to see he'd been accosted by another girl who was quite pretty even to Cress's untrickable eyes. She was smiling at Thorne through her long lashes in a way that was both sultry and vicious.

For his part, Thorne just looked surprised.

"I thought I sensed an Earthen boy," said the girl. Reaching up, she traced the glowing lights on Thorne's bow tie, then trailed her finger down his chest. "And a well-dressed one at that. What a lucky find."

Pulse thumping, Cress surveyed the corridor. The crowd was beginning to trickle toward the great hall, but plenty of guests were still fluttering around one another in no apparent hurry. No one was paying them any attention. This woman, too, seemed to have eyes only for Thorne. Cress racked her brain for some way to get him away from her without raising suspicion or drawing attention to herself.

Then the woman wrapped her arms around Thorne's neck and every thought flew out of Cress's head. Dumbfounded, Thorne offered no resistance as she pulled him into a kiss.

Seventy-One

CRESS'S SPINE STIFFENED INDIGNANTLY, AT THE SAME TIME A group of Lunar women chortled not far away. "Good eye, Luisa," one of them called, followed by another: "If you spot any more pretty Earthens like that one, send them my way!"

Neither Thorne nor Luisa seemed to hear them. In fact, as Cress watched, aghast, Thorne slid his arms around Luisa's body and drew her closer.

Cress clenched her fists, her shoulders, her entire body. She was appalled. Then annoyed. Then logic began to creep in and she realized that, while they were probably just toying with Thorne, they would not be so kind to her if they figured out she was immune to their glamours and manipulation.

Shaking with contempt, Cress backed into an alcove behind a pillar. There she waited, arms crossed and red sparks in her vision, as Thorne kissed the girl.

And kissed her.

And *kissed* her.

Cress's fingernails had left painful crescent moon imprints in her skin by the time they finally pulled apart.

Luisa fluttered her lashes, breathless. "You've been wanting that awhile, haven't you?"

Cress rolled her eyes skyward.

And Thorne said . . .

Thorne said . . .

"I think I'm in love with you."

A nail pierced Cress's heart, and she gasped, actually *gasped* from the pain of it. Her jaw fell, but she quickly lifted it again. The puncture wound in her chest quickly filled with resentment.

If she had to watch him swoon over anyone else she was going to scream. How was it possible that *she* was the only girl in the galaxy he didn't try to kiss and woo and flirt with?

Well, he had kissed her that one time on the rooftop, but it had been as a favor to her and hardly counted.

She withdrew farther into the alcove, seething, but also hurt. That was it, then. He never would desire her, not like these other girls who caught his eye. Cress had to accept the fact that their kiss—the most passionate, romantic moment of her life—had been nothing more than a gesture made out of pity.

"Oh, aren't you just *darling*?" said the woman. "And not a bad kisser, either. Maybe we can enjoy more of each other's company later?" Without waiting for a response, she patted Thorne on the chest and winked, before swaying away down the hall.

The adoring peanut gallery, too, meandered off, leaving Thorne in the middle of the corridor, stunned. His cheeks were flushed, his eyes dark with what Cress assumed was lust, and his hair was messed where Luisa had clawed her hands into it.

Luisa. Who he *loved.*

Cress squeezed her arms tight over her chest.

After a long, bewildered minute, Thorne shook off the

lingering effects of the manipulation and looked around, turning in a full circle. His hand smoothed down his unkempt hair.

"Cress?" he asked, not too loudly at first, but then, with growing worry, "Cress!"

"I'm here."

He spun toward her and his body sagged with relief. "Spades. I'm sorry. I don't know what happened. That was—"

"I don't want to know." Pushing herself away from the wall, Cress started down the hallway.

Thorne chased after her. "Whoa, hey, hold on. Are you mad?"

"Why would I be mad?" She swung her hands in a wild gesture. "You have the right to flirt with and kiss and proclaim your love for whoever you want to. Which is good, because you *do*. All the time."

Thorne kept pace easily beside her, which irritated her even more given that she was already winded from walking so fast.

"So . . . ," Thorne said, his tone teasing. "You're jealous?"

Cress bristled. "You do realize that all she wanted was to get a laugh at your expense, right?"

He chuckled, annoyingly good-natured when Cress was so furious. "Yeah, I get that *now*. Cress, wait." Thorne grabbed her elbow and forced her to stop. "I know they can't do it to you, but the rest of us can't *choose* not to be controlled by them. She manipulated me. It wasn't my fault."

"And I suppose you're going to say that you didn't enjoy it?"

He opened his mouth, but hesitated. "Er. Well . . ."

Cress ripped her arm away from him. "I know it wasn't your fault. But that doesn't excuse *everyone else*. I mean, take Iko!"

"What about Iko?"

She dropped her voice to mimic Thorne. "'*I really know how to pick them, don't I?*'"

He chuckled, his eyes glinting at her mockery. "It's the truth, isn't it? Her new body is gorgeous."

Cress fixed one moment's worth of intensive glaring on him.

"That was clearly not the right thing to say. Sorry. But I'd just gotten my eyesight back."

"Yeah, and all you wanted to look at was *her.*"

Thorne blinked, and sudden comprehension dawned in his eyes, but Cress stormed away before he could reply. "Never mind. Let's just—"

"Pardon me."

A palace guard blocked their path, one arm held out, stopping Cress in her tracks. She gasped and backed into Thorne, who latched on to her elbow. Her mouth ran dry. She'd been so incensed she hadn't noticed the two guards stationed in the hall.

"We are asking that all guests begin to make their way to the great hall so the coronation ceremony can begin without delay." The guard nodded in the direction they'd come. "Please proceed this way."

Cress's heart was hammering, but Thorne, calm as ever, pulled her away with a casual smile. "Of course, thank you. We must have gotten turned around."

As soon as they turned a corner, Cress yanked her arm out of Thorne's hold. He let his hand fall without argument. They were in a hallway that was quieter than the main corridor, though there were still a handful of guests drifting about.

"Stop here," Thorne said, and she did, letting him back her against a wall. He towered too close to her, and to anyone it would look like they were in some intimate conversation, which only served to make Cress's anger flare again. She clenched her fists and stared resolutely at his shoulder.

Thorne sighed.

"Cress. I know you're upset, but could you pretend not to be for a second?"

She shut her eyes and took a deep breath. She was not angry. She was not hurt. She was not heartbroken.

When she opened her eyes again, she morphed her expression into what she hoped looked like cheerful flirtation.

Thorne raised an eyebrow. "That's uncanny."

Her voice still had a sting to it, though, when she said, "I'm a girl too, you know. I may not be as pretty as Iko, or brave like Cinder or bold like Scarlet—"

"Wait, Cress—"

"And I don't even want to know what dumb thing you said when you met Princess Winter for the first time."

Thorne clamped his mouth shut, confirming her suspicion that he had said something dumb indeed.

"But I'm not invisible! And yet you flirt with every *single* one of them. You'll flirt with anyone who so much as *looks* at you."

"You've made your point." The teasing glint in his eye was gone, and Cress's contrived smile had left her too. Though he had one hand near her hip, he was no longer touching her.

"This is what you were trying to tell me, wasn't it?" Her voice wavered. "In the desert. When you were going on and on about how I'm so *sweet* and how you didn't want to hurt me and . . . You were trying to warn me, but I was too much of a . . . a naïve, hopeless romantic to even listen to you."

His eyes softened. "I didn't want to hurt you."

She crossed her arms defensively over her chest. Tears were blurring her vision. "I know. It's my own fault I've been this stupid."

Thorne flinched, but the movement was coupled with a glance around, which prompted Cress to do the same, swiping at her eyes before the tears could gather. The hallway had almost cleared, and the few remaining guests weren't looking their way.

Reaching around Cress, Thorne pulled open a door that she hadn't even noticed and within half a blink ushered her inside. She stumbled from the quickness of it, catching herself on a plant stand beside the door. They were surrounded by flowers and greenery of every imaginable color, their perfume thick and steaming in her throat. The ceiling rose several stories high and was made of the same leaded glass as the windows in the main corridor. Sofas and reading chairs were set in small groupings throughout the room and straight ahead they faced a series of desks overlooking the lake beyond.

"Good," said Thorne. "I thought I remembered seeing something about an atrium. We'll wait here until the halls clear. I'm hoping we can cross into one of the servant halls and avoid any more run-ins with guards for a while."

Cress filled her lungs to near bursting and let it all out, but the breath did nothing to refresh her. She stepped into the room, putting much-needed space between her and Thorne.

She was an idiot. He had never once given her any indication that a real relationship could be in their future. He'd given her every chance to get used to this fact. But despite all his attempts to dissuade her from falling in love with him, her heart was still shattered.

What was worse, a kiss from a Lunar, of all things, had shattered it—and Thorne really couldn't be blamed for that.

"Cress . . . listen . . ."

His fingers brushed her wrist, but she jerked away. "Don't. I'm sorry. That wasn't fair of me. I shouldn't have said anything."

She wiped her nose with the flimsy wing material of her ridiculous costume.

Thorne sighed and from the corner of her eye she caught him running a hand through his hair. She could feel his gaze burning into the back of her neck, so she turned away and pretended to inspect an enormous purple blossom.

He knew now, of course. She had given all her feelings away—had probably given them away a long time ago, but he'd been too concerned with *hurting* her to let on that he knew.

She could tell he wanted to talk more. She could feel unspoken words hovering in the air between them, suffocating her. He would apologize. He would tell her how much he cared for her—as a friend. As a member of his crew.

She didn't want to hear it. Not now. Not *ever*, but especially not now, when there were more pressing issues to deal with.

"How long are we waiting here?" she asked, and though her voice was tinted with emotion, it had stopped shaking.

She heard a rustle and a quiet click of a portscreen. "A few more minutes, just to make sure they've rounded up the slower guests."

She nodded.

A second later, she heard another sigh. "Cress?"

She shook her head. The little antenna balls bounced in the corner of her eyes—she'd forgotten she was wearing them. She dared to face him, hoping her face didn't convey the misery underneath. "I'm all right. I just don't want to talk about it."

Thorne had situated himself against the closed door, his hands stuck in his pockets. His expression was tumultuous. Shame, maybe, mixed with doubt and nerves, and something else that was dark and heady and made her toes tingle.

He considered her for a long moment. "All right," he said, finally. "I don't want to talk about it, either."

She started to nod, but was surprised when Thorne pushed

away from the door. Cress blinked and stumbled back, startled by the sudden movement. Three, four steps. The backs of her thighs hit one of the desks.

"What—?"

In one movement, Thorne lifted her onto the desk and pressed her back against an enormous potted fern and—*oh.*

Cress had built a thousand fantasies around their rooftop kiss, but *this* kiss was something new.

Where before, the kiss had been gentle and protective, now there was something passionate. Determined. Cress's body dissolved into nothing but sensation. His hands burned her waist through the skirt's thin fabric. Her knees pressed against his hips, and he pulled her closer, closer, like he couldn't get her close enough. A whimper escaped her mouth, only to be swallowed by his. She heard a moan, but it could have come from either of them.

And where, on the rooftop, the kiss had been cut too short by the battle raging on around them, this kiss went on, and on, and on . . .

Finally, when Cress was starting to feel faint, the kiss was broken with a needy inhale. Cress was trembling and she hoped he wasn't about to set her back on her feet and inform her it was time to get on with their work, because she doubted she could walk for two steps, much less to the other side of the palace.

Thorne didn't pull away. Rather, he slipped his arms around her back, and here was the gentle protectiveness she remembered. His breathing was as erratic as hers.

"*Cress.*" He said her name like a vow.

Cress shivered. Licking her tender lips, she forced her hands to un-bury themselves from his hair and moved them instead to his chest.

Then she forced herself to push him away.

Not enough to break out of his embrace, but enough that she could breathe and think and brace for the lifetime of regret she was about to bring on herself.

"This . . ." Her voice caught. She tried again. "This isn't what I wanted."

It took Thorne a moment, but then his dazed look hardened and he pushed himself back even farther.

"I mean, it *is*," she amended. "Obviously, it is."

His relief was obvious, and warmed every inch of her body. The quick, teasing grin spoke volumes. Of course this was what she wanted. Of *course* it was.

"But . . . not to be just another girl," she said. "I never wanted to be just another one of your girls."

The smile vanished again. "Cress . . ." He seemed torn, but also hopeful and unguarded. He took a deep breath. "She looked like you."

She hadn't realized she was watching his mouth until her eyes snapped up to meet his. "What?"

"The girl in the hallway, the one that kissed me. She looked like you."

The kiss with the Lunar girl felt like eons ago. The memory caused a surge of envy, but Cress did her best to stomp it back down.

"That's ridiculous. She was brunette, and tall, and—"

"Not to me." Thorne tucked a strand of Cress's hair behind an ear. "She must have seen us walking together. Maybe she saw how I looked at you or something, I don't know, but she knew . . . she made her glamour look like you."

Lips parting, Cress envisioned herself hidden in that alcove again. Watching Thorne's expression of bewilderment. Of desire. The way he'd kissed her, and held her . . .

"I thought I was kissing you," he confirmed, brushing her lips with his again. And again. Cress's fingers found his lapels and she pulled him closer.

It didn't last long, though, as another memory resurfaced.

She yanked away. "But . . . you told her you loved her."

His expression froze, desire giving way to alarm. They hovered in that moment for an eternity.

Finally, Thorne gulped. "Right. That." He shrugged. "I mean, I was . . . we were—"

Before he could finish, the door swung open behind him.

Seventy-Two

THEY BOTH FROZE.

Jaw tightening, Thorne whispered, "To be continued?"

She nodded, having some difficulty trying to remember where they were.

Thorne spun back to the door, his body shielding Cress from whoever had entered. Peering around his elbow, she caught sight of a palace guard outlined in the hallway's light.

The guard was scowling as he raised a device to his mouth. "It's just a couple of guests," he said, his voice gruff. He nudged his chin toward Thorne and Cress. "I need to ask you to move along. All corridors and public spaces need to be cleared prior to the start of the ceremony."

Clearing his throat, Thorne tugged down his jacket and adjusted his bow tie. "So sorry. I guess we just . . . got carried away."

Cress plucked a fern leaf off Thorne's sleeve. Heat singed her cheeks, but it was only part from mortification, and mostly from the lingering feel of his arms, his kisses, the hazy reality of the past few minutes.

"We'll just be moving along, then." Thorne grabbed the

bug-antenna hat that had ended up on the floor and handed it to Cress, then helped her back down to the floor.

Her shaking hands fumbled to strap the antennae back onto her head.

"Thanks for letting us borrow the place," Thorne said to the guard, winking, as they scooted into the hallway. Only once the guard was behind them did he show the slightest crack in his composure, releasing a slow breath. "Try to act natural."

The words echoed in Cress's head for a long moment before she could make sense of them. Act natural? Act *natural*? When her legs were made of noodles and her heart was about to pound right out of her chest and he'd said that he *loved* her, at least, in a sense. What did it even mean to act natural in the first place? When had she ever in her life known how to act natural?

So she started to laugh. A stifled snort, first. Then a rush of giggles crawling up her throat, until she was half falling over herself in an effort to walk straight. The laughter nearly choked her.

Thorne kept an arm locked around her waist. "Not quite what I had in mind," he muttered, "but sort of charming all the same."

"I'm sorry." She gasped out the words, coughed a little, and tried to mold her face into *natural*, but another giggle fit was rumbling her stomach, spasming in her chest. She buckled over again.

"Um. Cress. You're adorable, but I need you to focus for a second. We're lucky that guard didn't recognize either of us, but if he—"

"Hey! Stop!"

Thorne cursed.

Cress's laughter was doused with panic.

"Run!"

She did, gripping Thorne's hand. Around one corner, then

another. He led them to an inconspicuous alcove with a small door and shoved her through—into the servants' halls.

"Left!" he ordered, yanking the door shut and grabbing a service tray that had been left in the corridor. He wedged it into place while Cress ran, past pallets of supplies and maintenance equipment, storage cabinets and broken sculptures. Thorne caught up to her easily. He had pulled the handgun from inside his jacket. "Still have that chip?"

She pressed a hand against her bodice, detecting the small chip with Cinder's video tucked against her skin. She nodded, running too hard to speak.

"Good."

Without warning, Thorne slammed into Cress, pushing them both behind an enormous wheel of electrical cording. She hit the wall hard, panting.

"Two corridors back there was an elevator," he said. "Find a place to hide, then get to the security center. I'll draw them off and circle back around to find you."

Cress started to shake her head. "No. You can't leave me, not again. I can't do this without you."

"Sure you can. It won't be as much fun, but you'll figure it out."

Footsteps thundered in the distance. She squeaked.

"I'll find you," Thorne whispered. He pressed a hasty kiss against her mouth, wrapping her hand around something heavy and warm. "Be heroic."

He took off running again, just as she heard the footsteps catching up.

"There!" someone yelled.

Thorne disappeared around a corner.

Cress stared at the gun he'd given her. This small contraption, so solid in her grip, terrified her more than the guards. She ached to put it down on the floor and step away.

Instead, she flattened herself against the electrical cording and pried her finger from the trigger, where it had landed instinctively. *Just like a computer,* she told herself. *Computers only do what you tell them to do. The gun will only fire if you pull the trigger.*

It wasn't particularly comforting.

Two guards ran past, not even glancing in her direction.

She considered staying where she was, out in the open as it may be. She was shaking from head to toe and every fiber of her body told her that to move would be to get caught.

But logic told her that her body was lying. They would come back. They would send reinforcements. She would be seen.

Distant gunshots made her jump, spurring her into action. The shots were followed by grunts and the sounds of a struggle.

Cress pushed herself out of the corner and turned back in the direction she and Thorne had come from. Two corridors back, he'd said. An elevator.

She went quietly this time, pressing her free hand into the stitch in her side. She passed one corridor and heard more footsteps, but couldn't tell which direction they were coming from. She froze, scanned her surroundings, and yanked open one of the storage cabinets.

Rolls of decorative fabric were stood on end, many of them taller than she was, and all of them lush and glistening in metallics and jewel tones.

Cress climbed inside, squeezing her body into the space created from the fabric bolts that had toppled to one side. Pulling the door shut, she set the gun on the cabinet's floor. She was very careful to aim it away from her.

The footsteps grew louder and she was sure she'd been seen, but no one yelled.

Until—

"*Stop!*"

Another gunshot, this one followed by an instantaneous grunt and a body crashing onto the floor. It sounded close. Cress squeezed her eyes shut, pressing her chin onto her knees. *Not Thorne. Please not Thorne.*

A heavy sigh was followed by a soothing male voice. "All this over a pesky Earthen? You guards are pathetic."

Cress pressed her hands against her mouth to keep any sounds from escaping. She stared into the darkness, attempting to shallow her breathing, though she worried she might pass out if she didn't get more air soon.

Someone groaned. Not far away from where she was hiding.

"He is definitely one of the cyborg's allies. The question is, what are you doing in the palace?"

A beat, then Thorne's voice. "Just kissing my girl," he said, wheezing a little. Cress scrunched up her whole face and buried it against her knees, choking back a sob. "I didn't realize that was a . . . a capital offense around here."

The man sounded unamused. "Where is the girl you were with?"

"I think you scared her off."

Another sigh. "We don't have time for this. Put him in a holding cell—we'll deal with him after the coronation. I'm sure he'll make a delightful Earthen pet for one of the families. And keep looking for that girl—alert me the moment you find her. Increase security around the great hall. They're plotting something, and Her Majesty will kill us all if the ceremony is interrupted."

There was a thud and another grunt. Cress flinched, her head filling with all the things they could have done to Thorne to cause that grunt—all the things they could still do to him.

She bit her lip until she tasted blood, the pain alone keeping her from crying as she listened to them drag him away.

Seventy-Three

"*JACIN.*" CINDER'S TONE WAS FULL OF WARNING. "IKO DID NOT sacrifice herself so you could crash us into a crater and kill us both."

"Calm down. I know what I'm doing," he responded, pretending to be calm while his heart was a hammer pounding against his chest.

"I thought you said you've never driven one of these before."

"I haven't." He banked hard and the terrain-speeder careened to the left, fast and smooth.

Cinder gasped and reached for a bar overhead. A hiss of pain followed—probably her shoulder wound acting up again—but she didn't say anything and Jacin didn't slow down.

The vehicle was by far the slickest Jacin had ever piloted. Little more than a risky toy to some rich Artemisian, it hovered close to the rocky, uneven surface of Luna, soaring so fast the white ground blurred beneath them. The roof was see-through, making it feel as if they were out in the airless terrain rather than in a protective vehicle.

Though *protective* was a subjective word. Jacin had the feeling that if he clipped any rocks, this thing would crumple around them like an aluminum can.

Hell, maybe it *was* aluminum.

They launched off a cliff and the speeder engaged antigravity mode, keeping them on a smooth trajectory as they sailed over the crater below, before descending toward the other side and continuing on as if nothing had happened. Jacin's stomach flipped—a product of both the high speed and not quite having adjusted to the weightlessness outside of the gravity-controlled domes.

"Just an observation," Cinder said through her teeth, "but we have a *lot* of fragile and important vials in the back of this thing. Maybe we don't want to crash?"

"We're fine." His attention dropped to the holographic map above the controls. Any other day this would have been a daring game, but now they were on a mission. Every spare corner of the speeder was full of antidote vials and every moment that passed meant people were dying.

And one of them was Winter.

A dome appeared on the horizon. Even from here he could see the lines of tree trunks on one side and the clear-cut stumps on the other.

Jacin maneuvered the speeder around a series of jagged rock formations. Cinder adjusted the holograph, repositioning the map so Jacin could see the best route to their destination. Most of the domes were clumped together in groups—both because they had been easier to build that way back when Luna was being colonized, but also so they could share ports that connected them to the outside terrain of Luna and allow for supply deliveries independent of the underground shuttle system.

The barrenness of the landscape made distances deceptive. It felt like hours had gone by since the lumber sector had first come into view, and every moment that ticked by drowned Jacin in anxiety. He kept seeing those soldiers carrying the suspended-animation tank between them like pallbearers. He tried to tell himself that he wasn't too late. Surely they'd put Winter into the tank because they believed there was a chance to save her. Surely the tank would slow down the disease enough to keep her safe until he got there. It *had* to.

"Whoa, whoa, *whoa—wall!*" Cinder screamed, bracing for impact.

Jacin swerved at the last moment, tilting the speeder on its side as he careened along the dome's exterior curve. The holograph magnified their destination—the dock's entry flickering in the corner of Jacin's vision. He considered his timing. *Straighten the ship, reduce the propulsion, toggle the hoverblades.* He jolted forward against the harness as the speeder slowed.

Slowed.

Slowed.

And dropped. A rock plummeting from a cliff.

Cinder yelped.

The dome and the rocky landscape disappeared as dark cave walls surrounded them. Jacin resumed auto-power and their descent turned from death-defying to gradual, bringing them to a steady, controlled hover. A lit landing strip and holding chamber opened before them and Jacin coaxed the speeder inside.

"I'm never getting into a vehicle with you again," Cinder said, panting.

Jacin ignored her, his nerves still electrified, and not from the fall. Behind them, the holding door slammed shut, and another door opened, an enormous iron beast. Jacin coaxed the speeder forward, relieved when there was no sign of opposition to stop them.

The holographic map changed from the exterior layout of Luna to a map of this port and the surrounding sectors. Jacin gripped the flight controls, mentally tracing their route up to the clinic where Winter was waiting.

This was where they were supposed to get out and go the rest of the way on foot, hauling as many trays of antidote as they could up into the sectors.

Tearing his attention from the coordinates, he eyed the emergency evacuation stairwell that led to the surface. A sign indicated the nearest domes. LW-12 was the third on the list, complete with a helpful arrow indicating which stairwell would take them there.

Jacin calculated. His thumb caressed the power switch.

"Jacin," said Cinder, following his gaze. "I don't think we can—"

Her warning dissolved into a scream.

She was wrong. The terrain-speeder *did* fit up the stairwell, and he only nicked the walls a few times as they soared upward and emerged beneath the biodome of LW-12. By the time he leveled out, Cinder had slumped into the copilot seat with her hand over her eyes and her opposite knuckles tight around the bar.

"We're here," he said, adjusting the holograph again. It guided them beneath the canopy of trees toward the outer edge of the dome where a single street of residences and supply shops encircled the forest.

He noticed the thinning of the trees first, then the staggered shapes of people.

A lot of people.

An entire crowd of people was gathered at the forest's edge.

They were gawking at the neon-yellow terrain-speeder as it emerged from their peaceful woods. The crowd retreated, making space, or maybe afraid of being hit. Jacin lowered the speeder to the ground and cut the power.

His finger reached for the release button.

"Wait." Cinder reached toward her feet and drew two vials from a rack that was secured there. "We're no longer immune, either," she said, handing one to him.

They each tossed back the antidote without ceremony. Jacin was opening the vehicle before he could swallow. There was a whoosh of air as the bubbled ceiling of the terrain-speeder split down the middle and peeled open like a cracked nutshell.

Unsnapping his harness, Jacin hauled himself over the top of the vehicle, landing on a squishy patch of moss. Cinder climbed out not quite as gracefully on the other side.

Jacin hadn't given much thought to this moment. No doubt there were people in this sector who needed the antidote, but to tell them they had entire pallets of it could lead to a brawl.

Snatching a single vial from a tray that was padded against the back floorboards, Jacin tucked it into his palm and strode toward the crowd.

He'd gone four steps when, suddenly, he was not facing a bedraggled assortment of lumberjacks, but a wall of spears and slingshots and a whole lot of sticks.

He froze.

Either he'd been far too distracted to notice they were all armed, or they'd been practicing for a moment like this. A man stepped out of the crowd, gripping a wooden club. "Who are—?"

Recognition was already pooling in their eyes, though, as Cinder wobbled up to Jacin's side. She held up both hands, showing the metal plating.

"I have no way of proving to you that I'm not using a glamour," she started, "but I *am* Princess Selene, and we're not here to hurt you. Jacin here is a friend of Princess Winter's. He's the one who helped her escape the palace when Levana tried to have her killed." She paused. "The first time."

"No friend of ours has Artemisian toys like that," said the man, pointing his club at the speeder.

Jacin snarled. "She didn't say I was a friend of *yours*. Where's the princess?"

"Jacin, don't try to help." Cinder cast him an annoyed look. "We know Princess Winter is ill, along with many of your friends and family—"

"What's going on out here?"

A familiar face emerged from the crowd, her cheeks dirty and her red curls limp with grease. There were dark circles beneath her eyes and an unhealthy pallor to her skin.

Scarlet froze. "Cinder!" But as soon as she started to smile, suspicion crept in and she held up a finger. "Where did you and I first meet?"

Cinder hesitated, but only for a moment. "In Paris, outside the opera house. I tranquilized Wolf because I thought he was attacking you."

Scarlet's grin was back before Cinder had finished speaking. She pulled her into a hug, then cursed and stepped back. Half a dozen wolf soldiers had followed in her wake and were crowding around her like overeager security guards. They looked tame, for the moment, but also like they could tear apart every person in this crowd in all of ten seconds if they chose to.

"Sorry—you shouldn't be here. Levana—" Scarlet started to cough into her elbow, nearly doubling over with the cough's unexpected force. When she caught her breath, there were dark spots of blood on her sleeve. "It's not safe here," she finished, as if it wasn't obvious.

"Is Winter alive?" Jacin said.

Scarlet crossed her arms, but not in a defiant way. More that she wanted to hide the evidence of the disease. "She's alive," said Scarlet, "but sick. A lot of us are sick. Levana poisoned her with letumosis and it spread fast. We have Winter in a suspended—"

"We know," said Cinder. "We brought the antidote."

Jacin held up the vial he'd grabbed from the speeder.

Scarlet's eyes widened, and those clustered around them stirred. Many weapons had lowered once Scarlet and Cinder had embraced, but not all.

Jacin jerked a thumb over his shoulder. "Get some of your muscle to help empty the speeder."

"And take one for yourself," added Cinder. "There should be enough for every person who's showing symptoms, and we'll make sure to ration extras for anyone who might still become ill."

Squeezing the vial, Jacin neared Scarlet and lowered his voice. "Where is she?"

Scarlet turned to the soldiers surrounding her. "Let him see the princess. He won't hurt her. Strom, let's organize a team to distribute the antidote."

Jacin had stopped listening. As the crowd parted he could see the daylight glinting off the glass of the suspended-animation tank, and he was already forcing his way toward it.

Here, in the dirt pathway that separated the nondescript medical clinic from the shadowed forest, they had created a shrine around her. Crisscrossed twigs and branches formed a lattice around the metal base of the tank, hiding the chamber that contained all the life-giving fluids and chemicals that were being recycled in and out of her system. Daisies and buttercups were strewn over the glass top, though many had slid off and now littered the ground around her.

Jacin paused to take in the sight, thinking maybe Levana wasn't paranoid after all. Maybe the people really did love Winter enough that she was a threat to her stepmother's crown, despite not having royal blood.

The vial grew warm in his palm. All the voices muffled in his ears, replaced with the tinny ring of the tank's machinery, the constant hum of the life support, a beep from the screen that displayed her vitals.

Jacin swiped his arm across the top, scattering the flowers. Beneath the glass, Winter looked like she was sleeping, except the preservation liquid gave her skin a bluish tinge, making her appear sickly and drawing attention to the scars on her face.

Then there was the rash. Raised rings of darkened flesh scattered across her hands and up her arms and neck. A few had appeared on her chin and around her ears. Jacin focused again on her hands, and though it was difficult to tell with her brown skin and the tinted liquid, he could see a shadow around her fingernails. The last fatal mark of the blue fever.

Despite everything, she still looked like perfection, at least to him. Her curly hair was buoyant in the tank's gel and her full lips were turned upward. It was like she was going to open her eyes and smile at him, any minute now. That teasing, taunting, irresistible smile.

"The tank has slowed down her biological systems, including the progression of the disease."

Jacin started. An elderly man stood on the other side of the tank with a mask over his mouth and nose. At first Jacin assumed the mask was to keep him from catching the disease, but then he saw the bruises creeping out from beneath the man's sleeves and realized it was to keep himself from contributing to its spread.

"But it hasn't stopped the disease entirely," the man added.

"Are you a doctor?"

He nodded. "If we open the tank, and your antidote doesn't work, she will die, probably within the hour."

"How long will she live if we leave her in there?"

The doctor's eyes fell down to the princess's face, then darted to the screen embedded at the foot of the tank. "A week, optimistically."

"Pessimistically?"

"A day or two."

Clenching his teeth, Jacin held up the vial. "This is the antidote from Her Majesty's own labs. It will work."

The man's eyes crinkled and he glanced past Jacin. Turning, Jacin saw that Cinder and Scarlet had followed him, though they were standing a respectful distance back.

"Winter would trust him with her life," said Scarlet. "I say we open it."

The doctor hesitated a moment longer before moving to the foot of the tank and tapping some commands into the screen.

Jacin tensed.

It took a moment to notice any difference, but then he saw a bubble of air form against the glass encasement as the liquid drained out through the bottom, complete with the quiet sound of it being sucked through some invisible tubing. Winter's profile emerged above the blue-tinted liquid. The difference was striking, to see the lingering redness in her lips and the occasional flutter beneath her eyelids.

She was not a corpse.

She was not dead.

He was going to save her.

Once the liquid had drained, the doctor tapped at the screen again and the lid opened, sliding off the base on skinny rails, leaving a shallow bed where Winter lay.

Her hair, damp from the gel, had settled in limp clumps around her face, and her skin glistened where the light struck her. Jacin reached for her hands, unlacing her fingers so he could slip his own palm beneath hers. Her skin was slick and the blue tinge around her fingernails was obvious now.

The doctor started to remove the needles and tubes from her body, the life forces that had kept her blood oxygenated without breath, that had kept her brain and heart functioning while she slept in peaceful stasis. Jacin's gaze followed his deft, wrinkled hands, ready to knock the old man away if he thought he was doing something wrong. But his hands were steady and practiced.

Slowly, Winter's body began to recognize that it was no longer being assisted. Her chest started to rise and fall. Her cold fingers twitched. Jacin set the vial beside her body and lowered himself to his knees amid the scattered branches and flowers. He placed two fingers against her wrist. The pulse was there, growing stronger.

His gaze returned to her face, waiting for the moment when her eyelids would open. When she would be awake and alive and, once again, completely unattainable.

He flinched. It was all too surreal, and he'd almost forgotten. Winter, crowned with flowers and resting upon a bower of tree branches. She was still a princess, and he was still nothing.

The reminder haunted him as he waited. Memorizing her sleeping face, the feel of her hand in his, the fantasy of what it would be like to witness her still, sleeping form each day.

A footstep padded behind him and he remembered that they had an audience. The crowd was pushing in, not so close as to be suffocating, but closer than he would have liked, given that he'd forgotten they were there at all.

And here he'd been thinking of bedrooms and daybreaks.

Scrambling to his feet, Jacin waved his hand at the crowd. "Don't you have an uprising to plan or something?"

"We just want to know she's all right," said Scarlet. She was holding an empty vial in one hand.

"She's waking up," said the doctor.

Jacin swiveled back around in time to see her eyelashes twitch.

The doctor had one hand on Winter's shoulder, the other holding a portscreen over her body to monitor her systems. "Organs are reacting normally to the reanimation process. Her throat and lungs will be sore for a while, but I suggest we go ahead and give her the antidote now."

Winter's eyes opened, her pupils dilated. Jacin gripped the edge of the tank. "Princess?"

She blinked rapidly a few times, as if trying to shake the remnants of oil from her lashes. She focused on Jacin.

Though he tried to stifle it, Jacin grinned, overwhelmed with relief. There had been so many moments when he'd been sure he would never see her again.

"Hey, Trouble," he whispered.

Her lips stretched into a tired smile. Her hand bumped into the walls of the tank as if she wanted to reach for him, and Jacin scooped it up and squeezed. With his other hand, he lifted the vial of antidote. His thumb unscrewed the top.

"I need you to drink this."

Seventy-Four

WINTER VAGUELY RECALLED JACIN HELPING HER SIT UP AND tipping a vial against her mouth and a tasteless liquid spilling in. It was difficult to swallow, but she squeezed Jacin's hand and forced her throat muscles to cooperate. The world smelled like chemicals and her skin felt oily and she was sitting on a bed of some sort of slimy gel.

Where was she? She remembered the regolith caves and the wolf soldiers, the thaumaturges and Scarlet. She remembered the people and the trees. She remembered a crooked old woman and a box of candies.

"Princess? How do you feel?"

She slumped against Jacin's arm. "Hungry."

"Right. We'll get you some food." It was strange to see him showing so much concern. Usually his emotions were written in a code she couldn't break. But now he looked past her and asked, "What does it say?"

Following the look, Winter saw an old man wearing a face mask and holding a portscreen. "Her vitals are returning to normal, but it's too early to tell if this is a result of being awoken from stasis or because of the antidote."

It occurred to her, like a muddled puzzle fitting together, that they were outside and surrounded by people. Winter listed her head and a curl of damp hair slithered across her shoulder. There was vivacious Scarlet and there were the wolf soldiers that had failed to eat them and there were many, many strangers, all curious and worried and hopeful.

And there was her cousin, her metal hand gleaming.

"Hello, friends," she whispered, to no one in particular.

It was Scarlet who smiled first. "Welcome back, crazy."

"How long before we know for sure if it worked?" asked Jacin.

The doctor glided the portscreen back and forth above Winter's arm. She followed the device, noting how it seemed to be scanning the rash of bumps and blisters on her skin. "It shouldn't be long now."

Running her tongue around her parched mouth, Winter lifted her hand toward the false daylight. False now—but not for long. Sun rays could be seen brightening the horizon. Sunrise was upon them.

The rash was thick on her skin, rings of raised flesh piled on top of one another, some ready to burst. It was horrifying and grotesque.

If her lungs had been functioning, she might have laughed.

For the first time in her life, no one could say she was beautiful.

Her attention caught on a particularly large spot, as wide as her thumb was long, situated between her wrist and the base of her palm. It was wiggling. As she stared, it grew little legs and crawled up her arm, dodging its brethren like an obstacle course, skittering over the tender skin of her inner elbow. A fat spider scurrying up her flesh.

"*Winter.*"

She jumped. Scarlet had moved closer and was standing at the foot of the tank, arms akimbo. She, too, had dark spots, and though there were not as many of them as Winter had, they stood out more on her pale skin.

"The doctor asked you a question."

"Don't snap at her," said Jacin.

"Don't coddle her," snapped Scarlet.

Winter glanced down to check that the rogue spot had returned to her wrist before looking up at the masked doctor.

"I apologize, Your Highness. May I take a sample of your blood?"

She nodded, and watched with interest as he inserted a needle into her arm and drew out a sample. Her manufacturing plant had been busy while she slept.

He put the sample into a specialized plug on the side of the portscreen. "Oh, and drink this," he said, as an afterthought, gesturing to a paper cup with an orange liquid in it. "It should help with your throat."

Jacin tried to hold the cup for her, but she took it from him. "I'm getting stronger," she whispered.

He did not look comforted.

"Yes. Excellent," said the doctor. "The pathogens appear to be neutralized. Your immune system is rebounding at an impressive rate." He grinned. "I believe it's safe to say the antidote worked. You should be feeling much better within . . . oh, an hour or two, I think, will make a notable difference, though it may take a few days to feel entirely yourself again."

"Oh, do not worry," Winter said, her voice faint even in her own head. "I never feel entirely myself." She held up her arm. "Will I forever be a leopard?"

"The spots will fade with time."

"Will they leave scars?"

He hesitated. "I don't know."

"It's all right, Winter," said Scarlet. "The important thing is that you're alive."

"I am not sad about it." She traced a finger over the raised flesh. How alien it felt. How imperfect. She could get used to imperfection.

"That's proof then," said Cinder, appearing at Jacin's side. "The antidote works. I need two volunteers to assist with the rest of the distribution. Anyone who's showing symptoms can form a line over there—if anyone has blue fingers, they move to the front of the line. No running, and help people who are too weak to help themselves. Let's move." She clapped her hands and the people hurried to obey.

Jacin pulled some of the gunk out of Winter's hair, his gaze absent like he wasn't aware he was doing it. In response, Winter reached up and tugged at a clump of his own blond hair.

"Are you real?" she asked.

He smiled, but only a little. "Do I seem real?"

She shook her head. "Never." Her attention darted to the crowd. "Has Selene had her revolution?"

"Not yet. The coronation is this evening. But we're . . ." He paused. "Things are happening."

She chewed her lip, fighting off the disappointment. This was not over. They had not yet won.

"Is there somewhere we can go to get this stuff off her?" Jacin asked.

"There are two washrooms inside the clinic, one down each hallway," said the doctor.

Scooping Winter into his arms, Jacin carried her inside the clinic. She tucked her head beneath his chin, even though she was leaving slimy goop all over him. It felt good to be together, for a moment at least.

He found the washroom, which contained a toilet and a large utilitarian sink and a shallow bathtub. Jacin paused in the doorway, surveying his options with an unhappy look.

"Your face is bruised." She brushed a knuckle against the wound. "Were you in a brawl?"

"Thorne hit me." His lips twitched. "But I guess I deserved it."

"It makes you look very tough. No one would ever suspect you're just a gentle goose on the inside."

He snorted and held her gaze. Suddenly she was feeling his heartbeat, but she didn't know if it was beating harder, or if she'd just become attuned to it in that moment. She started to feel shy.

The last time she'd seen Jacin, she'd kissed him. She'd confessed her love for him.

She flushed. Losing her courage, she looked away first. "You can put me in the bathtub. I'm strong enough to wash myself."

He reluctantly settled her on the edge of the metal tub and began fidgeting with the water controls. The water had a sulfuric smell. When the temperature was right, he searched through a cabinet and found a bottle of liquid soap. He set it within reaching distance.

Winter pulled at her hair, gathering a handful of chemical-scented grime in her palm. "You don't see the disease when you look at me."

Dipping his fingers into the tub, Jacin adjusted the waterspout again. He helped steady Winter with one hand as she spun on the tub's edge and dunked her feet into the water.

"Have I ever seen the disease when I looked at you?"

She knew he was talking about Lunar sickness, not some engineered plague. The disease in her head came with its own scars.

Scars, scars. She was coming to have so many. She wondered if it was wrong to be proud of them.

"How does it feel?" Jacin asked, and it took her a moment to realize he was asking about the water.

She inspected the pocked, darkened base of the tub and the cloudy water. "Am I to bathe fully dressed?"

"Yes, you are. I'm not leaving you alone."

"Because you can't stand to be parted from me?" She fluttered her lashes at him, but the teasing suggestion was quickly replaced with a realization. "Oh. Because you think I'll have a vision and drown."

"It can't be both? Come on, slide in."

She held his neck while he lowered her into the water, just a few degrees above lukewarm and stinging against her raw skin. An oily film rose to the water's surface.

"I'll get a wash—"

Jacin paused, stuck in place when her arms didn't unwind from his neck. He was kneeling on the other side of the tub, his arms elbow deep in water.

"Jacin. I'm sorry that I'm not sort of pretty anymore."

One eyebrow lifted and he looked like he might laugh.

"I mean it." Her stomach tightened with sadness. "And I'm sorry you have to worry about me all the time."

His almost-smile faded. "I like worrying about you. It gives me something to think about during those long, boring shifts in the palace." Tilting her chin down, Jacin pressed a kiss on top of Winter's head. Her arms fell away from him.

He stood, giving her an illusion of privacy while he scrounged for more towels.

"Will you stay a royal guard after Selene becomes the queen?"

"I don't know," he said, tossing a washcloth at her. "But I'm pretty sure that as long as you're a princess in need of protecting, you're going to be stuck with me."

Seventy-Five

IT HAD GROWN HOT INSIDE THE CABINET AND CRESS'S LEFT leg was tingling from too little blood flow when she finally forced herself to move. She didn't want to. Uncomfortable as the cabinet was, it felt safe, and she was convinced that the moment she moved someone would shoot her.

But she couldn't stay there forever, and time was not going to move any slower to accommodate her failing courage. Wiping her nose with the faux butterfly wing, she forced herself to nudge open the door.

The hallway light blinded her and Cress shrank back, hiding behind her arm. She was drained of emotions as she crawled out of the cabinet, peering each way down the servants' hall.

Her eye caught on a smear of blood not far from the cupboard. *Thorne.* She flinched away and tried to erase the sight from her memory before it paralyzed her.

Cress pounded life back into her leg and slowly stood. She listened, but heard nothing but distant machines and the hum of whatever heating and water systems were working in these walls.

Steeling herself, she checked that the chip was still tucked in her dress before she picked up the gun. The antennae had fallen off again and she left them in the bottom of the cabinet.

Her stomach was in ropes, her heart in tatters, but she managed to backtrack to the corridor Thorne had mentioned. She paused at the corner, peeked her head around, and drew back, her heart pummeling her rib cage.

A guard was there.

She should have expected it. Would all of the elevators be under guard now? The stairwells too?

Hopelessness seeped into her already-delirious thoughts. They were looking for her, and she was vulnerable without Thorne, and she had no plan.

This wouldn't work. She couldn't do it alone. She was going to be caught and imprisoned and killed, and Thorne would be killed, and Cinder would fail, and they would all—

She balled her fists into her eyes, pressing them there until she felt the panic subside.

Be heroic, Thorne had said.

She had to be heroic.

Hardly daring to breathe for fear of drawing attention, she strained to think of another way to get to the fourth floor.

Footsteps approached. She scrambled behind a statue with a missing arm and curled into a ball.

Be heroic.

She had to focus. She had to think.

The coronation would begin soon. She had to be in the control center before it was over.

When the guard had gone, and she was relatively sure she wasn't going to hyperventilate, Cress lifted her head and peeked around the statue. The hall wasn't wide but it was crammed full of stuff, from cabinets and framed paintings to rolled area rugs and cleaning buckets.

An idea forming, she used the wall for support as she stood and took a few steps away from the statue. She braced herself, then ran at the statue and shoved her shoulder into it as hard as she could.

Her foot slipped from the force and she landed hard on one knee, clenching her teeth against a grunt. The statue tilted on its base. Back. Forth. Back—

Cress covered her head as the statue toppled toward her, hitting her on the hip before shattering on the floor. She pressed a silent scream into her knuckles, but forced herself to hobble back toward the elevator bank, crawling behind a stack of rolled-up area rugs.

It wasn't long before the guard came running, darting past Cress's hiding space.

She shoved down the pain in her bruised knee and hip and scurried out from behind the rugs. She ran as hard as she could toward the abandoned elevators. A yell of surprise echoed behind her. She collided into the wall and jabbed her finger into the call button. The doors slid open.

She stumbled inside. "Door, close!"

The doors drew shut.

A gun fired. Cress screamed as one bullet buried itself in the wall behind her. Another pinged off the closing doors before they clamped shut.

She fell against the wall and groaned, pressing her hand against her injured hip. She could already tell it was going to leave one enormous bruise.

The elevator started to rise and she realized after a moment that she hadn't selected a floor. No doubt, the guard below would be monitoring it to see which floor she arrived at, anyway.

She had to be strategic. She had to think like a criminal mastermind.

Cress tried to prepare herself for whatever she would be faced with when the doors opened again. More guards. More guns. More endless corridors and desperate hiding places.

Squeezing her eyes shut, she struggled to picture the palace map she'd studied back at the mansion. She could envision the throne room easily, situated in the center of the palace, its balcony overhanging the lake below. The rest started to fill in as she focused. The private quarters for the thaumaturges and the court. A banquet hall. Drawing rooms and offices. A music room. A library.

And the queen's system control center, including the broadcasting suite where the crown recorded their propaganda in comfort and security.

The elevator stopped at the third floor. Trembling, Cress hid the gun in the frilly folds of her skirt. The doors opened.

A crowd of strangers stood before her. Cress squeaked. Her feet itched to run, her brain screamed at her to hide—but there was no space to disappear into as the men and women eyed her with contempt and suspicion. Those closest to the elevator hesitated, like they were considering waiting for another. But then one person grumbled something and filed in, and the others followed.

Cress pressed her back against the far wall, but the crush of bodies didn't come. Despite how crowded the elevator was, everyone was being careful not to get too close to her.

Her anxiety began to shrivel up. These people weren't Lunar.

These were the Earthen guests and, judging from their formal attire, they were heading down to the coronation.

The last thing she wanted was to be caught in a crowd of people heading to the coronation.

As the doors started to close, Cress cleared her throat. "Pardon me, but I'd like to get out here."

She squeezed through, her crinkled skirt catching against the fine suits and gowns. Though there were many frowns cast in her direction, they gladly parted for her.

Because they thought *she* was Lunar. A real Lunar, with the ability to manipulate them, not just a shell.

"Thank you," Cress muttered to the person who had stopped the doors from closing. She slipped into the elevator bank, pulse thumping.

Another beautiful hall. More striking views. A dozen pedestals showcasing statues and painted vases.

Cress found herself yearning for the rugged interior of the Rampion.

She tucked herself against a wall and waited until she was sure the elevator had gone before calling for a new one. She needed to go up one more floor. She had to find some stairs, or escape back into the servants' halls. She felt too out in the open here. Too exposed.

A chime announced the arrival of a new elevator, and Cress spooked, darting out of sight. When the doors opened, they were filled with laughter and giggles, and Cress held her breath until the doors had closed again.

At the sound of voices coming from her left, Cress turned and headed right. She passed a series of black doors, their darkness sharply contrasted against the white walls. Each one was marked with a name and affiliation in gold script letters.

REPRESENTATIVE MOLINA, ARGENTINA, AMERICAN REPUBLIC. PRESIDENT VARGAS, AMERICAN REPUBLIC. PRIME MINISTER BROMSTAD, EUROPEAN FEDERATION. REPRESENTATIVE ÖZBEK, SOUTH RUSSIA PROVINCE, EUROPEAN FEDERATION.

A door swung open and a woman with gray-blonde hair and a floor-length navy gown stepped out—Robyn Gliebe, Australia's speaker of the house. When Cress had worked for Levana, she'd spent hours listening to Gliebe's speeches regarding trade agreements and labor disputes. They had not been exciting hours.

Gliebe paused, startled to see Cress standing there. Cress hid the gun behind her back.

"Can I help you?" she said, asserting herself with narrowed, scolding eyes.

Of course, Cress would have to run into the only Earthen diplomat who wasn't intimidated by a dodgy Lunar girl sneaking around her wing.

"No," said Cress, ducking her head in apology. "You startled me, that's all." She moved past the woman, eyes lowered.

"Are you supposed to be up here?"

Hesitating, Cress glanced back. "I'm sorry?"

"Her Majesty guaranteed we would not be pestered during our stay. I think you should leave."

"Oh. I'm ... I have a message to deliver. I'll just be a minute. I'm sorry to have bothered you."

Cress scooted backward, but the woman persisted, pulling her penciled eyebrows into a tight frown. Stepping forward, she held out her hand. "Who is your message for? I will see that he or she receives it."

Cress stared down at the open palm, soft and wrinkled. "It's ... confidential."

The woman pursed her lips. "Well, I'm afraid if you don't leave immediately, I will have to call a guard to confirm your story. We were promised our privacy and I don't—"

"Cress?"

Her heart hiccuped.

Kai.

He stood there blinking at her as if he thought she might be a trick.

An ocean's worth of relief crashed into Cress, nearly knocking her off her feet. She braced herself with one hand against the wall. "Kai!" Shaking herself, she amended, "I mean, Emperor—Your Majesty." She dipped into a flustered curtsy.

Brow drawn, Kai looked at the speaker. "Gliebe-dàren, you haven't gone down yet?"

"I was just on my way," said the woman, and though Cress didn't meet her gaze, she could sense her distrust. "But I saw this girl and . . . as you know, we were guaranteed privacy on this floor, and I don't think she should—"

"It's all right," said Kai. "I know this girl. I'll take care of it."

Cress studied the floor, listening to the crinkle of the taffeta skirt.

"With all due respect, Your Majesty, how can I be sure she isn't manipulating you into siding with her?"

"With all due respect," said Kai, sounding exhausted, "if she wanted to manipulate someone, why wouldn't she have manipulated *you* into leaving her alone?"

Cress chewed on the inside of her cheek while a moment stretched out between them. Finally, the woman bowed. "Of course, you would know best. Congratulations on your forthcoming coronation."

The woman's footsteps clipped toward the elevator bank. When she had gone, Cress waited three whole seconds before launching herself into Kai's arms with a sob she hadn't known she'd been holding in.

Kai stumbled back in surprise, but returned the embrace, letting her cry into his very fine silk shirt.

The adviser made a strangled noise and Cress felt the handgun being lifted from her hand. She was glad to let it go.

"Calm down," Kai said, stroking her hair. "You're all right now."

She shook her head. "They took Thorne. They shot him and they took him and I don't know if he's alive and I don't know . . . I don't know what they're going to do to him."

Cress gave up on speaking until the flood of sobs started to wane. Ducking her head, she pulled her hands back and swiped at her hot cheeks. "I'm sorry." She sniffed. "I'm sorry. It's just . . . really, really good to see you."

"It's all right." Kai gently held Cress away so he could see her face. "Start from the beginning. Why are you here?"

She was trying to rein in the stampede of emotions when she saw the damp spot she'd left on his shirt. "Oh—aces. I'm so sorry." She swiped at it with her fingers.

He gave her a little shake. "It's fine. Cress. Look at me."

She looked at him, rubbing her wrist across her eyes again. Despite the splotch she'd left, Kai was quite dapper in a cream-colored silk tunic. It was fastened with gold frogs and a sash striped with the colors of the Eastern Commonwealth flag: sea-foam green, teal blue, sunset orange. If the sash had been red, it would have been an exact replica of the outfit he'd been wearing when Cinder and the others had kidnapped him.

But no. He was already married. He was Queen Levana's husband now, the man who was on his way to be crowned king consort of Luna.

Her focus darted to the side. Royal Adviser Konn Torin was

wearing a basic black tuxedo and Cress could sense his concern despite his composure. He was holding the gun's handle between two pinched fingers, looking about as comfortable with it as Cress had been.

"Cress?" said Kai, stealing back her attention.

She licked her lips. "Thorne and I were supposed to get to the system control center, but he was captured. They said something about taking him to a holding cell? And I got away, but now I—"

"Why are you trying to get to the control center?"

"To play another video Cinder recorded. It shows the queen— oh! You probably don't know that Cinder is alive!"

Kai's expression froze for a moment, before he tilted his head back and let out a long, slow breath. His eyes had a new light in them when he glanced at Konn Torin, but the adviser was watching Cress, unwilling to be relieved just yet.

"Cinder's alive," Kai repeated to himself. "Where is she?"

"She's with Iko and Jacin and . . . it's a long story." Scrunching up her face, Cress felt the weight of time pressing down on her. She started to speak faster. "Jacin was going to see if he could find the letumosis antidote and distribute it to the outer sectors, because a lot of people are sick, including Princess Winter, and Scarlet too. Oh, and Levana took Wolf and we don't know where he is, and now they have Thorne—!" Cress hid her face behind her hands in an effort to refrain from sullying Kai's shirt any more than she already had. Kai rubbed her arms, but even in this sympathetic touch she could tell he was distracted.

Konn Torin cleared his throat. Sniffling, Cress lowered her hands and found a handkerchief being held out to her, extended at arm's length as if Torin were afraid that her hysteria would rub off on him if he got much closer.

Cress took the handkerchief and held it to her nose. "Thank you."

"What do you need?"

She dragged her attention back to Kai. "To rescue Thorne," she said, without thinking. But then she remembered his last words to her. *Be heroic.* She gulped. "No, I ... I need to get to the control center. I need to play this video over Levana's broadcasting system. Cinder's counting on it."

Kai ran a hand through his hair. Cress flinched as he went from neat-and-tidy emperor to concerned teenage boy with that one movement. She could see his indecision. How badly he wanted to help, in contrast to how much danger his involvement could put his country in.

Cress felt time ticking away.

"Your Majesty."

Kai nodded at his adviser. "I know. They'll probably send a search party if I don't show up soon. But I just need a minute to ... to think."

"What is there to think about?" said Torin. "You asked this girl what she needed, and she gave you a very concise answer. We all know you're going to help her, so it seems like a waste of time to argue the pros and cons of such a decision."

Cress fidgeted with her gloves, feeling the butterfly wings graze her arms. The adviser looked both stern and kind as he handed the gun back to her, handle first.

Cress shuddered. "You can keep it, if you want."

"I don't," said Torin. "Neither do I intend to put myself into any situations in which I *might* want it."

With a resigned sigh, Cress took it from him. She spent a moment considering where she might be able to store it, but her outfit didn't offer any good solutions.

"Here." Torin removed his tuxedo jacket and handed it to her. Cress hesitated, hearing Iko's voice in her head—*that doesn't match at all!*—before casting the voice away and allowing him to help her into the sleeves. She was drowning in the jacket, but already she felt more composed, less vulnerable.

"Thank you," she said, finding an inside pocket and sliding the gun into it with an enormous sense of relief.

"His Majesty is expected to be in the main hall within the next two minutes," Torin said, then passed his attention to a baffled Kai. "I'm confident I can delay them for at least fifteen more."

Seventy-Six

KAI WASN'T SURE IF HE OR CRESS WAS IN THE LEAD AS THEY rushed through the abandoned corridors, their footsteps loud and brisk. When Cress started to fall behind, struggling to keep up, he forced himself to slow his pace.

"We're going to try to accomplish this without the gun," he said, as if they'd been discussing it, although they'd hardly spoken since parting ways with Torin. "We're going to take care of this diplomatically. Or ... at least, sneakily. If we can."

"I have no problem with that," said Cress. "However, I don't think that just because you're an emperor and you're about to become their king they're going to let you waltz into their broadcasting room and start fiddling with their equipment."

Each door they passed had a different design carved into the wood. A beautiful woman holding up a long-eared rabbit. A falcon-headed man with a crescent moon balanced on his head. A young girl dressed in the mantle of a fox and carrying a hunting spear. Kai knew they were symbolic of the moon and its importance in Earthen cultures, many of them lost and forgotten. Even Kai no longer recognized the significance.

They turned down another hallway and passed over a sky-bridge made of glass. A silver stream passed beneath their feet.

"You're right," said Kai, "but I think I can at least get you inside." He hesitated, before adding, "Cress, I won't be able to stay. If I'm absent for too long, Levana will get suspicious, and that's the last thing we need right now. You understand, right?"

"I understand." She dropped her voice, although the hallways were empty—every guest, every guard, every servant waiting for the coronation to begin. "I suspect the door locks will be coded. The plan was to hack them, but Thorne had the portscreen with him . . ."

Kai unclipped his portscreen from his belt. "Can you use mine?"

She stared at the device. "You won't . . . need it?"

"Not like you will. I couldn't have brought it into the ceremony, anyway. All recording devices are prohibited." He rolled his eyes and handed the port to her. Though it once would have felt like giving up one of his limbs, he'd gotten used to being without it after Levana had it confiscated.

Besides, a part of him was giddy with the knowledge that he was helping to undermine the queen.

"How do you know where we're going?" Cress asked, tucking the port into one of the pockets in Torin's jacket.

Kai scowled. "I had the great experience of partaking in one of her propaganda videos a while back."

As they neared the palace wing on the opposite side of the lake from the great hall, where the coronation was set to start, oh, six minutes ago, Kai held up a hand, bringing them to a stop.

"Wait here," he whispered, holding a finger to his lips.

Cress pressed herself against a wall. She looked tiny and terrified and preposterous in that poufy orange skirt, and some chivalrous instinct told Kai he shouldn't abandon her here, of all places. But he shoved that instinct down, reminding himself that she was also the genius who had single-handedly shut down the entire security system of New Beijing Palace.

Straightening his patriotic sash, Kai stepped around the corner. This wing was sealed off, and as far as Kai knew, there was only this one door in and out. As expected, a guard stood in front of the door at mute attention. The same guard, Kai thought, who had been on duty when Levana had dragged him here before.

The guard's eyes narrowed upon seeing Kai in his white silk tunic. "This area is not open to the public," he said in a bored tone.

"I'm hardly 'the public.'" Kai tucked his hands into his pockets, trying to look both accommodating and defiant. "My understanding is that the coronation regalia are held in this wing, are they not?"

The guard squinted suspiciously.

"I've been sent to obtain the Brooch of . . . Eternal Starlight. I'm sure you'll understand that I'm rather short on time."

"I'm sure you're used to getting your way on Earth, *Your Emperorship*, but you will not be permitted past these doors, and to see the crown jewels, no less, without official documentation from the queen."

"I understand, and I would gladly obtain that documentation if Her Majesty wasn't at this very moment in the opposite wing of the palace, dressed in full coronation garb, having already been anointed with a concoction of sacred Eastern Commonwealth oils in order to purify her for the ceremony in which she will become empress of my country. So she's just a little preoccupied at the moment, and I need to find that brooch before the ceremony is delayed even more than it already is."

"Do you think I'm an idiot?"

"I'm beginning to, actually. Only an idiot would stall Her Majesty's coronation. Would you like me to go to her now and explain how we cannot proceed because of your obstinacy?"

"I've never even heard of this 'Brooch of Eternal Starlight.'"

"Of course you haven't. It was designed specifically to represent an alliance between Luna and Earth and gifted to one of the queen's great ancestors over a century ago. Unfortunately, as you may be aware, there hasn't been an alliance between us in that time, so the brooch hasn't been necessary. Until tonight—and the moron who was in charge of preparing the regalia forgot about it."

"And they sent *you* to pick it up? Shouldn't you be getting anointed with oils yourself?"

Kai let out a slow breath and dared to put himself in arm's reach of the guard. "Unfortunately, I seem to be the only person on this little moon who has any clue what it looks like. Now—by the end of this night, I will be your king, and if you want to still have your job by tomorrow morning, I suggest you let me through."

The guard's jaw clenched. He still didn't move.

Kai threw his arms up. "Stars above, I'm not asking you to open the door, close your eyes, and count to ten. Obviously, you'll come in with me and make sure I don't steal anything. But time is running out. I'm ten minutes late already. Perhaps you'd like to comm Her Majesty and explain the delay?"

With a huff, the guard stepped back and yanked open the door. "Fine. But if you touch anything other than this supposed *brooch* of yours, I will chop off your hand."

"Fine." Kai rolled his eyes in a way he hoped indicated a total lack of concern and followed the guard. Not that the guard was traveling far from his post—the vault that housed the crown jewels, when they weren't being used for a coronation, was immediately on the left, behind an enormous vault door.

Kai averted his eyes while the guard pressed a code into a screen and scanned his fingerprints, then twisted the unlock mechanism.

The door, when it opened, was as thick as the guard's skull.

The vault was lined with velvet and spotlights that shined on empty pedestals. Most of the crowns and orbs and scepters that usually lived there were already down in the great hall.

But it wasn't empty, either.

Kai took in a deep breath and started pacing around the vault. He inspected every ring, scabbard, coronet, and cuff, all the pieces the Lunar crown had collected over the years to be used in a variety of ceremonies. Most of them, Kai knew, had been gifts from Earth a long, long time ago. A show of goodwill, before the relationship between Earth and Luna had been severed.

He heard a padded footstep outside the vault door but he dared not look up. "Here!" he yelled, turning his back on the guard, his heart lodged in his throat, as he imagined Cress scurrying past the door. He pulled the medallion from his pocket, the one Iko had given him aboard the Rampion, what felt like ages ago. He rubbed his thumb over the tarnished insignia and the faded words. *The American Republic 86th Space Regiment.* "Found it," he said, holding the medallion up so the guard could see he was holding something without getting a very good look at it. Cress was gone, and Kai wasn't faking his relief as he said, "Whew. Great. We couldn't have done the coronation without it. Her Majesty will be thrilled. I'll see if we can't get you a promotion, all right?" He slapped the guard on the arm. "I guess that's it, then. Thanks for your help. I'd better hurry back."

The guard grunted, and Kai knew he was anything but convinced, but it didn't matter.

When he and the guard stepped back into the corridor, Cress had already disappeared.

CRESS HURRIED AROUND THE FIRST CORNER AND PRESSED HER back against the wall, her heart in her throat. She waited until she heard the guard shutting the vault door, then she started to run, hoping the noise of the vault's locking mechanism would cover the sound of her footsteps.

She remembered this hall from when Sybil used to bring her before, and it was easy to find the door to the control center once she had her bearings. She slid to a stop and hesitantly tested the handle. She was relieved to find it locked, a good indication that no one was inside. She'd been confident the security staff would have located themselves to a satellite control room nearer the great hall—that had been the procedure during important events when she worked for Sybil—but being confident wasn't being certain. The gun, heavy in Torin's jacket pocket, offered no comfort at all should she run into more opposition now.

Cress crouched before the security panel and retrieved Kai's portscreen. She unwound the universal connector cable.

It took her twenty-eight seconds to break into the room, which was an eternity, but she was distracted, jumping at every distant noise. Sweat was snaking down her spine by the time she heard the door unlatch.

Her breath was shaky but relieved. No one was inside. The door shut behind her.

Cress's adrenaline was pumping like jet fuel through her veins as she scanned the room. She was surrounded by invisi-screens and holographs and programming, and the familiarity of it all made the knot in her stomach loosen. Instinct and habit. She formed a checklist in her mind.

The room was big, but crowded with desks and chairs and equipment, panels that switched from video footage of the outer sectors to the underground shuttle map to surveillance feeds of different sections of the palace. A separate recording suite was accessed through a soundproof door. Lights and re-cording equipment surrounded a replica of the queen's throne. A sheer veil was draped over a mannequin head and the sight gave Cress a chill down her spine. It felt like it was watching her.

She turned away from the mannequin and settled herself into one of the controller's chairs. She removed the gun from the jacket pocket and set it and the portscreen on the desk, both within easy reach. She felt the press of time as keenly as Kai had. She'd already wasted too much of it. Kissing Thorne in the atrium. Hiding in that cabinet. Dodging in and out of corridors like a lost rabbit.

But she was here. She'd made it. She'd been heroic—almost.

Her objectives spooled through her thoughts.

Placing her fingertips across the nearest invisi-screen, she began to count them off, one by one.

First, she reconfigured the security codes for the queen's broadcasting transmitter. She put the palace's armory under lockdown. She scheduled a retraction for the tunnel barricades surrounding Artemisia.

Breaking through the codes, navigating the protocols—it felt like a choreographed dance, and though her muscles were weary, they still remembered the steps.

Finally, she pulled the chip from her bodice. She envisioned the transmitter on top of the palace, sending the crown's official feed to receivers throughout the dome. A closed feed, protected by a complex labyrinth of internal firewalls and security codes.

Five minutes could have passed. Eight. Nine, at the most.

Check. Check. Check—

She heard footsteps in the hallway as she was inserting the chip with Cinder's video into the port. She felt the satisfying click.

Download, data transfer, translate the encryption.

Her fingers danced over the screens, daring the coding to keep up.

Boots outside, pounding faster now.

Her hair clung to the back of her neck.

Check. Check.

Done.

Cress cleared the screens, disguising her motives with a few hasty commands.

The door crashed open. Guards filed in.

Confused silence.

Squeezed into the alcove between the bank of screens and the transmitter's mainframe, Cress held her breath.

"Spread out—and get tech up here to find out what she did!"

"She left a portscreen," said someone else, and she heard a subtle clacking on the desk as they picked it up. Trembling, Cress looked down at the gun cradled in her hands. Her stomach was knotted again. She couldn't help feeling like she'd grabbed the wrong thing. They would know the portscreen was Kai's easy enough. They would know he'd helped her. "Maybe she was planning on coming back."

"You, stay here and wait for tech. And I want a guard posted at every door in this wing until she's found. Go!"

The door slammed shut and Cress released a shaky breath, wilting from the surge of adrenaline.

She was trapped. Thorne was captured.

But they had been heroic.

Seventy-Seven

JACIN HAD GONE BACK OUTSIDE BY THE TIME WINTER finished cleaning the slippery gel-like substance out of her hair. She changed into the dry clothes someone had brought for her.

She could not stop smiling. Jacin was back and he was alive.

And yet, at the same time, her heart ached. People were going to die today.

She checked her arms. The rash was already receding. At least, some of the bruises looked not quite as dark, and the blue had disappeared from beneath her fingernails.

When she left the security of the washroom, she found the clinic crammed full of people—the one doctor and a dozen civilians checking on the patients who had been too ill to line up for the antidote outside. Seven deaths, she'd been told. In the short time since Levana had infected Winter, seven people in this sector had died from letumosis.

It would have been many more if Jacin and Cinder hadn't arrived, but Winter was hardly comforted. Seven deaths. Seven people who could have been in the suspension tank if they hadn't given it to her.

Winter passed the patients slowly, taking the time to smile and offer a comforting squeeze of a shoulder as she made her way to the exit. She emerged on the little wooden step.

A whooping cheer swelled up in the dome, hundreds of voices buffeting her.

Winter froze, then backed into the building's overhang again. The crowd continued to cheer, shaking their makeshift weapons over their heads. The wolf soldiers started to howl. Winter wondered if she, too, should cheer. Or howl. Or if they expected her to speak—though her throat still felt chapped and her brain was still muddled.

Scarlet appeared beside her, waving her arms in an attempt to quiet the crowd. She looked both pleased and annoyed as she faced Winter. The evidence of the plague still lingered on Scarlet's pale skin—freckles mixed with bruises and irritated flesh. Though there were still a few dark blisters, the disease had not escalated as quickly on Scarlet as it had on Winter and those seven poor residents. They all knew she'd gotten lucky.

"What's happening?" Winter asked.

"Cinder and the alphas are discussing strategy," said Scarlet. "The coronation is scheduled to begin any minute now. People are getting restless. Plus, everyone loves you—surprise, surprise—and they've been waiting to see that you're all right."

Winter risked a smile, and the people cheered again. Someone whistled and another soldier howled.

Winter caught sight of a figure in the corner of her eye— Jacin was leaning against the clinic's wall, watching her with a knowing smirk. "They haven't started composing ballads in your honor yet," he said, "but I'm sure it's just a matter of time."

"Cress did it!" Cinder yelled. She came charging through the crowd, a cluster of soldiers in tow. The people parted for her.

"The barriers in the maglev tunnels are down. There's nothing else to bar our way into Artemisia. There's nothing stopping us from demanding that Levana be brought to justice!"

Another cheer, twice as loud as before, billowed up and vibrated through the ground and echoed off the dome.

Winter cast her gaze over the crowd, her heart expanding like a balloon. The people stared at Cinder with awe and clarity and the faint glow of hope. She'd never seen that before in the eyes of the citizens of Luna. Their faces were always obscured by fear and uncertainty. Or, even worse, gazing at her stepmother with dazed adoration. Love for their ruler forced upon them—a reminder that they had no freedom, not even in their own minds or hearts.

This was different. The people weren't blinded by Cinder's glamour or being manipulated into seeing her as their rightful queen. They were seeing her as she truly was.

"Alpha Strom, the map," said Cinder, with an excited gesture.

Strom handed her a holograph node and Cinder pulled up an image that everyone could see, outlining the path they would take into the capital.

"We're going to divide into two groups to allow for faster passage through the tunnels," she said, indicating the routes on the map. "When we reach AR-4 and AR-6, we'll divide our numbers further to disperse between the eight entrances into Artemisia. At every sector we pass, we'll need volunteers to rally as many people to our cause as possible. Gather weapons and supplies, then keep moving. Remember, our safety lies in numbers. She keeps the sectors divided for a reason. She knows that she's powerless if we all stand together, and that's exactly what we're going to do!"

Another roar from the crowd, but Cinder—wild-eyed and exhilarated—had already turned toward the steps.

Winter straightened, for once proud to be standing before her queen.

"We've seen evidence that at least eighty-seven other sectors have joined our cause, and I have every reason to believe that number has continued to increase. With the shuttles down, that terrain-speeder is the best method we have for spreading our news quickly and ensuring that all civilians are joined into one solid force moving into Artemisia. Jacin, I've made a list of sectors I want you to go to—those that showed evidence of rebellion already and should have access to weapons. Also those closest to Artemisia that offer a solid hope for increasing our numbers fast. Hit as many as you can in the next two hours, then meet us in the tunnels beneath AR-4 at—"

"No."

Cinder blinked. Her lips stayed half-wrapped around an unspoken word. She blinked again. "Excuse me?"

"I won't leave Winter."

A shiver coursed over Winter's skin, but Jacin didn't look at her.

Mouth still open, Cinder looked at Winter, then Scarlet, then back at Jacin. She shut her mouth with a scowl and turned to Scarlet again. "Can *you* fly it?"

"I've never even seen one of those things before. Does it fly like a spaceship?"

Cinder's withering glare returned to Jacin. "I need you to do it. I trust you, and—"

"I said no."

She shook her head, disbelieving. Then angry. "What do you think is going to happen to Winter, to *any* of us, if we lose?"

Jacin crossed his arms, ready to argue again, when Winter placed a hand on his shoulder.

"I'll go with him," she said lightly, so her words might defuse some of the tension.

It didn't work. Jacin's glower turned on her. "No, you will stay here and recover from almost *dying*. Besides, Levana's been given enough chances to kill you. You're not going anywhere near Artemisia."

She fixed her eyes on him, feeling the stir of determination she'd had when she decided to find her stepmother's army and bring them to her side. "I may not be able to fight, but I *can* be useful. I'll come with you and talk to the people. They'll listen to me."

"Princess, we don't have to—"

"I've already made my decision. I have as much to lose as any of them."

"She makes some good points," said Cinder.

"Surprisingly," added Scarlet.

Jacin pushed Winter out of their little circle, into a semblance of privacy. "Look," he whispered, gripping her elbows. She could feel the calluses on his hands, more poignant than she'd ever felt them before. Her pulse galloped at the unexpected intimacy. "If you want me to do this thing for Cinder, then I'll do it. For *you*. But I won't—I *can't* lose you again."

Winter smiled and pressed her palms against his cheeks. "There is no safer place for me than at your side."

His jaw tightened. She could see the war in his thoughts, but she was already resolved.

"I have lived in fear of her my entire life," she continued. "If this is the only chance I'm given to stand against her, then I have to take it. I don't want to hide. I don't want to be afraid. And I *don't* want to be separated from you, ever again."

His shoulders started to droop, the first indication she'd won.

He raised a finger between them. "Fine. We'll go together. But you are not to touch *any* weapons, understand?"

"What would I do with a weapon?"

"Exactly."

"Jacin, Winter." Cinder was tapping her foot, her eyes wild with growing impatience. "We're sort of on a tight—"

As if the sky itself were listening, the dome overhead darkened, and three enormous screens lit up against the black backdrop.

"People of Luna," said a feminine voice, "please give your full attention now to this mandatory broadcast, live from Artemisia Palace. The royal coronation ceremony is about to begin."

A wicked grin pulled at Winter's lips. She stepped away from Jacin, faced the people, and raised her arms to her sides. "People of Luna," she said, echoing the broadcast and pulling the crowd's attention away from the dome, "please give your full attention now to the true heir to the Lunar throne, Princess Selene, live from your very own sector." Her eyes flashed as she swooped an arm toward Cinder. "Our revolution is about to begin."

BOOK
Five

The mirror answered: "You, my queen, are fair; it's true.

But the young queen is far more fair than you."

Seventy-Eight

KAI BARRELED DOWN THE HALLWAY, GLAD NO ONE WAS around to see him sprinting in his coronation finery, though his thoughts were too full to worry about appearances. Cinder was alive. Thorne was captured. Cinder was going to invade Artemisia.

Today. *Now.*

He still felt guilty for leaving Cress alone. He should have done more. He shouldn't have cared how late he was to this coronation, a ceremony he had no desire to be a part of to begin with. He should have taken more pleasure in making Levana wait. He should have faked another kidnapping.

He cursed inside, wishing he would have thought of that sooner.

But, no—his going missing would set off alarms and the last thing Cress and the others needed were alarms. The best thing he could do to quell Levana's suspicions was to go forward as if nothing had changed.

The best thing he could do was crown her empress of his country.

It made him sick to think it, but he would stick to the plan. He would play his part.

He spun around a corner, nearly toppling a statue of some chisel-muscled moon god. Kai grabbed the statue, righting it while his heart launched into his throat. When both he and the statue had calmed, he shoved his way through the double doors that led into a series of private waiting chambers.

Two guards flanked the doorway into the great hall. Torin was seated on a cushioned bench beside a woman with gold, poufed hair, who gasped with such fervor Kai thought she might pass out.

"Oh, thank you, Artemis!" she said, pressing a cloth to her brow. "Where have you *been*?"

"I told you he was on his way," said Torin.

The woman ignored him, already speaking into a device attached to her wrist. "The emperor has arrived. Ceremony to commence in thirty seconds." She shoved the port onto her belt and focused on Kai, scanning him with a mix of anxiety and disgust. "*Earthens,*" she muttered, straightening his sash and brushing his hair away from his face. "You never take any pride in your appearance."

He gulped back a quick retort involving gold hair and accepted a glass of water from a servant.

Torin stood from the bench and slipped his hands into his pockets. He looked alarmingly casual without a jacket, and Kai wondered if he, too, had already been criticized by this woman, whoever she was. "Is everything all right, Your Majesty?"

The words were said with calm indifference, but Kai could see tense curiosity beneath Torin's expression.

Although he didn't know whether it was true, he nodded. "Everything's fine."

Beyond the double doors he could hear the chatter of hundreds of voices and he wondered what rumors were already circulating as to the ceremony's delay. "I'm ready."

"So is Her Majesty," said the woman. She shoved Torin toward another entrance. "You—go take your seat! Your Majesty, follow me."

Kai followed her between the guards, through the double doors, into a short hallway lined with ornamental pillars.

Levana was waiting, outfitted in a dress that matched Kai's sash—the colors of the Eastern Commonwealth. She looked like a giant walking flag, with a row of stars along the base of her gown's hem and a white lotus blossoming across her side. She, too, wore a sash, this in burnt orange—on Earth, the color of the rising sun.

The sight of her showing so much fake patriotism for the Commonwealth made him want to tear off that sash and strangle her with it.

She held her hands toward him as he approached. Though he bristled, he had no choice but to take them. Her fingers were icy cold.

"My dear husband," she cooed. "I feel we were parted for too long."

He scowled. "How long are you planning on keeping up this charade, exactly?"

"'Charade'?" Levana tittered. "Surely a wife is allowed to long for her husband without her emotions being considered suspect?"

"Unless you want me to be physically ill during these proceedings, I suggest we change the topic."

Her expression hardened. "Our marriage union is final and binding. It is *your* choice how you react to the situation."

"You're giving me a choice about something?" Kai flashed his most diplomatic smile. "How generous of you."

Levana matched the look. "There. That wasn't so difficult, was it?" She turned so they were facing the great hall, arm in arm. Kai caught a glimpse of the scratch on her forearm where he had cut her with the scissors during their wedding.

The sight strengthened him as the horns blared.

The doors were pulled back, revealing masses of onlookers. Kai found it a strain on his eyes to look at the vibrant colors and sparkling lights and flouncy materials spilling out of the audience and into the aisle.

"All rise for Her Royal Majesty, Queen Levana Blackburn of Luna, direct descendant of First King Cyprus Blackburn, and His Imperial Majesty, Emperor Kaito of the Eastern Commonwealth of Earth."

The Lunar anthem began to play. Kai and Levana paced down the aisle. If it weren't for the gaudy clothing in the pews, the mood would have felt somber.

"I was given an interesting piece of information before you arrived," said Levana, keeping her expression pleasant for the crowd, "involving a traitor that was recently detained in our underground holding cells."

Kai's stomach tightened. "Do go on."

"It seems they found one of Linh Cinder's accomplices prowling around our palace. That Earthen criminal—Carswell Thorne, I believe is his name."

"That *is* interesting."

"I don't suppose you know what he was attempting to accomplish here?"

"Perhaps he felt slighted at not receiving an invitation."

Levana nodded to the crowd. "No matter. We caught him before he could cause too much trouble."

"I'm glad to hear it."

"I thought, as you will soon be Luna's king consort and he was your prisoner before he was mine, I might allow you to decide how best to execute him."

He set his jaw. "How my wife does honor me."

Though in reality, while Levana was trying to goad his temper, she'd given him a gift. It was a relief to hear that Thorne wasn't already dead.

As they neared the end of the aisle, he spotted his Earthen peers near the front. Torin was already there—they must have sneaked him in through some other entrance—along with dozens of representatives from the Commonwealth and the other nations. He even saw, with some surprise, Linh Adri and Linh Pearl standing beside an American representative. They both wore frozen smiles, and though Kai had a particular kind of hatred for those two women, he also felt a sting of sympathy. Levana had been toying with them like a cat toys with a mouse before devouring it. Offering favors, then punishing them, then offering favors again. No wonder they both looked stricken with fear, afraid to make any sudden movements.

A dozen people stood on the raised dais, a mix of thaumaturges and royal guards and one bioengineered soldier dressed up in a pretty uniform that was at odds with his malformed face and body.

Kai grimaced, wondering what Levana was thinking to bring one of those creatures to the coronation. Their presence hadn't worked out for *either* side at the wedding feast.

Then the light caught on the creature's eyes, blazing green, and Kai frowned. If he didn't know better—

He jolted, his feet stumbling on the first step. He caught himself, successfully navigating the rest of the steps without falling on his face. His heart continued to thump inside his chest and he remembered Cress telling him they'd taken Wolf, but she didn't know what had become of him.

Now he knew.

This creature was Wolf, but not. His eyes were turbulent and dark, boring into Kai, hinting at the ferocity that simmered beneath the surface.

With a snarl, Wolf looked away first.

"You recognize my prized soldier?" said Levana as they reached the altar full of regalia. "I should think he's changed a great deal since last you saw him."

Kai's fury writhed inside him. She only wanted a reaction. She only wanted him to know that she was in control—of his fate, of the fate of his country, of the fate of his friends.

Kai braced himself as he and Levana turned to face the audience. This was the moment in which he would be handing Levana half his power. This was when he would tell his country that, should he die, this woman would become their sole ruler.

His body throbbed with refusal, but he knew there were no more options left to him.

Please let Cinder come, a voice repeated in the back of his head. *Please let her come.*

"People of Luna and of Earth," said Levana, holding her hands toward the crowd. "You are here to witness a momentous event in our history. Today, we shall crown an Earthen as our king— my husband, Emperor Kaito of the Eastern Commonwealth. And today, I shall be crowned an empress, the first of our royal bloodline to form a binding alliance with our Earthen brethren."

The people cheered.

Well, the Lunars cheered. The Earthens clapped sort of politely.

"I ask that you be seated," said Levana.

As the people took their seats, Kai and Levana paced to the two bejeweled cases set upon the altar. Kai released a slow breath and undid the latch on the case.

Inside, settled on a bed of silk, was the empress crown, molded into the shape of a phoenix and studded with flaming jewels.

His heart caught, overwhelming him with emotion he hadn't been prepared for. The last time he'd seen this crown it had been worn by his mother. She had worn it during the annual ball celebrating world peace every year. She had always been so beautiful.

He shivered at the memory, and at the blasphemy he was about to commit.

On the other side of the altar, Levana emerged with her own crown. In comparison to the Earthen jewels, the crown for Luna's king was simple. Seven spindly tines carved of moon rock, the white stone shimmering in the candlelight. It was ancient. The monarchy of Luna had been formed long before the Fourth World War had led to the formation of the Eastern Commonwealth and its own royal family.

Steeling himself, Kai lifted his mother's crown from its protective box, and together, he and Levana faced the crowd again, holding their symbolic crowns overhead. Kai found Torin and saw sadness mirrored in his expression. Perhaps he, too, was thinking of Kai's mother.

Before Levana could launch into her speech about the symbolic importance of this crown and how it symbolized the sovereign's power and so on and so forth, the doors at the back of the room crashed open.

The gold-haired woman marched down the aisle, and though

her expression was horrified, her movements were robotic, keeping her heading toward the queen.

Kai lowered the crown, his palms growing warm. Hope expanded in his chest. As the crowd turned to watch the woman's approach, a titter spread through them. Something was happening. Kai did not sense fear from the crowd so much as excitement, like this was nothing but a fictional drama to them.

The woman arrived at the stairs and dropped to one knee. "Forgive me, My Queen," she stammered. "We have received notice that there is a disturbance in several nearby sectors, including the outlying domes of Artemisia City."

Kai risked a glance at Wolf, but Wolf was still twitching and snarling. He looked ready to snap his enormous jaws around the first throat that passed too close.

"What sort of disturbance?" Levana growled.

"We don't know how, but the barricades around the rebellious sectors have been lifted, and the people are . . . they are coming here. Swarming the maglev tunnels. There is word that . . . that Princess Winter is among them."

Levana's face reddened. "That is not possible."

"I . . . I do not know, My Queen. That's only what I was told. And . . . and also, supposedly, the cyborg is with them as well."

Kai grinned. He couldn't help it, and he did nothing to hide it when Levana turned a scowl on him. With a shrug, he told her, "She *did* warn you."

Levana's jaw clenched. She turned back to the woman. "The cyborg is dead and I will not tolerate any rumors to the contrary."

The woman's mouth hung.

"Are the barricades holding around Artemisia?"

"Y-yes, My Queen. To my knowledge they've been unable to breach—"

"Then we are not under any immediate threat, are we?"

"I . . . I suppose not, My Queen."

"Then *why* are you interrupting this ceremony?" Levana flicked her wrist. "Guards, escort this woman to a prison cell. I will suffer no more interruptions."

Her eyes were flaming, merciless, as the woman stood and stumbled back. Two of the guards caught her.

The crowd was trying to stifle their enthusiasm, but was failing. Kai saw a number of mocking looks cast toward the woman as she was dragged away, even though surely it had not been *her* idea to bring news of the insurrection to Levana.

Kai's own thoughts were teeming. He bit down hard on the inside of his cheek, while Levana's face untwisted, transforming back into pleasant serenity.

"Now then," she said, raising the Lunar crown over her head. "Let us proceed."

Seventy-Nine

CINDER STAYED AT THE FRONT OF THEIR SMALL ARMY, ALONG with Alpha Strom. The subway tunnels were wide enough to walk in rows of five and Strom had made sure everyone knew this was to be their formation—to deviate in such confined quarters could lead to panic and confusion. They tried to be quiet, but it was impossible. They progressed like a roll of thunder. Thousands of feet pounding against the rocky terrain inside the lava tubes.

The mutant soldiers stayed near the front, the first line of defense, while the people from the outer sectors followed behind.

It had become a numbers game, and their numbers were growing. Every sector they passed through had new civilians joining their cause, many who had been preparing from the moment Cinder's first message had broadcast.

Cinder kept running the calculations over and over in her head, but there were still too many variables to factor. They needed enough civilians to overthrow the queen and her thaumaturges, and enough un-manipulated fighters left to take on the guards and any wolf soldiers Levana brought to her defense.

She was relying on Jacin and Winter to spread the word, and fast. If they failed, it would become a massacre, and not in their favor. If they succeeded . . .

The tunnels were pitch-black but for the lanterns scavenged by the people in the outer sectors and a handful of flashlights. Cinder wished she had a map in her head telling her how far they'd gone and how much farther they had to go. She'd become accustomed to having infinite data within her grasp, and it was disconcerting now to be without it. After five years of wishing she was like everyone else, now she missed all those conveniences that had come with being cyborg.

Four times they came across stalled trains and shuttles that filled up the confined space of the tunnel. These had at first seemed like insurmountable obstacles, but the soldiers went forward with zeal, prying off the panels, tearing up the interior seats, trampling their way through the other side. They made for an efficient, destructive machine, and their makeshift army was given passage through.

Although the maglev system had been shut down, power was still being sent out on the grid and the platforms they passed were well lit with a holograph of the mandatory-viewing video feed of the coronation. Unable to record the ceremony itself, as the queen would not be donning her veil, a broadcaster was relaying a moment-by-moment breakdown of the event.

As they entered into AR-4, one of the sectors adjacent to Artemisia Central, Cinder heard Kai's voice and paused. He was reciting the vows to become the king consort of Luna.

Their army divided into four regiments. Each would enter the capital through a different tunnel. As the alphas led their packs and the civilians in opposite directions, Cinder caught sight of Strom, watching her.

"We should keep moving," he said. "My men are hungry and restless, and you've put us in a confined space with a lot of sweet-smelling flesh."

Cinder raised an eyebrow. "If they need a snack, tell them to chew on each other for a while. I just want to make sure Jacin has enough time to reach as many sectors as possible."

Strom smirked, as if impressed at Cinder's inability to be bullied. "It's time to move," he repeated. "Our people are almost in position. The queen and her entourage are all in one place. We may be sitting down here for weeks waiting for more civilians that never show up."

Cinder believed they would come. They *had* to come. But she also knew he was right.

The coronation was almost over.

They started creeping through the tunnels again. Hands tightened on their weapons. Paces slowed with mounting anxiety. They hadn't gone much farther when Cinder's flashlight caught on iron bars in the distance. Strom held up a hand, signaling for everyone to stop.

"The barricade." Cinder sent her flashlight beam into the wall around the iron grate. It would take weeks to dig around it.

"There's no way through," said Strom. He was snarling as he looked at Cinder, as if this were her fault. "If this is a trap, it's a good one. They could kill us all in a heartbeat while we're stuffed like sausages in these tunnels."

"Cress was supposed to open them," she said. "They should have been down by now. Unless . . ." Unless Cress and Thorne had failed. Unless they'd been caught. "What time is it?"

She looked at Strom, but he had no idea. He didn't have a clock in his head, either.

Cress was supposed to set all of the barricades surrounding the city to open at once, to keep enthusiastic revolutionaries from sneaking into the city too soon and winding up dead or giving away their surprise. Had Cress failed, or were they early? Kai was still reciting his vows. Cinder shoved down her rising panic.

Strom started to growl. "I smell something."

The surrounding soldiers turned their noses up, sniffing the air.

"Something synthetic," said Strom. "Something Earthen. A machine."

Cinder pressed a hand against the bars, but the soldiers pulled her away, forming a protective wall between her and the barricade. As if she was worth protecting.

Cinder tried not to be annoyed.

Footsteps thumped in the tunnel beyond the gate, growing louder. A kicked pebble skittered along the ground. A flashlight came into view, though the carrier was still cast in shadow.

The beam darted over the gathered soldiers and the figure froze.

The soldiers snarled.

"Well," she said. "What a menacing bunch *you* are."

Cinder's heart sputtered. "Iko!" she cried, trying to shove her way through, but the bodies blocking her were unshovable.

Iko moved closer and Cinder was able to catch her in the beam of her own light. She gasped and stopped struggling. Iko's right arm was hanging limp again and there were bullet holes and ripped synthetic tissue and dead wires all over her body. Her left ear was missing.

"Oh, Iko . . . what happened?"

"More stupid Lunar guards, that's what happened. He cornered me in the basement of the med-clinic and did this. I had to play dead until he left me alone. Good thing they have no idea how to kill an android here."

"Iko. I'm so sorry."

Iko waved her away with her good arm. "I don't feel like talking about it. Are you being held prisoner right now, or are these bullies on our side?"

"They're on our side."

Iko's attention swooped over the wolves again. "Are you sure?"

"Not entirely," said Cinder. "But they're the army Scarlet and Winter recruited and they're the best we've got. They haven't eaten anybody yet."

Strom smirked at her around his protruding fangs.

"Iko, what time is it? Shouldn't the gates be open by now?"

"We're right on schedule. T minus seventeen seconds, by my—"

The sound of machinery groaned and creaked inside the stone walls. The grate began to descend into the rocky ground.

Iko's lips puckered. "Cress's timing is off, not mine."

Cinder exhaled with relief.

While the grate disappeared, the wolves returned to formation, hands locked behind their backs, chins lifted. It was the most professional Cinder had seen them, making them look more like men than monsters. And very, very much like soldiers.

As soon as the grate was low enough, Iko hurled herself over it and fell into Cinder's arms, her good hand flopping against Cinder's back. "You will fix me again, won't you?"

Cinder squeezed her back. "Of course I will. Broken isn't the same as unfixable."

Pulling away, Iko beamed, and the smile was punctuated by a spark flying out of her empty ear cavity. "I love you, Cinder."

Cinder grinned. "I love you too."

"Why are we not moving?" said Strom, his voice rumbling through the tunnel. "We grow impatient to shred Levana and her court into tiny, bite-size pieces. We will suck the marrow from their bones and drink their blood as if it were fine wine."

Iko fixed an uncomfortable look on Cinder. "Good thing they're on our side."

Eighty

WOLF HAD BEEN STRAINING THROUGHOUT THE CORONATION
ceremony. His head ached with the effort, the constant struggle
to control his hunger, but he felt like it was gnawing at him from
the inside out. Though he had devoured the meat given him, it
still raged on. A thousand scents filled his nostrils. Every Earthen.
Every Lunar. Every guard and every thaumaturge, each one
smelling delicious enough that he couldn't help but envision
sinking his teeth into their flesh, tearing their muscles off their
bones, gorging himself on their fat—

The only instinct stronger than his ravenous hunger was the
fear of what the thaumaturge would do to him if he misbehaved.
He could not stand to be subjected to that agony again. The
knife-sharp pain that shot through every muscle and ripped at
every tendon.

His mouth watered, but he swallowed the saliva back. He did
not move.

His attention locked on the queen. Already Emperor Kaito had
knelt before her and accepted the Lunar crown and the title of

king consort, to enthusiastic applause, although by the emperor's expression he could have been accepting a vial of poison.

Now it was the queen's turn.

The emperor raised the crown of the Eastern Commonwealth and repeated the queen's speech, ruminating on the political power held by this position, the obligations and duties, the honors and expectations, the symbolism and history contained within that hunk of metal and a hundred glittering jewels.

Levana knelt. She glowed with anticipation. Her lips trembled with a restrained smile. Her eyes were feasting on the crown as Kai turned toward her.

Wolf swallowed another mouthful of saliva. The queen's flesh was the most tempting of any of them, sweetened by the knowledge that she was his mistress and his enemy. She had commanded that Wolf be taken from his family. She had ordered that he become this monster. It was at her word that the thaumaturges tortured him.

He would devour her heart if ever he had the chance.

"Do you swear," said Kai, "to govern the peoples of the Eastern Commonwealth according to the laws and customs as laid down by generations of past rulers, to use all the power bestowed on you to further justice, to be merciful, to honor the inherent rights of all peoples, to respect the peace between all nations, to rule with kindness and patience, and to seek the wisdom and council of our peers and brethren? Do you promise all this to do today and for all the days of your reign as empress of the Eastern Commonwealth, before all the witnesses of the earth and heavens?"

She was watching the crown, not the emperor. "I do," she breathed.

Kai's expression was dark. He hesitated, holding the crown aloft. His arms were shaking.

Wolf watched as Kai forced himself to set the crown on Levana's head. She shut her eyes, her expression tantamount to euphoria.

"By the power given to me by the citizens of the Eastern Commonwealth and our allies in the Earthen Union, as the emperor of the Eastern Commonwealth, I do proclaim you—" He paused. Waited. Wolf could hear the hope shriveling inside him and he thought he understood the temptation to wait a second more, *one second more…*

The second passed, and Kai set his face in stone.

"—Empress Levana of the Eastern Commonwealth. From this day until the day that one or both of us shall die, you are my wife and I will share with you my throne."

His voice cracked on the last word. Kai tore his hands away from the crown as if it had burned him.

The crowd erupted, streamers and flower petals emerging from hidden pockets, turning the somber, sacred affair into a cacophony of noise. Levana stood. Arms outstretched, she paced to the edge of the dais, accepting the torrential praise of the Lunar aristocrats.

Before she could speak, the triumphant cheers were interrupted by a shrill screech, the sound stabbing at Wolf's ears like needles burrowing into his brain. He crouched down, snarling. The audience cowered. The noise erupted from everywhere at once.

Wolf lifted his head. This was his chance. Though the sound had turned his vision white, his oversensitive ears making him want to fall to the ground in convulsions, his hatred for the queen was stronger than the pain.

He lunged forward, his vision full of her and her most fragile spots. Her throat. Her stomach.

He heard a war cry. A guard dove in front of him, blocking his path. Wolf slashed at him with his newly sharpened nails and grabbed the guard's knife from the scabbard at his side. He raised the knife over his shoulder.

The guard's yell had drawn attention, even over the screeching. The queen spun as Wolf's hand whipped forward.

Agony locked down on him all at once, like searing metal vises clamping around his fingers, his wrist, his arm. He released the knife half a moment too soon, knowing it was wrong the second his frozen fingers were empty. The blade grazed the queen's neck when it should have lodged into her heart, and buried itself in the heavy draperies behind the altar.

Wolf crumpled to the ground, blinded by the torrent of pain that cut through his flesh, ripping his mind apart.

The noise stopped and, with it, the torment.

The sudden absence was like a vacuum sucking out every other sound from the great hall. They were left in crystallized silence, hundreds of bodies paralyzed from shock.

Wolf lay gasping on the ground, wishing he were dead.

He knew the chance would not come again. He knew his punishment had only begun.

Levana was also panting, her eyes ablaze. Her lips looked more red than usual, matched by the blood that was beading up on the side of her neck. "Control him!"

"Yes, My Queen," said Mistress Bement. "It won't happen again, My Queen."

Then, cutting through the heady silence, came a voice. The palace paused to listen. Wolf focused on the ceiling, wondering if the pain had made him delirious.

It was Cinder's voice.

"Hello, dearest Aunt Levana," she said, her tone light and taunting. "I'm sorry to interrupt, but I wanted to make sure I had your *full* attention. First, allow me to congratulate you. It seems you finally have everything you've always wanted. Now, it's my turn."

There was a long pause. The speakers crackled.

Cinder's voice was no longer jovial when she said, "You have ten minutes to come to the front gates of your palace and surrender."

That was all.

The people waited for more. More taunting. More threats. More explanation. But the message was over.

Levana looked visibly shaken, while the emperor looked ready to burst out laughing.

Then Kai's gaze landed on Wolf and the grin fell. His brow twitched with concern.

Wolf glowered and moved to stand on his weak legs, glad when the thaumaturge didn't prevent it.

"It's a trick!" Levana screamed, her voice fragmented. "She can do *nothing* to me!"

A patter of hurried footsteps broke through the queen's outrage. They came through one of the side entrances, Head Thaumaturge Aimery Park flanked by two guards.

A snarl tried to rip out of Wolf's throat and he barely slammed it down again. This man had killed his mother.

"What?" snapped the queen.

"We've been informed that since the security breach occurred, our system has been neglecting to relay information from the tunnels—"

"*Quickly*, Aimery."

His mouth turned down. "They are inside the city, My Queen. All eight of our barricades are down."

"Who is inside the city?"

"The cyborg. Civilians from the outer sectors. Even some of our own soldiers have joined them."

Levana was hyperventilating, burning with rage. "The next person who uses the word *cyborg* in my presence will be losing a limb." She took in a sharp breath. "Why haven't they been stopped?"

"Our resources are thin, Your Majesty. So many of our men were sent to the outer sectors to tame the uprisings. We cannot send reinforcements to meet these rebels without weakening our position here in the palace."

Gathering her skirt in her hands, Levana drew her shoulders so close to her neck that a spot of blood was left in the crease. "Fine," she hissed. "This little rebellion will end here."

"Also, My Queen, we found this in the system control center after we discovered that our security had been tampered with." Aimery held up a portscreen. "It would appear that it belongs to none other than our honored king consort."

Levana's gaze spoke of murder as she turned to Emperor Kaito.

"I was wondering where that had gotten off to," he said, his mouth twitching with a challenge. "And here I spent all morning looking for it."

Levana's nostrils flared, her expression vicious and calculating. She grabbed the portscreen from Aimery and threw it at the altar. The plastic casing shattered.

"This celebration is over," she said, her voice amplified by speakers around the great hall as she faced the audience. "It appears that some of my subordinates have chosen this night to incite what they see as a rebellion. But do not be alarmed—I am sure it's little more than a silly demonstration." She was slowly claiming control over her emotions again. "For your safety, I must ask that all of you, as my distinguished guests, remain seated while I see to the disturbance."

A rustle passed through the crowd.

"Wait," said a man's voice, speaking from the rows of Earthens. "You can't expect us to stay in this room while the palace is under attack. This is your war, not ours. I demand to be allowed to return to my ship at once."

The man had an Earthen-European accent, and a vision of the red-haired girl flashed through Wolf's thoughts. He frowned, searching for the man in the crowd as a thrum of agreement rose up from the other Earthens.

Levana's lips drew back. "You will stay here," she said, each word hard and cold as an ice cube, "until I give you permission to leave."

All at once, the Earthen dissent hushed. Levana directed her attention to the guards. "Bar all the doors. No one is to leave this room until I allow it." She glanced at Wolf and snapped her fingers. "That one stays at my side. He will make the perfect shield should I need one."

"My Queen," said one of the guards, "we must insist that you allow us to escort you to safety. The lava tubes beneath the city—"

"Absolutely not," Levana seethed. "These are my people. This is my kingdom. I will not abandon them now."

She started marching toward the main exit, but Kai followed beside her. "These Earthens aren't yours to lock up. We aren't *hostages.*"

"Are you sure about that, Husband?" Levana snapped her fingers at two of the nearest guards. "Take him back to the others."

They hastened to obey, dragging Kai away from the queen and toward the group of brainwashed Earthens. "Release me!" Kai yelled. "I have as much right to give orders now as you do, to any Lunar guard or soldier."

Levana laughed, and she would have sounded entertained if it hadn't been borderline hysterical. "I hope you don't believe *that*."

Wolf was standing right next to Kai as he was pulled away from the queen, but the knowledge of the thaumaturge watching his movements kept him from stepping forward in the emperor's defense. A shudder rumbled through him at the mere thought of earning her disapproval again.

When the queen beckoned him to follow, he did.

Eighty-One

THEY SENT SCOUTS AHEAD TO CONFIRM THERE WASN'T AN ambush waiting for them at the maglev's platform. It was Strom's idea, and while Cinder was a little annoyed to see someone else taking charge, it also felt nice to have another leader considering strategy and making sure Cinder wasn't about to make a stupid tactical error. It was the sort of thing Wolf would have done, if he'd been there.

No, she didn't want to think about Wolf. She'd had to tell Scarlet about how they were separated as soon as they were brought back to Artemisia and how she didn't have any idea what had become of him. The memory opened up a wound that was still too fresh, one she didn't have time to let heal.

She tried to still her thrumming pulse, focusing on the allies she still had. Iko was by her side again. Scarlet was off in one of the other tunnels along with another group of soldiers and civilians. Thorne and Cress were in the palace and, if the removal of the barricades was an indication, they were still safe. Winter and Jacin were making their way through the nearby sectors, recruiting as many reinforcements as they could.

She felt like she was playing one of Cress's strategy games. All her pawns were in place and her final attack was about to begin.

A hand slipped into hers. Iko, offering one last moment of comfort.

A low howl echoed down the stifling tunnel.

The signal.

Cinder gave Iko's hand a squeeze, then waved her arm. Time to move.

They slipped forward onto the empty platform, where the netscreens were announcing that the coronation had ended. Levana was empress.

They entered the stairwell, pushing toward the daylight. Though manufactured evening would soon be forced upon the domes, real daylight could be seen off the horizon, a faint sliver of their burning sun.

Sunrise.

It was beautiful.

Their footsteps pounded against the stone streets of Artemisia. She had expected the streets to be as empty as they had been before, but as the sound of their march echoed off the mansion walls and through the manicured gardens, silhouettes were drawn to the windows.

She tensed, readying for a surprise attack. But one of the wolves muttered, "Servants."

Looking closer, she saw that he was right. Dressed in simple clothing, eyes overflowing with fear, these were the lower classes who lived in the shadows of the white city and attended to the needs and whims of their masters.

Cinder hoped some of them might be brave enough to fight. After all, now was the time to show it. But to her disappointment, most of the servants disappeared back into seclusion. She tried not to be resentful. No doubt they'd suffered from years of punishments and brainwashing.

It occurred to her that this might be the first they'd heard of the insurgence at all.

The palace came into view, shimmering and majestic.

"Alphas!" yelled Strom, his voice carrying over the clomping footsteps. "Spread out and surround the palace. We'll come at it from every open street."

They were a well-oiled machine, and watching the certainty with which the packs divided, each leading their regiment of civilians down various side streets, gave Cinder a chill. Though the people looked afraid, they also took confidence from the beastly men leading them. It was the type of confidence she wasn't sure she could have inspired on her own.

As they reached the gates of the palace, the clomp of their footsteps halted.

No one was in sight. Even the guard tower was empty. The heavy iron gates were wide open, beckoning them forward. It was as if Levana had no idea she was under siege—or like she was too confident to heed Cinder's threats.

Or maybe it was a trap.

The gilded doors of the castle were shut tight.

Cinder emerged from the front line of her army, stepping before the open gates. There was an energy coursing through her, an impatience humming across her skin. Strom and Iko stayed at her side, ready to protect her if an attack came from one of the palace windows.

Cinder scanned the sparkling windows but saw no sign of life. Anticipation wrapped around her body like a rope, growing tighter by the moment. She felt as if she were teetering on the edge of a cliff, waiting to be pushed off.

Glancing down the front line, she watched as the groups that had split off emerged, filling up the intersections of every city street. The soldiers waited in perfect military formation. Training and willpower turned them into ferocious statues, but she noticed the twitch of a muscle, the flexing of a fist, eagerness sizzling beneath their skin.

Behind them, thousands of civilians waited. Less intimidating, less prepared, but no less determined. She saw Scarlet's red hair in the crowd.

Not everyone who had joined them had come from LW-12. Some had come on faith, because of a couple videos and a promise that their true queen had returned. Some had been encouraged by the messengers Cinder had sent. Some, she hoped, were still coming.

Inhaling deeply, Cinder stretched her thoughts thin, reaching for all the electrical pulses within her reach, and slipped her will into her allies. It was what she should have done in RM-9, before Aimery had seized control. She told herself it was a protection against Levana and her thaumaturges. So long as a civilian was under *her* control, then the queen could not have them.

But she also knew that she would use them, if she had to.

She would sacrifice them, even. If she had to.

She had ordered the strongest of her allies to do the same thing—to seize control of their comrades now, before Levana and her court had the chance. They couldn't control everyone, but she had to believe that neither could Levana. Cinder needed enough people to overwhelm her defenses. It had to be enough. They had to be enough.

"If Levana does not surrender," Cinder yelled into the eerie silence, "we will take the palace by force. There are multiple entrances on this main floor. Take them all. Break the windows. But do not forget that the queen and her entourage are inside." She scanned the windows again, unnerved that there was still no sign of opposition. A feeling of dread stirred in the pit of her stomach.

She was confident in their plan, but not *that* confident. They had made it to the queen's doorstep without a hint of resistance beyond the barricaded tunnels. Something should have happened by now.

"Thaumaturges will try to manipulate you," she continued. "Kill them if you have the chance, as they will not hesitate to kill you, or use you to kill your own friends and neighbors. The queen's guards are trained soldiers, but their minds are weak. Use that to your advantage. Above all else, remember why you are here today. By this night, I will be your queen, and you will no longer be slaves!"

A cheer pulsed through the courtyard, coupled with a bone-chilling howl that coursed through Cinder's body. She raised an arm, telling her allies to hold. She prepared herself to let it fall— the signal to charge. She watched Iko from the corner of her eye, waiting for her to say that the ten minutes were up.

Her eye caught on movement.

The palace doors were opening.

The soldiers dropped into fighting stances. A low growl rumbled through the ground, shaking the soles of Cinder's stolen boots. As the doors spread, they revealed a glowing silhouette. Not a long-coated thaumaturge or even the slender figure of the queen.

A mutant. One of the queen's soldiers.

A hand grabbed Cinder's elbow and hauled her back behind the front line.

The soldier stepped onto the palace steps. His movements were graceful and precise. There was a familiarity to him that Cinder struggled to place, something different from the soldiers surrounding her now. The same malformed face. The same protruding teeth. Angry eyes flashing at the crowd. He was dressed not in the drab, utilitarian uniforms of the regiment, but in a uniform more fitting to the royal guard—all decorum.

Her breath caught.

It was Wolf. Wolf, repugnant and beastly, who stopped at the edge of the steps.

Her thoughts darted to Scarlet, but she dared not turn to see Scarlet's reaction.

Another form emerged from the castle. Queen Levana herself. Thaumaturge Aimery followed and, spilling out behind them, thaumaturges in red and black, forming a line of haughty expressions and amused sneers, hands tucked into their belled sleeves. The embroidered runes glinted in the first natural daylight they had seen in weeks.

For the first time, Cinder had no lie detector to tell her that the queen's glamour was an illusion. She had no evidence that this was really Wolf, either, and not someone glamoured to look like him.

But she also had no reason to doubt it.

She felt again for the strings of power connecting her to the men and women she had taken control of. She had never controlled so many at once, and her grip felt delicate and weak.

"'By this night, I will be your queen,'" Levana quoted, smiling her wicked smile, "'and you will no longer be slaves.' What spirited words from the girl who causes death and chaos everywhere she goes." Levana held out her hands, like a peace offering that meant nothing. "Here I am, girl who claims to be Princess

Selene. I will not make you go in search of me. Go ahead. Try to take my crown."

Cinder's eye twitched. Her pulse was racing beneath the surface, but there was calmness at the center of her mind. Maybe because, for the first time, her cyborg brain wasn't breaking down the statistics of the world around her. She could guess that her adrenaline levels were spiking and her blood pressure was worrisome, but without the red stream of warning text, she didn't care.

Arm still raised, she spread her fingers, indicating that her people should hold their attack.

Levana was betting on Cinder's loyalty to Wolf. She must believe that Cinder would not attack so long as he could get caught in the crossfire. That she would not dare to put her friend in danger.

But she couldn't even be sure he was her friend anymore. Was he still Wolf, or was he something else now? A monster, a predator?

She clenched her jaw, recognizing the hypocrisy of her thoughts. He was the same now as the soldiers who stood beside her, ready to fight and die for their freedoms. Whatever Wolf had become, she had to believe he was still her ally.

The true question was whether or not Wolf, her friend, her ally, her teacher, was a worthwhile sacrifice to win this war.

"*Princess*," Strom growled, "she's brought reinforcements."

Cinder dared not take her gaze from Levana, though curiosity twitched inside her.

"I smell them approaching. A dozen packs, maybe more, along with their masters. We'll soon be surrounded."

Cinder kept her expression composed. "This is your last chance," she said, holding her aunt's gaze across the courtyard.

"Proclaim before all these witnesses that I am Selene Blackburn, the rightful heir to the Lunar throne. Give me your crown, and I will let you and your followers live. No more lives have to be lost."

Levana's lips curved, bloodred against her pale skin. "Selene is dead. I am the queen of Luna, and you are nothing but an impostor."

Cinder waited one full breath before she returned the smile. "I thought you'd say that."

Then she let her arm fall.

Eighty-Two

CINDER'S ARMY SURGED FORWARD, THE CIVILIANS POOLING through the open gates while the soldiers ran for the fence, scaling to the top and hurling themselves into the gardens on the other side.

The queen did not flinch. Her thaumaturges did not stir.

They had reached the base of the marble steps when Levana raised her hand. Her thaumaturges closed their eyes.

It was a moment of contrasts.

The mutant soldiers, their first line of attack, fell as one. Their enormous bodies crumpled to the ground like forgotten toys, and a hundred men howled from what pain Cinder could only imagine. She had heard such inhuman noises only once, when she herself had tortured Thaumaturge Sybil Mira—driving her to insanity.

The civilians whose minds were protected by Cinder and those who were strongest with their gift pushed forward, heaving themselves over the wolf soldiers as well as they could. But the others began to stumble and halt as the queen claimed them. Many collapsed, their weapons thudding to the ground. Those under Cinder's control swarmed around them and over them, tripping over fallen bodies, charging forward with weapons raised.

The thaumaturges, Cinder thought, mentally coaxing them toward the distinctive red and black coats. Every dead thaumaturge would equal a dozen soldiers or citizens returned to their side.

But the rush of civilians was met with resistance as the queen's palace guards formed a wall, dividing the queen and her entourage from the attackers who barreled toward them.

They crashed into one another like a river into a dam. Steel rang. Wooden spears thumped and splintered. Cries of war and pain reverberated down the streets.

Cinder shuddered and moved to step forward, to join the melee and cut her own path through to the queen—but her body wouldn't move. Her limbs seemed stuck in mud.

Her pulse skipped.

No.

She had not expected—had not thought—

Clenching her teeth, she tried to shake off the manipulation that was being pressed into her thoughts. She imagined the sparks of electricity lighting up inside her brain, the twist of energy as Levana turned her own mind against her. She had always shaken it off before. She had always managed to escape, to be stronger. Her cyborg brain could override the effects of—

A shiver raced down her brain.

Her cyborg brain was broken.

No. *No.* How could she defend the minds of others when she couldn't protect her own thoughts from the queen?

She gritted her teeth. If she could free one limb, prove to her body that it could be done . . .

She groaned and fell to one knee. Her body pulsed with unspent energy and she felt the sudden snap. Her tenuous control over the citizens dissolved. The surrounding howls of pain burrowed into Cinder's ears.

Within seconds, those allies were taken from her too.

The battle ended before it had truly begun.

Cinder sat panting from the exertion of trying to rid herself of Levana's mind control, and even still her limbs felt heavy and uncoordinated. The screams of her soldiers dwindled into whimpers and groans of the dying. Even from that brief collision, the iron smell of blood tainted the air.

Levana started to laugh. Delighted and shrill, the sound was as painful to listen to as the screams of a hundred warriors.

"What is this?" said the queen, clapping her hands together. "Why, I had been looking forward to a battle of skill, young *princess*. But it seems you will not put up the fight I'd been expecting." She laughed again. Raising a hand, she stroked her fingernails through Wolf's hair, a gesture that was both endearing and possessive.

"There is an easy treat for you, my pet. Already caught in a snare."

He growled, his enlarged teeth flashing as he prowled down the steps. The guards parted for him and he stepped over the collapsed citizens as if he didn't even see them.

Cinder shivered. She had lost count of how many times she'd faced those vibrant green eyes, both as an enemy and as a friend. But never before had she been helpless.

She tried to shake her head. To plead with Wolf, or whatever piece of Wolf was left inside the creature.

"Hey, your queenliness! Over here!"

Cinder's eyes widened. *Iko.*

A gunshot ricocheted through the crowd. Levana stumbled.

Cinder saw the blood spray on the massive golden doors and there was a moment—the tiniest of moments—in which she was overjoyed. She'd been shot—the queen was shot!

But it was Wolf who roared. Levana had ducked behind him. The bullet had hit near his hip and already his fine uniform was darkening with blood.

Iko cried out, horrified.

Levana snarled and her anger tightened around Cinder and the crowd like a noose. Her control was strangling. Suffocating.

Wolf charged, not toward Cinder, but Iko. She could see it in his eyes, the animal instinct. Attacking his attacker.

Cinder's stomach roiled. She couldn't move. Couldn't do anything. Could hardly even breathe. Her lungs burned, but she was trapped.

Wolf reached Iko while she stood gripping the gun, unsure what to do. His claws swiped at her, tearing more skin fibers from her already-shredded abdomen. She shrieked and scrambled backward, unwilling to shoot him again. He tackled her to the ground. His jaws sank into her synthetic arm and the gun clattered beside her. A wire sparked in his mouth and he let go.

Cinder pleaded with her control panel to wake up, to fight back, to be stronger than her, to *win*—

"*I am Princess Selene.*"

The disembodied voice fell over the crowd. Determined. Familiar, yet not.

The dome above them darkened. Like a storm moving in, the glass tinted to near blackness. On the surface, a series of squares brightened. Blue light at first, before the video began to crystallize.

Levana's voice screeched all around them. "*You are an impostor!*"

Levana looked up. Her guards and thaumaturges tensed.

"And I am ready to claim what's mine. People of Artemisia, this is your chance. Renounce Levana as your queen and swear fealty to me, or I swear that when I wear that crown, every person in this room will be punished for their betrayal."

The throne room came into view, seen from Cinder's perspective. The servants and the thaumaturges had not changed position. Neither had Kai, in the front row, terrified and desperate.

"That is enough. Kill her."

Then there was Levana, but not Levana. She was recognizable only by the red wedding gown.

Beneath the glamour, her face was disfigured from ridges and scars, sealing shut her left eye. The destroyed skin continued down her jaw and neck, disappearing beneath the collar of her dress. Her hair was thinner and a lighter shade of brown, and great chunks were missing where the scars had reached around to the back of her head. More scars could be seen on her left arm where her silk sleeve didn't hide them.

Burns.

They were scars created from burns.

Cinder knew it with absolute certainty.

A wretched scream sent a shock of cold water over Cinder's body.

"Turn it off! Turn it off!" Levana shrieked. She spun away from the video in the sky, grasping the arms and faces of the thaumaturges nearest her and forcing them to turn away. "Don't look! Stop looking! I'll have your eyes ripped out, every one of you!"

Cinder realized she was no longer paralyzed from Levana's mind control—it was her own shock keeping her rooted to the ground.

It was working. The queen was losing control. She was being forced to see the truth beneath her own glamour, and she could do nothing to stop it.

The video dissolved into a chaos of bullets and screams, blood and bodies.

Levana stared out at the people who were no longer under her control. Her glamour was gone. She was wretched and disfigured and, in that moment, afraid.

A gun fired, but missed. The bullet embedded itself in the palace doors. Someone behind Cinder cursed. Eyes widening, she swiveled her head around. It was Scarlet, her red hair like a spotlight in the crowd. She reloaded her gun and took aim again.

Levana stumbled back two, three steps, then she turned and ran back into her palace, leaving her entourage of shocked thaumaturges behind. Leaving Wolf too, still hunkered over Iko's body, though she was no longer moving. His focus was on Scarlet, his deformed face twisted in recognition and horror.

For a moment, Cinder found herself immobilized by her own scattered thoughts. She didn't know what to do. Iko wasn't moving. She didn't know if she could trust Wolf. The queen had run, but her path to the palace was still blocked, and there were still enough thaumaturges to control most of the soldiers and the civilians, but everyone was shocked, motionless, reeling from the video—

A howl silenced her racing thoughts.

Cinder gasped, unable to tell where it had come from. She didn't know if it was one of the soldiers who had joined her side, or if it was one of the other packs Strom had mentioned would soon be surrounding them.

The howl was joined by another, and another. Then everything dissolved into chaos.

Eighty-Three

STANDING ON THE DAIS ON WHICH HE'D BEEN CROWNED THE king of Luna, Kai crossed his arms and scowled into the audience. The leaders and diplomats from the Earthen Union were stone-faced in an attempt to hide the anger lurking under the surface. Levana had locked them in the great hall with guards posted outside each door along with hundreds of Lunar aristocrats, who smirked and tittered at the Earthens as though they were exotic animals—adorable and fascinating and harmless.

He could hear the distant sounds of fighting and stampeding feet, but they were muffled by the thick stone walls.

The threat of revolt and the massacre of thousands of their countrymen was not enough to taint the Lunars' revelry. They were acting as though they were at a circus. Cheering when the sounds of fighting got louder outside. Placing bets on different thaumaturges and who would have the highest death count when it was done. Making crude jokes about who among them would be going without cashmere wraps and blueberry wine next season if the laborers from the outer sectors didn't stop playing at war games and get back to work, lazy buffoons that they were.

Listening to it had Kai's vision blazing red. He didn't realize his hands had been tightened into trembling fists until Torin settled a hand on his shoulder. Kai started, then forced his fists open and took in a calming breath. "They have no idea," he said. "They have no clue what it's like in the outer sectors, no gratitude at all for the workers that allow them to have the luxuries they do. They believe they're entitled to everything they've been given."

"I agree, it's sickening and perhaps even unforgivable," said Torin, "but we should consider that they have been kept in ignorance as much as those in the outer sectors have."

Kai snarled. He was not in the mood to feel sympathetic toward these people. "It would appear the honeymoon is over."

"I must say, the queen does have a flair for the dramatic." Torin cast a sly grin toward Kai. "So, it seems, does her niece."

He smothered a twitch of pride. Cinder did have a knack for making an entrance. "What have we learned?"

"All of the exits have been bolted shut from the outside, and if the Lunars are to be believed, there are two guards posted at each exit."

"Guards are easily manipulated, aren't they?" Kai gestured toward the audience. "These Lunars—do you think they could control the guards through the doors? Cinder always said she could detect people through doors, but I don't know if she could also manipulate them. But if we could get some of these Lunars to manipulate the guards into unlatching the doors, then clear a path down to the docks ... maybe we could get everyone to safety."

"The docks would offer shelter and the potential for escape should Linh-dàren fail," said Torin, "but I can't imagine these Lunars choosing to help us anytime soon."

Kai blinked. It was the first time he'd heard anyone refer to Cinder as Linh-dàren—a title of high honor.

"You're right," he said. "They won't help us, and they're idiots for it. Have they even stopped to think why Levana locked them in here too? They think they're invincible because they're under her protection, but Levana doesn't care about them. She'll use them as quickly as anyone if she thinks it will further her cause."

A distant rumble shook the palace, followed by yelling, throaty and furious, from what could have been thousands of voices. Then there was a rain of gunfire.

Kai shuddered. Even knowing Levana had gone to meet Cinder and whatever allies she'd persuaded to join her, it hadn't seemed real. A revolution, a battle . . . it was incomprehensible. But now there were guns and people were dying and they were trapped.

"That was a bomb!" screamed a representative from Eastern Europe. "They're bombing the palace! They're going to kill us all!"

A group of nearby Lunars started to titter and cry out in mocking fear, "*A bomb, oh stars, not a bomb!*"

Kai narrowed his eyes. He didn't know if the sound had been caused by an explosive or not, but his companion's fear had given him an idea.

The portscreen Levana had thrown was still on the floor beside the altar. He marched toward it and gathered together the pieces. A couple plastic panels had snapped off and there was a permanent dent in the corner, but it hummed to life when he turned it on.

As the screen brightened, though, it was jumbled and pixilated, full of black spots and broken icons. He cursed, sweeping his fingers over the screen, jabbing at the controls. Nothing changed.

"Your Majesty?" Torin crouched beside him.

Kai held up the broken portscreen. "What would Cinder do? How would she fix it?"

A crease formed across Torin's brow. "You want to comm for help?"

"Sort of." He buried a hand in his hair, thinking, thinking. He pictured Cinder at her booth at the market. She would have been surrounded by tools and spare parts. She would have known what to do. She would have—

He hopped to his feet, his pulse racing, and whapped the corner of the portscreen hard on the top of the altar. Torin jerked back.

Kai looked again and let out an excited whoop. Half the screen had cleared.

He opened a comm.

"How did you do that?" said Torin.

"I don't know," he said, typing in a hasty message, "but you'd be surprised how often that works."

A bout of laughter pulled his attention back to the audience. A group of Lunars had formed a circle around one of the servants who had been locked inside with them. The servant girl was dancing, but with jerky, uncomfortable movements. There were tears on her face, even though her eyes were shut and her expression was twisted in an attempt to imagine herself elsewhere. The look made Kai's heart shrivel in his chest.

Somehow he knew this was not an unusual occurrence for the girl. He wondered if she had ever gone an entire day without someone else's will being forced upon her limbs.

"That's not a waltz at all!" a Lunar cried, smacking his companion on a shoulder. "Let me have a try at it. I can make her much more graceful than that."

"She needs a partner, doesn't she?" someone else said. "Let's get one of those Earthens up here and have ourselves a bit of puppet theater while we wait."

"Hey—how about that sweet young girl from the Commonwealth, the one that's related to the cyborg? Remember her from the trial? Where is she?"

Kai heard a whimper. Cinder's stepmother and stepsister were kneeling on the floor between two rows of chairs, clutching each other in an attempt to go unnoticed.

He ripped his gaze away and clipped the port back to his belt. "That's enough," he said, stalking toward the group. "Release the servant at once!"

"Ah, it looks as though the pretty emperor wants to dance too."

The cheers that greeted Kai sounded cruel, but to his relief, no one took control of his body, even as he put an arm around the servant girl and hugged her against his side. She stopped dancing at once and slumped against his body, exhausted.

"You are addressing your king," he said, enunciating each word. He was glad that he still wore the spindly Lunar crown, even though *king consort* was not a title that carried much power. He could hope that not everyone knew that, though. "You don't seem to comprehend the situation. We are all prisoners in this room, each and every one of us. That also makes us allies, whether we like it or not." He jabbed a finger toward the back wall. "Once Levana realizes she's overpowered—and *she is*—she will retreat. And where do you think she's going to come?"

He fixed his gaze on those closest to him. They were smirking. Humored by Kai's outrage.

"She didn't lock us in here for our *protection*, or because she wanted us to go on having a big party. She's keeping us here as her reserves. Once her guards fall, you are going to be her next line of defense. She will use your bodies as shields. She will turn you into weapons. She will sacrifice every person in this room and she won't feel a hint of remorse so long as *she* survives. Don't you get it? She doesn't care about you. All she cares about is having more bodies at her disposal when she needs them."

The eyes around him still glimmered. It was impossible to tell if his words were having an impact, but he continued, "We don't have to sit here and wait for her to come back. With your help, we can get out of this room. We can all get down to the royal port where we'll be safe and where Levana won't be able to use us to fight her battles."

A man standing not far away clicked his tongue. "Oh, poor pathetic Earthen king, talking to us as if we are powerless little children who will bow to him just because he wears a crown. We are not allies, Your Grace, nor would we ever stoop to consider ourselves *equals* with your kind. Our queen may have seen the benefit of making you her husband and crowning you our king, but in truth, you and your companions are hardly worthy of washing the spaces between our toes."

The room erupted into laughter. The man who had spoken smirked at Kai while his words were rewarded with shouted suggestions of all sorts of other vile things the Earthens were not worthy of.

"Fine," Kai growled, his tone icy. "Allow me to persuade you."

Unlatching his portscreen, he pulled up a holographic map of Luna, enlarging it to hang over their heads. The image filled up the space within the great hall, the moon's cratered surface touching the lofted ceilings. Kai adjusted the map so everyone had a good view of Artemisia Central and the eight city sectors surrounding it. Then he lit up the space fleet that he had ordered to take up position in neutral space earlier that day—sixty ships that had reacted swiftly to his comm. Sixty ships that were making their way toward Luna's capital.

"Each of these Earthen spaceships is carrying weapons capable of destroying your biodomes. We have enough ammunition to reduce your entire country to rubble."

It was a lie. Not every ship was armed, but there was enough, he hoped, to still do significant damage. To make them afraid. The energy in the room changed. The smiles became hesitant. The laughter uncertain.

"While you were busy taunting this poor servant, I sent a comm to my military with the order to open fire as soon as they're within range. But I will revoke that command once my people have been safely relocated to the ports."

A woman giggled, but it was high-pitched and anxious. "You would not dare risk an attack while you yourself are in the palace! You and all your Earthen friends would be dead."

Kai grinned. "You're right. I wouldn't attack Artemisia Central. But if I'm not mistaken, most of *your* homes aren't in the central dome, are they? Most of them are in one of these outlying city sectors, right?"

The glowing ships in the holograph ticked closer. Closer.

The aristocrats exchanged looks, showing the first signs of nervousness. It was as if they were silently daring one another to call his bluff, but no one wanted to be the one to do it.

"If I'm not mistaken," Kai said, "we have less than twenty minutes before the ships arrive. If you ever want to see your homes again, I suggest we move fast."

"THIS IS NOT GOOD," SAID THE NASALLY VOICE CRESS HAD come to think of, somewhat unoriginally, as Sinus, the queen's moronic computer technician.

Honestly. If Sybil had let her stay on Luna, Cress could have taken over this guy's job when she was ten.

"This is very, very bad," he continued, his voice trembling with impending doom.

"Just make it stop," yelled a deeper masculine voice. Cress was pretty sure it was the same guard who had been stationed outside the hall before.

"I can't! The video already played. Do you want me to *unplay* it?" Sinus groaned. "She . . . she's going to kill me. The queen will have me executed for this."

Withholding a sigh, Cress tried her best to roll her ankle. A cramp was starting to develop in her left calf and she had a feeling it was going to come on quick if she didn't have a chance to stretch the muscle soon. She managed to move her ankle a little, but the small movement only reminded her muscles how enclosed they were in this tiny alcove.

The technician knew it was too late. He knew he couldn't stop the video from playing. Why didn't he *leave* already?

"Well?" said the guard. "Did she set up any more surprises for us?"

"What more do you need? That video—the queen will be . . ." He didn't finish, but Cress sensed the shudder in his voice.

Having seen the video herself at the mansion, Cress knew the vision wouldn't soon leave them. Levana's scarred face, her empty eye socket, her nub of an ear. It was not a face one looked away from, no matter how they wanted to. It was not a face one forgot.

And now they'd all seen it. Cress hoped Levana herself had seen it. She suspected it wouldn't be easy to recover her glamour after a shock like that.

Maybe not, though. Levana had been practicing her deception for a long, long time.

"Have they caught her?" Sinus asked. "The girl who did this? She's . . . she really knew what she was doing."

The comment might have flattered Cress if she hadn't been so uncomfortable. As it was, she just wanted them to go talk about her elsewhere. She was still gripping the handle of the gun Thorne had given to her, and it had imprinted her palm with painful red grooves.

"That's not your problem," the guard growled. "Just get it back to normal. And get rid of that video before—"

He didn't finish. There was no *before*. They were already in the after.

"I'm trying," said Sinus, "but the crossfeeds have all been restructured and it could take days to . . ."

Cress stopped listening, her attention stolen by the cramp in her right calf. She gasped, wrapping her hands around the muscle in an attempt to rub out the tightness.

"What was that?" Sinus asked.

Cress flinched and crawled out of the alcove. The second she was on her feet, she aimed the gun at the technician, then the guard, then back at the technician. For as puny as his voice sounded, she'd been imagining a guy not much older than her, but he looked like he might be in his fifties.

The technician pushed back his chair. The guard reached for his weapon.

"Don't mo—ah!" Cress grimaced as the muscle in her leg tightened again and she fell into the desk. The corner dug into the hip that was still sore from where the statue had fallen on her in the servants' halls. Groaning, she reached down to knead the muscles.

Remembering the gun, she started to lift it again, at the same moment the guard snatched it from her hand. Cress cried out and grabbed for it, but the gun was already out of reach. Whimpering, she went back to rubbing the muscle and raised the now-empty hand in exhausted surrender.

The guard kept his own weapon pinned on her.

"I'm unarmed," she said meekly.

He didn't seem to care.

"Are you . . ." Sinus looked from her to the screens. "Did *you* do this?"

"Yes, sir." She breathed a sigh of relief as the pain began to recede. "And, can I make a suggestion? Because I've been listening to you talk and I have to wonder, if you're sure Levana is going to have you executed for failing to stop the video . . . have you considered joining the other side?"

They both stared at her.

Fisting her hands, Cress pounded at the sides of her leg. She was going to have to start working on her exercise regimes again after this. Or at least stop hiding in such confined spaces.

"I mean it," she said. "I happen to know Princess Selene and she's really nice. She wouldn't have you executed, especially for something that wasn't your fault."

"I'm taking you into custody," said the guard, grabbing her elbow.

"Wait!" she cried, unable to tug away from his grip. "You're not even going to think about it? You would choose execution at the hands of Levana over . . . not execution?"

The guard smirked as he pulled her away from the bank of invisi-screens. "This rebellion is not going to succeed."

"Yes, it is. Levana will be overthrown and Selene will be our new ruler and—"

She was interrupted by an alarm blaring from a screen on the other side of the control center. The guard swiveled toward the sound, pinning Cress against his chest, as if she were a threat with her cramping leg and puffy orange skirt.

"Now what's happening?" the guard yelled.

Sinus was already at the warning screen. He stared slack-jawed for a moment, before he muttered, "I think ... I think we're under attack."

"Obviously we're under attack!"

Sinus shook his head and enlarged a holograph. Above the glittering domes of Artemisia, a regiment of spaceships had breached neutral space and were moving fast toward the city. "Not from the civilians," he said. A drop of sweat fell down his temple. "These are militarized Earthen ships."

They all stared at the ships, watching their blinking lights draw steadily closer. It was Cress who managed to gather her thoughts first. She tried to stand straighter, but the guard had too firm of a grip on her.

"That's right," she said, relieved when her voice didn't tremble. "Princess Selene has allied herself with Earth. If Levana doesn't surrender, we're prepared to destroy you all." She ran her tongue over her parched lips and craned her neck to look at the guard. She hoped she was convincing when she said, "But it's not too late for you to join the winning side."

Eighty-Four

IKO WAS BEGINNING TO COMPREHEND WHY HUMANS CURLED
into the fetal position when they were afraid. On the ground, on
her side, with her nose tucked against her knees and her one
good arm flopped over her head, she never wanted to move again.
Wolf had bitten her already-damaged arm and she could tell
he'd done a fair amount of damage to her abdomen and thighs
too, not that they were in great shape to begin with.

What *was* it about her that attracted razor-sharp claws
and teeth? Bullets too, for that matter. This was an android injus-
tice that needed to be dealt with as soon as this whole revolution
thing was behind them.

A boot stomped inches from her head and she cringed, bundling herself tighter. She didn't want to get up. She didn't want to
move. She wanted her power cell to wind on down so she could
wake fully formed once again, after Cinder had fixed her and—

Cinder.

Cinder didn't have the option of lying comatose in the middle
of her revolution. Cinder was out there, now, in danger.

Whimpering, Iko dared to lower her arm and scan her

surroundings. All around, war cries and screams barraged her audio sensor, and the rumble of charging footsteps thundered into her limbs. She peered through the torrent of legs and weapons—first the wolf soldiers, then the men and women from the outer sectors, gripping their spears and knives. All crashing toward the castle as the thaumaturges tried to take control again.

But there were too many, and the wolves were too difficult to control. That's what Wolf had been telling them from the beginning, hadn't he? The soldiers were meant to be unleashed on Earth—a scourge of death and terror. They were not meant to be prim, proper, well-organized soldiers.

And there were so many of them. More than Cinder had brought through the tunnels. Iko grimaced as a new regiment of soldiers charged into the fray, teeth gnashing. Grabbing at anyone who moved. All around her, mutants wrestled with one another. Blades slashed across throats. Spears bit into flesh.

"All right, Cinder," she whispered, forcing herself to sit up. "I'm coming."

Her internal systems were frayed, her processor a mix of scrambled messages, and she could feel at least two disconnected wires sparking in her stomach. She picked her gun off the ground.

It took forever to find Cinder as Iko weaved in and out of the chaos with her bad arm dangling at her side. She held the gun ready, shooting when she thought she could save someone, ignoring the countless scratches that appeared like magic on her clothes and synthetic skin. What were a few more scratches at this point, anyway? For once she was glad not to have nerve endings. She just hoped her body didn't shut down on her with all the sustained injuries.

By the time she made it to Cinder, she was out of bullets. Thank the stars, Cinder was staying out of the fight for once.

Some of the stone statues lining the courtyard had been knocked over and Cinder was hunkered behind one, watching the battle like she was waiting for the right opportunity to move into it.

Iko slipped down beside her, pressing her back against the statue. "Nice speech earlier."

Starting, Cinder whipped her head around, nearly taking out Iko's button nose with an instinctive punch. She froze just in time. Relief clouded her eyes. "You're all right," she gasped. "Wolf?"

"May have anger management issues. Scarlet?"

Cinder shook her head. "I lost her."

An enemy soldier came from nowhere. Cinder pushed Iko aside and shoved the soldier's head into the statue with her metal fist. The statue cracked, a chunk of stone clattering to the ground, and the soldier collapsed unconscious.

"Cinder, you're bleeding," said Iko.

Cinder glanced down at her shoulder, where the wound they'd bandaged up at the mansion had bled through. She looked unbothered by it as she grabbed Iko's elbow and tugged her into what protective cover the statue could offer. "Levana went back in the palace. I need to get in there."

"Do you think Kai's in there too?"

"Probably."

Iko nodded. "Then I'm going with you."

A trembling scream drew Iko's attention back into the skirmish in time to see a woman from the lumber sector turn her own knife on herself and plunge it into her chest. Iko's eyes widened. She couldn't look away as the woman dropped to her knees, staring openmouthed at her own traitorous hands.

Beside her, Cinder let out a battle cry and rushed toward a thaumaturge. She grabbed a knife out of a guard's hand right before he swung and in the same movement—

Iko recoiled. She'd witnessed enough death already, even if this one was an enemy.

"Iko, come on!"

Lifting her head again, she saw Cinder leap over the fallen thaumaturge and keep running, straight for the palace doors. She was still gripping the guard's knife, but Iko wasn't sure how much of the blood on it was new.

"Right. We'll just kill all the bad guys." Iko looked down at her limp hand, shook it out a little, and watched her fingers wobble uselessly. "Good plan."

Bracing herself, she rushed into the melee, weaving her way between those fallen and fighting. She caught up with Cinder as she sprinted through the yawning doors of the palace. Iko followed her, then skidded to a stop. Her gaze traveled up and up and up, to the top of the massive goddess sculpture centered in the main hall. "Whoa."

"*Iko.*"

She found Cinder panting on the other side of the statue, her attention darting one way and then the other. The bloodied knife was still gripped in her whitened knuckles.

"Which way do you think she went?" Cinder asked.

"Down to the spaceship ports so she could run away, never to be seen again?"

Cinder cut her an unamused look.

"Or maybe to call for backup?"

"Maybe. We need to find Kai. Levana will use him against me if she can."

Iko tugged on a braid, glad that, no matter how bad of a shape her body was in, her hair still looked good. "The coronation was supposed to take place in the great hall. We could start there."

Cinder nodded. "I don't have access to the palace blueprints anymore. Can you lead?"

Iko's internal synapses fired for a few moments before they managed to compute Cinder's words. She recalled all of their planning and plotting, all the diagrams and maps and strategies they'd drawn up. She raised her good hand and pointed. "The great hall is that way."

SCARLET COULD HEAR HER GRANDMOTHER'S VOICE, GENTLE yet firm, as the battle raged around her. She'd already gone through two magazines and she had seen more claw-torn abdomens and tooth-ripped throats than even her nightmares could have shown her. Still, the soldiers kept coming. She knew they had one regiment on their side, but she couldn't begin to guess how many of the soldiers were fighting with her and how many against her, and no matter how many fell, more were always there, ready to replace them.

Afraid she might shoot an ally when every blood-soaked civilian looked like an enemy, Scarlet focused on the obvious targets. The thaumaturges in their maroon and black jackets were easy to spot even in the fray. Every time Scarlet felt her conscience creeping up on her—it was a life, a *human life* she was about to take—she would see one of the civilians put a gun to their own head or stab one of their family members to death, and she would pick a thaumaturge whose face was tight with concentration and all her qualms would disappear.

Hold the gun with both hands, her grandma would tell her. *I know they do it differently in the dramas, but they're idiots. Line up your target using the front and back sights. Don't pull the trigger—squeeze it. It will fire when it's ready.*

The thaumaturge in her sight line stumbled back, a dark spot appearing on her red coat.

Click. Click.

Scarlet reached for her back pocket.

Empty.

She cursed. Shoving the gun into her waistband, she spun around, searching the ground for another weapon. Having been so focused on targeting her enemies, she was surprised to find herself in a sea of bodies and blood.

A drop of sweat slid down her temple.

How many had they lost? It seemed like the fighting had just started. How were there so many already dead? Dismay filled her lungs.

This was a battlefield. A massacre. And she was caught in the middle of it.

She released a shaky breath, wishing she could release her terror along with it. Her grand-mère's voice had disappeared as soon as she'd put away the gun. Now there was only the sound of killing. Screams and war cries. The stench of blood.

Spotting an axe, she bent to pick it up, and didn't realize until she found resistance that the blade was buried in a body. Grimacing, she shut her eyes, gritted her teeth, and pulled it free. She didn't check to see who the body belonged to.

She was exhausted in every way, exhausted halfway to delirium. Her attention fell on a middle-aged woman who at first glance reminded her of Maha, but older. The woman was trembling from shock and her arm was cut and torn—by teeth, Scarlet guessed—and she was using her good hand to drag an injured man to safety.

Scarlet stumbled forward, gripping the axe handle. She should help her.

She went to drop the axe, but then her fingers twitched, which was her first warning. Eyes widening, she looked down at her hand. Her knuckles whitened on the axe handle, gripping it tighter. A shudder ripped through her body.

Someone else had control of her hands.

But they hadn't thought to take her tongue, at least.

"Get away from me!" she screamed, to no one in particular. To anyone close enough to hear. "*Run!*"

The woman paused and looked up. There wasn't enough time. Scarlet's disjointed legs stumbled toward her and she took the axe in both hands and raised it overhead, her muscles flexing under its weight. "*Run!*" she yelled again, panic clawing at her throat, her mind overcome with the horrible reality of being under a thaumaturge's control.

Comprehension filled the woman's face and she scrambled backward. She turned to run, but tripped.

Scarlet screamed in anguish. The woman threw her hands up to protect herself. Scarlet slammed her eyes shut, pushing out tears she hadn't known were there, and her arms swung the axe toward the woman's stomach.

The axe came to a jarring stop, halting mid-swing.

Gasping around her own heartbeat, Scarlet dared to look up.

A form, massive and dark and covered in blood, towered over her. Scarlet whimpered. In relief, in gratitude, in a thousand feelings that didn't come with words. "*Wolf.*"

His eyes were as vibrant green as ever, despite being more sunken than before—a result of his protruding nose and jaw.

Scarlet's arm tried to pull the axe away, but he tore it from her grip.

Her mindless fingers changed tactics, scrabbling for a weakness, though there weren't many. Her thumbs dove for his eye sockets.

Wolf caught her easily, still gripping the axe while his arms came around to smother Scarlet, pinning her arms to her sides. She screamed with frustration, and she wasn't sure if it was her own frustration or that of a thaumaturge screaming through her. Her legs jostled and kicked and stamped, her body writhing against Wolf's iron grip. He was immovable and merciless, bending his body around her like a cocoon.

The thaumaturge gave up, moving on to control an easier victim. Scarlet felt the release like a rubber band snapping inside her limbs. She shivered, melting into Wolf's embrace with a sob.

"Oh stars, oh stars," she cried, burying her face in his chest. "I almost—I would have—"

"You didn't."

His voice a little rougher, but still his.

Planting her hands on his chest, Scarlet pushed herself away and peered up at him. Her breaths were still rattling inside her lungs, the sounds of battle were still echoing in her ears, but she hadn't felt less afraid in days. She reached up, hesitant at first, and brushed her fingers over the prominent new cheekbones, along the unfamiliar ridge of his brow. Wolf grimaced. It was the same face he'd made when she'd first discovered his fangs.

She found the scar on his left eyebrow, and the scar on his mouth, and they were right where she remembered them on the night she'd kissed him aboard the train heading to Paris.

"It is still you, isn't it? They haven't ... changed you?"

She saw his jaw working. "Yes," he choked. Then, "I don't know. I think so." His face crumpled, as if he might start crying, but he didn't. "*Scarlet*. I am so sick of the taste of blood."

She dragged the pad of her thumb along his lower lip, until it collided with one of the sharp canine teeth. "That's good," she said. "We don't serve a whole lot of blood on the farm, so we were going to have to work on your diet, anyway." Noting a smear of dried blood on his cheek, she tried to scrub it away, but quickly gave up. "Have you seen Cinder? We should find—"

"Scarlet." His voice trembled with desperation and fear. "They did change me. I'm dangerous now. I'm—"

"Oh, please. We don't have time for this." Digging her hands into his hair—the same soft, wild, unkempt hair—she pulled him toward her. She wasn't quite sure what a kiss would be like, and it was different and awkward in that hasty stolen moment, but she was confident they could perfect it later. "You have *always* been dangerous. But you're my alpha and I'm yours and that's not going to change because they gave you a new jawline. Now come on. We should—"

Behind Wolf, a soldier let out a cry of pain and crumpled to the ground, bleeding from a dozen different wounds. Wolf pulled Scarlet back, shielding her. There was blood coating his side, and she remembered that Iko had shot him, but he hardly seemed to notice the wound.

She looked again, scouring the weapons, the limbs, the bodies.

Less chaos than before. The battle was beginning to dwindle.

There were not so many people left to fight and still she could see the thaumaturges gathered in the distance. Some had fallen, certainly, but their numbers were holding. It was too easy for them to take control of the civilians, and with the wolf soldiers keeping one another occupied . . .

Was it possible they were losing?

A controlled civilian came running at her, a spear held over his head. Wolf swiped him away and snapped the spear in half before Scarlet could react. Turning, he growled, and yanked Scarlet to one side moments before a knife slashed through the empty air. With a single throw of Wolf's fist, the unsuspecting man fell unconscious. Though he was still holding the axe, Wolf didn't raise it. After all, these were their allies, even if they had become weapons for the enemy.

The more that fell, the easier it would be for the thaumaturges to take control . . .

"Stay down!" Wolf yelled, pushing Scarlet to the ground and hunkering over her body. A living shield. His instinct was still there, at least. The desire to protect her above all else.

That was all the confirmation she needed.

Feeling more safe than she should have, Scarlet stayed low and scanned the chaos for any sign of Cinder or Iko or Alpha Strom or—

She spotted a wolf soldier, one she didn't recognize, about ready to launch himself at them. "Wolf!"

Wolf snarled, baring his teeth.

The soldier hesitated. He sniffed once at the air, looking from Wolf to Scarlet and back again. Then he turned and rushed off to find some other victim.

Wetting her chapped lips, Scarlet placed a hand on Wolf's elbow. "Are we losing?" she said, trying to count, but it was impossible to tell how many of the wolf soldiers were theirs and how many Levana's. She did know the civilians were falling faster and faster as the scales tipped in the thaumaturges' favor.

"Not for long," said Wolf.

She craned her head up. His eyes were still flashing dangerously, scanning for immediate threats. "What do you mean?"

His nose twitched. "Princess Winter is close, and . . . she's brought reinforcements."

Eighty-Five

"WE'RE ALMOST THERE," SAID IKO, AS SHE AND CINDER CREPT
down the main corridor of the palace. They could still hear the
sounds of the battle raging in the distance, but the palace was
quiet in comparison. There had been no sign of Levana since
they'd entered and Iko almost expected the crazed queen to
jump out from behind a corner and try to stab them with her
pointy-heeled shoes.

Seeing Levana on the palace steps was the first time Iko had
ever seen the Lunar queen, and her scarred face made Iko wish
she wasn't immune to glamours. After years of hearing about the
queen's famous beauty, the truth had been something of a
letdown.

But the truth was out. Thanks to Cinder's video, now everyone
knew what lurked beneath the illusion. Hopefully they would be
able to find the queen while she was still shaken from it.

Cinder's grip tightened on her bloody knife. "Two guards up
ahead."

They rounded a corner, and she was right—two guards stood in
front of a set of ornate doors, huge guns already trained on them.

Iko froze and raised her good hand in a show of innocence. She tried to smile sweetly, but with her missing ear and a twitching cheek muscle, she was not performing at the height of her abilities.

Then recognition sparked through her processor. "*You!*" she screamed. "He's ... that's the guy that saved Winter."

Though the guard was immobile, probably thanks to Cinder, his face was free to twist with disgust as his eyes traveled the length of Iko's battered body, dead wires, loose parts, and all.

"And you're that disturbing robot."

Iko bristled. "The correct term is *escort-droid,* you ignorant, inconsiderate—"

"Iko."

She clamped her mouth shut, though her synapses were still firing.

Cinder cocked her head to the side. "So you're the one who killed Levana's captain of the guard?"

"I did," he said.

The second guard snarled, casting his glare between his companion and Cinder. "*Traitor.*"

A low, humorless laugh echoed through the first guard's throat—Kinney, Iko remembered. "You're wasting your energy controlling me. I have no intention of shooting you."

"Fine," Cinder drawled, though Iko could tell she didn't fully trust him. "So long as you don't try to harm us, I have no reason to manipulate you." It wasn't a real concession. If he tried anything, Iko knew Cinder could stop him.

The muscles in Kinney's arms relaxed. "So you're the cyborg that's been causing so much trouble."

"Wow," Iko mused. "He's pretty *and* smart."

His wrinkling nose made her wonder if she was starting to

overdo it on the sarcasm, but her smarting ego made her irate. She'd gotten used to people looking at her like she was human. Not only human, but *beautiful*. But now she was stuck with a flopping arm and shredded skin tissue and a missing ear, and all this guard saw was a broken machine.

Not that his opinion mattered. He was clearly a jerk.

Except for the whole saving-Winter's-life thing, which was probably a fluke.

"Is Levana in there?" Cinder asked, gesturing to the barred doors.

"No, just the coronation guests. Our orders were to contain them until either the queen or a thaumaturge retrieves them—I suspect she's preparing to slaughter all the Earthens if you don't surrender."

"Sounds like her," said Cinder, "but I doubt she has the strength to glamour so many people at once right now. Otherwise, I think she would have come straight here."

Kinney frowned, speculative. He wouldn't have seen the video. He didn't know that the truth beneath Levana's glamour had been revealed.

"Where else would she go?" asked Cinder. "If she was trying to lure me somewhere, somewhere she feels safe and powerful."

He shrugged. "The throne room, I guess."

Cinder's jaw flexed. "That's where the feast was the other night? With the balcony over the lake?"

Kinney had started to nod when the second guard reeled his head back and spat. Literally *spat* on this gorgeous tile floor.

"Oh!" Iko cried. "You heathen!"

"When she catches you," the guard snarled, "my queen will eat your heart with salt and pepper."

"Well," said Cinder, unconcerned, "my heart is half synthetic, so it'll probably give her indigestion."

Kinney looked almost amused. "We guards tend to be treated well here. You'll find that a lot of us will stay loyal to Her Ma—to Levana." The queen's given name was awkward and Iko wondered if he'd ever said it before.

"Why aren't you?" Cinder asked.

"Something tells me I'm going to like your offer more." His gaze slipped toward Iko. "Even if you do keep strange company."

She huffed.

Stepping forward, Cinder reached for the holster on the second guard's hip, taking his handgun for herself. "Maybe when this is over I can convince them that I intend to treat you pretty well too."

Cinder turned, and Iko could make out the conflict warring across her facial muscles. "Stay with Kai. In case she does send a thaumaturge after them, I want someone there who can't be controlled. And try to get him and any Earthens away from here." She inhaled sharply. "I'm going after Levana."

"No, wait," said Iko. "I should come with you."

Ignoring her, Cinder jutted a finger toward Kinney. "If you're loyal to me, then you'll be loyal to the Earthen emperor. Protect him with your life."

The guard hesitated, but then brought a fist to his heart.

Her new gun in one hand and her knife in the other, Cinder turned and started running back the direction they'd come from.

"Cinder, wait!" Iko yelled.

"Stay with Kai!"

"But . . . *be careful!*"

When Cinder turned the corner, Iko swiveled back to the guards, just as the second guard realized he had control of his body. Gaze darkening, he lifted the large gun again, aiming for Iko.

Kinney clubbed him over the head with the butt of his own rifle. Iko jumped back as the guard sprawled face-first on the ground.

"I feel like I should be going with her," said Kinney.

Snarling, Iko stepped over the fallen guard and jabbed a finger at his chest. "I have known her a lot longer than you have, mister, and if there's one of us who should be going with her, it's *me*. Now open these doors."

One eyebrow—dark and thick—shot upward. She could see him struggling to say something, or *not* say something. He gave up and turned away, shoving the wooden board through the handles. He hauled open the door.

Iko took two steps into the great hall and froze.

The room was not filled with hundreds of Lunar aristocrats and Earthen leaders and her handsome emperor. In fact, only a few dozen vibrantly dressed Lunars stood at the far end of the room. The rest of the floor was littered with chairs, many of them on their sides so there was hardly any space to walk in, making it difficult to traverse.

"He made us!" a Lunar woman cried, drawing Iko's attention. "We didn't want to help the Earthens but he threatened to bomb the city. Oh, please don't tell the queen."

Iko glanced back, but judging from the way Kinney's mouth had fallen open, he was as surprised as she was. She started forging a path through the fallen chairs, and it occurred to Iko that whoever had scattered them had likely done it intentionally, to slow down anyone who tried to pursue them.

As they got closer, Iko saw an open door behind an enormous altar—a curtain pulled across it would normally have kept it hidden.

"That door leads into the servants' halls," said Kinney, "but they should have been guarded too."

"Oh, you look *terrible!*" the first woman screamed, covering her mouth as she took in Iko's injuries. "Why would anyone glamour themselves to look like *that?*"

Before Iko could process an indignant response, Kinney said, "Emperor Kaito is taking the other Earthens to the ports?"

The Lunars nodded, a few pointing to the open door. "That way," said the offensive woman. "You can catch them if you hurry. And don't forget to tell Her Majesty that *we* stayed behind!"

They ignored her and barreled toward the door.

Iko started to look up the most direct route to the ports, but it became obvious that Kinney knew which way to go, so she allowed him to lead. They hadn't been running for long before her audio sensor picked up on voices echoing down the corridor.

They turned a corner and Iko saw the source of the noise up ahead—here were the hundreds of Lunar aristocrats, staggered in a messy line, waiting to pass through a doorway into a stairwell that would lead them down, down to the sublevels beneath the palace.

Among the chatter, her audio input recognized a voice.

Kai.

She picked up her speed. The Lunars, who didn't notice her until she was right behind them, cried out with surprise, many throwing themselves against the walls to let her pass.

"Kai!"

The crowd shifted. Kai and his adviser, Konn Torin, stood beside the stairwell door, urging the crowd to move faster, to keep pace.

His eyes collided with her. Relief. Happiness. "Iko?"

She threw herself into Kai's arms, for once not caring about the singed paneling on the side of her face or the holes in her torso. He squeezed her back. "Iko. Thank the stars."

Just as fast as he had embraced her, he pushed her back to arm's distance and glanced past her shoulder, but his joy fell when he saw only Kinney at her side. "Where's Cinder?"

Iko, too, glanced back. Kinney was sneering contemptuously at Kai's hand on Iko's broken arm. She pressed her lips into her own sneer. "She's looking for Levana. We think she went to the throne room."

"Alone?"

She nodded. "She wanted me to make sure you were all right."

Heaving a frustrated breath, Kai nudged Iko and Kinney against the wall, clearing a path for those Lunars still waiting to descend.

"We're moving everyone down to the spaceship ports. It will be the safest place while the fighting continues and keep any more puppets out of Levana's hands." He squeezed Iko's hand, and her wiring buzzed with delight. "Do you think you'd be able to open the ports to let the ships out if I got you down there?"

Kinney answered before she could. "I know the access code."

Iko turned to him.

"I've had pilot training," he said, with a nonchalant shrug.

Kai gave him an appreciative nod, and if he was stunned that a royal guard was helping them, it didn't show. "Then let's finish this, and go find Cinder."

Eighty-Six

JACIN WAS HOLDING HER HAND, HIS FINGERS STRONG AND tense, like he was afraid she would vanish if he loosened his grip. They emerged with the flood of people out of the maglev tunnels into Artemisia Central. Winter's childhood home. Jacin's too. She felt like a ghost. She felt like a conqueror.

It had taken hours for them to traverse Luna's terrain, visiting dozens of the nearest sectors, spreading the word of Selene's survival and the call to arms and asking the people to stand with them. It had taken less coercing than she'd expected. Already spurred on by the first video Cinder had broadcast and incensed by Levana's attempt to have the princess murdered—again—the people were in a frenzy by the time Jacin and Winter arrived to tell them their news. Many were already on their way to the capital.

No sooner had she and Jacin broken onto the surface than the people took off sprinting toward the palace, roaring and gripping their weapons. Winter tried to keep pace with them, but Jacin's grip tightened and pulled her to the side, keeping her sheltered from the teeming crowd.

The courtyard in front of the palace was already a graveyard, though there were still people struggling to go on fighting. A battalion of thaumaturges and countless wolf soldiers wasted no time launching themselves at the new arrivals, and those brave war cries from the front lines were quickly turned into screams. There were more coming still, pouring out of the tunnels and into the streets, and Winter recognized many of her own soldiers trying to rip the mutants away from their allies. Confusion reigned. Thaumaturge-controlled civilians turned into enemies, and it was sometimes impossible to tell which of the wolf soldiers were on their side.

Claws ripping open a person's chest.

A bullet tearing through the side of a woman's face.

A spear impaling a man's abdomen.

Howls of pain and victory, indistinguishable. The tangy smell of blood. Still the people came and came and came. The people she had brought there.

Winter's head rang with it all. Her feet were rooted to the ground. She was glad Jacin had stopped her.

"The palace will be soaked through with blood," she whispered. "The waters of Artemisia Lake will run red, and even the Earthens will see it."

Jacin's eyes flashed with alarm. "Winter?"

She barely heard Jacin over the din inside her skull. Prying herself away from him, she stumbled forward and collapsed over the body of one of the wolf soldiers. There was a familiarity to the set of his jaw, the dead eyes staring upward.

Brushing a lock of bloodstained hair away from the man's brow, Winter began to wail.

It was Alpha Strom.

And it was her fault, *her fault* he was here. She had asked him to fight for her and now he was dead and—

Jacin took her elbow. "Winter, what are you doing?"

She collapsed, sobbing over Strom's body. "I'm dying," she whimpered, digging her fingers into the filth-crusted fabric of Strom's shirt.

Jacin cursed. "I knew this was a bad idea." He tugged at her, but she ripped her arm away and scanned the raging battle around them.

"I am destroyed," she said. Tears were on her cheeks, mixing with all the blood. "I do not know that even a sane person could recover from this. So how can I?"

"Precisely why we should leave. Come on." This time he didn't give her a choice, just hooked his hands under her arms and hauled her to her feet. Winter slid against him, allowing him to fit her to his body. A surprising cheer called her attention toward the palace and she saw the thaumaturges fleeing back inside. Many had fallen and were lying dead or dying on the palace stairs. They were overwhelmed. There were too many people now for the queen's minions to hold their own, just as Cinder had hoped.

Armies were falling—on both sides.

So many deaths.

Spurred on by their victory, the people rushed the palace, streaming in through the enormous doors, chasing the thaumaturges.

Winter spotted a flash of vivid red hair and her heart leaped.

"*Scarlet!*" she screamed, struggling against Jacin, though he held her firm. "No, Scarlet! Don't go in there! The walls are bleeding!" Her word turned into shudders, but it worked. Scarlet had frozen and turned. She searched the crowd for the source of her name.

Jacin dragged Winter beneath the overhang of a dress shop and pressed her into the alcove.

"It's not safe!" Winter screamed, reaching past him for her friend, but she could no longer see Scarlet in the swarm. She met Jacin's panicked eyes. "It isn't safe in there. The walls . . . the blood. She'll be hurt and she'll die and they're all going to die."

"All right, Winter. Calm down," he said, smoothing back Winter's hair. "Scarlet is strong. She'll be all right."

She whimpered. "It isn't just Scarlet. Everyone is going to die, and nobody knows, nobody sees it but me—" Her voice cracked and she started sobbing. Hysterical. She started to collapse, but Jacin caught her and held her against him, letting her cry against his chest. "I'm going to lose them all. They'll be drowned in their own blood."

The sounds of fighting were distant and muffled now within the palace walls, replaced in the streets and courtyard with the moans of death and bloodied coughing. Winter's vision was blurred as she peered over Jacin's shoulder. Mostly bodies and blood, but also some stragglers. A few dozen people picking their way through the destruction. Trying to tend to those who were still alive. Pulling bodies off other bodies. A girl in an apron— surprisingly clean—pulled the buttons off one of the thaumaturges' black coats.

"I should have left you with the lumberjacks," Jacin muttered.

The girl in the apron noticed them, startled, then scampered off to the other side of the courtyard to rifle through some other victims' pockets. A servant from the city, Winter guessed, though she didn't recognize her.

"I could have been you," Winter whispered after her. Jacin's fingers dug into her back. "The lowly daughter of a guard and a seamstress. I should have been her, scavenging for scraps. Not royalty. Not this."

Sandwiching Winter's face in both hands, Jacin forced her gaze up to his. "Hey," he said, somehow stern and gentle at the same time. "You're my princess, right? You were always going to be my princess, no matter what you were born, no matter who your dad married."

Her eyes misted. Reaching up, she folded her fingers over Jacin's forearms. "And you are always my guard."

"That's right." The faintest touch. His calloused thumb against her temple. Winter's whole body quivered. "Come on. I'm getting you out of here."

He started to pull away, but she dug her fingertips into his arms. "You need to help Selene and Scarlet and the others."

"No. Either she's winning or she's losing. My presence won't sway it at this point. But you—I can take care of you. For once."

"You always take care of me."

His lips tightened and his attention dipped toward her scars, before he looked away altogether. He was about to speak again when Winter's eye caught on movement.

The servant in her apron had sneaked up on them and now had an empty look in her face. She raised a bloodied knife over her head.

Winter gasped and yanked Jacin to the side. The tip of the knife slashed through the back of his arm, ripping through his shirt. Snarling, he spun to face the attacker and grabbed her wrist before she could swipe at him again.

"Don't hurt her!" Winter screamed. "She's being manipulated!"

"I noticed," he growled, prying the woman's fingers back until she dropped the knife. It landed with a clatter on the stone ground. Jacin shoved her away and she fell, collapsing on her side.

In the same movement, Jacin yanked the shoulder straps that held his gun and knife over his head and threw them as hard as he could toward the obstacle course of fallen bodies. Before they could be used against him. Before his own hands could turn the weapons against him.

"I hope you don't think *that* will make a difference."

Whimpering, Winter pressed herself back into the doorway.

Aimery. He was standing in the street—not smiling. For once, not even pretending to smile. Not smug or cruel or taunting.

He looked unhinged.

The servant girl, released from his control, scrambled away on her hands and knees and escaped as fast as she could into an alleyway. Winter heard her crawling turn into the hurried beat of running. Aimery let her go. He didn't even look at her.

Jacin placed himself between Winter and Aimery, though she didn't know why. Aimery could have forced Jacin to move aside with a tiny little thought. Aimery could toy with them as easily as pawns on the queen's game board.

"As you are useless with your own gift," Aimery drawled, dark eyes burning, "perhaps you do not understand that we do not require guns and knives to do damage. When you have been given the power that I have, all the world is an armory, and everything in it a weapon."

Aimery tucked his hands into his sleeves, although he was lacking his normal composure. His expression was frazzled and angry.

"You could be strangled with your own belt," he continued, still speaking slowly. "You could impale yourself with a serving fork. You could plunge your own thumbs into your eye sockets."

"You think *I* don't know the sort of things you can do?" Jacin's body was taut, but Winter didn't think Aimery had taken control of him.

Not yet.

But he would.

There was Aimery's nightmare smile, but it was crossed with a snarl. "You are as inferior to me as a rat." His attention switched to Winter. His lip curled in disgust. "Yet she still made her choice, didn't she?"

Winter's heart pummeled against her rib cage, Aimery's words echoing inside her frazzled skull. *Strangle. Impale. Plunge.*

He would. Not yet. But he would.

A chill crawled over her skin from the pure hatred she saw in Aimery's face.

"You should have accepted me when you had the chance," he said.

She tried to swallow, but her saliva felt like paste. "I could have," she said, "but it would have been no more real than the visions that plague me."

"So you chose a pathetic guard."

Her lips quivered. "You don't understand. He is the *only thing* that is real."

Aimery's expression darkened. "And soon he will be dead, little princess." He spat the title like an insult. "Real or not, I will have you. If not as a wife or a willing mistress, then as a possession to be displayed in a pretty bejeweled case." His eyes took on a hint of madness. "I have waited too many years to let you go now."

Jacin's back was to Winter, his shoulders knotted. A line of blood curled down his elbow and dripped along his wrist. Splattered to the ground below. He was powerless to do anything but stand there and say cold and callous things and hope no one detected how afraid and frustrated he really was.

But Winter knew. She had lived her life with that fear too.

Aimery looked pleased as he focused again on Jacin. "I have been waiting for this since you were brought before the court. I should have watched you bleed on the throne room floor that day."

Winter convulsed.

"That must have been such a disappointment for you," said Jacin.

"It was," agreed Aimery, "but I do think I will enjoy this moment even more." His cheek twitched. "How shall it be done? By my hand? By your own?" His eyes glistened. "By *hers*? Ah—how inconsolable she would be then, to be the instrument of her own beloved's death. Perhaps I will have her bash in your skull with a rock. Perhaps I will have her choke you with her pretty fingers."

Nausea rolled over her.

Jacin—

Jacin.

"I rather like that idea," Aimery mused.

Winter's hands stirred. She did not know if they would be strangling or choking or bashing or impaling. She knew Aimery had her now and Jacin was in danger and this was the end. There was no gray area. There were no winners. She was a fool, a fool, a fool.

Winter kept her eyes open against the hot tears.

Jacin turned to face her as her hands wrapped around his neck. Her thumbs pressed into the flesh of his throat. There was a gasp, and if he wanted to push her away, Aimery wouldn't let him.

Winter couldn't look. Couldn't watch. She was crying uncontrollably and the awful feel of Jacin's throat under her thumbs was too awful, too fragile, too—

A flash of red sparked through the pooling tears.

Scarlet, creeping behind Aimery. Inching over the fallen bodies. A knife in her hand.

Seeing that Winter had spotted her, Scarlet raised a finger to her lips.

Aimery turned his head.

Not toward Scarlet, but toward an enormous, roaring figure.

Aimery laughed, waving one hand through the air. Wolf was steps away when he collapsed, howling in pain. "I am the queen's own thaumaturge!" Aimery yelled, eyes blazing as he snarled down at Wolf's twitching body. "You think I cannot feel you sneaking up on me? You think I cannot handle one pathetic mutant and a weak-minded guard and an *Earthen*?"

He pivoted to face Scarlet. She was still half a dozen paces away from him and she froze, her knuckles clenched around the knife handle.

Aimery's smile faded. His brow twitched as he realized that the bioelectricity around Scarlet's body was already claimed.

His eyes narrowed and he searched the graveyard they stood on, but there was no one there to be controlling Scarlet. No one who could have undermined his own powers. Except . . .

Scarlet lumbered closer to him. Her gait was stunted and awkward. Her arm trembling as she raised the knife.

Aimery stepped back and his attention turned and locked on to Winter. In the moment he'd been distracted by Wolf—poor, tortured Wolf—he had released Winter's hands and mind. Jacin was still rubbing his throat and struggling for breath and Winter . . .

Winter was staring at Scarlet. Horrified. Trembling. But fierce.

Jacin's hand whipped out, backhanding Winter across her face. She crashed against the building wall, but didn't feel the force of it. Her focus was on Scarlet, only Scarlet, Scarlet and her knife.

Winter was crying and hating herself. She was wretched and cruel but she didn't relent as she forced Scarlet into battle. Aimery stumbled back again and raised his hands to his own defense. Scarlet hurled herself at him. Aimery tripped over the leg of a dead civilian man and sprawled backward. Scarlet landed on her knees beside him and scrambled forward. Her eyes were confused, her mouth slack with disbelief, but her body was vicious and determined and sure as she plunged the knife into his flesh.

Eighty-Seven

REALITY DISINTEGRATED. THE WORLD WAS A THOUSAND cumbersome pixels tearing apart, leaving black spaces in between, then smashing back together in blinding sparks.

Winter had made herself as small as she could, huddled in the shop's doorway off the main thoroughfare of Artemisia. Her own shaking arms made for a protective shield around her body and her feet were pulled in tight. She'd lost a shoe. She didn't know how or when.

Aimery was dead.

Scarlet-friend had stabbed him nine times.

Winter had stabbed him nine times.

Dear Scarlet. Vicious, stubborn, weak-minded Scarlet.

Once she had started, Winter couldn't make it stop. *Nine times.* It had been years since she'd manipulated anyone and never with violent intentions. Aimery, in his determination to subdue them all with his gift, had not tried to get away until after the second stab. By that time Winter was already lost. She couldn't make it stop. She thought only of erasing forever that awful, charming grin. Of destroying his mind so she would not be forced to wrap her hands around Jacin's neck again and finish what she'd started.

Now Aimery was dead.

The streets were full of his blood. They reeked with the stench of it.

"What's wrong with her?" some far-off voice shrieked. "Why is she acting this way?"

"Give her some space." This command was followed by a grunt. Jacin? Could it be her guard, so near, always so near?

Jacin had been the one to tackle Scarlet and rip the knife away, snapping the hold Winter had taken over her. Otherwise she knew she would have kept stabbing and stabbing and stabbing and stabbing and stabbing until Aimery was nothing but chopped bits of flesh and smiles.

Winter's head was full of distraction, too much to comprehend. The shop's sign overhead swung on its hinges. There was a torn curtain behind broken glass. Bullet holes in the walls. Roofs caving in. Glass shattered beneath her feet.

"We have to find Cinder." The voice was insistent, but terrified. "We have to make sure she's okay, but I can't . . . I don't want to leave Winter . . ."

Winter arched her back and clawed her hands into her hair, gasping from an onslaught of sensation. Every inch of her skin was a hive of stinging bees.

Arms circled around her. Or maybe they had been there for a long time. She could hardly feel them outside of the cocoon she'd erected, even though it was covered in hairline fractures. "It's all right. I've got Winter. Go."

A cocoon.

An encasement of ice.

A spaceship harness strangling her, the belt cutting into her flesh.

"Go!"

Winter clawed at the straps, struggling to get out. Those same strong arms tried to hold her still. Tried to secure her thrashing. She snapped her teeth, and the body shifted out of her reach. She was pulled away from the door, their bodies repositioned, so the arms could restrain her without being in danger themselves. She struggled harder. Kicked and writhed.

And screamed.

stabbing and stabbing and stabbing and stabbing and stabbing and

Her throat was hoarse.

Maybe she'd been screaming for a long time.

Maybe the sound was imprisoned inside this cocoon, trapped like she was. Maybe no one would ever hear her. Maybe she would scream until her throat bled and no one would ever know.

Her heart split in two. She was an animal. A killer and a predator.

The screams turned to howls.

Sad and broken howls.

Haunting and furious howls.

"Winter? Winter!"

The arms around her were unrelenting. She thought there might be a voice, familiar and kind, somewhere far in the distance. She thought there might be good intentions in that voice. She thought that if she could follow the sound, it would lead her to somewhere safe and calm, where she was no longer a murderer.

But she was already suffocating beneath the weight of her crimes.

Animal. Killer. Predator. *And the wolves all howl, aa-ooooooooooh...*

Eighty-Eight

CINDER CHECKED THE GUN'S AMMUNITION, COUNTING THE bullets while she ran. She was breathing hard, but she didn't feel tired or even sore. Adrenaline was pumping hot through her veins and for once she was aware of it only because she could feel herself trembling with the surge of it, not because her brain interface was telling her so.

The sounds of battle were echoing in the palace, dim and far away. Many floors below. They were inside, she could tell. There would be a lot of casualties, she knew.

She felt like they might be winning. *She could win.*

But it would fall apart if she didn't finish what she'd come to do. If she didn't find a way to end Levana's tyranny for good, the people would be back under her control by morning.

She took the stairs two at a time. Her hair prickled on the back of her neck as she arrived in the fourth floor corridor. She peered down the empty hall with its artwork and tapestries and shimmering white tiles, listening for any sound indicating an ambush.

Not that ambushes came with warning sounds.

Everything was eerie and haunted after the chaos of the courtyard.

It was no comfort to Cinder that she had reached the throne room without incident. It wasn't like Levana to make things easy for her, which meant that either Levana was so distraught from the video she was no longer thinking straight, or—more likely—Cinder was walking into a trap.

She held the gun with one hand, the knife in the other, and tried to calm her stampeding heart. She did her best to come up with some sort of plan for when she reached the throne room, assuming Levana was in there, probably with an entire envoy of guards and thaumaturges.

If the guards weren't already under someone's control, she would steal them away and form a protective barrier around herself. The moment an opportunity presented itself, she would shoot Levana. No hesitation allowed.

Because Levana wouldn't hesitate to kill *her*.

She found herself standing outside the throne room doors, the Lunar insignia carved across their surface. She gulped, wishing she could sense how many people were inside, but the room was too well sealed. Whatever lay beyond these doors was a mystery.

An ambush, common sense whispered to her. *A trap*.

Licking the salt from her lips, she braced herself and kicked one of the doors open, wedging inside before it could slam back on her. Her body was tense, braced for an impact, a punch, a bullet, anything other than the stillness that greeted her.

Only two people were in the room, making it feel infinitely larger than it had during the wedding feast. The audience chairs were still there, but many of them had been shoved against the walls or crushed in the destruction she had wreaked.

The throne, though, had not moved, and Levana was seated on it like before. Rather than looking smug and cruel as usual, she was slumped on the enormous throne with an air of defeat around her. She wore the colors of the Eastern Commonwealth flag in her gown, a mockery of everything Kai and his country stood for. Her glamour had returned. She had her face turned away from Cinder, hiding behind her wall of glossy hair, and Cinder could see only the tip of her nose and a hint of ruby lips.

The second person in the room was Thorne. Her heart sank, but was lifted by a slim hope. Perhaps it was only a Lunar glamoured to *look* like Thorne. She narrowed her eyes in suspicion, not daring to go any farther into the room.

"Well, it's about time," said Thorne, his voice comfortingly sardonic. "You have no idea how awkward these last few minutes have been."

Cinder's heart squeezed, her hope fading. It was definitely Thorne and he was standing precariously close to the ledge of the throne room, the one Cinder had jumped from. His hands were behind his back, most likely bound. The glowing bow tie was gone and his purple suit reduced to just the dress shirt, now unbuttoned at the collar. There was a hole in the thigh of his pants and dried blood above his knee. A lump beneath the fabric suggested hasty bandaging.

Cinder reached for him with her thoughts, but Levana had already claimed him, holding his feet as tight-gripped as iron shackles.

Thorne's gaze swooped down over Cinder's bloodstained clothes and the weapon in each of her hands. One eyebrow tilted up. "Rough day?"

Cinder didn't respond. She was still waiting for that surprise attack. A shot through the heart. A guard appearing out of the shadows and tackling her to the ground.

Nothing happened.

No sound but her own heavy breathing.

"Your leg?" she asked.

Thorne shrugged. "Hurts like hell, but it won't kill me. Unless the prisons were full of grimy bacteria and the wound gets infected, which, let's face it, is entirely plausible."

Glancing behind her to make sure no one was sneaking up from the corridor, Cinder took a hesitant step forward.

Thorne took a step back. One step closer to the edge.

Cinder paused.

"Do not come any closer," said Levana. Her voice was meek and tired, a far cry from the haughty glee with which she'd ordered Cinder's execution. She still did not lift her head. "I suggest you do not raise your weapons, either. Unless you think he is as lucky as you are."

"I'm pretty sure he's luckier."

Thorne nodded in agreement, but said nothing, and Cinder didn't move. Peering at him, she mouthed a single word—*Cress?*

His indifference dissolved and he gave the smallest shake of his head. She didn't know if this meant that he didn't know where she was, or if something bad had happened and he didn't want to discuss it at the moment.

Cinder was distracted from her curiosity by her hand twitching. She was lifting the gun toward her own head.

It was halfway there when she gritted her teeth and forced her limb to stop. To her relief, it did.

Snarling, she lowered the weapon back to her side.

Levana laughed, but the sound came off as more brittle than

charmed. "I thought that might be the case," she said, rubbing her forehead. "I am...not myself at the moment. Though it seems, neither are you."

Cinder frowned, wondering why Levana could control her in the courtyard, but failed now. Was it because her own mental strength had been too fragile then, while trying to maintain control of so many people, or was the queen growing weak? Perhaps the video showing her true face had fragmented her abilities.

It did not seem to be affecting her ability to manipulate Thorne, but, to be fair, Cinder was pretty sure a Lunar toddler could have manipulated Thorne.

Levana sighed. "Why, Selene? Why do you want to take everything from me?"

Cinder narrowed her eyes. "You're the one who tried to kill *me*, remember? You're the one sitting on *my* throne. You're the one who married *my* boyfriend!" The word was out before she'd contemplated it, and Cinder thought it was the first time she'd ever said it aloud. She wasn't even sure if it was true. But it felt sort of right, except for the whole being-married-to-her-aunt thing.

But Levana didn't seem to be listening.

"You don't understand how hard I worked for all this. How many years of planning, of laying the foundation. The disease, the shells, the antidote, the soldiers, the operatives, the carefully orchestrated attacks." She pressed a pale hand against her temple. She looked miserable. "It was done. It was *perfect*. He would have announced our engagement at the ball, but, no—you had to be there. Back from the dead to haunt me. And you come here, and you ask my people to hate me, and you show that... that horrid video, and fill their head with your lies."

"*My* lies! You're the one who brainwashes them. I just showed them the truth."

Levana flinched, turning her head even farther away like she couldn't stand to be reminded of what she was hiding underneath the illusion of beauty.

Exhaling sharply, Cinder stepped forward.

Thorne stepped back.

She grimaced. So much for hoping Levana was caught up enough in her own delusions to stop paying attention.

"What I can't understand," Cinder said, easing her tone, "is how you could have done that to me. I was just a kid, and you ..." Her heart twisted. "I know those are burn scars you have. I have the same scar tissue where I lost my leg. Knowing what it's like, living with that—how could you do it to someone else?"

"You weren't supposed to *survive*," Levana snapped, as if that made it better. "At least I would have had the mercy to kill you, to be done with it."

"But I didn't die."

"Yes, I've noticed. It is not my fault someone thought you might be worth saving. It is not my fault they turned you into ... into *that*." She cast a halfhearted gesture toward Cinder.

Cinder clenched her teeth, wanting to argue the point, but she bit her tongue. Levana had been living with her excuses for a long time.

She stole a glance at Thorne. He was sucking on his teeth and staring up at the ceiling. He looked bored.

Cinder tried taking a step backward, like a show of peace, but Thorne stayed where he was.

"Who did it to you, anyway?" she asked, aiming for gentle. "Who hurt you like that?"

Levana sniffed and, finally, dared to look at Cinder. There was all the beauty glistening on the surface, but now that Cinder had seen beneath it, she couldn't unsee the truth. Whether it was her cyborg programming or Levana's own weakness, she could see her as she was now. Scarred and deformed.

There was a twinge of sympathy in her stomach, but only a twinge.

"You don't know?" Levana asked.

"Why should I?"

"You stupid child." A lock of hair fell over Levana's face. "Because it was your mother."

Eighty-Nine

THE WORD *MOTHER* WAS FOREIGN TO CINDER'S EAR. *MOTHER*.
A woman who had given birth to her, but that was all. She had no
memories of her, only rumors—horrifying tales that said Queen
Channary was more cruel even than Levana, though her reign
had been much shorter.

"My own sweet sister," Levana purred. "Would you like to hear
how it happened?"

No.

But Cinder couldn't form the word.

"She was thirteen and I was six. She was learning how to use
her gift, taking great amounts of pleasure in manipulating those
around her—though I was always her favorite target. She was
very good. As I am. As you are. It is in our blood."

Cinder shivered. *It is in our blood.* She hated to think that she
shared blood with anyone in this family.

"At that age, it was her favorite trick to convince me that she
loved me dearly. Having never felt love from our parents, it was
not a hard thing to get me to believe. And then, when she was
sure I would do anything for her, she would torture me. On this

particular day, she told me to put my hand into a fireplace. When I refused, she made me do it anyway." Levana smiled as she told the story, a deranged look. "As you've seen, by the time she let me go, it was not only my hand that suffered."

Bile was filling Cinder's mouth. A child so young, so impressionable.

It would have been so *easy*.

Yet a cruelty too impossible to fathom.

Her *mother*?

"After that, they started to call me the ugly princess of Artemisia, the sad little deformed creature. While Channary was the beautiful one. Always the beautiful one. But I practiced my glamour, and I told myself that someday they would forget about the fire and the scars. Someday I would be queen and I would make sure the people loved me. I would be the most beautiful queen Luna had ever known."

Cinder tightened her grip on her weapons. "Is that why you killed her? So you could be queen? Or was it because she . . . did that. To you."

One of Levana's perfect eyebrows lifted. "Who says that I killed her?"

"Everyone says it. Even down on Earth we've heard the rumors. That you killed your sister, and your own husband, and *me*, all for your own ambitions."

A coolness passed over Levana's face and she leaned slowly back against her throne. "What I have done, I have done for Luna. My struggles, my sacrifices. Everything has been for Luna. All my life I've been the only one who cared, the only one who could see the potential of our people. We are destined for something so much greater than this *rock*, but all Channary cared about were her dresses and her conquests. She was a horrible queen.

She was a monster." She paused, nostrils flaring. "But no. I did not kill her, though I've wished a thousand times that I had. I should have killed her before she ruined everything. Before she had *you*, a healthy baby girl who would grow up to be just like her!"

Cinder snarled. "I don't know who I would have become if I'd grown up here," she said, "but I am *not* like her."

"Oh, yes," Levana mused, skipping from word to word like a stream over rocks. "On that note, I believe you are correct. When I first saw your glamour at the Commonwealth ball, I was surprised at how much you resembled her, once the dirt and grime and awful metal extremities were removed. But that seems to be where the similarities end." Her lips stretched, bloodred, curving around perfect pearl teeth. "No, little niece. You are much more like me. Willing to do anything to be admired. To be wanted. To be *queen*."

Cinder's body went rigid. "I'm not like you, either. I'm doing this because you've given me no choice. You *had* your chance. You couldn't have just been fair. Been a good ruler who treats her people with respect. And Earth! You wanted an alliance, Earth wanted peace . . . why couldn't you just . . . agree to it? Why the disease? Why the attacks? Did you honestly believe that was the way to get them to love you?"

Levana peered at her, furious and hateful. But then her lips twitched into something resembling a grin. A furious, hateful grin. "Love," she whispered. "Love is a conquest. Love is a war. That is all it is."

"No. You're wrong."

"Fine." Levana dragged her fingers along the arm of her throne. "Let us see how much your love is worth. Relinquish all rights to my throne, and I will not kill your friend."

Cinder's lips tightened. "How about we put it to a vote? Let the people decide who they want to rule them."

Thorne took a step back. His left heel was on the edge now, and there was an expression of dismay as he glanced down at the lake below.

Cinder flinched. "Wait. I could promise to relinquish my throne to you, but there are still going to be tens of thousands of people outside demanding for you to abdicate. The secret is out. They know I'm Selene. I can't take that back."

"Tell them you lied."

She exhaled sharply. "Also, the second you kill him, I'm going to kill you."

Levana cocked her head to one side, and though she had her glamour, Cinder was seeing the woman from the video. That was her good eye, she realized.

"Then I will change the terms of my offer," said Levana. "Sacrifice yourself, and I will not kill him."

Cinder glanced at Thorne, who seemed indifferent to the fact they were negotiating with his life. He clicked his tongue at her. "Even I can see that's a bad deal."

"Thorne..."

"Do me a favor?"

She frowned.

"Tell Cress I meant it."

Her gut tightened. "Thorne—"

He met Levana's gaze. "All right, Your Queenliness. I'll call your bluff if she won't."

"I am not negotiating with *you*," Levana snapped.

"If you kill me, you've lost your last bargaining chip and Cinder wins. So let's talk about your options. You can either accept that your time as queen is over and let us both go, and maybe

Cinder will take mercy and not have you executed as a traitor. Or you can throw me off this ledge and—"

"Fine."

Thorne's eyes widened. He stepped off the overhang. With a cry, he threw up his arms—one wrist still bound, the opposite hand gripping the kitchen knife he'd swiped from the mansion. Gasping, his arms cartwheeled, his balance precarious.

Cinder dropped her weapons and rushed toward him.

Thorne fell—throwing his body forward at the last minute. One hand grabbed the ledge. He grunted. Cinder dove.

Levana leaned forward.

Thorne's fingers let go, just in time for Cinder to reach over the edge and latch on to his arm. Her injured shoulder screamed, but she held tight.

Thorne looked up at her, and it was by far the most fear she'd ever known him to reveal. "Thanks," he panted. Then his free hand swung upward, punching Cinder on the jaw. She flinched, ducking away without letting go.

"Sorry! That's not me."

"I know," she grunted. Planting her other hand on the floor, she pushed herself backward, dragging Thorne with her until his torso was on the ledge, his feet scrabbling for purchase. She dared not let go, even as he shoved his body onto the floor.

Cinder knew that the second she let go of him, Levana would send him careening to his death again.

Too late, it occurred to her that he'd actually managed to get out of his bindings. He must've spent the whole time she was arguing with Levana trying to work himself free. The fall might not have killed him, and with his arms free he'd have been able to swim. But now he was—

Thorne jabbed the knife into her thigh.

Cinder screamed.

"Still not me," he said, breathless, as his fist ripped the knife back out. He raised his arm overhead, preparing to stab her again.

Cinder tackled him, knocking the knife out of his grip.

Thorne threw his elbow into her throat. The air left her, white spots flecking her vision. Thorne scrambled away, but he didn't run back to the ledge.

Wrapping a hand around her throat, Cinder massaged the muscles, urging them to take in air again. Still dizzy, she forced herself onto her wobbling legs, ready to lunge at Thorne again.

She heard the click of a gun's safety being released.

She froze. Thorne had gone a lot farther than she'd expected and now he was standing near the room's entrance, holding the knife and gun she'd dropped when she'd tried to save him. The barrel of the gun was aimed at her head.

Cinder swayed. Stumbled once. Regained her footing.

A gunshot echoed off the room's stone walls. Cinder recoiled, expecting a jolt of pain, but instead she heard a bellowed curse. The gun Thorne had grabbed skittered across the floor. Cinder shook away the light-headedness and gawked at Thorne, who was in turn staring, horrified, at his hand. His arm was still raised, but his hand was now empty and covered in blood.

"I'm sorry!" Cress cried. She was on the floor against the door-way, struggling to get back up. The kickback had knocked her off balance. "I'm sorry, Captain!"

Thorne cursed again. Sweat was beading on his brow. But when he looked at Cress, jaw hanging, he bit back the pain and shouted, "Nice shot!"

"Cress," Cinder croaked. "The queen, Cress. Shoot the queen!"

Though Cress whimpered, she did change her aim, leveling the gun at Levana.

Cinder ran for the gun that had been shot from Thorne's hand.

Thorne ran too, yanking Cress's attention back to him. In one movement, he knocked Cress's arm up with his elbow while simultaneously, with his noninjured hand, driving the knife into her stomach, burying it to the hilt.

Cinder snatched her gun off the floor. Cress dropped hers. Blood seeped through her dress. She gaped up at Thorne and it was impossible to tell which of them was filled with more horror. Thorne's hand was still wrapped around the knife's hilt.

Turning toward the throne, Cinder fired, but Levana threw herself to the floor and the bullet ricocheted off the carved back of the throne. As Cinder loaded another bullet into the chamber, Levana scrambled off the floor, slipping on her billowing skirt as she pulled herself behind the throne. Cinder fired again, barely missing the queen's leg as she disappeared.

"*No*," Cress gasped.

A searing pain sliced through Cinder's side. She collapsed onto her hands and knees. Flopping onto her back, she pushed herself away, one hand pressed against the wound. Thorne stood over her, gripping the knife. Cress was dangling from his arm in an attempt to pull him away, but he was too strong and she was trying to keep one hand on her stomach wound. Her entire front was already covered in blood.

"I'm sorry," Thorne sobbed. All signs of his usual confidence were gone. "I'm sorry, I'm so sorry—"

Cress bit him then, digging her teeth into the flesh of his hand in an attempt to get him to release the knife. He stifled a scream behind his teeth, but didn't let go.

Snatching the gun again, Cinder launched herself off the floor, trying to wrestle the knife out of Thorne's grip. With a grunt, she planted a foot on his chest and kicked, ripping the knife away. He fell back, catching one of the audience chairs between his shoulders. His face barely registered the pain. His actions were becoming less graceful, more stilted.

Maybe because of his injuries, but more likely because Levana was growing too tired to go on controlling him.

Cress collapsed to her knees, clutching her stomach. Her cheeks were streaked with tears. "Cinder ..."

Cinder stood over them, the gun in her left hand and the blood-slicked knife in her right, every muscle trembling.

"Stars ..."

She whipped her head toward the doorway. Scarlet and Wolf had arrived.

"No. Run! Get out of here!"

Scarlet met her gaze and started to shake her head. "Wha—?"

More weapons. More potential enemies. More people she loved that Levana could take from her. Gritting her teeth, Cinder reached out, trying to lock on to their bioelectricity.

Too late. Wolf could no longer be controlled, and Scarlet was already taken.

Ninety

CINDER GLANCED TOWARD LEVANA, WHO WAS PEERING AT the newcomers over one of the throne's carved arms. Then Levana looked at the second gun, lying forgotten near the doorway.

Scarlet gasped as her body lurched forward of its own accord.

Cinder dove for it too, sliding across the slick floor. There were too many weapons, too many threats, and she did not have enough hands.

Instead of grabbing the gun, she shoved it and watched as it went careening past Scarlet, toward the audience's raised dais. A second later the weight of Scarlet's body landed on top of her. Scarlet grabbed her by the hair and yanked her head back, nearly snapping her neck. Cinder cried in pain and rolled over, shoving Scarlet off her. Maintaining her grip on the gun, she whipped her arm around, sending the back of her metal hand into Scarlet's temple.

She grimaced at the impact, but it worked. Letting go, Scarlet skidded halfway across the room and lay sprawled across the floor.

The guilt didn't have time to sink in—when she heard a roar, fear drew her attention back toward Wolf. Snarling, furious. He was already charging toward her.

The gun. The knife. It was Wolf but it wasn't Wolf and she didn't have the strength to fight him off, not now, not again …

Cinder scrunched up her face as a drop of sweat slid into her eyes and raised the gun.

But Wolf's focus was on Scarlet's fallen body, and when he leaped, he cleared Cinder entirely. She spun around, stunned, as Wolf scooped Scarlet into his arms and cradled her against him.

Wolf, who was a monster, who was one of the queen's uncontrollable beasts …

He was still Wolf after all.

Gulping, choking, gulping again, Cinder raised herself up. She lost balance and fell onto one knee. "Wolf," she stammered. "Please … help Cress, and Thorne … *Please* … "

He raised his head, green eyes burning at first, but then he looked over to where Cress was clutching her stomach, deathly pale. To where Thorne was crumpled against a fallen chair, looking like he wanted to go to Cress but was terrified that his own body couldn't be trusted if he got close enough.

Wolf gave an understanding nod.

Relieved that, if nothing else, she could trust Wolf to get her friends out of here and start tending to their wounds, Cinder tried again to stand. This time she succeeded. She stumbled toward the throne, gripping the gun in one hand and the knife in the other. When she rounded the dais, she saw Levana on her knees, one hand dug into the folds of her dress while she clung to the back of the throne with the other. Her coronation gown billowed around her, elegant and distinguished, a sharp contrast to her grotesque face. She had given up on trying to use her glamour.

Cinder hated her own mind for labeling the queen as grotesque. She had once been a victim, as Cinder had once been a victim. And how many had labeled Cinder's own metal limbs as grotesque, unnatural, disgusting?

No. Levana was a monster, but it wasn't because of the face she'd kept hidden all these years. Her monstrosities were buried much deeper than that.

Another drop of sweat fell into Cinder's lashes and she swiped it away with the back of her wrist. Then she lifted the gun, aiming at Levana's heart.

At the same time, Levana lifted the hand that had been tucked into the luxurious fabric. She held the gun that Cinder had shoved toward the dais. Her arm trembled as if the weapon were impossibly heavy and it was clear from the way she held it that she had never held a gun before. She was a queen, after all. She had minions to do the killing for her.

The queen locked her teeth in concentration, and Cinder felt the muscles in her right arm pull in tight against her bones. The tendons started to cramp, the ligaments tightened.

She grimaced and looked at the gun in her hand. At her finger on the trigger.

She tried to pull the trigger.

Urged her finger to pull. Begged it.

Pull the trigger.

Pull it.

Her hand began to shake, the gun wobbling at the end of her arm. Her breaths came in short, stifled gasps as the trigger dug into the pad of her finger.

But she couldn't pull it. She couldn't.

Levana's terror began to melt away. Her lips twitched in what could have been relief if her brow hadn't been furrowed with so much concentration. She kept a firm hold of Cinder's arm, the finger, the gun.

Levana's tongue snaked out of her mouth, wetting her parched lips.

"Ah," she whispered, gaze flashing with pride. "You are tired too, I see."

Cinder snarled. An earthquake rumbled inside her body. She settled her focus on the queen's trembling hand and lashed out with her thoughts.

Levana's eyes widened. Her hair clung to the scar tissue on her face. She looked down at her own hand, as much a traitor as Cinder's.

Cinder forced Levana's arm to bend. She guided the gun upward, every centimeter a battle. Every moment a struggle.

Levana flushed red. She pinched her teeth in renewed concentration, and Cinder felt her own arm following suit. Her traitor of a hand lifted the gun and pressed the barrel against her own temple. She was the mirror image of her aunt, each of them primed to shoot.

"This is how it should have ended the night of the ball," Levana whispered. "This is how it should be." She smiled a mad woman's smile and stared at the place where the gun pressed against Cinder's damp skin.

Cinder remembered the night clearly, like a nightmare she'd never forget. Levana had controlled her arm, forcing her to take Jacin's gun and hold it against her temple. Cinder had been sure she was going to die, but her cyborg programming had saved her.

It would not save her this time.

"Good-bye, niece."

Cinder could not take back her own arm, but her body

burned with resolve. She would keep her finger from squeezing the trigger. She would not let Levana pull it. She would *not*.

The finger twitched. Throbbed, torn between two masters. Such a tiny limb. A tiny, tiny finger.

The rest of her willpower tightened around Levana's own hand. She could feel the bioelectricity sizzling in the air between them. She listened to the crackle of energy. There was an ebb and flow to their strengths and their weaknesses. Cinder would think she was making progress, curling Levana's finger inward, only to feel her own finger twitch against her control. A drop of sweat tickled the inside of her elbow. A stray hair clung to her lips. The smell of iron assaulted her nostrils. Every sense was a distraction. Every moment she could feel herself growing weaker.

But Levana's brow was drawn too. Levana was sweating too, her face contorted with the strain. They were both struggling for breath, and then—

A *snap* cracked loud inside Cinder's head.

She gasped, and her hand dropped to her side. Her muscles ached from the strain, but they were her muscles again. She gulped down a breath, dizzy from the effort.

Levana sobbed with frustration. Her body sagged. "Fine. Fine. I surrender." She spoke so quietly, Cinder wasn't sure she'd heard right. Though she was still controlling Levana's hand and still had the gun poised at Levana's temple, the queen seemed to have forgotten it was there. Her face crumpled, her body wilting into the enormous gown. "I relinquish my crown to you, my country, my throne. Take it all. Just . . . just let me be. Let me have my beauty again. *Please.*"

Cinder studied her aunt. Her scars and her matted hair and her sealed-shut eyelid. Her trembling lip and defeated shoulders.

She was too exhausted for even her glamour. Too weak to fight anymore.

A shock of pity stole through her.

This miserable, awful woman still had no idea what it meant to be truly beautiful, or truly loved.

Cinder doubted she ever would.

She gulped, though it was difficult around her parched tongue.

"I accept," Cinder said, dazed. She kept hold of Levana's trigger finger but allowed Levana to lower the gun. Cinder held out her hand and Levana stared at it for a moment before reaching forward and setting the gun into Cinder's palm.

In the same movement, she grabbed the forgotten knife and lurched forward, driving the blade into Cinder's heart.

The breath left her all at once, like her lungs imploding on themselves. Like a lightning bolt striking her from her head to her toes. Shock exploded through her chest and she fell backward. Levana fell with her, her face tight with rage. She had both hands on the knife handle now and when she twisted it, every nerve in Cinder's head exploded with agony. The world went foggy, vague, blurred in her vision.

Instinct alone prompted her to raise the gun and fire.

The blast knocked Levana away. Cinder didn't see where the bullet had gone, but she saw a line of blood arc across the back of the throne.

Her vision glazed over, all white and dancing stars. Her body was pain and blackness and hot and sticky with blood. *Stars.* It wasn't just in her head, she realized. Someone had painted stars on the throne room ceiling. A galaxy spread out before her.

In the silence of space, she heard a million noises at once.

Faraway and inconsistent. A scream. A roar, like an angered animal. Pounding footsteps. A door crashing against a wall.

Her name.

Muddled. Echoing. Her lungs twitched, or maybe it was her whole body, convulsing. She tasted blood on the back of her tongue.

A shadow passed in front of her. Brown eyes, filled with terror. Messy black hair. Lips that every girl in the Commonwealth had admired a thousand times.

Kai looked at her, the wound, the knife handle, the blade still buried. She saw his mouth forming her name. He turned and screamed something over his shoulder, but his voice was lost to her—so loud, but far, far, *far away.*

Ninety-One

"I TOLD YOU, I'M *FINE*," SCARLET INSISTED, THOUGH HER TONE
was weary. "It's just been a really long few months."

"'*Fine*'?" Émilie screeched. By the way her eyes blurred and
her blonde curls took up the screen, Scarlet could tell that the
waitress—the only friend she had back in Rieux—was holding
her port far too close to her face. "You have been missing for
weeks! You were gone during the attacks, and then the war broke
out, and I found those convicts in your house and then—*nothing!*
I was sure you were dead! And now you think you can send me a
comm and ask me to go throw some mulch on the garden like
everything is . . . is fine?"

"Everything *is* fine. Look—I'm not dead."

"I can see you're not dead! But, Scar, you are *all over* the news
down here! It's all anyone will talk about. This . . . this Lunar revolution, and our little Scarling in the center of it all. They're
calling you a hero in town, you know. Gilles is talking about putting up a plaque in the tavern, about how Rieux's own hero,
Scarlet Benoit, stood on this *very bar* and yelled at us all, and

we're so proud of her!" Émilie craned her head, as if that would allow her to see more in Scarlet's background. "Where are you, anyway?"

"I'm . . ." Scarlet glanced around the lavish suite of Artemisia Palace. The room was a thousand times more extravagant than her little farmhouse, and she hated it with a great passion. "I'm still on Luna, actually."

"*Luna!* Can I see? Is it even safe up there?"

"Ém, please stop screaming." Scarlet rubbed her temple.

"Don't you tell me to stop screaming, Mademoiselle Too-Busy-to-Send-a-Comm-and-Let-Me-Know-You're-Not-Dead."

"I was a prisoner!" Scarlet yelled.

Émilie gasped. "A prisoner! Did they hurt you? Is that a black eye or is it just my port, because my screen's been acting up lately . . ." Émilie scrubbed her sleeve over the screen.

"Listen, I promise I will tell you the whole story when I get home. Just, please tell me you're still watching the farm. Please tell me I have a home to go back to?"

Émilie scowled. Despite her hysteria, she'd been a welcome sight. Pretty and bubbly and so far removed from everything Scarlet had been through. Hearing her voice reminded Scarlet of home.

"Of course I'm still watching the farm," said Émilie, in a tone that suggested she was hurt Scarlet had doubted it. "You asked me to, after all, and I didn't want to think you were dead, even though . . . even though everyone believed it, and I did too for a while. I'm so glad you're not dead, Scar."

"Me too."

"The animals are fine and your android rentals are still coming . . . you must have paid them very far in advance."

Scarlet smiled tightly, recalling something about how Cress had set up a few payments in her absence.

"Scar?"

She raised her eyebrows.

"Did you ever find your grand-mère?"

Her heart had built up a strong-enough wall that the question didn't knock the breath out of her, but Scarlet still felt the pang of remembering. It was impossible to keep away the memories of the prisons beneath the opera house. Her grandmother's broken body. Her murder, as Scarlet watched and could do nothing.

This and this alone was the one thing she dreaded about returning home. The house wouldn't be the same without her grandmother's bread rising in the kitchen or her muddy boots left in the entry.

"She's dead," Scarlet said. "She died in the first attacks on Paris."

Émilie's face pinched. "I'm so sorry."

A silence crept in, that moment when there was nothing appropriate to say.

Scarlet straightened her spine, needing to change the subject. "Do you remember that street fighter who was coming into the tavern for a while?"

Émilie's expression lit up. "With the *eyes*?" she asked. "How could a girl forget?"

Scarlet laughed. "Yeah, well. It turns out he's Lunar."

Émilie gasped. "*No.*"

"Also, I'm kind of dating him."

The view on the screen shook as Émilie clasped a hand over her mouth. "Scarlet Benoit!" She stammered for a moment, before—"It's going to take weeks for you to explain this all to me, isn't it?"

"Probably." Scarlet brushed her hair over one shoulder. "But I will. I promise. Look, I should go. I just wanted you to know I'm all right, and to check on the farm—"

"I'll tell everyone you're safe. But when are you coming home?"

"I don't know. Soon, I hope. And, Ém? Please don't let Gilles put up a plaque about me."

The waitress shrugged. "I make no promises, Scarling. You are our little hero."

Scarlet clicked off the portscreen and tossed it onto the bed. Sighing, she glanced out the window. Below, she could see the destruction of the courtyard and hundreds of people trying to put it back together.

Artemisia was beautiful in its own way, but Scarlet was ready for fresh air and home-cooked food. She was ready to go home.

A knock sounded at the door and it opened, just a bit at first, Wolf hesitant on the other side. Scarlet smiled and he dared to come in, shutting the door behind him. He was holding a bouquet of blue daisies and looking immensely guilty.

"I was eavesdropping," he confessed, hunching his shoulders beside his ears.

She smirked, teasingly. "What's the point of superhuman hearing if you don't eavesdrop once in a while? Come in. I didn't expect you back so soon."

Wolf took another step and paused. He had a slight limp from the bullet that had hit his side, but it was healing fast. That was one thing to be said for the alterations—Wolf had certainly been made to be tough.

On the outside, at least.

He frowned at the flowers, his ferocious teeth digging into his lower lip.

He'd left to go back to the house that morning—his child-hood home. Though his mother's body had already been taken out to one of the great graveyards in the wasteland of Luna, it had been important to him that he see the house one last time. To see if there was anything worth saving there, anything to re-member his parents by, or even his brother.

Scarlet had offered to go with him but he wanted to do it alone.

She understood. Some things had to be done alone.

"Did you . . . find anything?"

"No," he said. "There was nothing I wanted. Everything from my childhood was gone, and . . . she didn't have much, you know. Except these."

He approached her, unable to hold eye contact, and handed her the bouquet of flowers. Over half of their delicate stems had been crushed or snapped in Wolf's indelicate fists.

"When I was a kid, I used to pick wildflowers for my grand-mère. She would keep them in a jar until they started to wilt, then press them between parchment paper so they'd last forever. I bet she has an entire box full of dried flowers some-where." She trailed a finger around some of the soft petals. "That's what we'll do with these. In honor of Maha." She arranged the flowers in a half-full water glass that had been brought with her breakfast.

When she turned back, Wolf had nudged aside the portscreen and lowered himself onto the edge of the enormous bed. Scarlet was pretty sure the linens had been made by slave labor, and the thought made her uncomfortable every time she crawled into them.

As soon as he was sitting, Wolf's leg started bouncing with anxious energy. Scarlet squinted at it. This wasn't mourning.

He was nervous.

"What is it?" she said, sinking beside him. She set her hand on his knee and it froze.

His bright eyes found her. "You told your friend we're dating."

Scarlet blinked, and a sudden laugh tickled her throat, but at Wolf's distraught face she held it back. "It seemed easier than trying to explain the whole alpha mate system."

He looked down at his fidgeting hands. "And . . . you told her you'll be going back to the farm."

"Of course I'm going back to the farm." She cocked her head, starting to grow anxious herself. "I mean, not *tomorrow*, but once things have calmed down."

Wolf's opposite knee started to bounce instead.

"Wolf?"

"Do you still—" He scratched behind his ear. "Do you still want me to come back with you? Now that I'm . . . that I . . ." He sucked in a quick breath. "Do you still want me?"

Wolf seemed like he was in pain. Actual pain. Her heart softened.

"Wol—" She paused and swallowed. "Ze'ev."

His eyes snapped to her, surprised. The portscreen chimed, but Scarlet ignored the comm. She shifted on the bed so she could face him and tucked one foot beneath his thigh. She said firmly, "I still want you."

His jogging leg slowly stilled. "It's just . . . I know I'm not what you had in mind."

"Is that so? Because I was envisioning a big strapping fellow who can chop firewood and master the post-hole digger, and you certainly fit that description. I mean, my grandma and I got along just fine, but honestly . . . I'm looking forward to having the help."

"Scarlet—"

"*Ze'ev.*" She tilted his face toward her. She didn't flinch when she looked at him. Not at his enormous teeth or his monstrous hands. Not at the inhuman slope to his shoulders or the way his jaw protruded from his cheekbones. It was all superficial. They hadn't changed *him.* "You're the only one, Ze'ev Kesley. You'll always be the only one."

His eyebrows rose in recognition of the words he'd once said to her.

"I'm not going to say it won't take some getting used to. And it might be a while before we can convince the neighbor kids not to be terrified of you." She smoothed down a lock of his hair. It popped right back up. "But we'll figure it out."

His body sagged. "I love you," he whispered.

Scarlet slipped her hands through his crazy hair. "Really? I couldn't tell."

The portscreen chimed again. Scowling, she reached over and silenced it, then leaned into Wolf, nudging his nose with hers. Wolf hesitated for only a moment before kissing her. Scarlet sank against him. It was as tender a kiss as any half-man, half-wolf mutant had ever given.

When he pulled away, though, he was frowning. "Do you really think the neighbor kids will be afraid of me?"

"Definitely," she said. "But I have a feeling you'll win them over in the end."

His eyes crinkled. "I'll do my best." Then his smile turned wicked. His hand gathered the material at the small of Scarlet's back and he fell back on the bed, pulling her down beside him.

"*Scarlet!* Scar—oh."

They both froze. Groaning, Scarlet pushed herself up onto her elbows. Iko was half inside her suite, gripping the door handle. Her android body was covered in bandages, which were purely aesthetic, but there weren't a whole lot of android supply shops on Luna and she'd told Scarlet she was sick of everyone staring at her.

"Sorry! 1 should have knocked. But you weren't answering your comms and—" Iko beamed, with more happiness than a person who ran on wires and power cells should have possessed. "Cinder's awake!"

Ninety-Two

DIAGNOSTICS CHECK COMPLETE. ALL SYSTEMS
STABILIZED. REBOOTING IN 3 . . . 2 . . .
1 . . .

Cinder's eyes sprang open, met with a white ceiling and blinding lights. She jerked upward and hissed at the shock of pain in her chest.

The woman who had been hunkered over Cinder's hand cried out and fell off her rolling stool, landing hard on the ground. Metal fuse pullers clattered beside her.

Kai jumped up from a chair in the room's corner and rushed to Cinder's side, pushing his messy hair out of his eyes. "It's all right," he said, supporting Cinder as she pressed both hands against her chest. She could feel a lump of bandaging there, on top of the ache.

She pried her startled attention off the woman—a stranger—and turned to Kai.

Blinked. Noticed first how handsome he looked, and second how exhausted.

A spurt of data began to scroll against her vision in sterile green text.

EMPEROR KAITO OF THE EASTERN
COMMONWEALTH
ID #0082719057
BORN 7 APR 108 T.E.
FF 107,448 MEDIA HITS, REVERSE CHRON
POSTED 13 NOV T.E.: *IN A STATEMENT
RELEASED THIS MORNING, EMPEROR KAITO
INFORMED THE PRESS THAT HE HAS DELAYED
HIS RETURN TO EARTH FOR AN INDETERMINATE
AMOUNT OF TIME, STATING THAT HIS PRESENCE
IS NECESSARY AT THIS TIME TO OVERSEE THE
RECONSTRUCTION OF THE LUNAR CAPITAL—*

Cinder squeezed her eyes shut and willed the text to descend out of her vision. She waited for her heart rate to calm before opening her eyes again.

Her lap was draped with a white linen blanket so thin she could see a groove in the fabric where the flesh of her left thigh met the top of her prosthetic leg. Her left hand was splayed out, palm up, on top of the blanket. The palm chamber was open, revealing a multitude of disconnected wires inside.

"What are you doing to my hand?" she croaked.

The woman climbed to her feet and straightened her white lab coat. "Fixing it."

"Here, drink this." Kai held out a glass of water. Cinder stared at it for longer than she should have, her brain working through mud, before she took it from him. "This is Dr. Nandez," Kai said, watching her drink. "She's one of Earth's best cybernetic surgeons.

I had her flown up yesterday to ... to look at you." His lips tightened, as if he wasn't sure if he'd overstepped some boundary between them.

Handing the glass back to Kai, Cinder studied the doctor, who stood with her arms crossed, tapping the fuse pullers against her forearm. Cinder reached for the back of her head, where her panel was shut tight.

"I'm not dead?"

"You almost were," said Kai. "The knife penetrated one of your prosthetic heart chambers, which drove your body into survival mode. That chamber shut down while the rest of your heart was able to keep functioning ... more or less." Kai glanced at the doctor. "Did I get that right?"

"Close enough," said Dr. Nandez with a weak smile.

Cinder's heart throbbed with every breath. "My retina display is functioning again."

The doctor nodded. "You were in need of a new processing unit—the one you were installed with wasn't designed for full underwater submersion. You were lucky it went into preservation mode, otherwise you wouldn't have had any function over your hand or leg either."

"I didn't, for a while." Cinder tried to move her cybernetic fingers, but they sat unmoving on the bedspread. "I'm sorry I scared you."

"Your reaction was warranted." Dr. Nandez gestured at Cinder's hand. "May I?"

An awkwardness started to creep up Cinder's spine—her palm open and vulnerable, right in front of Kai.

But then she felt silly and vain, so she nodded.

Dr. Nandez wheeled herself back to Cinder's side and set a portscreen on the bed. A holograph flickered in the air above the screen—an exact replica of Cinder's hand and internal wiring. The doctor adjusted the image and bent over Cinder's hand again.

"You should lie back down," Kai said. "You were stabbed, you know."

"I remember." Grimacing, she pressed her hand harder against her wound. The pressure eased some of the throbbing.

"Forty-two stitches, and something tells me you may have just pulled some of them out. Here, lie down."

She allowed Kai to guide her back onto the pillows. She sank into the soft, crisp bedding with a sigh, though the doctor's surgical light was once again blinding her and Kai had taken on a supernatural glow.

"Levana's dead?" she murmured.

"Levana's dead."

With that confirmation, and the stark memory of a gunshot and a splatter of blood burned into her mind, she opened her brain to all the other questions. They tumbled like a waterfall into her thoughts. *Cress, Thorne, Scarlet, Wolf, Winter, Jacin, Iko*—

"Everyone's alive," Kai said as if her thoughts were written in plain green text on her irises. "But Cress is . . . her vitals are stable, and they're hopeful for a recovery, but she hasn't come out of suspension yet. Scarlet had a mild concussion, but she's all right. Thorne lost two fingers, but he's a prime candidate for prostheses if he wants them. Wolf is . . . well, they can't undo the bioengineering without risking serious damage, but he's alive and seems, you know, like Wolf. Jacin suffered some injuries, but nothing life threatening, and Princess Winter . . ." His gaze dropped.

Cinder felt a jolt in her wrist, and her thumb twitched uncontrollably for a moment before there was another zing and it stopped.

"She's been inconsolable since the revolt. They've had to keep her restrained. And a lot of people died, on both sides, but . . . it worked. The outer sectors responded in droves, far too many for the thaumaturges to control at once. People were still coming in from the outer sectors for hours after the fighting was over."

Another zap of electricity, then the snap of a metal latch. "Give that a try," said Dr. Nandez, turning off the holograph.

Cinder lifted her hand. It had been polished to a sparkling finish and she could see echoes of her dark hair in the surface. She curled her fingers one at a time, then rolled her wrist back and forth. Spreading her fingers, she tested the functionality of the tools inside them—all except the gun, which she hoped to never fire again.

Resealing her fingertips, she peered at the doctor. "Thank you."

"My pleasure," said Dr. Nandez, standing. "I'll be back to check on you in a few hours."

As soon as she left, Cinder felt the air change. A sudden tension, a sudden stillness.

She licked her parched lips. "Are you the king of Luna now?"

Kai looked surprised at the question. "No. As Levana was never the true queen, she didn't have the legal power to appoint anyone as king consort. I am technically a widower, but I think I can get that little mishap annulled."

"'Little mishap'?" For something she had risked her life to prevent multiple times, Cinder wasn't sure she could consider Kai's marriage a "little mishap."

"A temporary mistake," he said, shoving away the surgeon's light so it was no longer blinding Cinder. "With all that was going on, we never even had time to consummate."

Cinder coughed. "Unnecessary information."

"Really? You weren't curious?"

"I'd been trying not to think about it."

"Well—think no more. I'm still thanking all the stars, one by one."

Cinder would have laughed, except it hurt too much.

Pacing around the bed, Kai claimed the doctor's stool. The wheels clacked on the floor as he pulled himself so close his knees pressed against the bed frame. "What else do you need to know before I let you get some rest?"

She ran her tongue against the roof of her mouth, wishing she would have drank more water. "Am I ... do they think I'm ...?"

"The queen?"

She nodded.

"Yes, Cinder. You're the queen of Luna." The words were unrelenting. So unapologetic. "They ran your DNA while you were unconscious and you're definitely Selene. According to Lunar law, that means you were the princess regent until your thirteenth birthday, at which time you became the queen of Luna. Levana was the impostor. They're calling you 'the lost queen.' They've been celebrating your return since the night of the battle. Of course, they will want to have a ceremony eventually—more for tradition than anything else."

Cinder bit her lip, thinking of the years she'd spent under Adri's care. A mechanic, a servant, a piece of property. All that time she'd been royalty, and she had no idea.

"Even the thaumaturges, the ones who are still alive, say their loyalty is to the Lunar throne and whoever sits on it. At least, that's what they're saying now. We'll see how they feel once things start to change around here." Kai scratched behind his ear. "The army is being problematic. We're recalling all those who were sent to Earth, but some of the soldiers are ... well, not convinced the war is over. Some have gone rogue on Earth and the Earthen militaries are doing their best to track them down, but we're hoping to—"

She reached for his hands, silencing him.

She was still working through the fact that she was the queen.

She was the queen of Luna.

She reminded herself that this was what she wanted. This responsibility, this duty, this *right* was what she'd been fighting for all along. The chance to rid the world of Levana and change the country she'd been born to. To change it for the better.

Kai's fingers covered hers. Only then did she realize she'd grabbed him with her cyborg hand.

"I'm sorry," said Kai. "You don't need to worry about all that right now. Torin and I are taking care of everything. Making sure the injured are taken care of, getting the city cleaned up . . . oh, and the antidote. We're preparing some big shipments for Earth, and the technicians have been working to produce more batches. We've already sent more than a thousand doses home with the diplomats and they say we'll have triple that amount ready to go out tomorrow evening, although . . ." He hesitated, a shadow crossing his face. "The antidote is produced using shell blood, and there's a whole complicated mess of laws surrounding the shells, and the antidote, and I didn't feel comfortable doing anything without you. That's something we're going to have to deal with, when you're ready." He trailed off, though Cinder could see the struggle warring in his eyes. The relief of having the antidote at his disposal, coupled with the horrible things Levana had been doing to obtain it.

She tried to smile, but she knew how drained she must look. "Thank you, Kai."

He shifted his head, chunks of hair falling across his brow.

"I'm sorry. I should let you sleep. It's just . . . it's really good to see you awake. To talk to you about all this."

"How long was I out?"

"Almost three days."

She turned her eyes toward the ceiling. "Three days. What a luxury."

"A much deserved one." Kai lifted her hand and pressed his lips against her knuckles. "Take your time recovering. The hard part is over."

"Is it?"

He hesitated. "Well. The *dangerous* part is over."

"Can you do something for me?"

Kai frowned, like he didn't want to encourage any crazy ideas, but the moment was brief. "Anything."

"Have all the Earthen leaders gone back to Earth?"

"No. We were able to sneak all the Earthens out of Artemisia during the fighting, once we got the ports open, but most of them came back after they learned you succeeded. I think they're all waiting to meet you."

"Can you call a meeting? You, me, the Earthen leaders . . . and . . . does Luna . . . do I have a cabinet, or a prime minister or anything?"

His lip twitched like he wanted to tease her, but he withheld the urge. "Normally the head thaumaturge would act as second in command, but Thaumaturge Aimery is dead. Your court is in sad disarray right now, I'm afraid."

"Well, whoever you think should be invited then, to an official meeting. An important one."

"Cinder . . ."

"And my stepmother. Is she still here?"

He frowned. "Actually, yes. She and her daughter have been given a spot aboard one of our representatives' ships, but it won't be leaving until tomorrow."

"Bring her too. And maybe that doctor that was just here."

"Cinder, you need to rest."

"I'm fine. I have to do this—as soon as possible, before anyone else tries to kill me."

He grinned, but it was a tender look. "You have to do what, exactly?"

"Sign the Treaty of Bremen." Saying the words brought a real smile to her lips. "I want to make our alliance official."

Ninety-Three

JACIN SLUMPED IN THE VISITOR CHAIR, WATCHING THE doctor check Winter's vitals with no small amount of envy. He wished he was the one to administer to her needs, to know from a readout of life statistics how she was faring and what he could do to make her better. Instead he had to sit there and pretend to be patient and wait for the doctor to inform him, once again, there was nothing to be done. They just had to wait and see if she would recover.

Recover.

Jacin hated the word. Every time it was said he could hear Winter's voice, haunted and afraid. *I do not know that even a sane person could recover from this. So how can I?*

"Her heartbeat is still accelerated," said the doctor, putting away his portscreen, "but at least she's sleeping. We'll check on her again when she wakes up."

Jacin nodded, holding back any of the multiple retorts he had. When she wakes up kicking and screaming. When she wakes up crying. When she wakes up *howling* again like a sad, lonely wolf. When she wakes up and nothing has changed.

"I don't get it," Jacin grumbled, letting his gaze rest on Winter's forehead—at least she was calm in her sleep. "It should have made her better, using her gift. Not worse. She shouldn't be like this, after so many years of fighting it."

"All those years are precisely what caused it." The doctor sighed, and he too looked wistfully down on the princess. *Too* wistfully. Jacin bristled. "It might help to think of the brain and our gift like a muscle. If you don't use that muscle for many years, and then one day you decide to push it to its full potential, you're more likely to strain it than strengthen it. She did too much, too quickly, and it . . . damaged her mind, quite extensively."

I am destroyed, she'd said. Not damaged. *Destroyed.*

And that was before Aimery had even shown up.

As soon as the doctor left, Jacin scooted his chair closer to Winter's bed. He checked the padded restraints on her limbs—they were secure, but not too tight. She had often woken up with violent thrashing and clawing, and one medical assistant had nearly lost an eye before they decided it was best to secure her. Jacin hated watching them do it, but even he agreed it was for the best. She had become a danger to others and to herself. Her teeth had even left an impressive gash on his own shoulder, yet he still couldn't fathom that it was Winter lashing out. Sweet, gentle Winter.

Broken, destroyed Winter.

Jacin let his fingers lie on her wrists longer than was necessary, but there was no one to chastise him now, other than himself.

The rash from the disease grew fainter every day. He doubted it would leave many scars, and what it did leave would be largely unnoticeable on her dark skin. Not like the scars on her cheek that had paled over time.

He both hated and admired those scars. On one hand, they reminded him of a time she'd been suffering. Of a time when he hadn't been able to protect her.

On the other hand, they also reminded him of her bravery and the courage that so few people saw in her. In her subtly defiant way, she had dared to go against Levana's wishes and the expectations of their society time and again. She had been forced to choose her battles, but choose them she had, and both her losses and her victories had cost her so much.

The doctors were at a loss for what to do with her. They had little experience with Lunar sickness. Few people chose to let their sanity deteriorate like she had, and they could only guess what the long-term effects might be.

And all because she refused to be like Levana and Aimery and all the rest of the Lunars who abused and manipulated and used others to fulfill their own selfish desires.

Even in her last desperate act, when she had used Scarlet's hand to kill Aimery, Jacin knew she had done it to save him, not herself. Never herself.

Just like he would do anything to save her.

He dragged a hand down his face, overcome with exhaustion. He'd spent every night since the fight at her side and was surviving on little nourishment and even less sleep.

His parents, he had been shocked to learn, were not dead. He had been certain that his defying Levana's order and helping Winter escape would end in their public executions, like Levana had threatened, but a twist of irony had spared their lives. His father had been transferred to a lumber sector years ago. When Cinder's call for revolution broadcast, the civilians rioted, imprisoning all of their guards and the guards' families. By the time Levana's order to have them killed had come through, Jacin's parents were no longer under her domain. The lumber sector, it turned out, was the same one where Winter had been poisoned.

He hadn't seen them yet, as all guards were waiting to be granted trials under the new regime. Most would be offered a chance to swear fealty to Queen Selene and join the new royal guard she was building. He knew his father, a good man who had long suffered under Levana's thumb, would be happy at the change.

Jacin himself was nervous to be reunited with his family. After years of pushing everyone he loved away, it was difficult to imagine a life in which he was free to care for people without fear of them becoming pawns to be used against him.

He knew they would love to see Winter again too, who had been like a part of their family growing up. But . . . not like this. Seeing her like this would break their hearts.

Seeing her like this . . .

Winter whimpered, a pathetic sound like that of a dying animal. Jacin jumped to his feet and settled a hand on her shoulder in what he hoped was a comforting gesture. She whipped her head back and forth a few times, her eyes jerking beneath her closed lids, but she didn't wake up. When she had settled down again, Jacin breathed a heavy sigh.

He wanted her to be better. He wanted this to be over. He wanted her to open her eyes and not thrash or bite or howl. He wanted her to look at him with recognition and happiness and that hint of mischief that had captured his heart long before she'd been the most beautiful girl on Luna.

He pulled a coiled spring of hair away from her lips, brushing it back off her face.

"I love you, Princess," he whispered, hovering over her for a long time, tracing the planes of her face and the curve of her lips and remembering how she had kissed him in the menagerie. She'd told him then that she loved him, and he hadn't been brave enough to say it back.

But now ...

He placed one hand on the other side of her body, leaning into it for balance. His heart was racing, and he felt like an idiot. If anyone saw him, they'd think he was one of Winter's creepy admirers.

It would change nothing—every bit of logic told him so. A stupid, idealistic kiss could not put her mind back together.

But he had nothing to lose.

Winter went on sleeping, her chest rising. Falling.

Rising and falling and rising.

Jacin realized he was stalling. Building up hope, but also erecting a wall around himself for when nothing happened. Because nothing would happen.

He leaned over her, leaving a hint of space between them, and dug his fingers into the thin hospital blankets. "I love you, Winter. I always have."

He kissed her. One-sided as it was, it had little of the passion there'd been in the menagerie, but so much more hope. And a whole lot of foolishness.

Pulling away, he swallowed hard and dared to open his eyes.

Winter was staring at him.

Jacin snapped backward. "Dammit, Winter. You ... how long ..." He rubbed the back of his neck. "Were you just pretending to be asleep?"

Winter stared up at him, a dreamy half smile on her lips.

Jacin's pulse skittered at that look, his attention dipping back to her lips. *Was it possible—?*

"Win—Princess?"

"Hello," she said, her voice parched, but no less sweet than usual. "Do you see the snow?"

His brow twitched. "Snow?"

Winter peered up at the ceiling. Though her wrists were bound tight, she opened up a palm, like trying to catch something. "It is more beautiful than I'd ever imagined," she whispered. "I am the girl of ice and snow, and I think I'm very glad to meet you."

Disappointment tried to burrow into Jacin's chest, but the walls he'd thrown up did their job, and it was repelled as quickly as it came.

At least she wasn't trying to bite him.

"Hello, snow girl," he said, folding her fingers around an imaginary snowflake. "I'm glad to meet you too."

Ninety-Four

STILL WEAK-LEGGED, CINDER HELD ON TO KAI'S ARM AS HE guided her through Artemisia Palace for the first time since the insurrection. All around her, enormous windows and tiled walls glittered in the sunlight. It was so beautiful. She was having trouble believing it was hers.

Her palace, her kingdom, her *home.*

She wondered how long it would take before it felt real.

Iko had chosen her dress, a simple gown taken from Winter's wardrobe, and done her hair in some fancy updo. Cinder was afraid to move her head for fear it would all come tumbling down. She knew she was supposed to feel regal and powerful, but instead she felt like a feeble girl playing dress-up.

She drew strength from Kai's presence on one side and Iko on the other, even though Iko wouldn't stop reaching up and mucking with her hair. Cinder batted her away again.

At least Iko's arm was working again. Dr. Nandez had managed to return most of her body's functionality, but there was still a lot of damage to be repaired.

As they turned a corner, she spotted her new personal guard,

Liam Kinney, along with Kai's adviser, Konn Torin. Beside them were Adri and Pearl.

Cinder hesitated, her pulse speeding up.

"Cinder."

She met Kai's gaze, his encouraging smile, and felt her heart tumbling for another reason entirely.

"I know this is weird," he said, "but I'm here if you need me. You won't need me, though. You're going to be great."

"Thanks," she murmured, fighting the urge to embrace him, to crawl into his arms and hide from the rest of the galaxy. Maybe forever.

"Also"—his voice lowered—"you look beautiful."

It was Iko who responded, "Thank you for noticing."

Kai laughed, while Cinder, her thoughts fluttering in all different directions, ducked her head.

Cinder limped along, making a point not to look at her stepfamily. When she was close enough, Konn Torin bowed to her. Diplomatic respect, Cinder thought, remembering all the many glares she'd received from this man since she'd first seen him at the annual ball. But when he raised his head, he was smiling. In fact, he seemed downright friendly.

"Your Majesty," he said. "On behalf of the people of the Eastern Commonwealth, I want to thank you for all you've done, and all you will do."

"Oh, um. Yeah. Anytime." With a difficult swallow, she dared to look at Adri.

Her stepmother's face had a gauntness about it. Her number of gray hairs had tripled these past weeks.

There was a moment in which Cinder thought of a thousand things she could say to this woman, but none of them seemed important anymore.

Adri's gaze dropped to the floor. She and Pearl both lowered into uncomfortable curtsies.

"Your Majesty," said Adri, sounding like she was chewing on a bitter lemon. Beside her, Pearl also mumbled, almost unintelligibly, "Your Majesty."

Iko snorted—a derisive sound that Cinder hadn't even thought escorts were capable of making.

Staring at the tops of Pearl's and Adri's heads, she attempted to come up with a gracious response—something Kai would have said. Things a good queen would have done to ease the tension. To offer forgiveness.

Instead, she turned away.

Kinney fisted a hand against his chest and Cinder gave him what she hoped was a regal nod, before Kai led her through a pair of double doors. She had asked him to find a neutral place to host this meeting—not the throne room that had seen so much blood, or the queen's solar, or wherever Levana would have conducted such a thing. She entered into a conference room with an enormous marble table and two holograph nodes, turned off.

The room was already full. She gulped, the uncanny silence nearly pushing her back into the hallway. She recognized most of them, but her brain interface wasted no time in pulling up their profiles from the net database anyway.

President Vargas of the American Republic.

Prime Minister Kamin of the African Union.

Queen Camilla of the United Kingdom.

Governor-General Williams of Australia.

Prime Minister Bromstad of the European Federation.

Dr. Nandez—the acclaimed cybernetic surgeon, and Nainsi, the android that Cinder had fixed for Kai a long time ago. She had been brought to Luna to record this occasion for Earth's official records.

Adri and Pearl were escorted around the table.

Which left only Iko, Kai, Konn Torin, and Cinder herself—or, Her Royal Majesty, Queen Selene Channary Jannali Blackburn of Luna. She wondered if it was all right for her to ask that everyone just call her Cinder.

Before she could speak, the world's leaders rose to their feet and started to applaud. Cinder recoiled.

One by one, they went around the room, bowing and curtsying in turn.

Suddenly panicked, Cinder looked at Kai. He gave her a one-shouldered shrug, suggesting that, yeah, it's weird, but you get used to it.

When the circle came around to him, he too pressed one hand to his chest and inclined his head, the best bow he could give while still supporting her with one arm.

"Th-thank you," she stammered, wondering if she should curtsy, but she couldn't perform a graceful curtsy on her best of days, and it would be disastrous with all her injuries. Instead she held her cyborg hand out to them. "Um, please, be seated?"

The clapping had faded, but no one sat.

Kai led Cinder to the head of the table and eased her into a seat. Only then did the others follow, Kai taking the seat to Cinder's right. Adri and Pearl were sandwiched between Konn Torin and President Vargas. They looked supremely uncomfortable.

"Um. Thank you all for coming on such short notice," Cinder began. She tried folding her hands on top of the table, but that felt strange, so she instead curled them in her lap. "I'm sure you're all eager to return home."

"I'm so sorry to interrupt," said Queen Camilla, not looking at all sorry, "but might I take this moment to say *congratulations* on the reclamation of your throne."

Another fit of clapping started at the queen's words, and Cinder had the impression they weren't so much congratulating her on becoming a queen as they were congratulating themselves on no longer having to deal with Levana.

"Thanks. Thank you. I hope you'll understand that I...um. I hope you'll be patient with me. This is all new for me and I'm not..."

I'm not really a queen.

She glanced around the table, at the eager, hopeful faces staring at her like she was some sort of hero. Like she had done something great. Her gaze swept around the table, feeling more nervous and inadequate with every person she crossed—older, wiser, experienced—until Kai.

As soon as he had her attention, he winked.

Her stomach flipped.

She turned away and squared her shoulders.

"I asked you here today because the relationship between Earth and Luna has been strained for a long time, and my first act as ..." She hesitated and moved her hands to the top of the table again, lacing her fingers together. A few gazes dropped to her cyborg prosthetic, but all tried to pretend they hadn't noticed. "As my first act as queen of Luna, I want to forge a peaceful alliance with the Earthen Union. Even if it's only symbolic at first, I hope it will be the start of a fruitful and mutually beneficial ... political ... um ..." She glanced at Kai.

"Relationship?" he suggested.

"Relationship." She straightened her spine, hoping she didn't sound as stupid as she felt. Around her, though, the diplomats were nodding, all respect and agreement. "I'm aware that a peaceful alliance will begin with all Lunar military units being removed from Earthen soil, and I will try to ensure that the transition is completed as quickly as possible."

A breath of relief washed over those gathered.

"In fact," Cinder continued, "my understanding is that, under Kai—Emperor Kai—Kaito?" She raised her eyebrows at him, realizing this was the first time she'd ever been expected to be formal in his presence.

In response, Kai looked like he wanted to laugh. She glared at him.

"Under Emperor Kaito's instruction," she continued, "some of those military units are already en route back to Luna."

A round of nods. They had heard this already.

She swallowed, hard. Her wounds were starting to itch on top of the constant, drug-dulled aching. She hoped that her first act as queen wouldn't be passing out.

"Luna will also continue to produce and distribute the letumosis antidote as it's necessary and our resources allow. As you know, the antidote was being obtained from ungifted Lunars who had been forced into a permanent comatose state in order to have their blood extracted, which is a violation of their rights. I'm told it might be possible to manufacture lab-grown blood platelets to mimic those of the shell—um, ungifted Lunars, and I hope to redirect Luna's research efforts in that direction, and find a solution that will be fair to everyone. Of course, all samples of the antidote that we already have in stock will be dispersed to Earth immediately."

Nodding. Smiles. Relief and gratitude.

Cinder braced herself. "That said, I do have a few . . . requests to make of you."

As the air of victory around the table gave way to masked patience, and a hint of tension, Cinder tucked a strand of fallen hair behind her ear.

"I want to make clear that these requests are just that—requests. Your answer won't change my mind about any of the promises I've made. This isn't a negotiation." She pulled herself closer to the table.

"First." She tried to hold eye contact with those around her, but found it impossible, her gaze sinking down to her hands while she spoke. "For years, cyborgs have been treated as secondary citizens..." She cleared her throat, feeling Kai's presence, burning, beside her. "I experienced it firsthand growing up in the Commonwealth. Underage cyborgs are seen more as property than people, with hardly any more rights than androids. There's a prejudice surrounding us, that because we've been given unnatural abilities—*man-made* abilities—we're a danger to society. But it isn't true. We just want acceptance, like anybody else. And so, my request is that all laws regarding cyborgs be reexamined, and we be given the same equality and basic rights as everybody else."

Daring to look up, she saw more than one flushed face, and no one daring to make eye contact with her. The new cyborg queen of Luna.

Except Kai, who looked ashamed to be included with the others. But despite his decision to stop the cyborg draft for letumosis testing, the Commonwealth continued to have many of the same injustices as the rest of the planet.

Kai was the first to nod. "The Commonwealth agrees to your request. These laws are unfair and antiquated."

After another long silence, Queen Camilla cleared her throat. "The UK agrees as well. We will begin the reexamination of the laws in earnest upon my return."

Prime Minister Bromstad bashfully admitted that he would need to set up a parliamentary vote before any changes could be made into law, as did the other republics, but there was general agreement around the table. It was by no means a hearty agreement, Cinder could tell, and she tried to disguise how much this irked her. She knew that just because one cyborg had saved the world didn't mean they were ready to give up generations of prejudices, but Cinder hoped it was a start.

"Second. I ask that all restrictions on Lunar emigration be removed. Lunars should be free to come and go between Luna and Earth as they please—I don't want Luna to feel like a prison to its citizens anymore. Likewise, once we're prepared for it, I will open Luna's ports to Earthen travel and emigration. Like it used to be, when Luna first became a country and trade and travel were encouraged. I feel like it's the only way our two societies will begin to start trusting each other."

As she spoke, she noticed many glances being passed between the other leaders.

It was the Australian governor-general who dared to speak. "While I understand your motives, how can we trust that the Lunars who come into our countries won't . . ." He hesitated.

"Manipulate you?" said Cinder. "Brainwash your people? Commit unspeakable crimes against humanity, knowing how easy it will be for them to get away with it?"

He flashed a wry smile. "Exactly."

"I believe that Earthens and Lunars can coexist peacefully," said Cinder. "We've seen it in Farafrah and other north African towns over the past decade, where close to fifteen percent of the population is made up of Lunar immigrants. They work together. They trust each other."

"Fifteen percent?" said Africa's Prime Minister Kamin. "I've never heard this statistic."

"They don't publicize it, but it didn't seem to be a secret, even

· 788 ·

to the Earthen locals. They had formed a mutually beneficial relationship."

"As lovely as that thought is," said Kamin, "with all due respect, you are very young, Your Majesty. You may not be aware that there was a time when travel was encouraged between Earth and Luna, and in that time, we experienced episodes of mass brainwashing put upon our people, forced suicides, rapes . . . Not only is it difficult to prove when a Lunar has manipulated an Earthen, but half the time, we can't even tell a crime was committed." She stopped herself as her voice started to rise. "I of course mean no disrespect to you, Your Majesty."

"No disrespect taken," said Cinder. "I am, in fact, quite familiar with the Massacre at New Haven, 41 T.E., the Mindless Marches of 18 T.E., the highly publicized case of Roget v. Caprice in the second era, and, oh, about a thousand other notable examples of Lunars exerting their gift on the people of Earth."

Kamin looked taken aback. In fact, the whole table seemed more than a little surprised.

Leaning forward, Cinder spoke very clearly. "I have a computer in my *brain*," she said. "So while I'm not going to tell you that I am the smartest or, by any means, the most experienced person in this room, I would suggest that no one use my youth to believe that I am also *ignorant*."

"Of course," said Kamin, newly tense. "Forgive me. I meant no offense."

"Your concerns are legitimate," said Cinder. "If I could offer you a solution—a promise that no Earthen would ever be manipulated again, or would at least be given an opportunity to protect themselves against that manipulation—would you agree to my request?"

"It would be worth considering," said President Vargas. "And I, for one, am dying to know what this solution might be."

"Right." Cinder flicked her hand toward her stepmother. "This is Linh Adri, a citizen of the Eastern Commonwealth."

Adri started, whipping her gaze around the table of very important people.

"Adri's husband, a man named Linh Garan, was an inventor who specialized in android systems and cybernetics. He's deceased now, but when he was alive, he invented a...device. It attaches to a person's nervous system and can protect them from being manipulated by the Lunar gift. Levana learned of this device recently and did her best to have all patents and blueprints concerning the device destroyed, even going so far as to have Adri, the rightful owner of the technology, imprisoned here on Luna."

Adri had gone pale. "I'm sorry, but I don't know anything about it. This device, if it ever existed, is long gone—"

"Well, it's sort of long gone," interrupted Cinder. "As far as I know, there were only two working prototypes. One was in an Earthen woman named Michelle Benoit, who was killed during the attacks in Paris. The other is inside me." She turned to Dr. Nandez, whose interest seemed piqued for the first time since the meeting had started.

Leaning forward, the doctor cupped her chin in one hand. "On your axis vertebra?" she said. "I saw it on your holograph, but I didn't know what it was."

Cinder nodded. "I hope you'll tell me the device can be safely removed, and the hardware reproduced. If we can copy it, there could come a time when everyone who wants to avoid bioelectrical manipulation would have the power to do so."

A rustle of disbelief.

"Is that possible?" said President Vargas.

"Absolutely," said Cinder. "It worked on me, and it worked on Michelle Benoit."

"I hate to be pessimistic," said Dr. Nandez, "but your installed device appeared to have severe damage. Though it's possible we could use it to create a blueprint for the hardware, I have to assume that any programming has been damaged beyond repair. If Queen Levana really did have the data destroyed, I don't know how easily it can be reproduced."

"You're right. Mine was destroyed." Cinder risked a glance at Adri and Pearl, who were frowning as they tried to follow the conversation. "Luckily, Linh Garan created a backup for the device's internal software. He was clever enough to hide it in an obscure place where no one would think to look for it. Do *you* know, Linh-jiě?"

Startled at the formal greeting, Adri shook her head.

"He hid it inside the personality chip of a lowly Serv9.2."

Iko squeaked.

Redness crept into Adri's cheeks. Dawning comprehension, and horror. "Oh—but I . . . but the android . . . I didn't know she was—"

"Valuable?" Cinder smiled wryly. "I know. Adri had the android in question dismantled and sold off as spare parts."

There was more than one gasp around the table, and a lot of furious glances passed toward Adri and Pearl.

"Everything," Cinder added, "except the faulty personality chip that no one else wanted. No one except Linh Garan . . . and me." She nodded at Iko. "The chip is inside my escort-droid friend here, and I have no doubt we'll be able to extract the information stored there."

"Huh," said Iko, pressing her finger into her temple. "I remember when he uploaded those files. I thought they were for malware protection."

"Of course," said Cinder, "Linh Adri is the owner of the patent and the technology, so it's fair she be compensated. I expect you can work out some sort of royalty from the manufacturing of the device."

A round of agreement rumbled through the table—all but Adri. "Royalty?" Her gaze darted to Pearl, then back to Cinder. "How . . . how much of a royalty?"

Iko lowered her hand, grumbling, "Too much."

Cinder bit back a smile. "That's between you and the government entities you're selling it to." Leaning across the table, she fixed a glare on her stepmother. "I suggest you *don't* get greedy."

Scolded, Adri sank back in her chair. But there was a brightness in her eye, as someone across the table mentioned the potential market for such a device. Millions, possibly billions could be reproduced over the next decade . . .

Adri reached for her daughter's hand. Pearl glanced at her mother, and she, too, seemed to finally understand.

Linh Garan's device had the potential to make them very, very wealthy.

Cinder realized, with some surprise, that she didn't feel as bitter about it as she'd thought she would. Let Adri have her riches and royalties, her daughter and her life. After this day, Cinder intended never to think of either of them again.

Her only regret was that Peony wasn't here to see it. She would never play dress-up with Iko in the royal closets. Her eyes wouldn't sparkle as Cinder put on her crown for the first time. She had never met Kai, who had become so much more to Cinder than her prince or her emperor or an impossible dream.

"That brings me to my final request," Cinder said, determined to get through this meeting before any emotions, good or bad, overwhelmed her. "This one relates to only two of you. President Vargas and Governor-General Williams." Cinder adjusted herself in her chair. "It involves a man named Carswell Thorne."

Ninety-Five

THE NURSE KEPT APOLOGIZING AS SHE ESCORTED CRESS FROM the med-clinic to the palace. Far from being fully healed, Cress had to be transported on a maglev chair, which was the oddest floating contraption she'd ever seen. Not quite a gurney, but not a wheelchair, either. For the moment in which Cress let her imagination carry her away, she'd been an exotic first-era princess being carried around on a lavish throne on the shoulders of very strong men.

Then the nurse had launched into her apologies again, destroying the daydream. The clinic was so overcrowded, she explained, the doctors spread so thin, and now that Cress was out of critical status . . .

Cress didn't mind the change. She was glad to be out of the sterile clinic.

Though Cress had only been brought out of suspended animation four hours ago, she'd already seen Iko, Scarlet, Wolf, and even a weary Jacin, who told her of their victory and how Cinder had signed the Treaty of Bremen and how the shells had been awakened and how researchers were figuring out the best way to get them adjusted to life on Luna while also meeting Earth's antidote needs. It left Cress's head spinning.

At the top of her thoughts, however—always, always—was Thorne.

He hadn't been there.

No one had even mentioned his name, and Cress had felt like they were all holding their breath. Wanting to say something, but waiting, uncertain.

She'd shot off two of his fingers. It may have been a minor injury compared with what she and Cinder had suffered, but still—*she* had done it. Of her own will and volition.

The nurse guided her into a familiar guest wing. This was where she had run into Kai.

"Here we are," said the nurse, opening a door. "If you need anything at all—"

"I'm fine." Cress used the controls on the chair's arm to guide it into the room. A canopied bed was covered in shining silks, the stone floors were polished to a glossy finish. The window looked out on some of the palace's flowering gardens, full of gazebos and statues. "Thank you."

"We've taken care to make sure you're close to your friends," said the woman. "Mr. Kesley and Miss Benoit are two doors down on the left, and Emperor Kaito is around the corner. Mr. Thorne is staying across the hall."

Cress spun her chair around. Her door was still open and she could see Thorne's closed door from where she sat. "He is?"

"Would you like me to see if he's in?"

Cress flushed. "Oh. No, that's all right. Thank you."

"Then I should be getting back to the clinic. Would you like to be helped into bed before I go?"

"No, I think I'm going to sit and enjoy the view for a while. Thank you."

The nurse left, shutting the door behind her.

Cress took in a deep breath. The fine guest quarters smelled of lemon cleaner and a bouquet of white lilacs that sat on a desk. They were already wilting, though, and Cress wondered how long they'd been there. Perhaps this room had been set up for someone else, perhaps one of the Earthen diplomats who had already gone home.

Mr. Thorne is staying across the hall.

She stared at the door, willing him to appear.

Her stomach was throbbing where Thorne had stabbed her, when he'd been under Levana's control. She pressed her fingers against the bandages over her stitches, trying to ease the ache. She wondered if she should have asked the nurse to leave her some pain medicine.

She took in a deep breath, feeling the sting in her ribs as her lungs pressed against them. She would be brave. She would be heroic. She would make her own destiny.

She urged her floating chair to the door and yanked it open.

Thorne stood in the hallway.

He jumped, clasping his hands behind his back, a rigidly formal stance. He was clean-shaven with his hair neatly combed, and he was wearing brand-new clothes: a blue collared shirt rolled to the elbows and khaki pants tucked into brown boots.

Cress squeezed herself against the back of the chair, feeling inadequate. Though she'd showered away the suspension tank's goop, she still wore the paper-thin gown from the clinic and hadn't even had a chance to comb her hair.

"Captain," she breathed.

"Sorry," he said, clicking his heels. "Were you leaving?"

"No. I . . . I thought I'd come see you."

Thorne looked caught off guard, but then an edge of relief turned up one side of his mouth. He leaned down and placed his hands on her armrests. His right hand was cocooned in a cast. "You're supposed to be *resting*," he said, pushing her backward and shutting the door with his foot. He took her back to the window, then glanced around. "What can I get you? A portscreen? A masseuse? Whiskey on the rocks?"

She couldn't take her eyes off him. Even knowing he was alive, she hadn't completely believed it until then. "You look . . ." She couldn't finish. Her eyes started to water.

A grin in expectation of a compliment quickly turned to panic. "Oh, hey, what are you doing that for?" He crouched in front of her. "I don't think crying will feel very good in your condition."

She bit her lip, hard. He was right. Already her warbling breaths were making her abdomen throb. She forced the tears to subside.

Thorne took her hands, snaking his cast beneath her fingers. His skin looked tan and rugged against hers.

"I'm sorry," he said. "I wanted to be there when they brought you out of the tank, but I was in a meeting when Scarlet commed to tell me, and I couldn't leave, and I thought . . . I didn't know . . ." He exhaled, a frustrated set to his mouth.

"A meeting?" Cress said, not sure if this explanation made her feel better or worse.

His expression brightened. "You'll never believe this. President Vargas himself wanted to meet me. The *actual* president of the American Republic. Guess what he said."

She considered. "He's giving you a medal of honor for your bravery?"

"Close enough." Thorne's blue eyes gleamed. "He's giving me the Rampion."

Her eyes widened.

Launching to his feet, Thorne started to pace. "Well, I mean, he's *leasing* me the Rampion, but I can start making payments to purchase it from the military. Cinder asked him to pardon me if I promised not to steal anymore, yadda yadda, *and* she recommended me and my crew to head the efforts of distributing the letumosis antidote. But I need a ship to do it, which is why President Vargas made the deal. You should have seen how unhappy he looked about it. I don't think he's my biggest fan, but—he still did it."

Cress clapped. "I'm so happy for you."

"Can you imagine, me, in a legitimate job?"

"And a job that's helping people." She beamed. "I can imagine it very easily."

"I'm sure you're the only one." He stopped pacing long enough to grin at her.

Warmth flooded her face, and she looked down, noticing his cast again. He would have to retrain himself how to fly with his injuries. "I'm—I'm sorry about your hand," she stammered.

"Don't," he said quickly, as if he'd been expecting this apology. "Scarlet and I are going to start a missing-fingers club. We might let Cinder be an honorary member." Sinking onto the edge of the bed, he stared at his cast, twisting it in the light. "Plus, I'm thinking of getting some cyborg replacements. You know how Cinder's hand does all sorts of tricks? I thought it might be nice to always have a toothpick handy. Or maybe a comb." He sounded distracted, like his words and thoughts weren't lining up with each other. When he dared to look up again, there was anxiety behind his eyes. "I'm sorry too, Cress. I . . . I nearly killed you and—"

"Levana almost killed me."

His jaw flexed. "I was the one holding the knife. I felt it. I felt it happening, and there was nothing I could do ..."

"There was nothing you could do," she agreed.

Settling his elbows on his knees, he leaned over, his head hanging between his shoulders. "No. I know." He dragged his good hand through his hair. "I know, logically, that it was her, not me. But ... Cress." He sighed. "I will have nightmares about that moment for the rest of my life."

"It wasn't your fault."

"Cress, that's not ..." Massaging the back of his neck, he peered up at her, but the look was so intense she had trouble holding it. Her blush deepened. "I ..." He planted his hands on his knees, bracing himself. "Will you stay on my crew?"

Her thoughts scattered. "Your ... crew?"

"I know." He cleared his throat. "You've spent your entire life in space, removed from civilization. I understand if you say no. If you want to stay here on Luna, or even ... even if you want me to take you to Earth. I'm sure you could stay with Kai for a while, who, you know, lives in a palace." Thorne's expression darkened. "Which is probably really tempting compared with the cargo ship I'm offering."

He started to pace again. "But Wolf and Scarlet are staying on—just temporarily, until the disease is under control. And I had an idea. This assignment will take us all over the Republic. Not that we'll be doing much sightseeing, but there'll be ... um. Forests. And mountains. And all sorts of things. And when we're done, if there's anywhere you want to go back to, we could do that. And stay for a while. Or I could take you ... anywhere. Anywhere you want to see."

His pacing was making her dizzy. "You're offering me a . . . job."

"Ye—no." He hesitated. "I mean, sort of. You know, this went a lot smoother when I practiced last night."

She shut one eye, squinting. "Captain, I'm still on a lot of medication, and I'm not sure I'm following you."

He took in the hospital gown and hovering chair as if he'd forgotten about them. "Spades, I am bad at this, aren't I? Do you want to lie down? You should lie down."

Without waiting for a response, he swept an arm beneath her knees and lifted her out of the chair, gentle, as if he were picking up a priceless dream doll. She buried a hiss of pain in her throat as he carried her to the bed.

"Better?" he said, easing her on top of the covers.

"Better," she admitted.

But he didn't let go, and he was awfully close when she met his eyes. "Cress, look. I'm obviously no good at this. At least not when it's . . . when it's *you*." He seemed frustrated. His fingers curled, gathering up the flimsy material of the hospital gown. "But I am good at *this*."

He leaned closer and his lips found hers, pressing her into the soft pillows. She gasped and dug her fingers into his shirt, afraid he would pull away before she could memorize this moment. But he didn't pull away, and Cress gradually dared to kiss him back. The mattress shifted—Thorne bringing a knee up to keep from crushing her. His cast brushed her hip, clumsy at first, but less so when he raised it to the side of her face to trace his bare thumb against her jaw. And his lips followed. To her chin. Her neck. The dip of her clavicle.

Her body became liquid, and she thought, if they could bottle him, he would make the best pain medication.

Thorne stopped kissing her, but she could still feel the brush of his hair against her jaw, the warmth of his breath on her shoulder.

"Twenty-three," he said.

"Mm?" She opened her dazed eyes. Thorne pulled back, looking guilty and worried, which made some of her euphoria fade away.

"You once asked me how many times I'd told a girl I loved her. I've been trying to remember them all, and I'm pretty sure the answer is twenty-three."

She blinked, a slow, fluttering stare. Her lips pursed in a question that took a while to form. "Including the Lunar girl who kissed you?"

His brow furrowed. "Are we counting her?"

"You said it, didn't you?"

His gaze darted to the side. "Twenty-four."

Cress gaped. *Twenty-four girls.* She didn't even know twenty-four *people.*

"Why are you telling me this?"

"Because I need you to know I never meant it. I said it because I thought that's what you're supposed to say, but it didn't mean anything. And it's different with you. This is the first time I've been scared. Scared you'll change your mind. Scared I'll screw it up. Aces, Cress, I'm *terrified* of you."

Her stomach fluttered. He didn't *look* terrified.

"Here's the thing." Thorne crawled over her legs and lay down beside her, boots and all. "You deserve better than some thief who's going to end up in jail again. Everyone knows it. Even *I* know it. But you seem determined to believe I'm actually a decent guy who's halfway worthy of you. So, what scares me most"—he twisted a lock of her hair between his fingers—"is that someday even you will realize that you can do better."

"Thorne..."

"Not to worry." He kissed the lock of hair. "I am a criminal mastermind, and I have a plan." Clearing his throat, he started to check things off in the air. "First, get a legitimate job—*check*. Legally buy my ship—*in progress*. Prove that I'm hero material by helping Cinder save the world—oh, wait, I did that already." He winked. "Oh, and I have to stop stealing things, but that's probably a given. So I figure, by the time you realize how much I don't deserve you...I might kind of deserve you." His grin turned smug. "And *that's* how that speech was supposed to go."

"That was a good speech," she said.

"I know." Scooting closer, he kissed her shoulder. Goose bumps erupted down her arm.

"Captain?"

"Cress."

She couldn't *not* say it, although she realized he was right. It was sort of scary. Much scarier than it had been the first time she'd told him, out in the desert. It was different now. It was real. "I'm in love with you."

He chuckled. "I should hope so, after all that." He leaned forward and pressed a kiss against her temple. "And I love you too."

Ninety-Six

WINTER PICKED UP A STICK FROM THE GROUND AND TOSSED it toward the protective fence around the enclosure, but the ghost Ryu just tilted his head to one side.

Sighing, she dropped her hands into her lap.

Her fits still came and went, but she'd been deemed lucid enough that the doctors allowed her to make the decision: Would she rather remain in the med-clinic, where she could be restrained when her outbursts came, or would she rather be outfitted with shock bracelets that could incapacitate her when needed? She had chosen this imaginary freedom, thinking of Ryu and how his own collar would never let him leave the enclosure that must have seemed very escapable at first.

Jacin hated the idea. He had argued that her mind was fragile enough without fearing random shocks. But Winter had needed to get out of the clinic. She had needed to get away from the nightmares that haunted her.

She came to the menagerie often since her release, finding it one of the few serene places in a city that was fluttering with talk of reconstruction and political change. This was all very important, of course. She had always wanted her country to be a place where the people could speak their mind and be treated fairly, where people were given choices over the life they wanted to live. But the talk of it made her head hurt. When the world started to spin out of control she found it best to remove herself to somewhere peaceful and solitary, where she couldn't hurt anyone but herself.

The delusions were no longer constant like they had been in the days following the battle, although her mind still tricked her into seeing her stepmother's shadow in the palace, waiting with a sharpened knife and cruelly kind words. Or the flash of Aimery's eyes following her down the corridors. Too often she smelled the blood dripping down the walls.

The first time she'd come to the menagerie, Ryu's ghost had been waiting for her.

In the uncertainty of the revolution, the gamekeepers had run away, and had yet to be found. The animals had been hungry and restless, and Winter had spent the whole day hunting down the storage rooms where the food was kept, cleaning out the cages, and turning the menagerie back into the sanctuary she'd always known it to be. When Jacin had come looking for her, he conscripted servants to help too.

Staying busy helped. It was not a cure, but it helped. As far as anyone cared, she was the gamekeeper now, though everyone still called her *Princess* and pretended she didn't smell like manure.

Ryu laid his head in Winter's lap and she stroked him between the ears, this sad ghost who wouldn't play fetch anymore.

"Princess."

Ryu evaporated. Jacin was leaning against the enclosure wall, not far from where he'd faked her murder. Where she'd kissed him and he'd kissed her back.

With that memory, Winter was submerged. In water and ice, in hot and cold. She shivered.

Jacin's brow twitched with concern, but she stuffed the memory down. Not a hallucination. Just a normal fantasy, like a normal girl might have when she had a normal crush on her best friend.

"You don't have to call me that, you know," she said, brushing her hair back from her shoulders. "There was a time when you called me *Winter.*"

He leaned his elbows on the enclosure wall. "There was also a time when 1 could come visit you without feeling like 1 was supposed to toss bread crumbs to earn your favor."

"Bread crumbs? Do 1 look like a goose?"

He tilted his head to the side. "You don't look like an arctic wolf, either, but that's what the plaque tells me I'm looking at."

Winter leaned back on her hands. "I will not play fetch," she said, "but 1 might howl if you ask nicely."

He grinned. "I've heard your howl. It's not very wolf-like, either."

"I've been practicing."

"You won't bite me if 1 come in there, will you?"

"I make no guarantees."

Jacin hopped over the rail and came to sit beside her. She raised an eyebrow. "You don't look like an arctic wolf, either."

"I also don't howl." He considered. "Though 1 might play fetch, depending on the prize."

"The prize is another game of fetch."

"You drive a hard bargain."

Her lips curled upward, but when it seemed like Jacin was going to return the smile, he looked away. "You and 1 have had a request from Cin—Selene. Now that the treaty's signed, she wants to start discussing trade agreements between Luna and Earth. Along with open communication, travel, access to Earthen media, stuff like that."

Ryu bumped his head between Winter's shoulder blades. Pulling back her arm, she tried to scratch under his ear, but as soon as she touched him, he faded away.

Jacin was watching her. "The wolf again?"

"Don't worry. He's forgiven you."

He frowned.

"What can we do to help Selene with her politics?"

"Well, given that you're so regrettably charming, and you did such a great job getting the wolf soldiers to join us, and everyone likes you so much . . ."

"So many compliments in a row? I feel like I must be walking into a trap."

"Exactly. Cinder thinks you might make a good ambassador. Her *first* ambassador."

She cocked her head to the side. "What would I have to do?"

"I'm not sure. Go to Earth. Have dinner with fancy people. Show them we Lunars aren't all monsters."

She grinned, feeling wolfish.

"I told her I would ask," Jacin added, "but you're not obligated to say yes. You need to take care of yourself first."

"Would you be with me?"

"Of course." He crossed one ankle over the other. "But you could say no, and I'll be with you then too. I'm done serving everyone else." He leaned back onto his elbows. "Who knows. Maybe someday I'll take up studying to be a doctor again. But until then, I'm your guard, to do with as you will."

"So it will be like playing the Princess and the Guard," she said—a game they'd played when they were kids. She'd act out a much bossier version of herself, while Jacin would model himself after their fathers, all stoic and serious and scrambling to do her bidding. When Winter ran out of commands to give him, they would pretend there were murderers and kidnappers coming for the princess and he would protect her from them.

Jacin grinned. "Hopefully with fewer kidnappings."

She pressed her cheek against his shoulder. "If Cinder wishes it, I would be honored to charm the people of Earth."

"I had a feeling you'd say that." Lying all the way back, he rubbed a hand over his forehead.

Ryu howled, crying his soul up to the menagerie's vine-covered glass ceiling. He was not usually so restless. Maybe it was Jacin's presence. Maybe Ryu was trying to speak to her.

Maybe this was her own insanity, signifying nothing.

Winter started to speak, but hesitated. She looked down at Jacin, but he had his hand covering his eyes. She wondered if he'd been sleeping much lately.

"Dr. Nandez says she may have a prototype of Cinder's device ready within the next week."

Jacin's hand lifted. "Already?"

"She doesn't know yet if it will work. She needs a test subject first."

"Princess—"

"I've already volunteered. You can try to talk me out of it, but I'm fully prepared to ignore you."

Jaw tensing, Jacin sat up again. "The *test* subject? We don't know what the side effects will be. We don't know if it will even work. Let someone else try it first."

"I want to do it. I am one of the most severe cases of Lunar sickness to date." She lost her fingers in the wolf's fur. "But it's occurred to me that, if it works, I won't see Ryu again." She smiled sadly. "And what if . . . what if people don't like me anymore?"

Jacin shook his head. "They don't like you because you're crazy. They like you because . . ."

She waited.

"Because you were good to them when no one else was. Because you care. This device won't change who you are."

"You want me to be fixed, don't you?"

Jacin drew back, as if she'd thrown something at him. "You're not *broken*."

Her vision began to blur. "Yes, Jacin. I am."

"No, you're—" He growled, a throaty, frustrated sound that made her feel giddy. "Look, I would love to not have to worry about you anymore. That you'll hurt yourself or that someone will take advantage of you. But *you're* not—you're—"

"I'm delusional, and crazy, and damaged. I've known it a long time, we both have. Scarlet tells me all the time."

"You're perfect," he said, finishing his thought as if she hadn't interrupted. "I don't care if you see dead wolves and turn into a living ice sculpture when you're having a bad day. I don't care if I have an imprint of your teeth on my shoulder. I don't care if you're . . . *fixed*." He spat the word like it tasted bad. "I want you to be safe and happy. That's all."

Winter fluttered her lashes at him, and he turned away. "Don't look at me like that."

"I want to be the test subject." She reached for his hand. "I'll be safe and happy when I'm no longer afraid of my own mind."

Pressing his lips into a thin line, Jacin nodded. Slowly. "I just don't like the idea of you going first," he grumbled.

"Jacin?"

He met her gaze again.

Winter scooted closer and linked her arm with his. "You think I'm perfect?"

He didn't look away. Didn't look bashful or even nervous. Just stared at her, like she'd asked him if Luna orbited the Earth.

Then he leaned over and brushed a kiss against her forehead. "Just sort of," he said. "You know. On a good day."

Ninety-Seven

"*ALL* OF THEM?"

Cinder smiled at Iko's exuberance. She had already gotten more joy out of the way Iko was beaming at the rows and rows and *rows* of dresses than she ever would have gotten from the dresses themselves.

"Every last one," said Cinder. "I never want to look at them again."

She had already spent more time surrounded by Levana than she'd intended. Her perfume, her gowns, her jewelry. She had no interest in her aunt's wardrobe—but Iko did, so Iko could have them all.

She had never seen Iko so pleased. Not even when Thorne had brought her that escort-droid body he'd found in the desert. Not even when the shipment from Earth had finally arrived with the spare parts to fix her near-destroyed body. Cinder had told her that with so much damage it would be more cost effective to install her personality chip into a brand-new body. She could have had her pick of any model she wanted. But Iko had refused. She had grown attached to this one, she'd said, and besides—none of her friends' bodies were disposable, so why should hers be?

Cinder had no argument for that.

The only upgrade Iko had requested was a pair of brand-new eyes that changed colors based on her moods. Today her eyes were sunburst yellow. Happy, happy, happy.

"You won't mind seeing them on me, will you?" asked Iko, pulling a slinky orange piece off its hanger and holding it against her chest.

"Not if they make you that happy."

"Where will I wear them?" Before Cinder could answer, she waved her hand. "Never mind. Where *wouldn't* I wear them?" Hanging the slinky dress back up, Iko scanned the wardrobe again. Her eyes darkened—more buttercup now, with a tinge of lime around the edges. "I think I feel guilty."

"Guilty?"

Huffing, Iko planted her hands on her hips. Her concern lasted for a few moments before she beamed again. "I know. I'll choose my ten favorites and sell the rest on escort-droid costuming feeds. We can use the proceeds to build schools in the outer sectors, or something charitable like that." Fingering a fine lace sleeve, she glanced at Cinder. "What do you think?"

If Cinder's eyes reflected *her* moods, they would have been sapphire-blue proud. "I think that's a great idea."

Iko beamed and started working her way through the racks again, narrowing down her favorites, while Cinder turned to face her reflection in the mirror that had been loaned to her from one of the Earthen spaceships. She was still getting used to seeing herself looking so . . . *queenly*.

Her own gown was brand-new. Although she had intended to wear one of Winter's dresses again, a few Artemisian

seamstresses had pleaded to be allowed to design her coronation dress, proclaiming what an honor it would be. Cinder hadn't
even known she had expectations until the dress surpassed
them.

Done up in Luna's official colors of white, red, and black, the
gown was made of more material than she'd ever seen in her life.
The heavy white skirt draped around her like a bell, with a massive train that would follow her down the long, long aisle. Red
and black gems were beaded along the skirt's hem and woven
through the bodice. A modest neckline with capped sleeves fit
her perfectly.

She had expected the seamstresses to also make gloves to
cover her cyborg hand, but they didn't. "No gloves," one of the
seamstresses said when she asked. "And no veil."

A knock drew her attention to the door and the guard, Kinney, entered. "Your Majesty," he greeted. His respectful expression turned sour as he addressed Iko, "Madame Counselor."

Iko's eyes went coppery with pride at her new title, even
though she met the guard with a sour glare of her own.

"Yes, Kinney?" said Cinder.

"The captain and his crew are requesting an audience."

"Ha!" Thorne's voice carried from the corridor. "I told you I
could get him to call me the captain."

Cinder rolled her eyes. "Let them in."

They poured in before Kinney could admit them, all grinning
and dressed formally for the occasion. Even Wolf was wearing a
suit, though Cinder couldn't imagine it had been easy to find one
to fit his altered body on such short notice. His red shirt matched
Scarlet's stunning red dress, the fabric clashing spectacularly
with her hair. Thorne was in a tuxedo and bow tie. He came in
pushing Cress along on her floating contraption—Cinder had

heard that her wounds were healing well and she was expected to be walking in short bursts by the end of the week. She was wearing one of Winter's gauzy yellow dresses, hemmed to fit her. Jacin was in his guard uniform, but had replaced the normal shoulder armor with dashing epaulets, making him almost prince-like beside Winter, who was even more breathtaking than usual in a white gown that would have looked plain on anyone else. Kai followed the group in a black dress shirt with a mandarin collar.

He was carrying a silver platter topped with a round, single-tiered cake covered in swirls of pale yellow frosting. Cinder knew immediately that it wasn't from the royal pastry chefs, whose creations were almost too immaculate to touch. This cake, with its messy frosting and lack of decoration, was remarkably unpretentious.

With a bow, the guard slipped out the door. Iko stuck her tongue out at his retreating back.

"What's going on?" said Cinder. "The coronation starts in twenty minutes. You should all be seated by now."

"It was my idea," said Iko, bouncing on her toes. "I knew you'd be nervous, so I thought we'd have a celebration first."

"And you made a cake?"

"Scarlet did," said Thorne.

Scarlet brushed her hair off her shoulder. "It's a lemon cake. My grandmother's special recipe. But"—her gaze swooped down Cinder's dress—"you might want to wait until after the coronation so you don't get frosting all over yourself."

Winter snorted and grabbed the tray away from Kai. "Let's not be cruel. One should never save cake for later when it can be eaten now." She slid the cake onto a priceless silk divan.

"I've never had cake before," said Cress, drawing plenty of

surprised looks. She was holding Thorne's hand, but for once she didn't shrink closer to him, even being the center of attention.

Iko crossed her arms. "Can we please not start listing all the wonderful, marvelous food we've never had?"

"That settles it, then," said Thorne. "Who brought the silverware?"

No one had, so Jacin offered his dagger instead. They took turns cutting off bite-size chunks of cake and frosting and eating it with their fingers until the cake resembled little more than the crater-pocked surface of the moon.

Naturally, Cinder got some on her gown—a smear of yellow frosting on the enormous skirt. She was mortified until Iko adjusted the skirt so the folds would hide it.

"It was inevitable," Iko said with a wink. "It's part of your charm."

Cinder started to laugh, but was startled into silence by a sudden hiccup in her chest.

She looked around, at the smiles and the arms draped over shoulders and Winter daintily licking buttercream from her fingers. At the homemade cake. A gathering of friends. A celebration, for *her*. They were silly things to be floored by, but she couldn't help it. She'd never had these things before.

Gratitude swelled behind her sternum, and though she was still nervous—still *terrified*—she realized that she felt lighter than she had in days.

"Your Majesty?"

She looked up. Kinney had returned.

"It's time."

Cinder gulped and stood, her heart thumping. The festive mood turned serious.

Wolf, who had been holding the knife last, gobbled down a few extra bites before passing the knife back to Jacin. Jacin took one look at the frosting- and crumb-covered blade and stuck it back in the cake for safekeeping.

"I'm ready," said Cinder. Breathing became difficult as the dress constricted against her stomach. "I am ready, aren't I?"

"Hold on." Iko turned Cinder to face her. "Smile."

Cinder gave her a nervous smile, and Iko nodded proudly. "Nothing in your teeth. I'd say you're ready."

Her friends gathered around her, pulling her into embrace after embrace.

Until she reached Kai, who wrapped his arms around her waist and kissed her. He tasted like lemon frosting.

Thorne whistled. Iko swooned. The kiss ended too quickly.

"What was that for?" Cinder whispered against him.

Kai scooped his arm around her shoulders and led her out of the queen's chambers. "I was just thinking about the good future," he said. "The one with you in it."

THE OFFICIAL CORONATION OF QUEEN SELENE CHANNARY Jannali Blackburn was in some ways an intimate affair, and in others an intergalactic sensation. Cinder had held a lottery for tickets so all of Luna's sectors would be represented, and all the guests combined made for a crowd a few hundred strong, which barely filled up half the seats that had been set out for Levana and Kai's ceremony a few weeks prior.

The footage was broadcast, not only to every sector on Luna but also to all Earthen newsfeeds that chose to run it. It became the most viewed netfeed of the third era.

While Cinder walked down the endless black-carpeted aisle, she tried not to think of all the people in the universe who were watching her. She tried not to wonder whether they were judging her or admiring her, afraid of her or impressed by her. She tried not to guess how many saw her as a lost princess or a pathetic cyborg, a vigilante or a criminal, a revolutionary or a lowly mechanic that had gotten lucky.

She tried not to think about the smear of yellow frosting on her priceless gown.

Kai and Winter stood at the altar encased in the light of glowing orbs, Winter holding the queen's crown and Kai a ceremonial scepter. Together, they represented how both Earth and Luna would accept her right to rule. The rest of her friends were in their reserved seats in the front row. Thorne, on the aisle, held out his hand as Cinder passed. She snorted and accepted the high five before floating up the stairs.

Winter winked at her. "Well done, Cinder-friend. You didn't trip. The hard part is over."

Kai gave a smile meant for only Cinder, even though the entire universe was watching. "She's right, that really is the hard part."

"Thank the stars," Cinder whispered back. "Now let's get this over with."

Taking in a long, shaky breath, she turned to face her kingdom.

THE BLOOD HAD BEEN SCRUBBED FROM THE THRONE ROOM floor, but the room was still a disaster. Toppled chairs and broken rails, cracked tiles and wall panels where bullets had hit them. Even the throne itself had a fracture in the stone from when Cinder had tried to shoot Levana. It smelled of chemicals and bleach from the cleaning.

The horrors of the rebellion were starting to fade. Not, perhaps, for those who had lost friends and family, and Cinder knew there was still so much to be done in order for Luna to pick up the pieces of Levana's rule. But they were eager to start picking up those pieces right away.

She'd begun compiling councils made up of both members from the Artemisian court and nominated citizens from the outer sectors to begin bridging the gap between the classes and figuring out how best to reallocate funds and labor. Already the "families" and the thaumaturges were starting to fight against her, but that was all right. It would take time, but they would adjust.

She'd been sitting on her throne in the silent, chemical-filled air for what could have been hours, watching the city of Artemisia shimmering before her and Earth turning above the horizon.

The doors opened. Kai poked his head in and Cinder tensed, feeling guilty to be caught on the throne—even if it was *her* throne—all alone in the darkness.

"There you are," he said.

"Sorry," she said. "I'm kind of hiding. Would you believe that when you're royalty, it is *really* difficult to find a moment of privacy?"

Smirking, Kai shut the door behind him. He kept a hand behind his back as he came toward her. "Might I suggest getting yourself a hooded sweatshirt? It makes a surprisingly adequate disguise." He paused when he spotted Earth over the balcony, all beautiful and enormous in the dark sky. "That's quite a view."

Cinder nodded. "Not to justify what Levana did, but I can kind of understand why she wanted it so much."

When Kai said nothing, she slid her gaze back to him and she knew what he'd come there to say. Her heart sank. "You're leaving, aren't you?"

He turned away from the view. "In two days. Two *Earthen* days." He frowned apologetically. "I've been gone for too long already."

She tried to smother the despair that knocked into her. Kai would be gone. Thorne, Cress, Wolf, and Scarlet had already left, and Winter and Jacin would be leaving on their first ambassadorial trip in the next few days, and then she would be alone.

Well, she and Iko would be alone.

She'd been expecting it. She had known he couldn't stay forever. He had his own country to rule.

"Right," she said, feigning confidence. "I understand. You've been a huge help, you and Konn-dàren. Is ... is he leaving too?"

Kai grimaced. "He is. I'm sorry."

"No. You ... you have to go home. Of course you do."

"You should come visit," he said, speaking fast. "Soon. It would be symbolic, I think, of the new alliance ..." He trailed off and scratched behind his neck, one hand still hidden. "Or I could make up a political dilemma we need to work through if that would help."

Cinder forced a smile. "I'd like to come visit. I'm ... Iko and I are going to miss you."

"I think you'll find that being a queen doesn't leave a whole lot of time for being lonely."

"We'll see about that." Suddenly, it felt awkward to be sitting on her throne while Kai stood below her. She stood and crossed her arms over her chest, drifting toward the balcony ledge.

Anxiety was already growing inside her. *Two days. Two more days and he'll be gone.*

There was so much she wanted to say to him, and two days wasn't enough time to get it all out—especially when all the words remained locked up in her throat.

"It's strange," Kai said, joining her on the glass overhang, his gaze fixed on Earth again. "I spent all that time trying to avoid a marriage alliance with Luna. And now that the treaty is signed and the war is over...somehow, a marriage alliance doesn't sound so bad."

Her heart flipped. Kai's gaze danced back to her and then he was smiling in a way that was both bashful and confident. The same smile he'd given her the day they'd met in the market-place. After a long, awkward moment, he laughed. "You really *can't* blush, can you?"

A mix of relief and disappointment rolled through her and she tucked her hands under her arms to hide their shaking. "That wasn't nice."

"Only if you think I didn't mean it."

Her brow twitched.

"Here, I have something for you."

"It had better not be an engagement ring."

He paused, his lips puckering as if the thought hadn't occurred to him and he was regretting it.

"Or gloves," added Cinder. "That didn't work out too well last time."

Grinning, Kai took a step closer to her and dropped to one knee.

Her eyes widened.

"Cinder ..."

Her heart thumped. "Wait."

"I've been waiting a long time to give this to you."

"Kai—"

With an expression as serious as politics, he pulled his hand from behind his back. In it was cupped a small metal foot, frayed wires sticking up from the cavity and the joints packed with grease.

Cinder released her breath, then started to laugh. "You—*ugh*."

"Are you terribly disappointed, because I'm sure Luna has some great jewelry stores if you wanted me to—"

"Shut up," she said, taking the foot. She turned it over in her palms, shaking her head. "I keep trying to get rid of this thing, but somehow it keeps finding its way back to me. What made you keep it?"

"It occurred to me that if I could find the cyborg that fit this foot, it must be a sign we were meant to be together." He twisted his lips to one side. "But then I realized it would probably fit an eight-year-old."

"Eleven, actually."

"Close enough." He hesitated. "Honestly, I guess it was the only thing I had to connect me to you when I thought I'd never see you again."

She slid her gaze off the foot. "Why are you still kneeling?"

Kai reached for her prosthetic hand and brushed his lips against her newly polished knuckles. "You'll have to get used to people kneeling to you. It kind of comes with the territory."

"I'm going to make it a law that the correct way to address your sovereign is by giving a high five."

Kai's smile brightened. "That's genius. Me too."

Cinder pulled her hand away from him and sat down, letting

her legs hang over the edge. Her thoughts grew serious again as she stared at the metal foot. "Actually, there's something I wanted to get your opinion on."

Kai settled beside her. His expression turned curious, and she looked away, bracing herself. "I think—" She stopped. Gulped. Started again. "I've decided to dissolve the Lunar monarchy."

Pressing her lips together, she waited. The silence became solid in the space between them. But Kai didn't ask "Why?" or "How?" or "Are you insane?"

Instead, he said, "When?"

"I don't know. When things have calmed down. When I think they can handle it." She took in a deep breath. "It will happen again. Some king or queen is going to brainwash the people, use their power to enslave them . . . There has to be some division of power, some checks and balances . . . so I've decided to change Luna into a republic, elected officials and all." She bit her lip. She still felt silly talking politics like she had a clue, and it wasn't until Kai nodded, thoughtful, that she realized how important his approval had been to her. She swallowed around the lump in her throat. "You think it's a good idea?"

"I think it will be difficult. People don't like change, and even the citizens who were oppressed under Levana immediately accepted you as their new queen. Plus, they have that whole superstition thing about the royal bloodline. But . . . I think you're right. I think it's what Luna needs."

She felt as though an entire moon had been lifted off her shoulders.

"What will you do then? After you abdicate?"

"I don't know. I hear Thorne is looking for a full-time mechanic." She shrugged, but Kai went on looking pensive. "What?"

"I think you should come back to the Commonwealth. You

could stay in the palace, as a Lunar ambassador. It would be a show of good faith. Proof that Earth and Luna can work together, *coincide* together."

Cinder chewed on the inside of her cheek. "I thought the people of the Commonwealth hated me," she said. "For the kidnapping. And all that other stuff that happened."

"Please. You're the lost princess that saved them from the reign of *Empress* Levana. I heard there's a toy company that wants to make action figures of you. And they want to put up a statue where your booth used to be at the market."

She grimaced.

Chuckling, Kai took her hand. "Whenever you come back, you will be welcomed with open arms. And after everything that's happened, you're probably going to have about two hundred thousand guys wanting to take you to the Annual Peace Ball next year. I expect the offers to start rolling in any day now."

"I highly doubt that."

"Just wait, you'll see." He tilted his head, clumps of hair falling into his eyes. "I figured it couldn't hurt to get my name on the list before anyone else steals you away. If we start now, and plan frequent visits between Earth and Luna, I might even have time to teach you to dance."

Cinder bit her lip to disguise a budding smile.

"Please say yes," said Kai.

Fiddling with the dead wires of her old foot, she asked, "Do I have to wear a dress?"

"I don't care if you wear military boots and cargo pants."

"I just might."

"Good."

"Iko would kill me." She pretended to be considering it as she cast her gaze toward the sky. "Can I bring my friends?"

"I will personally extend invitations to the entire Rampion crew. We'll make a reunion out of it."

"Even Iko?"

"I'll find her a date."

"Because there's a rule against androids coming to the ball, you know."

"I think I know someone who can change that rule."

Grinning, she scooted a bit closer. The idea of going back to the ball and facing all those people who had stared at her with such horror and contempt filled her with copious amounts of everything from anxiety to dread to unspeakable joy.

"I would be honored," she said.

His eyes warmed. "And those dance lessons?"

"Don't press your luck."

Kai tilted her chin toward him and kissed her. She didn't know what number it was—she'd finally figured out how to turn off her brain's auto-count function and she didn't care how many times he kissed her. She did care that every kiss no longer felt like their last.

Except, when Kai pulled away, a hint of sadness had slipped into his expression. "Cinder, I believe you would make a great ruler. I believe this decision is proof of that." He hesitated. "But I also know you never wanted to be queen. Not really."

Cinder had never told him that, and she wondered if it had been obvious this whole time.

"But I have to ask if"—Kai hesitated—"if you think, *someday*, you might consider being an empress."

Cinder forced herself to hold his gaze, and to swallow the lighthearted joke that rose to the tip of her tongue. He wasn't teasing her about engagement rings and dance lessons. This was a real question, from a real emperor, who had the real future of his country to consider.

If she wanted to be a part of his future, she'd have to be a part of it all.

"I would consider it," she said, then took in the first full breath she'd taken in days. "Someday."

His grin returned, full force and full of relief.

He put an arm around her and Cinder couldn't smother her own smile as she leaned against him, staring at Artemisia Lake and the white city and planet Earth surrounded by stars. She spun the cumbersome, hateful foot in her fingers. Ever since she could remember, it had been a burden. A constant reminder that she was worthless, she was unimportant, she was nothing but a cyborg.

She held the foot over the water and let go.

And they all lived happily to the end of their days.

Acknowledgments

My heart overfloweth with gratitude . . .

For everyone at Macmillan Children's, including, but not limited to: Jean Feiwel, Liz Szabla, Jon Yaged, Nicole Banholzer, Molly Brouillette, Lauren Burniac, Mariel Dawson, Lucy Del Priore, Liz Fithian, Courtney Griffin, Angus Killick, Johanna Kirby, Anna Roberto, Caitlin Sweeny, Mary Van Akin, Allison Verost, Ksenia Winnicki, and countless more behind-the-scenes advocates for these books. You are all so brilliant and creative and I'm so lucky to be working with you. I also want to give special thanks to the cover designer, Rich Deas, and illustrator, Michael O, who together have created some of the most gorgeous book covers an author could hope for. Thanks also to my copyeditor, Anne Heausler, for your careful attention and surprisingly excellent knowledge of moon geology.

For Rebecca Soler, the ridiculously talented audiobook narrator, along with Samantha Edelson and the whole crew at Macmillan Audio for bringing these stories to life in such a lively and tangible way.

For my intrepid agent and her team: Jill Grinberg, Cheryl Pientka, Katelyn Detweiler, and Denise St. Pierre. Thank you for your constant faith, guidance, and zeal for toasting every milestone. (*Winter* is done—cheers!)

For my beta readers, Tamara Felsinger, Jennifer Johnson, and Meghan Stone-Burgess, who have been with me since the start of this crazy journey. Time and again you've forced me to dig deeper and push harder, and your invaluable feedback has made such a tremendous difference to this series and for me as a writer. Plus, I just really adore you all.

For the Sailor Moon fandom, from those who gave me courage back when I was a fledgling fanfiction writer, to some of my dearest friends who still make me laugh with your hijinks. (There, I put Jacin in a towel. *Are you happy??*)

We often talk about writing being a solitary profession, but it's hard to tell when you're surrounded by wonderful fellow writers as I've been. I'm grateful for my local partners-in-crime—Gennifer Albin (we miss you!), Martha Brockenbrough, Corry Lee, Lish McBride, Ayesha Patel, and Rori Shay—for keeping me inspired and focused during our many writing dates and retreats. I'm so glad to have met each of you. Thanks also to Mary Christine Weber and Jay Asher, who joined me for a super-fun interview in the *Cress* paperback, and to so many writers who have joked, inspired, commiserated, motivated, taught, toured with, and encouraged me throughout this epic book-writing quest: Anna Banks, Leigh Bardugo, Stephanie Bodeen, Jennifer Bosworth, Jessica Brody, Alexandra Coutts, Jennifer Ellision, Elizabeth Eulberg, Elizabeth Fama, Nikki Kelly, Robin LaFevers, Emmy Laybourne, Beth Revis, Leila Sales, and Jessica Spotswood, with sincere apologies to anyone I might have missed.

For the librarians, teachers, booksellers, and bloggers who've rallied around this series. From book talks to art assignments, staff picks to GoodReads reviews, your enthusiasm has introduced countless readers to the Lunar Chronicles and I am enormously grateful for all you've done.

For my friends and family, who plan launch parties, take photos, make dinners, babysit, pitch my books to random people at the supermarket, do my hair, make crowns, share book recommendations, help me shop for event outfits, and constantly remind me of the important things in life. Thank you; I love you.

For Jesse, who does so much so I can stay focused on writing and dreaming, dreaming and writing. I love you with my whole heart. And for Sarah and Emily, whose smiles have made this the brightest year of my life.

Lastly, I have infinite gratitude for the readers (yes, you!). Over the past years, you've made fanart and written letters, held in-depth discussions on the merits of various OTPs, shared with me your struggles and joys, hosted read-a-thons, donned costumes and red high heels, driven for hours to attend book signings, dreamed up movie fancastings, baked Lunar Chronicles cupcakes, started Tumblrs and compiled Pinterest boards, and so so so much more. This tale belongs to you now, as much as to me, and I couldn't feel as though I'm putting it in better hands. If you need me, I'll be thanking all the stars for each of you, one by one.

Photo credit © Julia Scott

MARISSA MEYER is the author of the #1 *New York Times*–bestselling Lunar Chronicles series: *Cinder, Scarlet, Cress, Winter, Stars Above*, and *Fairest*. She is also the author of the Lunar Chronicles graphic novels, *Wires and Nerve* and *Wires and Nerve, Volume 2: Gone Rogue*, and *Renegades*, Book 1 of the Renegades Trilogy, as well as the book *Heartless*. She lives in Tacoma, Washington, with her family.

marissameyer.com